ED
McBAIN

ED McBAIN

Cop Hater

Give the Boys a Great Big Hand

Doll

Eighty Million Eyes

The Heckler

Ten Plus One

Octopus/Heinemann

Cop Hater was first published in the United States
by Permabooks in 1956
Give the Boys a Great Big Hand was first published in the United States
by Simon & Schuster, Inc in 1960
Doll was first published in the United States
by Delacorte Press in 1965
Eighty Million Eyes was first published in the United States
by Delacorte Press in 1966
The Heckler was first published in the United States
by Simon & Schuster, Inc in 1960
Ten Plus One was first published in the United States
by Simon & Schuster, Inc in 1963

This edition first published in the United States of America
in 1981 jointly by

William Heinemann Inc

and

Octopus Books, Inc.
One Madison Avenue
New York, N.Y. 10010

ISBN 0 905712 63 3

Printed in the United States of America
by R. R. Donnelley and Sons Company

CONTENTS

COP HATER

"The alarm
sounded at
eleven p.m.
He reached
out for it,
groping in
the dark-
ness, find-
ing the
lever and
pressing it
against the
back of the
clock...."

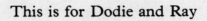

This is for Dodie and Ray

Chapter One

The alarm sounded at eleven p.m.

He reached out for it, groping in the darkness, finding the lever and pressing it against the back of the clock. The buzzing stopped. The room was very silent. Beside him, he could hear May's even breathing. The windows were wide open, but the room was hot and damp, and he thought again about the air conditioning unit he'd wanted to buy since the summer before. Reluctantly, he sat up and rubbed hamlike fists into his eyes.

He was a big man, his head topped with straight blond hair that was unruly now. His eyes were normally grey, but they were virtually colourless in the darkness of the room, puffed with sleep. He stood up and stretched. He slept only in pyjama pants, and when he raised his arms over his head, the pants slipped down over the flatness of his hard belly. He let out a grunt, pulled up the pants, and then glanced at May again.

The sheet was wadded at the foot of the bed, a soggy lifeless mass. May lay curled into a sprawling C, her gown twisted up over her thigh. He went to the bed and put his hand on her thigh for an instant. She murmured and rolled over. He grinned in the darkness and then went into the bathroom to shave.

He had timed every step of the operation, and so he knew just how long it took to shave, just how long it took to dress, just how long it took to gulp a quick cup of coffee. He took off his wrist watch before he began shaving, leaving it on the wash-basin where he could glance at it occasionally. At eleven-ten, he began dressing. He put on an Aloha shirt his brother had sent him from Hawaii. He put on a pair of tan gabardine slacks, and a light poplin windbreaker. He put a handkerchief in his left hip pocket, and then scooped his wallet and change off the dresser.

He opened the top drawer of the dresser and took the .38 from where it lay next to May's jewellery box. His thumb passed over the hard leather of the holster, and then he shoved the holster and gun into his right hip pocket, beneath the poplin jacket. He lighted a cigarette, went into the kitchen to put up the coffee water, and then went to check on the kids.

Mickey was asleep, his thumb in his mouth as usual. He passed his hand over the boy's head. He was sweating like a pig. He'd have to talk to May about the air conditioning again. It wasn't fair to the kids, cooped up like this in a sweat box. He walked to Cathy's bed and went through the same ritual. She wasn't as perspired as her brother. Well, she was a girl, girls didn't sweat as much. He heard the kettle in the kitchen whistling loudly. He glanced at his watch, and then grinned.

He went into the kitchen, spooned two teaspoonfuls of instant coffee into a large cup, and then poured the boiling water over the powder. He drank the coffee black, without sugar. He felt himself coming awake at last, and he vowed for the hundredth time that he wouldn't try to catch any sleep before this tour, it was plain stupid. He should sleep when he got home, hell, what did he average this way? A couple of hours? And then it was time to go in. No, it was foolish. He'd have to talk to May about it. He gulped the coffee down, and then went into his bedroom again.

He liked to look at her asleep. He always felt a little sneaky when he took advantage of her that way. Sleep was a kind of private thing, and it wasn't right to pry when somebody was completely unaware. But, God, she was beautiful when she was asleep, so what the hell, it wasn't fair. He watched her for several moments, the dark hair spread out over the pillow, the rich sweep of her hip and thigh, the femaleness of the raised gown and the exposed white flesh. He went to the side of the bed, and brushed the hair back from her temple. He kissed her very gently, but she stirred and said, 'Mike?'

'Go back to sleep, honey.'

'Are you leaving?' she murmured hoarsely.

'Yes.'

'Be careful, Mike.'

'I will.' He grinned. 'And you be good.'

'Uhm,' she said, and then she rolled over into the pillow. He sneaked a last look at her from the doorway, and then went through the living room and out of the house. He glanced at his watch. It was eleven-thirty. Right on schedule, and damn if it wasn't a lot cooler in the street.

At eleven forty-one, when Mike Reardon was three blocks away from his place of business, two bullets entered the back of his skull and ripped away half his face when they left his body. He felt only impact and sudden unbearable pain, and then vaguely heard the shots, and then everything inside him went dark, and he crumpled to the sidewalk.

He was dead before he struck the ground.

He had been a citizen of the city, and now his blood poured from his broken face and spread around him in a sticky red smear.

Another citizen found him at eleven fifty-six, and went to call the police. There was very little difference between the citizen who rushed down the street to a phone booth, and the citizen named Mike Reardon who lay crumpled and lifeless against the concrete.

Except one.

Mike Reardon was a cop.

Chapter Two

The two Homicide cops looked down at the body on the sidewalk. It was a hot night, and the flies swarmed around the sticky blood on the sidewalk. The Assistant Medical Examiner was kneeling alongside the body, gravely studying it. A photographer from the Bureau of Identification was busily popping flash bulbs. Cars 23 and 24 were parked across the street, and the patrolmen from those cars were unhappily engaged in keeping back spectators.

The call had gone to one of the two switchboards at Headquarters where a sleepy patrolman had listlessly taken down the information and then shot it via pneumatic tube to the radio room. The dispatcher in the radio room, after consulting the huge precinct map on the wall behind him, had sent Car 23 to investigate and report on the allegedly bleeding man in the street. When Car 23 had reported back with a homicide, the dispatcher had contacted Car 24 and sent it to the scene. At the same time, the patrolman on the switchboard had called Homicide North and also the 87th Precinct, in which territory the body had been found.

The body lay outside an abandoned, boarded-up theatre. The theatre had started as a first-run movie house, many years back when the neighbourhood had still been fashionable. As the neigbourhood began rotting, the theatre began showing second-run films, and then old movies, and finally foreign language films. There was a door to the left of the movie house, and the door had once been boarded, too, but the planks had been ripped loose and the staircase inside was littered with cigarette butts, empty pint whisky bottles, and contraceptives. The marquee above the theatre stretched to the sidewalk, punched with jagged holes, the victim of thrown rocks, tin cans, hunks of pipe, and general debris.

Across the street from the theatre was an empty lot. The lot had once owned an apartment house, and the house had been a good one with high rents. It had not been unusual, in the old days, to see an occasional mink coat drifting from the marbled doorway of that apartment house. But the crawling tendrils of the slum had reached out for the brick, clutching it with tenacious fingers, pulling it into the ever-widening circle it called its own. The old building had succumbed, becoming a part of the slum, so that people rarely remembered it had once been a proud and elegant dwelling. And then it had been condemned, and the building had been razed to the ground, and now the lot was clear and open, except for the scattered brick rubble that still clung to the ground in some places. A City housing project, it was rumoured, was going up in the lot. In the meantime, the kids used the lot for various purposes. Most of the purposes were concerned with bodily functions, and so a stench hung on the air over the lot, and the stench was particularly strong on a hot summer night, and it drifted towards the theatre, captured beneath the canopy of the overhanging marquee, smothering the sidewalk with its smell of life, mingling with the smell of death on the sidewalk.

One of the Homicide cops moved away from the body and began scouring the sidewalk. The second cop stood with his hands in his back pockets. The Assistant M.E. went through the ritual of ascertaining the death of a man who was certainly dead. The first cop came back.

'You see these?' he asked.

'What've you got?'

'Couple of ejected cartridge cases.'

'Mm?'

'Remington slugs. .45 calibre.'

'Put 'em in an envelope and tag 'em. You about finished, Doc?'

'In a minute.'

The flash bulbs kept popping. The photographer worked like the press agent for a hit musical. He circled the star of the show, and he snapped his pictures from different angles, and all the while his face showed no expression, and the sweat streamed down his back, sticking his shirt to his flesh. The Assistant M.E. ran his hand across his forehead.

'What the hell's keeping the boys from the 87th?' the first cop asked.

'Big poker game going probably. We're better off without them.' He turned to the Assistant M.E. 'What do you say, Doc?'

'I'm through.' He rose wearily.

'What've you got?'

'Just what it looks like. He was shot twice in the back of the head. Death was probably instantaneous.'

'Want to give us a time?'

'On a gunshot wound? Don't kid me.'

'I thought you guys worked miracles.'

'We do. But not during the summer.'

'Can't you even guess?'

'Sure, guessing's free. No rigor mortis yet, so I'd say he was killed maybe a half-hour ago. With this heat, though ... hell, he might maintain normal body warmth for hours. You won't get us to go out on a limb with this one. Not even after the autopsy is ...'

'All right, all right. Mind if we find out who he is?'

'Just don't mess it up for the Lab boys. I'm taking off.' The Assistant M.E. glanced at his watch. 'For the benefit of the timekeeper, it's 12:19.'

'Short day today,' the first Homicide cop said. He jotted the time down on the time table he'd kept since his arrival at the scene.

The second cop was kneeling near the body. He looked up suddenly. 'He's heeled,' he said.

'Yeah?'

The Assistant M.E. walked away, mopping his brow.

'Looks like a .38,' the second cop said. He examined the holstered gun more closely. 'Yeah. Detective's Special. Want to tag this?'

'Sure.' The first cop heard a car brake to a stop across the street. The front doors opened, and two men stepped out and headed for the knot around the body. 'Here's the 87th now.'

'Just in time for tea,' the second cop said drily. 'Who'd they send?'

'Looks like Carella and Bush.' The first cop took a packet of rubber-banded tags from his right hand jacket pocket. He slipped one of the tags free from the rubber band, and then returned the rest to his pocket. The tag was a three-by-five rectangle of an oatmeal colour. A hole was punched in one end of the tag, and a thin wire was threaded through the hole and twisted to form two loose ends. The tag read POLICE DEPARTMENT, and beneath that in bolder type: EVIDENCE.

Carella and Bush, from the 87th Precinct, walked over leisurely. The Homicide cop glanced at them cursorily, turned to the *Where found* space on the tag, and began filling it out. Carella wore a blue suit, his grey tie neatly clasped to his white shirt. Bush was wearing an orange sports shirt and khaki trousers.

'If it ain't Speedy Gonzales and Whirlaway,' the second Homicide cop said. 'You guys certainly move fast, all right. What do you do on a bomb scare?'

'We leave it to the Bomb Squad,' Carella said drily. 'What do you do?'

'You're very comical,' the Homicide cop said.

'We got hung up.'

'I can see that.'

'I was catching alone when the squeal came in,' Carella said. 'Bush was out with Foster on a bar knifing. Reardon didn't show.' Carella paused. 'Ain't that right, Bush?' Bush nodded.

'If you're catching, what the hell are you doing here?' the first Homicide cop said.

Carella grinned. He was a big man, but not a heavy one. He gave an impression of great power, but the power was not a meaty one. It was, instead, a fine-honed muscular power. He wore his brown hair short. His eyes were brown, with a peculiar downward slant that gave him a clean-shaven Oriental appearance. He had wide shoulders and narrow hips, and he managed to look well-dressed and elegant even when he was dressed in a leather jacket for a waterfront plant. He had thick wrists and big hands, and he spread the hands wide now and said, 'Me answer the phone when there's a homicide in progress?' His grin widened. 'I left Foster to catch. Hell, he's practically a rookie.'

'How's the graft these days?' the second Homicide cop asked.

'Up yours,' Carella answered drily.

'Some guys get all the luck. You sure as hell don't get anything from a stiff.'

'Except *tsores*,' the first cop said.

'Talk English,' Bush said genially. He was a soft-spoken man, and his quiet voice came as a surprise because he was all of six feet four inches and weighed at least two-twenty, bone dry. His hair was wild and unkempt, as if a wise Providence had fashioned his unruly thatch after his surname. His hair was also red, and it clashed violently against the orange sports shirt he wore. His arms hung from the sleeves of the shirt, muscular and thick. A jagged knife scar ran the length of his right arm.

The photographer walked over to where the detectives were chatting.

'What the hell are you doing?' he asked angrily.

'We're trying to find out who he is,' the second cop said. 'Why? What's the matter?'

'I didn't say I was finished with him yet.'

'Well, ain't you?'

'Yeah, but you should've asked.'

'For Pete's sake, who are you working for? Conover?'

'You Homicide dicks give me a pain in the ...'

'Go home and emulsify some negatives or something, will you?'

The photographer glanced at his watch. He grunted and withheld the time purposely, so that the first cop had to glance at his own watch before jotting down the time on his time table. He subtracted a few minutes, and indicated a t.o.a. for Carella and Bush, too.

Carella looked down at the back of the dead man's head. His face remained expressionless, except for a faint, passing film of pain which covered his eyes for a moment, and then darted away as fleetingly as a jack-rabbit.

'What'd they use?' he asked. 'A cannon?'

'A .45,' the first cop said. 'We've got the cartridge cases.'

'How many?'

'Two.'

'Figures,' Carella said. 'Why don't we flip him over?'

'Ambulance coming?' Bush asked quietly.

'Yeah,' the first cop said. 'Everybody's late tonight.'

'Everybody's drowning in sweat tonight,' Bush said. 'I can use a beer.'

'Come on,' Carella said, 'give me a hand here.'

The second cop bent down to help Carella. Together they rolled the body over. The flies swarmed up angrily, and then descended to the sidewalk again, and to the bloody broken flesh that had once been a face. In the darkness, Carella saw a gaping hole where the left eye should have been. There was another hole beneath the right eye, and the cheek bone was splintered outward, the jagged shards piercing the skin.

'Poor bastard,' Carella said. He would never get used to staring death in the face. He had been a cop for twelve years now, and he had learned to stomach the sheer, overwhelming, physical impact of death – but he would never get used to the other thing about death, the invasion of privacy that came with death, the reduction of pulsating life to a pile of bloody, fleshy rubbish.

'Anybody got a flash?' Bush asked.

The first cop reached into his left hip pocket. He thumbed a button, and a circle of light splashed onto the sidewalk.

'On his face,' Bush said.

The light swung up onto the dead man's face.

Bush swallowed. 'That's Reardon,' he said, his voice very quiet. And then, almost in a whisper, 'My God, that's Mike Reardon.'

Chapter Three

There were sixteen detectives assigned to the 87th Precinct, and David Foster was one of them. The precinct, in all truth, could have used a hundred and sixteen detectives and even then been understaffed. The precinct area spread South from the River Highway and the tall buildings which still boasted doormen and elevator operators to the Stem with its delicatessens and movie houses, on South to Culver Avenue and the Irish section, still South to the Puerto Rican section and then into Grover's Park, where muggers and rapists ran rife. Running East and West, the precinct covered a long total of some thirty-five streets. And packed into this rectangle – North and South from the river to the park, East and West for thirty-five blocks – was a population of 90,000 people.

David Foster was one of those people.

David Foster was a Negro.

He had been born in the precinct territory, and he had grown up there, and when he'd turned 21, being of sound mind and body, being four inches over the minimum requirement of five feet eight inches, having 20/20 vision without glasses, and not having any criminal record, he had taken the competitive Civil Service examination and had been appointed a patrolman.

The starting salary at the time had been $3,725 per annum, and Foster had earned his salary well. He had earned it so well that in the space of five years he had been appointed to the Detective Division. He was now a 3rd Grade Detective, and his salary was now $5,230 per annum, and he still earned it.

At one a.m., on the morning of July 24th, while a colleague named Mike Reardon lay spilling his blood into the gutter, David Foster was earning his salary by interrogating the man he and Bush had picked up in the bar knifing.

The interrogation was being conducted on the second floor of the precinct house. To the right of the desk on the first floor, there was an inconspicuous and dirty white sign with black letters which announced DETECTIVE DIVISION, and a pointing hand advised any visitor that the bulls hung out upstairs.

The stairs were metal, and narrow, but scrupulously clean. They went up for a total of sixteen risers, then turned back on themselves and continued on up for another sixteen risers, and there you were.

Where you were was a narrow, dimly-lighted corridor. There were two doors on the right of the open stairway, and a sign labelled them LOCKERS. If you turned left and walked down the corridor, you passed a wooden slatted bench on your left, a bench without a back on your right (set into a narrow alcove before the sealed doors of what had once been an elevator shaft), a door on your right marked MEN'S LAVATORY, and a door on your left over which a small sign hung, and the sign simply read CLERICAL.

At the end of the corridor was the detective squadroom.

You saw first a slatted rail divider. Beyond that, you saw desks and telephones, and a bulletin board with various photographs and notices on it, and a hanging light globe and beyond that more desks and the grilled windows that opened on the front of the building. You couldn't see very much that went on beyond the railing on your right because two huge metal filing cabinets blocked the desks on that side of the room. It was on that side of the room that Foster was interrogating the man he'd picked up in the bar earlier that night.

'What's your name?' he asked the man.

'*No hablo inglés,*' the man said.

'Oh, hell,' Foster said. He was a burly man with a deep chocolate colouring and warm brown eyes. He wore a white dress shirt, open at the throat. His sleeves were rolled up over muscular forearms.

'*Cuál es su nombre?*' he asked in hesitant Spanish.

'Thomas Perillo.'

'Your address?' He paused, thinking. '*Dirección?*'

'*Tres-tres-cuatro Mei-son.*'

'Age? *Edad?*'

Perillo shrugged.

'All right,' Foster said, 'where's the knife? Oh, God, we'll never get anywhere tonight. Look, *dónde está el cuchillo? Puede usted decirme?*'

'*Creo que no.*'

'Why not? For God's sake, you had a knife, didn't you?'

'*No sé.*'

'Look, you son of a bitch, you know damn well you had a knife. A dozen people saw you with it. Now how about it?'

Perillo was silent.

'*Tiene usted un cuchillo?*' Foster asked.

'*No.*'

'You're a liar!' Foster said. 'You *do* have a knife. What'd you do with it after you slashed that guy in the bar?'

'*Dónde está el servicio?*' Perillo asked.

'Never mind where the hell the men's room is,' Foster snapped. 'Stand up straight. What the hell do you think this is, the pool room? Take your hands out of your pockets.'

Perillo took his hands from his pockets.

'Now where's the knife?'

'*No sé.*'

'You don't know, you don't know,' Foster mimicked. 'All right, get the hell out of here. Sit down on the bench outside. I'm gonna get a cop in here who really speaks your language, pal. Now go sit down. Go ahead.'

'*Bien,*' Perillo said. '*Dónde está el servicio?*'

'Down the hall on your left. And don't take all night in there.'

Perillo went out. Foster grimaced. The man he'd cut hadn't been cut bad at all. If they knocked themselves out over every goddamn knifing they got, they'd be busy running down nothing but knifings. He wondered what it would be like to be stationed in a precinct where carving was something you did to a turkey. He grinned at his own humour, wheeled a typewriter over, and began typing up a report on the burglary they'd had several days back.

When Carella and Bush came in, they seemed in a big hurry. Carella walked directly to the phone, consulted a list of phone numbers beside it, and began dialling.

'What's up?' Foster said.

'That homicide,' Carella answered.

'Yeah?'

'It was Mike.'

'What do you mean? Huh?'

'Mike Reardon.'

'What?' Foster said. 'What?'

'Two slugs at the back of his head. I'm calling the Lieutenant. He's gonna want to move fast on this one.'

'Hey, is he kidding?' Foster said to Bush, and then he saw the look on Bush's face, and he knew this was not a joke.

Lieutenant Byrnes was the man in charge of the 87th Detective Squad. He had a small, compact body and a head like a rivet. His eyes were blue and tiny, but those eyes had seen a hell of a lot, and they didn't miss very much that went on around the lieutenant. The lieutenant knew his precinct was a trouble spot, and that was the way he liked it. It was the bad neighbourhoods that needed policemen, he was fond of saying, and he was proud to be a part of a squad that really earned its keep. There had once been sixteen men in his squad now there were fifteen.

Ten of those fifteen were gathered around him in the squadroom, the remaining five being out on plants from which they could not be yanked. The men sat in their chairs, or on the edges of desks, or they stood near the grilled windows, or they leaned against filing cabinets. The squadroom looked the way it might look at any of the times when the new shift was coming in to relieve the old one, except that there were no dirty jokes now. The men all knew that Mike Reardon was dead.

Acting Lieutenant Lynch stood alongside Byrnes while Byrnes filled his pipe. Byrnes had thick capable fingers, and he wadded the tobacco with his thumb, not looking up at the men.

Carella watched him. Carella admired and respected the lieutenant, even though many of the other men called him 'an old turd'. Carella knew cops who worked in precincts where the old man wielded a whip instead of a cerebellum. It wasn't good to work for a tyrant. Byrnes was all right, and Byrnes was also a good cop and a smart cop, and so Carella gave him his undivided attention, even though the lieutenant had not yet begun speaking.

Byrnes struck a wooden match and lighted his pipe. He gave the appearance of an unhurried man about to take his port after a heavy meal, but the wheels were grinding furiously inside his compact skull, and every fibre in his body was outraged at the death of one of his best men.

'No pep talk,' he said suddenly. 'Just go out and find the bastard.' He blew out a cloud of smoke and then waved it away with one of his short, wide hands. 'If you read the newspapers, and if you start believing them, you'll know that cops hate cop killers. That's the law of the jungle. That's the law of survival. The newspapers are wrong if they think any revenge motive is attached. We can't let a cop be killed because a cop is a symbol of law and order. If you take away the symbol, you get animals in the streets. We've got enough animals in the streets now.

'So I want you to find Reardon's killer, but not because Reardon was a cop assigned to this precinct, and not even because Reardon was a good cop. I want you to find that bastard because Reardon was a *man* – and a damned fine man.

'Handle it however you want to, you know your jobs. Give me progress reports on whatever you get from the files, and whatever you get in the streets. But find him. That's all.'

The lieutenant went back into his office with Lynch, and some of the cops went to the *modus operandi* file and began digging for information on thugs who used .45's. Some of the cops went to the Lousy File, the file of known criminals in the precinct, and they began searching for any cheap thieves who may have crossed Mike Reardon's path at one time or another. Some of the cops went to the Convictions File and began a methodical search of cards listing every conviction for which the precinct had been responsible, with a special eye out for cases on which Mike Reardon had worked. Foster went out into the corridor and told the suspect he'd questioned to get the hell home and to keep his nose clean. The rest of the cops took to the streets, and Carella and Bush were among them.

'He gripes me,' Bush said. 'He thinks he's Napoleon.'

'He's a good man,' Carella said.

'Well, *he* seems to think so, anyway.'

'Everything gripes you,' Carella said. 'You're maladjusted.'

'I'll tell you one thing,' Bush said. 'I'm getting an ulcer in this goddamn precinct. I never had trouble before, but since I got assigned to this precinct, I'm getting an ulcer. Now how do you account for that?'

There were a good many possible ways to account for Bush's ulcer and none of them had anything whatever to do with the precinct. But Carella didn't feel like arguing at the moment, and so he kept his peace. Bush simply nodded sourly.

'I want to call my wife,' he said.

'At two in the morning?' Carella asked incredulously.

'What's the matter with that?' Bush wanted to know. He was suddenly antagonistic.

'Nothing. Go ahead, call her.'

'I just want to check,' Bush said, and then he said, 'Check in.'

'Sure.'

'Hell, we may be going for days on this one.'

'Sure.'

'Anything wrong with calling her to let her know what's up?'

'Listen, are you looking for an argument,' Carella asked, smiling.

'No.'

'Then go call your wife, and get the hell off my back.'

Bush nodded emphatically. They stopped ouside an open candy store on Culver, and Bush went in to make his call. Carella stood outside, his back to the open counter at the store's front.

The city was very quiet. The tenements stretched grimy fingers towards the soft muzzle of the sky. Occasionally, a bathroom light winked like an opening eye in an otherwise blinded face. Two young Irish girls walked past the candy store, their high heels clattering on the pavement. He glanced momentarily at their legs and the thin summer frocks they wore. One of the girls winked unashamedly at him, and then both girls began giggling, and for no good reason he remembered something about lifting the skirts of an Irish lass, and the thought came to him full-blown so that he knew it was stored somewhere in his memory, and it seemed to him he had read it. Irish lasses, *Ulysses*? That had been one hell of a book to get through, pretty little lasses and all. I wonder what Bush reads? Bush is too busy to read. Bush is too busy worrying about his wife. God, does that man worry.

He glanced over his shoulder. Bush was still in the booth, talking rapidly. The man behind the counter leaned over a racing form, a toothpick angling up out of his mouth. A young kid sat at the end of the counter drinking an egg cream. Carella sucked in a breath of fetid air. The door to the phone booth opened, and Bush stepped out, mopping his brow. He nodded at the counterman, and then went out to join Carella.

'Hot as hell in that booth,' he said.

'Everything okay?' Carella asked.

'Sure,' Bush said. He looked at Carella suspiciously. 'Why shouldn't it be?'

'No reason. Any ideas where we should start?'

'This isn't going to be such a cinch,' Bush said. 'Any stupid son of a bitch with a grudge could've done it.'

'Or anybody in the middle of committing a crime.'

'We ought to leave it to Homicide. We're in over our heads.'

'We haven't even started yet, and you say we're in over our heads. What the hell's wrong with you, Hank?'

'Nothing,' Bush said, 'only I don't happen to think of cops as masterminds, that's all.'

'That's a nice thing for a cop to say.'

'It's the truth. Look, this detective tag is a laugh, and you know it as well as I do. All you need to be a detective is a strong pair of legs, and a stubborn streak. The legs take you around to all the various dumps you have to go to, and the stubborn streak keeps you from quitting. You follow each separate trail mechanically, and if you're lucky, one of the trails pays off. If you're not lucky, it doesn't. Period.'

'And brains don't enter into it at all, huh?'

'Only a little. It doesn't take much brains to be a cop.'

'Okay.'

'Okay what?'

'Okay, I don't want to argue. If Reardon got it trying to stop somebody in the commission of a crime ...'

'That's another thing that burns me up about cops,' Bush said.

'You're a regular cop hater, aren't you?' Carella asked.

'This whole goddamn city is full of cop haters. You think anybody respects a cop? Symbol of law and order! The old man ought to get out there and face life. Anybody who ever got a parking tag is automatically a cop hater. That's the way it is.'

'Well, it sure as hell shouldn't be that way,' Carella said, somewhat angrily.

Bush shrugged. 'What burns me up about cops is they don't speak English.'

'What?'

'In the commission of a crime!' Bush mocked. 'Cop talk. Did you ever hear a cop say "We caught him"? No. He says, "We apprehended him".'

'I never heard a cop say "We apprehended him",' Carella said.

'I'm talking about for official publication,' Bush said.

'Well, that's different. Everybody talks fancy when it's for official publication.'

'Cops especially.'

'Why don't you turn in your shield? Become a hackie or something?'

'I'm toying with the idea.' Bush smiled suddenly. His entire tirade had been delivered in his normally hushed voice, and now that he was smiling, it was difficult to remember that he'd been angry at all.

'Anyway, I thought the bars,' Carella said. 'I mean, if this *is* a grudge kind of thing, it might've been somebody from the neighbourhood. And we may be able to pick up something in the bars. Who the hell knows?'

'I can use a beer, anyway,' Bush said. 'I've been wanting a beer ever since I come on tonight.'

The Shamrock was one of a million bars all over the world with the same name. It squatted on Culver Avenue between a pawn shop and a Chinese laundry. It was an all-night joint, and it catered to the Irish clientele that lined Culver. Occasionally, a Puerto Rican wandered into *The Shamrock*, but such offtrail excursions were discouraged by those among *The Shamrock*'s customers who owned quick tempers and powerful fists. The cops stopped at the bar often, not to wet their whistles – because drinking on duty was strictly forbidden by the rules and regulations – but to make sure that too many quick tempers did not mix with too much whisky or too many fists. The flareups within the gaily decorated walls of the bar were now few and far between, or – to be poetic – less frequent than they had been in the good old days when the neighbourhood had first succumbed to the Puerto Rican assault wave. In those days, not speaking English too well, not reading signs too well, the Puerto Ricans stumbled into *The Shamrock* with remarkably ignorant rapidity. The staunch defenders of America for the Americans, casually ignoring the fact that Puerto Ricans were and are Americans, spent many a pugilistic evening proving their point. The bar was often brilliantly decorated with spilled blood. But that was in the good old days. In the bad new days, you could go into *The Shamrock* for a week running, and not see more than one or two broken heads.

There was a Ladies Invited sign in the window of the bar, but not many ladies accepted the invitation. The drinkers were, instead, neighbourhood men who tired of the four walls of their dreary tenement flats, who sought the carefree camaraderie of other men who had similarly grown weary of their own homes. Their wives were out playing Bingo on Tuesdays, or at the movies collecting a piece of china on Wednesdays, or across the street with the Sewing Club ('We so and so and so and so') on Thursdays, and so it went. So what was wrong with a friendly brew in a neighbourhood tavern? Nothing.

Except when the cops showed.

Now there was something very disgusting about policemen in general, and bulls in particular. Sure, you could go through the motions of saying, 'How are yuh, this evenin', Officer Dugan?' and all that sort of rot, and you could really and truly maybe hold a fond spot in the old ticker for the new rookie, but you still couldn't deny that a cop sitting next to you when you were half-way towards getting a snootful was a somewhat disconcerting thing and would likely bring on the goblins in the morning. Not that anyone had anything against cops. It was just that cops should not loiter around bars and spoil a man's earnest drinking. Nor should cops hang around book joints and spoil a man's earnest gambling. Nor should they hang around brothels and spoil a man's earnest endeavours too, cops simply shouldn't hang around, that was all.

And bulls, bulls were cops in disguise, only worse.

So what did those two big jerks at the end of the bar want?

'A beer, Harry,' Bush said.

'Comin' up,' Harry the bartender answered. He drew the beer and brought it over to where Bush and Carella were seated. 'Good night for a beer, ain't it?' Harry said.

'I never knew a bartender who didn't give you a commercial when you ordered a beer on a hot night,' Bush said quietly.

Harry laughed, but only because his customer was a cop. Two men at the shuffleboard table were arguing about an Irish free state. The late movie on television was about a Russian empress.

'You fellows here on business?' Harry asked.

'Why?' Bush said. 'You got any for us?'

'No, I was just wonderin'. I mean, it ain't often we get the bu ... it ain't often a detective drops by,' Harry said.

'That's because you run such a clean establishment,' Bush said.

'Ain't none cleaner on Culver.'

'Not since they ripped your phone booth out,' Bush said.

'Yeah, well, we were gettin' too many phone calls.'

'You were taking too many bets,' Bush said, his voice even. He picked up the glass of beer, dipped his upper lip into the foam, and then downed it.

'No, no kiddin',' Harry said. He did not like to think of the close call he'd had with that damn phone booth and the State Attorney's Commission. 'You fellows lookin' for somebody?'

'Kind of quiet tonight,' Carella said.

Harry smiled, and a gold tooth flashed at the front of his mouth. 'Oh, always quiet in here, fellows, you know that.'

'Sure,' Carella said, nodding. 'Danny Gimp drop in?'

'No, haven't seen him tonight. Why? What's up?'

'That's good beer,' Bush said.

'Like another?'

'No, thanks.'

'Say, are you sure nothing's wrong?' Harry asked.

'What's with you, Harry? Somebody do something wrong here?' Carella asked.

'What? No, hey, no I hope I didn't give you that impression. It's just kind of strange, you fellows dropping in. I mean, we haven't had any trouble here or anything.'

'Well, that's good,' Carella said. 'See anybody with a gun lately.'

'A gun?'

'Yeah.'

'What kind of gun?'

'What kind did you see?'

'I didn't see any kind.' Harry was sweating. He drew a beer for himself and drank it hastily.

'None of the young punks in with zip guns or anything?' Bush asked quietly.

'Oh, well zip guns,' Harry said, wiping the foam from his lip, 'I mean, you see them all the time.'

'And nothing bigger?'

'Bigger like what? Like you mean a .32 or a .38?'

'Like we mean a .45,' Carella said.

'The last .45 I seen in here,' Harry said, thinking, 'was away back in ...' He shook his head. 'No, that wouldn't help you. What happened? Somebody get shot?'

'Away back *when*?' Bush asked.

'Fifty, fifty-one, it must've been. Kid discharged from the Army. Come in here wavin' a .45 around. He was lookin' for trouble all right, that kid. Dooley busted it up. You remember Dooley? He used to have this beat before he got transferred out to another precinct. Nice kid. Always used to stop by and ...'

'He still live in the neighbourhood?' Bush asked.

'Huh? Who?'

'The guy who was in here waving the .45 around.'

'Oh, him.' Harry's brows swooped down over his eyes. 'Why?'

'I'm asking you,' Bush said. 'Does he or doesn't he?'

'Yeah. I guess. Why?'

'Where?'

'Listen,' Harry said, 'I don't want to get nobody in trouble.'

'You're not getting anybody in trouble,' Bush said. 'Does this guy still own the .45?'

'I don't know.'

'What happened that night? When Dooley busted it up.'

'Nothing. The kid had a load on. You know, just out of the Army, like that.'

'Like what?'

'Like he was wavin' the gun around. I don't even think it was loaded. I think the barrel was leaded.'

'Are you sure it was?'

'Well, no.'

'Did Dooley take the gun away from him?'

'Well ...' Harry paused and mopped his brow. 'Well, I don't think Dooley even saw the gun.'

'If he busted it up ...'

'Well,' Harry said, 'one of the fellows saw Dooley comin' down the street, and they kind of calmed the kid down and got him out of here.'

'*Before* Dooley came in?'

'Well, yeah. Yeah.'

'And the kid took the gun with him when he left?'

'Yeah,' Harry said. 'Look, I don't want no trouble in my place, you follow?'

'I follow,' Bush said. 'Where does he live?'

Harry blinked his eyes. He looked down at the bar top.

'Where?' Bush repeated.

'On Culver.'

'Where on Culver?'

'The house on the corner of Culver and Mason. Look, fellows ...'

'This guy mention anything about not liking cops?' Carella asked.

'No, no,' Harry said. 'He's a fine boy. He just had a couple of sheets to the wind that night, that's all.'

'You know Mike Reardon?'

'Oh, sure,' Harry said.

'This kid know Mike?'

'Well, I can't say as I know. Look, the kid was just squiffed that night, that's all.'

'What's his name?'

'Look, he was only tanked up, that's all. Hell, it was away back in 1950.'

'What's his name?'

'Frank. Frank Clarke. With an "e".'

'What do you think Steve?' Bush asked Carella.

Carella shrugged. 'It came too easy. It's never good when it comes that easy.'

'Let's check it, anyway,' Bush said.

Chapter Four

There are smells inside a tenement, and they are not only the smell of cabbage. The smell of cabbage, to many, is and always will be a good wholesome smell and there are many who resent the steady propaganda which links cabbage with poverty.

The smell inside a tenement is the smell of life.

It is the smell of every function of life, the sweating, the cooking, the elimination, the breeding. It is all these smells, and they are wedded into one gigantic smell which hits the nostrils the moment you enter the downstairs doorway. For the smell has been inside the building for decades. It has seeped through the floorboards and permeated the walls. It clings to the banister and the linoleum-covered steps. It crouches in corners and it hovers about the naked light bulbs on each landing. The smell is always there, day and night. It is the stench of living, and it never sees the light of day, and it never sees the crisp brittleness of starlight.

It was there on the morning of July 24 at 3:00 a.m. It was there in full force because the heat of the day had baked it into the walls. It hit Carella as he and

Bush entered the building. He snorted through his nostrils and then struck a match and held it to the mailboxes.

'There it is,' Bush said. 'Clarke. 3B.'

Carella shook out the match and they walked towards the steps. The garbage cans were in for the night, stacked on the ground floor landing behind the steps. Their aroma joined the other smells to clash in a medley of putridity. The building slept, but the smells were awake. On the second floor, a man – or a woman – snored loudly. On each door, close to the floor, the circular trap for a milk bottle lock hung despondently, awaiting the milkman's arrival. On one of the doors hung a plaque, and the plaque read IN GOD WE TRUST. And behind that door, there was undoubtedly the unbending steel bar of a police lock, embedded in the floor and tilted to lean against the door.

Carella and Bush laboured up to the third floor. The light bulb on the third floor landing was out. Bush struck a match.

'Down the hall there.'

'You want to do this up big?' Carella asked.

'He's got a .45 in there, hasn't he?'

'Still.'

'What the hell, my wife doesn't need my insurance money,' Bush said.

They walked to the door and flanked it. They drew their service revolvers with nonchalance. Carella didn't for a moment believe he'd need his gun, but caution never hurt. He drew back his left hand and knocked on the door.

'Probably asleep,' Bush said.

'Betokens a clear conscience,' Carella answered. He knocked again.

'Who is it?' a voice answered.

'Police. Want to open up?'

'Oh, for God's sake,' the voice mumbled. 'Just a minute.'

'We won't need these,' Bush said. He holstered his gun, and Carella followed suit. From within the apartment, they could hear bed springs creaking, and then a woman's voice asking 'What is it?' They heard footsteps approaching the door, and then someone fumbled with the police lock on the inside, and the heavy steel bar clattered when it was dropped to the floor. The door opened a crack.

'What do you want?' the voice said.

'Police. We'd like to ask you a few questions.'

'At this time of the morning? Can't it wait?'

'Afraid it can't.'

'Well, what's the matter? There a burglar in the building?'

'No. We'd just like to ask you some questions. You're Frank Clarke, aren't you?'

'Yeah.' Clarke paused. 'Let me see your badge.'

Carella reached into his pocket for the leather case to which his shield was pinned. He held it up to the crack in the door.

'I can't see nothing,' Clarke said. 'Just a minute.'

'Who is it?' the woman asked.

'The cops,' Clarke mumbled. He stepped away from the door, and then a light flashed inside the apartment. He came back to the door. Carella held up the badge again.

'Yeah, okay,' Clarke said. 'What do you want?'

'You own a .45, Clarke?'

'What?'

'A .45. Do you own one?'

'My God, is that what you want to know? Is that what you come banging on the door for in the middle of the night? Ain't you guys got any sense at all? I got to go to work in the morning.'

'Do you have a .45, or don't you?'

'Who said I had one?'

'Never mind who. How about it?'

'Why do you want to know? I been here all night.'

'Anybody to swear for that?'

Clarke's voice lowered. 'Hey, look, fellows, I got somebody with me, you know what I mean? Look, give me a break, will you?'

'What about the gun?'

'Yeah. I got one.'

'A .45?'

'Yeah. Yeah, it's a .45.'

'Mind if we take a look at it?'

'What for? I've got a permit for it.'

'We'd like to look at it anyway.'

'Hey, look, what the hell kind of a routine is this, anyway? I told you I got a permit for the gun. What did I do wrong? Whattya want from me, anyway?'

'We want to see the .45,' Bush said. 'Get it.'

'You got a search warrant?' Clarke asked.

'Never mind that,' Bush said. 'Get the gun.'

'You can't come in here without a search warrant. And you can't bulldoze me into gettin' the gun, either. I don't want to get that gun, then you can whistle.'

'How old's the girl in there?' Bush asked.

'What?'

'You heard me. Wake up, Clarke!'

'She's 21, and you're barkin' up the wrong tree,' Clarke said. 'We're engaged.'

From down the hall, someone shouted, 'Hey, shut up, willya? For Christ's sake! Go down to the poolroom, you want to talk!'

'How about letting us in, Clarke?' Carella asked gently. 'We're waking your neighbours.'

'I don't have to let you in noplace. Go get a search warrant.'

'I know you don't, Clarke. But a cop's been killed, and he was killed with a .45, and if I were you I wouldn't play this so goddamn cosy. Now how about opening that door and showing us you're clean? How about it, Clarke?'

'A cop? You say, a cop! Why didn't you say so? Just a ... just a minute, willya? Just a minute.' He moved away from the door. Carella could hear him talking to the woman, and he could hear the woman's whispered answer. Clarke came back to the door and took off the night chain. 'Come on in,' he said.

There were dishes stacked in the kitchen sink. The kitchen was a six-by-eight rectangle, and adjoining that was the bedroom. The girl stood in the bedroom doorway. She was a short blonde, somewhat dumpy. She wore a man's bathrobe. Her eyes were puffed with sleep, and she wore no makeup.

She blinked her eyes and stared at Carella and Bush as they moved into the kitchen.

Clarke was a short man with bushy black brows and brown eyes. His nose was long, broken sharply in the middle. His lips were thick, and he needed a shave badly. He was wearing pyjama pants and nothing else. He stood bare-chested and bare-footed in the glare of the kitchen light. The water tap dripped its tattoo on the dirty dishes in the sink.

'Let's see the gun,' Bush said.

'I got a permit for it,' Clarke answered. 'Okay if I smoke?'

'It's your apartment.'

'Gladys,' Clarke said, 'there's a pack on the dresser. Bring some matches, too, willya?' The girl moved into the darkness of the bedroom, and Clarke whispered, 'You guys sure picked a hell of a time to come calling, all right.' He tried a smile, but neither Carella or Bush seemed amused, and so he dropped it instantly. The girl came back with the package of cigarettes. She hung one on her lip, and then handed the pack to Clarke. He lighted his own cigarette and then handed the matches to the blonde.

'What kind of a permit?' Carella asked. 'Carry or premises?'

'Carry,' Clarke said.

'How come?'

'Well, it used to be premises. I registered the gun when I got out of the Army. It was a gift,' he said quickly. 'From my captain.'

'Go ahead.'

'So I got a premises permit when I was discharged. That's the law, ain't it?'

'You're telling the story,' Bush said.

'Well, that's the way I understood it. Either that, or I had to get the barrel leaded up. I don't remember. Anyway, I got the permit.'

'*Is* the barrel leaded?'

'Hell, no. What do I need a permit for a dead gun for? I had this premises permit, and then I got a job with a jeweller, you know? Like I had to make a lot of valuable deliveries, things like that. So I had it changed to a carry permit.'

'When was this?'

'Couple of months back.'

'Which jeweller do you work for?'

'I quit that job,' Clarke said.

'All right, get the gun. And get the permit, too, while you're at it.'

'Sure,' Clarke said. He went to the sink, held his cigarette under the dripping tap, and then dropped the soggy butt in with the dishes. He walked past the girl and into the bedroom.

'This is some time of night to be asking questions,' the girl said angrily.

'We're sorry, Miss,' Carella said.

'Yeah, I'll bet you are.'

'We didn't mean to disturb your beauty sleep,' Bush said nastily.

The girl raised one eyebrow. 'Then why did you?' She blew out a cloud of smoke, the way she had seen movie sirens do. Clarke came back into the room holding the .45. Bush's hand moved imperceptibly towards his right hip and the holster there.

'Put it on the table,' Carella said.

Clarke put the gun on the table.

'Is it loaded?' Carella asked.

'I think so.'

'Don't you know?'

'I ain't even looked at the thing since I quit that job.'

Carella draped a handkerchief over his spread fingers and picked up the gun. He slid the magazine out. 'It's loaded, all right,' he said. Quickly, he sniffed the barrel.

'You don't have to smell,' Clarke said. 'It ain't been fired since I got out of the Army.'

'It came close once, though, didn't it?'

'Huh?'

'That night in *The Shamrock*.'

'Oh, that,' Clarke said. 'Is that why you're here? Hell, I was looped that night. I didn't mean no harm.'

Carella slammed the magazine back into place. 'Where's the permit, Clarke?'

'Oh, yeah. I looked around in there. I couldn't find it.'

'You're sure you've got one?'

'Yeah, I'm sure. I just can't find it.'

'You'd better take another look. A good one, this time.'

'I did take a good look. I can't find it. Look, I got a permit. You can check on it. I wouldn't kid you. Who was the cop got killed?'

'Want to take another look for the permit?'

'I already told you, I can't find it. Look, I got one.'

'You *had* one, pal,' Carella said. 'You just lost it.'

'Huh? What? What'd you say?'

'When a cop asks you for your permit, you produce it or you lose it.'

'Well, hell, I just misplaced it temporarily. Look, you can check all this. I mean . . . look, what's the matter with you guys, anyway? I didn't do nothing. I been here all night. You can ask Gladys. Ain't that right, Gladys?'

'He's been here all night,' Gladys said.

'We're taking the gun,' Carella said. 'Give him a receipt for it, Hank.'

'That ain't been fired in years,' Clarke said. 'You'll see. And you check on that permit. I got one. You check on it.'

'We'll let you know,' Carella said. 'You weren't planning on leaving the city were you?'

'Hell, no. Where would I go?'

'Back to sleep is as good a place as any,' the blonde said.

Chapter Five

The pistol permit was on Steve Carella's desk when he reported for work at 4:00 p.m. on the afternoon of July 24. He had worked until eight in the morning, gone home for six hours' sleep, and was back at his desk now, looking a little bleary-eyed but otherwise none the worse for wear.

The heat had persisted all day long, a heavy yellow blanket that smothered the city in its woolly grip. Carella did not like the heat. He had never liked summer, even as a kid, and now that he was an adult and a cop, the only memorable characteristic summer seemed to have was that it made dead bodies decompose more quickly.

He loosened his collar the instant he entered the squadroom, and when he got to his desk, he rolled up his sleeves, and then picked up the pistol permit. Quickly, he scanned the printed form.

License No.	Date	Police Department	Year	

PISTOL LICENSE APPLICATION

(APPLICATION MUST BE MADE IN DUPLICATE)

I Hereby Apply for License to Carry a Revolver or Pistol upon my person or Possession on premises

37-12 Culver Avenue

For the following reasons: Make deliveries for jewelry firm.

    Clarke   Francis D.   37 -12 Culver Ave.

(PRINT)	Surname	Given Name	Initials	Number	Street

There was more, a lot more, but it didn't interest Carella. Clarke had indeed owned a pistol permit – but that didn't mean he hadn't used the pistol on a cop named Mike Reardon.

Carella shoved the permit to one side of his desk, glanced at his watch, and then reached for the phone automatically. Quickly, he dialled Bush's home number and then waited, his hand sweating on the receiver. The phone rang six times, and then a woman's voice said, 'Hello?'

'Alice?'

'Who's this?'

'Steve Carella.'

'Oh. Hello, Steve.'

'Did I wake you?'

'Yes.'

'Hank's not here yet. He's all right, isn't he?'

'He left a little while ago,' Alice said. The sleep was beginning to leave her voice already. Alice Bush was a cop's wife who generally slept when her husband did, adjusting her schedule to fit his. Carella had spoken to her on a good many mornings and afternoons, and he always marvelled at the way she could come almost instantly awake within the space of three or four sentences. Her voice invariably sounded like the first faint rattle of impending death when she picked up the receiver. As the conversation progressed, it modulated into the dulcet whine of a middle-aged Airedale, and then into the disconcertingly sexy voice which was the normal speaking voice of Hank's wife. Carella had met her on one occasion, when he and Hank had shared a late snack with her, and he knew that she was a dynamic blonde with a magnificent figure and the brownest eyes he'd ever seen. From what Bush had expansively delivered about personal aspects of his home life, Carella knew that Alice slept in clinging black, sheer nightgowns. The knowledge was unnerving, for whenever Carella roused her out of bed, he automatically formed a mental picture of the well-rounded blonde he'd met, and the picture was always dressed as Hank had described it.

He generally, therefore, cut his conversations with Alice short, feeling somewhat guilty about the artistic inclinations of his mind. This morning, though, Alice seemed to be in a talkative mood.

'I understand one of your colleagues got knocked off,' she said.

Carella smiled, in spite of the topic's grimness. Alice sometimes had a peculiar way of mixing the King's English with choice bits of underworld and police vernacular.

'Yes,' he said.

'I'm awfully sorry,' she answered, her voice changing. 'Please be careful, you and Hank. If a cheap hood is shooting up the streets ...'

'We'll be careful,' he said. 'I've got to go now, Alice.'

'I leave Hank in capable hands,' Alice said, and she hung up without saying goodbye.

Carella grinned and shrugged, and then put the receiver back into the cradle. David Foster, his brown face looking scrubbed and shining, ambled over to the desk. 'Afternoon Steve,' he said.

'Hi, Dave. What've you got?'

'Ballistics report on that .45 you brought in last night.'

'Any luck?'

'Hasn't been fired since Old King Cole ordered the bowl.'

'Well, that narrows it down,' Carella said. 'Now we've only got the nine million, nine hundred ninety-nine thousand other people in this fair city to contend with.'

'I don't like it when cops get killed,' Foster said. His brow lowered menacingly, giving him the appearance of a bull ducking his head to charge at the *muleta*. 'Mike was my partner. He was a good guy.'

'I know.'

'I been trying to think who,' Foster said. 'I got my personal I.B. right up here, and I been leafing through them mug shots one by one.' He tapped his temple. 'I been turning them over and studying them, and so far I haven't got anything, but give me time. Somebody musta had it in for Mike, and when that face falls into place, that guy's gonna wish he was in Alaska.'

'Tell you the truth,' Carella said, 'I wish I was there right now.'

'Hot, ain't it?' Foster said, classically understating the temperature and humidity.

'Yeah.' From the corner of his eye, Carella saw Bush walk down the corridor, push through the railing, and sign in. He walked to Carella's desk, pulled over a swivel chair and plopped into it disconsolately.

'Rough night?' Foster asked, grinning.

'The roughest,' Bush said in his quiet voice.

'Clarke was a blank,' Carella told him.

'I figured as much. Where do we go from here?'

'That's a good question.'

'Coroner's report in yet?'

'No.'

'The boys picked up some hoods for questioning,' Foster said. 'We might give them the once over.'

'Where are they? Downstairs?' Carella asked.

'In the Waldorf Suite,' Foster said, referring to the detention cells on the first floor of the building.

'Why don't you call down for them?'

'Sure,' Foster said.

'Where's the Skipper?'

'He's over at Homicide North. He's trying to goose them into some real action on this one.'

'You see the paper this morning?' Bush asked.

'No,' Carella said.

'Mike made the front page. Have a look.' He put the paper on Carella's desk. Carella held it up so that Foster could see it while he spoke on the phone.

'Shot him in the back,' Foster mumbled. 'That lousy bastard.' He spoke into the phone and then hung up. The men lighted cigarettes, and Bush phoned out for coffee, and then they sat around gassing. The prisoners arrived before the coffee did.

There were two men, both unshaven, both tall, both wearing short-sleeved sports shirts. The physical resemblance ended there. One of the men owned a handsome face, with regular features and white, even teeth. The other man looked as if his face had challenged a concrete mixer and lost. Carella recognized both of them at once. Mentally, he flipped over their cards in the Lousy File.

'Were they picked up together?' he asked the uniformed cop who brought them into the squadroom.

'Yeah,' the cop said.

'Where?'

'13th and Shippe. They were sitting in a parked car.'

'Any law against that?' the handsome one asked.

'At three in the morning,' the uniformed cop added.

'Okay,' Carella said. 'Thanks.'

'What's your name?' Bush asked the handsome one.

'You know my name, cop.'

'Say it again. I like the sound.'

'I'm tired.'

'You're gonna be a lot more tired before this is finished. Now cut the comedy, and answer the questions. Your name?'

'Terry.'

'Terry what?'

'Terry McCarthy. What the hell is this, a joke? You know my name.'

'How about your buddy?'

'You know him, too. He's Clarence Kelly.'

'What were you doing in that car?' Carella asked.

'Looking at dirty pictures,' McCarthy said.

'Possession of pornography,' Carella said dully. 'Take that down, Hank.'

'Hey, wait a minute,' McCarthy said. 'I was only wisecrackin'.'

'DON'T WISECRACK ON MY TIME!!' Carella shouted.

'Okay, okay, don't get sore.'

'What were you doing in that car?'

'Sitting.'

'You always sit in parked cars at three in the a.m.?' Foster asked.

'Sometimes,' McCarthy said.

'What else were you doing?'

'Talking.'

'What about?'

'Everything.'

'Philosophy?' Bush asked.

'Yeah,' McCarthy said.

'What'd you decide?'

'We decided it ain't wise to sit in parked cars at three in the morning. There's always some cop who's got to fill his pinch book.'

Carella tapped a pencil on the desk. 'Don't get me mad, McCarthy,' he said. 'I just come from six hours' sleep, and I don't feel like listening to a vaudeville routine. Did you know Mike Reardon?'

'Who?'

'Mike Reardon. A detective attached to this precinct.'

McCarthy shrugged. He turned to Kelly. 'We know him, Clarence?'

'Yeah,' Clarence said. 'Reardon. That rings a bell.'

'How big a bell?' Foster asked.

'Just a tiny tinkle so far,' Kelly said, and he began laughing. The laugh died when he saw the bulls weren't quite appreciating his humour.

'Did you see him last night?'

'No.'

'How do you know?'

'We didn't run across any bulls last night,' Kelly said.

'Do you usually?'

'Well, sometimes.'

'Were you heeled when they pulled you in?'

'What?'

'Come on,' Foster said.

'No.'

'We'll check that.'

'Yeah, go ahead,' McCarthy said. 'We didn't even have a water pistol between us.'

'What were you doing in the car?'

'I just told you,' McCarthy said.

'The story stinks. Try again,' Carella answered.

Kelly sighed. McCarthy looked at him.

'Well?' Carella said.

'I was checkin' up on my dame,' Kelly said.

'Yeah?' Bush said.

'Truth,' Kelly said. 'So help me God, may I be struck dead right this goddamn minute.'

'What's there to check up on?' Bush asked.

'Well, you know.'

'No, I don't know. Tell me.'

'I figured she was maybe slippin' around.'

'Slipping around with who?' Bush asked.

'Well, that's what I wanted to find out.'

'And what were you doing with him, McCarthy?'

'I was helping him check,' McCarthy said, smiling.

'Was she?' Bush asked, a bored expression on his face.

'No, I don't think so,' Kelly said.

'Don't check again,' Bush said. 'Next time we're liable to find you with the burglar's tools.'

'Burglar's tools!' McCarthy said, shocked.

'Gee, Detective Bush,' Kelly said, 'you know us better than that.'

'Get the hell out of here,' Bush said.

'We can go home?'

'You can go to hell, for my part,' Bush informed them.

'Here's the coffee,' Foster said.

The released prisoners sauntered out of the squadroom. The three detectives paid the delivery boy for the coffee and then pulled chairs up to one of the desks.

'I heard a good one last night,' Foster said.

'Let's hear it,' Carella prompted.

'This guy is a construction worker, you see?'

'Yeah.'

'Working up on a girder about sixty floors above the street.'

'Yeah?'

'The lunch whistle blows. He knocks off, goes to the end of the girder, sits down, and puts his lunch box on his lap. He opens the box, takes out a sandwich and very carefully unwraps the waxed paper. Then he bites into it. "Goddamn!" he says, "peanut butter!" and he throws the sandwich down the sixty floors to the street.'

'I don't get it,' Bush said, sipping his coffee.

'I'm not finished yet,' Foster said, grinning, hardly able to contain his glee.

'Go ahead,' Carella said.

'He reaches into the box,' Foster said, 'for the next sandwich. He very carefully unwraps the waxed paper. He bites into the sandwich. "Goddamn!" he says again, "peanut butter!" and he flings that second sandwich down the sixty floors to the street.'

'Yeah,' Carella said.

'He opens the third sandwich,' Foster said. 'This time it's ham. This time he likes it. He eats the sandwich all up.'

'This is gonna go on all night,' Bush said. 'You shoulda stood in bed, Dave.'

'No wait a minute, wait a minute,' Foster said. 'He opens the fourth sandwich. He bites into it. "Goddamn!" he says again, "peanut butter!" and he flings that sandwich too down the sixty floors to the street. Well, there's another construction worker sitting on a girder just a little bit above this fellow. He looks down and says, "Say, fellow, I've been watching you with them sandwiches."

'"So what?" the first guy says.'

'"You married?" the second guy asks.'

'"Yes, I'm married."'

'The second guy shakes his head, "How long you been married?"'

'"Ten years," the first guy says.'

'"And your wife still doesn't know what kind of sandwiches you like?"'

'The first guy points his finger up at the guy above him and yells, "You leave my wife out of this. I made those goddamn sandwiches myself!"'

Carella burst out laughing, almost choking on his coffee. Bush stared at Foster dead-panned.

'I still don't get it,' Bush said. 'What's so funny about a guy married ten years whose wife doesn't know what kind of sandwiches he likes? That's not funny. That's a tragedy.'

'He made the sandwiches *himself*,' Foster said.

'So then it's a psycho joke. Psycho jokes don't appeal to me. You got to be nuts to appreciate a psycho joke.'

'I appreciate it,' Carella said.

'So? That proves my point,' Bush answered.

'Hank didn't get enough sleep,' Carella said to Foster. Foster winked.

'I got plenty of sleep,' Bush said.

'Ah-ha,' Carella said. 'Then that explains it.'

'What the hell do you mean by that?' Bush said, annoyed.

'Oh, forget it. Drink your coffee.'

'A man doesn't get a joke, right away his sex life gets dragged in. Do I ask you how much sleep you get or don't get?'

'No,' Carella said.

'Okay. Okay.'

One of the patrolmen walked into the squadroom. 'Desk sergeant asked me to give you this,' he said. 'Just came up from Downtown.'

'Probably that Coroner's report,' Carella said, taking the manila envelope. 'Thanks.'

The patrolman nodded and went out. Carella opened the envelope.

'Is it?' Foster asked.

BULLET

Calibre	Weight	Twist	No. of Grooves
.45	230grms.	16L	6

Width of land marks		Width of groove marks	
	.071		.158

Metal Case		Half Metal		Soft Point	
	Brass				No

Deceased	Michael Reardon		Date	July 24th

Remarks: Remington bullet taken from wooden booth

behind body of Michael Reardon

'Yeah. Something else, too.' He pulled a card from the envelope. 'Oh, report on the slugs they dug out of the theatre booth.'

'Let's see it,' Hank said.

Carella handed him the card.

'Argh, so what does it tell us?' Bush said, still smarting from the earlier badinage.

'Nothing,' Carella answered, 'until we get the gun that fired it.'

'What about the Coroner's report?' Foster asked.

Carella slipped it out of the envelope.

CORONER'S PRELIMINARY

AUTOPSY REPORT

MICHAEL REARDON

Male, apparent age 42; chronological age 38. Approximate weight 210 pounds; height 289 cm.

GROSS INSPECTION

HEAD: 1.0 × 1.25 cm circular perforation visible 3.1 centimetres laterally to the left of external occipital protuberance (inion). Wound edges slightly inverted. Flame zone and second zone reveal heavy embedding of powder grains. A number 22 catheter inserted through the wound in the occipital region of the skull transverses ventrally and emerges through the right orbit. Point of emergence has left a gaping rough-edged wound measuring 3.7 centimetres in diameter.

There is a second perforation located 6.2 centimetres laterally to the left of the tip of the right mastoid process of the temporal bone, measuring 1.0 × 1.33 centimetres. A number 22 catheter inserted through this second wound passes anteriorly and ventrally and emerges through a perforation measuring approximately 3.5 centimetres in diameter through the right maxilla. The edges of the remaining portion of the right maxilla are splintered.

BODY: Gross inspection of remaining portion of body is negative for demonstrable pathology.

REMARKS: On craniotomy with brain examination, there is evidence of petechiae along course of projectile; splinters of cranial bone are embedded within the brain substance.

MICROSCOPIC: Examination of brain reveals minute petechiae as well as bone substance within brain matter. Microscopic examination of brain tissue is essentially negative for pathology.

'He did a good job,' Foster said.

'Yeah,' Bush answered.

Carella sighed and looked at his watch. 'It's going to be a long night, fellers,' he said.

Chapter Six

He had not seen Teddy Franklin since Mike took the slugs.

Generally, in the course of running down something, he would drop in to see her spending a few minutes with her before rushing off again. And, of course, he spent all his free time with her because he was in love with the girl.

He had met her less than six months ago, when she'd been working addressing envelopes for a small firm on the fringe of the precinct territory. The firm reported a burglary, and Carella had been assigned to it. He had been taken instantly with her buoyant beauty, asked her out, and that had been the beginning. He had also, in the course of investigation, cracked the burglary – but that didn't seem important now. The important thing now was Teddy. Even the firm had gone the way of most small firms, fading into the abyss of a corporate dissolution, leaving her without a job but with enough saved money to maintain herself for a while. He honestly hoped it would only be for a while, a short while at that. This was the girl he wanted to marry. This was the girl he wanted for his own.

Thinking of her, thinking of the progression of slow traffic lights which kept him from racing to her side, he cursed Ballistics Reports and Coroner's Reports, and people who shot cops in the back of the head, and he cursed the devilish instrument known as the telephone and the fact that the instrument was worthless with a girl like Teddy. He glanced at his watch. It was close to midnight, and she didn't know he was coming, but he'd take the chance, anyway. He wanted to see her.

When he reached her apartment building in Riverhead, he parked the car and locked it. The street was very quiet. The building was old and sedate, covered with lush ivy. A few windows blinked wide-eyed at the stifling heat of the night, but most of the tenants were asleep or trying to sleep. He glanced up at her window, pleased when he saw the light was still burning. Quickly, he mounted the steps, stopping outside her door.

He did not knock.

Knocking was no good with Teddy.

He took the knob in his hand and twisted it back and forth, back and forth. In a few moments, he heard her footsteps, and then the door opened a crack, and then the door opened wide.

She was wearing prisoner pyjamas, white-and-black striped cotton top and pants she'd picked up as a gag. Her hair was raven black, and the light in the foyer put a high sheen onto it. He closed the door behind him, and she went instantly into his arms, and then she moved back from him, and he marvelled at the expressiveness of her eyes and her mouth. There was joy in her eyes, pure soaring joy. Her lips parted, edging back over small white teeth, and then she lifted her face to his, and he took her kiss, and he felt the warmth of her body beneath the cotton pyjamas.

'Hello,' he said, and she kissed the words on his mouth and then broke away, holding only his hand, pulling him into the warmly-lighted living room.

She held her right index finger alongside her face, calling for his attention.

'Yes?' he said, and then she shook her head, changing her mind, wanting him to sit first. She fluffed a pillow for him, and he sat in the easy chair, and she perched herself on the arm of the chair and cocked her head to one side, repeating the extended index finger gesture.

'Go ahead,' he said, 'I'm listening.'

She watched his lips carefully, and then she smiled. Her index finger dropped. There was a white tag sewed onto the prisoner pyjama top close to the mound of her left breast. She ran the extended finger across the tag. He looked at it closely.

'I'm not examining your feminine attributes,' he said, smiling, and she shook her head, understanding. She had inked numbers onto the tag, carrying out the prison garb motif. He studied the numbers closely.

'My shield numbers,' he said, and the smile flowered on her mouth. 'You deserve a kiss for that,' he told her.

She shook her head.

'No kiss?'

She shook her head again.

'Why not?'

She opened and closed the fingers on her right hand.

'You want to talk?' he asked.

She nodded.

'What about?'

She left the arm of the chair suddenly. She went to an end-table and picked up a newspaper. She carried it back to him and then pointed to the picture of Mike Reardon on page one, his brains spilling out onto the sidewalk.

'Yeah,' he said dully.

There was sadness on her face now, an exaggerated sadness because Teddy could not give tongue to words, Teddy could neither hear words, and so her face was her speaking tool, and she spoke in exaggerated syllables, even to Carella, who understood the slightest nuance of expression in her eyes or on her mouth. But the exaggeration did not lie, for there was genuineness to the grief she felt. She had never met Mike Reardon, but Carella had talked of him often, and she felt that she knew him well.

She raised her eyebrows and spread her hands simultaneously, asking Carella 'Who?' and Carella, understanding instantly, said, 'We don't know yet. That's why I haven't been around. We've been working on it.' He saw puzzlement in her eyes. 'Am I going too fast for you?' he asked.

She shook her head.

'What then? What's the matter?'

She threw herself into his arms and she was weeping suddenly and fiercely, and he said, 'Hey, hey, come on, now,' and then realized she could not read his lips because her head was buried in his shoulder. He lifted her chin.

'You're getting my shirt wet,' he said.

She nodded, trying to hold back the tears.

'What's the matter?'

She lifted her hand slowly, and she touched his cheek gently, so gently that it felt like the passing of a mild breeze, and then her fingers touched his lips and lingered there, caressing them.

'You're worried about me?'

She nodded.

'There's nothing to worry about.'

She tossed her hair at the first page of the newspaper again.

'That was probably some crackpot,' Carella said.

She lifted her face, and her eyes met his fully, wide and brown, still moist from the tears.

'I'll be careful,' he said. 'Do you love me?'

She nodded, and then ducked her head.

'What's the matter?'

She shrugged and smiled, an embarrassed, shy smile.

'You missed me?'

She nodded again.

'I missed you, too.'

She lifted her head again, and there was something else in her eyes this time, a challenge to him to read her eyes correctly this time, because she had truly missed him but he had not uncovered the subtlety of her meaning as yet. He studied her eyes, and then he knew what she was saying, and he said only, 'Oh.'

She knew that he knew then, and she cocked one eyebrow saucily and slowly gave one exaggerated nod of her head, repeating his 'oh,' soundlessly rounding her lips.

'You're just a fleshpot,' he said jokingly.

She nodded.

'You only love me because I have a clean, strong, young body.'

She nodded.

'Will you marry me?'

She nodded.

'I've only asked you about a dozen times so far.'

She shrugged and nodded, enjoying herself immensely.

'When?'

She pointed at him.

'All right, I'll set the date. I'm getting my vacation in August. I'll marry you then, okay?'

She sat perfectly still, staring at him.

'I mean it.'

She seemed ready to cry again. He took her in his arms and said, 'I mean it, Teddy. Teddy, darling, I mean it. Don't be silly about this, Teddy, because I honestly, truly mean it. I love you, and I want to marry you, and I've wanted to marry you for a long, long time now, and if I have to keep asking you, I'll go nuts. I love you just the way you are, I wouldn't change any of you, darling, so don't get silly, please don't get silly again. It ... it doesn't matter to me, Teddy. Little Teddy, little Theodora, it doesn't matter to me, can you understand that? You're *more* than any other woman, so much more, so please marry me.'

She looked up at him, wishing she could speak because she could not trust her eyes now, wondering why someone as beautiful as Steve Carella, as wonderful as Steve Carella, as brave and as strong and as marvellous as Steve Carella would want to marry a girl like her, a girl who could never say, 'I love you, darling, I adore you.' But he has asked her again, and now, close in the circle of his arms, now she could believe that it didn't really matter to him, that to him she was as whole as any woman, 'more than any other woman,' he had said.

'Okay?' he asked. 'Will you let me make you honest?'

She nodded. The nod was a very small one.

'You mean it this time?'

She did not nod again. She lifted her mouth, and she put her answer into her lips, and his arms tightened around her, and she knew that he understood her. She broke away from him, and he said, 'Hey!' but she trotted away from his reach and went to the kitchen.

When she brought back the champagne, he said, 'I'll be damned!'

She sighed, agreeing that he undoubtedly would be damned, and he slapped her playfully on the fanny.

She handed him the bottle, did a deep curtsy which was ludicrous in the prisoner pyjamas and then sat on the floor cross-legged while he struggled with the cork.

The champagne exploded with an enormous pop, and though she did not hear the sound, she saw the cork leave the neck of the bottle and ricochet off the ceiling, and she saw the bubbly white fluid overspilling the lip and running over his hands.

She began to clap, and then she got to her feet and went for glasses, and he poured first a little of the wine into his saying, 'That's the way it's done, you know. It's supposed to take off the skim and the bugs and everything,' and then filling her glass, and then going back to pour his to the brim.

'To us,' he toasted.

She opened her arms slowly, wider and wider and wider.

'A long, long, happy love,' he supplied.

She nodded happily.

'And our marriage in August.' They clinked glasses, and then sipped at the wine, and she opened her eyes wide in pleasure and cocked her head appreciatively.

'Are you happy?' he asked.

Yes, her eyes said, yes, yes.

'Did you mean what you said before?'

She raised one brow inquisitively.

'About . . . missing me?'

Yes, yes, yes, yes, her eyes said.

'You're beautiful.'

She curtsied again.

'Everything about you. I love you, Teddy. God, how I love you.'

She put down the wine glass and then took his hand. She kissed the palm of his hand, and the back, and then she led him into the bedroom, and she unbuttoned his shirt and pulled it out of his trousers, her hands moving gently. He lay down on the bed, and she turned off the light and then, unselfconsciously, unembarrassedly, she took off the pyjamas and went to him.

And while they made gentle love in a small room in a big apartment house, a man named David Foster walked towards his own apartment, an apartment he shared with his mother.

And while their love grew fierce and then gentle again, a man named David Foster thought about his partner Mike Reardon, and so immersed in his thoughts was he that he did not hear the footsteps behind him, and when he finally did hear them, it was too late.

He started to turn, but a .45 automatic spat orange flame into the night, once, twice, again, again, and David Foster clutched at his chest, and the red blood burst through his brown fingers, and then he hit the concrete – dead.

Chapter Seven

There is not much you can say to a man's mother when the man is dead. There is not much you can say at all.

Carella sat in the doilied easy chair and looked across at Mrs Foster. The early afternoon sunlight seeped through the drawn blinds in the small, neat living room, narrow razor-edge bands of brilliance against the cool dimness. The heat in the streets was still insufferable, and he was thankful for the cool living room, but his topic was death, and he would have preferred the heat.

Mrs Foster was a small, dried-up woman. Her face was wrinkled and seamed, as brown as David's had been. She sat hunched in the chair, a small withered woman with a withered face and withered hands, and he thought *A strong wind would blow her away, poor woman*, and he watched the grief that lay quietly contained behind the expressionless withered face.

'David was a good boy,' she said. Her voice was hollow, a narrow sepulchral voice. He had come to talk of death, and now he could smell death on this woman, could hear death in the creak of her voice, and he thought it strange that David Foster, her son, who was alive and strong and young several hours ago was now dead – and his mother, who had probably longed for the peaceful sleep of death many a time, was alive and talking to Carella.

'Always a good boy. You raise 'em in a neighbourhood like this one,' Mrs Foster said, 'and you fear for how they'll turn out. My husband was a good worker, but he died young, and it wasn't always easy to see that David wasn't needing. But he was a good boy, always. He would come home and tell me what the other boys were doing, the stealing and all the things they were doing, and I knew he was all right.'

'Yes, Mrs Foster,' Carella said.

'And they all liked him around here, too,' Mrs Foster went on, shaking her head. 'All the boys he grew up with, and all the old folks, too. The people around here, Mr Carella, they don't take much to cops. But they liked my David because he grew up among them, and he was a part of them, and I guess they were sort of proud of him, the way I was proud.'

'We were all proud of him, Mrs Foster,' Carella said.

'He was a good cop, wasn't he?'

'Yes, he was fine cop.'

'Then why should anyone want to kill him?' Mrs Foster asked. 'Oh, I know his job was a dangerous one, yes, but this is different, this is senseless. He wasn't even on duty. He was coming home. Who would want to shoot my boy, Mr Carella? Who would want to shoot my boy?'

'That's what I wanted to talk to you about, Mrs Foster. I hope you don't mind if I ask a few questions.'

'If it'll help you find the man who killed David, I'll answer questions all day for you.'

'Did he ever talk about his work?'

'Yes, he did. He always told me what happened around the precinct, what you were working on. He told me about his partner being killed, and he told me he was leafing through pictures in his mind, just waiting until he hit the right one.'

'Did he say anything else about the pictures? Did he say he suspected anyone?'

'No.'

'Mrs Foster, what about his friends?'

'Everyone was his friend.'

'Did he have an address book or anything in which their names might be listed?'

'I don't think he had an address book, but there's a pad near the telephone he always used.'

'May I have that before I leave?'

'Certainly.'

'Did he have a sweetheart?'

'No, not anyone steady. He went out with a lot of different girls.'

'Did he keep a diary?'

'No.'

'Does he have a photograph collection?'

'Yes, he liked music a lot. He was always playing his records whenever he . . .'

'No, not phonograph. Photograph.'

'Oh. No. He carried a few pictures in his wallet, but that's all.'

'Did he ever tell you where he went on his free time?'

'Oh, lots of different places. He like the theatre a lot. The stage, I mean. He went often.'

'These boyhood friends of his. Did he pal around with them much?'

'No, I don't think so.'

'Did he drink?'

'Not heavily.'

'I mean, would you know whether or not he frequented any of the bars in the neighbourhood? Social drinking, of course.'

'I don't know.'

'Had he received any threatening letters or notes that you know of?'

'He never mentioned any.'

'Ever behave peculiarly on the telephone?'

'Peculiarly? What do you mean?'

'Well, as if he were trying to hide something from you. Or as if he were worried ... anything like that. I'm thinking of threatening calls, Mrs Foster.'

'No, I don't ever remember him acting strange on the phone.'

'I see. Well ...' Carella consulted his notes. 'I guess that's about it. I want to get going, Mrs Foster, because there's a lot of work to do. If you could get me that telephone pad ...'

'Yes, of course.' She rose, and he watched her slight body as she moved out of the cool living room into one of the bedrooms. When she returned, she handed him the pad and said, 'Keep it as long as you like.'

'Thank you. Mrs Foster, please know that we all share your sorrow,' he said lamely.

'Find my boy's killer,' Mrs Foster said. She extended one of her withered hands and took his hand in a strong, firm grip, and he marvelled at the strength of the grip, and at the strength in her eyes and on her face. Only when he was in the hallway, with the door locked behind him, did he hear the gentle sobs that came from within the apartment.

He went downstairs and out to the car. When he reached the car, he took off his jacket, wiped his face, and then sat behind the wheel to study his worksheet:

STATEMENT OF EYEWITNESSES: None.

MOTIVE: Revenge? Con? Nut? Tie-in with Mike? Check Ballistics report.

NUMBER OF MURDERERS: Two? One Mike, one David. Or tie-in? B.R. again.

WEAPONS: .45 automatic.

ROUTE OF MURDERER: ?

DIARIES, JOURNALS, LETTERS, ADDRESSES, TELEPHONE NUMBERS, PHOTO-GRAPHS: Check with David's mthr.

ASSOCIATES, RELATIVES, SWEETHEARTS, ENEMIES, ETC: Ditto.

PLACES FREQUENTED, HANG-OUTS: Ditto.

HABITS: Ditto.

TRACES AND CLUES FOUND ON THE SCENE: Heelprint in dog faeces. At lab now. Four shells. Two bullets. Ditto.

FINGERPRINTS FOUND: None.

Carella scratched his head, sighed against the heat, and then headed back for the precinct house to see if the new Ballistics report had come in yet.

The widow of Michael Reardon was a full-breasted woman in her late thirties. She had dark hair and green eyes, and an Irish nose spattered with a clichéful of freckles. She had a face for merry-go-rounds and roller-coaster rides, a face that could split in girlish glee when water was splashed on her at the seashore. She was a girl who could get drunk sniffing the vermouth cork before it was passed over a martini. She was a girl who went to church on Sundays, a girl who'd belonged to the Newman Club when she was younger. She had good legs, very white, and a good body, and her name was May.

She was dressed in black on the hot afternoon of July 25, and her feet were planted firmly on the floor before her, and her hands were folded in her lap, and there was no laughter on the face made for roller-coaster rides.

'I haven't told the children yet,' she said to Bush. 'The children don't know. How can I tell them? What can I say?'

'It's a rough thing,' Bush said in his quiet voice. His scalp felt sticky and moist. He needed a haircut, and his wild red hair was shrieking against the heat.

'Yes,' May said. 'Can I get you a beer or something? It's very hot. Mike used to take a beer when he got home. No matter what time it was, he always took a beer. He was a very well-ordered person. I mean, he did things carefully and on schedule. I think he wouldn't have been able to sleep if he didn't have that glass of beer when he got home.'

'Did he ever stop in the neighbourhood bars?'

'No. He always drank here, in the house. And never whisky. Only one or two glasses of beer.'

Mike Reardon, Bush thought. *He used to be a cop and a friend. Now he's a victim and a corpse, and I ask questions about him.*

'We were supposed to get an air-conditioning unit,' May said. 'At least, we talked about it. This apartment gets awfully hot. That's because we're so close to the building next door.'

'Yes,' Bush said. 'Mrs Reardon, did Mike have any enemies that you know of? I mean, people he knew outside his line of duty?'

'No, I don't think so. Mike was a very easy-going sort. Well, you worked with him. You know.'

'Can you tell me what happened the night he was killed? Before he left the house?'

'I was sleeping when he left. Whenever he had the twelve-to-eight tour, we argued about whether we should try to get any sleep before he went in.'

'Argued?'

'Well, you know, we discussed it. Mike preferred staying up, but I have two children, and I'm beat when it hits ten o'clock. So he usually compromised on those nights, and we both got to bed early – at about nine, I suppose.'

'Were you asleep when he left?'

'Yes. But I woke up just before he went out.'

'Did he say anything to you? Anything that might indicate he was worried about an ambush? Had he received a threat or anything?'

'No.' May Reardon glanced at her watch. 'I have to be leaving soon, Detective Bush. I have an appointment at the funeral parlour. I wanted to ask you about that. I know you're doing tests on ... on the body and all ... but the family ... Well, the family is kind of old-fashioned and we want to ... we want to make arrangements. Do you have any idea when ... when you'll be finished with him?'

'Soon, Mrs Reardon. We don't want to miss any bets. A careful autopsy may put us closer to finding his killer.'

'Yes, I know. I didn't want you to think ... it's just the family. They ask questions. They don't understand. They don't know what it means to have him gone, to wake up in the morning and not ... not have him here.' She bit her lip and turned her face from Bush. 'Forgive me. Mike wouldn't ...

wouldn't like this. Mike wouldn't want me to . . .' She shook her head and swallowed heavily. Bush watched her, feeling sudden empathy for this woman who was Wife, feeling sudden compassion for all women everywhere who had ever had their men torn from them by violence. His thoughts wandered to Alice, and he wondered idly how she would feel if he stopped a bullet, and then he put the thought out of his mind. It wasn't good to think like that. Not these days. Not after two in a row. Was it possible there was a nut loose? Somebody who'd marked the whole goddamn precinct as his special target?

Yes, it was possible.

It was very damn possible, and so it wasn't good to think about things like Alice's reaction to his own death. You thought about things like that, and they consumed your mind, and then when you needed a clear mind which could react quickly to possible danger, you didn't have it. And that's when you were up the creek without a paddle.

What had Mike Reardon been thinking of when he'd been gunned down?

What had been in the mind of David Foster when the four slugs ripped into his body?

Of course, it was possible the two deaths were unrelated. Possible, but not very probable. The m.o. was remarkably similar, and once the Ballistics report came through they'd know for sure whether they were dealing with one man or two.

Bush's money was on the one-man possibility.

'If there's anything else you want to ask me,' May said. She had pulled herself together now, and she faced him squarely, her face white, her eyes large.

'If you'll just collect any address books, photographs, telephone numbers, newspaper clippings he may have saved, anything that may give us a lead onto his friends or even his relatives, I'd be much obliged.'

'Yes, I can do that,' May said.

'And you can't remember anything unusual that may have some bearing on this, is that right?'

'No, I can't. Detective Bush, what am I going to tell the kids? I sent them off to a movie. I told them their daddy was out on a plant. But how long can I keep it from them? How do you tell a pair of kids that their father is dead? Oh God, what am I going to do?'

Bush remained silent. In a little while, May Reardon went for the stuff he wanted.

At 3:42 p.m. on July 25, the Ballistics report reached Carella's desk. The shells and bullets found at the scene of Mike Reardon's death had been put beneath the comparison microscope together with the shells and bullets used in the killing of David Foster.

The Ballistics report stated that the same weapon had been used in both murders.

Chapter Eight

On the night that David Foster was killed, a careless mongrel searching for food in garbage cans, had paused long enough to sully the sidewalk of the city. The dog had been careless, to be sure, and a human being had been just as careless, and there was a portion of a heelprint for the Lab boys to work over, solely because of this combined record of carelessness. The Lab boys turned to with something akin to distaste.

The heelprint was instantly photographed, not because the boys liked to play with cameras, but simply because they knew accidents frequently occurred in the making of a cast. The heelprint was placed on a black-stained cardboard scale, marked off in inches. The camera, supported above the print by a reversible tripod, the lens parallel to the print to avoid any false perspectives, clicked merrily away. Satisfied that the heelprint was now preserved for posterity – photographically, at least – the Lab boys turned to the less antiseptic task of making the cast.

One of the boys filled a rubber cup with half a pint of water. Then he spread plaster of Paris over the water, taking care not to stir it, allowing it to sink to the bottom of its own volition. He kept adding plaster of Paris until the water couldn't absorb any more of it, until he'd dumped about ten ounces of it into the cup. Then he brought the cup to one of the other boys who was preparing the print to take the mixture.

Because the print was in a soft material, it was sprayed first with shellac and then with a thin coat of oil. The plaster of Paris mixture was stirred and then carefully applied to the prepared print. It was applied with a spoon in small portions. When the print was covered to a thickness of about one-third of an inch, the boys spread pieces of twine and sticks onto the plaster to reinforce it, taking care that the debris did not touch the bottom of the print and destroy its details. They then applied another coat of plaster to the print, and allowed the cast to harden. From time to time, they touched the plaster, feeling for warmth, knowing that warmth meant the cast was hardening.

Since there was only one print, and since it was not even a full print, and since it was impossible to get a Walking Picture from this single print, and since the formula $H\dfrac{r}{1} - BS\dfrac{ra\ rv\ raa\ ll\ lb}{la\ lv\ laa\ rl\ rb}X$, a formula designed to give the complete picture of a man's walk in terms of step length, breadth of step length of left foot, right foot, greatest width of left foot, right foot, wear on heel and sole – since the formula could not be applied to a single print, the Lab boys did all they could with what they had.

And they decided, after careful study, that the heel was badly worn on the outside edge, a peculiarity which told them the man belonging to that heel undoubtedly walked with a somewhat duck-like waddle. They also decided that the heel was not the original heel of the shoe, that it was a rubber heel which had been put on during a repair job, and that the third nail from the shank side of the heel, on the left, had been bent when applying the new heel.

And – quite coincidentally *if* the heelprint happened to have been left by the murderer – the heel bore the clearly stamped trade name 'O'Sullivan', and everyone knows that O'Sullivan is America's Number One Heel.

The joke was an old one. The Lab boys hardly laughed at all.

The newspapers were not laughing very much, either.

The newspapers were taking this business of cop-killing quite seriously. Two morning tabloids, showing remarkable versatility in headlining the same incident, respectively reported the death of David Foster with the words SECOND COP SLAIN and KILLER SLAYS 2ND COP.

The afternoon tabloid, a newspaper hard-pressed to keep up with the circulation of the morning sheets, boldly announced KILLER ROAMS STREETS. And then, because this particular newspaper was vying for circulation, and because this particular newspaper made it a point to 'expose' anything which happened to be in the public's eye at the moment – anything from Daniel Boone to long winter underwear, anything which gave them a free circulation ride on the then-popular bandwagon – their front page carried a red banner that day, and the red banner shouted 'The Police Jungle – What Goes On In Our Precincts' and then in smaller white type against the red, 'See Murray Schneider, p. 4.'

And anyone who had the guts to wade through the first three pages of cheesecake and chest-thumping liberalism, discovered on page four that Murray Schneider blamed the deaths of Mike Reardon and David Foster upon 'the graft-loaded corruptness of our filth-ridden Gestapo.'

In the graft-loaded squadroom of the corrupt 87th Precinct, two detectives named Steve Carella and Hank Bush stood behind a filth-ridden desk and pored over several cards their equally corrupt fellow-officers had dug from the Convictions File.

'Try this for size,' Bush said.

'I'm listening,' Carella said.

'Some punk gets pinched by Mike and Dave, right?'

'Right.'

'The judge throws the book at him, and he gets room and board from the State for the next five or ten years. Okay?'

'Okay.'

'Then he gets out. He's had a lot of time to mull this over, a lot of time to build up his original peeve into a big hate. The one thing in his mind is to get Mike and Dave. So he goes out for them. He gets Mike first and then he tries to get Dave quick, before this hate of his cools down. Wham, he gets Dave, too.'

'It reads good,' Carella said.

'That's why I don't buy this Flannagan punk.'

'Why not?'

'Take a look at the card. Burglary, possession of burglary tools, a rape

NAME OF PRISONER

Precinct	(Surname)	(First Name and Init.)
87th	ORDIZ	LUIS "DIZZY"

Date & Time of Arrest	Address of Prisoner
May 2, 1952 7.00PM	635 6th St. South

Sex	Colour	Date of Birth Mo. Day Year	Place of Birth	Alien ~~Citizen~~
M	White	8 12 1912	San Juan Puerto Rico	

Social Condition	Read and Write	Occupation	Employed
Married (Single)	Yes (No)	Dishwasher	Yes (No)

Charge	Specific Offense	Date-Time Occurrence
Violation PL 1751 Subdiv. 1	Poss. of nar- cotics with intent to sell.	5/2/52 7:00 PM

Pct. Complaint No.	Place of Occurrence	Precinct
33A-411	635 6th St. South	87th

D.B. Complaint No.

DD179-52

Name of Complainant	Address of Complainant

Arresting Officer(s) (Name-s) Michael Reardon & David Foster

(Rank)	(Command)
Det. 3rd & Det. 2nd Gr.	Det. Bureau

Authority

(Pickup)   Complaint   Warrant   F.O.A.

Action of Court

Sentenced for four years at state
penitentiary, Ossining, New York

Date	Judge	Court
7/6/52	Fields	

away back in '47. Mike and Dave got him on the last burglary pinch. This was the first time he got convicted, and he drew ten, just got out last month on parole after doing five years.'

'So.'

'So I don't figure a guy with a big hate is going to be good enough to cut ten years to five. Besides, Flannagan never carried a gun all the while he was working. He was a gent.'

'Guns are easy to come by.'

'Sure. But I don't figure him for our man.'

'I'd like to check him out, anyway,' Carella said.

'Okay, but I want to check this other guy out first. Ordiz. Luis "Dizzy" Ordiz. Take a look at the card.'

Carella pulled the conviction card closer. The card was a 4 × 6 white rectangle, divided into printed rectangles of various sizes and shapes.

'A hophead,' Carella said.

'Yeah. Figure the hate a hophead can build in four years' time.'

'He went the distance?'

'Got out the beginning of the month,' Bush said. 'Cold turkey all that time. This don't build brotherly love for the cops who made the nab.'

'No, it doesn't.'

'Figure this, too. Take a look at his record. He was picked up in '51 on a dis cond charge. This was before he got on the junk, allegedly. But he was carrying a .45. The gun had a busted hammer, but it was still a .45. Go back to '49. Again, dis cond, fighting in a bar. Had a .45 on him, no busted hammer this time. He got off lucky that time. Suspended sentence.'

'Seems to favour .45's.'

'Like the guy who killed Mike and Dave. What do you say?'

'I say we take a look. Where is he?'

Bush shrugged. 'Your guess is as good as mine.'

Danny Gimp was a man who'd had polio when he was a child. He was lucky in that it had not truly crippled him. He had come out of the disease with only a slight limp, and a nickname which would last him the rest of his life. His real surname was Nelson, but very few people knew that, and he was referred to in the neighbourhood as Danny Gimp. Even his letters came addressed that way.

Danny was fifty-four years old, but it was impossible to judge his age from his face or his body. He was very small, small all over, his bones, his features, his eyes, his stature. He moved with the loose-hipped walk of an adolescent, and his voice was high and reedy, and his face bore hardly any wrinkles or other telltale signs of age.

Danny Gimp was a stool pigeon.

He was a very valuable man, and the men of the 87th Precinct called him in regularly, and Danny was always ready to comply – whenever he could. It was a rare occasion when Danny could not supply the piece of information the bulls were looking for. On these occasions, there were other stoolies to talk to. Somewhere somebody had the goods. It was simply a question of finding the right man at the right time.

Danny could usually be found in the third booth on the right hand side of a bar name *Andy's Pub*. He was not an alcoholic, nor did he even drink to excess. He simply used the bar as a sort of office. It was cheaper than paying rent someplace downtown, and it had the added attraction of a phone booth which he used regularly. The bar, too, was a good place to listen – and listening was one-half of Danny's business. The other half was talking.

He sat opposite Carella and Bush, and first he listened.

Then he talked.

'Dizzy Ordiz,' he said. 'Yeah, yeah.'

'You know where he is?'

'What's he do?'

'We don't know.'

'Last I heard, he was on the state.'

'He got out at the beginning of the month.'

'Parole?'

'No.'

'Ordiz, Ordiz. Oh, yeah. He's a junkie.'

'That's right.'

'Should be easy to locate. What'd he do?'

'Maybe nothing,' Bush said. 'Maybe a hell of a lot.'

'Oh, you thinking of these cop kills?' Danny asked.

Bush shrugged.

'Not Ordiz. You're barkin' up the wrong tree.'

'What makes you say so?'

Danny sipped at his beer, and then glanced up at the rotating fan. 'You'd never know there was a fan going in this dump, would you? If this heat don't break soon. I'm headin' for Canada. I got a friend up there. Quebec. You ever been to Quebec?'

'No,' Bush said.

'Nice there. Cool.'

'What about Ordiz?'

'Take him with me, he wants to come,' Danny said, and then he began laughing at his own joke.

'He's cute today,' Carella said.

'I'm cute all the time,' Danny said.

'How much love you got for Ordiz?'

'Don't know him from a hole in the wall. Don't care to, either. Hopheads make me want to vomit.'

'Okay, then where is he?'

'I don't know yet. Give me some time.'

'How much time?'

'Hour, two hours. Junkies are easy to trace. Talk to a few pushers, zing, you're in. He got out at the beginning of the month, huh? That means he's back on it strong by now. This should be a cinch.'

'He may have kicked it,' Carella said. 'It may not be such a cinch.'

'They never kick it,' Danny said. 'Don't pay attention to fairy tales. He was probably gettin' the stuff sneaked in even up the river. I'll find him. But if you think he knocked off your buddies, you're wrong.'

'Why?'

'I seen this jerk around. He's a nowhere. A real *trombenik*, if you dig foreign. He don't know enough to come in out of an atom bomb attack. He got one big thing in his life. Horse. That's Ordiz. He lives for the White God. Only thing on his mind.'

'Reardon and Foster sent him away,' Carella said.

'So what? You think a junkie bears a grudge? All part of the game. He ain't got time for grudges. He only got time for meetin' his pusher and makin' the buy. This guy Ordiz, he was always half-blind on the stuff. He couldn't see straight enough to shoot off his own big toe. So he's gonna cool two cops? Don't be ridic.'

'We'd like to see him, anyway,' Bush said.

'Sure. Do I tell you how to run headquarters? Am I the commissioner? But this guy is from Squaresville, fellas, I'm telling you. He wouldn't know a .45 from a cement mixer.'

'He's owned a few in his life,' Carella said.

'Playing with them, playing with them. If one of them things ever went off within a hundred yards of him, he'd be scared for a week. Take it from me, he don't care about nothin' but heroin. Listen, they don't call him Dizzy for nothin'. He's dizzy. He's got butterflies up here. He chases them away with H.'

'I don't trust junkies,' Bush said.

'Neither do I,' Danny answered. 'But this guy ain't a killer, take it from me. He don't even know how to kill time.'

'Do us a favour,' Carella said.

'Sure.'

'Find him for us. You know our number.'

'Sure. I'll buzz you in an hour or so. This is gonna be a cinch. Hopheads are a cinch.'

Chapter Nine

The heat on that July 26 reached a high of 95.6 at twelve noon. At the precinct house, two fans circulated the soggy air that crawled past the open windows and the grilles behind them. Everything in the Detective squad-room seemed to wilt under the steady, malignant pressure of the heat. Only the file cabinets and the desks stood at strict attention. Reports, file cards, carbon paper, envelopes, memos, all of these were damp and sticky to the touch, clinging to wherever they were dropped, clinging with a moist limpidity.

The men in the squadroom worked in their shirt sleeves. Their shirts were stained with perspiration, large dark amoeba blots which nibbled at the cloth, spreading from beneath the armpits, spreading from the hollow of the spinal column. The fans did not help the heat at all. The fans circulated the suffocating breath of the city, and the men sucked in the breath and typed up their reports in triplicate, and checked their worksheets, and dreamt of summers in the White Mountains or summers in Atlantic City with the ocean slapping their faces. They called complainants, and they called suspects, and their hands sweated on the black plastic of the phone, and they

feel Heat like a living thing which invaded their bodies and seared them with
a million white-hot daggers.

Lieutenant Byrnes was as hot as any man in the squadroom. His office was
just to the left of the slatted dividing railing, and it had a large corner
window, but the window was wide open and not a breath of a breeze came
through it. The reporter sitting opposite him looked cool. The reporter's
name was Savage, and the reporter was wearing a blue seersucker suit and a
dark blue Panama, and the reporter was smoking a cigarette and casually
puffing the smoke up at the ceiling where the heat held it in a solid blue-grey
mass.

'There's nothing more I can tell you,' Byrnes said. The reporter annoyed
him immensely. He did not for a moment believe that any man on this earth
had been born with a name like 'Savage'. He further did not believe that any
man on this earth, on this day, could actually be as cool as Savage pretended
he was.

'Nothing more, Lieutenant?' Savage asked, his voice very soft. He was a
handsome man with close-cropped blond hair and a straight, almost-
feminine nose. His eyes were grey, cool. Cool.

'Nothing,' the Lieutenant said. 'What the hell did you expect? If we knew
who did it, we'd have him in here, don't you think?'

'I should imagine so,' Savage said. 'Suspects?'

'We're working on it.'

'Suspects?' Savage repeated.

'A few. The suspects are our business. You splash them on your front
page, and they'll head for Europe.'

'Think a kid did it?'

'What do you mean, a kid?'

'A teen-ager.'

'Anybody could've done it,' Brynes said. 'For all I know *you* did it.'

Savage smiled, exposing bright white teeth. 'Lots of teen-age gangs in this
precinct, aren't there?'

'We've got the gangs under control. This precinct isn't the garden spot of
the city, Savage, but we like to feel we're doing the best job possible here.
Now I realize your newspaper may take offence at that, but we really try,
Savage, we honestly try to do our little jobs.'

'Do I detect sarcasm in you voice, Lieutenant?' Savage asked.

'Sarcasm is a weapon of the intellectual, Savage. Everybody, especially
your newspaper, knows that cops are just stupid, plodding beasts of
burden.'

'My paper never said that, Lieutenant.'

'No?' Byrnes shrugged. 'Well, you can use it in tomorrow's edition.'

'We're trying to help,' Savage said. 'We don't like cops getting killed any
more than you do.' Savage paused. 'What about the teen-age gang idea?'

'We haven't even considered it. This isn't the way those gangs operate.
Why the hell do you guys try to pin everything that happens in this city on
the teen-agers? My son is a teen-ager, and he doesn't go around killing cops.'

'That's encouraging,' Savage said.

'The gang phenomenon is a peculiar one to understand,' Byrnes said. 'I'm
not saying we've got it licked, but we do have it under control. If we've
stopped the street rumbles, and the knifings and shootings, then the gangs

have become nothing more than social clubs. As long as they stay that way, I'm happy.'

'Your outlook is a strangely optimistic one,' Savage said coolly. 'My newspaper doesn't happen to believe the street rumbles have stopped. My newspaper is of the opinion that the death of those two cops may be traced directly to these "social clubs".'

'Yeah?'

'Yeah.'

'So what the hell do you want me to do about it? Round up every kid in the city and shake him down? So your goddamn newspaper can sell another million copies?'

'No. But we're going ahead with our own investigation. And if we crack this, it won't make the 87th Precinct look too good.'

'It won't make Homicide North look too good, either. And it won't make the Police Commissioner look good. It'll make everybody in the department look like amateurs as contrasted with the super-sleuths of your newspaper.'

'Yes, it might,' Savage agreed.

'I have a few words of advice for you, Savage.'

'Yes?'

'The kids around here don't like questions asked. You're not dealing with Snob Hill teen-agers who tie on a doozy by drinking a few cans of beer. You're dealing with kids whose code is entirely different from yours or mine. Don't get yourself killed.'

'I won't,' Savage said, smiling resplendently.

'And one other thing.'

'Yes?'

'Don't foul up my precinct. I got enough headaches without you and your half-witted reporters stirring up more trouble.'

'What's more important to you, Lieutenant?' Savage asked. 'My not fouling up your precinct – or my not getting killed?'

Byrnes smiled and then began filling his pipe. 'They both amount to about the same thing,' he said.

The call from Danny Gimp came in fifty minutes. The desk Sergeant took the call, and then plugged it in to Carella's line.

'87th Detective Squad,' he said. 'Carella here.'

'Danny Gimp.'

'Hello, Danny, what've you got?'

'I found Ordiz.'

'Where?'

'This a favour, or business?' Danny asked.

'Business,' Carella said tersely. 'Where do I meet you?'

'You know *Jenny's*?'

'You kidding?'

'I'm serious.'

'If Ordiz is a junkie, what's he doing on Whore Street?'

'He's blind in some broad's pad. You're lucky you get a few mumbles out of him.'

'Whose pad?'

'That's what we meet for, Steve. No?'

'Call me "Steve" face-to-face, and you'll lose some teeth, pal,' Carella said.

'Okay, *Detective* Carella. You want this dope, I'll be in Jenny's in five minutes. Bring some loot.'

'Is Ordiz heeled?'

'He may be.'

'I'll see you,' Carella said.

La Vi de Putas was a street which ran North and South for a total of three blocks. The Indians probably had their name for it, and the teepees that lined the path in those rich days of beaver pelts and painted beads most likely did a thriving business even then. As the Indians retreated to their happy hunting grounds and the well-worn paths turned to paved roads, the teepees gave way to apartment buildings, and the practitioners of the world's oldest profession claimed the plush-lined cubby holes as their own. There was a time when the street was called *Piazza Putana* by the Italian immigrants, and *The Hussy Hole* by the Irish immigrants. With the Puerto Rican influx, the street had changed its language – but not its sole source of income. The Puerto Ricans referred to it as *La Via de Putas*. The Cops called it 'Whore Street.' In any language, you paid your money, and you took your choice.

The gals who ran the sex emporiums called themselves Mama-this or Mama-that. Mama Theresa's was the best-known joint on the Street. Mama Carmen's was the filthiest. Mama Luz's had been raided by the cops sixteen times because of some of the things that went on behind its crumbling brick façade. The cops were not above visiting any of the various Mamas on social calls, too. The business calls included occasional raids and occasional rake-offs. The raids were interesting sometimes, but they were usually conducted by members of the Vice Squad who were unfamiliar with the working arrangements some of the 87th Precinct cops had going with the madams. Nothing can mess up a good deal like an ignorant cop.

Carella, perhaps, was an ignorant cop. Or an honest one, depending how you looked at it. He met Danny Gimp at Jenny's, which was a small cafe on the corner of Whore Street, a cafe which allegedly served old world absinthe, complete with wormwood and water to mix the stuff in. No old-world absinthe drinker had ever been fooled by Jenny's stuff, but the cafe still served as a sort of no-man's land between the respectable workaday world of the proletariat, and the sinful shaded halls of the brothels. A man could hang his hat in Jenny's, and a man could have a drink there, and a man could pretend he was on a fraternity outing there, and with the third drink, he was ready to rationalize what he was about to do. Jenny's was something necessary to the operation of the Street. Jenny's, to stretch a point, served the same purpose as the shower stall does in a honeymoon suite.

On July 26, with the heat baking the black paint that covered the lower half of Jenny's front window – a window which had been smashed in some dozen times since the establishment was founded – Carella and Danny were not interested in the Crossing-the-Social-Barrier aspect of Jenny's bistro. They were interested in a man named Luis 'Dizzy' Ordiz, who may or may not have pumped a total of six bullets into a total of two cops. Bush was out checking on the burglar named Flannagan. Carella had come down in a squad car driven by a young rookie named Kling. The squad car was parked outside now, with Kling leaning against the fender, his head erect, sweltering even in his Summer blues. Tufts of blond hair stuck out of his lightweight hat. He was hot. He was hot as hell.

Inside, Carella was hot, too. 'Where is he?' he asked Danny.

Danny rolled the ball of his thumb against the ball of his forefinger. 'I haven't had a square meal in days,' he said.

Carella took a ten spot from his wallet and fed it to Danny.

'He's at Mama Luz's,' Danny said. 'He's with a broad they call La Flamenca. She ain't so hot.'

'What's he doing there?'

'He copped from a pusher a couple of hours back. Three decks of H. He stumbled over to Mama Luz with amorous intentions, but the H won the battle. Mama Luz tells me he's been dozing for the past sixty.'

'And La Flamenca?'

'She's with him, probably cleaned out his wallet by this time. She's a big red-headed job with two gold teeth in the front of her mouth, damn near blind you with them teeth of hers. She's got mean hips, a big job, real big. Don't get rough with her, less she swallow you up in one gobble.'

'Is he heeled?' Carella asked.

'Mama Luz don't know. She don't think so.'

'Doesn't the red-head know?'

'I didn't ask the red-head,' Danny said. 'I don't deal with the hired help.'

'Then how come you know about her hips?' Carella asked.

'Your ten spot don't buy my sex life,' Danny said, smiling.

'Okay,' Carella said, 'thanks.'

He left Danny at the table and went over to where Kling was leaning on the fender.

'Hot,' Kling said.

'You want a beer, go ahead,' Carella told him.

'No, I just want to go home.'

'Everybody wants to go home,' Carella said. 'Home is where you pack your rod.'

'I never understand detectives,' Kling said.

'Come on, we have a visit to make,' Carella said.

'Where?'

'Up the street, Mama Luz. Just point the car; it knows the way.'

Kling took off his hat and ran one hand through his blond hair. 'Phew,' he said, and then he put on his hat and climbed in behind the wheel. 'Who are we looking for?'

'Man named Dizzy Ordiz.'

'Never heard of him.'

'He never heard of you either,' Carella said.

'Yeah,' Kling said drily, 'well, I'd appreciate it if you introduced us.'

'I will,' Carella said, and he smiled as Kling set the car in motion.

Mama Luz was standing in the doorway when they pulled up. The kids on the sidewalk wore big grins, expecting a raid. Mama Luz smiled and said, 'Hello, Detective Carella. Hot, no?'

'Hot,' Carella agreed, wondering why in hell everybody and his brother commented about the weather. It was certainly obvious to anyone but a half-wit that this was a very hot day, that this was a suffocatingly hot day, that this was probably hotter than a day in Manilla, or even if you thought Calcutta hotter, this was still a lotta hotter heat than that.

Mama Luz was wearing a silk kimono. Mama Luz was a big fat woman with a mass of black hair pulled into a bun at the back of her head. Mama Luz used to be a well-known prostitute, allegedly one of the best in the city, but now she was a madam. She was scrupulously clean, and always smelled of lilacs. Her complexion was as white as any complexion can be, more white because it rarely saw the sun. Her features were patrician, her smile was angelic. If you didn't know she ran one of the wildest brothels on the Street, you might have thought she was somebody's mother.

She wasn't.

'You come on a social call?' she asked Carella, winking.

'If I can't have you, Mama Luz,' Carella said, 'I don't want anybody.'

Kling blinked, and then wiped the sweatband of his hat.

'For you, *toro*,' Mama Luz said, winking again, 'Mama Luz does anything. For you, Mama Luz is a young girl again.'

'You've always been a young girl,' Carella said, and he slapped her on the backside, and then said, 'Where's Ordiz?'

'With *la roja*,' Mama Luz said. 'She has picked his eyes out by now.' She shrugged. 'These new girls, all they are interested in is money. In the old days ...' Mama Luz cocked her head wistfully. 'In the old days, *toro*, there was sometimes love, do you know? What has happened to love nowadays, eh?'

'It's all locked up in that fat heart of yours,' Carella said. 'Does Ordiz have a gun?'

'Do I shake down my guests?' Mama Luz said. 'I don't think he has a gun, Stevie. You will not shoot up the works, will you? This has been a quiet day.'

'No, I will not shoot up the works,' Carella said. 'Show me where he is.'

'This way. Upstairs.'

The stairs shook beneath her. She turned her head over her shoulder, winked at Carella, and said, 'I trust you behind me, Stevie.'

'*Gracias*,' Carella said.

'Don't look up my dress.'

'It's a temptation, I'll admit,' Carella said, and behind him he heard Kling choke back a cross between a sob and a gasp.

Mama Luz stopped on the first landing. 'The door at the end of the hall. No blood, Stevie, please. With this one, you do not need blood. He is half-dead already.'

'Okay,' Carella said. 'Get downstairs, Mama Luz.'

'And later, when the work is done,' Mama Luz said suggestively, and she bumped one fleshy hip against Carella, almost knocking him off his feet. She went past Kling, laughing, her laughter trailing up the stairwell.

Carella sighed and looked at Kling. 'What're you gonna do, kid,' he said, 'I'm in love.'

'I never understand detectives,' Kling said.

They went down the hallway. Kling drew his service revolver when he saw Carella's was already in his hand.

'She said no shooting,' he reminded Carella.

'So far, she only runs a whore house,' Carella said. 'Not the Police Department.'

'Sure,' Kling said.

Carella rapped on the door with the butt of his .38.

'*Quién es?*' a girl's voice asked.

'Police,' Carella said. 'Open up.'

'*Momento,*' the voice said.

'She's getting dressed,' Kling advised Carella.

In a few moments, the door opened. The girl standing there was a big redhead. She was not smiling, so Carella did not have the opportunity to examine the gold teeth in the front of her mouth.

'What you want?' she asked.

'Clear out,' Carella said. 'We want to talk to the man in there.'

'Sure,' she said. She threw Carella a look intended to convey an attitude of virginity offended, and then she swivelled past him and slithered down the hallway. Kling watched her. When he turned back to the door, Carella was already in the room.

There was a bed in the room, and a night table, and a metal washbasin. The shade was drawn. The room smelled badly. A man lay in the bed in his trousers. His shoes and socks were off. His chest was bare. His eyes were closed, and his mouth was open. A fly buzzed around his nose.

'Open the window,' Carella said to Kling. 'This place stinks.'

The man on the bed stirred. He lifted his head and looked at Carella.

'Who are you?' he said.

'Your name Ordiz?' Carella asked.

'Yeah. You a cop?'

'Yes.'

'What did I do wrong now?'

Kling opened the window. From the streets below came the sound of children's voices.

'Where were you Sunday night?'

'What time?'

'Close to midnight.'

'I don't remember.'

'You better, Ordiz. You better start remembering damn fast. You shoot up just now?'

'I don't know what you mean.'

'You're an H-man, Ordiz, and we know it, and we know you copped three decks a little while back. Are you stoned now, or can you read me?'

'I hear you,' Ordiz said.

He passed a hand over his eyes. He owned a thin face with a hatchet nose and thick, rubbery lips. He needed a shave badly.

'Okay, talk.'

'Friday night, you said?'

'I said Sunday.'

'Sunday. Oh yeah. I was at a poker game.'

'Where?'

'South 4th. What's the matter, you don't believe me?'

'You got witnesses?'

'Five guys in the game. You can check with any one of them.'

'Give me their names.'

'Sure. Louie DeScala, and his brother, John. Kid named Pete Diaz. Another kid they call Pepe. I don't know his last name.'

'That's four,' Carella said.

'I was the fifth.'

'Where do these guys live?'

Ordiz reeled off a string of addresses.

'Okay, what about Monday night?'

'I was home.'

'Anybody with you?'

'My landlady.'

'What?'

'My landlady was with me. What's the matter, don't you hear good?'

'Shut up, Dizzy. What's her name?'

'Olga Pazio.'

'Address?'

Ordiz gave it to him. 'What am I supposed to done?' he asked.

'Nothing. You got a gun?'

'No. Listen, I been clean since I got out.'

'What about those three decks?'

'I don't know where you got that garbage. Somebody's fooling you, cop.'

'Sure. Get dressed, Dizzy.'

'What for? I paid for the use of this pad.'

'Okay, you used it already. Get dressed.'

'Hey, listen, what for? I tell you I've been clean since I got out. What the hell, cop?'

'I want you at the precinct while I check these names. You mind?'

'They'll tell you I was with them, don't worry. And that junk about the three decks, I don't know where you got that from. Hell, I ain't been near the stuff for years now.'

'That's plain to see,' Carella said. 'Those scabs on you arm are from beriberi or something, I guess.'

'Huh?' Ordiz asked.

'Get dressed.'

Carella checked with the men Ordiz had named. Each of them was willing to swear that he'd been at the poker game from ten-thirty on the night of July 23, to four a.m. on the morning of July 24. Ordiz' landlady reluctantly admitted she had spent the night of the 24th and the morning of the 25th in Ordiz' room. Ordiz had solid alibis for the times someone had spent killing Reardon and Foster.

When Bush came back with his report on Flannagan, the boys were right back where they'd started.

'He's got an alibi as long as the Texas panhandle,' Bush said.

Carella sighed, and then took Kling down for a beer before heading over to see Teddy.

Bush cursed the heat, and then went home to his wife.

Chapter Ten

From where Savage sat at the end of the bar, he could plainly see the scripted lettering on the back of the boy's brightly coloured jacket. The boy had caught his eye the moment Savage entered the bar. He'd been sitting in a booth with a dark-haired girl, and they'd both been drinking beer. Savage had seen the purple and gold jacket and then sat at the bar and ordered a gin and tonic. From time to time, he'd glanced over at the couple. The boy was thin and pale, a shock of black hair crowning his head. The collar of the jacket was turned up, and Savage could not see the lettering across the back at first because the boy sat with his back tight against the padded cushioning of the booth.

The girl finished her beer and left, but the boy did not vacate the booth. He turned slightly, and that was when Savage saw the lettering, and that was when the insistent idea at the back of his mind began to take full shape and form.

The lettering on the jacket read: The Grovers.

The name had undoubtedly been taken from the name of the park that hemmed in the 87th Precinct, but it was a name that rang a bell in Savage's head, and it didn't take long for that bell to begin echoing and re-echoing. The Grovers had been responsible for a good many of the street rumbles in the area, including an almost titanic struggle on one section of the park, a struggle featuring knives, broken bottles, guns, and sawed-off stickball bats. The Grovers had made their peace with the cops, or so the story went, but the persistent idea that one of the gangs was responsible for the deaths of Reardon and Foster would not leave Savage's mind.

And here was a boy to talk to.

Here was a Grover.

Savage finished his gin and tonic, left his stool, and walked over to where the boy was sitting alone in the booth.

'Hi,' he said.

The boy did not move his head. He raised only his eyes. He said nothing.

'Mind if I sit down?' Savage asked.

'Beat it, mister,' the boy said.

Savage reached into his jacket pocket. The boy watched him silently. He took out a package of cigarettes, offered one to the boy and, facing the silent refusal, hung one on his own lip.

'My name's Savage,' he said.

'Who cares?' the boy answered.

'I'd like to talk to you.'

'Yeah? What about?'
'The Grovers.'
'Mister, you don't live around here, do you?'
'No.'
'Then, Dad, go home.'
'I told you. I want to talk.'
'I don't. I'm waitin' for a deb. Take off while you still got legs.'
'I'm not scared of you, kid, so knock off the rough talk.'
The boy appraised Savage coolly.
'What's your name?' Savage asked.
'Guess, Blondie.'
'You want a beer?'
'You buying?'
'Sure,' Savage said.
'Then make it a rum-coke.'
Savage turned towards the bar. 'Rum-coke,' he called, 'and another gin and tonic.'
'You drink gin, huh?' the boy said.
'Yes. What's your name, son?'
'Rafael,' the boy said, still studying Savage closely. 'The guys call me Rip.'
'Rip. That's a good name.'
'Good as any. What's the matter, you don't like it?'
'I like it,' Savage said.
'You a nab?'
'A what?'
'A cop.'
'No.'
'What then?'
'I'm a reporter.'
'Yeah?'
'Yes.'
'So whatya want from me?'
'I only want to talk.'
'What about?'
'Your gang.'
'What gang?' Rip said. 'I don't belong to no gang.'
The waiter brought the drinks. Rip tasted his and said, 'That bartender's a crook. He cuts the juice here. This tastes like cream soda.'
'Here's luck,' Savage said.
'You're gonna need it,' Rip replied.
'About the Grovers ...'
'The Grovers are a club.'
'Not a gang?'
'Whatta we need a gang for? We're a club, that's all.'
'Who's president?' Savage asked.
'That's for me to know and you to find out,' Rip answered.
'What's the matter? You ashamed of the club?'
'Hell, no.'
'Don't you want to see it publicized in a newspaper? There isn't another

club in the neighbourhood that ever got a newspaper's full treatment.'
'We don't need no treatment. We got a big rep as it is. Ain't nobody in this city who ain't heard of The Grovers. Who you tryin' to snow, mister?'
'Nobody. I just thought you'd like some public relations work.'
'What the hell's that?'
'A favourable press.'
'You mean . . .' Rip furrowed his brow. 'What do you mean?'
'An article telling about your club.'
'We don't need no articles. You better cut out, Dad.'
'Rip. I'm trying to be your friend.'
'I got plenty of friends in The Grovers.'
'How many?'
'There must be at least . . .' Rip stopped short. 'You're a wise bastard, ain't you?'
'You don't have to tell me anything you don't want to, Rip. Why do the boys call you "Rip"?'
'We all got nicknames. That's mine.'
'But why?'
'Because I can handle a blade good.'
'Did you ever have to?'
'Handle one? You're kidding? In this neighbourhood, you don't carry a knife or a piece, you're dead. Dead, man.'
'What's a piece, Rip?'
'A gun.' Rip opened his eyes wide. 'You don't know what a piece is? Man, you ain't been.'
'Do The Grovers have many pieces?'
'Enough.'
'What kind?'
'All kinds. What do you want? We got it.'
'.45's?'
'Why do you ask?'
'Nice gun, a .45.'
'Yeah, it's big,' Rip said.
'Do you ever use these pieces?'
'You got to use them. Man, you think these diddlebops are for fun? You got to use whatever you can get you hands on. Otherwise, you wind up with a tag on your toe.' Rip drank a little more of the rum. 'This neighbourhood ain't a cream puff, Dad. You got to watch yourself all the time. That's why it helps to belong to The Grovers. They see this jacket comin' down the street, they got respect. They know if they mess with me, they got *all* The Grovers to mess with.'
'The police, you mean?'
'Naw, who wants Law trouble? We steer away from them. Unless they bother us.'
'Any cops bother you lately?'
'We got a thing on with the cops. They don't bother us, we don't bother them. Man, there ain't been a rumble in months. Things are very quiet.'
'You like it that way?'
'Sure, why not? Who wants his skull busted? The Grovers want peace. We never punk out, but we never go lookin' for trouble, either. Only time we

get involved is when we're challenged, or when a stud from another club tries to make it with one of our debs. We don't go for that.'
  'So you've had no trouble with the police lately?'
  'Few little skirmishes. Nothing to speak of.'
  'What kind of skirmishes?'
  'Agh, one of the guys was on mootah. So he got a little high, you know. So he busted a store window, for kicks, you know? So one of the cops put the arm on him. He got a suspended sentence.'
  '*Who* put the arm on him?'
  'Why you want to know?'
  'I'm just curious.'
  'One of the bulls, I don't remember who.'
  'A detective?'
  'I said a bull, didn't I?'
  'How'd the rest of The Grovers feel about this?'
  'How do you mean?'
  'About this detective pulling in one your boys?'
  'Agh, the kid was a Junior, didn't know his ass from his elbow. Nobody shoulda given him a reefer to begin with. You don't handle a reefer right . . . well, you know, the guy was just a kid.'
  'And you felt no resentment for the cop who'd pulled him in?'
  'Huh?'
  'You had nothing against the cop who pulled him in?'
  Rip's eyes grew suddenly wary. 'What're you drivin' at, mister?'
  'Nothing, really.'
  'What'd you say your name was?'
  'Savage.'
  'Why you askin' about how we feel about cops?'
  'No reason.'
  'Then why you askin'?'
  'I was just curious.'
  'Yeah,' Rip said flatly. 'Well, I got to go now, I guess that deb ain't comin' back.'
  'Listen, stick around a while,' Savage said. 'I'd like to talk some more.'
  'Yeah?'
  'Yes, I would.'
  'That's tough pal,' Rip said. 'I wouldn't.' He got out of the booth. 'Thanks for the drink. I see you around.'
  'Sure,' Savage said.
  He watched the boy's shuffling walk as he moved out of the bar. The door closed behind him, and he was gone.
  Savage studied his drink. There *had* been trouble between The Grovers and a cop – a detective, in fact. So his theory was not quite as far-fetched as the good lieutenant tried to make it.
  He sipped at his drink, thinking, and when he'd finished it, he ordered another. He walked out of the bar about ten minutes later, passing two neatly dressed men on his way out.
  The two men were Steve Carella and a patrolman in street clothes – a patrolman named Bert Kling.

Chapter Eleven

Bush was limp when he reached the apartment.

He hated difficult cases, but only because he felt curiously inadequate to cope with them. He had not been joking when he told Carella he felt detectives weren't particularly brilliant men. He thoroughly believed this, and whenever a difficult case popped up, his faith in his own theory was reaffirmed.

Legwork and stubbornness, that was all it amounted to.

So far, the legwork they'd done had brought them no closer to the killer than they originally were. The stubbornness? Well, that was another thing again. They would keep at it of course. Until the break came. When would the break come? Today? Tomorrow? Never?

The hell with the case, he thought. I'm home. A man is entitled to the luxury of leaving his goddamn job at the office. A man is entitled to a few peaceful hours with his wife.

He pushed his key into the lock, twisted it, and then threw the door open.

'Hank?' Alice called.

'Yes.' Her voice sounded cool. Alice always sounded cool. Alice was a remarkable woman.

'Do you want a drink?'

'Yes. Where are you?'

'In the bedroom. Come on in, there's a nice breeze here.'

'A breeze? You're kidding.'

'No, seriously.'

He took off his jacket and threw it over the back of a chair He was pulling off his shirt as he went into the bedroom. Bush never wore undershirts. He did not believe in the theory of sweat absorption. An undershirt, he held, was simply an additional piece of wearing apparel, and in this weather the idea was to get as close to the nude as possible. He ripped off his shirt with almost savage intensity. He had a broad chest matted with curling red hair that matched the thatch on his head. The knife scar ran its crooked path down his right arm.

Alice lay in chaise near the open window. She wore a white blouse and a straight black skirt. She was barefoot, and her legs were propped up on the window sill, and the black skirt rustled mildly with the faint breeze that came through the window, She had drawn her blonde hair back into a pony tail. He went to her, and she lifted her face for his kiss, and he noticed the thin film of perspiration on her upper lip.

'Where's that drink?' he asked.

'I'll mix it,' she said. She swung her feet off the window sill, and the skirt pulled back for an instant, her thigh winking at him. He watched her silently, wondering what it was about this woman that was so exciting, wondering if all married men felt this way about their wives even after ten years of marriage.

'Get that gleam out of your eyes,' she said, reading his face.

'Why?'

'It's too damn hot.'

'I know a fellow who claims the best way ...'

'I know about that fellow.'

'Is in a locked room on the hottest day of the year with the windows closed under four blankets.'

'Gin and tonic?'

'Good.'

'I heard that vodka and tonic is better.'

'We'll have to get some.'

'Busy day at the mine?'

'Yes. You?'

'Sat around and worried about you,' Alice said.

'I see all those grey hairs sprouting.'

'He belittles my concern,' Alice said to the air. 'Did you find that killer yet?'

'No.'

'Do you want a lime in this?'

'If you like.'

'Means going into the kitchen. Be a doll and drink it this way.'

'I'm a doll,' Bush said.

She handed him the drink. Bush sat on the edge of the bed. He sipped at the drink, and then leaned forward, the glass dangling at the ends of his muscular long arms.

'Tired?'

'Pooped.'

'You don't look very tired.'

'I'm so pooped, I'm peeped.'

'You always say that,' Alice said. 'I wish you wouldn't always say that. There are things you always say.'

'Like what?'

'Well, like that, for one.'

'Name another.'

'When we're driving in the car and there are fixed traffic signals. Whenever you begin hitting the lights right, you say "We're in with the boys".'

'So what's wrong with that?'

'Nothing, the first hundred times.'

'Oh, hell.'

'Well, it's true.'

'All right, all right. I'm not peeped. I'm not even pooped.'

'I'm hot,' Alice said.

'So am I.'

She began unbuttoning her blouse, and even before he looked up, she said, 'Don't get ideas.'

She took off the blouse and draped it over the back of the chaise.
'What'd you do all day?' he asked.
'Nothing much.'
'Were you in?'
'Most of the time.'
'So what'd you do?'
'Sat around, mostly.'
'Mmmm.' He could not take his eyes from her brassiere. 'Did you miss me?'
'I always miss you,' she said flatly.
'I missed you.'
'Drink your drink.'
'No, really.'
'Well, good,' she said, and she smiled fleetingly. He studied the smile. It was gone almost instantly, and he had the peculiar feeling that it had been nothing more than a duty smile.
'Why don't you get some sleep?' she asked.
'Not yet,' he said, watching her.
'Hank, if you think ...'
'What?'
'Nothing.'
'I've got to go in again later,' he said.
'They're really pushing on this one, aren't they?'
'Lots of pressure,' he said. 'I think the Old Man is scared he's next.'
'I'll bet it's all over,' Alice said. 'I don't think there'll be another killing.'
'You can never tell,' Bush said.
'Do you want something to eat before you turn in?' she asked.
'I'm not turning in yet.'
Alice sighed. 'You can't escape this damn heat,' she said. 'No matter what you do, it's always with you.' Her hand went to the button at the side of her skirt. She undid it, and then pulled down the zipper. The skirt slid to her feet, and she stepped out of it. She walked to the window, and he watched her. Her legs were long and clean.
'Come here,' he said.
'No. I don't want to, Hank.'
'All right,' he said.
'Do you think it'll cool off tonight?'
'I doubt it.' He watched her closely. He had the distinct impression that she was undressing for him, and yet she'd said ... He tweaked his nose, puzzled.
She turned from the window. 'You need a haircut,' she said.
'I'll try to get one tomorrow. We haven't had a minute.'
'Oh, goddamn this heat, anyway.' She walked to mix herself another drink, and he could not take his eyes from her. *What's she trying to do?* he wondered. *What the hell is she trying to do to me?*
He rose swiftly, walking to where she stood. He put his arms around her.
'Don't,' she said.
'Baby ...'
'Don't.' Her voice was firm, a cold edge to it.
'Why not?'

'Because I say so.'

'Well, then why the hell are you parading around like ...'

'Take you hands off me, Hank. Let me go.'

'Aw, baby ...'

She broke away from him. 'Get some sleep,' she said. 'You're tired.'
There was something strange in her eyes, an almost malicious gleam.

'Can't ...'

'No.'

'For God's sake. Alice ...'

'No!'

'All right.'

She smiled quickly. 'All right,' she repeated.

'Well ...' Bush paused. 'I'd ... I'd better get to bed.'

'Yes. You'd better.'

'What I can't understand is why ...'

'You won't even need a sheet in this weather,' Alice interrupted.

'No, I guess not.'

He went to the bed and took off his shoes and socks. He didn't want to
undress because he didn't want to give her the satisfaction, now that he'd
been denied, of knowing how she'd affected him. He took off his trousers
and quickly got into the bed, pulling the sheet to his throat.

Alice watched him, smiling. 'I'm reading *Anapurna*,' she said.

'So?'

'I just happened to think of it.'

Bush rolled over onto his side.

'I'm still hot,' Alice said. 'I think I'll take a shower. And then maybe I'll
catch an air-conditioned movie. You don't mind, do you?'

'No,' Bush mumbled.

She walked to the side of the bed and stood there for a moment, looking
down at him. 'Yes, I think I'll take a shower.'

He did not move. He kept his eyes on the floor, but he could see her feet
and her legs, but he did not move.

'Sleep tight, darling,' she whispered, and then she went into the
bathroom.

He heard the shower when it began running. He lay on the soggy sheet and
listened to the steady machine-gunning of the water. Then, over the sound
of the shower, came the sound of the telephone, splitting the silence of the
room.

He sat up and reached for the instrument.

'Hello?'

'Bush?'

'Yes?'

'This is Havilland. You better get down here right away.'

'What's the matter?' Bush asked.

'You know that young rookie Kling?'

'Yeah?'

'He was just shot in a bar on Culver.'

Chapter Twelve

The squadroom of the 87th resembled nothing so much as the locker room of the Boys' Club when Bush arrived. There must have been at least two dozen teen-agers crammed in behind the dividing rail and the desks beyond it. Add to this a dozen or so detectives who were firing questions, the answers to which were coming in two languages, and the bedlam was equivalent to the hush of a hydrogen bomb explosion.

The boys were all wearing brilliantly contrasting purple and gold jackets, and the words 'The Grovers' decorated the back of each jacket. Bush looked for Carella in the crowded room, spotted him, and walked over towards him quickly. Havilland, a tough cop with a cherubic face, shouted at one of the boys, 'Don't give me any guff, you little punk, or I'll break your goddamn arm.'

'You try it, dick,' the kid answered, and Havilland cuffed him across the mouth. The boy staggered back, slamming into Bush as he went by. Bush shrugged his shoulders, and the boy flew back into Havilland's arms, as if he'd been brushed aside by a rhinoceros.

Carella was talking to two boys when Bush approached him.

'Who fired the gun?' he asked.

The boys shrugged.

'We'll throw you all in jail as accessories,' Carella promised.

'What the hell happened?' Bush wanted to know.

'I was having a beer with Kling. Nice and peaceful off-duty beer. I left him there, and ten minutes later, when he's leaving the joint, he gets jumped by these punks. One of them put a slug in him.'

'How is he?'

'He's at the hospital. The slug was a .22, went through his right shoulder. We figure a zip gun.'

'You think this ties with the other kills?'

'I doubt it. The m.o.'s 'way off.'

'Then why?'

'How the hell do I know? Looks like the whole city figures it's open season on cops.' Carella turned back to the boys. 'Were you with the gang when the cop was jumped?'

The boys would not answer.

'Okay, fellas,' Carella said, 'play it smart. See what that gets you. See how long The Grovers are gonna last under a rap like this one.

'We din' shoot no cop,' one of the boys said.

'No? What happened, he shoot himself?'

'You ting we crazy?' the other boy said. 'Shoot a bull?'
'This was a patrolman,' Carella said, 'not a detective.'
'He wass wear a suit,' the first boy said.
'Cops wear suits off-duty,' Bush said. 'Now how about it?'
'Nobody shoot a cop,' the first boy said.
'No, except somebody did.'
Lieutenant Byrnes came out of his office and shouted, 'All right, knock it off! KNOCK IT OFF!'
The room fell immediately silent.
'Who's your talk man?' Byrnes asked.
'I am,' a tall boy answered.
'What's your name?'
'Do-Do.'
'What's your full name?'
'Salvador Jesus Santez.'
'All right, come here, Salvador.'
'The guys call me Do-Do.'
'Okay, come here.'
Santez walked over to where Byrnes was standing. He walked with a shuffle which was considered both hip and cool. The boys in the room visibly relaxed. This was their talk man, and Do-Do was a real gone stud. Do-Do would know how to handle this jive.
'What happened?' Byrnes asked.
'Little skirmish, that's all,' Santez said.
'Why?'
'Jus' like that. We got the word passed down, so we joined the fray.'
'What word?'
'You know, like a scout was out.'
'No, I don't know. What the hell are you talking about?'
'Look, Dad ...' Santez started.
'You call me "Dad" again,' Byrnes warned, 'and I'll beat you black and blue.'
'Well, gee, Da ...' Santez stopped dead. 'What you want to know?'
'I want to know why you jumped a cop.'
'What cop? What're you talkin' about?'
'Look, Santez, don't play this too goddamn cute. You jumped one of our patrolmen as he came out of a bar. You beat him up, and one of your boys put a bullet in his shoulder. Now what the hell's the story?'
Santez considered Byrnes' question gravely.
'Well?'
'He's a cop?'
'What the hell did you think he was?'
'He was wearing a light blue summer suit!' Santez said, his eyes opening wide.
'What the hell's that got to do with it? Why'd you jump him? Why'd you shoot him?'
A mumbling was starting behind Santez. Byrnes heard the mumble and shouted. 'Shut up! You've got your talk man, let *him* talk!'
Santez was still silent.
'What about it, Santez?'

'A mistake,' Santez said.

'That's for damn sure.'

'I mean, we didn't know he was a cop.'

'Why'd you jump him?'

'A mistake, I tell you.'

'Start from the beginning.'

'Okay,' Santez said. 'We been giving you trouble lately?'

'No.'

'Okay. We been minding our own business, right? You never hear from The Grovers, except when we protectin' our own, right? The last rumble you get is over there in The Silver Culvers' territory when they pick on one of our Juniors. Am I right?'

'Go ahead, Santez.'

'Okay. Early today, there's a guy snooping around. He grabs one of our Seniors in a bar, and starts pumpin' him.'

'Which Senior?'

'I forget,' Santez said.

'Who was the guy?'

'Said he was from a newspaper.'

'What?'

'Yeah. Said his name was Savage, you know him?'

'I know him,' Byrnes said tightly.

'Okay, so he starts askin' like how many pieces we got, and whether we got .45's and whether we don't like the Law, things like that. This Senior, he's real hip. He tips right off this guy is trying to mix in The Grovers with the two bulls got knocked off around here. So he's on a newspaper, and we got a rep to protect. We don't want Law trouble. If this jerk goes back to his paper and starts printing lies about how we're mixed in, that ain't good for our rep.'

'So what'd you do, Santez?' Byrnes asked wearily, thinking of Savage, and thinking of how he'd like to wring the reporter's neck.

'So this Senior comes back, and we planned to scare off the reporter before he goes printing any story. We went back to the bar and waited for him. When he come out, we jumped him. Only he pulled a gun, so one of the boys plugged him in self defence.'

'Who?'

'Who knows?' Santez said. 'One of the boys burned him.'

'Thinking he was Savage.'

'Sure. How the hell we supposed to know he's a cop instead? He had on a light blue suit, and he had blond hair, like this reporter creep. So we burned him. It was a mistake.'

'You keep saying that, Santez, but I don't think you know just how big a mistake it was. Who fired that shot?'

Santez shrugged.

'Who was the Senior Savage talked to?'

Santez shrugged.

'Is he here?'

Santez had stopped talking, it seemed.

'You know we've got a list of every damn member in your gang, don't you, Santez?'

'Sure.'

'Okay. Havilland, get the list. I want a roll call. Whoever's not here, pick him up.'

'Hey, wait a minute,' Santez said. 'I told you it was all a mistake. You going to get somebody in trouble just 'cause we mistake a cop?'

'Listen to me, Santez, and listen hard. Your gang hasn't been in any trouble recently, and that's fine with us. Call it a truce, call it whatever you want to. But don't ever think and mean *ever*, Santez, that you or your boys can shoot anybody in this goddamn precinct and get away with it. You're a bunch of hoods as far as I'm concerned, Santez. You're a bunch of hoods with fancy jackets, and a seventeen-year-old hood is no less dangerous than a fifty-year-old hood. The only reason we haven't been bearing down on you is because you've been behaving yourself. All right, today you stopped behaving yourself. You shot a man in my precinct territory – and that means you're in trouble. That means you're in big trouble.'

Santez blinked.

'Put them all downstairs and call the roll there,' Byrnes said. 'Then get whoever we missed.'

'All right, let's go,' Havilland said. He began herding the boys out of the room.

Miscolo, one of the patrolmen from Clerical, pushed his way through the crowd and walked over to the Lieutenant.

'Lieutenant, fella outside wants to see you,' he said.

'Who?'

'Guy named Savage. Claims he's a reporter. Wants to know what the rumble was about this aft ...'

'Kick him down the steps,' Byrnes said, and he went back into his office.

Chapter Thirteen

Homicide, if it doesn't happen too close to home, is a fairly interesting thing.

You can really get involved in the investigation of a homicide case because it is the rare occurrence in the everyday life of a precinct. It is the most exotic crime because it deals with the theft of something universal – a man's life.

Unfortunately, there are other less interesting and more mundane matters to deal with in a precinct, too. And in a precinct like the 87th, these mundane matters can consume a lot of time. There are the rapes, and the muggings, and the rollings, and the knifings, and the various types of disorderly conducts, and the breakings and entries, and the burglaries, and the car thefts, and the street rumbles, and the cats caught in sewers, and oh, like that. Many of these choice items of crime are promptly turned over to special squads within the department, but the initial squeal nonetheless goes to the precinct in which the crime is being committed, and these squeals can keep a man hopping.

It's not so easy to hop when the temperature is high.

For cops, shocking as the notion may sound at first, are human beings. They sweat like you and me, and they don't like to work when it's hot. Some of them don't like to work even when it's cool. None of them like to draw Lineup, especially when it's hot.

Steve Carella and Hank Bush drew Lineup on Thursday, July 27.

They were especially displeased about it because Lineup is held only from Mondays to Thursdays, and if they had missed it this Thursday, chances were they would not pull the duty until the following week and perhaps – just perhaps the heat would have broken by then.

The morning started the way most mornings were starting that week. There was a deceptive coolness at first, a coolness which – despite the prognostications of television's various weather men and weather women – seemed to promise a delightful day ahead. The delusions and flights of fancy fled almost instantly. It was apparent within a half-hour of being awake that this was going to be another scorcher, that you would meet people who asked, 'Hot enough for you?' or who blandly and informatively remarked, 'It's not the heat; it's the humidity.'

Whatever it was, it was hot.

It was hot where Carella lived in the suburb of Riverhead, and it was hot in the heart of the city – on High Street, where Headquarters and the line-up awaited.

Since Bush lived in another suburb – Calm's Point, west a little south of Riverhead – they chose to meet at Headquarters at 8:45, fifteen minutes before the linup began. Carella was there on the dot.

At 8:50, Bush strolled up. That is to say, he more or less crawled onto the pavement and slouched over to where Carella was standing and puffing on a cigarette.

'Now I know what Hell is like,' he said.

'Wait until the sun really starts shining,' Carella said.

'You cheerful guys are always good for an early-morning laugh,' Bush answered. 'Let me have a cigarette, will you?'

Carella glanced at his watch. 'Time we were up there.'

'Let it wait. We've got a few minutes yet.' He took the cigarette Carella offered, lighted it, and blew out a stream of smoke. 'Any new corpses today?'

'None yet.'

'Pity. I'm getting so I miss my morning coffee and corpse.'

'The city,' Carella said.

'What?'

'Look at it. What a goddamn monster.'

'A hairy bastard,' Bush agreed.

'But I love her.'

'Yeah,' Bush said noncommittally.

'It's too hot to work today. This is a day for the beach.'

'The beaches'll be jammed. You're lucky you've got a nice lineup to attend.'

'Sure, I know. Who wants a cool, sandy beach with the breakers rolling in and ...'

'You Chinese?'

'Huh?'

'You know your torture pretty good.'

'Let's go upstairs.'

They flipped their cigarettes away and entered the Headquarters building. The building had once boasted clean red brick and architecture which was modern. The brick was now covered with the soot of five decades, and the architecture was as modern as a suit of armour.

They walked into the first-floor marbled entryway, past the dick squadroom, past the lab, past the various records rooms. Down a shaded hallway, a frosted glass door announced 'Commissioner of Police.'

'I'll bet *he's* at the beach,' Carella said.

'He's in there hiding behind his desk,' Bush said. 'He's afraid the 87th's maniac is going to get him next.'

'Maybe he's not at the beach,' Carella amended. 'I understand this building has a swimming pool in the basement.'

'Two of them,' Bush said. He rang for the elevator. They waited in hot, suffering silence for several moments. The elevator doors slid open. The patrolman inside was sweating.

'Step into the iron coffin,' he said.

Carella grinned. Bush winced. Together they got into the car.

'Lineup?' the patrolman asked.

'No, the swimming pool,' Bush cracked.

'Jokes I can't take in this heat,' the patrolman said.

'Then don't supply straight lines,' Bush said.

'Abbott and Costello I've got with me,' the patrolman said, and he lapsed into silence. The elevator crawled up the intestinal tract of the building. It creaked. It whined. Its walls were moist with the beaded exhalations of its occupants.

'Nine,' the patrolman said.

The doors slid open. Carella and Bush stepped into a sunlit corridor. Simultaneously, they reached for the leather cases to which their shields were pinned. Again simultaneously, they pinned the tin to their collars and then walked towards the desk behind which another patrolman was seated.

The patrolman eyed the tin, nodded, and they passed the desk and walked into a large room which served many purposes at Headquarters. The room was built with the physical proportions of a gymnasium, and did indeed have two basketball hoops, one at each end of the room. The windows were wide and tall, covered with steel mesh. The room was used for indoor sport, lectures, swearing in of rookies, occasional meetings of the Police Benevolent Association or the Police Honor Legion and, of course, the lineups.

For the purpose of these Monday-to-Thursday parades of felony offenders, a permanent stage had been set up at the far end of the room, beneath the balcony there, and beyond the basketball hoop. The stage was brilliantly lighted. Behind the stage was a white wall, and upon the wall in black numerals was the graduated height scale against which the prisoners stood.

In front of the stage, and stretching back towards the entrance doorways for about ten rows, was an array of folding chairs, most of which were occupied by detectives from all over the city when Bush and Carella entered. The blinds at the windows had already been drawn, and a look at the raised dais and speaking stand behind the chairs showed that the Chief of Detectives was already in position and the strawberry festival would start in a few moments. To the left of the stage, the felony offenders huddled in a group, lightly guarded by several patrolmen and several detectives, the men who had made the arrests. Every felony offender who'd been picked up in the city the day before would be paraded across the stage this morning.

The purpose of the lineup, you see – despite popular misconception about the identification of suspects by victims, a practice which was more helpful in theory than in actual usage – was simply to acquaint as many detectives as possible with the men who were doing evil in their city. The ideal set-up would have been to have each detective in each precinct at each scheduled lineup, but other pressing matters made this impossible. So two men were chosen each day from each precinct, on the theory that if you can't acquaint all of the people all of the time, you can at least acquaint some of them some of the time.

'All right,' the Chief of Detectives said into his microphone, 'let's start.'

Carella and Bush took seats in the fifth row as the first two offenders walked onto the stage. It was the practice to show the offenders as they'd been picked up, in pairs, in a trio, a quartet, whatever. This simply for the purpose of establishing an m.o. If a crook works in a pair once, he will generally work in a pair again.

The police stenographer poised his pen above his pad. The Chief of Detectives intoned, 'Diamondback, One,' calling off the area of the city in which the arrest had been made, and the number of the case from that area that day. 'Diamondback, One. Anselmo, Joseph, 17 and Di Palermo, Frederick, 16. Forced the door of an apartment on Cambridge and Gribble. Occupant screamed for help, bringing patrolman to scene. No statement. How about it, Joe?'

Joseph Anselmo was a tall, thin boy with dark black hair and dark brown eyes. The eyes seemed darker than they were because they were set against a pale, white face. The whiteness was attributable to one emotion, and one emotion alone. Joseph Anselmo was scared.

'How about it, Joe?' the Chief of Detectives asked again.

'What do you want to know?' Anselmo said.

'Did you force the door to that apartment?'

'Yes.'

'Why?'

'I don't know.'

'Well, you forced a door, you must have had a reason for doing it. Did you know somebody was in the apartment?'

'No.'

'Did you force it alone.'

Anselmo did not answer.

'How about it, Freddie? Were you with Joe when you broke that lock?'

Frederick Di Palermo was blond and blue-eyed. He was shorter than Anselmo, and he looked cleaner. He shared two things in common with his friend. First, he had been picked up on a felony offence. Second, he was scared.

'I was with him,' Di Palermo said.

'How'd you force the door?'

'We hit the lock.'

'What with.'

'A hammer.'

'Weren't you afraid it would make a noise?'

'We only give it a quick rap,' Di Palermo said. 'We didn't know somebody was home.'

'What'd you expect to get in that apartment?' the Chief of Detectives asked.

'I don't know,' Di Palermo said.

'Now, look,' the Chief of Detectives said patiently, 'you both broke into an apartment. Now we know that, and you just admitted it, so you must have had a reason for going in there. What do you say?'

'The girls told us,' Anselmo said.

'What girls?'

'Oh, some chicks,' Di Palermo answered.

'What'd they tell you?'

'To bust the door.'

'Why?'

'Like that,' Anselmo said.

'Like what?'

'Like for kicks.'

'Only for kicks?'

'I don't know why we busted the door,' Anselmo said, and he glanced quickly at Di Palermo.

'To take something out of the apartment?' the Chief asked.

'Maybe a ...' Di Palermo shrugged.

'Maybe what?'

'A couple of bucks. You know, like that.'

'You were planning a burglary then, is that right?'

'Yeah, I guess.'

'What'd you do when you discovered the apartment was occupied?'

'The lady screamed,' Anselmo said.

'So we run,' Di Palermo said.

'Next case,' the Chief of Detectives said.

The boys shuffled off the stage to where their arresting officer was waiting for them. Actually, they had said a hell of a lot more than they should have. They'd have been within their rights if they'd insisted on not saying a word at the lineup. Not knowing this, not even knowing that their position was fortified because they'd made no statement when they'd been collared, they had answered the Chief of Detectives with remarkable naïveté. A good lawyer, with a simple charge of unlawfully entering under circumstances or in a manner not amounting to a burglary, would have had his clients plead guilty to a misdemeanor. The Chief of Detectives, however, had asked the boys if they were planning to commit a burglary, and the boys had answered in the affirmative. And the Penal Law, Section 402, defines Burglary in first degree thusly:

A person, who, with intent to commit some crime therein, breaks and enters, in the night time, the dwelling-house of another, in which there is at the time a human being:

1. Being armed with a dangerous weapon; or

2. Arming himself therein with such a weapon: or
3. Being assisted by a confederate actually present; or . . .

Well, no matter. The boys had very carelessly tied the knot of a felony about their youthful necks, perhaps not realizing that burglary in the first degree is punishable by imprisonment in a state prison for an indeterminate term the minimum of which shall not be less than ten years and the maximum of which shall not be more than thirty years.

Apparently, 'the girls' had told them wrong.

'Diamondback, Two,' the Chief of Detectives said. 'Pritchett, Virginia, 34. Struck her quote husband unquote about the neck and head with a hatchet at three a.m. in the morning. No statement.'

Virginia Pritchett had walked onto the stage while the Chief of Detectives was talking. She was a small woman, barely clearing the five-foot-one-inch marker. She was thin, narrow-boned, with red hair of the fine, spider-webby type She wore no lipstick. She wore no smile. Her eyes were dead.

'Virginia?' the Chief of Detectives said.

She raised her head. She kept her hands close to her waist, one fist folded over the other. Her eyes did not come to life. They were grey, and she stared into the glaring lights unblinkingly.

'Virginia?'

'Yes, sir?' Her voice was very soft, barely audible. Carella leaned forward to catch what she was saying.

'Have you ever been in trouble before, Virginia?' the Chief of Detectives asked.

'No, sir.'

'What happened, Virginia?'

The girl shrugged, as if she too could not comprehend what had happened. The shrug was a small one, a gesture that would have been similar to passing a hand over the eyes.

'What happened, Virginia?'

The girl raised herself up to her full height, partly to speak into the permanently fixed microphone which dangled several inches before her face on a solid steel pipe, partly because there were eyes on her and because she apparently realized her shoulders were slumped. The room was deathly still. There was not a breeze in the city. Beyond the glaring lights, the detectives sat.

'We argued,' she said sighing.

'Do you want to tell us about it?'

'We argued from the morning, from when we first got up. The heat. It's . . . it was very hot in the apartment. Right from the morning. You . . . you lose your temper quickly in the heat.'

'Go on.'

'He started with the orange juice. He said the orange juice wasn't cold enough. I told him I'd had it in the ice box all night, it wasn't my fault it wasn't cold. Diamondback isn't ritzy, sir. We don't have refrigerators in Diamondback, and with this heat, the ice melts very fast. Well, he started complaining about the orange juice.'

'Were you married to this man?'

'No, sir.'

'How long have you been living together?'

'Seven years, sir.'

'Go on.'

'He said he was going down for breakfast, and I said he shouldn't go down because it was silly to spend money when you didn't have to. He stayed, but he complained about the orange juice all the while he ate. It went on like that all day.'

'About the orange juice, you mean?'

'No, other things. I don't remember what. He was watching the ball game on TV, and drinking beer, and he'd pick on little things all day long. He was sitting in his undershorts because of the heat. I had hardly anything on myself.'

'Go on.'

'We had supper late, just cold cuts. He was picking on me all that time. He didn't want to sleep in the bedroom that night, he wanted to sleep on the kitchen floor. I told him it was silly, even though the bedroom is very hot. He hit me.'

'What do you mean, he hit you?'

'He hit me about the face. He closed one eye for me. I told him not to touch me again, or I would push him out the window. He laughed. He put a blanket on the kitchen floor, near the window, and he turned on the radio, and I went into the bedroom to sleep.'

'Yes, go ahead, Virginia.'

'I couldn't sleep because it was so hot. And he had the radio up loud. I went into the kitchen to tell him to please put the radio a little lower, and he said to go back to bed. I went into the bathroom, and I washed my face, and that was when I spied the hatchet.'

'Where was the hatchet?'

'He keeps tools on a shelf in the bathroom, wrenches and a hammer, and the hatchet was with them. I thought I would go out and tell him to put the radio lower again, because it was very hot and the radio was very loud, and I wanted to try to get some sleep. But I didn't want him to hit me again, so I took the hatchet, to protect myself with, in case he tried to get rough again.'

'Then what did you do?'

'I went out into the kitchen with the hatchet in my hands. He had got up off the floor and was sitting in a chair near the window, listening to the radio. His back was to me.'

'Yes.'

'I walked over to him, and he didn't turn around, and I didn't say anything to him.'

'What did you do?'

'I struck him with the hatchet.'

'Where?'

'On his head and on his neck.'

'How many times?'

'I don't remember exactly. I just kept hitting him.'

'Then what?'

'He fell off the chair, and I dropped the hatchet, and I went next door to Mr Alanos, he's our neighbour, and I told him I had hit my husband with a hatchet, and he didn't believe me. He came into the apartment, and then he called the police, and an officer came.'

'Your husband was taken to the hospital, did you know that?'

'Yes.'

'Do you know the disposition of his case?'

Her voice was very low. 'I heard he died,' she said. She lowered her head and did not look out past the lights again. Her fists were still folded at her waist. Her eyes were still dead.

'Next case,' the Chief of Detectives said.

'She *murdered* him,' Bush whispered, his voice curiously loaded with awe. Carella nodded.

'Majesta, One,' the Chief of Detectives said. 'Bronckin, David, 27. Had a lamp outage report at 10:24 p.m. last night, corner of Weaver and 69th North. Electric company notified at once, and then another lamp outage two blocks south reported, and then gunfire reported. Patrolman picked up Bronckin on Dicsen and 69th North. Bronckin was intoxicated, was going down the street shooting out lamp-post fixtures. What about it, Dave?'

'I'm only Dave to my friends,' Bronckin said.

'What about it?'

'What do you want from me? I got high, I shot out a few lights. I'll pay for the goddamn lights.'

'What were you doing with the gun?'

'You *know* what I was doing. I was shooting at lamp-posts.'

'Did you start out with that idea? Shooting at the lamp-posts?'

'Yeah. Listen, I don't have to say anything to you. I want a lawyer.'

'You'll have plenty opportunity for a lawyer.'

'Well, I ain't answering any questions until I get one.'

'Who's asking questions? We're trying to find out what possessed you to do a damn fool thing like shooting at light fixtures.'

'I was high. What the hell, you never been high?'

'I don't go shooting at lamp-posts when I'm high,' the Chief said.

'Well, I do. That's what makes horse races.'

'About the gun.'

'Yeah, I knew we'd get down to the gun sooner or later.'

'Is it yours?'

'Sure, it's mine.'

'Where'd you get it?'

'My brother sent it home to me.'

'Where's your brother?'

'In Korea.'

'Have you got a permit for the gun?'

'It was a gift.'

'I don't give a damn if you *made* it! Have you got a permit?'

'No.'

'Then what gave you the idea you could go around carrying it?'

'I just got the idea. Lots of people carry guns. What the hell are you picking on me for? All I shot was a few lights. Why don't you go after the bastards who are shooting people?'

'How do we know you're not one of them, Bronckin?'

'Maybe I am. Maybe I'm Jack the Ripper.'

'Maybe not. But maybe you were carrying that .45 and planning a little worse mischief that shooting out a few lights.'

'Sure. I was gonna shoot the Mayor.'

'A .45,' Carella whispered to Bush.

'Yeah,' Bush said. He was already out of his chair and walking back to the Chief of Detectives.

'All right, smart guy,' the Chief of Detectives said. 'You violated the Sullivan Law, do you know what that means?'

'No, what does it mean, smart guy?'

'You'll find out,' the Chief said. 'Next case.'

At his elbow, Bush said, 'Chief, we'd like to question that man further.'

'Go ahead,' the Chief said. 'Hillside, One. Matheson, Peter, 45 ...'

Chapter Fourteen

David Bronckin did not apreciate the idea of being detained from his visit to the Criminal Courts Building, whereto he was being led for arraignment when Carella and Bush intercepted him.

He was a tall man, at least six-three, and he had a very loud voice and a very pugnacious attitude, and he didn't like Carella's first request at all.

'Lift your foot,' Carella said.

'What?'

The men were seated in the Detective squadroom at Headquarters, a room quite similar to the room of the same name back at the 87th. A small fan atop one of the filing cabinets did its best to whip up the air, but the room valiantly upheld its attitude of sleazy limpidity.

'Lift your foot,' Carella repeated.

'What for?'

'Because I say so,' Carella answered tightly.

Bronckin looked at him for a moment and then said, 'You take off that badge and I'll ...'

'I'm not taking it off,' Carella said. 'Lift your foot.'

Bronkin mumbled something and then raised his right foot; Carella held his ankle and Bush looked at the heel.

'Cat's Paw,' Bush said.

'You got any other shoes?' Carella asked.

'Sure, I got other shoes.'

'Home?'

'Yeah. What's up?'

'How long have you owned that .45?'

'Couple of months now.'

'Where were you Sunday night?'

'Listen, I want a lawyer.'

'Never mind the lawyer,' Bush said. 'Answer the question.'

'What was the question?'

'Where were you Sunday night?'

'What time Sunday night?'

'About 11:40 or so.'

'I think I was at a movie.'

'Which movie?'

'The Strand. Yeah. I was at a movie.'

'Did you have the .45 with you?'

'I don't remember.'

'Yes or no.'

'I don't remember. If you want a yes or no, it'll have to be no. I'm no dope.'

'What picture did you see?'

'An old one.'

'Name it.'

'The Creature from the Black Lagoon.'

'What was it about?'

'A monster that comes up from the water.'

'What was the co-feature?'

'I don't remember.'

'Think.'

'Something with John Garfield.'

'What?'

'A prize-fight picture.'

'What was the title?'

'I don't remember. He's a bum, and then he gets to be champ, and then he takes a dive.'

'Body and Soul?'

'Yeah, that was it.'

'Call The Strand, Hank,' Carella said.

'Hey, what're you gonna do that for?' Bronckin asked.

'To check and see if those movies were playing Sunday night.'

'They were playing, all right.'

'We're also going to check that .45 with Ballistics, Bronckin.'

'What for?'

'To see how it matches up against some slugs we've got. You can save us a lot of time.'

'How?'

'What were you doing Monday night?'

'Monday, Monday? Who remembers?'

Bush had located the number in the directory, and was dialling.

'Listen,' Bronckin said, 'you don't have to call them. Those were the pictures, all right.'

'What were you doing Monday night?'

'I ... I went to a movie.'

'Another movie? Two nights in a row?'

'Yeah. The movies are air-conditioned. It's better than hanging around and suffocating, ain't it?'

'What'd you see?'

'Some more old ones.'

'You like old movies, don't you?'

'I don't care about the picture. I was only tryin' to beat the heat. The places showing old movies are cheaper.'

'What were the pictures?'

'Seven Brides for Seven Brothers and Violent Saturday.'

'You remember those all right, do you?'

'Sure, it was more recent.'

'Why'd you say you couldn't remember what you did Monday night?'

'I said that?'

'Yes.'

'Well, I had to think.'

'What movie house was this?'

'On Monday night, you mean?'

'Yeah.'

'One of the RKO's. The one on North 80th.'

Bush put the receiver back into its cradle. 'Checks out, Steve,' he said. 'Creature from the Black Lagoon, and Body and Soul. Like he said.' Bush didn't mention that he'd also taken down a timetable for the theatre, or that he knew exactly what times each picture started and ended. He nodded briefly at Carella, passing on the information.

'What time did you go in?'

'Sunday or Monday?

'Sunday.'

'About 8:30.'

'Exactly 8:30?'

'Who remembers exactly? It was getting hot, so I went into The Strand.'

'What makes you think it was 8:30?'

'I don't know. It was about that time.'

'What time did you leave?'

'About – musta been about a quarter to twelve.'

'Where'd you go then?'

'For some coffee and ...'

'Where?'

'The White Tower.'

'How long did you stay?'

'Half-hour, I guess.'

'What'd you eat?'

'I told you. Coffee and ...'

'Coffee and *what*?'

'My God, a jelly doughnut,' Bronckin said.

'This took you a half-hour?'

'I had a cigarette while I was there.'

'Meet anybody you know there?'

'No.'

'At the movie?'

'No.'

'And you didn't have the gun with you, that right?'

'I don't think I did.'

'Do you usually carry it around?'

'Sometimes.'

'You ever been in trouble with the Law?'

'Yeah.'

'Spell it.'

'I served two at Sing Sing.'

'What for?'

'Assault with a deadly weapon.'

'What was the weapon?'

Bronckin hesitated.

'I'm listening,' Carella said.

'A .45.'

'This one?'

'No.'

'Which?'

'Another one I had.'

'Have you still got it?'

Again, Bronckin hesitated.

'Have you still got it?' Carella repeated.

'Yes.'

'How come? Didn't the police ...'

'I ditched the gun. They never found it. A friend of mine picked it up for me.'

'Did you use the business end?'

'No. The butt.'

'On who?'

'What difference does it make?'

'I want to know. Who?'

'A ... a lady.'

'A woman?'

'Yes.'

'How old?'

'Forty. Fifty.'

'Which?'

'Fifty.'

'You're a nice guy.'

'Yeah,' Bronckin said.

'Who collared you? Which precinct?'

'Ninety-second, I think.'

'Was it?'

'Yes.'

'Who were the cops?'

'I don't know.'

'The ones who made the arrest, I mean.'

'There was only one.'

'A dick?'

'No.'

'When was this?' Bush asked.

'Fifty-two.'

'Where's that other .45?'

'Back at my room.'

'Where?'

'831 Haven.'

Carella jotted down the address.

'What else have you got there?'

'You guys going to help me?'

'What help do you need?'

'Well, I keep a few guns.'

'How many?'

'Six,' Bronckin said.

'What?'

'Yeah.'

'Name them.'

'The two .45's. Then there's a Luger, and a Mauser, and I even got a Tokarev.'

'What else?'

'Oh, just a .22.'

'All in your room?'

'Yeah, it's quite a collection.'

'Your shoes there, too?'

'Yeah. What's with my shoes?'

'No permits for any of these guns, huh?'

'No. Slipped my mind.'

'I'll bet. Hank, call the Ninety-second. Find out who collared Bronckin in '52. I think Foster started at our house, but Reardon may have been a transfer.'

'Oh,' Bronckin said suddenly.

'What?'

'That's what this is all about, huh? Those two cops.'

'Yes.'

'You're way off,' Bronckin said.

'Maybe. What time'd you get out of that RKO?'

'About the same. Eleven-thirty, twelve.'

'The other one check, Hank?'

'Yep.'

'Better call the RKO on North 8oth and check this one, too. You can go now, Bronckin. Your escort's in the hall.'

'Hey,' Bronckin said, 'how about a break? I helped you, didn't I? How about a break?'

Carella blew his nose.

None of the shoes in Bronckin's apartment owned heels even faintly resembling the heel-print cast the Lab boys had.

Ballistics reported that neither of the .45's in Bronckin's possession could have fired any of the fatal bullets.

The 92nd Precinct reported that neither Michael Reardon or David Foster had ever worked there.

There was only one thing the investigators could bank on.

The heat.

Chapter Fifteen

At seven twenty-six that Thursday night, the city looked skyward.

The city had heard a sound, and it paused to identify the sound. The sound was the roll of distant thunder.

And it seemed, simultaneously, as if a sudden breeze sprang up from the North and washed the blistering face of the city. The ominous rolling in the sky grew closer, and now there were lightning flashes, erratic, jagged streaks that knifed the sky.

The people of the city turned their faces upward and waited.

It seemed the rain would never come. The lightning was wild in its fury, lashing the tall buildings, arcing over the horizon. The thunder answered the spitting anger of the lightning, booming its own furious epithets.

And then, suddenly, the sky split open and the rain poured down. Huge drops, and they pelted the sidewalks and the gutters and the streets; and the asphalt and concrete sizzled when the first drops fell; and the citizens of the city smiled and watched the rain, watched the huge drops – God, how big the drops were! – splattering against the ground. And the smiles broadened, and the people slapped each other on the back, and it looked as if everything was going to be all right again.

Until the rain stopped.

It stopped as suddenly as it had begun. It had burst from the sky like water that had broken through a dam. It rained for four minutes and thirty-six seconds. And then, as though someone had suddenly plugged the broken wall of the dam, it stopped.

The lightning still flashed across the sky, and the thunder still growled in response, but there was no rain.

The cool relief the rain had brought lasted no more than ten minutes. At the end of that time, the streets were baking again, and the citizens were swearing and mumbling and sweating.

Nobody likes practical jokes.

Even when God is playing them.

She stood by the window when the rain stopped.

She swore mentally, and she reminded herself that she would have to teach Steve sign language, so that he'd know when she was swearing. He had promised to come tonight, and the promise filled her now, and she wondered what she should wear for him.

'Nothing' was probably the best answer. She was pleased with her joke. She must remember it. To tell him when he came.

The street was suddenly very sad. The rain had brought gaiety, but now the rain was gone, and there was only the solemn grey of the street, as solemn as death.

Death.

Two dead, two men he worked with and knew well, why couldn't he have been a streetcleaner or a flagpole sitter or something, why a policeman, why a cop?

She turned to look at the clock wondering what time it was, wondering how long it would be before he came, how long it would be before she spotted the slow, back-and-forth twisting of the knob, before she rushed to the door to open it for him. The clock was no comfort. It would be hours yet. If he came, of course. If nothing else happened, something to keep him at the station house, another killing, another . . .

No, I mustn't think of that.

It's not fair to Steve to think that.

If I think of harm coming to him . . .

Nothing will happen to him . . . no. Steve is strong, Steve is a good cop, Steve can take care of himself. But Reardon was a good cop, and Foster, and they're dead now, how good can a cop be when he's shot in the back with a .45? How good is any cop against a killer in ambush?

No, don't think these things.

The murders are over now. There will be no more. Foster was the end. It's done. Done.

Steve, hurry.

She sat facing the door, knowing it would be hours yet, but waiting for the knob to turn, waiting for the knob to tell her he was there.

The man rose.

He was in his undershorts. They were gaily patterned, and they fitted him snugly, and he walked from the bed to the dresser with a curiously ducklike motion. He was a tall man, excellently built. He examined his profile in the mirror over the dresser, looked at the clock, sighed heavily, and then went back to bed.

There was time yet.

He lay and looked at the ceiling, and then he suddenly desired a cigarette. He rose and walked to the dresser again, walking with the strange ducklike waddle which was uncomplimentary to a man of his physique. He lighted the cigarette and then went back to bed, where he lay puffing and thinking.

He was thinking about the cop he would kill later that night.

Lieutenant Byrnes stopped in to chat with Captain Frick, commanding officer of the precinct, before he checked out that night.

'How's it going?' Frick asked.

Byrnes shrugged. 'Looks like we've got the only cool thing in this city.'

'Huh?'

'This case.'

'Oh. Yeah,' Frick said. Frick was tired. He wasn't as young as he used to be, and all this hullaballoo made him tired. If cops got knocked off, those were the breaks. Here today, gone tomorrow. You can't live forever, and you can't take it with you. Find the perpetrator, sure, but don't push a man too hard. You can't push a man too hard in this heat, especially when he's not as young as he used to be, and tired.

To tell the truth, Frick was a tired man even when he was twenty, and Byrnes knew it. He didn't particularly care for the captain, but he was a conscientious cop, and a conscientious cop checked with the precinct commander every now and then, even if he felt the commander was an egghead.

'You're really working the boys, aren't you?' Frick asked.

'Yes,' Byrnes said, thinking that should have been obvious even to an egghead.

'I figure this for some screwball,' Frick said. 'Got himself a peeve, figured he'd go out and shoot somebody.'

'Why cops?' Byrnes asked.

'Why not? How can you figure what a screwball will do? Probably knocked off Reardon by accident, not even knowing he was a cop. Then saw all the publicity the thing got in the papers, figured it was a good idea, and purposely gunned for another cop.'

'How'd he know Foster was a cop? Foster was in street clothes, same as Reardon.'

'Maybe he's a screwball who's had run-ins with the law before, how do I know? One thing's for sure, though. He's a screwball.'

'Or a mighty shrewd guy,' Byrnes said.

'How do you figure that? What brains does it take to pull a trigger?'

'It doesn't take any brains,' Byrnes said. 'Unless you get away with it.'

'He won't,' Frick answered. He sighed expansively. He was tired. He was getting old. Even his hair was white. Old men shouldn't have to solve mysteries in hot weather.

'Hot, ain't it?' Frick said.

'Yes indeed,' Byrnes replied.

'You heading for home now?'

'Yes.'

'Good for you. I'll be taking off in a little while, too. Some of the boys are out on an attempted suicide, though. Want to find out how it turns out. Some dame on the roof, supposed to be ready to jump.' Frick shook his head. 'Screwballs, huh?'

'Yeah,' Byrnes said.

'Sent my wife and kids away to the mountains,' Frick said. 'Damn glad I did. This heat ain't fit for man nor beast.'

'No, it's not,' Byrnes agreed.

The phone on Frick's desk rang. Frick picked it up.

'Captain Frick,' he said. 'What? Oh. Okay, fine. Right.' He replaced the receiver. 'Not a suicide at all,' he said to Byrnes. 'The dame was just drying her hair, had it sort of hanging over the edge of the roof. Screwball, huh?'

'Yes. Well, I'm taking off.'

'Better keep your gun handy. Might get you next.'

'Who?' Byrnes asked, heading for the door.

'Him.'

'Huh?'

'The screwball.'

Roger Havilland was a bull.

Even the other bulls called him a bull. A real bull. He was a 'bull' as differentiated from a 'bull' which was a detective. Havilland was built like a bull, and he ate like a bull, and he even snorted like a bull. There were no two ways about it. He was a real bull.

He was also not a very nice guy.

There was a time when Havilland was a nice guy, but everyone had forgotten that time, including Havilland. There was a time when Havilland could talk to a prisoner for hours on end without once having to use his hands. There was a time when Havilland did not bellow every other syllable to leave his mouth. Havilland had once been a gentle cop.

But Havilland had once had a most unfortunate thing happen to him. Havilland had tried to break up a street fight one night, being on his way home at the time and being, at the time, that sort of conscientious cop who recognized his duty twenty-four hours a day. The street fight had not been a very big one, as street fights go. As a matter of fact, it was a friendly sort of argument, more or less, with hardly a zip gun in sight.

Havilland stepped in and very politely attempted to bust it up. He drew his revolver and fired a few shots over the heads of the brawlers and somehow or other one of the brawlers hit Havilland on the right wrist with a piece of lead pipe. The gun left Havilland's hand, and then the unfortunate thing happened.

The brawlers, content until then to be bashing in their own heads, suddenly decided a cop's head would be more fun to play upon. They turned on the disarmed Havilland, dragged him into an alley, and went to work on him with remarkable dispatch.

The boy with the lead pipe broke Havilland's arm in four places.

The compound fracture was a very painful thing to bear, more painful in that the damned thing would not set properly and the doctors were forced to rebreak the bones and set them all over again.

For a while there, Havilland doubted if he'd be able to keep his job on the force. Since he'd only recently made Detective 3rd Grade, the prospect was not a particularly pleasant one to him. But the arm healed, as arms will, and he came out of it just about as whole as he went into it – except that his mental attitude had changed somewhat.

There is an old adage which goes something like this: 'One guy can screw it up for the whole company.'

Well, the fellow with the lead pipe certainly screwed it up for the whole company, if not the whole city. Havilland became a bull, a real bull. He had learned his lesson. He would never be cornholed again.

In Havilland's book, there was only one way to beat down a prisoner's resistance. You forgot the word 'down', and you concentrated on beating in the opposite direction: 'up'.

Not many prisoners liked Havilland.

Not many *cops* liked him either.

It is even doubtful whether or not Havilland liked himself.

'Heat,' he said to Carella, 'is all in the mind.'

'My mind is sweating the same as the rest of me,' Carella said.

'If I told you right this minute that you were sitting on a cake of ice in the middle of the Arctic Ocean, you'd begin to feel cool.'

'I don't feel any cooler,' Carella said.

'That's because you're a jackass,' Havilland said, shouting. Havilland always shouted. When Havilland whispered, he shouted. 'You don't want to feel cool. You want to feel hot. It makes you think you're working.'

'I am working.'

'I'm going home,' Havilland shouted abruptly.

Carella glanced at his watch. It was 10:17.

'What's the matter?' Havilland shouted.

'Nothing.'

'It's a quarter after ten, that's what you're looking sour about?' Havilland bellowed.

'I'm not looking sour.'

'Well, I don't care how you look,' Havilland roared. 'I'm going home.'

'So go home. I'm waiting for my relief.'

'I don't like the way you said that,' Havilland answered.

'Why not?'

'It implied that *I* am *not* waiting for my relief.'

Carella shrugged and blithely said, 'Let your conscience be your guide, brother.'

'Do you know how many hours I've been on this job?'

'How many?'

'Thirty-six,' Havilland said. 'I'm so sleepy I could crawl into a sewer and not wake up until Christmastime.'

'You'll pollute our water supply,' Carella said.

'Up yours!' Havilland shouted. He signed out and was leaving when Carella said, 'Hey!'

'What?'

'Don't get killed out there.'

'Up yours,' Havilland said again, and then he left.

The man dressed quietly and rapidly. He put on black trousers and a clean white shirt, and a gold-and-black striped tie. He put on dark blue socks, and then he reached for his shoes. His shoes carried O'Sullivan heels.

He put on the black jacket to his suit, and then he went to the dresser and opened the top drawer. The .45 lay on his handkerchiefs, lethal and blue-black. He pushed a fresh clip into the gun, and then put the gun into his jacket pocket.

He walked to the door in a ducklike waddle, opened it, took a last look around the apartment, flicked out the lights, and went into the night.

Steve Carella was relieved at 11:33 by a detective named Hal Willis. He filled Willis in on anything that was urgent, left him to catch and then walked downstairs.

'Going to see the girlfriend, Steve?' the desk sergeant asked.

'Yep,' Carella answered.

'Wish I was as young as you,' the sergeant said.

'Ah, come on,' Carella replied. 'You can't be more than seventy.'

The sergeant chuckled. 'Not a day over,' he answered.

'Good night,' Carella said.

'Night.'

Carella walked out of the building and headed for his car, which was parked two blocks away in a 'No Parking' zone.

Hank Bush left the precinct at 11:52 when his relief showed up.
'I thought you'd never get here,' he said.
'I thought so, too.'
'What happened?'
'It's too hot to run.'
Bush grimaced, went to the phone, and dialled his home number. He waited several moments. The phone kept ringing on the other end.
'Hello?'
'Alice?'
'Yes.' She paused. 'Hank?'
'I'm on my way, honey. Why don't you make some iced coffee?'
'All right, I will.'
'Is it very hot there?'
'Yes. Maybe you should pick up some ice cream.'
'All right.'
'No, never mind. No. Just come home. The iced coffee will do.'
'Okay. I'll see you later.'
'Yes, darling.'
Bush hung up. He turned to his relief. 'I hope you don't get relieved 'til nine,' he said.
'The heat's gone to his head,' the detective said to the air.
Bush snorted, signed out, and left the building.

The man with the .45 waited in the shadows.
His hand sweated on the walnut stock of the .45 in his jacket pocket. Wearing black, he knew he blended with the void of the alley mouth, but he was nonetheless nervous and a little frightened. Still, this had to be done.
He heard footsteps approaching. Long firm strides. A man in a hurry. He stared up the street. Yes.
Yes, this was his man.
His hand tightened on the .45.
The cop was closer now. The man in black stepped out of the alleyway abruptly. The cop stopped in his tracks. They were almost of the same height. A street lamp on the corner cast their shadows onto the pavement.
'Have you got a light, Mac?'
The cop was staring at the man in black. Then, suddenly, the cop was reaching for his back pocket. The man in black saw what was happening, and he brought up the .45 quickly, wrenching it free from his pocket. Both men fired simultaneously.
He felt the cop's bullet rip into his shoulder, but the .45 was bucking now, again and again, and he saw the cop clutch at his chest and fall for the pavement. The Detective's Special lay several feet from the cop's body now.
He backed away from the cop, ready to run.
'You son of a bitch,' the cop said.
He whirled. The cop was on his feet, rushing for him. He brought up the .45 again, but he was too late. The cop had him, his thick arms churning. He fought, pulling free, and the cop clutched at his head, and he felt hair wrench

loose, and then the cop's fingers clawed at his face, ripping, gouging.

He fired again. The cop doubled over and then fell to the pavement, his face colliding with the harsh concrete.

His shoulder was bleeding badly. He cursed the cop, and he stood over him, and his blood dripped onto the lifeless shoulders, and he held the .45 out at arm's length and squeezed the trigger again. The cop's head gave a sideways lurch and then was still.

The man in black ran off down the street.

The cop on the sidewalk was Hank Bush.

Chapter Sixteen

Sam Grossman was a police lieutenant. He was also a lab technician. He was tall and angular, a man who'd have looked more at home on a craggy New England farm than in the sterile orderliness of the Police Laboratory which stretched almost half the length of the first floor at Headquarters.

Grossman wore glasses, and his eyes were a guileless blue behind them. There was a gentility to his manner, a quiet warmth reminiscent of a long-lost era, even though his speech bore the clipped stamp of a man who is used to dealing with cold scientific fact.

'Hank was a smart cop,' he said to Carella.

Carella nodded. It was Hank who'd said that it didn't take much brain power to be a detective.

'The way I figure it,' Grossman went on, 'Hank thought he was a goner. The autopsy disclosed four wounds altogether, three in the chest, one at the back of the head. We can safely assume, I think, that the head shot was the last one fired, a *coup de grâce*.'

'Go ahead,' Carella said.

'Figure he'd been shot two or three times already, and possibly knew he'd be a dead pigeon before this was over. Whatever the case, he knew we could use more information on the bastard doing the shooting.'

'The hair, you mean?' Carella asked.

'Yes. We found clumps of hair on the sidewalk. All the hairs had living roots, so we'd have known they were pulled away by force even if we hadn't found some in the palms and fingers of Hank's hands. But he was thinking overtime. He also tore a goodly chunk of meat from the ambusher's face. That told us a few things, too.'

'And what else?'

'Blood. Hank shot this guy, Steve. Well, undoubtedly you know that already.'

'Yes. What does it all add up to?'

'A lot,' Grossman said. He picked up a report from his desk, 'This is what we know for sure, from what we were able to piece together, from what Hank gave us.'

Grossman cleared his throat and began reading.

'The killer is a male, white, adult, not over say fifty years of age. He is a mechanic, possibly highly skilled and highly paid. He is dark complexioned, his skin is oily, he has a heavy beard which he tries to disguise with talc. His hair is dark brown, and he is approximately six feet tall. Within the past two days, he took a haircut and a singe. He is fast, possibly indicating a man who is not overweight. Judging from the hair, he should weigh about 180. He is wounded, most likely above the waist, and not superficially.'

'Break it down for me,' Carella said, somewhat amazed – as he always was – by what the Lab. boys could do with a rag, a bone, and a hank of hair.

'Okay,' Grossman said. 'Male. In this day and age, this sometimes poses a problem, especially if we've got only hair from the head. Luckily, Hank solved that one for us. The *head* hairs of either a male or a female will have an average diameter of less than 0.08 mm. Okay, having only a batch of head hairs to go on, we've got to resort to other measurements to determine whether or not the hair came from a male or a female. Length of the hair used to be a good gauge. If the length was more than 8 cm., we could assume the hair came from a woman. But the goddamn women nowadays are wearing their hair as short as, if not shorter than, the men. So we could have been fooled on this one, if Hank hadn't scratched this guy's face.'

'What's the scratch have to do with it?'

'It gave us a skin sample, to begin with. That's how we knew the man was white, dark complexioned, and oily. But it also gave us a beard hair.'

'How do you know it was a beard hair?'

'Simple,' Grossman said. 'Under the microscope, it showed up in cross-section as being triangular, with concave sides. Only beard hairs are shaped that way. The diameter, too, was greater than 0.1 mm. Simple. A beard hair. Had to be a man.'

'How do you know he was a mechanic?'

'The head hairs were covered with metal dust.'

'You said possibly a highly skilled and highly paid one. Why?'

'The head hairs were saturated with a hair preparation. We broke it down and checked it against our sample sheets. It's very expensive stuff. Five bucks the bottle when sold singly. Ten bucks when sold in a set with the after-shave talc. This customer was wearing both the hair gook *and* the talc. What mechanic can afford ten bucks for such luxuries – unless he's highly paid? If he's highly paid, chances are he's highly skilled.'

'How do you know he's not over fifty?' Carella asked.

'Again, by the diameter of the hair and also the pigmentation. Here, take a look at this chart.' He extended a sheet to Carella.

Age	Diameter
12 days	0.024 mm.
6 months	0.037 mm.
18 months	0.038 mm.
15 years	0.053 mm.
Adults	0.07 mm.

'Fellow's head hair had a diameter of 0.071,' Grossman said.

'That only shows he's an adult.'

'Sure. But if we get a hair with a living root, and there are hardly any pigment grains in the cortex, we can be pretty sure the hair comes from an old person. This guy had plenty of pigment grains. Also, even though we rarely make any age guesses on such single evidence, an older person's hair has a tendency to become finer. This guy's hair is coarse and thick.'

Carella sighed.

'Am I going too fast for you?'

'No,' Carella said. 'How about the singe and the haircut?'

'The singe was simple. The hairs were curled, slightly swelled, and greyish in colour. Not naturally grey, you understand.'

'The haircut?'

'If the guy had had a haircut just before he did the shooting, the head hairs would have shown clean-cut edges. After forty-eight hours, the cut begins to grow round. We can pretty well determine just when a guy's had his last haircut.'

'You said he was six feet tall.'

'Well, Ballistics helped us on that one.'

'Spell it,' Carella said.

'We had the blood to work with. Did I mention the guy has type O blood?'

'You guys . . .' Carella started.

'Aw come on, Steve, that was simple.'

'Yeah.'

'Yeah,' Grossman said. 'Look, Steve, the blood serum of one person has the ability to agglutinate . . .' He paused. 'That means clump, or bring together the red blood cells of certain other people. There are four blood groups: Group O, Group A, Group B, Group AB. Okay?'

'Okay,' Carella said.

'We take the sample of blood, and we mix a little of it with samples from the four groups. Oh, hell, here's another chart for you to look at.' He handed it to Carella.

1. Group O – no agglutination in either serum.
2. Group A – agglutination in serum B only.
3. Group B – agglutination in serum A only.
4. Group AB – agglutination in both serums.

'This guy's blood – and he left a nice trail of it when he was running away, in addition to several spots on the back of Hank's shirt – would not agglutinate, or clump, in any of the samples. Hence, type O. Another indication that he's white incidentally. A and O are most common in white people. 45% of all white people are in the O group.'

'How do figure he's six feet tall? You still haven't told me.'

'Well, as I said, this is where Ballistics came in. In addition to what we had, of course. The blood spots on Hank's shirt weren't of much value in determining from what height they had fallen since the cotton absorbed them when they hit. But the blood stains on the pavement told us several things.'

'What'd they tell you?'

'First that he was going pretty fast. You see, the faster a man is walking, the narrower and longer will be the blood drops and the teeth on those drops. They look something like a small gear, if you can picture that, Steve.'

'I can.'

'Okay. These were narrow and also sprinkled in many small drops, which told us that he was moving fast and also that the drops were falling from a height of somewhere around two yards or so.'

'So?'

'So, if he was moving fast, he wasn't hit in the legs or the stomach. A man doesn't move very fast under those conditions. If the drops came from a height of approximately two yards, chances are the man was hit high above the waist. Ballistics pried Hank's slug out of the brick wall of the building, and from the angle – assuming Hank only had time to shoot from a draw – they figured the man was struck somewhere around the shoulder. This indicates a tall man, I mean when you put the blood drops and the slug together.'

'How do you know he wasn't wounded superficially?'

'All the blood, man. He left a long trail.'

'You said he weighs about 180. How ...'

'The hair was healthy hair. The guy was going fast. The speed tells us he wasn't overweight. A healthy man of six feet should weigh about 180, no?'

'You've given me a lot, Sam,' Carella said. 'Thanks.'

'Don't mention it. I'm glad I'm not the guy who has to check on doctors' gunshot wound reports, or absentee mechanics. Not to mention this hair lotion and talc. It's called "Skylark", by the way.'

'Well, thanks, anyway.'

'Don't thank me,' Grossman said.

'Huh?'

'Thank Hank.'

Chapter Seventeen

The teletype alarm went out to fourteen states.

It read:

XXXXX APPREHEND SUSPICION OF MURDER XXX UNIDENTIFIED MALE WHITE CAUCASIAN ADULT BELOW FIFTY XXXXX POSSIBLE HEIGHT SIX FEET OR OVER XXX POSSIBLE WEIGHT ONE HUNDRED EIGHTY XXX DARK HAIR SWARTHY COMPLEXION HEAVY BEARD XXXX USES HAIR PREPARATION AND TALC TRADENAME 'SKYLARK' XXXX SHOES MAY POSSIBLY CARRY HEELS WITH 'O'SULLIVAN' TRADENAME XXXX MAN ASSUMED TO BE SKILLED MECHANIC MAY POSSIBLY SEEK SUCH WORK XXXXX GUNWOUND ABOVE WAIST POSSIBLE SHOULDER HIGH MAN MAY SEEK DOCTOR XXXX THIS MAN IS DANGEROUS AND ARMED WITH COLT .45 AUTOMATIC XX

'Those are a lot of "possiblys",' Havilland said.

'Too damn many,' Carella agreed. 'But at least it's a place to start.'

It was not so easy to start.

They could, of course, have started by calling all the doctors in the city, on the assumption that one or more of them had failed to report a gunshot wound, as specified by law. However, there were quite a few doctors in the city. To be exact, there were:

4,283 doctors in Calm's Point
1,975 doctors in Riverhead
8,728 doctors in Isola (including the Diamondback and Hillside sectors)
2,614 doctors in Majesta
and 264 doctors in Bethtown
for a grand total of

COUNT 'EM!

17,864 DOCTORS 17,864

Those are a lot of medical men. Assuming each call would take approximately five minutes, a little multiplication told the cops it would take them approximately 89,320 minutes to call each doctor in the classified directory. Of course, there were 22,000 policemen on the force. If each cop took on the job of calling four doctors, every call could have been made before twenty minutes had expired. Unfortunately, many of the other cops had other tidbits of crime to occupy themselves with. So, faced with the overwhelming number of healers, the detectives decided to wait – instead – for one of them to call with a gunshot wound report. Since the bullet had exited the killer's body, the wound was in all likelihood a clean one, anyway, and perhaps the killer would *never* seek the aid of a doctor. In which case the waiting would all be in vain.

If there were 17,864 doctors in the city, it was virtually impossible to tally the number of mechanics plying their trade there. So this line of approach was also abandoned.

There remained the hair lotion and talc with the innocent-sounding name 'Skylark'.

A quick check showed that both masculine beauty aids were sold over the counter of almost every drug store in the city. They were as common as – if higher-priced than – aspirin tablets.

Good for a cold.

If you don't like them . . .

The police turned, instead, to their own files in the Bureau of Identification, and to the voluminous files in the Federal Bureau of Investigation.

And the search was for a male, white Caucasian, under fifty years in age, dark-haired, dark-complexioned, six feet tall, weighing one-hundred-eighty pounds, addicted to the use of a Colt .45 automatic.

The needle may have been in the city.

But the entire United States was the haystack.

'Lady to see you, Steve,' Miscolo said.

'What about?'

'Said she wanted to talk to the people investigating the cop killer.' Miscolo wiped his brow. There was a big fan in the Clerical Office, and he hated leaving it. Not that he didn't enjoy talking to the DD men. It was simply that Miscolo was a heavy sweater, and he didn't like the armpits of his uniform shirts ruined by unnecessary talk.

'Okay, send her in,' Carella said.

Miscolo vanished, and then reappeared with a small bird-like woman whose head jerked in short arcs as she surveyed first the dividing railing and then the file cabinets and then the desks and the grilled windows and then the detectives on phones everywhere in the squadroom, most of them in various stages of sartorial inelegance.

'This is Detective Carella,' Miscolo said. 'He's one of the detectives on the investigation.' Miscolo sighed heavily and then fled back to the big fan in the small Clerical office.

'Won't you come in, ma'am?' Carella said.

'*Miss*,' the woman corrected. Carella was in his shirt sleeves, and she noticed this with obvious distaste, and then glanced sharply around the room again and said, 'Don't you have a private office?'

'I'm afraid not,' Carella said.

'I don't want them to hear me.'

'Who?' Carella asked.

'Them,' she said. 'Could we go to a desk somewhere in the corner?'

'Certainly,' Carella said. 'What did you say your name was, Miss?'

'Oreatha Bailey,' the woman said. She was at least fifty-five or so, Carella surmised, with the sharp-featured face of a sterotyped witch. He led her through the gate in the railing and to an unoccupied desk in the far right corner of the room, a corner which – unfortunately – did not receive any ventilation from the windows.

When they were seated, Carella asked, 'What can I do for you, Miss Bailey?'

'You don't have a bug in this corner, do you?'

'A ... bug?'

'One of them dictaphone things.'

'No.'

'What did you say your name was?'

'Detective Carella.'

'And you speak English?'

Carella suppressed a smile. 'Yes, I ... I picked up the language from the natives.'

'I'd have preferred an American policeman,' Miss Bailey said in all seriousness.

'Well, I sometimes pass for one,' Carella answered, amused.

'Very well.'

There was a long pause. Carella waited.

Miss Bailey showed no signs of continuing the conversation

'Miss ... ?'

'Shh!' she said sharply.

Carella waited.

After several moments, the woman said. 'I know who killed those policemen.'

Carella leaned forward, interested. The best leads sometimes came from the most unexpected sources. 'Who?' he asked.

'Never you mind,' she answered.

Carella waited.

'They are going to kill a lot more policemen,' Miss Bailey said. 'That's their plan.'

'Whose plan?'

'If they can do away with law enforcement, the rest will be easy,' Miss Bailey said. 'That's their plan. First the police, then the National Guard, and then the regular Army.'

Carella looked at Miss Bailey suspiciously.

'They've been sending messages to me,' Miss Bailey said. 'They think I'm one of them, I don't know why. They come out of the walls and give me messages.'

'Who comes out of the walls?' Carella asked.

'The cockroach-men. That's why I asked if there was a bug in this corner.'

'Oh, the ... the cockroach-men.'

'Yes.'

'I see.'

'Do I look like a cockroach?' she asked.

'No,' Carella said. 'Not particularly.'

'Then why have they mistaken me for one of them? They look like cockroaches, you know.'

'Yes, I know.'

'They talk by radio-nuclear thermics. I think they must be from another planet, don't you?'

'Possibly,' Carella said.

'It's remarkable that I can understand them. Perhaps they've overcome my mind, do you think that's possible?'

'Anything's possible,' Carella agreed.

'They told me about Reardon the night before they killed him. They said they would start with him because he was the Commissar of Sector Three. They used a thermo-disintegrator on him, you know that, don't you?' Miss Bailey paused, and then nodded. '.45 calibre.'

'Yes,' Carella said.

'Foster was the Black Prince of Argaddon. They had to get him. That's what they told me. The signals they put out are remarkably clear, considering the fact that they're in an alien tongue. I do wish you were an American, Mr Carella. There are so many aliens around these days that one hardly knows who to trust.'

'Yes,' Carella said. He could feel the sweat blotting the back of his shirt. 'Yes.'

'They killed Bush because he wasn't a bush, he was a tree in disguise. They hate all plant life.'

'I see.'

'Especially trees. They need the carbon dioxide, you see, and plants consume it. Especially trees. Trees consume a great deal of carbon dioxide.'

'Certainly.'

'Will you stop them, now that you know?' Miss Bailey asked.

'We'll do everything in our power,' Carella said.

'The best way to stop them ...' Miss Bailey paused and rose, clutching her purse to her narrow bosom. 'Well, I don't want to tell you how to run your business.'

'We appreciate your help,' Carella said. He began walking her to the railing. Miss Bailey stopped.

'Would you like to know the best way to stop these cockroach-men? Guns are no good against them, you know. Because of the thermal heat.'

'I didn't know that,' Carella said. They were standing just inside the railing. He opened the gate for her, and she stepped through.

'There's only one way to stop them,' she said.

'What's that?' Carella asked.

Miss Bailey pursed her mouth. 'Step on them!' she said, and she turned on her heel and walked past Clerical, and then down the steps to the first floor.

Bert Kling seemed to be in high spirits that night.

When Carella and Havilland came into the hospital room, he was sitting up in bed, and aside from the bulky bandage over his right shoulder, you'd never know anything was wrong with him. He beamed a broad smile, and then sat up to talk to the two visiting detectives.

He chewed on the candy they'd brought him, and he said this hospital duty was real jazzy, and that they should get a look at some of the nurses in their tight white uniforms.

He seemed to bear no grudge whatever against the boy who'd shot him. Those breaks were all part of the game, he supposed. He kept chewing candy, and joking, and talking until it was almost time for the cops to leave.

Bert Kling seemed to be in high spirits that night.

Chapter Eighteen

The three funerals followed upon each other's heels with remarkable rapidity. The heat did not help the classical ceremonies of death. The mourners followed the caskets and sweated. An evil, leering sun grinned its blistering grin, and freshly turned soil – which should have been cool and moist – accepted the caskets with dry, dusty indifference.

The beaches that week were jammed to capacity. In Calm's Point at Mott's Island, the scorekeeper recorded a record-breaking crowd of two million four hundred and seventy thousand surf seekers. The police had problems. The police had traffic problems because everyone who owned any sort of a jalopy had put it on the road. The police had fire-hydrant problems, because kids all over the city were turning on the johnny pumps, covering the spout with a flattened coffee can, and romping beneath the improvised shower. The police had burglary problems, because people were sleeping with their windows open; people were leaving parked cars unlocked, windows wide; shopkeepers were stepping across the street for a moment to catch a quick Pepsi Cola. The police had 'floater' problems, because the scorched and heat-weary citizens sometimes sought relief in the polluted currents of the rivers that bound Isola – and some of them drowned, and some of them turned up with bloated bodies and bulging eyes.

On Walker Island, in the River Dix, the police had prisoner problems because the cons there decided the heat was too much for them to bear, and they banged their tin cups on the sweating bars of their hot cells, and the cops listened to the clamour and rushed for riot guns.

The police had all sorts of problems.

Carella wished she were not wearing black.

He knew this was absurd. When a woman's husband is dead, the woman wears black.

But Hank and he had talked a lot in the quiet hours of the midnight tour, and Hank had many times described Alice in the black nightgowns she wore to bed. And try as he might, Carella could not disassociate the separate concepts of black: black as sheer and frothy raiment of seduction; black as the ashy garment of mourning.

Alice Bush sat across from him in the living room of the Calm's Point apartment. The windows were wide open, and he could see the tall Gothic structures of the Calm's Point College campus etched against the merciless, glaring blue of the sky. He had worked with Bush for many years, but this was the first time he'd been inside his apartment, and the association of Alice Bush in black cast a feeling of guilt over his memories of Hank.

The apartment was not at all what he would have expected for a man like Hank. Hank was big, rough-hewn. The apartment was somehow frilly, a woman's apartment. He could not believe that Hank had been comfortable in these rooms. His eyes had scanned the furniture, small-scaled stuff, stuff in which Hank could never have spread his legs. The curtains at the windows were ruffled chintz. The walls of the living room were a sickeningly pale lemon shade. The end tables were heavy with curlicues and inlaid patterns. The corners of the room contained knick-knack shelves, and the shelves were loaded with fragile glass figurines of dogs and cats and gnomes and one of Little Bo Peep holding a delicately blown, slender glass shepherd's crook.

The room, the apartment, seemed to Carella to be the intricately cluttered design for a comedy of manners. Hank must have been as out of place here as a plumber at a literary tea.

Not so Mrs Bush.

Mrs Bush lounged on a heavily padded chartreuse love-seat, her long legs tucked under her, her feet bare. Mrs Bush belonged in this room. This room had been designed for Mrs Bush, designed for femininity, and the Male Animal be damned.

She wore black silk. She was uncommonly big-busted, incredibly narrow-waisted. Her hip bones were wide, flesh-padded, a woman whose body had been designed for the bearing of children – but somehow she didn't seem the type. He could not visualize her squeezing life from her loins. He could only visualize her as Hank had described her – in the role of a seductress. The black silk dress strengthened the concept. The frou-frou room left no doubt. This was a stage set for Alice Bush.

The dress was not low-cut. It didn't have to be.

Nor was it particularly tight, and it didn't have to be that, either.

It was not expensive, but it fitted her figure well. He had no doubt that anything she wore would fit her figure well. He had no doubt that even a potato sack would look remarkably interesting on the woman who had been Hank's wife.

'What do I do now?' Alice asked. 'Make up beds at the precinct? That's the usual routine for a cop's widow, isn't it?'

'Did Hank leave any insurance?' Carella asked.

'Nothing to speak of. Insurance doesn't come easily to cops, does it? Besides . . . Steve, he was a young man. Who thinks of things like this? Who thinks these things are going to happen?' She looked at him wide-eyed. Her eyes were very brown, her hair was very blonde, her complexion was fair and unmarred. She was a beautiful woman, and he did not like considering her such. He wanted her to be dowdy and forlorn. He did not want her looking fresh and lovely. Goddamnit, what was there about this room that suffocated a man? He felt like the last male alive, surrounded by bare-breasted beauties on a tropical island surrounded by man-eating sharks. There was no place to run to. The island was called Amazonia or something, and the island was female to the core, and he was the last man alive.

The room and Alice Bush.

The femaleness reached out to envelop him in a cloying clinging embrace.

'Change your mind, Steve,' Alice said. 'Have a drink.'

'All right, I will,' he answered.

She rose, displaying a long white segment of thigh as she got to her feet, displaying an almost indecent oblivion to the way she handled her body. She had lived with it for a long time, he supposed. She no longer marvelled at its allure. She accepted it, and lived with it, and others could marvel. A thigh was a thigh, what the hell! What was so special about the thigh of Alice Bush?

'Scotch?'

'All right.'

'How does it feel, something like this?' she asked. She was standing at the bar across from him. She stood with the loose-hipped stance of a fashion model, incongruous because he always pictured fashion models as willowy and thin and flat-chested. Alice Bush was none of these.

'Something like what?'

'Investigating the death of a colleague and friend.'

'Weird,' Carella said.

'I'll bet.'

'You're taking it very well,' Carella said.

'I have to,' Alice answered briefly.

'Why?'

'Because I'll fall all to pieces if I don't. He's in the ground, Steve. It's not going to help for me to wail and moan all over the place.'

'I suppose not.'

'We've got to go on living, haven't we? We can't simply give up because someone we love is gone, can we?'

'No,' Carella agreed.

She walked to him and handed him the drink. Their fingers touched for an instant. He looked up at her. Her face was completely guileless. The contact, he was sure, had been accidental.

She walked to the window and looked out towards the college. 'It's lonely here without him,' she said.

'It's lonely at the house without him, too,' Carella said, surprised. He had not realized, before this, how really attached he had become to Hank.

'I was thinking of taking a trip,' Alice said, 'getting away from things that remind me of him.'

'Things like what?' Carella asked.

'Oh, I don't know,' Alice said. 'Like . . . last night I saw his hair brush on the dresser, and there was some of the wild red hair of his caught in the bristles, and all at once it reminded me of him, of the wildness of him. He was a wild person, Steve.' She paused. 'Wild.'

The word was female somehow. He was reminded again of the word portrait Hank had drawn, of the real portrait before him, standing by the window, of the femaleness everywhere around him on this island. He could not blame her, he knew that. She was only being herself, being Alice Bush, being Woman. She was only a pawn of fate, a girl who automatically embodied womanhood, a girl who . . . hell!

'How far have you come along on it?' she asked. She whirled from the window, went back to the love seat and collapsed into it. The movement was not a gracious one. It was feline, however. She sprawled in the love seat like a big jungle cat, and then she tucked her legs under her again, and he would not have been surprised if she'd begun purring in that moment.

He told her what they thought they knew about the suspected killer. Alice nodded.

'Quite a bit to go on,' she said.

'Not really.'

'I mean, if he should seek a doctor's aid.'

'He hasn't yet. Chances are he won't. He probably dressed the wound himself.'

'Badly shot?'

'Apparently. But clean.'

'Hank should have killed him,' she said. Surprisingly, there was no viciousness attached to the words. The words themselves bore all the lethal potential of a coiled rattler, but the delivery made them harmless.

'Yes,' Carella agreed. 'He should have.'

'But he didn't.'

'No.'

'What's your next step?' she asked.

'Oh, I don't know. Homicide North is up a tree on these killings, and I guess we are, too. I've got a few ideas kicking around, though.'

'A lead?' she asked.

'No. Just ideas.'

'What kind of ideas?'

'They'd bore you.'

'My husband's been killed,' Alice said coldly. 'I assure you I will not be bored by anything that may lead to finding his killer.'

'Well, I'd prefer not to air any ideas until I know what I'm talking about.'

Alice smiled. 'That's different. You haven't touched your drink.'

He raised the glass to his lips. The drink was very strong.

'Wow!' he said. 'You don't spare the alcohol, do you?'

'Hank liked his strong,' she said. 'He liked everything strong.'

And again, like an interwoven thread of personality, a personality dictated by the demands of a body that could look nothing but blatantly inviting, Alice Bush had inadvertently lighted another fuse. He had the feeling that she would suddenly explode into a thousand flying fragments of breast and hip and thigh, splashing over the landscape like a Dali painting.

'I'd better be getting along,' he said. 'The City doesn't pay me for sipping drinks all morning.'

'Stay a while,' she said. 'I have a few ideas myself.'

He glanced up quickly, almost suspecting an edge of *double entendre* in her voice. He was mistaken. She had turned away from him and was looking out the window again, her face in profile, her body in profile.

'Let me hear them,' he said.

'A cop hater,' she replied.

'Maybe.'

'It has to be. Who else would senselessly take three lives? It has to be a cop hater, Steve. Doesn't Homicide North think so?'

'I haven't talked to them in the past few days. That's what they thought in the beginning, I know.'

'What do they think now?'

'That's hard to say.'

'What do *you* think now?'

'Maybe a cop hater. Reardon and Foster, yes, a cop hater. But Hank . . . I don't know.'

'I'm not sure I follow you.'

'Well, Reardon and Foster were partners, so we could assume that possibly some jerk was carrying a grudge against them. They worked together . . . maybe they rubbed some idiot the wrong way.'

'Yes?'

'But Hank *never* worked with them. Oh, well maybe not never. Maybe once or twice on a plant or something. He never made an important arrest with either of them along, though. Our records show that.'

'Who says it has to be someone with a personal grudge, Steve? This may simply be some goddamned lunatic.' She seemed to be getting angry. He didn't know why she was getting angry because she'd certainly been calm enough up to this point. But her breath was coming heavier now, and her breasts heaved disconcertingly. 'Just some crazy, rotten, twisted fool who's taken it into his mind to knock off every cop in the 87th Precinct. Does that sound so far-fetched?'

'No, not at all. As a matter of fact, we've checked all the mental institutions in the area for people who were recently released who might possibly have had a history of . . .' He shook his head. 'You know, we figured perhaps a paranoiac, somebody who'd go berserk at the sight of a uniform. Except these men weren't in uniform.'

'No, they weren't. What'd you get?'

'We thought we had one lead. Not anyone with a history of dislike for policemen, but a young man who had a lot of officer trouble in the Army. He was recently released from Bramlook as cured, but that doesn't mean a goddamned thing. We checked with the psychiatrists there, and they felt his illness would never break out in an act of violence, no less a prolonged rampage of violence.'

'And you let it drop?'

'No, we looked the kid up. Harmless. Alibis a mile long.'

'Who else have you checked?'

'We've got feelers out to all our underworld contacts. We thought this might be a gang thing, where some hood has an alleged grievance against something we've done to hamper him, and so he's trying to show us we're not so high and mighty. He hires a torpedo and begins methodically putting us in our places. But there's been no rumble so far, and underworld revenge is not something you can keep very quiet.'

'What else?'

'I've been wading through FBI photos all morning. You'd never realize how many men there are who fit the possible description we have.' He sipped at the scotch. He was beginning to feel a little more comfortable with Alice. Maybe she wasn't so female, after all. Or maybe her femaleness simply enveloped you after a while, causing you to lose all perspective. Whatever it was, the room wasn't as oppressive now.

'Turn up anything? From the photos?'

'Not yet. Half of them are in jail, and the rest are scattered all over the country. You see, the hell of this thing is ... well ...'

'What?'

'How'd the killer know that these men were cops? They were all in plainclothes. Unless he'd had contact with them before, how could he know?'

'Yes, I see what you mean.'

'Maybe he sat in a parked car across from the house and watched everyone who went in and out. If he did that for a while, he'd get to know who worked there and who didn't.'

'He could have done that,' Alice said thoughtfully. 'Yes he could have.' She crossed her legs unconsciously. Carella looked away.

'Several things against that theory, though,' Carella said. 'That's what makes this case such a bitch.' The word had sneaked out, and he glanced up apprehensively. Alice Bush seemed not to mind the profanity. She had probably heard enough of it from Hank. Her legs were still crossed. They were very good legs. Her skirt had fallen into a funny position. He looked away again.

'You see, if somebody had been watching the house, we'd have noticed him. That is, if he'd been watching it long enough to know who worked there and who was visiting ... that would take time. We'd surely have spotted him.'

'Not if he were hidden.'

'There are no buildings opposite the house. Only the park.'

'He could have been somewhere in the park ... with binoculars, maybe.'

'Sure. But how could he tell the detectives from the patrolmen, then?'

'What?'

'He killed three detectives. Maybe it was chance. I don't think so. All right, how the hell could he tell the patrolmen from the detectives?'

'Very simply,' Alice said. 'Assuming he was watching, he'd see the men when they arrived, and he'd see them after muster when they went out to their beats. They'd be in uniform then. I'm talking about the patrolmen.'

'Yes, I suppose.' He took a deep swallow of the drink. Alice moved on the love seat.

'I'm hot,' she said.

He did not look at her. He knew that his eyes would have been drawn downward if he did, and he did not want to see what Alice was unconsciously, obliviously showing.

'I don't suppose this heat has helped the investigation any,' she said.

'This heat hasn't helped *anything* any.'

'I'm changing to shorts and a halter as soon as you get out of here.'

'There's a hint if ever I heard one,' Carella said.

'No, I didn't mean ... oh hell, Steve, I'd change to them now if I thought you were going to stay longer. I just thought you were leaving soon. I mean ...' She made a vague motion with one hand. 'Oh, nuts.'

'I am leaving, Alice. Lots of photos to look through back there.' He rose. 'Thanks for the drink.' He started for the door, not looking back when she got up, not wanting to look at her legs again.

She took his hand at the door. Her grip was firm and warm. Her hand was fleshy. She squeezed his hand.

'Good luck, Steve. If there's anything I can do to help ...'

'We'll let you know. Thanks again.'

He left the apartment and walked down to the street. It was very hot in the street.

Chapter Nineteen

'Now here's what I call a real handsome one,' Hal Willis said. Hal Willis was the only really small detective Carella had ever known. He passed the minimum height requirement of five eight, of course, but just barely. And contrasted against the imposing bulk of the other bulls in the division, he looked more like a soft shoe dancer than a tough cop. That he was a tough cop, there was no doubt. His bones were slight, and his face was thin, and he looked as if he would have trouble swatting a fly, but anyone who'd ever tangled with Hal Willis did not want the dubious pleasure again. Hal Willis was a Judo expert.

Hal Willis could shake your hand and break your backbone in one and the same motion. Were you not careful with Hal Willis, you might find yourself enwrapped in the excruciating pain of a Thumb Grip. Were you even less careful, you might discover yourself hurtling through space in the fury of either a Rugby or a Far-Eastern Capsize. Ankle Throws, Flying Mares, Back Wheels, all were as much a part of Hal Willis's personality as the sparkling brown eyes in his face.

Those eyes were amusedly turned now towards the FBI photo which he shoved across the desk towards Carella.

The photo was of a man who was indeed a 'real handsome one.' His nose had been fractured in at least four places. A scar ran the length of his left cheek. Scar tissue hooded his eyes. He owned cauliflower ears and hardly any teeth. His name, of course, was 'Pretty-Boy Krajak'.

'A doll,' Carella said. 'Why'd they send him to us?'

'Dark hair, six feet two, weight one-eighty-five. How'd you like to run across him some dark and lonely night?'

'I wouldn't. Is he in the city?'

'He's in L.A.,' Willis said.

'Then we'll leave him to Joe Friday,' Carella cracked.

'Have another Chesterfield,' Willis countered. 'The only living cigarette with 60,000 filter dragnets.'

Carella laughed. The phone rang. Willis picked it up.

'87th Squad,' he said. 'Detective Willis.'

Carella looked up.

'What?' Willis said. 'Give me the address.' He scribbled something hastily on his pad. 'Hold him there, we'll be right over.' He hung up, opened the desk drawer and removed his holster and service revolver.

'What is it?' Carella asked.

'Doctor on 35th North. Has a man in his office with a bullet wound in his left shoulder.'

A squad car was parked in front of the brownstone on 35th North when Carella and Willis arrived.

'The rookies beat us here,' Willis said.

'So long as they've got him,' Carella answered, and he made it sound like a prayer. A sign on the door read, 'DOCTOR IS IN. RING BELL AND PLEASE BE SEATED.'

'Where?' Willis asked. 'On the doorstep?'

They rang the bell, opened the door, and entered the office. The office was situated off the small courtyard on the street level of the brownstone. A patrolman was seated on the long leather couch, reading a copy of *Esquire*. He closed the magazine when the detective entered and said, 'Patrolman Curtis, sir.'

'Where's the doctor?' Carella asked.

'Inside, sir. Country is asking him some questions.'

'Who's Country?'

'My partner, sir.'

'Come on,' Willis said. He and Carella went into the doctor's office. Country, a tall gangling boy with a shock of black hair, snapped to attention when they entered.

'Goodbye, Country,' Willis said drily. The patrolman eased himself towards the door and left the office.

'Dr Russell?' Willis asked.

'Yes,' Dr Russell replied. He was a man of about fifty, with a head of hair that was silver white, giving the lie to his age. He stood as straight as a telephone pole, broad-shouldered, immaculate in his white office tunic. He was a handsome man, and he gave an impression of great competence. For all Carella knew, he may have been a butcher, but he'd have trusted this man to cut out his heart.

'Where is he?'

'Gone,' Dr Russell said.

'How ...'

'I called as soon as I saw the wound. I excused myself, went out to my private office and placed the call. When I came back, he was gone.'

'Nuts,' Willis said. 'Want to tell us from the beginning, doctor?'

'Certainly. He came in ... oh, not more than twenty minutes ago. The office was empty, unusual for this time of day, but I rather imagine people with minor ailments are curing them at the seashore.' He smiled briefly. 'He said he'd shot himself while cleaning his hunting rifle. I took him into the Examination Room – that's *this* room, gentlemen – and asked him to take off his shirt. He did.'

'What happened then?'

'I examined the wound. I asked him when he had had the accident. He said it had occurred only this morning. I knew instantly that he was lying. The wound I was examining was not a fresh one. It was already highly infected. That was when I remembered the newspaper stories.'

'About the cop killer?'

'Yes. I recalled having read something about the man having a pistol wound above the waist. That was when I excused myself to call you.'

'Was this definitely a gunshot wound?'

'Without a doubt. It had been dressed, but very badly. I didn't examine it very closely, you understand, because I rushed off to make the call. But it seemed to me that iodine had been used as a disinfectant.'

'Iodine?'

'Yes.'

'But it was infected nonetheless?'

'Oh, definitely. That man is going to have to find another doctor, sooner or later.'

'What did he look like?'

'Well, where should I begin?'

'How old?'

'Thirty-five or thereabouts.'

'Height?'

'A little over six feet, I should say.'

'Weight?'

'About one-ninety.'

'Black hair?' Willis asked.

'Yes.'

'Colour of eyes?'

'Brown.'

'Any scars, birthmarks, other identifying characteristics?'

'His face was very badly scratched.'

'Did he touch anything in the office?'

'No. Wait, yes.'

'What?'

'I had him sit on the table here. When I began probing the wound, he winced and gripped the stirrups here at the foot of the table.'

'This may be a break, Hal,' Carella said.

'It sounds like one. What was he wearing, Dr Russell?'

'Black.'

'Black suit?'

'Yes.'

'What colour shirt?'

'White. It was stained over the wound.'

'Tie.'

'A striped tie. Gold and black.'

'Tie clasp?'

'Yes. Some sort of design on it.'

'What kind?'

'A bugle? Something like that.'

'Trumpet, hunting horn, horn of plenty?'

'I don't know. I couldn't identify it. It only stuck in my mind because it was an unusual clasp. I noticed it when he was undressing.'

'What colour shoes?'

'Black.'

'Clean-shaven?'

'Yes. That is, you meant was he wearing a beard?'

'Yes.'

'Well then, yes, he was clean-shaven. But he needed a shave.'

'Uh-huh. Wearing any rings?'

'None that I noticed.'

'Undershirt?'

'No undershirt.'

'Can't say I blame him in this heat. Mind if I make a call, Doc?'

'Please help yourself. Do you think he's the man?'

'I hope so,' Willis said. 'God, I hope so.'

When a man is nervous, he perspires – even if the temperature is not hovering somewhere in the nineties.

There are sweat pores on the fingertips, and the stuff they secrete contains 98.5 per cent water and 0.5 to 1.5 per cent solid material. This solid material breaks down to about one-third of inorganic matter – mainly salt – and two-thirds of organic substances like urea, albumin and formic, butyric and acetic acids. Dust, dirt, grease cling to the secretion from a man's fingertips.

The perspiration, mixed with whatever happens to be clinging to it at the moment, leaves a filmy impression on whatever the man happens to touch.

The suspected killer happened to touch the smooth chromium surfaces of the stirrups in Dr Russell's office.

The tech crew dusted the latent fingerprints with one of the commercial black powders. The excess powder was allowed to fall on a sheet of paper. The prints were lightly brushed with an ostrich feather. They were then photographed.

There were two good thumbprints, one for each hand where the suspect had pressed down on the top surfaces of the stirrups. There were good second-joint prints for each hand where the suspect had gripped the undersides of the stirrups.

The prints were sent to the Bureau of Identification. A thorough search was made of the files. The search proved fruitless, and the prints were sent to the Federal Bureau of Investigation while the detectives sat back to wait.

In the meantime, a police artist went to see Dr Russell. Listening to Dr Russell's description, he began drawing a picture of the suspect. He made changes as Dr Russell suggested them – 'No, the nose is a little too long; yes, that's better. Try to give a little curl to his lip there, yes, yes, that's it' – and he finally came up with a drawing which tallied with Dr Russell's recollection of the man he had examined. The picture was sent to each metropolitan daily and to each television station in the area, together with a verbal description of the wanted man.

All this while, the detectives waited for the FBI report. They were still waiting the next day.

Willis looked at the drawing on the first page of one of the morning tabloids.

The headline screamed: HAVE YOU SEEN THIS MAN?

'He's not bad-looking,' Willis said.

'Pretty-Boy Krajak,' Carella said.

'No, I'm serious.'

'He may be handsome, but he's a killer,' Carella said. 'I hope his arm falls off.'

'It very well might,' Willis said drily.

'Where the hell's that FBI report?' Carella asked edgily. He had been answering calls all morning, calls from citizens who reported having seen the killer. Each call had to be checked out, of course, but thus far the man had been seen all over the city at simultaneous times. 'I thought those G-men were supposed to be fast.'

'They are,' Willis said.

'I'm going to check with the Lieutenant.'

'Go ahead,' Willis said.

Carella went to the Lieutenant's door. He knocked and Byrnes called, 'Come.' Carella went into the office. Byrnes was on the phone. He signalled for Carella to stand by. He nodded then and said, 'But, Harriet, I can't see anything wrong with that.'

He listened patiently.

'Yes, but ...'

Carella walked to the window and stared out at the park.

'No, I can't see any reason for ...'

Marriage, Carella thought. And then he thought of Teddy. *It'll be different with us.*

'Harriet, let him go,' Byrnes said. 'He's a good boy, and he won't get into any trouble. Look, take my word for it. For God's sake, it's only an amusement park.'

Byrnes sighed patiently.

'All right, then.' He listened. 'I'm not sure yet, honey. We're waiting for an FBI report. If I'll be home, I'll call you. No, nothing special. It's too damn hot to eat, anyway. Yes, dear, 'bye.'

He hung up. Carella came from the window.

'Women,' Byrnes said, not disagreeably. 'My son wants to go out to Jollyland tonight with some of the boys. She doesn't think he should. Can't see why he wants to go there in the middle of the week. She says she's read newspaper stories about boys getting into fights with other boys at these places. For Pete's sake, it's just an amusement park. The kid is seventeen.'

Carella nodded.

'If you're going to watch them every minute, they'll feel like prisoners. Okay, what are the odds on a fight starting at a place like that? Larry knows enough to avoid trouble. He's a good kid. You met him, didn't you, Steve?'

'Yes,' Carella said. 'He seemed very level-headed.'

'Sure, that's what I told Harriet. Ah, what the hell! These women never cut the apron strings. We get raised by one woman, and then when we're ripe, we get turned over to another woman.'

Carella smiled. 'It's a conspiracy,' he said.

'Sometimes I think so,' Byrnes said. 'But what would we do without them, huh?' He shook his head sadly, a man trapped in the labial folds of a society structure.

'Anything from the Feds yet?' Carella asked.

'No, not yet. I'm praying for a break.'

'Mmmm.'

'We deserve a break, don't we?' Byrnes asked. 'We've worked this one right into the ground. We deserve a break.'

There was a knock on the door.

'Come,' Byrnes said.

Willis entered the room with an envelope. 'This just arrived, sir,' he said.

'FBI?'

'Yes.'

Byrnes took the envelope. Hastily, he tore open the flap and pulled out the folded letter.

'Hell!' he erupted. 'Hell and damnation!'

'Bad?'

'They've got nothing on him!' Byrnes shouted. 'Goddamnit! Goddamnit to hell!'

'Not even Service prints?'

'Nothing. He was probably 4-F!'

'We know *everything* about this guy,' Willis said vehemently, beginning to pace the office. 'We know what he looks like, we know his height, his weight, his blood type, when he got his last haircut.' He slammed his fist into the opposite hand. 'The only thing we don't know is who the hell he is! Who is he, damnit, who is he?'

Neither Carella or Byrnes answered.

That night, a boy named Miguel Aretta was taken to Juvenile House. The police had picked him up as one of the boys who'd been missing from the roundup of The Grovers. It did not take the police long to discover that Miguel was the boy who'd zip-gunned Bert Kling.

Miguel had been carrying a zip-gun on the night that Kling got it. When a Senior Grover named Rafael 'Rip' Desanga had reported to the boys that a smart guy had been around asking questions, Miguel went with them to teach the smart guy a lesson.

As it turned out, the smart guy – or the person they assumed to be the smart guy – had pulled a gun outside the bar. Miguel had taken his own piece from his pocket and burned him.

Bert Kling, of course, had not been that smart guy. He turned out to be, of all things, a cop. So Miguel Aretta was now in Juvenile House, and the people there were trying to understand what made him tick so that they could present his case fairly when it came up in Children's Court.

Miguel Aretta was fifteen years old. It could be assumed that he just didn't know any better.

The real smart guy – a reporter named Cliff Savage – was thirty-seven years old, and he should have know better.

He didn't.

Chapter Twenty

Savage was waiting for Carella when he left the precinct at 4:00 p.m. the next day.

He was wearing a brown Dupioni silk suit, a gold tie, and a brown straw with a pale yellow band. 'Hello,' he said, shoving himself off the side of the building.

'What can I do for you?' Carella asked.

'You're a detective, aren't you?'

'If you've got a complaint,' Carella said, 'take it to the desk sergeant. I'm on my way home.'

'My name's Savage.'

'Oh,' Carella said. He regarded the reporter sourly.

'You in the fraternity, too?' Savage asked.

'Which one?'

'The Fraternity against Savage. Eeta Piecea Cliff.'

'I'm Phi Beta Kappa myself,' Carella said.

'Really?'

'No.' He began walking towards his car. Savage fell in step with him.

'Are you sore at me, too, is what I meant,' Savage said.

'You stuck your nose in the wrong place,' Carella answered. 'Because you did, a cop is in the hospital and a kid is in Juvenile House, awaiting trial. What do you want me to do, give you a medal?'

'If a kid shoots somebody, he deserves whatever he gets.'

'Maybe he wouldn't't've shot anybody if you'd kept you nose out of it.'

'I'm a reporter. My job is getting facts.'

'The lieutenant told me he'd already discussed the possibility of teen-agers being responsible for the deaths. He said he told you he considered the possibility extremely remote. But you went ahead and put your fat thumb in the pie, anyway. You realize Kling could have been killed?'

'He wasn't. Do you realize *I* could have been killed?' Savage said.

Carella made no comment.

'If you people cooperated more with the press ...'

Carella stopped walking. 'Listen,' he said, 'what are you doing in this neighbourhood? Looking for more trouble? If any of The Grovers recognize you, we're going to have another rhubarb. Why don't you go back to your newspaper office and write a column on garbage collection?'

'Your humour doesn't ...'

'I'm not trying to be funny,' Carella said, 'nor do I particularly feel like discussing anything with you. I just came off duty. I'm going home to shower and then I have a date with my fiancée. I'm theoretically on duty twenty-four hours a day, every day of the week, but fortunately that duty does not include extending courtesy to every stray cub reporter in town.'

'Cub?' Savage was truly offended. 'Now, listen . . .'

'What the hell do you want from me?' Carella asked.

'I want to discuss the killings.'

'I don't.'

'Why not?'

'You're a real leech, aren't you?'

'I'm a reporter, and a damned good one. Why don't you want to talk about the killings?'

'I'm perfectly willing to discuss them with anyone who knows what I'm talking about.'

'I'm a good listener,' Savage said.

'Sure. You turned a fine ear towards Rip Desanga.'

'Okay, I made a mistake, I'm willing to admit that. I thought it was the kids, and it wasn't. We know now it was an adult. What else do we know about him? Do we know why he did it?'

'Are you going to follow me all the way home?'

'I'd prefer buying you a drink,' Savage said. He looked at Carella expectantly. Carella weighed the offer.

'All right,' he said.

Savage extended his hand. 'My friends call me Cliff. I didn't get your name.'

'Steve Carella.'

They shook. 'Pleased to know you. Let's get that drink.'

The bar was air-conditioned, a welcome sanctuary from the stifling heat outdoors. They ordered their drinks and then sat opposite each other at the booth alongside the left-hand wall.

'All I want to know,' Savage said, 'is what you think.'

'Do you mean me personally, or the department?'

'You, or course. I can't expect you to speak for the department.'

'Is this for publication?' Carella asked.

'Hell, no. I'm just trying to jell my own ideas on it. Once this thing is broken, there'll be a lot of feature coverage. To do a good job, I want to be acquainted with every facet of the investigation.'

'It'd be a little difficult for a layman to understand every facet of police investigation,' Carella said.

'Of course, of course. But you can at least tell me what you think.'

'Sure. Provided it's not for publication.'

'Scout's honour,' Savage said.

'The department doesn't like individual cops trying to glorify . . .'

'Not a word of this will get into print,' Savage said. 'Believe me.'

'What do you want to know?'

'We've got the means, we've got the opportunity,' Savage said. 'What's the motive?'

'Every cop in the city would like the answer to that one,' Carella said.

'A nut maybe.'

'Maybe.'

'You don't think so?'

'No. Some of us do. I don't.'

'Why not?'

'Just like that.'

'Do you have a reason?'

'No, just a feeling. When you've been working on a case for any length of time, you begin to get feelings about it. I just don't happen to believe a maniac's involved here.'

'What *do* you believe?'

'Well, I have a few ideas.'

'Like what?'

'I'd rather not say right now.'

'Oh, come on, Steve.'

'Look, police work is like any other kind of work – except we happen to deal with crime. If you run an import-export business, you play certain hunches and others you don't. It's the same with us. If you have a hunch, you don't go around making a million dollar deal on it until you've checked it.'

'Then you do have a hunch you want to check?'

'Not even a hunch, really. Just an idea.'

'What kind of an idea?'

'About motive.'

'What about motive?'

Carella smiled. 'You're a pretty tenacious guy, aren't you?'

'I'm a good reporter. I already told you that.'

'All right, look at it this way. These men were cops. Three of them were killed in a row. What's the automatic conclusion?'

'Somebody doesn't like cops.'

'Right. A cop hater.'

'So?'

'Take off their uniforms. What have you got then?'

'They weren't wearing uniforms. None of them were uniform cops.'

'I know. I was speaking figuratively. I meant, make them ordinary citizens. Not cops. What do you have then? Certainly not a cop hater.'

'But they *were* cops.'

'They were men first. Cops only coincidentally and secondarily.'

'You feel, then, that the fact that they were cops had nothing to do with the reason they were killed.'

'Maybe. That's what I want to dig into a little deeper.'

'I'm not sure I understand you.'

'It's this,' Carella said. 'We knew these men well, we worked with them every day. Cops. We knew them as cops. We didn't know them as *men*. They may have been killed because they were men, and not because they were cops.'

'Interesting,' Savage said.

'It means digging into their lives on a more personal level. It won't be fun because murder has a strange way of dragging skeletons out of the neatest closets.'

'You mean, for example ...' Savage paused. 'Well, let's say Reardon was playing around with another dame, or Foster was a horse player, or Bush was taking money from a racketeer, something like that.'

'To stretch the point, yes.'

'And somehow, their separate activities were perhaps tied together to one person who wanted them all dead for various reasons. Is that what you're saying?'

'That's a little complicated,' Carella said. 'I'm not sure the deaths are connected in such a complicated way.'

'But we do know the same person killed all three cops.'

'Yes, we're fairly certain of that.'

'Then the deaths are connected.'

'Yes, of course. But perhaps...' Carella shrugged. 'It's difficult to discuss this with you because I'm not sure I know what I'm talking about. I only have this idea, that's all. This idea that motive may go deeper than the shield these men wore.'

'I see.' Savage sighed. 'Well, you can console yourself with the knowledge that every cop in the city probably has his own ideas on how to solve this one.'

Carella nodded, not exactly understanding Savage, but not willing to get into a lengthier discussion. He glanced at his watch.

'I've got to go soon,' he said. 'I've got a date.'

'Your girlfriend?'

'Yes.'

'What's her name?'

'Teddy. Well, Theodora really.'

'Theodora what?'

'Franklin.'

'Nice,' Savage said. 'Is this a serious thing?'

'As serious as they come.'

'These ideas of yours,' Savage said. 'About motive. Have you discussed them with your superiors?'

'Hell, no. You don't discuss every little pang of inspiration you get. You look into it, and then if you turn up anything that looks remotely promising, well, then you air the idea.'

'I see. Have you discussed it with Teddy?'

'Teddy? Why, no not yet.'

'Think she'll go for it?'

Carella smiled uneasily. 'She thinks I can do no wrong.'

'Sounds like a wonderful girl.'

'The best. And I'd better get to her before I lose her.'

'Certainly,' Savage said understandingly. Carella glanced at his watch again. 'Where does she live?'

'Riverhead,' Carella said.

'Theodora Franklin of Riverhead,' Savage said.

'Yes.'

'Well, I've appreciated listening to your ideas.'

Carella rose. 'None of that was for print, remember,' he said.

'Of course not,' Savage assured him.

'Thanks for the drink,' Carella said.

They shook hands. Savage stayed in the booth and ordered another Tom Collins. Carella went home to shower and shave for his date with Teddy.

She was dressed resplendently when she opened the door. She stood back, waiting for him to survey her splendour. She was wearing a white linen suit, white straw pumps, a red-stoned pin on the collar of the suit, bright scarlet oval ear-rings picking up the scream of the pin.

'Shucks,' he said, 'I was hoping I'd catch you in your slip.'

She made a motion to unbutton her jacket, smiling.

'We have reservations,' he said.

Where? her face asked.

'Ah Lum Fong,' he replied.

She nodded exuberantly.

'Where's your lipstick?' he asked.

She grinned and went to him, and he took her in his arms and kissed her, and then she clung to him as if he were leaving for Siberia in the next ten minutes.

'Come on,' he said, 'put on your face.'

She went into the other room, applied her lipstick and emerged carrying a small red purse.

'They carry those on the Street,' he said. 'It's a badge of the profession,' and she slapped him on the fanny as they left the apartment.

The Chinese restaurant boasted excellent food and an exotic decor. To Carella, the food alone would not have been enough. When he ate in a Chinese restaurant, he wanted it to look and feel Chinese. He did not appreciate an expanded, upholstered version of a Culver Avenue diner.

They ordered fried wonton soup, and lobster rolls, and barbecued spare ribs and Hon Shu Gai and Steak Kew and sweet and pungent pork. The wonton soup was crisp with Chinese vegetables; luscious snow peas, and water chestnuts, and mushrooms, and roots he could not have named if he'd tried. The wontons were brown and crisp, the soup itself had a rich tangy taste. They talked very little while they ate. They dug into the lobster rolls, and then they attacked the spare ribs, succulently brown.

'Do you know that Lamb thing?' he asked 'A Dissertation on . . .'

She nodded, and then went back to the spare ribs.

The chicken in the Hon Shu Gai was snappingly crisp. They polished off the dish. They barely had room for the Steak Kew, but they did their best with it, and when Charlie – their waiter – came to collect their dishes, he looked at them reproachfully because they had left over some of the delicious cubes of beef.

He cut a king pineapple for them in the kitchen, cut it so that the outside shell could be lifted off in one piece, exposing the ripe yellow meat beneath the prickly exterior, the fruit sliced and ready to be lifted off in long slender pieces. They drank their tea, savouring the aroma and the warmth, their stomachs full, their minds and their bodies relaxed.

'How's August nineteenth sound to you?'

Teddy shrugged.

'It's a Saturday. Would you like to get married on a Saturday?'

Yes, her eyes said.

Charlie brought them their fortune cookies and replenished the teapot.

Carella broke open his cookie. Then, before he read the message on the narrow slip of paper, he said, 'Do you know the one about the man who opened one of these in a Chinese restaurant?'

Teddy shook her head.

'It said, "Don't eat the soup. Signed, a friend."'

Teddy laughed and then gestured to his fortune slip. Carella read it aloud to her:

'You are the luckiest man alive. You are about to marry Theodora Franklin.'

She said 'Oh!' in soundless exasperation, and then took the slip from him. The slender script read: 'You are good with figures.'

'Your figure,' he said.

Teddy smiled and broke open her cookie. Her face clouded momentarily.

'What is it?' he asked.

She shook her head.

'Let me see it.'

She tried to keep the fortune slip from him, but he got it out of her hand and read it.

'Leo will roar – sleep no more.'

Carella stared at the printed slip. 'That's a hell of a thing to put in a cookie,' he said. 'What does it mean?' He thought for a moment. 'Oh, Leo. Leo the Lion. July 22 to August something, isn't it?'

Teddy nodded.

'Well, the meaning here is perfectly clear then. Once we're married, you're going to have a hell of a time sleeping.'

He grinned, and the worry left her eyes. She smiled, nodded, and then reached across the table for his hand.

The broken cookie rested alongside their hands, and beside that the curled fortune slip.

Leo will roar – sleep no more.

Chapter Twenty-One

The man's name was not Leo.

The man's name was Peter.

His last name was Byrnes.

He was roaring.

'What the hell kind of a story is this, Carella?'

'What?'

'Today's issue of this ... this goddamn rag!' he shouted, pointing to the afternoon tabloid on his desk. 'August 4th!'

Leo, Carella thought. 'What ... what do you mean, Lieutenant?'

'What do I mean?' Byrnes shouted. 'WHAT DO I MEAN? Who the hell gave you the authority to reel off this nonsense to that idiot Savage?'

'What?'

'There are cops walking beats in Bethtown because they spouted off nonsense like ...'

'Savage? Let me see that ...' Carella started.

Byrnes flipped open the newspaper angrily. 'Cop Defies Department!' he shouted. 'That's the headline. COP DEFIES DEPARTMENT! What's the matter, Carella, aren't you happy here?'

'Let me see . . .'

'And under that "MAY KNOW MURDERER," DETECTIVE SAYS.'

'May know . . .'

'Did you tell this to Savage?'

'That I may know who the murderer is? Of course not. Honest, Pete . . .'

'Don't call me Pete! Here, read the goddamn story.'

Carella took the newspaper. For some strange reason, his hands were trembling.

Sure enough, the story was on page four, and it was headlined:

COP DEFIES DEPARTMENT

'MAY KNOW MURDERER,'

DETECTIVE SAYS

'But this is . . .'

'Read it,' Byrnes said.

Carella read it.

The bar was cool and dim.

We sat opposite each other, Detective Stephen Carella and I. He toyed with his drink, and we talked of many things, but mostly we talked of murder.

'I've got an idea I know who killed those three cops,' Carella said. 'It's not the kind of idea you can take to your superiors, though. They wouldn't understand.'

And so came the first ray of hope in the mystery which has baffled the masterminds of Homicide North and tied the hands of stubborn, opinionated Detective-Lieutenant Peter Byrnes of the 87th Precinct.

'I can't tell you very much more about it right now,' Carella said, 'because I'm still digging. But this cop-hater theory is all wrong. It's something in the personal lives of these three men, of that I'm sure. It needs work, but we'll crack it.'

So spoke Detective Carella yesterday afternoon in a bar in the heart of the Murder Belt. He is a shy, withdrawn man, a man who — in his own words — is 'not seeking glory.'

'Police work is like any other kind of work,' he told me, 'except that we deal in crime. When you've got a hunch, you dig into it. If it pans out, then you bring it to your superiors, and maybe they'll listen, and maybe they won't.'

Thus far, he had confided his 'hunch' only to his fiancée, a lovely young lady named Theodora Franklin, a girl from Riverhead. Miss Franklin feels that Carella can 'do no wrong,' and is certain he will crack the case despite the inadequate fumblings of the department to date.

'There are skeletons in the closets,' Carella said. 'And those skeletons point to our man. We've got to dig deeper. It's just a matter of time now.'

We sat in the cool dimness of the bar, and I felt the quiet strength emanating from this man who has the courage to go ahead with his investigation in spite of the Cop-Hater Theory which pervades the dusty minds of the men working around him.

This man will find the murderer, I thought.

This man will relieve the city of its constant fear, its dread of an unknown killer roaming the streets with a wanton .45 automatic in his blood-stained fist. This man ...

'Good God!' Carella said.

'Yeah,' Byrnes answered. 'Now what about it?'

'I never said these things. I mean, not this way. And he said it wasn't for print!' Carella suddenly exploded. 'Where's the phone? I'm going to sue this son of a bitch for libel! He can't get away with ...'

'Calm down,' Byrnes said.

'Why'd he drag Teddy into this? Does he want to make her a sitting duck for that stupid bastard with the .45? Is he out of his mind?'

'Calm down,' Byrnes repeated.

'Calm down? I never said I knew who the murderer was! I never ...'

'What did you say?'

'I only said I had an idea that I wanted to work on.'

'And what's the idea?'

'That maybe this guy wasn't after cops at all. Maybe he was just after men. And maybe not even that. Maybe he was just after *one* man.'

'Which one?'

'How the hell do I know? Why'd he mention Teddy? What's the matter with this guy?'

'Nothing that a head doctor couldn't cure,' Byrnes said.

'Listen, I want to go up and see Teddy. God knows ...'

'What time is it?' Byrnes asked.

Carella looked at the wall clock. 'Six-fifteen.'

'Wait until six-thirty. Havilland will be back from supper by then.'

'If I ever meet this guy Savage again,' Carella promised, 'I'm going to rip him in half.'

'Or at least give him a speeding ticket,' Byrnes commented.

The man in the black suit stood outside the apartment door, listening. A copy of the afternoon newspaper stuck up from the right-hand pocket of his jacket. His left shoulder throbbed with pain, and the weight of the .45 automatic tugged at the other pocket of his jacket, so that – favouring the wound, bearing the weight of the gun – he leaned slightly to his left while he listened.

There was no sound from within the apartment.

He had read the name very carefully in the newspaper, Theodora Franklin, and then he had checked the Riverhead directory and come up with the address. He wanted to talk to this girl. He wanted to find out how much Carella knew. He had to find out.

She's very quiet in there, he thought. *What's she doing?*

Cautiously, he tried the door knob. He wiggled it slowly from side to side. The door was locked.

He heard footsteps. He tried to back away from the door too late. He reached for the gun in his pocket. The door was opening, wide, wider.

The girl stood there, surprised. She was a pretty girl, small, dark-haired, wide brown eyes. She wore a white chenille robe. The robe was damp in spots. He assumed she had just come from the shower. Her eyes went to his face, and then to the gun in his hand. Her mouth opened, but no sound came from it. She tried to slam to door, but he rammed his foot into the wedge and then shoved it back.

She moved away from him, deeper into the room. He closed the door and locked it.

'Miss Franklin?' he asked.

She nodded, terrified. She had seen the drawing on the front pages of all the newspapers, had seen it broadcast on all the television programmes. There was no mistake, this was the man Steve was looking for.

'Let's have a little talk, shall we?' he asked.

His voice was a nice voice, smooth, almost suave. He was a good-looking man, why had he killed those cops? Why would a man like this . . . ?

'Did you hear me?' he asked.

She nodded. She could read his lips, could understand everything he said, but . . .

'What does your boyfriend know?' he asked.

He held the .45 loosely, as if he were accustomed to its lethal power now, as if he considered it a toy more than a dangerous weapon.

'What's the matter, you scared?'

She touched her hands to her lips, pulled them away in a gesture of futility.

'What?'

She repeated the gesture.

'Come on,' he said, 'talk, for God's sake! You're not that scared!'

Again, she repeated the gesture, shook her head this time. He watched her curiously.

'I'll be damned,' he said at last. 'A dummy!' He began laughing. The laugh filled the apartment, reverberating from the walls. 'A dummy! If that don't take the cake! A dummy!' His laughter died. He studied her carefully. 'You're not trying to pull something, are you?'

She shook her head vigorously. Hands went to the opening of her robe, clutching the chenille to her more tightly.

'Now this has definite advantages, doesn't it?' he said, grinning. 'You can't scream, you can't use the phone, you can't do a damned thing, can you?'

Teddy swallowed, watching him.

'What does Carella know?' he asked.

She shook her head.

'The paper said he's got a lead. Does he know about me? Does he have any idea who I am?'

Again she shook her head.

'I don't believe you.'

She nodded, trying to convince him that Steve knew nothing. What paper was he referring to? What did he mean? She spread her hands wide, indicating innocence, hoping he would understand.

He reached into his jacket pocket and tossed the newspaper to her.

'Page four,' he said. 'Read it. I've got to sit down. This goddamn shoulder . . .'

He sat, the gun levelled at her. She opened the paper and read the story, shaking her head as she read.

'Well?' he asked.

She kept shaking her head. No, *this is not true. No. Steve would never say things like these. Steve would ...*

'What'd he tell you?' the man asked.

Her eyes opened wide with pleading. *Nothing, he told me nothing.*

'The newspaper says ...'

She hurled the paper to the floor.

'Lies, huh?'

Yes, she nodded.

His eyes narrowed. 'Newspapers don't lie,' he said.

They do, they do!

'When's he coming here?'

She stood motionless, controlling her face, not wanting her face to betray anything to the man with the gun.

'Is he coming?'

She shook her head.

'You're lying. It's all over your face. He's coming here, isn't he?'

She bolted for the door. He caught her arm and flung her back across the room. The robe pulled back over her legs when she fell to the floor. She pulled it together quickly and stared up at him.

'Don't try that again,' he said.

Her breath came heavily now. She sensed a coiled spring within this man, a spring which would unleash itself at the door the moment Steve opened it. But he'd said he would not be there until midnight. He had told her that, and there were a lot of hours between now and midnight. In that time ...

'You just get out of the shower?' he asked.

She nodded.

'Those are good legs,' he said, and she felt his eyes on her. 'Dames,' he said philosophically. 'What've you got on under that robe?'

Her eyes widened.

He began laughing. 'Just what I thought. Smart. Good way to beat the heat. When's Carella coming?'

She did not answer.

'Steve, eight, nine? Is he on duty today?' He watched her. 'Nothing from you, huh? What's he got, the four to midnight? Sure, otherwise he'd probably be with you right this minute. Well, we might as well make ourselves comfortable, we got a long wait. Anything to drink in this place?'

Teddy nodded.

'What've you got? Gin? Rye? Bourbon?' He watched her. 'Gin? You got tonic? No, huh? Club soda? Okay, mix me a Collins. Hey, where you going?'

Teddy gestured to the kitchen.

'I'll come with you,' he said. He followed her into the kitchen. She opened the refrigerator and took out an opened bottle of club soda.

'Haven't you got a fresh one?' he asked. Her back was to him, and so she could not read his lips. He seized her shoulder and swung her around. His hand did not leave her shoulder.

'I asked you if you had a fresh bottle,' he said.

She nodded and bent, taking an unopened bottle from the lowest shelf of the refrigerator. She took lemons from the fruit drawer, and then went to the cupboard for the bottle of gin.

'Dames,' he said again.

She poured a double shot of gin into a tall glass. She spooned sugar into the glass, and then she went to one of the drawers.

'Hey!'

He saw the knife in her hand.

'Don't get ideas with that. Just slice the lemon.'

She sliced the lemon and squeezed both halves into the glass. She poured club soda until the glass was three-quarters full, and then she went back to the refrigerator for the ice cubes. When the drink was finished, she handed it to him.

'Make one for yourself,' he said.

She shook her head.

'I said make one for yourself! I don't like to drink alone.'

Patiently, wearily, she made herself a drink.

'Come on. Back in the living room.'

They went into the living room, and he sat in an easy chair, wincing as he adjusted himself so that his shoulder was comfortable.

'When the knock comes on that door,' he said, 'you just sit tight, understand? Go unlock it now.'

She went to the door and unlocked it. And now, knowing that the door was open, knowing that Steve would enter and be faced with a blazing .45, she felt fear crawl into her head like a nest of spiders.

'What are you thinking?' he asked.

She shrugged. She walked back into the room and sat opposite him, facing the door.

'This is a good drink,' he said. 'Come on, drink.'

She sipped at the Collins, her mind working ahead to the moment of Steve's arrival.

'I'm going to kill him, you know,' he said.

She watched him, her eyes wide.

'Won't make any difference now, anyway, will it? One cop more or less. Make it look a little better, don't you think?'

She was puzzled, and the puzzlement showed on her face.

'It's the best way,' he explained. 'If he knows something, well, it won't do to have him around. And if he doesn't know anything, it'll round out the picture.' He struggled in the chair. 'I've got to get this shoulder fixed. How'd you like that lousy doctor? That was something, wasn't it? I thought they were supposed to be healers.'

He talks the way anyone does, she thought. *Except that he talks so casually of death. He is going to kill Steve.*

'We were figuring on Mexico, anyway. Going to leave this afternoon, until your boyfriend came up with his bright idea. We'll take off in the morning, though. Soon as I take care of this.' He paused. 'Do you suppose I can get a good doctor in Mexico? The things a guy will do, huh?' He watched her face carefully. 'You ever been in love?'

She studied him, puzzled, confused. He did not seem like a killer. She nodded.

'Who with? This cop?'

She nodded again.

'Well, that's a shame.' He seemed sincerely sorry. 'It's a damn shame, honey, but what hasta be hasta be. There's no other way, you can see that, can't you? I mean, there was no other way right from the start, from the minute I started this thing. And when you start something, you've got to see it through right to the finish. It's a matter of survival now, you realize that? The things a guy will do. Well, you know.' He paused. 'You'd kill for him, wouldn't you?'

She hesitated.

'To keep him, you'd kill for him, wouldn't you?' he repeated.

She nodded.

'So? So there.' He smiled. 'I'm not a professional, you know. I'm a mechanic. That's my line. I'm a damn good mechanic, too. Think I'll be able to get work in Mexico?'

Teddy shrugged.

'Sure, they must have cars down there. They've got cars everywhere. Then, later, when things have cooled down, we'll come back to the States. Hell, things should cool down sooner or later. But what I'm trying to tell you, I'm not a professional killer, so don't get that idea. I'm just a regular guy.'

Her eyes did not believe him.

'No, huh? Well, I'm telling you. Sometimes, there's no other way out. If you see something's hopeless, and somebody explains to you where there's some hope, okay, you take it. I never harmed nobody until I killed those cops. You think I wanted to kill them? Survival, that's all. Some things, you've got to do. Agh, what the hell do you understand? You're just a dummy.'

She sat silent, watching him.

'A woman gets under your skin. Some women are like that. Listen, I've been around. I've been around plenty. I had me more dames than you could count. But this one – different. Different right from the beginning. She just got under my skin. Right under it. When it gets you like that, you can't eat, you can't sleep, nothing. You just think about her all day long. And what can you do when you realize you can't really have her ... well ... unless you ... hell, didn't she ask him for a divorce? Is it my fault he was stubborn? Well, he's still stubborn – only now he's dead.'

Teddy's eyes moved from his face. They covered the door behind him, and then dropped to the doorknob.

'And he took two of his pals with him.' He stared into his glass. 'Those are the breaks. He should've listened to reason. A woman like her ... You'd do anything for a woman like her. Anything! Just being in the same room with her, you want to ...'

Teddy watched the knob with fascination. She rose suddenly. She brought back her glass and then threw it at him. It grazed his forehead, the liquid splashing out of the glass and cascading over his shoulder. He leaped to his feet, his face twisted in fury, the .45 pointed at her.

'You stupid bitch!' he bellowed. 'Why the hell did you do that?'

Chapter Twenty-Two

Carella left the precinct at 6:30 on the button. Havilland had not yet come back from supper, but he could wait no longer. He did not want to leave Teddy alone in that apartment, not after the fool stunt Savage had pulled.

He drove to Riverhead quickly. He ignored traffic lights and full stop signs. He ignored everything. There was an all-consuming thought in his mind, and that thought included a man with a .45 and a girl with no tongue.

When he reached her apartment building, he glanced up at the window. The shades were not drawn. The apartment looked very quiet. He breathed a little more easily, and then entered the building. He climbed the steps, his heart pounding. He knew he shouldn't be alarmed but he could not shake the persistent feeling that Savage's column had invited danger for Teddy.

He stopped outside her door. He could hear the persistent drone of what sounded like the radio going inside. He reached for the knob. In his usual manner, he twisted it slowly from side to side, waiting for her footsteps, knowing she would come to the door the moment she saw his signal. He heard the sound of a chair scraping back and then someone shouted, 'You stupid bitch! Why the hell did you do that?'

His brain came alive. He reached for his .38 and snapped the door open with his other hand.

The man turned.

'You ...!' he shouted, and the .45 bucked in his hand.

Carella fired low, dropping to the floor the instant he entered the room. His first two shots took the man in the thigh. The man fell face forward, the .45 pitching out of his fist. Carella kicked back the hammer on the .38, waiting.

'You bastard,' the man on the floor said. 'You bastard.'

Carella got to his feet. He picked up the .45 and stuck it into his back pocket.

'Get up,' he said. 'You all right, Teddy?'

Teddy nodded. She was breathing heavily, watching the man on the floor.

'Thanks for the warning,' Carella said. He turned to the man again. 'Get up!'

'I can't, you bastard. Why'd you shoot me? For God's sake, why'd you shoot me?'

'Why'd you shoot three cops?'

The man went silent.

'What's your name?' Carella asked.

'Mercer. Paul Mercer.'

'Don't you like cops?'

'I love them.'

'What's the story then?'

'I suppose you're going to check my gun with what you've already got.'

'Damn right,' Carella said. 'You haven't got a chance, Mercer.'

'She put me up to it,' Mercer said, a scowl on his dark face. 'She's the real murderer. All I done was pull the trigger. She said we had to kill him, said it was the only way. We threw the others in just to make it look good, just to make it look as if a cop hater was loose. But it was her idea. Why should I take the rap alone?'

'Whose idea?' Carella asked.

'Alice's,' Mercer said. 'You see ... we wanted to make it look like a cop hater. We wanted ...'

'It was,' Carella said.

When they brought Alice Bush in, she was dressed in grey, a quiet grey. She sat in the squadroom, crossing her legs.

'Do you have a cigarette, Steve?' she asked.

Carella gave her one. He did not light it for her. She sat with the cigarette dangling from her lips until it was apparent she would have to light it herself. Unruffled, she struck a match.

'What about it?' Carella asked.

'What about it?' she repeated, shrugging. 'It's all over, isn't it?'

'You must have really hated him. You must have hated him like poison.'

'You're directing,' Alice said. 'I'm only the star.'

'Don't get glib, Alice!' Carella said angrily. 'I've never hit a woman in my life, but I swear to God ...'

'Relax,' she told him. 'It's all over. You'll get your gold star, and then you'll ...'

'Alice ...'

'What the hell do you want me to do? Break down and cry? I hated him, all right? I hated his big, pawing hands and I hated his stupid red hair, and I hated everything about him, all right?'

'Mercer said you'd asked for a divorce. Is that true?'

'No, I didn't ask for a divorce. Hank would've never agreed to one.'

'Why didn't you give him a chance?'

'What for? Did he ever give me a chance? Cooped up in that goddamned apartment, waiting for him to come off some burglary or some knifing or some mugging? What kind of life is that for a woman?'

'You knew he was a cop when you married him.'

Alice didn't answer.

'You could've asked for a divorce, Alice. You could've tried.'

'I didn't want to, damnit. *I wanted him dead.*'

'Well, you've got him dead. Him and two others. You must be tickled now.'

Alice smiled suddenly. 'I'm not too worried, Steve.'

'No?'

'There have to be *some* men on the jury.' She paused. 'Men like me.'

There were, in fact, eight men on the jury.

The jury brought in a verdict in six minutes flat.

Mercer was sobbing as the jury foreman read off the verdict and the judge gave sentence. Alice listened to the judge with calm indifference, her shoulders thrown back, her head erect.

The jury had found them both guilty of murder in the first degree, and the judge sentenced them to death in the electric chair.

On August nineteenth, Stephen Carella and Theodora Franklin listened to their own sentence.

'Do either of you know of any reason why you both should not be legally joined in marriage, or if there be any present who can show any just cause why these parties should not be legally joined together, let him now speak or hereafter hold his peace.'

Lieutenant Byrnes held his peace. Detective Hal Willis said nothing. The small gathering of friends and relatives watched, dewy-eyed.

The city clerk turned to Carella.

'Do you, Stephen Louis Carella, take this woman as your lawfully wedded wife to live together in the state of matrimony? Will you love, honour and keep her as a faithful man is bound to do, in health, sickness, prosperity and adversity, and forsaking all others keep you alone unto her as long as you both shall live?'

'Yes,' Carella said. 'Yes, I will. I do. Yes.'

'Do you, Theodora Franklin, take this man as your lawfully wedded husband to live together in the state of matrimony? Will you love, honour, and cherish him as a faithful woman is bound to do, in health, sickness, prosperity and adversity, and forsaking all others keep you alone unto him as long as you both shall live?'

Teddy nodded. There were tears in her eyes, but she could not keep the ecstatic smile off her face.

'For as you both have consented in wedlock and have acknowledged it before this company, I do by virtue of the authority vested in me by the laws of this state now pronounce you husband and wife. And may God bless your union.'

Carella took her in his arms and kissed her. The clerk smiled. Lieutenant Byrnes cleared his throat. Willis looked up at the ceiling. The clerk kissed Teddy when Carella released her. Byrnes kissed her. Willis kissed her. All the male relatives and friends came up to kiss her.

Carella smiled idiotically.

'You hurry back,' Byrnes said to him.

'Hurry back? I'm going on my honeymoon, Pete!'

'Well, hurry anyway. How are we going to run that precinct without you? You're the only cop in the city who has the courage to buck the decisions of stubborn, opinionated Detective-Lieutenant Byrnes of the ...'

'Oh, go to hell,' Carella said, smiling.

Willis shook his hand. 'Good luck, Steve. She's a wonderful gal.'

'Thank you, Hal.'

Teddy came to him. He put his arm around her.

'Well,' he said, 'let's go.'

They went out of the room together.

Byrnes stared after them wistfully.

'He's a good cop,' he said.

'Yeah,' Willis answered.

'Come on,' Byrnes said, 'let's go see what's brewing back at the house.'
They went down into the street together.

'Want to get a paper,' Byrnes said. He stopped at a news-stand and picked
up a copy of Savage's tabloid. The trial news had been crowded right off the
front pages. There was more important news.

The headlines simply read:

HEAT WAVE BREAKS!
HAPPY DAY!

GIVE THE BOYS A GREAT BIG HAND

"It was raining.
It had been rain-
ing for three days
now, an ugly March
rain that
washed the
brilliance of
near-spring
with a mono-
chromatic,
unrelenting grey...."

This is for Phyllis and Rick

Chapter One

It was raining.

It had been raining for three days now, an ugly March rain that washed the brilliance of near-spring with a monochromatic, unrelenting grey. The television forecasters had correctly predicted rain for today and estimated that it would rain tomorrow also. Beyond that, they would not venture an opinion.

But it seemed to Patrolman Richard Genero that it had been raining forever, and that it would continue to rain forever, and that eventually he would be washed away into the gutters and then carried into the sewers of Isola and dumped unceremoniously with the other garbage into either the River Harb or the River Dix. North or south, it didn't make a damn bit of difference: both rivers were polluted; both stank of human waste.

Like a man up to his ankles in water in a rapidly sinking rowboat, Genero stood on the corner and surveyed the near-empty streets. His rubber rain cape was as black and as shining as the asphalt that stretched before him. It was still early afternoon, but there was hardly a soul in sight, and Genero felt lonely and deserted. He felt, too, as if he were the only human being in the entire city who didn't know enough to come in out of the rain. I'm going to drown here in the goddamn streets, he thought, and he belched sourly, consoling himself with the fact that he would be relieved on post at 3:45. It would take him about five minutes to get back to the station house and no more than ten minutes to change into his street clothes. Figure a half hour on the subway to Riverhead, and he would be home at 4:30. He wouldn't have to pick up Gilda until 7:30, so that gave him time for a little nap before dinner. Thinking of the nap, Genero yawned, tilting his head.

A drop of cold water ran down his neck, and he said, 'Oh hell!' out loud, and then hurriedly glanced around him to make sure he hadn't been overheard by any conscientious citizen of the city. Satisfied that the image of the pure American law-enforcer had not been destroyed, Genero began walking up the street, his rubber-encased shoes sloshing water every inch of the way.

Rain, rain, go away, he thought.

Oddly, the rain persisted.

Well, rain isn't so bad, he thought. It's better than snow, anyway. The thought made him shudder a little, partially because the very thought of snow was a chilling one, and partially because he could never think of snow or winter without forming an immediate association with the boy he had found in the basement so long ago.

Now cut that out, he thought. It's bad enough it's raining. We don't have to start thinking of creepy cadavers.

The boy's face had been blue, really blue, and he'd been leaning forward on the cot, and it had taken Genero several moments to realize that a rope was around the boy's neck and that the boy was dead.

Listen, let's not even think about it. It makes me itchy.

Well, listen, you're a cop, he reminded himself. What do you think cops do? Turn off fire hydrants all the time? Break up stickball games? I mean, now let's face it, every now and then a cop has got to find a stiff.

Listen, this makes me itchy.

I mean, that's what you get paid for, man. I mean, let's face it. A cop has every now and then got to come up against a little violence. And besides, that kid was a long time ago, all water under the ...

Water. Jesus, ain't it never going to stop raining?

I'm getting out of this rain, he thought. I'm going over to Max's tailor shop and maybe I can get him to take out some of that sweet Passover wine, and we'll drink a toast to Bermuda. Man, I wish I was in Bermuda. He walked down the street and opened the door to the tailor shop. A bell tinkled. The shop smelled of steam and clean garments. Genero felt better the moment he stepped inside.

'Hello, Max,' he said.

Max was a round-faced man with a fringe of white hair that clung to his balding pate like a halo. He looked up from his sewing machine and said, 'I ain't got no wine.'

'Who wants wine?' Genero answered, grinning a bit sheepishly. 'Would you kick me out of your shop on a miserable day like this?'

'On any day, miserable or otherwise, I wouldn't kick you out mine shop,' Max said, 'so don't make wisecracks. But I warn you, already, even before you begin, I ain't got no wine.'

'So who wants wine?' Genero said. He moved closer to the radiator and pulled off his gloves. 'What are you doing, Max?'

'What does it look like I'm doing? I'm making a plan for the White House. I'm going to blow it up. What else would I be doing on a sewing machine?'

'I mean, what's that thing your working on?'

'It's a Salvation Army uniform,' Max said.

'Yeah? How about that?'

'There's still a few *tailors* left in this city, you know,' Max said. 'It ain't by all of us a matter of cleaning and pressing. Cleaning and pressing is for machines. Tailoring is for men. Max Mandel is a tailor, not a pressing machine.'

'And a damn good tailor,' Genero said, and he watched for Max's reaction.

'I still ain't got no wine,' Max said. 'Why ain't you in the street stopping crime already?'

'On a day like this, nobody's interested in crime,' Genero said. 'The only crime going on today is prostitution.'

Genero watched Max's face, saw the quick gleam of appreciation in the old man's eyes and grinned. He was getting closer to that wine all the time. Max was beginning to enjoy his jokes, and that was a good sign. Now all he had to do was work up a little sympathy.

'A rain like today's,' Genero said, 'it seeps right into a man's bones. Right into his bones.'

'So?'

'So nothing. I'm just saying. Right to the marrow. And the worst part is, a man can't even stop off in a bar or something to get a shot. To warm him up, I mean. It ain't allowed, you know.'

'So?'

'So nothing. I'm just saying.' Genero paused. 'You're sure doing a fine job with that uniform, Max.'

'Thanks.'

The shop went silent. Outside, the rain spattered against the sidewalk in continuous drumming monotony.

'Right to the marrow,' Genero said.

'All right already. Right to the marrow.'

'Chills a man.'

'All right, it chills a man.'

'Yes, sir,' Genero said, shaking his head.

'The wine is in the back near the pressing machine,' Max said without looking up. 'Don't drink too much, you'll get drunk already and I'll be arrested for corrupting an officer.'

'You mean you have wine, Max?' Genero asked innocently.

'Listen to Mr Baby-Blue Eyes, he's asking if I got wine. Go, go in the back. Drink, choke, but leave some in the bottle.'

'That's awfully nice of you, Max,' Genero said, beaming. 'I had no idea you –'

'Go, go before I change my mind.'

Genero went into the back room and found the bottle of wine on the table near the pressing machine. He uncapped it, rinsed a glass at the sink near the small grime-smeared window and poured it full to the brim. He tilted the glass to his mouth, drank until it was empty, and then licked his lips.

'You want some of this, Max?' he called.

'The Salvation Army doesn't like I should drink when I'm sewing their uniforms.'

'It's very good, Max,' Genero said teasingly.

'So have another glass and stop bothering me. You're making my stitches go all *fermisht*.'

Genero drank another glassful, recapped the bottle, and came out into the shop again, rubbing his hands briskly.

'Now I'm ready for anything,' he said, grinning.

'What is there to be ready for? On a day like this, you already said there's nothing but prostitution.'

'I'm ready for that, too,' Genero answered. 'Come on, Max. Close up the shop, and we'll go find two delicious broads. What do you say?'

'Stop giving an old man ideas. My wife should only find me with a delicious broad. A knife she'll stick in my back. Get out, get out, go walk your beat. Go arrest the other drunkards and vagrants. Leave me in peace. I'm running here a bar and grill instead of a tailor shop. Every drunkard cop on the beat, he stops in for wine. The government should allow me to deduct the wine as part of my overhead. One day, in the wine bottle, I'm going to put poison instead of wine. Then maybe the *fercockteh* cops of the 87th will leave me alone, already. Go. Get lost. Go.'

'Ahhh, you know you love us, Max.'

'I love you like cockroaches.'

'Better than cockroaches.'

'That's right. I love you like water rats.'

Genero pulled on his gloves. 'Well, back to the bridge,' he said.

'What bridge?'

'The bridge of the ship. That's a joke, Max. The rain, get it? Water. A ship. Get it?'

'Already the television world lost a great comic when you decided to be a cop,' Max said, shaking his head. 'Back to the bridge.' He shook his head again. 'Do me a favour, will you?'

'What's that?' Genero asked, opening the door.

'From the bridge of this ship . . .'

'Yeah?'

'Jump!'

Genero grinned and closed the door behind him. It was still pouring outside, but he felt a lot better now. The sweet wine fumed in his stomach, and he could feel a warm lassitude seeping through his limbs. He sloshed through the puddles in an almost carefree manner, squinting through the driving rain, whistling tunelessly.

The man – or perhaps the tall woman, it was difficult to tell – was standing at the bus stop. The tall woman – or perhaps the man, it was impossible to see clearly in the rain – was dressed entirely in black. Black raincoat, black slacks, black shoes, black umbrella which effectively hid the head and hair. The bus pulled to the kerb, spreading a huge canopy of water. The doors snapped open. The person – man or woman – boarded the bus and the rain-streaked doors closed again, hiding the black-shrouded figure from view. The bus pulled away from the kerb, spreading another canopy of water which soaked Genero's trouser legs.

'You stupid . . .' he shouted, and he began brushing water from his trousers, and that was when he saw the bag resting on the sidewalk alongside the bus stop sign.

'Hey! Hey!' he yelled after the bus. 'You forgot your bag!'

His words were drowned in the gunning roar of the bus's engine and the steady drumming of the rain.

'Damnit,' he muttered, and he walked to the sign and picked up the bag. It was a small, blue overnight bag, obviously issued by an airline. In a white circle on the side of the bag, stencilled there in red letters, were the words: CIRCLE AIRLINES.

Beneath that, in white script lettering, was the slogan: *We circle the globe.*

Genero studied the bag. It was not very heavy. A small leather fob was attached to the carrying straps, and an identification tag showed behind a celluloid panel. But whoever owned the bag had neglected to fill in the NAME and ADDRESS spaces. The identification tag was blank.

Sourly, Genero unzipped the bag and reached into it.

He drew back his hand in terror and revulsion. An instant thought rushed across his mind – God, not again – and then he gripped the bus stop sign for support because he was suddenly dizzy.

Chapter Two

In the detective squadroom of the 87th Precinct, the boys were swapping
reminiscences about their patrolman days.

Now you may quarrel with the use of the word 'boys' to describe a group
of men who ranged in age from twenty-eight to forty-two, who shaved daily,
who went to bed with various and assorted mature and immature women,
who swore like pirates, and who dealt with some of the dirtiest humans since
Neanderthal. The word 'boys', perhaps, connotes a simplicity, an innocence
which would not be entirely accurate.

There was, however, a spirit of boyish innocence in the squadroom on
that dreary, rainy March day. It was difficult to believe that these men who
stood in a fraternal knot around Andy Parker's desk, grinning, listening in
attentiveness, were men who dealt daily with crime and criminals. The
squadroom, in effect, could have been a high-school locker room. The
chatter could have been that of a high-school football team on the day of the
season's last game. The men stood drinking coffee from cardboard containers, completely at ease in the grubby shopworn comfort of the squadroom. Andy Parker, like a belligerent fullback remembering a difficult time
in the game against Central High, kept his team huddled about him, leaned
back in his swivel chair, and shook his head dolefully.

'I had a pipperoo one time, believe me,' he said. 'I stopped her coming off
the River Highway. Right near Pier 17, do you know the spot?'

The boys nodded.

'Well, she crashed the light at the bottom of the ramp, and then made a U-
turn under the highway. I blew the whistle, and she jammed on the brakes,
and I strolled over to the car and said, "Lady, you must be the Mayor's
daughter to be driving like that."'

'Was she?' Steve Carella asked. Sitting on the edge of the desk, a lean
muscular man with eyes that slanted peculiarly downward to present an
Oriental appearance, he held his coffee container in big hands and studied
Parker intently. He did not particularly care for the man or his methods of
police investigation, but he had to admit he told a story with gusto.

'No, no. Mayor's daughter, my eye. What she was – well, let me tell the
story, will you?'

Parker scratched his heavy beard. He had shaved that morning, but five
o'clock shadow came at an earlier hour for him, so that he always looked
somewhat unkempt, a big shaggy man with dark hair, dark eyes, dark beard.
In fact, were it not for the shield Parker carried pinned to his wallet, he could
easily have passed for many of the thieves who found their way into the 87th.
He was so much the Hollywood stereotype of the gangster that he'd often

been stopped by over-zealous patrolmen seeking suspicious characters. On those occasions, he immediately identified himself as a detective and then proceeded to bawl out the ambitious rookie, which pastime – though he never admitted it to himself – gave him a great deal of pleasure. In truth, it was possible that Andy Parker purposely roamed around in other precincts hoping to be stopped by an unsuspecting patrolman upon whom he could then pull his rank.

'She was sitting in the front seat with a two-piece costume on,' Parker said, 'a two-piece costume and these long black net stockings. What the costume was, it was these little black panties covered with sequins, and this tiny little bra that tried to cover the biggest set of bubs I ever seen on any woman in my entire life I swear to God. I did a double take, and I leaned into the car and said, "You just passed a stop light, lady, and you made a U-turn over a double white line. And for all I know, we got a good case against you for indecent exposure. Now how about that?"'

'What did she say?' Cotton Hawes asked. He alone of the detectives surrounding Parker's desk was not drinking coffee. Hawes was a tea drinker, a habit he'd picked up as a growing boy. His father had been a Protestant minister, and having members of the congregation in for tea had been a daily routine. The boy Hawes, for reasons best known to his father, had been included in the daily congregational tea-drinking visits. The tea, hefty, hot and hearty, had not stunted his growth at all. The man Hawes stood six feet two inches in his stocking feet, a red-headed giant who weighed in at a hundred and ninety pounds.

'She looked at me with these big blue eyes set in a face made for a doll,' Parker said, 'and she batted her eyelashes at me and said, "I'm in a hurry. If you're going to give me the goddamn ticket, give it to me!"'

'Wow!' Hawes said.

'So I asked her what the hurry was, and she said she had to be on stage in five minutes flat.'

'What kind of stage? One of the burly houses?'

'No, no, she was a dancer in a musical comedy. A big hit, too. And it was just about eight-thirty, and she was breaking her neck to catch the curtain. So I pulled out my fountain pen and my pad, and she said, "Or would you prefer two tickets to the biggest hit in town?" and she started digging into her purse, those bubs about to spill out of that tiny little bra and stop traffic away the hell up to the Aquarium.'

'So how was the show?' Carella asked.

'I didn't take the tickets.'

'Why not?'

'Because this way I had a private show of my own. It took me twenty minutes to write that ticket, and all that time she was squirming and wiggling on the front seat with those gorgeous pineapples ready to pop. Man, what an experience!'

'You're not only mean,' Carella said, 'you're also horny.'

'That I am,' Parker admitted proudly.

'I caught a guy once on Freeman Lewis Boulevard,' Carella said. 'He was doing eighty miles an hour. I had to put on the siren before he'd stop. I got out of the squad car and was walking over to his car when the door popped open, and he leaped out and started running towards me.'

'A hood?' Hawes asked.

'No, but that's just what I thought. I figured I'd stumbled on a guy who was running from the law. I expected him to pull a gun any minute.'

'What *did* he do?'

'He came up to me hopping up and down, first one leg, then the other. He said he knew he was speeding, but he'd just had an acute attack of diarrhoea, and he had to find a gas station with a men's room in a hurry.'

Parker burst out laughing. 'Oh, brother, that takes it,' he said.

'Did you let him go?' Hawes asked.

'Hell, no. I just wrote the ticket in a hurry, that's all.'

'I'll tell you one I let go,' Hawes said. 'This was when I was a patrolman with the 30th. The guy was clipping along like a madman, and when I stopped him he just looked at me and said, "You going to give me a ticket?" So I looked right back at him and said, "Damn right, I'm going to give you a ticket." He stared at me for a long time, just nodding his head. Then he said, "That's it, then. You give me a ticket, and I'll kill myself."'

'What the hell did he mean?'

'That's just what I said. I said, "What do you mean, mister?" But he just kept staring at me, and he didn't say another word, just kept staring and nodding his head, over and over again, as if this ticket was the last straw, do you know what I mean? I had the feeling that this had just been one of those days where everything in the world had gone wrong for him, and I knew – I just knew as sure as I was standing there – that if I slapped a summons on him, he would actually go home and turn on the gas or jump out the window or slit his throat. I just knew it. I could just sense it about the guy.'

'So you let him go. The Good Samaritan.'

'Yeah, yeah, Samaritan,' Hawes said. 'You should have seen that guy's eyes. You'd have known he wasn't kidding.'

'I had a woman once,' Kling, the youngest of the detectives started, and Patrolman Dick Genero burst into the squadroom carrying the small, blue overnight bag. One look at his eyes, and anyone would have known he wasn't kidding. He carried the bag in his right hand, far away from his body, as if afraid to be contaminated by it. He pushed his way through the gate in the slatted railing which separated the squadroom from the corridor outside, went directly to Parker's desk, and plunked the bag down in the middle of it with a finality that indicated he had done his duty and was now glad to be rid of it.

'What have you got, Dick?' Hawes asked.

Genero could not speak. His face was white, his eyes were wide. He swallowed several times, but no words came from his mouth. He kept shaking his head and pointing at the bag. Hawes stared at the bag in puzzlement, and then began to unzip it. Genero turned away. He seemed ready to vomit momentarily.

Hawes looked into the bag and said, 'Oh Jesus, where'd you get this?'

'What is it?' Kling asked.

'Oh, Jesus,' Hawes said. 'What a goddamn thing. Get it out of here. Jesus, get it out of the squadroom. I'll call the morgue.' The rugged planes of his face were twisted in pain. He could not look into the bag again. 'I'll call the morgue,' he said again. 'Jesus, get it out of here. Take it downstairs. Get it out of here.'

Carella picked up the bag and started out of the room.
He did not look into it. He did not have to.

He had been a cop for a long time now, and he knew instantly from the expression on Hawes's face that the bag must contain a segment of a human body.

Chapter Three

Now that's pretty damn disgusting.

But let's get something straight. Death *is* pretty damn disgusting, and there are no two ways about it. If you are one of those people who like motion pictures where a man fires a gun and a small spurt of dust explodes on the victim's chest — just a small spurt of dust, no blood – then police work is not the line for you. Similarly, if you are one of those people who believe that corpses look 'just like they're sleeping', it is fortunate you are not a cop. If you are a cop, you know that death is seldom pretty, that it is in fact the ugliest and most frightening event that can overtake a human being.

If you are a cop, you have seen death at its ugliest because you have seen it as the result of violent upheaval. You have, more than likely, puked more than once at the things you have seen. You have, more than likely, trembled with fear, because death has a terrifying way of reminding the strongest human that his flesh can bleed and his bones can break. If you are a cop, you will never get used to the sight of a corpse or a part of a corpse – no matter how long you deal with them, no matter how strong you are, no matter how tough you become.

There is nothing reassuring about the sight of a man who has been worked over with a hatchet. The skull, a formidable piece of bone, assuming the characteristics of a melon, the parallel wounds, the criss-crossing wounds, the bleeding ugly wounds covering the head and the face and the neck, the windpipe exposed and raw, throbbing with colour so bright, but throbbing only with colour because life is gone, life has fled beneath the battering rigidity of an impersonal hatchet blade; there is nothing reassuring.

There is nothing beautiful about the post-mortem decomposition of a body, man or woman, child or adult, the gas formation, the discoloration of head and trunk tissues, the separation of epidermis, the staining of veins, the protrusion of tongue, decomposed liquefied fat soaking through the skin resulting in large yellow-stained areas; there is nothing beautiful.

There is nothing tender about bullet wounds, the smeared and lacerated flesh of contact wounds, the subcutaneous explosion of gases, the tissues seared and blackened by flame and smoke, the embedded powder grains, the gaping holes in the flesh; there is nothing tender.

If you are a cop, you learn that death is ugly, and frightening, and disgusting. If you are a cop, you learn to deal with what is ugly, frightening and disgusting or you quit the force.

The object in the overnight bag was a human hand, ugly, frightening and disgusting.

The man who received it at the morgue was an assistant medical examiner named Paul Blaney, a short man with a scraggly black moustache and violet eyes. Blaney didn't particularly enjoy handling the remains of dead people, and he often wondered why he – the junior member on the medical examiner's staff – was invariably given the most particularly obnoxious stiffs to examine, those who had been in automobile accidents, or fires, or whose remains had been chewed to ribbons by marauding rats. But he knew that he had a job to do. And that job was – given a human hand which has been severed at the wrist from the remainder of the body, how can I determine the race, sex, age, probable height and probable weight of the person to whom it belonged?

That was the job.

With a maximum of dispatch, and a minimum of emotional involvement, Blaney set to work.

Fortunately, the hand was still covered with skin. A lot of bodies he received simply weren't. And so it was quite simple to determine the race of the person to whom the hand had belonged. Blaney determined that race rather quickly, and then jotted the information on a slip of paper.

RACE: White.

Sex was another thing again. It was simple to identify the sex of an individual if the examiner was presented with remains of the breasts or sexual organs, but all Blaney had was a hand. Period. Just a hand. In general, Blaney knew, the female of the species usually had less body hair than the male, more delicate extremities, more subcutaneous fat and less musculature. Her bones, too, were smaller and lighter, with thinner shafts and wider medullary spaces.

The hand on the autopsy table was a huge one. It measured twenty-five centimetres from the tip of the middle finger to the base of the severed wrist, and that came to something more than nine and a half inches when translated into laymen's English. Blaney could not conceive of such a hand having belonged to a woman, unless she were a masseuse or a female wrestler. And even granting such exotic occupations, the likelihood was remote. He had, nonetheless, made errors in determining the sex of a victim from sex-unrelated parts in the past, and he did not wish to make such an error now.

The hand was covered with thick, black, curling hair, another fact which seemed to point towards a male identification; but Blaney carried the examination to its conclusion, measuring the bone shafts, studying the medullary spaces, and jotting down his estimate at last.

SEX: Male.

Well, we're getting someplace, he thought. We now know that this gruesome and severed member of a human body once belonged to a white male. Wiping his forehead with a towel, he got back to work again.

A microscopic examination of the hand's skin told Blaney that there had been no loss of elasticity due to the decrease of elastic fibres in the dermis. Since he was making his microscopic examination in an effort to determine the victim's age, he automatically chalked off the possibility of the man's having been a very old one. He knew, further, that he was not likely to get anything more from a closer examination of the skin. The changes in skin throughout the growth and decline of a human being very seldom provide accurate criteria of age. And so he turned to the bones.

The hand had been severed slightly above the wrist so that portions of the radius and ulna, the twin bones which run from the wrist to the elbow, were still attached to the hand. Moreover, Blaney had all the various bones of the hand itself to examine: the carpus, the metacarpal, the phalanx.

He mused, as he worked, that the average layman would – just about now – begin to consider all of his devious machinations as scientific mumbo jumbo, the aimless meanderings of a pseudo-wizard. Well, he thought, the hell with the average layman. I know damn well that the ossification centres of bones go through a sequence of growth and fusion, and that this growth and fusion takes place at certain age levels. I know further that by studying these bones, I can come pretty close to estimating the age of this dead white male, and that is just what I am going to do, average layman be damned.

The entire examination which Blaney conducted on the bones took close to three hours. His notes included such esoteric terms as 'proximal epiphysial muscle' and 'os magnum' and 'multangulum majus' and the like. His final note simply read:

AGE: 18–24.

When it came to the probable height and weight of the victim, Blaney threw up his hands in despair. If he had been presented with a femur, a humerus, or a radius in its entirety, he would have measured any one of them in centimetres from joint surface to joint surface with the cartilage in place, and then made an attempt at calculating the height using Pearson's formula. For the radius, if he'd had a whole one and not just a portion of one, the table would have read like this:

MALE	FEMALE
86.465 plus 3.271 times length of radius.	82.189 plus 3.343 times length of radius.

Then, to arrive at an estimate of the height of the *living* body, he'd have subtracted 1.5 centimetres from the final result for a male, and 2 centimetres for a female.

Unfortunately, he didn't have a whole radius, so he didn't even make an attempt. And although the hand gave him a good knowledge of the size of the victim's bones, he could not make a guess at the weight of the victim without a knowledge of the muscular development and the adipose tissue, so he quit. He wrapped the hand and tagged it for delivery to Lieutenant Samuel G. Grossman at the Police Laboratory. Grossman, he knew, would perform an iso-reaction test on a blood specimen in order to determine the blood group. And Grossman would undoubtedly try to get fingerprint impressions from the severed hand. In this respect, Blaney was positively certain that Grossman would fail. Each finger tip had been nearly sliced away from the rest of the hand by the unknown assailant. A magician couldn't have got a set of prints from that hand, and Grossman was no magician.

So Blaney shipped off the hand, and he concluded his notes; and what he finally transmitted to the bulls of the 87th was this:

RACE: White.
SEX: Male.
AGE: 18–24.

The boys had to take it from there.

Chapter Four

Detective Steve Carella was the first of the boys to take it from there.

He took it early the next morning. Sitting at his desk near the grilled squadroom windows, watching the rain ooze along the glass panes, he dialled Blaney's office and waited.

'Dr Blaney,' a voice on the other end of the wire said.

'Blaney, this is Carella up at the 87th.'

'Hello,' Blaney said.

'I've got your report on that hand, Blaney.'

'Yeah? What's wrong with it?' Blaney asked, immediately on the defensive.

'Nothing at all,' Carella said. 'In fact, it's very helpful.'

'Well, I'm glad to hear that,' Blaney said. 'It's very rare that anyone in the goddamn department admits a medical examination was helpful.'

'We feel differently here at the 87th,' Carella said smoothly. 'We've always relied very heavily upon information provided by the medical examiner's office.'

'Well, I'm certainly glad to hear that,' Blaney said. 'A man works here with stiffs all day long, he begins to have his doubts. It's no fun cutting up dead bodies, you know.'

'You fellows do a wonderful job,' Carella said.

'Well, thank you.'

'I mean it,' Carella said fervently. 'There isn't much glory in what you fellows do, but you can bet your life it's appreciated.'

'Well, thank you. Thank you.'

'I wish I had a nickel for every case you fellows made easier for us to crack,' Carella said, more fervently this time, almost carried away by himself.

'Well, gosh, thanks. What can I do for you, Carella?'

'Your report was an excellent one,' Carella said, 'and very helpful, too. But there was just one thing.'

'Yes?'

'I wonder if you can tell me anything about the person who did the job.'

'Did the job?'

'Yes. Your report told us a lot about the victim, and that's excellent . . .'

'Yes?'

'Yes, and very helpful. But what about the perpetrator?'

'The perpetrator?'

'Yes, the man or woman who did the surgery.'

'Oh. Oh, yes, of course,' Blaney said. 'You know, after you've been examining corpses for a while, you forget that someone was responsible for the corpse, do you know what I mean? It becomes ... well, sort of a mathematical problem.'

'I can understand that,' Carella said. 'But about the person responsible for this particular corpse, could you tell anything from the surgery?'

'Well, the hand was severed slightly above the wrist.'

'Could you tell what kind of a tool was used?'

'Either a meat cleaver or a hatchet, I would say. Or something similar.'

'Was it a clean job?'

'Fairly. Whoever did it had to hack through those bones. But there were no hesitation cuts anywhere on the hand, so the person who severed it from the body was probably determined and sure.'

'Skilful?'

'How do you mean?'

'Well, would you say the person had any knowledge of anatomy?'

'I wouldn't think so,' Blaney answered. 'The logical place for the cut would have been at the wrist itself, where the radius and ulna terminate. That certainly would have been easier than hacking through those bones. No, I would discount anyone with a real knowledge of anatomy. In fact, I can't understand why the hand was dismembered, can you?'

'I don't think I follow you, Blaney?'

'You've seen dismemberment cases before, Carella. We usually find the head, and then the trunk, and then the four extremities. But if a person is going to cut off an arm, why then cut off the hand? Do you know what I mean? It's an added piece of work that doesn't accomplish very much.'

'Yeah, I see,' Carella said.

'Most bodies are dismembered or mutilated because the criminal is attempting to avoid identification of the body. That's why the fingertips of that hand were mutilated.'

'Of course.'

'And sometimes your killer will cut up the body to make disposal easier. But cutting off a hand at the wrist? How would that serve either purpose?'

'I don't know,' Carella said. 'In any case, we're not dealing with a surgeon or a doctor here, is that right?'

'I would say not.'

'How about a butcher?'

'Maybe. The bones were severed with considerable force. That might imply a man familiar with his tools. The fingertips were neatly sliced.'

'Okay, Blaney, thanks a lot.'

'Any time,' Blaney said happily, and hung up.

Carella thought for a moment about dismembered bodies. There was suddenly a very sour taste in his mouth. He went into the Clerical Office and asked Miscolo to make a pot of coffee.

In Captain Frick's office downstairs a patrolman named Richard Genero was on the carpet. Frick, who was technically in command of the entire precinct – his command, actually, very rarely intruded upon the activities of the detective squad – was not a very imaginative man, nor in truth a very intelligent one. He liked being a policeman, he supposed, but he would rather have been a movie star. Movie stars got to meet glamorous women. Police captains only got to bawl out patrolmen.

'Am I to understand, Genero,' he said, 'that you don't know whether the person who left this bag on the sidewalk was a man or a woman, is that what I am made to understand, Genero?'

'Yes, sir,' Genero said.

'You can't tell a man from a woman, Genero?'

'No, sir. I mean, yes, sir, I can sir, but it was raining.'

'So?'

'And this person's face was covered. By an umbrella, sir.'

'Was this person wearing a dress?'

'No, sir.'

'A skirt?'

'No, sir.'

'Pants?'

'Do you mean trousers, sir?'

'Yes, of course I mean trousers!' Frick shouted.

'Well, sir, yes, sir. That is, they could have been slacks. Like women wear, sir. Or they could have been trousers. Like men wear, sir.'

'And what did you do when you saw the bag on the sidewalk?'

'I yelled after the bus, sir.'

'And then what?'

'Then I opened the bag.'

'And when you saw what was inside it?'

'I ... I guess I got a little confused, sir.'

'Did you go after the bus?'

'N ... n ... no, sir.'

'Are you aware that there was another bus stop three blocks away?'

'No, sir.'

'There was, Genero. Are you aware that you could have hailed a passing car, and caught that bus, and boarded it, and arrested the person who left this bag on the sidewalk? Are you aware of that, Genero?'

'Yes, sir. I mean, I wasn't aware of it at the time, sir. I am now, sir.'

'And saved us the trouble of sending this bag to the laboratory, or of having the detective division trot all the way out to International Airport?'

'Yes, sir.'

'Or of trying to find the other pieces of that body, of hoping we can identify the body *after* we have all the pieces, are you aware of all this, Genero?'

'Yes, sir.'

'Then how can you be so goddamn stupid, Genero?'

'I don't know, sir.'

'We contacted the bus company,' Frick said. 'The bus that passed that corner at two-thirty – was that the time, Genero?'

'Yes, sir.'

'– at two-thirty was bus number 8112. We talked to the driver. He doesn't remember anyone in black boarding the bus at that corner, man or woman.'

'There was a person, sir. I saw him. Or her, sir.'

'No one's doubting your word, Genero. A bus driver can't be expected to remember everyone who gets on and off his goddamn bus. In any case,

Genero, we're right back where we started. And all because you didn't think. Why didn't you think, Genero?'

'I don't know, sir. I was too shocked, I guess.'

'Boy, there are times I wish I was a movie star or something,' Frick said. 'All right, get out. Look alive, Genero. Keep on your goddamn toes.'

'Yes, sir.'

'Go on, get out.'

'Yes, sir.' Genero saluted and left the captain's office hurriedly, thanking his lucky stars that no one had discovered he'd had two glasses of wine in Max Mandel's shop just before finding the bag. Frick sat at his desk and sighed heavily. Then he buzzed Lieutenant Byrnes upstairs and told him he could deliver the bag to the lab whenever he wanted to. Byrnes said he would send a man down for it at once.

The photograph of the bag lay on Nelson Piat's desk.

'Yes, that's one of our bags, all right,' he said. 'Nice photograph, too. Did you take the photograph?'

'Me, personally, do you mean?' Detective Meyer Meyer asked.

'Yes.'

'No. A police photographer took it.'

'Well, it's our bag, all right,' Piat said. He leaned back in his leather covered swivel chair, dangerously close to the huge sheet of glass that formed one wall of his office. The office was on the fourth floor of the Administration Building at International Airport, overlooking the runway. The runway now was drenched with lashing curtains of rain that swept its slick surface. 'Damn rain,' Piat said. 'Bad for our operation.'

'Can't you fly when it rains?' Meyer asked.

'Oh, *we* can fly all right. *We* can fly in almost everything. But will the *people* fly, that's the question. The minute it begins raining, we get more damn cancellations than you can shake a stick at. Afraid. They're all afraid.' Piat shook his head and studied the photo of the bag again. It was an $8\frac{1}{2} \times 11$ glossy print. The bag had been photographed against a white backdrop. It was an excellent picture, the company's name and slogan leaping out of the print as if they were moulded in neon. 'Well, what about this bag, gentlemen?' Piat said. 'Did some burglar use it for his tools or something?' He chuckled at his own little joke and looked first to Kling and then to Meyer.

Kling answered for both of them. 'Well, not exactly, sir,' he said. 'Some murderer used it for part of a corpse.'

'Part of a . . . ?' Oh. I see. Well, that's not too good. Bad for our operation.' He paused. 'Or is it?' He paused again, calculating. 'Will this case be getting into the newspapers?'

'I doubt it,' Meyer said. 'It's a little too gory for the public, and so far it doesn't contain either a rape or a pretty girl in bloomers. It would make dull copy.'

'I was thinking . . . you know . . . a photo of the bag on the front pages of a mass circulation newspaper, that might not be bad for our operation. Hell, you can't buy that kind of advertising space, now can you? It might be very good for our operation, who knows?'

'Yes, sir,' Meyer said patiently.

If there was one virtue Meyer Meyer possessed, that virtue was patience. And it was, in a sense, a virtue he was born with or, at the very least, a virtue he was named with. Meyer's father, you see, was something of a practical joker, the kind of man who delighted in telling kosher dinner guests during the middle of a meat meal that they were eating off the dairy dishes. Oh, yes, he was a gasser, all right. Well, when this gasser was well past the age when changing diapers or wiping runny noses was a possibility, when his wife had in fact experienced that remarkable female phenomenon euphemistically known as change of life, they were both somewhat taken aback to learn that she was pregnant.

This was a surprising turn of events indeed, the practical joke supreme upon the king of the jesters. Meyer's father fretted, pouted and sulked about it. His jokes suffered while he planned his revenge against the vagaries of nature and birth control. The baby was born, a bouncing, blue-eyed boy delivered by a midwife and weighing in at seven pounds six ounces. And then Meyer's pop delivered the final hilarious thrust. The baby's first name would be Meyer, he decreed, and this handle when coupled with the family name would give the boy a title like a ditto mark: Meyer Meyer.

Well, that's pretty funny. Meyer's old man didn't stop laughing for a week after the briss. Meyer, on the other hand, found it difficult to laugh through bleeding lips. The family was, you understand, practising Orthodox Judaism and they lived in a neighbourhood which housed a large Gentile population, and if the kids in the neighbourhood needed another reason besides Meyer's Jewishness for beating him up every day of the week, his name provided that reason. 'Meyer Meyer, Jew on fire!' the kids would chant, and POW! Meyer got it in the kisser.

Over the years, he learned that it was impossible to fight twelve guys at once, but that it was sometimes possible to talk this even dozen out of administering a beating. Patiently, he talked. Sometimes it worked. Sometimes it didn't. But patience became a way of life. And patience is a virtue, we will all admit. But if Meyer Meyer had not been forced to sublimate, if he had for example just once, just once when he was a growing boy been called Charlie or Frank or Sam and been allowed to stand up against one other kid, not a dozen or more, and bash that kid squarely on the nose, well perhaps, just perhaps, Meyer Meyer would not have been completely bald at the tender age of thirty-seven.

On the other hand, who would have been so cruel as to deprive an ageing comedian of a small practical joke?

Patiently, Meyer Meyer said, 'How are these bags distributed, Mr Piat?'

'Distributed? Well, they're not exactly distributed. That is to say, they are given to people who fly with our airline. It's good for the operation.'

'These bags are given to every one of your passengers, is that correct?'

'No, not exactly. We have several types of flights, you see.'

'Yes?'

'Yes. We have our Luxury flight which gives more space between the seats, a big big twenty inches to stretch those legs in, and drinks en route, and a choice of several dinners, and special baggage accommodations – in short, the finest service our operation can offer.'

'Yes.'

'Yes. And then we have our First-Class flight which offers the same accommodations and the same seating arrangement except that drinks are not provided – you can buy them, of course, if you desire – and there is only one item on the dinner menu, usually roast beef, or ham, or something of the sort.'

'I see.'

'And then we have our Tourist flight.'

'Tourist flight, yes,' Meyer said.

'Our Tourist flight which gives only sixteen inches of leg room, but the same accommodations otherwise, including the same dinner as on the First-Class flight.'

'I see. And this bag ...'

'And then there is our Economy flight, same amount of leg room, but there are three seats on one side of the aisle, instead of two, and the dinner is not a hot meal, just sandwiches and, of course, no drinks.'

'And of all these flights, which ...'

'Then there's our Thrift flight which is not too comfortable, I'm afraid, that is to say not as comfortable as the other flights, but certainly comfortable enough, with only twelve inches of leg room, and ...'

'Is that the last flight?' Meyer asked patiently.

'We're now working on one called the Piggy Bank flight, which will be even less expensive. What we're trying to do, you see, we're trying to put our operation within reach of people who wouldn't ordinarily consider flying, who would take the old-fashioned means of conveyance, like trains, or cars, or boats. Our operation ...'

'Who gets the bags?' Kling asked impatiently.

'What? Oh, yes, the bags. We give them to all passengers on the Luxury or First-Class flights.'

'*All* passengers?'

'All.'

'And when did you start doing this?'

'At least six years ago,' Piat said.

'Then anyone who rode either Luxury or First-Class in the past six years could conceivably have one of these bags, is that right?' Meyer asked.

'That is correct.'

'And how many people would you say ...'

'Oh, thousands and thousands and thousands,' Piat said. 'You must remember, Detective Meyer ...'

'Yes?' ⠄

'We circle the globe.'

'Yes,' Meyer said. 'Forgive me. With all those flights zooming around, I guess I lost sight of the destinations.'

'Is there any possibility this might get into the newspapers?'

'There's always a possibility,' Meyer said, rising.

'If it does, would you contact me? I mean, if you know about it beforehand. I'd like to get our promotion department to work.'

'Sure thing,' Meyer said. 'Thank you for your time, Mr Piat.'

'Not at all,' Piat said, shaking hands with Meyer and Kling. 'Not at all.' As they walked across the room to the door, he turned to the huge window and looked out over the rain-soaked runway. 'Damn rain,' he said.

Chapter Five

Friday morning.

Rain.

When he was a kid, he used to walk six blocks to the library in the rain, wearing a mackinaw with the collar turned up, and feeling very much like Abraham Lincoln. Once there, he would sit in the warmth of the wood-panelled reading room, feeling strangely and richly rewarded while he read and the rain whispered against the streets outside.

And sometimes, at the beach, it would begin raining suddenly, the clouds sweeping in over the ocean like black horsemen in a clanging cavalry charge, the lightning scraping the sky like angry scimitar slashes. The girls would grab for sweaters and beach bags, and someone would reach for the portable record player and the stack of 45-rpms, and the boys would hold the blanket overhead like a canopy while they all ran to the safety of the boardwalk restaurant. They would stand there and look out at the rain-swept beach, the twisted, lipsticked straws in deserted Coca Cola bottles, and there was comfort to the gloom somehow.

In Korea, Bert Kling learned about a different kind of rain. He learned about a rain that was cruel and driving and bitter, a rain that turned the earth to a sticky clinging mud that halted machines and men. He learned what it was to be constantly wet and cold. And ever since Korea, he had not liked the rain.

He did not like it on that late Friday morning, either.

He had started the day by paying a visit to the Missing Persons Bureau and renewing his acquaintance there with Detectives Ambrose and Bartholdi.

'Well, well, look who is here,' Bartholdi had said.

'The Sun God of the 87th,' Ambrose added.

'The Blond Wonder himself.'

'In person,' Kling said drily.

'What can we do for you today, Detective Kling?'

'Who did you lose this week, Detective Kling?'

'We're looking for a white male between the ages of eighteen and twenty-four,' Kling said.

'Did you hear that, Romeo?' Ambrose said to Bartholdi.

'I heard it, Mike,' Bartholdi answered.

'That is an awful lot to go on. Now how many white males between the ages of eighteen and twenty-four do you suppose we have records on?'

'At a conservative estimate,' Bartholdi answered, 'I would say approximately six thousand seven hundred and twenty-three.'

'Not counting the ones we ain't had time to file yet.'

'With bulls from all over the city popping in here at every hour of the day, we don't get much time to do filing, Detective Kling.'

'That's a shame,' Kling said drily. He wished he could shake the feeling he constantly experienced in the presence of older cops who'd been on the force longer than he. He knew he was a young detective and a new detective, but he resented the automatic assumption that because of his age and inexperience he must, ipso facto, be an inept detective. He did not consider himself inept. In fact, he thought of himself as being a pretty good cop, Romeo and Mike be damned.

'Can I look through the files?' he asked.

'But of course!' Bartholdi said enthusiastically. 'That's why they're here! So that every dirty-fingered cop in the city can pore over them. Ain't that right, Mike?'

'Why, certainly. How else would we keep busy? If we didn't have dog-eared record cards to retype, we might have to go outside on a lousy day like this. We might have to actually use a gun now and then.'

'We prefer leaving the gunplay to you younger, more agile fellows, Kling.'

'To the heroes,' Ambrose said.

'Yeah,' Kling answered, and he searched for a more devastating reply, but none came to mind.

'Be careful with our cards,' Bartholdi cautioned. 'Did you wash your hands this morning?'

'I washed them,' Kling said.

'Good. Obey the sign.' He pointed to the large placard resting atop the green filing cabinets.

SHUFFLE THEM, JUGGLE THEM, MAUL THEM, CARESS THEM – BUT LEAVE THEM THE WAY YOU FOUND THEM!

'Got it?' Ambrose asked.

'I've been here before,' Kling said. 'You ought to change your sign. It gets kind of dull the hundredth time around.'

'It ain't there for entertainment,' Bartholdi said. 'It's there for information.'

'Take care of the cards,' Ambrose said. 'If you get bored, look up a dame named Barbara Cesare, also known as Bubbles Caesar. She was reported missing in February. That's over there near the window. She was a stripper in Kansas City, and she came here to work some of our own clubs. There are some very fine art photos in her folder.'

'He is just a boy, Mike,' Bartholdi said. 'You shouldn't call his attention to matters like that.'

'Forgive me, Romeo,' Ambrose said. 'You're right. Forget I mentioned Bubbles Caesar, Kling. Forget all about them lovely pictures in the February file over there near the window. You hear?'

'I'll forget all about her,' Kling said.

'We got typing to do,' Bartholdi said, opening the door. 'Have fun.'

'That's Caesar,' Ambrose said as he went out. 'C-A-E-S-A-R.'

'Bubbles,' Bartholdi said, and he closed the door behind him.

Kling, of course, did not have to look through 6,723 missing persons cards. If anything, the haphazard estimate given by Bartholdi was somewhat exaggerated. Actually, some 2,500 persons were reported missing annually in the city for which Kling worked. If this was broken down on a monthly basis, perhaps a little more than 200 people per month found their way into the files of the Missing Persons Bureau. The peak months for disappearances are May and September, but Kling, fortunately, was not particularly concerned with those months. He restricted himself to scouring the files covering January, February, and the early part of March, and so he didn't have very many folders to wade through.

The job, nonetheless, did get somewhat boring, and he did – since he was studying the February file, anyway – take a peek into the folder of the missing exotic dancer, Bubbles Caesar. He had to admit, after studying the several photos of her in the folder, that whoever had named this performer had a decided knack for the *mot juste*. Looking at the pictures of the stripper made him think of Claire Townsend, and thinking of Claire made him wish it was tonight instead of this morning.

He lighted another cigarette, ruefully put away Miss Caesar's folder, and got back to work again.

By eleven o'clock that morning, he had turned up only two possible nominations for the Missing Persons Award. He went down the hall and had both sheets photostated. Bartholdi, who did the job for him, seemed to be in a more serious frame of mind now.

'These what you were looking for, kid?' he asked.

'Well, they're only possibilities. We'll see how they turn out.'

'What's the case, anyway?' Bartholdi asked.

'One of our patrolmen found a severed hand in a bag.'

'Psssssss,' Bartholdi said and he pulled a face.

'Yeah. Right in the street. Near a bus stop.'

'Psssssss,' Bartholdi said again.

'Yeah.'

'A man or a woman? The hand, I mean.'

'A man,' Kling said.

'What kind of a bag? A shopping bag?'

'No, no,' Kling said. 'An airlines bag. You know these bags they give out? These little blue ones? This one came from an outfit called Circle Airlines.'

'A high-flying killer, huh?' Bartholdi said. 'Well, here are the stats, kid. Good luck with them.'

'Thanks,' Kling said. He took the proffered manila envelope and went down the corridor to a phone booth. He dialled Frederick 7–8024 and asked to talk to Steve Carella.

'Some weather, huh?' Carella said.

'The end,' Kling answered. 'Listen, I dug up two possibles from the files here. Thought I'd hit the first before lunch. You want to come with me?'

'Sure,' Carella said. 'Where shall I meet you?'

'Well, the first guy is a merchant seaman, vanished on February 14, Valentine's Day. His wife reported him missing. She lives on Detavoner, near South Eleventh.'

'Meet you on the corner there?'

'Fine,' Kling said. 'Were there any calls for me?'

'Claire called.'

'Yeah?'

'Said you should call her back as soon as you got a chance.'

'Oh? Okay, thanks,' Kling said. 'I'll see you in about a half-hour, okay?'

'Right. Stay out of the rain.' And he hung up.

Now, standing in the rain on what was probably the most exposed corner in the entire city, Kling tried to crawl deep into his trench coat, tried to form an airtight, watertight seal where his hands were thrust deep into his coat pockets, tried to pull in his neck like a turtle, but nothing worked against the goddamn rain, everything was wet and cold and clammy, and where the hell was Carella?

I wish I wore a hat, he thought. I wish I were that kind of American advertising executive who could feel comfortable in a hat.

Hatless, his blond hair soaked and plastered to his skull, Kling stood on the street corner observing:

a) the open parking lot on one corner.

b) the skyscraper under construction on the opposite corner.

c) the fenced-in park on the third corner.

d) the blank wall of a warehouse on the fourth corner.

No canopies under which to stand. No doorways into which a man could duck. Nothing but the wide open spaces of Isola and the rain driving across those spaces like a Cossack charge in an Italian-made spectacle. Damn you, Carella, where are you?

Aw, come on, Steve, he thought. Have a heart.

The unmarked police sedan pulled to the kerb. A sign on the lamp-post read NO PARKING OR STANDING 8:00 A.M. TO 6:00 P.M. Carella parked the car and got out.

'Hi,' he said. 'Been waiting long?'

'What the hell kept you?' Kling wanted to know.

'Grossman called from the lab just as I was leaving.'

'Yeah? So what ...?'

'He's working on both the hand and the bag now, says he'll have a report for us sometime tomorrow.'

'Will he get any prints from the hand?'

'He doubts it. The finger tips are cut to ribbons. Listen, can't we discuss this over a cup of coffee? Must we stand here in the rain? And I'd also like to take a look at that Missing Person sheet before we see this woman.'

'I can use a cup of coffee,' Kling said.

'Does she know we're coming? The guy's wife?'

'No. You think I should have called?'

'No, better this way. Maybe we'll find her with a body in a trunk and a meat cleaver in her dainty fist.'

'Sure. There's a diner in the middle of the block. Let's get the coffee there. You can look over the sheet while I buzz Claire.'

'Good,' Carella said.

They walked to the diner, sat in one of the booths, and ordered two cups of coffee. While Kling went to call his fiancée, Carella sipped at his coffee and studied the report. He read it through once, and then he read it through a second time. This is what it said:

POLICE DEPARTMENT
REPORT OF MISSING PERSON

DET. DISTRICT ___2nd___   SQD. ___26th___

CASE NO. ___DD25-1143___

BUS. NO. ___34A-1762___

DATE OF THIS REPORT ___2/16___

SURNAME ANDROVICH	FIRST NAME, INITIALS KARL F.		NATIVITY U.S.A.	SEX M	AGE 22	COLOR White
ADDRESS 537 Detavoner Avenue	LAST SEEN AT Home address		DATE AND TIME SEEN 2/14		6:30	A.M. P.M.
PROBABLE DESTINATION S.S. Farren, Pier 6	CAUSE OF ABSENCE ?		DATE AND TIME REPORTED 2/15		9:00	A.M. P.M.

PHYSICAL NOTE PECULIARITIES	CLOTHING—GIVE COLOR, FABRIC, STYLE, LABEL, WHERE POSSIBLE	STRIKE OUT IRRELEVANT WORDS	MISCELLANEOUS INFORMATION	
HEIGHT FT. 6 IN. 4½	HEADGEAR Watchcap, blue wool		OCCUPATION OR SCHOOL Wiper, S.S. Farren	
WEIGHT 210	OVER OR TOP COAT None		EVER FINGERPRINTED? WHERE AND WHEN? Yes. Morch-Mar. 2/4/58	
BUILD Husky	SUIT OR DRESS		DRY CLEANER MARKS In jacket. Detavoner Cleaners. 001 Detavoner Avenue	
COMPLEXION Sallow	JACKET Peajacket, Blue		LAUNDRY MARKS	
HAIR Brown	TROUSERS Dungarees, blue, faded		PHOTO RECEIVED Yes	PREVIOUSLY MISSING? No
EYES Brown	SHIRT white, cotton, long-sleeved,Manhatten label		PUBLICITY DESIRED? Yes	SOCIAL SECURITY NO. 119-16-4683
GLASSES, TYPE	TIE OR FUR PIECE SCARF		PRELIMINARY INVESTIGATION	Ptlm Ralph Cinnetar
MUSTACHE Brown, close trimmed	HOSE GLOVES Black socks, cotton dacron, Esquire		DESK OFFICER Lt. E. Neal	
TEETH No dental chart	SHOES Black, untrimmed		TELEGRAPH BUSINESS Sgt. N. Abronoff	
	HANDBAG		BUREAU OF INFORMATION Det. 1st/Or D. Nicholson	
SCARS	LUGGAGE Duffel bag, canvas, white, stenciled "K. F. ANDROVICH"		OTHERS	
	JEWELRY WORN			
DEFORMITIES				
	MONEY CARRIED $30		NOTIFICATION TO MISSING PERSONS BUR. BY Det./Lt.Franklin Canavan, 26DetSq	
TATTOO MARKS "MEG" in heart on left biceps	CHARACTERISTICS, HABITS, MANNERISMS Slight tic left eye. Stammers when excited. Very hot-tempered.		RECEIVED AT MISSING PERSONS BUREAU BY Sgt.Sean O'Rourke	
			ASSIGNED	SQUAD
CONDITION PHYSICAL MENTAL Good Good			ASSIGNED Det.2/Or Jonah Fredericks	
REPORTED BY Margaret Androvich	ADDRESS 537 Detavoner Avenue		TELEPHONE NO. IS 4-7361	RELATIONSHIP Wife

Androvich left his apartment at 537 Detavoner Avenue at 6:30 A.M. on February 14 apparently to board his ship, the SS Farren, wher it was docked at Pier 6. He was scheduled to sail for South America at 8:00 A.M. that morning, and gave every indication of wanting to catch the ship. His wife noticed nothing strange about his behavior at breakfast, which they ate together in the apartment. At 7:45 A.M., the chief officer of the Farren called to inquire of Androvich's whereabouts. His wife told the officer that Androvich had left the apartment at 6:30. She did not report his absence to the police during the remainder of that day, because she was hopeful he would return by morning. This was the first time, except when on cruises, that he had been gone for any prolonged period of time.

Det. Jonah Fredericks   _Lt. Samuel Barker_
Signature of Assigned Detective   Commanding Officer

When Kling came back to the table, there was a smile on his face.

'What's up?' Carella asked.

'Oh, nothing much. Claire's father left for New Jersey this morning, that's all. Won't be back until Monday.'

'Which gives you an empty apartment for the weekend, huh?' Carella said.

'Well, I wasn't thinking anything like that,' Kling said.

'No, of course not.'

'But it might be nice,' Kling admitted.

'When are you going to marry that girl?'

'She wants to get her master's degree before we get married.'

'Why?'

'How do I know? She's insecure.' Kling shrugged. 'She's psychotic. How do I know?'

'What does she want after the master's? A doctorate?'

'Maybe.' Kling shrugged. 'Listen, I ask her to marry me every time I see her. She wants the master's. So what can I do? I'm in love with her. Can I tell her to go to hell?'

'I suppose not.'

'Well, I can't.' Kling paused. 'I mean, what the hell, Steve, if a girl wants an education, it's not my right to say no, is it?'

'I guess not.'

'Well, would you have said no to Teddy?'

'I don't think so.'

'Well, there you are.'

'Sure.'

'I mean, what the hell else can I do, Steve? I either wait for her, or I decide not to marry her, right?'

'Right,' Carella said.

'And since I want to marry her, I have no choice. I wait.' He paused thoughtfully. 'Jesus, I hope she isn't one of those perennial schoolgirl types.' He paused again. 'Well, there's nothing I can do about it. I'll just have to wait, that's all.'

'That sounds like sound deduction.'

'Sure. The only thing is . . . well, to be absolutely truthful with you, Steve, I'm afraid she'll get pregnant or something, and then we'll *have* to get married, do you know what I mean? And that'll be different than if we just got married because we felt like it. I mean, even though we love each other and all, it'd be different. Oh, Jesus, I don't know what to do.'

'Just be careful, that's all,' Carella said.

'Oh, I am. I mean, we are, we are. You want to know something Steve?'

'What?'

'I wish I could keep my hands off her. You know, I wish we didn't have to . . . well, you know, my landlady looks at me cockeyed every time I bring Claire upstairs. And then I have to rush her home because her father is the strictest guy who ever walked the earth. I'm surprised he's leaving her alone this weekend. But what I mean is . . . well, damnit, what the hell does she need that master's for, Steve? I mean, I wish I could leave her alone until we were married, but I just can't. I mean, all I have to do is be with her, and my mouth goes dry. Is it that way with . . . well, never mind, I didn't mean to get personal.'

'It's that way,' Carella said.

'Yeah,' Kling said, and he nodded. He seemed lost in thought for a moment. Then he said, 'I've got tomorrow off, but not Sunday. Do you think somebody would want to switch with me? Like for a Tuesday or something? I hate to break up the weekend.'

'Where'd you plan to spend the weekend?' Carella asked.

'Well, you know ...'

'*All* weekend?' Carella said, surprised.

'Well, you know ...'

'Starting *tonight*?' he asked, astonished.

'Well, you know ...'

'I'd give you my Sunday, but I'm afraid ...'

'Will you?' Kling said, leaning forward.

'... you'll be a wreck on Monday morning.' Carella paused. '*All* weekend?' he asked again.

'Well, it isn't often the old man goes away. You know.'

'Flaming Youth, where have you gone?' Carella said, shaking his head. 'Sure, you can have my Sunday if the Skipper says okay.'

'Thanks, Steve.'

'Or did Teddy have something planned?' Carella asked himself.

'Now don't change your mind,' Kling said anxiously.

'Okay, okay.' He tapped the Missing Persons report with his forefinger. 'What do you think?'

'He looks good, I would say. He's big enough, anyway. Six-four and weighs two-ten. That's no midget, Steve.'

'And that hand belonged to a big man.' Carella finished his coffee and said, 'Come on, Lover Man, let's go see Mrs Androvich.'

As they rose, Kling said, 'It's not that I'm a great lover or anything, Steve. It's just ... well ...'

'What?'

Kling grinned. 'I *like* it,' he said.

Chapter Six

Margaret Androvich was a nineteen-year-old blonde who, in the hands of our more skilful novelists, would have been described as willowy. That is to say, she was skinny. The diminutive 'Meg' did not exactly apply to her because she was five feet seven and a half inches tall with all the cuddly softness of a steel cable. In the current fashion of naming particularly svelte women with particularly ugly names, 'Maggie' would have been more appropriate than the 'Meg' which Karl Androvich wore tattooed in a heart on his left arm. But Meg she was, all five feet seven and a half inches of her, and she greeted the detectives at the door with calm and assurance, ushered them into her living room, and asked them to sit.

They sat.

She was indeed skinny with that angular sort of femininity which is usually attributed to fashion models. She was not, at the moment, attired for the pages of *Vogue* Magazine. She was wearing a faded pink quilted robe and furry pink slippers which somehow seemed out of place on a girl so tall. Her face was as angular as her body, with high cheekbones and a mouth which looked pouting even without the benefit of lipstick. Her eyes were blue and large, dominating the narrow face. She spoke with a mild, barely discernible Southern accent. She carried about her the air of a person who knows she is about to be struck in the face with a closed fist but who bears the eventuality with calm expectation.

'Is this about Karl?' she asked gently.

'Yes, Mrs Androvich,' Carella answered.

'Have you heard anything? Is he all right?'

'No, nothing definite,' Carella said.

'But something?'

'No, no. We just wanted to find out a little more about him, that's all.'

'I see.' She nodded vaguely. 'Then you haven't heard anything about him.'

'No, not really.'

'I see.' Again she nodded.

'Can you tell us what happened on the morning he left here?'

'Yes,' she said. 'He just left, that was all. There was nothing different between this time and all the other times he left to catch his ship. It was just the same. Only this time he didn't catch the ship.' She shrugged. 'And I haven't heard from him since.' She shrugged again. 'It's been almost a month now.'

'How long have you been married, Mrs Androvich?'

'To Karl? Six months.'

'Had you been married before? I mean, is Karl your second husband?'

'No. He's my first husband. Only husband I ever had.'

'Where did you meet him, Mrs Androvich?'

'Atlanta.'

'Six months ago?'

'Seven months ago, really.'

'And you got married?'

'Yes.'

'And you came to this city?'

'Yes.'

'Where is your husband from originally?'

'Here. This city.' She paused. 'Do you like it here?'

'The city, do you mean?'

'Yes. Do you like it?'

'Well, I was born and raised here,' Carella said. 'Yes, I guess I like it.'

'I don't,' Meg said flatly.

'Well, that's what makes horse races, Mrs Androvich,' Carella said, and he tried a smile and then pulled it back quickly when he saw her face.

'Yes, that's what makes horse races, all right,' she said. 'I tried to tell Karl that I didn't like it here, that I wanted to go back to Atlanta. But he was born and raised here, too.' She shrugged. 'I guess it's different if you know the place. And with him gone so often, I'm alone a lot, and the streets confuse me. I mean, Atlanta isn't exactly a one-horse town, but it's small compared to here. I can never figure out how to *get* any place here. I'm always getting lost. I wander three blocks from the apartment, and I get lost. Would you like some coffee?'

'Well ...'

'Have some coffee,' Meg said. 'You're not going to rush right off, are you? You all are the first two people I've had here in a long time.'

'I think we can stay for some coffee,' Carella said.

'It won't take but a minute. Would you excuse me, please?'

She went into the kitchen. Kling rose from where he was sitting and walked to the television set. A framed photograph of a man rested atop the receiver. He was studying the photo when Meg came back into the room.

'That's Karl,' she said. 'That's a nice picture. That's the one I sent to the Missing Persons Bureau.' She paused. 'They asked me for a picture, you know.' She paused again. 'Coffee won't take a but a minute. I'm warming some rolls, too. You men must he half-froze, wandering about in that cold rain.'

'That's very nice of you, Mrs Androvich.'

She smiled fleetingly. 'Working man needs sustenance,' she said, and the smile vanished.

'Mrs Androvich, about that morning he left ...'

'Yes. It was Valentine's Day.' She paused. 'There was a big box of candy on the kitchen table when I woke up. And flowers came later. While we were having breakfast.'

'From Karl?'

'Yes. Yes, from Karl.'

'While you were having breakfast?'

'Yes.'

'But ... didn't he leave the house at 6:30?'

'Yes.'

'And flowers arrived before he left?'

'Yes.'

'That's pretty early, isn't it?'

'I guess he made some sort of arrangement with the florist,' Meg said. 'To have them delivered so early.' She paused. 'They were roses. Two dozen red roses.'

'I see,' Carella said.

'Anything out of the ordinary happen during breakfast?' Kling asked.

'No. No, he was in a very cheerful frame of mind.'

'But he wasn't always in a cheerful frame of mind, is that also right? You told someone earlier that he was very hot-tempered.'

'Yes. I told that to Detective Fredericks. At the Missing Persons Bureau. Do you know him?'

'No, not personally.'

'He's a very nice man.'

'And you told Detective Fredericks that your husband stammers, is that right? And he has a slight tic in the right eye, is that correct?'

'The left eye.'

'Yes, the left eye.'

'That's correct.'

'Is he a nervous person, would you say?'

'He's pretty tense, yes.'

'Was he tense on that morning?'

'The morning he left, do you mean?'

'Yes. Was he tense or nervous then?'

'No. He was very calm.'

'I see. And what did you do with the flowers when they arrived?'

'The flowers? I put them in a vase.'

'On the table?'

'Yes.'

'The breakfast table?'

'Yes.'

'They were there while you ate breakfast?'

'Yes.'

'Did he eat a good meal?'

'Yes.'

'His appetite was all right?'

'It was fine. He was very hungry.'

'And nothing seemed unusual or strange?'

'No.' She turned her head towards the kitchen. 'I think the coffee's perking,' she said. 'Will you excuse me, please?'

She went out of the room. Kling and Carella sat staring at each other. Outside, the rain slithered down the windowpane.

She came back into the living room carrying a tray with a coffeepot, three cups and saucers, and a dish of hot rolls. She put these down, studied the tray, and then said, 'Butter. I forgot butter.' In the doorway to the kitchen, she paused and said, 'Would you all like some jam or something?'

'No, this is fine, thanks,' Carella said.

'Would you pour?' she said, and she went out for the butter. From the kitchen, she called, 'Did I bring out the cream?'

'No,' Carella said.

'Or the sugar?'

'No.'

They heard her rummaging in the kitchen. Carella poured coffee into the three cups. She came into the room again and put down the butter, the cream and the sugar.

'There,' she said. 'Do you take anything in yours, Detective – Carella, was it?'

'Yes, Carella. No thank you, I'll have it black.'

'Detective Kling?'

'A little cream and one sugar, thank you.'

'Help yourself to the rolls before they get cold,' she said.

The detectives helped themselves. She sat opposite them, watching.

'Take your coffee, Mrs Androvich,' Carella said.

'Oh, yes. Thank you.' She picked up her cup, put three spoonfuls of sugar into it, and sat stirring it idly.

'Do you think you'll find him?' she asked.

'We hope so.'

'Do you think anything's happened to him?'

'That's hard to say, Mrs Androvich.'

'He was such a big man.' She shrugged.

'*Was*, Mrs Androvich?'

'Did I say "was"? I guess I did. I guess I think of him as gone for good.'

'Why should you think that?'

'I don't know.'

'It sounds as if he was very much in love with you.'

'Oh, yes. Yes, he was.' She paused. 'Are the rolls all right?'

'Delicious,' Carella said.

'Fine,' Kling added.

'I get them delivered. I don't go out much. I'm here most of the time. Right here in this apartment.'

'Why do you think your husband went off like that, Mrs Androvich?'

'I don't know.'

'You didn't quarrel or anything that morning, did you?'

'No. No, we didn't quarrel.'

'I don't mean a real fight or anything,' Carella said. 'Just a quarrel, you know. Anyone who's married has a quarrel every now and then.'

'Are you married, Detective Carella?'

'Yes, I am.'

'Do you quarrel sometimes?'

'Yes.'

'Karl and I didn't quarrel that morning,' she said flatly.

'But you did quarrel sometimes?'

'Yes. About going back to Atlanta mostly. That was all. Just about going back to Atlanta. Because I don't like this city, you see.'

'That's understandable,' Carella said. 'Not being familiar with it, and all. Have you ever been uptown?'

'Uptown where?'

'Culver Avenue? Hall Avenue?'

'Where the big department stores are?'

'No, I was thinking of a little further uptown. Near Grover Park.'

'No. I don't know where Grover Park is.'

'You've never been uptown?'

'Not that far uptown.'

'Do you have a raincoat, Mrs Androvich?'

'A what?'

'A raincoat.'

'Yes, I do. Why?'

'What colour is it, Mrs Androvich?'

'My *raincoat*?'

'Yes.'

'It's blue.' She paused. 'Why?'

'Do you have a black one?'

'No. Why?'

'Do you ever wear slacks?'

'Hardly ever.'

'But sometimes you do wear slacks?'

'Only in the house sometimes. When I'm cleaning. I never wear them in the street. Where I was raised, in Atlanta, a girl wore dresses and skirts and pretty things.'

'Do you have an umbrella, Mrs Androvich?'

'Yes, I do.'

'What colour is it?'

'Red. I don't think I understand all this, Detective Carella.'

'Mrs Androvich, I wonder if we could see the raincoat and the umbrella.'

'What for?'

'Well, we'd like to.'

She stared at Carella and then turned her puzzled gaze on Kling. 'All right,' she said at last. 'Would you come into the bedroom, please?' They followed her into the other room. 'I haven't made the bed yet, you'll have to forgive the appearance of the house.' She pulled the blanket up over the rumpled sheets as she passed the bed on the way to the closet. She threw open the closet door and said, 'There's the raincoat. And there's the umbrella.'

The raincoat was blue. The umbrella was red.

'Thank you,' Carella said. 'Do you have your meat delivered, too, Mrs Androvich?'

'My what?'

'Meat. From the butcher.'

'Yes, I do. Detective Carella, would you mind please telling me what this is all about? All these questions, you make it sound as if . . .'

'Well, it's just routine, Mrs Androvich, that's all. Just trying to learn a little about your husband's habits, that's all.'

'What's my raincoat and my umbrella got to do with Karl's habits?'

'Well, you know.'

'No, I don't know.'

'Do you own a meat cleaver, Mrs Androvich?'

She stared at Carella a long time before answering. Then she said, 'What's that got to do with Karl?'

Carella did not answer.

'Is Karl dead?' she said. 'Is that it?'

He did not answer.

'Did someone use a meat cleaver on him? Is that it? Is that it?'

'We don't know, Mrs Androvich.'

'Do you think I did it? Is that what you're saying?'

'We have no knowledge whatever about your husband's whereabouts, Mrs Androvich. Dead or alive. This is all routine.'

'Routine, huh? What happened? Did someone wearing a raincoat and carrying an umbrella hit my husband with a cleaver? Is that what happened?'

'No, Mrs Androvich. *Do* you own a meat cleaver?'

'Yes, I do,' she said. 'It's in the kitchen. Would you like to see it? Maybe you can find some of Karl's skull on it. Isn't that what you'd like to find?'

'This is just a routine investigation, Mrs Androvich.'

'Are all detectives as subtle as you?' she wanted to know.

'I'm sorry if I've upset you, Mrs Androvich. May I see that cleaver? If it's not too much trouble.'

'This way,' she said coldly, and she led them out of the bedroom, through the living room, and into the kitchen. The cleaver was a small one, its cutting edge dull and nicked. 'That's it,' she said.

'I'd like to take this with me, if you don't mind,' Carella said.
'Why?'
'What kind of candy did your husband bring you on Valentine's Day, Mrs Androvich?'
'Nuts. Fruits. A mixed assortment.'
'From where? Who made the candy?'
'I don't remember.'
'Was it a large box?'
'A pound.'
'But you called it a big box of candy when you first spoke of it. You said there was a big box of candy on the kitchen table when you woke up. Isn't that what you said?'
'Yes. It was in the shape of a heart. It looked big to me.'
'But it was only a pound box of candy, is that right?'
'Yes.'
'And the dozen red roses? When did they arrive?'
'At about six A.M.'
'And you put them in a vase?'
'Yes.'
'Do you have a vase big enough to hold a dozen roses?'
'Yes, of course I do. Karl was always bringing me flowers. So I bought a vase one day.'
'Big enough to hold a dozen red roses, right?'
'Yes.'
'They *were* red roses, a dozen of them?'
'Yes.'
'No *white* ones? Just a dozen red roses?'
'Yes, yes, a dozen red roses. All red. And I put them in a vase.'
'You said two dozen, Mrs Androvich. When you first mentioned them, you said there were two dozen.'
'What?'
'Two dozen.'
'I ...'
'Were there any flowers at all, Mrs Androvich?'
'Yes, yes. Yes, there were flowers. I must have made a mistake. It was only a dozen. Not two dozen. I must have been thinking of something else.'
'Was there candy, Mrs Androvich?'
'Yes, of course there was candy.'
'Yes, and you didn't quarrel at the breakfast table. Why didn't you report his absence until the next day?'
'Because I thought ...'
'Had he ever wandered off before?'
'No, he ...'
'Then this was rather unusual for him, wasn't it?'
'Yes, but ...'
'Then why didn't you report it immediately?'
'I thought he'd come back.'
'Or did you think he had reason for staying away?'
'What reason?'
'You tell me, Mrs Androvich.'

The room went silent.

'There was no reason,' she said at last. 'My husband loved me. There was a box of candy on the table in the morning. A heart. The florist delivered a dozen red roses at six o'clock. Karl kissed me goodbye and left. And I haven't seen him since.'

'Give Mrs Androvich a receipt for this meat cleaver, Bert,' Carella said. 'Thank you very much for the coffee and rolls. And for your time. You were very kind.'

As they went out, she said, 'He *is* dead, isn't he?'

Claire Townsend was easily as tall as Meg Androvich, but the similarity between the two girls ended there. Meg was skinny – or, if you prefer, willowy; Claire was richly endowed with flesh that padded the big bones of her body. Meg, in the fashion-model tradition, was flat-chested. Claire was not one of those over-extended cowlike creatures, but she was rightfully proud of a bosom capable of filling a man's hand. Meg was a blue-eyed blonde. Claire's eyes were brown and her hair was as black as sin. Meg, in short, gave the impression of someone living in the pallor of a hospital sickroom; Claire looked like a girl who would be at home on a sunwashed haystack.

There was one other difference.

Bert Kling was madly in love with Claire.

She kissed him the moment he entered the apartment. She was wearing black slacks and a wide, white, smocklike blouse which ended just below her waist.

'What kept you?' she said.

'Florists,' he answered.

'You bought me flowers?'

'No. A lady we talked to said her husband bought her a dozen red roses. We checked about ten florists in the immediate and surrounding neighbourhoods. Result? No red roses on Valentine's Day. Not to Mrs Karl Androvich, anyway.'

'So?'

'So Steve Carella is uncanny. Can I take off my shoes?'

'Go ahead. I bought two steaks. Do you feel like steaks?'

'Later.'

'How is Carella uncanny?'

'Well, he lit into this skinny, pathetic dame as if he were going to rip all the flesh from her bones. When we got outside, I told him I thought he was a little rough with her. I mean, I've seen him operate before, and he usually wears kid gloves with the ladies. So with this one, he used a sledge hammer, and I wondered why. And told him I disapproved.'

'So what did he say?'

'He said he knew she was lying from the minute she opened her mouth, and he began wondering why?'

'How did he know?'

'He just knew. That's what was so uncanny about it. We checked all those damn florists, and nobody made a delivery at six in the morning, and none of them were even *open* before nine.'

'The husband could have ordered the flowers anywhere in the city, Bert.'

'Sure, but that's pretty unlikely, isn't it? He's not a guy who works in an office some place. He's a seaman, and when he's not at sea, he's home. So the logical place to order flowers would be a neighbourhood florist.'

'So?'

'So nothing. I'm tired. Steve sent a meat cleaver to the lab.' He paused. 'She didn't look like the kind of a dame who'd use a meat cleaver on a man. Come here.'

She went to him, climbing into his lap. He kissed her and said, 'I've got the whole weekend. Steve's giving me his Sunday.'

'Oh? Yes?'

'You feel funny,' he said.

'Funny? How?'

'I don't know. Softer.'

'I'm not wearing a bra.'

'How come?'

'I wanted to feel free. Keep your hands off me!' she said suddenly, and she leaped out of his lap.

'Now you are the kind of a dame who would use a meat cleaver on a man,' Kling said, appraising her from the chair in which he sat.

'Am I?' she answered coolly. 'When do you want to eat?'

'Later.'

'Where are we going tonight?' Claire asked.

'No place.'

'Oh?'

'I don't have to be back at the squad until Monday morning,' Kling said.

'Oh, is that right?'

'Yes, and what I planned was ...'

'Yes?'

'I thought we could get into bed right now and stay in bed all weekend. Until Monday morning. How does that sound to you?'

'It sounds pretty strenuous.'

'Yes, it does. But I vote for it.'

'I'll have to think about it. I had my heart set on a movie.'

'We can always see a movie,' Kling said.

'Anyway, I'm hungry right now,' Claire said, studying him narrowly. 'I'm going to make the steaks.'

'I'd rather go to bed.'

'Bert,' she said, 'man does not live by bed alone.'

Kling rose suddenly. They stood at opposite ends of the room, studying each other. 'What did *you* plan on doing tonight?' he asked.

'Eating steaks,' she said.

'And what else?'

'A movie.'

'And tomorrow?'

Claire shrugged.

'Come here,' he said.

'Come get me,' she answered.

He went across the room to her. She tilted her head to his and then crossed her arms tightly over her breasts.

'All weekend,' he said.

'You're a braggart,' she whispered.

'You're a doll.'

'Am I?'

'You're a lovely doll.'

'You going to kiss me?'

'Maybe.'

They stood not two inches from each other, not touching, staring at each other, savouring this moment, allowing desire to leap between them in a mounting wave.

He put his hands on her waist, but he did not kiss her.

Slowly, she uncrossed her arms.

'You really have no bra on?' he asked.

'Big weekend lover,' she murmured. 'Can't even find out for himself whether or not I have a . . .'

His hands slid under the smock and he pulled Claire to him.

The next time anyone saw Bert Kling would be on Monday morning.

It would still be raining.

Sam Grossman studied the airlines bag for a long time, and then took off his eyeglasses. Grossman was a police lieutenant, a laboratory technician, and the man in charge of the police lab downtown on High Street. In his years of service with the lab, he had seen bodies or portions of bodies in trunks, valises, duffel bags, shopping bags, boxes, and even wrapped in old newspapers. He had never come across one in an airline's overnight bag, but he experienced no sensation of surprise or shock. The inside of the bag was covered with dried blood, but he did not reel back at the sight of it. He knew there was work to be done, and he set about doing it. He was somewhat like a New England farmer discovering that one of his fields would make an excellent pasture if only it were cleared of rocks and stumps. The only way to clear the field was to clear it.

He had already examined the severed hand, and reached the conclusion that it was impossible to get any fingerprint impressions from the badly mutilated fingertips. He had then taken a sampling of blood from the hand for an isoreaction test, and concluded that the blood was in the 'O' group.

Now he examined the bag for latent fingerprints, and found none. He had not, in all truth, expected to find any. The person who'd mutilated that hand was a person who was very conscious of fingerprints, a person who would have shown the same caution in handling the bag.

He checked the bag next for microscopic traces of hair or fibres or dust which might give some clue to either the killer's or the victim's identity, occupation, or hobby. He found nothing of value on the outside surface of the bag.

He slit the bag open with a scalpel and studied its inner surface and bottom with a magnifying glass. In one corner of the bag he found what appeared to be remnants of orange chalk dust. He collected several grains for a specimen, put them aside, and then studied the bloodstains on the bottom of the bag.

The average layman might have considered Grossman's examination absurd. He was, after all, examining a stain which had obviously been left in the bag by the severed hand. What in the hell was he trying to ascertain? That the hand had been in the bag? Everyone knew that already.

But Grossman was simply trying to determine whether or not the stain on the bottom of the bag was actually human blood; and if not blood, then what? There was the possibility, too, that an apparent bloodstain could have mingled with, or covered, another stain on the bag. And so Grossman really wasn't wasting his time. He was simply doing a thorough job.

The stain was a dark reddish brown in colour and, because of the nonabsorbent surface of the bag's bottom, it was somewhat cracked and chipped, resembling a dried mud flat. Grossman gingerly cut out a portion of the stain, and cut this into two smaller portions which he labelled Stain One and Stain Two, for want of a more imaginative nomenclature. He dropped his two specimens into an 0.9 per cent solution of physiologic salt, and then placed them on separate slides. The slides had to stand in a covered dish for several hours, so he left them and began performing his microscopic and spectroscopic tests on the orange chalk he had found in a corner of the bag. When he returned to the slides later that day, he covered one of them with a coverslip and studied it under a high-power microscope. What he saw was a number of non-nucleated discs, and he knew instantly that the suspect blood was mammalian in origin.

He then took the second slide and poured Wright's Stain onto the un-fixed smear, letting it stand for one minute while he timed the operation. Drop by drop, he added distilled water to the slide, waiting for a metallic scum to form on its surface. When the scum had formed, he again consulted his watch, waiting three minutes before he washed and dried the slide.

Using a micrometer eyepiece, he then measured the various cells on the slide. The human red blood corpuscle is about 1/3200 of an inch in diameter. The cell diameter will vary in other animals of the mammalian group, the erythrocyte of the dog – at 1/3500 of an inch – being closest to the human's.

The specimen Grossman examined under his microscope measured 1/3200 of an inch in diameter.

But where measurement dealt with error in thousandths of an inch, Grossman did not want to take any chances. And so he followed the usual laboratory procedure of using a precipitin reaction after either a chemical, microscopic, or spectroscopic test. The precipitin reaction would determine with certainty whether or not the stain was indeed human blood.

The precipitin reaction is a simple one. If you take a rabbit, and if you inject into this rabbit's blood a specimen of whole human blood or human blood serum, something is going to happen. The something that will happen is this: an antibody called a 'precipitin' will develop in the rabbit's own serum. This will then react with the proteins of the injected serum. If the reaction is a positive one, the proteins can then be identified as having come from a human being.

The specific reaction to Grossman's stain was positive.

The blood was human.

When he performed his isoreaction test, he learned that it was in the 'O' blood group, and he therefore made the logical assumption that the stain on the bottom of the bag had been left by blood dripping from the severed hand and by nothing else.

As for the bits of orange chalk dust, they turned out to be something quite other than chalk. The particles were identified as a woman's cosmetic, further identified through a chemical breakdown and a comparison with the cards in the files as a preparation called Skinglow.

Skinglow was a liquid powder base designed to retain face powder in a clinging veil, further designed to add a slight pink glow to very fair skin under makeup.

It was hardly likely that a man would have used it.

And yet the hand in the bag had definitely belonged to a man.

Grossman sighed and passed the information on to the boys of the 87th.

Chapter Seven

Saturday.

Rain.

Once, when he was a boy, he and some friends had crawled under the iceman's cart on Colby Avenue. It had been pouring bullets, and the three of them sat under the wooden cart and watched the spikes of rain pounding the cobblestones, feeling secure and impervious. Steve Carella caught pneumonia, and shortly afterwards the family moved from Isola to Riverhead. He'd always felt the move had been prompted by the fact that he'd caught pneumonia under the iceman's cart on Colby Avenue.

It rained in Riverhead, too. Once he necked with a girl named Grace McCarthy in the basement of her house while the record player oozed 'Perfidia' and 'Santa Fe Trail', and 'Green Eyes', and the rain stained the small crescent-shaped basement window. They were both fifteen, and they had started by dancing, and he had kissed her suddenly and recklessly in the middle of a dip, and then they had curled up on the sofa and listened to Glenn Miller and necked like crazy fools, expecting Grace's mother to come down to the basement at any moment.

Rain wasn't so bad, he supposed.

Sloshing through the puddles with Meyer Meyer on the way to question the second possibility Kling had pulled from the M.P.B. files, Carella cupped his hand around a match, lighted a cigarette, and flipped the match into the water streaming alongside the kerb.

'You know that cigarette commercial?' Meyer asked.

'Which one?'

'Where the guy is a Thinking Man. You know, a nuclear physicist really, but when we first see him he's developing snap-shots in a darkroom? You know the one?'

'Yeah, what about it?'

'I got a good one for their series.'

'Yeah, let's hear it,' Carella said.

'We see this guy working on a safe, you know? He's drilling a hole in the face of the safe, and he's got his safe-cracking tools on the floor, and a couple of sticks of dynamite, like that.'

'Yeah, go ahead.'

'And the announcer's voice comes in and says, "Hello there, sir." The guy looks up from his work and lights a cigarette. The announcer says, "It must take years of training to become an expert safe-cracker." The guy smiles politely. "Oh, I'm not a safe-cracker," he says. "Safe-cracking is just a hobby with me. I feel a man should have diversified interests." The announcer is very surprised. "Not a safe-cracker?" he asks. "Just a hobby? May I ask then, sir, what you actually do for a living?"'

'And what does the man at the safe answer?' Carella said.

'The man at the safe blows out a stream of smoke,' Meyer said, 'and again he smiles politely. "Certainly, you may ask," he says. "I'm a pimp."' Meyer grinned broadly. 'You like it, Steve?'

'Very good. Here's the address. Don't tell jokes to this lady or she may not let us in.'

'Who's telling jokes? I may quit this lousy job one day and get a job with an advertising agency.'

'Don't do it, Meyer. We couldn't get along without you.'

Together, they entered the tenement. The woman they were looking for was named Martha Livingston, and she had reported the absence of her son, Richard, only a week ago. The boy was nineteen years old, six feet two inches tall, and weighed a hundred and ninety-four pounds. These facts, and these alone, qualified him as a candidate for the person who had once owned the severed hand.

'Which apartment is it?' Meyer asked.

'Twenty-four. Second floor front.'

They climbed to the second floor. A cat in the hallway mewed and then eyed them suspiciously.

'She smells the law on us,' Meyer said. 'She thinks we're from the A.S.P.C.A.'

'She doesn't know we're really street cleaners,' Carella said.

Meyer stooped down to pet the cat as Carella knocked on the door. 'Come on, kitty,' he said. 'Come on, little kitty.'

'Who is it?' a woman's voice shouted. The voice sounded startled.

'Mrs Livingston?' Carella said to the door.

'Yes? Who is it?'

'Police,' Carella said. 'Would you open the door, please?'

'Po –'

And then there was silence.

The silence was a familiar one. It was the silence of sudden discovery and hurried pantomime. Whatever was going on behind that tenement door, Mrs Livingston was not in the apartment alone. The silence persisted. Meyer's hand left the cat's head and went up to the holster clipped to the right side of his belt. He looked at Carella curiously. Carella's .38 was already in his hand.

'Mrs Livingston?' Carella called.

There was no answer from within the apartment.

'Mrs Livingston?' he called again, and Meyer braced himself against the opposite wall, waiting. 'Okay, kick it in,' Carella said.

Meyer brought back his right leg, shoved himself off the wall with his left shoulder, and smashed his foot against the lock in a flat-footed kick that sent the door splintering inward. He rushed into the room behind the opening door, gun in hand.

'Hold it!' he yelled, and a thin man in the process of stepping out onto the fire escape, one leg over the sill, the other still in the room, hesitated for a moment, undecided.

'You'll get wet out there, mister,' Meyer said.

The man hesitated a moment longer, and then came back into the room. Meyer glanced at his feet. He was wearing no socks. He glanced sheepishly at the woman who stood opposite him near the bed. The woman was wearing a slip. There was nothing under it. She was a big blowsy dame of about forty-five with hennaed hair and a drunkard's faded eyes.

'Mrs Livingston?' Carella asked.

'Yeah,' she said. 'What the hell do you mean busting in here?'

'What was your friend's hurry?' Carella asked.

'I'm in no hurry,' the thin man answered.

'No? You always leave a room by the window?'

'I wanted to see if it was still raining.'

'It's still raining. Get over here.'

'What did I do?' the man asked, but he moved quickly to where the two detectives were standing. Methodically, Meyer frisked him, his hands pausing when he reached the man's belt. He pulled a revolver from the man's waist and handed it to Carella.

'You got a permit for this?' Carella asked.

'Yeah,' the man said.

'You'd better have. What's your name, mister?'

'Cronin,' he said. 'Leonard Cronin.'

'Why were you in such a hurry to get out of here, Mr Cronin?'

'You don't have to answer nothing, Lennie,' Mrs Livingston said.

'You a lawyer, Mrs Livingston?' Meyer said.

'No, but ...'

'Then stop giving advice. We asked you a question, Mr Cronin.'

'Don't tell him nothing, Lennie.'

'Look, Lennie,' Meyer said patiently, 'we got all the time in the world, either here or up at the squad, so you just decide what you're going to say, and then say it. In the meantime, go put on your socks, and you better put on a robe or something, Mrs Livingston, before we get the idea a little hanky-panky was going on in this room. Okay?'

'I don't need no robe,' Mrs Livingston said. 'What I got, you seen before.'

'Yeah, but put on the robe anyway. We wouldn't want you to catch cold.'

'Don't worry about me catching cold, you son-of-a-bitch,' Mrs Livingston said.

'Nice talk,' Meyer answered, shaking his head. Cronin, sitting on the edge of the bed, was pulling on his socks. He was wearing black trousers. A black raincoat was draped over a wooden chair in the corner of the room. A black umbrella dripped water onto the floor near the night-table.

'You were forgetting your raincoat and umbrella, weren't you, Lennie?' Carella said.

Cronin looked up from lacing his shoes. 'I guess so.'

'You'd both better come along with us,' Carella said. 'Put on some clothes, Mrs Livingston.'

Mrs Livingston seized her left breast with her left hand. She aimed it like a pistol at Carella, squeezed it briefly and angrily, and shouted, 'In your eye, cop!'

'Okay, then, come along the way you are. We can add indecent exposure to the prostitution charge the minute we hit the street.'

'Prosti – ! What the hell are you talking about? Boy, you got a nerve!'

'Yeah, I know,' Carella said. 'Let's go, let's go.'

'Why'd you have to bust in here anyway?' Mrs Livingston said. 'What do you want?'

'We come to ask you some questions about your missing son, that's all,' Carella said.

'My son? Is that what this is all about? I hope the bastard is dead. Is that why you broke down the door, for Christ's sake?'

'If you hope he's dead, why'd you bother to report him missing?'

'So I could get relief checks. He was my sole means of support. The minute he took off, I applied for relief. And I had to report him missing to make it legit. That's why. You think I care whether he's dead or alive? Some chance!'

'You're a nice lady, Mrs Livingston,' Meyer said.

'I am a nice lady,' she answered. 'Is there something wrong about a matinee with the man you love?'

'Not if your husband doesn't disapprove.'

'My husband is dead,' she said. 'And in hell.'

'You both behave as if there was a little more than that going on, Mrs Livingston,' Carella said. 'Get dressed. Meyer, take a look through the apartment.'

'You got a search warrant?' the little man asked. 'You got no right to go through this place without a warrant.'

'You're absolutely right, Lennie,' Carella said. 'We'll come back with one.'

'I know my rights,' Cronin said.

'Sure.'

'I know my rights.'

'How about it, lady? Dressed or naked, you're coming over to the station house. Now which will it be?'

'In your eye!' Lady Livingston said.

The patrolmen downstairs all managed to drop up to the Interrogation Room on one pretence or another to take a look at the fat red-headed slob who sat answering questions in her slip. Andy Parker said to Miscolo in the Clerical Office, 'We take a mug shot of her like that, and we'll be able to peddle the photos for five bucks apiece.'

'This precinct got glamour, that's what it's got,' Miscolo answered, and he went back to his typing.

Parker and Hawes went downtown for the search warrant. Upstairs, Meyer and Carella and Lieutenant Byrnes interrogated the two suspects. Byrnes, because he was an older man and presumably less susceptible to the mammalian display, interrogated Martha Livingston in the Interrogation Room off the corridor. Meyer and Carella talked to Leonard Cronin in a corner of the squadroom, far from Lennie's over-exposed paramour.

'Now, how about it, Lennie?' Meyer said. 'You really got a permit for this rod, or are you just snowing us? Come on, you can talk to us.'

'Yeah, I got a permit,' Cronin said. 'Would I kid you guys?'

'I don't think you'd try to kid us, Lennie,' Meyer said gently, 'and we won't try to kid you, either. I can't tell you very much about this, but it can be very serious, take my word for it.'

'How do you mean serious?'

'Well, let's say there could be a lot more involved here than just a Sullivan Act violation. Let's put it that way.'

'You mean because I was banging Martha when you come in? Is that what you mean?'

'No, not that, either. Let's say there is a very big juicy crime involved here maybe. And let's say you could find yourself right in the middle of it. Okay? So level with us from the start, and things may go easier for you.'

'I don't know what big juicy crime you're talking about,' Cronin said.

'Well, you think about it a little,' Carella said.

'You mean the gat? Okay, I ain't got a permit. Is that what you mean?'

'Well, that's not too serious, Lennie,' Meyer said. 'No, we're not thinking about the pistol.'

'Then what? You mean like because Martha's husband ain't really croaked? You mean like because you got us on adultery?'

'Well, even that isn't too serious, Lennie,' Carella said. '*That* we can talk about.'

'Then what? The junk?'

'The *junk*, Lennie?'

'Yeah, in the room.'

'Heroin, Lennie?'

'No, no, hey, no, nothing big like that. The mootah. Just a few sticks, though. Just for kicks. That ain't so serious, now is it?'

'No, that could be very minor, Lennie. Depending on how much marijuana you had there in the room.'

'Oh, just a few sticks.'

'Well then, you've only got a possession rap to worry about. You weren't planning on selling any of that stuff, were you, Lennie?'

'No, no, hey, no, it was just for kicks, just for me and Martha, like you know for kicks. We lit a few sticks before we hopped between the sheets.'

'Then that's not too serious, Lennie.'

'So what's so serious?'

'The boy.'

'What boy?'

'Martha's son. Richard, that's his name, isn't it?'

'How do I know? I never even met the kid.'

'You never met him? How long have you known Martha?'

'I met her last night. In a bar. A joint called The Short-Snorter, you know it? It's run by these two guys, they used to be in the China-Burma-India . . .'

'You only met her last night?'

'Sure.'

'She said you were the man she loved,' Carella said.

'Yeah, it was love at first sight.'

'And you never met her son?'

'Never.'

'You ever fly, Lennie?'

'Fly? How do you mean fly? You talking about the marijuana again?'

'No, fly. In an airplane.'

'Never. Just catch me dead in one of them things!'

'How long have you gone for black, Lennie?'

'Black? How do you mean black?'

'Your clothes. Your pants, your tie, your raincoat, your umbrella. Black.'

'I bought them for a funeral,' Cronin said.

'Whose funeral?'

'A buddy of mine. We used to run a crap game together.'

'You ran a crap game, too, Lennie? You've been a busy little man, haven't you?'

'Oh, this wasn't nothing illegal. We never played for money.'

'And your friend died recently, is that right?'

'Yeah. The other day. So I bought the black clothes. Out of respect. You can check. I can tell you the place where I bought them.'

'We'd appreciate that, Lennie. But you didn't own these clothes on Wednesday, did you?'

'Wednesday. Now let me think a minute. What's today?'

'Today is Saturday.'

'Yeah, that's right, Saturday. No. I bought the clothes Thursday. You can check it. They probably got a record.'

'How about you, Lennie?'

'How about me? How so you mean how about me?'

'Have *you* got a record?'

'Well, a little one.'

'How little?'

'I done a little time once. A stickup. Nothing serious.'

'You may do a little more,' Carella said. 'But nothing serious.'

In the Interrogation Room, Lieutenant Byrnes said, 'You're a pretty forthright woman, Mrs Livingston, aren't you?'

'I don't like being dragged out of my house in the middle of the morning,' Martha said.

'Weren't you embarrassed about going downstairs in your slip?'

'No. I keep my body good. I got a good body.'

'What were you and Mr Cronin trying to hide, Mrs Livingston?'

'Nothing. We're in love. I'll shout it from the rooftops.'

'Why did he try to get out of that room?'

'He wasn't trying to get out. He told them what he was trying to do. He wanted to see if it was still raining.'

'So he was climbing out on the fire escape to do that, right?'

'Yeah.'

'Are you aware that your son Richard could be dead at this moment, Mrs Livingston?'

'Who cares? Good riddance to bad rubbish. The people he was hanging around with, he's better off dead. I raised a bum instead of a son.'

'What kind of people was he hanging around with?'

'A gang, a street gang, it's the same story every place in this lousy city. You

try to raise a kid right, and what happens? Please, don't get me started.'
  'Did your son tell you he was leaving home?'
  'No. I already gave all this to another detective when I reported him missing. I don't know where he is, and I don't give a damn, as long as I get my relief cheques. Now that's that.'
  'You told the arresting officers your husband was dead. Is that true?'
  'He's dead.'
  'When did he die?'
  'Three years ago.'
  'Did he die, or did he leave?'
  'It's the same thing, isn't it?'
  'Not exactly.'
  'He left.'
  The room was suddenly very silent.
  'Three years ago?'
  'Three years ago. When Dickie was just sixteen. He packed up and left. It ain't so easy to raise a boy alone. It ain't so easy. And now he's gone, too. Men stink. They all stink. They all want one thing. Okay, I'll give it to them. But not here.' She tapped her chest. 'Not here inside, where it counts. They all stink. Every single one of them.'
  'Do you think your son might have run off with some of his friends?'
  'I don't know what he done, the little bastard, and I don't care. Gratitude. I raised him alone after his father left. And this is what I get. He runs out on me. Quits his job and runs out. He's just like all the rest of them, they all stink. You can't trust any man alive. I hope he drops dead, wherever he is. I hope the little bastard drops ...'
  And suddenly she was weeping.
  She sat quite still in the chair, a woman of forty-five with ridiculously flaming red hair, a big-breasted woman who sat attired only in a silk slip, a fat woman with the faded eyes of a drunkard, and her shoulders did not move, and her face did not move, and her hands did not move, she sat quite still in the hard-backed wooden chair while the tears ran down her face and her nose got red and her teeth clamped into her lips.
  'Running out on me,' she said, and then she didn't say anything else. She sat stiffly in the chair, fighting the tears that coursed down her cheeks and her neck and stained the front of her slip.
  'I'll get you a coat or something, Mrs Livingston,' Byrnes said.
  'I don't need a coat. I don't care who sees me. I don't care. Everybody can see what I am. One look, and everybody can see what I am. I don't need a coat. A coat ain't going to hide nothing.'
  Byrnes left her alone in the room, weeping stiffly in the hard-backed chair.

  They found exactly thirty-four ounces of marijuana in Martha Livingston's apartment. Apparently, Leonard Cronin was not a very good mathematician. Apparently, too, he was in slightly more serious trouble than he had originally presumed. If, as he'd stated, there had only been a stick or two of marijuana in the room – enough to have made at least two ounces of the stuff – he'd have been charged with possession, which particular crime was punishable by imprisonment of from two to ten years. Now *thirty-four* ounces ain't *two* ounces. And possession of sixteen ounces or more of narcotics other than heroin, morphine, or cocaine created a *rebuttable* presumption of intent to sell, the 'rebuttable' meaning that Cronin could claim he hadn't intended selling it at all, at all. And the maximum term of imprisonment for possession with intent to sell was ten years, the difference between the two charges being that a simple possession rap would usually draw a lesser prison term whereas an intent to sell rap usually drew the limit.

But Cronin had a few other things to worry about. By his own admission, he and Martha Livingston had lit a few sticks before hopping into bed together and Section 2010 of the Penal Law quite bluntly stated: 'Perpetration of an act of intercourse with a female not one's wife who is under the influence of narcotics is punishable by an indeterminate sentence of one day to life or a maximum of twenty years.'

When the gun charge was added to this, and the running of an illegal crap game considered, even if one wished to forget the simple charge of simple adultery – a misdemeanour punishable by imprisonment in a penitentiary or county jail for not more than six months, or by a fine of not more than two hundred and fifty bucks, or by both – even if one wished to forget this minor infraction, Leonard Cronin was going to be a busier little man than he had ever been.

As for Martha Livingston, she'd have been better off exploring Africa. Even allowing for her own conviction that all men stank, she had certainly chosen a prize this time. The narcotics, whomever they belonged to, had been found in her pad. The lady who'd fallen in love at first sight was going to have a hell of a tough row to hoe.

But whatever else lay ahead for the hapless lovers, homicide and butchery would not be included in the charges against them. A check with the clothing store Leonard Cronin named proved that he had indeed purchased his funeral outfit on Thursday. A further check of his rooming-house closet showed that he owned no other black garments. And neither did Mrs Livingston.

There must be a God, after all.

Chapter Eight

On Sunday morning, Cotton Hawes went to church in the rain before reporting to work.

When he came out, it was still raining and he felt much the same as he'd felt before the services. He didn't know why he expected to feel any different; he'd certainly never been washed by any of the great religious fervour which had possessed his minister father. But every Sunday, rain or shine, Cotton Hawes went to church. And every Sunday he sat and listened to the sermon, and he recited the psalms, and he waited. He didn't know exactly what he was waiting for. He suspected he was waiting for a bolt of lightning and an earsplitting crash of thunder which would suddenly reveal the face of God. He supposed that all he really wanted to see was a glimpse of something which was not quite so *real* as the things that surrounded him every day of the week.

For whatever else could be said about police work – and there were countless things to be said, and countless things being said – no one could deny that it presented its practitioners with a view of life which was as real as bread crumbs. Police work dealt with essentials, raw instincts and basic motives, stripped of all the hoop-dee-dah of the sterilized, compressed-in-a-vacuum civilization of the twentieth century. As he walked through the rain, Hawes thought it odd that most of the time consumed by people was spent in sharing the fantasies of another. A thousand escape hatches from reality were available to every manjack in the world – books, the motion pictures, television, magazines, plays, concerts, ballets, anything or everything designed to substitute a pretence of reality, a semblance of real life, a fantasy world for a flesh-and-blood one.

Now perhaps it was wrong for a cop to be thinking this way, Hawes realized, because a cop was one of the fantasy figures in one of the world's escapes: the mystery novel. The trouble was, he thought, that only the fantasy cop was the hero while the *real* cop was just a person. It seemed somehow stupid to him that the most honoured people in the world were those who presented the fantasies, the actors, the directors, the writers, all the various performers whose sole reason for being was to entertain. It was as if a very small portion of the world was actually alive, and these people were alive only in so far as they performed in created fantasies. The rest of the people were observing; the rest of the people were spectators. It would not have been half so sad if these people were viewing the spectacle of real life. Instead, they were observing only a representation of life, so that they became twice-removed from life itself.

Even conversation seemed to concern itself primarily with the fantasy world, and not the real. Did you see Jack Paar last night? Have you read *Doctor Zhivago*? Wasn't *Dragnet* exciting? Did you see the review of *Sweet Bird of Youth*? Talk, talk, talk, but all of the talk had as its nucleus the world of make-believe. And now the television programmes had carried this a step further. More and more channels were featuring people who simply talked about things, so that even the burden of talking about the make-believe world had been removed from the observer's shoulders – there were now other people who would talk it over *for* him. Life became thrice-removed.

And in the midst of this thrice-removed existence, there was reality, and reality for a cop was a hand severed at the wrist.

Now what the hell would they do with that hand on *Naked City*?

He didn't know. He only knew that every Sunday he went to church and looked for something.

On this Sunday, he came out feeling the same as when he'd gone in, and he walked along the shining wet sidewalk bordering the park, heading for the station house. The green globes had been turned on in defence against the rain, the numerals '87' glowing feebly against the slanting grey. He looked up at the dripping stone façade, climbed the low flat steps and entered the muster room. Dave Murchison was sitting behind the desk, reading a movie magazine. The cover showed a picture of Debbie Reynolds, and the headline asked the provocative question *What Will Debbie Do Now?*

He followed the pointing arrow of the DETECTIVE DIVISION sign, climbed the metal steps to the second story, and walked down the long, dim corridor. He shoved through the gate in the slatted railing, tossed his hat at the rack in the corner, and went to his desk. The squadroom was oddly silent. He felt almost as if he were in church again. Frankie Hernandez, a Puerto Rican cop who'd been born and raised in the precinct neighbourhood, looked up and said, 'Hi, Cotton.'

'Hello, Frankie,' he said. 'Steve come in yet?'

'He called in about ten minutes ago,' Hernandez answered. 'Said to tell you he was going straight to the docks to talk to the captain of the *Farren*.'

'Okay,' Hawes said. 'Anything else?'

'Got a report from Grossman on the meat cleaver.'

'What mea – oh yeah, yeah, the Androvich woman.' He paused. 'Any luck?'

'Negative. Not a thing on it but yesterday's roast.'

'Where is everybody, anyway?' Hawes asked. 'It's so quiet around here.'

'There was a burglary last night, grocery store on Culver. Andy and Meyer are out on it. The loot called in to say he'd be late. Wife's got a fever, and he's waiting for the doctor.'

'Isn't Kling supposed to be in today?'

Hernandez shook his head. 'Swapped with Carella.'

'Who's catching, anyway?' Hawes said. 'You got a copy of the duty sheet around?'

'I'm catching,' Hernandez said.

'Boy, it sure is quiet around here,' Hawes said. 'Is Miscolo around? I'd like some tea.'

'He was here a little while ago. I think he went down to talk to the Captain.'

'Days like this ...' Hawes started, and then let the sentence trail. After a while, he said, 'Frankie, you ever get the feeling that life just isn't real?'

Perhaps he'd asked the wrong person. Life, to Frankie Hernandez, was very real indeed. Hernandez, you see, had taken upon himself the almost impossible task of proving to the world at large that Puerto Ricans could be the *good* guys in life's little drama. He did not know who'd been handling his people's press relations before he happened upon the scene, but he did know that someone was handling it all wrong. He had never had the urge to mug anyone, or knife anyone, or even to have a single puff of a marijuana cigarette. He had grown up in the territory of the 87th Precinct, in one of the worst slums in the world, and he had never so much as stolen a postage stamp, or even a sidelong glance at the whores who paraded *La Via de Putas*. He was a devout Catholic whose father worked hard for a living, and whose mother was concerned solely with the proper upbringing of the four children she had brought into the world. When Hernandez decided to become a cop, his mother and father approved heartily. He became a rookie when he was twenty-two years old, after having served a four-year hitch in the Marines and distinguishing himself in combat during the hell that was Iwo Jima. In his father's candy store, a picture of Frankie Hernandez in full battle dress was pasted to the mirror behind the counter, alongside the Coca Cola sign. Frankie's father never failed to tell any stranger in the store that the picture was of his son Frankie who was now 'a detective in the city's police.'

It hadn't been easy for Hernandez to become a detective in the city's police. To begin with, he'd found a certain amount of prejudice within the department itself, brotherhood edicts notwithstanding. And, coupled with this was a rather peculiar attitude on the part of some of the citizens of the precinct. They felt, he soon discovered, that since he was 'one of them' he was expected to look the other way whenever they became involved in police trouble. Well, unfortunately, Frankie Hernandez was incapable of looking the other way. He had sworn the oath, and he was now wearing the uniform, and he had a job to perform.

And besides, there was The Cause.

Frankie Hernandez had to prove to the neighbourhood, the people of the neighbourhood, the police department, the city, and maybe even the world that Puerto Ricans were people. Colleagues the likes of Andy Parker sometimes made The Cause difficult. Before Andy Parker, there had been patrolmen colleagues who'd made The Cause just as difficult. Hernandez imagined that if he ever became Chief of Detectives or even Police Commissioner, there would be Andy Parker surrounding those high offices, too, ever ready to remind him that The Cause was something to be fought constantly, day and night.

So for Frankie Hernandez, life was always real. Sometimes, in fact, it got too goddamn real.

'No, I never got that feeling, Cotton,' he said.

'I guess it's the rain,' Hawes answered, and he yawned.

The *S.S. Farren* had been named after a famous and honourable White Plains gentleman called Jack Farren. But whereas the flesh-and-blood Farren was a kind, amiable, sympathetic, lovable coot who always carried a clean handkerchief, the namesake looked like a ship which was mean, rotten, rusty, dirty and snot-nosed.

The captain of the ship looked the same way.

He was a hulk of a man with a three-days' beard stubble on his chin. He picked his teeth with a matchbook cover all the while Carella talked to him, sucking air interminably in an attempt to loosen breakfast from his molars. They sat in the captain's cabin, a coffin of a compartment, the bulkheads of which dripped sweat and rust. The captain sucked at his teeth and prodded with his soggy matchbook cover. The rain slanted outside the single porthole. The compartment stank of living, of food, of human waste.

'What can you tell me about Karl Androvich?' Carella asked.

'What do you want to know?' the captain said. His name was Kissovsky. He sounded like a bear. He moved with all the subtle grace of a Panzer division.

'Has he been sailing with you long?'

Kissovsky shrugged. 'Two, three years. He in trouble? What did he get himself into since he jumped ship?'

'Nothing that we know of. Is he a good sailor?'

'Good as most. Sailors ain't worth a damn today. When I was a young man, sailors was sailors.' He sucked air between his teeth.

'Ships were made of wood,' Carella said, 'and men were made of iron.'

'What? Oh, yeah.' Kissovsky tried a smile which somehow formed as a leer. 'I ain't that old, buddy,' he said. 'But we had sailors when I was a kid, not beatniks looking for banana boats so they can practise that . . . what do you call it . . . Zen? And then come back to write about it. We had men! Men!'

'Then Androvich wasn't a good sailor?'

'Good as most until he jumped ship,' Kissovsky said. 'The minute he jumped ship, he became a bad sailor. I had to make the run down with a man short in the crew. I had the crew stretched tight as it was. One man short didn't help the situation any, I can tell you. A ship is like a little city, buddy. There's guys that sweep the streets, and guys that run the trains, and guys that turn on the lights at night, and guys that run the restaurants, and that's what makes the city go, you see. Okay. You lose the guy who turns on the lights, so nobody can see. You lose the guy who runs the restaurant, so nobody eats. Either that, or you got to find somebody else to do the job, and that means taking him away from another job, so no matter how you slice it, it screws up the china closet. Androvich screwed up the china closet real fine. Besides, he was a lousy sailor, anyway.'

'How so?'

'Out for kicks,' Kissovsky said, tossing one hand upward in a salute to God. 'Live, live, burn, burn, bright like a Roman candle, bullshit! Every port we hit, Androvich went ashore and come back drunk as a fish. And dames? All over the lot! It's a wonder this guy didn't come down with the Oriental Crud or something, the way he was knocking around. Kicks! That's all he was looking for. Kicks!'

'A girl in every port, huh?' Carella said.

'Sure, and drunk as a pig. I used to tell him you got a sweet little wife waiting for you home, you want to bring her back a present from one of these exotic tomatoes, is that what you want to do? He used to laugh at me. Ha, ha, ha. Big joke. Life was a big joke. So he jumps ship, and he screws up the chocolate pudding. That's a sailor, huh?'

'Did he have a girl in this city, too, Captain Kissovsky?'

'Lay off the captain crap, huh?' Kissovsky said. 'Call me Artie, okay, and I'll call you George or whatever the hell your name is, and that way we cut through the fog, okay?'

'It's Steve.'

'Okay. Steve. That's a good name. I got a brother named Steve. He's strong as an ox. He can lift a Mack truck with his bare hands, that kid.'

'Artie, did Androvich have a girl in this city?'

Kissovsky sucked air through his teeth, manoeuvred the matchbook folder around the back of his mouth, and thought. He spit a sliver of food onto the deck, shrugged, and said, 'I don't know.'

'Who *would* know?'

'Maybe the other guys in the crew, but I doubt it. Anything happens on this tub, I know about it. I can tell you one thing. He didn't spend his nights sitting around holding hands with little Lulu Belle or whatever the hell her name is.'

'Meg? His wife?'

'Yeah, Meg. The one he's got tattooed on his arm there. The one he picked up in Atlanta. Beats me how she ever got him to come up with a ring.' Kissovsky shrugged. 'Anyway, she did get him to marry her, but that don't mean she also got him to sit home tatting doilies. No, sir. This kid was out to live! No doilies for him. Doilies are for the Sands Spit commuters, not for the Karl Androviches. You know what he'd do?'

'What?' Carella asked.

'We'd pull into port, you know. I mean here, this city. So he'd wait like two weeks, living it up all over town, shooting his roll, before he'd call home to say we were in. And maybe this was like about two days before we were going to pull out again. Buddy, this kid was giving that girl the business in both ears. She seems like a nice kid, too. I feel a little sorry for her.' He shrugged and spit onto the deck again.

'Where'd he go?' Carella asked. 'When he wasn't home? Where'd he hang out?'

'Wherever there are dames,' Kissovsky said.

'There are dames all over the city.'

'Then that's where he hung out. All over the city. I'll bet you a five-dollar bill he's with some dame right now. He'll drop in on little Scarlett O'Hara or whatever the hell her name is, the minute he runs out of money.'

'He only had thirty dollars with him when he vanished,' Carella said.

'Thirty dollars, my eye! Who told you that? There was a big crap game on the way up from Pensacola. Androvich was one of the winners. Took away something like seven hundred bucks. That ain't hay, Steve-oh. Add to that all of January's pay, you know we were holding it until we hit port, and that adds up to quite a little bundle. And we were only in port here two days. We docked on the twelfth, and we were shoving off on the fourteenth, Valentine's Day. So a guy can't spend more than a grand in two days, can he?' Kissovsky paused thoughtfully. 'The way I figure it, he started back for the ship, picked up some floozie, and has been living it high on the hog with her for the past month or so. When the loot runs out, Androvich'll be home.'

'You think he's just having himself a fling, is that it?'

'Just running true to form, that's all. In Nagasaki, when we was there, this guy . . . well, that's another story.' He paused. 'You ain't worried about him, are you?'

'Well . . .'

'Don't be. Check the whore houses, and the strip joints, and the bars, and Skid Row. You'll find him, all right. Only thing is, I don't think he *wants* to be found. So what're you gonna do when you latch onto him? *Force* him to go back to Melissa Lee, or whatever the hell her name is?'

'No, we couldn't do that,' Carella said.

'So what the hell are you bothering for?' Kissovsky sucked air through his teeth and then spat on the deck. 'Stop worrying,' he said. 'He'll turn up.'

The garbage cans were stacked in the areaway between the two tenements, and the rain had formed small pools of water on the lid of each can. The old woman was wearing house slippers, and so she stepped gingerly into the areaway and tried to avoid the water underfoot, walking carefully to the closest garbage can, carrying her bag of garbage clutched to her breast like a sucking infant.

She lifted the lid of the can and shook the water free and was about to drop her bag into the can when she saw that it was filled. The old lady was Irish, and she unleashed a torrent of swear words which would have turned a leprechaun blue, replaced the lid and went to the second garbage can. She was thoroughly drenched now, and she cursed the fact that she hadn't thought to bring an umbrella down with her, cursed the lid of the second garbage can because it seemed to be stuck, finally wrenched it free, soaking herself anew with the water that had been resting on it, and prepared to toss her bag into it and run like hell for the building.

Then she saw the newspaper.

She hesitated for a moment.

The newspaper had been wrapped around something, but the wrapping had come loose. Curiously, the old lady bent closer to the garbage can.

And then she let out a shriek.

Chapter Nine

Everything happened on Monday.

To begin with, Blaney – the Assistant Medical Examiner – officially studied the delightful little package which the patrolman had dug out of the garbage can after a frantic call from the old lady.

The bloody newspaper contained a human hand.

And after duly examining this hand, Blaney phoned the 87th to say that it had belonged to a white male between the ages of 18 and 24, and that unless he was greatly mistaken, it was the mate to the hand he had examined the week before.

Bert Kling took the telephoned message. He barely had strength enough to hold the pencil in his hand as he wrote down the information.

That was the first thing that happened on Monday, and it happened at 9:30 in the morning.

The second thing happened at 11:30 a.m. and it seemed as if the second occurrence would solve once and for all the problem of identification. The second occurrence involved a body which had been washed ashore on the banks of the River Harb. The body had no arms and no head. It was promptly shipped off to the morgue where several things were learned about it.

To begin with, the body was clothed and a wallet in the right hip pocket of the trousers carried a sopping-wet identification card and a driver's licence. The man in the water was known as George Rice. A call to the number listed on the identification card confirmed Blaney's estimate that the body had been in the river for close to two weeks. Apparently, Mr Rice had failed to come home from work one night two weeks ago. His wife had reported him missing, and a sheet on him was allegedly in the files of the M.P.B. Mrs Rice was asked to come down to identify the remains as soon as she was able to. In the meantime, Blaney continued his examination.

And he decided, even though Mr Rice had been only twenty-six years old, and even though Mr Rice was lacking arms and a head, and even though Mr Rice was a good possibility for the person who had owned the two hands that had turned up – he decided after a thorough examination that the body had apparently lost its head and arms through contact with the propeller blades of either a ship or a large boat. And whereas the bloodstain on the bottom of the airline bag had belonged to the 'O' group, the blood of Mr Rice checked out as belonging to the 'AB' group. And whereas the hugeness of the two hands indicated a big fellow, Mr Rice, allowing for his missing head, added up to five feet eight and a half inches, and that is not big.

When Mrs Rice identified the remains through her husband's clothing and a scar on his abdomen – the clothing was not in such excellent shape after having been put through the rigorous test of contact with a boat's propeller and submersion for two weeks, but the scar was still intact – when she made the identification, she also stated that Mr Rice worked in the next state and that he took a ferry to work each morning and returned by ferry each evening, and it therefore seemed more than likely that Mr Rice had either jumped, been pushed, or had fallen from the stern of the ferry and thereby been mutilated by the boat's propellers. A thorough search of the Rice apartment that same day uncovered a suicide note.

And so it was Blaney's unfortunate duty to call the 87th once more and report to Kling, the weary weekend horseman, that the hands he'd been examining over the past few days did *not* belong to the body which had been washed ashore that morning.

So that was that, and the problem of identification still remained to be solved, with the young son of Martha Livingston and the young sailor Karl Androvich still shaping up as pretty good possibilities.

But it was still Monday, a very blue Monday at that because it was raining, and everything was going to happen on Monday.

At 2:00 p.m. the third thing happened.

Two hoodlums were picked up in the next state, and both gave the police an address in Isola. A teletype to City headquarters requesting information netted a B-sheet for one of them, but no record for the other. The boys, it seemed, had held up a Shell station and then tried a hasty escape in a beat-up automobile. So hasty was their departure that they neglected to notice a police car which was cruising along the highway, with the result that they smacked right into the front right fender of the approaching black-and-white sedan, and that was the end of *that* little caper. The boy carrying the gun, the one with the record, was named Robert Germaine.

The other boy, the sloppy driver who'd slammed into the motor patrol car, was named Richard Livingston.

No matter how sloppily you drive a car, it takes two hands – and Richard Livingston was in possession of both of his.

Kling got the information at 3:00 p.m. With weary, shaking fingers, he wrote it down and reminded himself to tell Carella to chalk off a possible victim.

At 4:10 p.m. the telephone rang again.

'Hello,' Kling said.

'Who's this?' a woman's voice asked.

'This is Detective Kling, 87th Squad. Who's this?'

'Mrs Androvich,' the voice said. 'Mrs Karl Androvich.'

'Oh. Hello, Mrs Androvich. What's wrong?'

'Nothing's wrong,' she said.

'I mean, what ...'

'My husband's back,' Meg Androvich said.

'Karl?'

'Yes.'

'He's back?'

'Yes.'

'When did he return?'

'Just a few minutes ago,' she said. She paused for a long time. Then she said, 'He brought me flowers.'

'I'm glad he's back,' Kling said. 'I'll notify the Missing Persons Bureau. Thank you for calling.'

'Not at all,' Meg said. 'Would you do me a favour, please?'

'What's that, Mrs Androvich?'

'Would you please tell that other detective? Carella? Was that his name?'

'Yes ma'am.'

'Would you please tell him?'

'That your husband's back? Yes, ma'am, I'll tell him.'

'No, not that. That's not what I want you to tell him.'

'What *do* you want me to tell him, Mrs Androvich?'

'That Karl brought me flowers. Tell him that, would you? That Karl brought me flowers.' And she hung up.

So that was what happened on Monday.

And that was everything.

The boys still had a pair of hands to work with, and nobody seemed to belong to those hands.

On Tuesday, there was a street rumble, and a fire in the neighbourhood, and a woman who clobbered her husband with a frying pan, and so everybody was pretty busy.

On Wednesday, Steve Carella came back to work. It was still raining. It seemed as if it would never stop raining. A week had gone by since Patrolman Genero had found the first hand.

A whole week had gone by, and the boys were right back where they'd started.

Chapter Ten

The old woman who'd discovered the second hand in the garbage can was named Colleen Brady. She was sixty-four years old, but there was about her a youthfulness which complied faithfully to her given name, so that indeed she seemed to be a colleen.

There is an image that comes instantly to mind whenever an Irish girl is mentioned, an image compounded of one part Saint Patrick's Day to three parts John Huston's *The Quiet One*. The girl has red hair and green eyes, and she runs through the heather beneath a sky of shrieking blue billowing with clouds of pure white, and there is a wild smile on her mouth and you know she will slap you silly if you try to touch her. She is Irish and wild and savage and pure and young, forever young, forever youthful.

And so was Colleen Brady.

She entertained Carella and Hawes as if they were beaux come to call on her with sprigs of hollyhock. She served them tea, and she told them jokes in a brogue as thick as good Irish coffee. Her eyes were green and bright and her skin was as smooth and as fair as a seventeen-year-old's. Her hair was white, but you knew with certainty that it had once been red, and her narrow waist could still be spanned by a man with big hands.

'I saw no one,' she told the detectives. 'Nary a soul. It was a day to keep indoors, it was. I saw no one in the hallway, and no one on the stairs, and no one in the courtyard. It was a right bitter day, and I should have carried down me umbrella, but I didn't. I like to have died from faint when I saw what was in that garbage can. Will y'have more tea?'

'No, thank you, Mrs Brady. You saw no one?'

'No one, aye. And I'm sorry I can't be of more help, for 'tis a gruesome thing to cut a man apart, a gruesome thing. 'Tis a thing for barbarians.' She paused, sipping at her tea, her green eyes alert in her narrow face. 'Have you tried the neighbours? Have you asked them? Perhaps they saw.'

'We wanted to talk to you first, Mrs Brady,' Hawes said.

She nodded. 'Are you Irish, young man?' she asked.

'Part.'

Her green eyes glowed. She nodded secretly and said nothing more, but she studied Hawes with the practised eye of a young girl who'd been chased around the village green more than once.

'Well, we'll be going now, Mrs Brady,' Carella said. 'Thank you very much.'

'Try the neighbours,' she told them. 'Maybe they saw. Maybe one of them saw.'

None of them had seen.

They tried every apartment in Mrs Brady's building and the building adjoining it. Then, wearily, they trudged back to the squadroom in the rain. Hernandez had a message for Carella the moment he walked in.

'Steve, got a call about a half-hour ago from a guy at the M.P.B. He asked for Kling, but I told him he was out, and he wanted to know who else was on the case of the hand in the airline bag, so I told him you were. He said either you or Kling should call him the minute either of you got in.'

'What's his name?'

'It's on the pad there. Bartholomew or something.'

Carella sat at his desk and pulled the pad over. 'Romeo Bartholdi,' he said aloud, and he dialled the Missing Persons Bureau.

'Hello,' he said, 'this is Carella at the 87th Precinct. We got a call here a little while ago from some guy named Bartholdi, said he . . .'

'This is Bartholdi.'

'Hi. What's up?'

'What'd you say your name was?'

'Carella.'

'Hello, *paisan*.'

'Hello,' Carella said, smiling. 'What's this all about?'

'Look, I know this is none of my business. But something occurred to me.'

'What is it?'

'A guy named Kling was in last week some time looking through the files. I got to talking to him later, and he told me how you guys found a hand in an airline overnight bag. A guy's hand.'

'Yeah, that's right,' Carella said. 'What about it?'

'Well, *paisan*, this is none of my business. Only he was looking for a possible connection with a disappearance, and he was working through the February stuff, you know.'

'Yeah?'

'He said the bag belonged to an outfit called Circle Airlines, am I right?'

'That's right,' Carella said.

'Okay. This may be reaching, but here it is anyway, for whatever it's worth. My partner and I have been trying to track down a dame who vanished about three weeks ago. She's a stripper, came here from Kansas City in January. Name's Bubbles Caesar. That's not the straight handle, Carella. She was born Barbara Cesare, the Bubbles is for the stage. She's *got* them, too, believe me.'

'Well, what about her?' Carella asked.

'She was reported missing by her agent, a guy named Charles Tudor, on February thirteenth, day before Valentine's Day. What's today's date, anyway?'

'The eleventh,' Carella said.

'Yeah, that's right. Well, that makes it longer than three weeks. Anyway, we've been looking for her all this time, and checking up on her past history, all that. What we found out is this. She flew here from K.C.'

'She did?'

'Yeah, and you can guess the rest. She flew with this Circle Airlines. Now this can be sheer coincidence, or it can amount to something, I don't know. But I thought I'd pass it on.'

'Yeah,' Carella said.

'It's a long shot, I'll admit it. Only there may be a tie-in.'

'How'd she fly?' Carella asked. 'Luxury, Tourist?'

'First Class,' Bartholdi said. 'That's another thing. They give them little bags to First Class passengers, don't they?'

'Yeah,' Carella said.

'Yeah. You know, this may be really far out, but suppose this dame vanished because she done some guy in? I mean, the hand *was* in a Circle Airlines ...' Bartholdi let the sentence trail. 'Well, I admit it's a long shot.'

'We've run out of the other kind,' Carella said. 'What's Tudor's address.'

The Creo Building was situated in midtown Isola, smack on The Stem, and served as an unofficial meeting place for every musician and performer in town. The building was flanked by an all-night cafeteria and a movie house, and its wide entrance doors opened on a marble lobby which would not have seemed out of place in St Peter's. Beyond the lobby, the upper storeys of the building deteriorated into the lesser splendour of unfurnished rehearsal halls and the cubbyhole offices of music publishers, composers, agents, and an occasional ambulance chaser renting telephone and desk space. The men and women who congregated before the entrance doors and in the lobby were a mixed lot.

Here could be seen the hip musicians with the dizzy kicks and the teno
sax cases and the trombone cases discussing openings on various bands
some of them passing around sticks of marijuana, others lost in the religio
that was music and needing no outside stimulation. Here, too, were the long
haired classicists carrying oboe cases, wearing soft felt hats, discussing th
season in Boston or Dallas, and wondering whether Bernstein would make i
at the Philharmonic. Here were the women singers, the canaries, th
thrushes whose grins were as trained as their voices, who – no matter hov
minuscule the band they sang with – entered the arcade like Hollywoo
movie queens.

Here were the ballet dancers and the modern dancers, wearing short blac
skirts which permitted freer movement, their high heels clicking on th
marble floor, walking with that peculiar duck waddle which seems to be th
stamp of all professional dancers. Here were the strippers, the big pal
women untouched by the sun, wearing dark glasses and lipstick slashes
Here were the publishers, puffing on cigars and looking like the Russia
concept of the American capitalist. And here were the unsuccessfu
composers, needing haircuts, and here were the slightly successful com
posers carrying demo records, and here were the really successful composer
who sang badly and who played piano more badly but who walked with th
cool assurance of jukebox loot spilling out of their ears.

Upstairs, everybody was rehearsing, rehearsing with small combos an
big bands, rehearsing with pianos, rehearsing with drums, rehearsin
dances and symphonies and improvised jam sessions. The only thing tha
wasn't rehearsed in the Creo Building was the dialogue going on in the lobb
and before the entrance doors.

The dialogue of Charles Tudor may or may not have been rehearsed, i
was difficult to tell. His small office was on the eighteenth floor of th
building. Two tall, pale, buxom girls carrying hatboxes were sitting on
wooden bench in the waiting room. A short, rosy-cheeked, flat-chested gi
was sitting behind a desk at the far end of the room. Carella went to her
flashed the tin, and said, 'We're from the police. We'd like to talk to M
Tudor, please.'

The receptionist studied first Hawes, then Carella. The two pale stripper
on the bench turned a few shades paler. The taller of the two rose abruptly
picked up her hatbox, and hastily departed. The second busied herself wit
a copy of *Variety*.

'What's this in reference to?' the receptionist asked.

'We'll discuss that with Mr Tudor,' Carella said. 'Would you mind tellin
him we're here?'

The girl pulled a face and pressed a stud in the phone on her desk. 'M
Tudor,' she said into the mouthpiece, 'there are a couple of gentlemen her
who *claim* to be detectives. Well, they said they'd discuss that with you, M
Tudor. I couldn't say, I've never met a detective before. Yes, he showed m
a badge. Yes, sir.' She hung up.

'You'll have to wait a minute. He's got somebody with him.'

'Thank you,' Carella said.

They stood near the desk and looked around the small waiting room. Th
second stripper sat motionless behind her *Variety*, not even daring to tur
the page. The walls of the room were covered with black-and-white photo

f strippers in various provocative poses. Each of the photographs was
igned. Most of them started with the words 'To Charlie, who . . .' and ended
vith exotic names like Flame or Torch or Maja or Exota or Bali. Hawes
valked around the room looking at the photos. The girl behind the copy of
Variety followed him with her eyes.

Finally, in a very tiny voice which seemed even smaller issuing from such
a big woman, she said, 'That's me.'

Hawes turned. 'Huh?' he asked.

'With the furs. The picture you were looking at. It's me.'

'Oh. Oh,' Hawes said. He turned to look at the picture again. Turning
back to the girl, he said, 'I didn't recognize you with your . . .' and then
stopped and grinned.

The girl shrugged.

'Marla? Is that your name? The handwriting isn't too clear.'

'Marla, that's it,' she said. 'It's really Mary Lou, but my first agent
changed it to Marla. That sounds exotic, don't you think?'

'Yes, yes, very,' Hawes agreed.

'What's your name?'

'Hawes.'

'That's all?'

'Well, no. Cotton is my first name. Cotton Hawes.'

The girl stared at him for a moment. Then she asked, 'Are *you* a stripper,
too?' and burst out laughing. 'Excuse me,' she said, 'but you have to admit
that's a pretty exotic name.'

'I guess so,' Hawes said, grinning.

'Is Mr Tudor in some trouble?' Marla asked.

'No.' Hawes shook his head. 'No trouble.'

'Then why do you want to see him?'

'Why do *you* want to see him?' Hawes asked.

'To get a booking.'

'Good luck,' Hawes said.

'Thank you. He's a good agent. He handles a lot of exotic dancers. I'm
sure he'll get me something.'

'Good,' Hawes said. 'I hope so.'

The girl nodded and was silent for a while. She picked up the copy of
Variety, thumbed through it, and then put it down again. 'You still haven't
told me why you want to see Mr Tudor,' she said, and at that moment the
door to the inner office opened and a statuesque brunette wearing heels
which made her four inches taller stepped into the waiting room, bust first.

'Thanks a lot, Charlie,' she yelled, almost colliding with Carella to whom
she hastily said, 'Oh, pardon me, dearie,' and then clattered out of the room.

The phone on the receptionist's desk buzzed. She lifted the receiver. 'Yes,
Mr Tudor,' she said, and then hung up. 'Mr Tudor will see you now,' she
said to Carella.

'Good luck,' Marla said to Hawes as he moved past the bench.

'Thank you,' Hawes said. 'The same to you.'

'If I ever need a cop or something,' she called after him, 'I'll give you a
ring.'

'Do that,' Hawes said, and he followed Carella into Tudor's office. The
office was decorated with more photographs of exotic dancers, so many

photographs that both Tudor and his desk were almost lost in the display
Tudor was a huge man in his late forties wearing a dark-brown suit and a
pale-gold tie. He possessed a headful of short black hair which was turning
white at the temples, and a black Ernie Kóvacs moustache. He was smoking
a cigarette in a gold-and-black cigarette holder. He gestured the detective
to chairs, and a diamond pinky ring glistened on his right hand.

'I understand you're policemen,' he said. 'Does this have anything to do
with Barbara?'

'Yes, sir,' Carella said. 'We understand that you were the gentleman who
reported Miss Caesar missing.'

'Yes,' Tudor said. 'You must forgive my rudeness when my receptionis
announced you. I sometimes get calls from policemen which have nothing
whatever to do with ... well, something as serious as Barbara.'

'What kind of calls, Mr Tudor?' Hawes asked.

'Oh, you know. A show is closed down someplace, and some of my girl
are in it, and immediately the police make an association. I only find
employment for these girls. I don't tell them how to observe the rules o
propriety.' Tudor shrugged. His speech was curious in that it was absolutely
phony. He spoke with the clipped precision of an Englishman, and one
received the impression that he chose his words carefully before allowing
them to leave his mouth. But the elegant tones and rounded vowels were
delivered in the harshest, most blatant city accent Carella had ever heard
And the odd part was that Tudor didn't seem at all aware of the accent tha
stamped him as a native of either Isola or Calm's Point. Blithely, he clipped
his words immaculately and seemed under the impression that he was a
member of the House of Lords delivering a speech to his fellow peers.

'I really am not responsible for whatever acts my clients wish to concoct,
Tudor said. 'I wish the police would realize that. I am a booking agent, not a
choreographer.' He smiled briefly. 'About Barbara,' he said. 'What have you
heard?'

'Nothing at all, Mr Tudor. We were hoping you could tell us a little more
about her.'

'Oh.'

Tudor uttered only that single word, but disappointment was evident in
it, and disappointment showed immediately afterward on his face.

'I'm sorry if we raised your hopes, Mr Tudor,' Carella said.

'That's all right,' Tudor said. 'It's just ...'

'She meant a lot to you, this girl?'

'Yes,' Tudor answered. He nodded his head. 'Yes.'

'In a business way?' Hawes asked.

'Business?' Tudor shook his head again. 'No, not business. I've handled
better strippers. *Am* handling better ones now. That little girl who just left
my office. Her name is Pavan, got here from Frisco last July and has jus
about set this metropolis on fire. Excellent. Absolutely excellent, and she's
only twenty years old, would you believe it? She has a long future ahead o
her, that girl. Barbara was no child, you know.'

'How old is she?'

'Thirty-four. Of course, there are strippers who keep performing until
they're well into their fifties. I don't know of any performers, or of any
women for that matter, who take as much pride in their bodies as exotic

dancers do. I suppose there's an element of narcissism involved. Or perhaps we're looking too deep. They know their bodies are their fortunes. And so they take care of themselves. Barbara, though she was thirty-four, possessed ...' Tudor stopped short. 'Forgive me. I must get out of the habit of using the past tense in speaking about her. It's simply that, when a person leaves, disappears, that person is thought of as being *gone*, and the tongue plays its trick. Forgive me.'

'Are we to understand, Mr Tudor, that there was something more than a strict business relationship between you and Miss Caesar?'

'More?' Tudor said.

'Yes, was there ...'

'I love her,' Tudor said flatly.

The room was silent.

'I see,' Carella said.

'Yes,' Tudor paused for a long time. 'I love her. I still love her. I must keep remembering that. I must keep remembering that I still love her, and that she is still here.'

'Here?'

'Yes. Here. Somewhere. In this city. She is still here.' Tudor nodded. 'Nothing has happened to her. She is the same Barbara, laughing, lovely ...' He stopped himself. 'Have you seen her picture, gentlemen?'

'No,' Carella said.

'I have some, I believe. Would they help you?'

'Yes, they would.'

'I have already given some to the Missing Persons Bureau. Are you from the Missing Persons Bureau?'

'No.'

'No, I didn't think you were. Then what is your interest in Barbara?'

'We're acting in an advisory capacity,' Carella lied.

'I see,' Tudor stood up. He seemed taller on his feet, a man bigger than six feet who walked with economy and grace to the filing cabinet in one corner of the room. 'I think there are some in here,' he said. 'I usually have pictures taken as soon as I put a girl under contract. I had quite a few taken of Barbara when she first came to me.'

'When was this, Mr Tudor?'

Tudor did not look up from the files. His hands worked busily as he spoke. 'January. She came here from Kansas City. A friend of hers in a show there recommended me to her. I was the first person she met in this city.'

'She came to you first, is that correct, Mr Tudor?'

'Straight from the airport. I helped her get settled. I fell in love with her the moment I saw her.'

'Straight from the airport?' Carella asked.

'What? Yes. Ah, here are the pictures.' He turned from the files and carried several glossy prints to his desk. 'This is Barbara, gentlemen. Bubbles Caesar. Beautiful, isn't she?'

Carella did not look at the pictures. 'She came straight from the airport, you say?'

'Yes. Most of these pictures ...'

'Was she carrying any luggage?'

'Luggage? Yes, I believe so. Why?'

'What kind of luggage?'

'A suitcase, I believe. A large one.'

'Anything else?'

'I don't remember.'

'Was she carrying a small, blue overnight bag?' Hawes asked.

Tudor thought for a moment. 'Yes, I think she was. One of those small bags the airlines give you. Yes, she was.'

'Circle Airlines, Mr Tudor?'

'I don't remember. I have the impression it was Pan American.'

Carella nodded and picked up the photographs. The girl Barbara 'Bubbles' Caesar did not seem to be thirty-four years old, not from the photographs, at any rate. The pictures showed a clear-eyed, smiling brunette loosely draped in what seemed to be a fisherman's net. The net did very little to hide the girl's assets. The girl had assets in abundance. And coupled with these was the provocative look that all strippers wore after they'd ceased to wear anything else. Bubbles Caesar looked out of the photographs with an expression that clearly invited trouble. Studying the photos, Carella was absolutely certain that this was the identical look which Eve had flashed at Adam after taking her midday fruit. The look spelled one thing and one thing alone and, even realizing that the look was an acquired one, a trick of the girl's trade, Carella studied the photos and found that his palms were getting wet.

'She's pretty,' he said inadequately.

'The pictures don't do her justice,' Tudor said. 'She has a complexion like a peach and . . . and a vibration that can only be sensed through knowing her. There are people who vibrate, gentlemen. Barbara is one of them.'

'You said you helped her get settled, Mr Tudor. What, exactly, did you do?'

'I got a hotel for her, to begin with. Until she found a place of her own. I advanced her some money. I began seeing her regularly. And, of course, I got a job for her.'

'Where?'

'The King and Queen. It's an excellent club.'

'Where's that, Mr Tudor?'

'Downtown, in The Quarter. I've placed some very good girls there. Pavan started there when she came here from Frisco. But, of course, Pavan had big-time quality, and I moved her out very fast. She's working on The Street now. A place called The String of Pearls. Do you know it?'

'It sounds familiar,' Carella said. 'Miss Caesar was not bigtime in your opinion, is that right?'

'No. Not bad. But not Big-time.'

'Despite those . . . vibrations.'

'The vibrations were a part of her personality. Sometimes they come over on the stage, sometimes they don't. Believe me, if Barbara could have incorporated this . . . this inner glow into her act, she'd have been the biggest ever, the biggest. Bar none. Gypsy Rose Lee, Margie Hart, Zorita, Lili St Cyr, I tell you Barbara would have outshone them all. But no.' He shook his head. 'She was a second-rate stripper. Nothing came across the footlights but that magnificent body and, of course, the look that all strippers wear. But not the glow, not the vibrations, not the . . . the life force, call it what you will.

These only came from knowing her. There is a difference, you understand.'
'Was she working at The King and Queen when she disappeared?'
'Yes. She didn't show up for the show on February twelfth. The owner of the club reported this to me as her agent, and I called her apartment. She was living at the time with two other girls. The one who answered the phone told me that she hadn't seen her since early that morning. I got alarmed, and I went out to look for her. This is a big city, gentlemen.'
'Yes.'
'The next morning, the thirteenth, I called the police.' Tudor paused. He looked past the detectives and through the window where the rain dripped steadily against the red brick of the Creo Building. 'I had bought her a necklace for Valentine's Day. I was going to give it to her on Valentine's Day.' He shook his head. 'And now she's gone.'
'What kind of a necklace, Mr Tudor?'
'A ruby necklace. She has black hair, you know, very black, and deep brown eyes. I thought rubies, I thought the fire of rubies ...' He paused again. 'But she's gone, isn't she?'
'Who owns The King and Queen, Mr Tudor?'
'A man named Randy Simms. Randolph is his full name, I believe, but everyone calls him Randy. He runs a very clean establishment. Do you plan to call on him?'
'Yes. Maybe he can give us some help.'
'Find her, would you?' Tudor said. 'Oh, God, please find her.'

Chapter Eleven

The King and Queen was actually on the outermost fringe of The Quarter, really closer to the brownstone houses which huddled in the side streets off Hall Avenue than to the restaurants, coffee houses, small theatres and art shops which were near Canopy Avenue.

The place was a step-down club, its entrance being one step down from the pavement. To the right of the entrance doorway was a window which had been constructed of pieces of coloured glass in an attempt to simulate a stained-glass window. The coloured panes showed a playing-card portrait of a king on the left, and a playing-card portrait of a queen on the right. The effect was startling, lighted from within so that it seemed as if strong sunlight were playing in the glass. The effect, too, was dignified and surprising. Surprising because one expected something more blatant of a strip joint, the life-sized placards out front featuring an Amazonian doll in the middle of a bump or a grind. There were no placards outside this club. Nor was there a bold display of typography announcing the name of the place. A small, round, gold escutcheon was set off centre in the entrance door, and this was the only indication of the club's name. The address – '12N.' – was engraved onto another round gold plaque set in the lower half of the door.

Hawes and Carella opened the door and walked in.

The club had that same slightly tired, unused look that most night clubs had during the daytime. The look was always startling to Carella. It was as if one suddenly came across a middle-aged woman dressed in black satin and wearing diamonds at ten o'clock in the morning in Schrafft's. The King and Queen looked similarly overdressed and weary during the daylight hours, and perhaps more lonely. There wasn't a sign of life in the place.

'Hello!' Carella called. 'Anybody home?'

His voice echoed into the long room. A window at the far end admitted a single grey shaft of rain-dimmed light. Dust motes slid down the shaft of light, settled silently on the bottoms of deserted chairs stacked on round tables.

'Hello?' he called again.

'Empty,' Hawes said.

'Looks that way. Anybody here?' Carella yelled again.

'Who is it?' a voice answered. 'We don't open until six p.m.'

'Where are you?' Carella shouted to the voice.

'In the kitchen. We're closed.'

'Come on out here a minute, will you?'

A man appeared suddenly in the gloom, wiping his hands on a dish towel. He stepped briefly into the narrow shaft of light and then walked to where the two detectives were standing.

'We're closed,' he said.

'We're cops,' Carella answered.

'We're still closed. Especially to cops. If I served you, I'd get my liquor licence yanked.'

'You Randy Simms?' Hawes asked.

'That's me,' Simms said. 'Why? What'd I do?'

'Nothing. Can we sit down and talk someplace?'

'Anyplace,' Simms said. 'Choose your table.'

They pulled chairs off one of the tables and sat. Simms was a sandy-haired man in his late forties, wearing a white dress shirt open at the throat, the sleeves rolled up. There was a faintly bored expression on his handsome face. He looked like a man who spent his summers at St Tropez at home among the girls in the bikinis, his winters at St Moritz skiing without safety bindings. Carella was willing to bet he owned a Mercedes-Benz and a collection of Oriental jade.

'What's this about?' Simms asked. 'Some violation? I had the other doors put in, and I put up the occupancy signs. So what is it this time?'

'We're not firemen,' Carella said. 'We're cops.'

'What difference does it make? Cops or firemen, whenever either of them come around, it costs me money. What is it?'

'You know a girl named Bubbles Caesar?'

'I do,' Simms said.

'She work for you?'

'She used to work for me, yes.'

'Any idea where she is?'

'Not the vaguest. Why? Did she do something?'

'She seems to have disappeared.'

'Is that a crime?'

'Not necessarily.'

'Then why do you want her?'

'We want to talk to her.'

'You're not alone,' Simms said.

'What do you mean?'

'Only that everybody who ever walked into this joint wanted to talk to Barbara, that's all. She's a very attractive girl. A pain in the ass, but very attractive.'

'She gave you trouble?'

'Yes, but not in a professional sense. She always arrived on time, and she did her act when she was supposed to, and she was friendly with the customers, so there was no trouble that way.'

'Then what way *was* there trouble?'

'Well, there were a couple of fights in here.'

'Over Barbara?'

'Yes.'

'Who?'

'What do you mean, who?'

'Who did the fighting?'

'Oh, I don't remember,' Simms said. 'Customers. It's a funny thing with strippers. A man watches a woman take off her clothes, and he forgets he's in a public place and that the girl is a performer. He enters a fantasy in which he is alone with this girl, and she's taking off her clothes only for *him*. Well, sometimes the fantasy persists after the lights go up. And when two guys share the same fantasy, there can be trouble. A man who thinks the girl belongs to *him*, is undressing for *him*, doesn't like the idea of another guy sharing the same impression. Bang, the fists explode. So we heave them out on the sidewalk. Or at least we did. No more now.'

'Now you let them fight?' Hawes asked.

'No. Now we don't give them a chance to fantasize.'

'How do you prevent that?'

'Simple. No strippers.'

'Oh? Have you changed the club's policy?'

'Yep. No strippers, no band, no dancing. Just a high-class jazz pianist, period. Drinks, dim lights, and cool music. You bring your own broad, and you hold hands with *her*, not with some dame wiggling on the stage. We haven't had a fight in the past two weeks.'

'What made you decide on this new policy, Mr Simms?'

'Actually, Barbara had a lot to do with it. She provoked a lot of the fights. I think she did it purposely. She'd pick out two of the biggest guys in the audience, and split her act between them. First one guy, then the other. Afterwards, when she came out front, she'd play up to both of them, and bang, came the fists. Then she didn't show up for work one night, so I was left with a string of second-run strippers and no headliner. It looked like amateur night at The King and Queen. And the trouble with the band, believe me, it wasn't worth it.'

'What kind of trouble with the band?'

'Oh, all kinds. One of the guys on the band was a hophead, the trombone player. So I never knew whether he was going to show up for work or be found puking in some gutter. And then the drummer took off without a word, just didn't show up one night. The drummer is a very important man

in a band that accompanies strippers. So I was stuck without a headliner
and without a drummer. So you can imagine what kind of a show I had that
night.'

'Let me get this straight,' Carella said. 'Are you saying that Barbara and
this drummer both disappeared at the same time?'

'The same night, yes.'

'This was when?'

'I don't remember when exactly. A few days before Valentine's Day, I
think.'

'What was this drummer's name?'

'Mike something. An Italian name. A real tongue twister. I can't
remember it. It started with a C.'

'Were Barbara and Mike very friendly?'

'They didn't seem to be, no. At least, I never noticed anything going on
between them. Except the usual patter that goes on between the girls in the
show and the band. But nothing special. Oh, I see,' Simms said. 'You think
they took off together, is that it?'

'I don't know,' Carella said. 'It's a possibility.'

'Anything's possible with strippers and musicians,' Simms agreed. 'I'm
better off without them, believe me. This piano player I've got now, he plays
very cool music, and everybody sits and listens in the dark, and it's great.
Quiet. I don't need fist fights and intrigue.'

'You can't remember this drummer's last name.'

'No.'

'Try.'

'It began with a C, that's all I can tell you. Italian names throw me.'

'What was the name of the band?' Carella said.

'I don't think it had a name. It was a pickup band.'

'It had a leader, didn't it?'

'Well, he wasn't exactly a leader. Not the type anybody would want to be
taken to, if you follow me. He was just the guy who rounded up a bunch of
musicians for the job.'

'And what was his name?'

'Elliot. Elliot Chambers.'

'One other thing, Mr Simms,' Carella said. 'Barbara's agent told us she
was living with two other girls when she disappeared. Would you know who
those girls were?'

'I know one of them,' Simms said without hesitation. 'Marla Phillips. She
used to be in the show, too.'

'Would you know where she lives?'

'She's in the book,' Simms said. He paused and looked at the detectives.
'Is that it?'

'That's it,' Carella said.

Outside, Hawes said, 'What do you make of it?'

Carella shrugged. 'I'm going to check with the musician's local, see if I
can't get a last name for this Mike the drummer.'

'Do drummers have big hands?'

'Search me. But it looks like more than coincidence, doesn't it? Both of
them taking a powder on the same night?'

'Yeah, it does,' Hawes said. 'What about Marla Phillips?'

'Why don't you drop in and pay a visit?'

'All right,' Hawes said.

'See what a nice guy I am? I tackle the musicians' union, and I leave the stripper to you.'

'You're a married man,' Hawes said.

'And a father,' Carella added.

'*And* a father, that's right.'

'If you need any help, I'll be back at the squad.'

'What help could I possibly need?' Hawes asked.

Marla Phillips lived on the ground floor of a brownstone four blocks from The King and Queen. The name plate on the mailboxes listed a hyphenated combination of three names: Phillips-Caesar-Smith. Hawes rang the bell, waited for the responding buzz that opened the inner door, and then stepped into the hallway. The apartment was at the end of the hall. He walked to it, rang the bell set in the door jamb, and waited. The door opened almost instantly.

Marla Phillips looked at him and said, 'Hey!'

He recognized her instantly, of course, and then wondered where his mind was today. He had made no connection with the name when Simms had first mentioned it.

'Aren't you the cop who was in Mr Tudor's office?' Marla asked.

'That's me,' he said.

'Sure. Cotton something. Well, come on in, Cotton. Boy, this is a surprise. I just got home a minute ago. You're lucky you caught me. I have to leave in about ten minutes. Come in, come in. You'll catch cold standing in the hallway.'

Hawes went into the apartment. Standing next to Marla, he realized how tall she truly was. He tried to visualize her on a runway, but the thought was staggering. He followed her into the apartment instead.

'Don't mind the underwear all over the place,' Marla said. 'I live with another girl. Taffy Smith. She's an actress. Legit. Would you like a drink?'

'No, thank you,' Hawes said.

'Too early, huh? Look, will you do me a favour?'

'Sure,' Hawes said.

'I have to call my service to see if there was anything for me while I was out. Would you feed the cat, please? The poor thing must be starved half to death.'

'The cat?'

'Yeah, he's a Siamese, he's wandering around here somewhere. He'll come running into the kitchen the minute he hears you banging around out there. The cat food is under the sink. Just open up a can and put some in his bowl. And would you heat some milk for him? He can't stand cold milk.'

'Sure,' Hawes said.

'You're a honey,' she told him. 'Go ahead now, feed him. I'll be with you in a minute.'

She went to the telephone and Hawes went into the kitchen. As he opened the can of cat food under the watchful eyes of the Siamese who had materialized instantly, he listened to Marla in the other room.

'A Mr Who?' she asked the telephone. 'Well, I don't know anybody by that name, but I'll give him a ring later in the afternoon. Anyone else? Okay, thank you.'

She hung up and walked into the kitchen.

'Are you still warming the milk?' she asked. 'It'll be too hot. You'd better take it off now.' Hawes took off the saucepan and poured the milk into the bowl on the floor.

'Okay, now come with me,' Marla said. 'I have to change, do you mind? I've got a sitting in about five minutes. I do modelling on the side. Cheesecake, you know. For the men's magazines. I've got to put on some fancy lingerie. Come on, come on, please hurry. This way.'

He followed her into a bedroom that held two twin beds, a huge dresser, several chairs, and an assortment of soiled cardboard coffee containers, wooden spoons, and clothing piled haphazardly on the floor and on the top of every available surface.

'Forgive the mess,' Marla said. 'My roommate is a slob.' She took off her suit jacket and threw it on the floor, slipping out of her pumps at the same time. She began pulling her blouse out of her skirt and then said, 'Would you mind turning your back? I hate to be a prude, but I am.'

Hawes turned his back, wondering why Marla Phillips thought it perfectly all right to take off her clothes in a night club before the eyes of a hundred men, but considered it indecent to perform the same act in a bedroom before the eyes of a single man. *Women*, he thought, and he shrugged mentally. Behind him, he could hear the frantic swishing of cotton and silk.

'I hate garter belts,' she said. 'I'm a big girl. I need something to hold me in. What's supposed to be so damn sexy about a garter belt, anyway, would you mind telling me? What was it you wanted, Cotton?'

'Somebody told us you used to room with Bubbles Caesar. Is that right?'

'Yes, that's right. Oh, goddamnit, I've got a run.' She pushed past him half-naked, bent over to pull a pair of stockings from the bottom drawer of the dresser, and then vanished behind his back again. 'Excuse me,' she said. 'What about Barbara?'

'Did she live with you?'

'Yes. Her name is still in the mailbox. There, that's better. Whenever I'm in a hurry, I tear stockings. I don't know what they make them out of these days. Tissue paper, I think. I'll have to take her name out, I suppose. When I get the time. Boy, if I only had time to do all the things I want to do. What about Barbara?'

'When did she move out?'

'Oh, you know. When there was that big fuss. When Mr Tudor reported her missing and all.'

'Around St Valentine's Day.'

'Yes, around that time.'

'Did she tell you she was going?'

'No.'

'Did she take her clothes with her?'

'No.'

'Her clothes are still here?'

'Yes.'

'Then she didn't really *move* out, she just never showed up again.'

'Yes, but she'll probably be back. Okay, you can turn now.'

Hawes turned. Marla was wearing a simple black dress, an offshade of black nylon stockings, and high-heeled black pumps. 'Are my seams straight?' she asked.

'Yes, they seem perfectly straight.'

'Do you like my legs? Actually, my legs are too skinny for the rest of me.'

'They seem okay to me,' Hawes said. 'What makes you think Barbara will be back?'

'I have the feeling she's shacking up with somebody. She likes men, Barbara does. She'll be back. I guess that's why I really haven't taken her name out of the mailbox.'

'These men she likes,' Hawes said. 'Was Mike the drummer one of them?'

'Not that I know of. At least, she never talked about him or anything. And he never called here. Excuse me, I have to put on a new face.'

She shoved Hawes aside and sat at the counter top before the large mirror. The counter was covered with cosmetics. Among the other jars and bottles, Hawes noticed a small jar labelled Skinglow. He picked it up and turned it over in his hands.

'This yours?' he asked.

'What?' Marla turned, lipstick brush in one hand. 'Oh. Yes. Mine, *and* Taffy's, *and* Barbara's. We all use it. It's very good stuff. It doesn't fade out under the lights. Sometimes, under the lights, your body looks *too* white, do you know? It's all right to look white, but not ghostly. So we use the Skinglow, and it takes off the pallor. A lot of strippers and actresses use it.'

'Do you know Mike's last name?'

'Sure. Chirapadano. It's a beaut, isn't it?'

'Does he have big hands?'

'All men have big hands,' Marla said.

'I mean, did you notice that his hands were unusually large?'

'I never noticed. The only thing I noticed about that band was that they all had six hands.'

'Mike included?'

'Mike included.' She turned to him. 'How do I look? What time is it?'

'You look fine. It's –' he glanced at his watch – 'twelve-fifteen.'

'I'm late,' she said flatly. 'Do I look sexy?'

'Yes.'

'Well, okay then.'

'Do you know any of the men Barbara saw?' Hawes asked. 'Any she might run away with?'

'Well, there was one guy who called her an awful lot. Listen, I'm sorry I'm giving you this bum's rush act, but I really have to get out of here. Why don't you call me sometime? You're awfully cute. Or if you're in the neighbourhood some night, drop in. She's always serving coffee, that goddamn screwy roommate of mine.'

'I might do that,' Hawes said. 'Who was this person who called Barbara a lot?'

'Oh, what was his name? He sounded like a Russian or something. Just a minute,' she said, 'I'll think of it.' She opened a drawer, took a black purse from it, and hastily filled it with lipstick, mascara, change, and a small woman's wallet. 'There, that's that,' she said. 'Do I have the address? Yes.'

She paused. 'Androvich, that was the name. Karl Androvich. A sailor or something. Look, Cotton, will you call me sometime? You're not married or anything, are you?'

'No. Did you say Androvich?'

'Yes. Karl Androvich. Will you call me? I think it might be fun. I'm not always in such a crazy rush.'

'Well, sure, but ...'

'Come on, I've got to go. You can stay if you want to, just slam the door on the way out, it locks itself.'

'No, I'll come with you.'

'Are you going uptown?'

'Yes.'

'Good, we can share a cab. Come on, hurry. Would you like to come to the sitting? No, don't, I'll get self-conscious. Come on, come on. Slam the door! Slam the door, Cotton!'

He slammed the door.

'I'm wearing this black stuff that's supposed to be imported from France. The bra is practically nonexistent. These pictures ought to ...'

'When did Androvich last call her?' Hawes asked.

'A few days before she took off,' Marla said. 'There's a cab. Can you whistle?'

'Yes, sure, but ...'

'Whistle!'

Hawes whistled. They got into the cab together.

'Oh, where the hell did I put that address?' Marla said. 'Just a minute,' she told the cabbie. 'Start driving uptown on Hall, I'll have the address for you in a minute. Do you think she ran off with Androvich? Is that possible, Cotton?'

'I doubt it. Androvich is home. Unless ...'

'Unless what?'

'I don't know. I guess we'll have to talk to Androvich.'

'Here's the address,' Marla said to the cabbie, '695 Hall Avenue. Would you hurry, please? I'm terribly late.'

'Lady,' the cabbie answered. 'I have never carried a passenger in this vehicle who *wasn't* terribly late.'

Chapter Twelve

At the squadroom, Hawes told Carella, 'I found out the drummer's name.'

'So did I. I got Chambers' number from the union, and I called him. Drummer's name is Mike Chirapadano. I called the union back and got an address and telephone number for him, too.'

'Call him yet?' Hawes asked.

'Yes. No answer. I'd like to stop by there later this afternoon. Have you had lunch yet?'

'No.'

'Let's.'

'Okay. We've got another stop to make, too.'

'Where?'

'Androvich.'

'What for? Lover Boy is back, isn't he?'

'Sure. But Bubbles' roommate told me Androvich was in the habit of calling her.'

'The roommate?'

'No. Bubbles.'

'Androvich? Androvich was calling Bubbles Caesar?'

'Uh-huh.'

'So *he's* back in it again, huh?'

'It looks that way. He called her a few days before she vanished, Steve.'

'Mmm. So what does that mean?'

'He's the only guy who would know, it seems to me.'

'Yeah. Okay. Lunch first, then Chirapadano – Jesus, that *is* a tongue twister – and then our amorous sailor friend. Cotton, there are times when I get very very weary.'

'Have you ever tried running a footrace with a stripper?' Hawes asked.

Mike Chirapadano lived in a furnished room on North Sixth. He was not in when the detectives dropped by, and his landlady told them he had not been around for the past month.

The landlady was a thin bird of a woman in a flowered housedress. She kept dusting the hall way while they spoke to her.

'He owes me almost two months' rent,' she said. 'Is he in some trouble?'

'When did you last see him, Mrs Marsten?' Hawes asked.

'In Feb-uary,' she answered. 'He owes me for Feb-uary, and he also owes me for March, if he's still living here. The way it looks to me, he ain't living here no more. Don't it look that way to you?'

'Well, I don't know. I wonder if we could take a look at his room.'

'Sure. Don't make no nevermind to me. What's he done? He a dope fiend? All these musicians are dope fiends, you know.'

'Is that right?' Carella asked as they walked upstairs.

'Sure. Main-liners. That means they shoot it right into their veins.'

'Is that right?'

'Sure. It's poison you know. That hero-in they shoot into their veins. That stuff. It's poison. His room is on the third floor. I was up there cleaning only yesterday.'

'Is his stuff still up there?'

'Yep, his clothes and his drums, too. Now why would a man take off like that and leave his belongs behind? He must be a dope fiend is the only way I can figure it. Here, it's down the end of the hall. What did you say he done?'

'Would you know exactly when in February he left, Mrs Marsten?'

'I would know exactly to the day,' the landlady said, but she did not offer the information.

'Well when?' Hawes asked.

'Feb-uary twelfth. It was the day before Friday the thirteenth, and that's how I remember. Friday the thirteenth, that's a hoodoo day if ever there was one. Here's his room. Just a second now, while I unlock the door.'

She took a key from the pocket of her dress and fitted it into the keyhole. 'There's something wrong with this lock; I have to get it fixed. There, that does it.' She threw open the door. 'Spic and span; I just cleaned it yesterday. Even picked up his socks and underwear from all over the floor. One thing I can't stand it's a sloppy-looking room.'

They went into the room together.

'There's his drums over there by the window. The big one is the bass drum, and that round black case is what they call the snare. The other thing there is the high hat. All his clothes is still in the closet and his shaving stuff is in the bathroom, just the way he left them. I can't figure it, can you? What'd you say it was that he done?'

'Did you see him when he left, Mrs Marsten?'

'No.'

'How old a man is he?'

'He's just a young fellow, it's a shame the way these young fellows get to be main-liners and dope fiends, shooting all that there hero-in poison into their systems.'

'How young, Mrs Marten?'

'Twenty-four, twenty-five, no older than that.'

'A big man?'

'More than six feet, I guess.'

'Big hands?'

'What?'

'His hands. Were they big, did you notice?'

'I never noticed. Who looks at a man's hands?'

'Well, some women do,' Carella said.

'All I know is he owes me almost two months' rent,' Mrs Marsten said, shrugging.

'Would you know whether or not he had a lot of girl friends, Mrs Marsten? Did he ever bring a girl here?'

'Not to my house,' the landlady said. 'Not to my house, mister! I don't allow any of that kind of stuff here. No, sir. If he had girl friends, he wasn't fooling around with them under my roof. I keep a clean house. Both the rooms *and* the roomers.'

'I see,' Carella said. 'You mind if we look around a little?'

'Go right ahead. Call me when you're done, and I'll lock the room. Don't make a mess. I just cleaned it yesterday.'

She went out. Carella and Hawes stared at each other.

'Do you suppose they went to Kansas City, maybe?' Hawes asked.

'I don't know. I'm beginning to wish both of them went to hell. Let's shake down the room. Maybe he left a clue.'

He hadn't.

Karl Androvich was a moustached giant who could have been a breathing endorsement for Marlboro cigarettes. He sat in a T-shirt at the kitchen table, his muscles bulging bronze against the clean white, the tattoo showing on his left biceps, 'Meg' in a heart. His hair was a reddish brown, and his moustache was a curious mixture of red, brown and blond hairs, a carefully trimmed, very elegant moustache which – reflecting its owner's pride – was constantly touched by Androvich during the course of the conversation. His hands were immense. Every time they moved up to stroke the moustache, Carella flinched as if he were about to be hit. Meg Androvich hovered about the kitchen, preparing dinner, her ears glued to the conversation.

'There are a few things we'd like to know, Mr Androvich,' Carella said.

'Yeah, what's that?'

'To begin with, where were you between February fourteenth and Monday when you came back to this house?'

'That's my business,' Androvich said. 'Next question.'

Carella was silent for a moment.

'Are you going to answer our questions here, Mr Androvich, or shall we go up to the squadroom where you might become a little more talkative?'

'You going to use a rubber hose on me? Man, I've been worked over with a hose before. You don't scare me.'

'You going to tell us where you were?'

'I told you that's my business.'

'Okay, get dressed.'

'What the hell for? You can't arrest me without a charge.'

'I've got a whole bagful of charges. You're withholding information from the police. You're an accessory before a murder. You're ...'

'A what? A murder? Are you out of your bloody mind?'

'Get dressed Androvich. I don't want to play around.'

'Okay,' Androvich said angrily. 'I was on the town.'

'On the town where?'

'Everywhere. Bars. I was drinking.'

'Why?'

'I felt like it.'

'Did you know your wife had reported you missing?'

'No. How the hell was I supposed to have known that?'

'Why didn't you call her?'

'What are you, a marriage counsellor? I didn't feel like calling her, okay?'

'He didn't have to call me if he didn't feel like it,' Meg said from the stove. 'He's home now. Why don't you all leave him alone?'

'Keep out of this, Meg,' Androvich warned.

'Which bars did you go to?' Hawes asked.

'I went all over the city. I don't remember the names of the bars.'

'Did you go to a place called The King and Queen?'

'No.'

'I thought you didn't remember the names.'

'I don't.'

'Then how do you know you *didn't* go to The King and Queen?'

'It doesn't sound familiar.' A slight tic had begun in Androvich's left eye.

'Does the name Bubbles Caesar sound familiar?'

'No.'

'Or Barbara Cesare?'

'No,' Androvich answered, the muscle of his eye jerking.

'How about Marla Phillips?'

'Never heard of her.'

'How about this phone number, Androvich? Sperling 7–0200. Mean anything to you?'

'No.' The muscle was twitching wildly now.

'Mrs Androvich,' Carella said, 'I think you'd better leave the room.'
'Why?'
'We're about to pull out a few skeletons. Go on in the other room.'
'My wife can hear anything you've got to say,' Androvich said.
'Okay. Sperling 7–0200 is the telephone number of three girls who share an apartment. One of them is named ...'
'Go on in the other room, M-M-Meg,' Androvich said.
'I want to stay here.'
'Do what I t-t-tell you to do.'
'Why is he asking you about that phone number? What have you got to do with those three ...?'
'G-G-Get the hell in the other room, Meg, before I slap you silly. Now do what I say!'
Meg Androvich stared at her husband sullenly, and then went out of the kitchen.
'Damn S-S-Southern t-t-trash,' Androvich muttered under his breath, the stammering more marked now, the tic beating at the corner of his eye.
'You ready to tell us a few things, Androvich?'
'Okay. I knew her.'
'Bubbles?'
'Bubbles.'
'How well did you know her?'
'Very well.'
'How well is that, Androvich?'
'You want a d-d-diagram?'
'If you've got one.'
'We were making it together. Okay?'
'Okay. When did you last see her?'
'February twelfth.'
'You remember the date pretty easily.'
'I ought to.'
'What does that mean?'
'I ... look, what the hell d-d-difference does all this make? The last time I saw her was on the t-t-twelfth. Last month. I haven't seen her since.'
'You sure about that?'
'I'm positive.'
'You sure you haven't been with her all this time?'
'I'm sure. Man, I wish I had been with her. I was *supposed* ...' Androvich cut himself off.
'Supposed to do what?' Hawes asked.
'N-N-Nothing.'
'You called her on the twelfth after your ship docked, is that right?'
'Yes.'
'And you saw her afterwards?'
'Yes, but only for about a half-hour or so.'
'That morning?'
'No. It was in the afternoon.'
'Where'd you see her?'
'At her p-p-p-place.'
'Was anybody else there? Either of her roommates?'

'No. I never met her roommates.'

'But you spoke to them on the telephone?'

'Yeah. I spoke to one of them.'

'Marla Phillips?'

'I d-d-don't know which one it was.'

'Did you speak to the roommate on the morning of the twelfth?'

'Yeah. I spoke to her, and then she called B-B-Bubbles to the phone.'

'And then you went to the apartment that afternoon, right?'

'Right. For a half-hour.'

'And then what?'

'Then I left. One of the r-r-r-roommates was supposed to be coming back. That d-d-damn place is like the middle of Main Street.'

'And you haven't seen her since that afternoon?'

'That's right.'

'Have you tried to contact her?'

Androvich hesitated. Then he said, 'No.'

'How come?'

'I just haven't. I figure she must have gone back to Kansas City.'

'What makes you figure that?'

'I just figure. She isn't around, is she?'

'How do you know?'

'Huh?'

'If you haven't tried contacting her, how do you know she isn't around?'

'Well, m-m-maybe I did try to reach her once or twice.'

'When?'

'I don't remember. During the past few weeks.'

'And you couldn't reach her?'

'No.'

'Who did you reach?'

'The g-g-goddamn answering service.'

'Now, let's go back a little, Androvich. You said you visited Miss Caesar in her apartment on the afternoon of the twelfth. All right, why?'

'I wanted to talk to her.'

'What about?'

'Various things.'

'Like what? Come on, Androvich, let's stop the teethpulling!'

'What d-d-difference does it make to you guys?'

'It may make a lot of difference. Miss Caesar has disappeared. We're trying to find her.'

'You're telling me she's disappeared! Boy, has she disappeared! Well, I d-d-don't know where she is. If I did know . . .' Again, he cut himself off.

'If you did know, then what?'

'Nothing.'

'What did you talk about that afternoon?'

'Nothing.'

'You spent a half-hour talking about nothing, is that right?'

'That's right.'

'Did you go to bed with her that afternoon?'

'No. I told you her r-r-roommate was expected back.'

'So you just sat and looked at each other, right?'

'More or less.'

'Get dressed, Androvich. We're going to have to take a little ride.'

'Ride, my ass! I don't know anything about where she is, dammit! If I knew, do you think I'd ...'

'What? Finish it, Androvich! Say what you've got to say!'

'Do you think I'd be here? Do you think I'd be playing hubby and wifey with that mealy-mouthed hunk of Southern garbage? Do you think I'd be listening to this molasses dribble day in and day out? Kahl, honeh, cain't we-all go back t'Atlanta, honeh? Cain't we, Kahl? Do you think I'd be here listening to that crap if I knew where Bubbles was?'

'What would you be doing, Androvich?'

'I'd be with her, goddamnit! Where do you think I spent the last month?'

'Where?'

'Looking for her. Searching this city, every c-c-corner of it. Do you know how big this city is?'

'We've got some idea.'

'Okay, I p-p-picked through it like somebody looking through a scalp for lice. And I didn't find her. And if I couldn't find her, she isn't here, believe me, because I covered every place, *every* place. I went to places you guys have never even heard of, l-l-looking for that broad. She's gone.'

'She was that important to you, huh?'

'Yeah, she was that important to me.'

Androvich fell silent. Carella stared at him.

'What did you talk about that afternoon, Karl?' he asked gently.

'We made plans,' Androvich said. His voice was curiously low now. The tic had stopped suddenly. The stammer had vanished. He did not look up at the detectives. He fastened his eyes on his big hands, and he twisted those hands in his lap, and he did not look up.

'What kind of plans?'

'We were going to run away together.'

'Where?'

'Miami.'

'Why there?'

'She knew of a job she could get down there. In one of the clubs. And Miami's a big port. Not as big as this city, but big enough. I could always get work out of Miami. Or maybe I could get a job on one of the yachts. Anyway, we figured Miami was a good place for us.'

'When were you supposed to leave?'

'Valentine's Day.'

'Why then?'

'Well, my ship was pulling out on the fourteenth, so we figured that would give us a head start. We figured Meg would think I was in South America, and then by the time she realized I wasn't, she wouldn't know where the hell I was. That was the way we figured it.'

'But instead, the chief officer called here to find out where you were.'

'Yeah, and Meg reported me missing.'

'Why *aren't* you in Miami, Karl? What happened?'

'She didn't show.'

'Bubbles?'

'Yeah. I waited at the train station all morning. Then I called her apartment, and all I got was the goddamn answering service. I called all that day, and all that day I got that answering service. I went down to The King and Queen, and the bartender there told me she hadn't showed up for work the past two nights. That was when I began looking for her.'

'Did you plan to marry this girl, Karl?'

'Marry her? How could I do that? I'm already married. Bigamy is against the law.'

'Then what did you plan to do?'

'Just have fun, that's all. I'm a young guy. I deserve a little fun, don't I? Miami is a good town for fun.'

'Do you think she could have gone to Miami without you?'

'I don't think so. I wired the club she mentioned, and they said she hadn't showed up. Besides, why would she do that?'

'Women do funny things.'

'Not Bubbles.'

'We'd better check with the Miami cops, Steve,' Hawes said. 'And maybe a teletype to Kansas City, huh?'

'Yeah.' He paused and looked at Androvich. 'You think she isn't here any more, huh? You think she's left the city?'

'That's the way I figure it. I looked everywhere. She couldn't be here. It'd be impossible.'

'Maybe she's hiding,' Carella said. 'Maybe she did something and doesn't want to be found.'

'Bubbles? No, not Bubbles.'

'Ever hear of a man called Mike Chirapadano?'

'No, Who's he?'

'A drummer.'

'I never heard of him.'

'Bubbles ever mention him?'

'No. Listen, she ain't in this city, that much I can tell you. She just ain't here. Nobody can hide that good.'

'Maybe not,' Carella said. 'But maybe she's here, anyway.'

'What sense does that make? If she ain't out in the open, and she ain't hiding, what does that leave?'

'The river,' Carella said.

Chapter Thirteen

It stopped raining that Thursday.

Nobody seemed to notice the difference.

It was strange. For the past nine days, it had rained steadily and everyone in the city talked about the rain. There were jokes about building arks and jokes about the rain hurting the rhubarb, and it was impossible to go anywhere or do anything without someone mentioning the rain.

On Thursday morning, the sun came out. There was no fanfare of trumpets heralding the sun's appearance, and none of the metropolitan dailies shrieked about it in four-point headlines. The rain just went, and the sun just came, and everyone in the city trotted about his business as if nothing had happened. The rain had been with them too long. It had become almost a visiting relative whose departure is always promised but never really expected. At last, the relative had left and – as with most promised things in life – there was no soaring joy accompanying the event. If anything, there was almost a sense of loss.

Even the bulls of the 87th who quite naturally detested legwork in the rain did not greet the sun with any noticeable amount of enthusiasm.

They had got their teletypes out to Miami and Kansas City, and they had received their answering teletypes, and the answering teletypes told them that Barbara 'Bubbles' Caesar was not at the moment gainfully employed in any of the various clubs in either of the cities. This did not mean that she wasn't living in either of the cities. It simply meant she wasn't working.

It was impossible to check bus or train transportation, but a call to every airline servicing both of the cities revealed that neither Bubbles Caesar nor a Mike Chirapadano had reserved passage out of Isola during the past month.

On Thursday afternoon, the Federal Bureau of Investigation delivered a photostatic copy of Mike Chirapadano's service record.

He had been born in Riverhead twenty-three years ago. He was white, and he was obviously male. Height, six feet three inches. Weight, 185. Eyes, blue. Hair, brown. When the Korean War broke out, he was only thirteen years old. When it ended, he was sixteen, and so he had been spared the Oriental bout. He had joined the Navy for a two-year hitch in July of 1956, had spent all of his service career – except for his boot training at the Great Lakes Naval Station – playing with the ComSerDiv band in Miami. When he got out of the navy in 1958, he came back to Isola. His record listed an honourable discharge in Miami, the Navy providing his transportation back to his home city. A copy of his fingerprint record was included in the data from the FBI but the prints were worthless for comparison purposes since the fingertips on both discovered hands had been mutilated. The Navy listed his blood as belonging to the 'O' group.

Carella studied the information and went home to his wife.

Teddy Carella was a deaf mute.

She was not a tall woman but she somehow managed to give the impression of height – a woman with black hair and brown eyes and a figure which, even after the bearing of twin children, managed to evoke street-corner whistles that – unfortunately – Teddy could not hear.

The twins, Mark and April, had been born on a Sunday in June. June 22, to be exact. Carella would never forget the date because, aside from it being the day on which he'd been presented with two lovely children, it had also been the day of his sister Angela's wedding, and there had been quite a bit of excitement on that day, what with a sniper trying to pick off the groom and all. Happily, the groom had survived. He had survived very well. Angela, less than a year after her marriage, was already pregnant.

Now the problems of the care and feeding of twins are manifold even for a mother who possesses the powers of speech and hearing. The feeding problem is perhaps the least difficult because the eventuality of twins was undoubtedly considered in the design of the female apparatus and allowances made therefore. For which, thank God. But any mother who has tried to cope with the infantile madness of even one child must surely recognize that the schizophrenic rantings of twins present a situation exactly doubled in potential frenzy.

When Steve Carella discovered that his wife was pregnant, he was not exactly the happiest man in the world. His wife was a deaf mute. Would the children be similarly afflicted? He was assured that his wife's handicap was not an inherited trait, and that in all probability a woman as healthy in all other respects as Teddy would deliver an equally healthy baby. He had felt somewhat ashamed of his doubts later. In all truth, he never really considered Teddy either 'handicapped' or 'afflicted'. She was, to him, the most beautiful and desirable woman on the face of the earth. Her eyes, her face, spoke more words to him than could be found in the languages of a hundred different nations. And when he spoke, she heard him, she heard him with more than ears, she heard him with her entire being. And so he'd felt some guilt at his earlier unhappiness, a guilt which slowly dissipated as the time of the birth drew near.

But he was not expecting twins, and when he was informed that he was now the father of a boy and a girl, the boy weighing in at six pounds four ounces, the girl being two ounces lighter than her brother, all of his old fears and anxieties returned. The fears became magnified when he visited the hospital the next morning and was told by the obstetrician that the firstborn, Mark, had broken his collarbone during delivery and that the doctor was placing him in an incubator until the collarbone healed. Apparently, the birth had been a difficult one and Mark had gallantly served as a trailblazer for his wombmate, suffering the fractured clavicle in his progress towards daylight. As it turned out, the fracture was simply a chipped bone, and it healed very rapidly, and the babies Carella and Teddy carried home from the hospital ten days later were remarkably healthy; but Carella was still frightened.

How will we manage? he wondered. How will Teddy manage to feed them and take care of them? How will they learn to speak? Wasn't speech a process of imitation? Oh, God, what will we do?

The first thing they had to do, they discovered, was to move. The Riverhead apartment on Dartmouth Road seemed to shrink the moment the babies and their nurse were put into the place. The nurse had been a gift from Teddy's father, a month's respite from the task of getting a household functioning again. The nurse was a marvellous woman in her fifties named Fanny. She had blue hair and she wore pincenez and she weighed a hundred and fifty pounds and she ran that house like an Army sergeant. She took an instant liking to Carella and his wife, and her fondness for the twins included such displays of affection as the embroidering of two pillow slips with their names, action clearly above and beyond the call of duty.

Whenever Carella had a day off, he and Teddy went looking for a house. Carella was a Detective 2nd/Grade and his salary – before the various deductions which decimated it – was exactly $5,555 a year. That is not a lot of loot. They had managed to save over the past years the grand total of two thousand bucks, and they were rapidly discovering that this paltry sum could barely cover the down payment on a lawn mower, much less a full-fledged house. For the first time in his life, Carella felt completely inadequate. He had brought two children into the world, and now he was faced with the possibility of being unable to house them properly, to give them the things they needed. And suddenly the Carellas discovered that their luck, by George, she was running good!

They found a house that could be had simply by paying the back taxes on it, which taxes amounted to ten thousand dollars. The house was a huge rambling monster in Riverhead, close to Donnegan's Bluff, a house which had undoubtedly held a large family and an army of servants in the good old days. These were the bad new days, however, and with servants and fuel costs being what they were, no one was very anxious to take over a white elephant like this one. Except the Carellas.

They arranged a loan through the local bank (a civil service employee is considered a good risk) and less than a month after the twins were born, they found themselves living in a house of which Charles Adams would have been ecstatically proud. Along about this time, their second stroke of good luck presented itself. Fanny, who had helped them move and helped them get settled, was due to terminate her month's employment when she offered the Carellas a proposition. She had, she told them, been making a study of the situation in the Carella household, and she could not visualize poor little Theodora (these were Fanny's words) raising those two infants alone, nor did she understand how the children were to learn to talk if they could not intimate their mother, and how was Theodora to hear either of the infants yelling, suppose one of them got stuck with a safety pin or something, my God?

Now she understood that a detective's salary was somewhere around five thousand a year – 'You *are* a 2nd/grade detective, aren't you, Steve?' – and that such a salary did not warrant a full-time nurse and governess. But at the same time, she had the utmost faith that Carella would eventually make 1st/grade – 'That *does* pay six thousand a year, doesn't it, Steve? – and until the time when the Carellas could afford to pay her a decent wage, she would be willing to work for room and board, supplementing this with whatever she could earn making night calls and the like.

The Carellas would not hear of it.

She was, they insisted, a trained nurse, and she would be wasting her time by working for the Carellas at what amounted to no salary at all when she could be out earning a damned good living. And besides, she was not a truck horse, how could she possibly work all day long with the children and then hope to take on odd jobs at night? No, they would not hear of it.

But neither would Fanny hear of their not hearing of it.

'I am a very strong woman,' she said, 'and all I'll be doing all day long is taking care of the children under the supervision of Theodora who is their mother. I speak English very well, and the children could do worse for someone to imitate. And besides, I'm fifty-three years old, and I've never had a family of my own, and I rather like this family and so I think I'll stay. And it'll take a bigger man than you, Steve Carella, to throw me into the street. So that settles that.'

And, that indeed, did settle that.

Fanny had stayed. The Carellas had sectioned off one corner of the house and disconnected the heating to it so that their fuel bills were not exorbitant.

Slowly but surely, the bank loan was being paid off. The children were almost a year old and showed every sign of being willing to imitate the sometimes colourful speech of their nurse. Fanny's room was on the second floor of the house, near the children's room, and the Carellas slept downstairs in a bedroom off the living room so that even their sex life went uninterrupted after that grisly six-weeks' postnatal wait. Everything was rosy.

But sometimes a man came home looking for an argument, and you can't very well argue with a woman who cannot speak. There are some men who might agree that such a state of matrimony is surely a state approaching paradise, but on that Thursday night, with the sky peppered with stars, with a springlike breeze in the air, Carella walked up the path to the old house bristling for a fight.

Teddy greeted him at the doorway. He kissed her briefly and stamped into the house, and she stared after him in puzzlement and then followed him.

'Where's Fanny?' he asked.

He watched Teddy's fingers as they rapidly told him, in sign language, that Fanny had left early for a nursing job.

'And the children?' he asked.

She read his lips, and then signalled that the children were already in bed, asleep.

'I'm hungry,' he said. 'Can we eat, please?'

They went into the kitchen, and Teddy served the meal – pork chops, his favourite. He picked sullenly at his food, and after dinner he went into the living room, turned on the television set, watched a show featuring a private eye who was buddy-buddy with a police lieutenant and who was also buddy-buddy with at least eighteen different women of assorted provocative shapes, and then snapped off the show and turned to Teddy and shouted, 'If any police lieutenant in the country ran his squad the way that jerk does, the thieves would overrun the streets! No wonder he needs a private eye to tell him what to do!'

Teddy stared at her husband and said nothing.

'I'd like to see what the pair of them would do with a real case. I'd like to see how they'd manage without a dozen clues staring them in the face.'

Teddy rose and went to her husband, sitting on the arm of his chair.

'I'd like to see what they'd do with a pair of goddamn severed hands. They'd probably both faint dead away,' Carella said.

Teddy stroked his hair.

'We're back to Androvich again,' he shouted. It occurred to him that it didn't matter whether or not he shouted because Teddy was only reading his lips and the decibels didn't matter one little damn. But he shouted nonetheless. 'We're right back to Androvich, and where does that leave us? You want to know where that leaves us?'

Teddy nodded.

'Okay. We've got a pair of hands belonging to a white male who is somewhere between the ages of eighteen and twenty-four. We've got a bum of a sailor who flops down with any girl he meets, bong, bong, there goes Karl Androvich, who allegedly made a date to run off with a stripper named Bubbles Caesar. You listening?'

Yes Teddy nodded.

'So they set the date for Valentine's Day, which is very romantic. All the tramps of the world are always very romantic. Only this particular tramp didn't show up. She left our sailor friend Androvich waiting in the lurch.' He saw the frown on Teddy's face. 'What's the matter? You don't like my calling Bubbles a tramp? She reads that way to me. She's provoked fights in the joint where she stripped by leading on two men simultaneously. She had this deal going with Androvich, and she also probably had something going with a drummer named Mike Chirapadano. At any rate, she and Chirapadano vanished on exactly the same day, so that stinks of conspiracy. And she's also got her agent, a guy named Charlie Tudor, all butterflies in the stomach over her. So it seems to me she was playing the field in six positions. And if that doesn't spell tramp, it comes pretty close.'

He watched his wife's fingers as she answered him.

He interrupted, shouting, 'What do you mean, maybe she's just a friendly girl? We know she was shacking up with the sailor, and probably with the drummer, and probably with the agent as well. All big men, too. She goes for them big. A tramp with ...'

The drummer and the agent are only supposition, Teddy spelled with her hands. *The only one you have any sure knowledge of is the sailor.*

'I don't need any sure knowledge. I can read Bubbles Caesar from clear across the bay on a foggy day.'

I thought sure knowledge was the only thing a detective used.

'You're thinking of a lawyer who never asks a question unless he's sure of what the answer will be. I'm not a lawyer, I'm a cop. I have to ask the questions.'

Then ask them, and stop assuming that all strippers are ...

Carella interrupted her with a roar that almost woke the children. 'Assuming! Who's assuming?' he bellowed, finally involved in the argument he'd been seeking ever since he came home, a curious sort of argument in that Teddy's hands moved unemotionally, filled with words, while he yelled and ranted to her silent fingers. 'What does a girl have to do before I figure her for rotten? For all I know, she knocked off this guy Chirapadano and won't be happy until she's dropped his hands and his legs and his heart and his liver into the little paper sacks all over town! I won't be surprised if she cuts off his ...'

Don't be disgusting, Steve, Teddy cautioned with her hands.

'Where the hell is she? That's what I'd like to know,' Carella said. 'And where's Chirapadano? And whose damn hands are those? And where's the rest of the body? And what's the motive in this thing? There has to be a motive, doesn't there? People just don't go around killing other people, do they?'

You're the detective. You tell me.

'There's always a motive,' Carella said, 'that's for sure. Always. Dammit, if we only *knew* more. Did Bubbles and the drummer go off together? Did she dump the sailor because she wanted the drummer? And if so, did she get tired of him and knock him off? Then why cut off his hands, and where's the rest of the body? And if they aren't his hands, then whose are they? Or are Bubbles and the drummer even connected with the hands? Maybe we're off on a wild goose chase altogether. Boy, I wish I was a shoemaker.'

You do not wish you were a shoemaker, Teddy told him.

'Don't tell me what I wish,' Carella said. 'Boy, you're the most argumentative female I've ever met in my life. Come here and kiss me before we start a real fight. You've been looking for one ever since I got home.'

And Teddy, smiling, went into his arms.

Chapter Fourteen

The very next day, Carella got the fight he was spoiling for.

Oddly, the fight was with another cop.

This was rather strange because Carella was a fairly sensible man who realized how much his colleague could contribute to his job. He had certainly avoided any trouble on the squad prior to this, so it could only be assumed that the Hands Case – as the men had come to call it – was really getting him down.

The fight started very early in the morning, and it was one of those fights which seem to come about full-blown, with nothing leading up to them, like a summer storm which suddenly blackens the streets with rain. Carella was putting a call in to Taffy Smith, the other girl who'd shared the apartment with Bubbles Caesar. He mused that this damned case was beginning to resemble the cases of television's foremost private eye, with voluptuous cuties popping out of the woodwork wherever a man turned. He could not say he objected to the female pulchritude. It was certainly a lot more pleasant than investigating a case at an old ladies' home. At the same time, all these broads seemed to be leading nowhere, and it was this knowledge which rankled in him, and which probably led to the fight.

Hernandez was sitting at the desk alongside Carella's, typing a report. Sunshine sifted through the grilled windows and threw a shadowed lacework on the squadroom floor. The door to Lieutenant Byrnes' office was open. Someone had turned on the standing electric fan, not because it was really hot but only because the sunshine – after so much rain – created an illusion of heat.

'Miss Smith?' Carella said into the phone.

'Yes. Who's this, please?'

'Detective Carella of the 87th Detective Squad.'

'Oh, my goodness,' Taffy Smith said.

'Miss Smith, we'd like to talk to you about your missing roommate, Bubbles Caesar. Do you suppose we could stop by sometime today?'

'Oh. Well, gee, I don't know. I'm supposed to go to rehearsal.'

'What time is your rehearsal, Miss Smith?'

'Eleven o'clock.'

'And when will you be through?'

'Gee, that's awfully hard to say. Sometimes they last all day long. Although maybe this'll be a short one. We got an awful lot done yesterday.'

'Can you give me an approximate time?'

'I'd say about three o'clock. But I can't be sure. Look, let's say three, and you can call here before you leave your office, okay? Then if I'm delayed or anything, my service can give you the message. Okay? Would that be okay?'

'That'd be fine.'

'Unless you want me to leave the key. Then you could go in and make yourself a cup of coffee. Would you rather do that?'

'No, that's all right.'

'Okay, then, I'll see you at three, okay?'

'Fine,' Carella said.

'But be sure to call first, okay? And if I can't make it, I'll leave a message. Okay?'

'Thank you, Miss Smith,' Carella said, and he hung up.

Andy Parker came through the slatted rail divider and threw his hat at his desk. 'Man, what a day,' he said. 'Supposed to hit seventy today. Can you imagine that? In March? I guess all that rain drove winter clear out of the city.'

'I guess so,' Carella said. He listed the appointment with Taffy on his pad and made a note to call her at 2:30 before leaving the squadroom.

'This is the kind of weather you got back home, hey, Chico?' Parker said to Hernandez.

Frankie Hernandez, who'd been typing, did not hear Parker. He stopped the machine, looked up, and said, 'Huh? You talking to me, Andy?'

'Yeah. I said this is the kind of weather you got back home, ain't it?'

'Back home?' Hernandez said. 'You mean Puerto Rico?'

'Sure.'

'I was born here,' Hernandez said.

'Sure, I know,' Parker said. 'Every Puerto Rican you meet in the streets, he was born here. To hear them tell it, none of them ever came from the island. You'd never know there was a place called Puerto Rico, to hear them tell it.'

'That's not true, Andy,' Hernandez said gently. 'Most Puerto Ricans are very proud to have come from the island.'

'But not you, huh? You deny it.'

'I don't come from the island,' Hernandez said.

'No, that's right. You were born here, right?'

'That's right,' Hernandez said, and he began typing again.

Hernandez was not angry, and Parker didn't seem to be angry, and Carella hadn't even been paying any attention to the conversation. He was making out a tentative schedule of outside calls which he hoped he and Hawes could get to that day. He didn't even look up when Parker began speaking again.

'So that makes you an American, right, Chico?' Parker said.

This time, Hernandez heard him over the noise of the typewriter. This time, he looked up quickly and said, 'You talking to me?' But whereas the words were exactly the words he'd used the first time Parker had spoken, Hernandez delivered them differently this time, delivered them with a tightness, an intonation of unmistakable annoyance. His heart had begun to pound furiously. He knew that Parker was calling upon him to defend The Cause once more, and he did not particularly feel like defending anything on a beautiful morning like this one, but the gauntlet had been dropped, and there it lay, and so Hernandez hurled back his words.

'You talking to me?'

'Yes, I am talking to you, Chico,' Parker said. 'It's amazing how you damn people never hear anything when you don't want to hear ...'

'Knock it off, Andy,' Carella said suddenly.

Parker turned towards Carella's desk. 'What the hell's the matter with you?' he said.

'Knock it off, that's all. You're disturbing my squadroom.'

'When the hell did this become *your* squadroom?'

'I'm catching today, and it looks like your name isn't even listed on the duty chart. So why don't you go outside and find some trouble in the streets, if trouble is what you want?'

'When did you become the champion of the people?'

'Right this minute,' Carella said, and he shoved back his chair and stood up to face Parker.

'Yeah?' Parker said.

'Yeah,' Carella answered.

'Well, you can just blow it out your ...'

And Carella hit him.

He did not know he was going to throw the punch until after he had thrown it, until after it had collided with Parker's jaw and sent him staggering backwards against the railing. He knew then that he shouldn't have hit Parker, but at the same time he told himself he didn't feel like sitting around listening to Hernandez take a lot of garbage on a morning like this, and yet he knew he shouldn't have thrown the punch.

Parker didn't say a word. He shoved himself off the railing and lunged at Carella who chopped a short right to Parker's gut, doubling him over. Parker grabbed for his midsection and Carella delivered a rabbit punch to the back of Parker's neck, sending him sprawling over the desk.

Parker got up and faced Carella with new respect and with renewed malice. It was as if he'd forgotten for a moment that his opponent was as trained and as skilled as he himself was, forgotten that Carella could fight as clean or as dirty as the situation warranted, and that the situation generally warranted the dirtiest sort of fighting, and that this sort of fighting had become second nature.

'I'm gonna break you in half, Steve,' Parker said, and there was almost a chiding tone in his voice, the tone of warning a father uses to a child who is acting up.

He feinted with his left and as Carella moved to dodge the blow, he slammed a roundhouse right into his nose, bringing blood to it instantly. Carella touched his nose quickly, saw the blood, and then brought up his guard.

'Cut it out, you crazy bastards,' Hernandez said, stepping between them. 'The skipper's door is open. You want him to come out here?'

'Sure. Steve-oh doesn't care, do you, Steve? You and the skipper are real buddies, aren't you?'

Carella dropped his fists. Angrily, he said, 'We'll finish this another time, Andy.'

'You're damn right we will,' Parker said, and he stormed out of the squadroom.

Carella took a handkerchief from his back pocket and began dabbing at his nose. Hernandez put a cold key at the back of his neck.

'Thanks, Steve,' he said.

'Don't mention it,' Carella answered.

'You shouldn't have bothered. I'm used to Andy.'

'Yeah, but I guess I'm not.'

'Anyway, thanks.'

Hawes walked into the squadroom, saw Carella's bloody handkerchief, glanced hastily at the lieutenant's door, and then whispered, 'What happened?'

'I saw red,' Carella said.

Hawes glanced at the handkerchief again. 'You're *still* seeing red,' he said.

Taffy Smith was neither voluptuous, overblown, *zoftik*, nor even pretty. She was a tiny little girl with ash blonde hair trimmed very close to her head. She had the narrow bones of a sparrow, and a nose covered with freckles, and she wore harlequin glasses which shielded the brightest blue eyes Carella or Hawes had ever seen.

There was, apparently, great Freudian meaning to this girl's penchant for making coffee for strangers. Undoubtedly, as a child, she had witnessed her mother clobbering her father with a coffeepot. Or perhaps a pot of coffee had overturned, scalding her, and she now approached it as a threat to be conquered. Or perhaps she had been raised by a tyrannical aunt in Brazil where, so the song says, coffee beans grow by the millions. Whatever the case, she trotted into the kitchen and promptly got a pot going while the detectives sat down in the living room. The Siamese cat, remembering Hawes, sidled over to him and purred idiotically against his leg.

'Friend of yours?' Carella asked.

'I fed him once,' Hawes answered.

Taffy Smith came back into the living room. 'Gee, I'm bushed,' she said. 'We've been rehearsing all day long. We're doing *Detective Story* at the Y. I'm playing the shoplifter. It's an exhausting role, believe me.' She paused. 'We're all Equity players, you understand. This is just between jobs.'

'I understand,' Carella said.

'How do you like living with a pair of strippers?' Hawes asked.

'Fine,' Taffy said. 'Gee, what's wrong with strippers? They're swell girls.' She paused. 'I've been out of work for a long time now. Somebody's got to keep up the rent. They've been swell about it.'

'They?' Carella said.

'Barbara and Marla. Of course, Barbara's gone now. You know that. Listen, what does a B-sheet look like?'

'Huh?' Carella said.

'A B-sheet. It's mentioned in the play, it takes place in a detective squadroom, you know.'

'Yes, I know.'

'Sure, and a B-sheet is mentioned, and our prop man is going nuts trying to figure out what it looks like. Could you send me one?'

'Well, we're not supposed to give out official documents,' Hawes said.

'Gee, I didn't know that.' She paused. 'But we got a real pair of handcuffs. *They're* official, aren't they?'

'Yes. Where'd you get them?'

'Some fellow who used to be a cop. He's got connections.' She winked.

'Well, maybe we can send you a B-sheet,' Carella said. 'If you don't tell anyone where you got it.'

'Gee, that would be swell,' Taffy answered.

'About your roommate. Barbara. You said she was nice to live with. Didn't she seem a little wild at times?'

'Wild?'

'Yes.'

'You mean, did she break dishes? Something like that?'

'No. I mean men.'

'Barbara? Wild?'

'Yes. Didn't she entertain a lot of men here?'

'Barbara?' Taffy grinned infectiously. 'She never had a man in this apartment all the while I've been living here.'

'But she received telephone calls from men, didn't she?'

'Oh, sure.'

'And none of these men ever came here?'

'I never saw any. Oh, excuse me. That's the coffee.'

She went into the kitchen and returned instantly with the coffeepot and three cardboard containers.

'You'll have to excuse the paper cups,' she said, 'but we try to keep from washing too many dishes around here. We usually get a mob in every night for coffee, kids from all over who feel like talking or who just feel like sitting on a comfortable chair. We've got a nice place, don't you think?'

'Yes,' Carella said.

'I love to make coffee,' Taffy said. 'I guess I got in the habit when I was first married. I used to think that was the dream of marriage, do you know? I had the idea that marriage meant you could make a cup of coffee in your own house whenever you wanted to.' She grinned again. 'I guess that's why I'm divorced right now. Marriage is a lot more than making coffee, I suppose. Still I like to make coffee.'

She poured, went back to the kitchen with the pot, and then returned with cream, sugar, and wooden spoons.

'At these midnight get-togethers,' Carella said, 'where you make coffee – did Barbara hang around?'

'Oh, sure.'

'And she was friendly?'

'Oh, sure.'

'But she never brought any men here?'

'Never.'

'Never entertained any men here?'

'Never. You see, we only have the three rooms. The kitchen, the living room, and the bedroom. The bedroom has two beds, and this sofa opens into a bed, so that makes three beds. So we had to figure out a sort of a schedule. If one of the girls had a date and she thought she might be asking him in for a drink later, we had to keep the living room free. This really wasn't such a problem because Barbara never brought anyone home. So only Marla and I had to worry about it.'

'But Barbara *did* date men?'

'Oh, sure. Lots of them.'

'And if she felt like asking someone in for a drink, she didn't ask them in here, is that right?'

'That's right. Some more coffee?'

'No, thank you,' Hawes said. He had only taken a sip of the first cup.

'Then where did she take them?' Carella asked.

'I beg your pardon?'

'Her boy friends. Where did she go with them?'

'Oh, all over. Clubs, theatres, wherever they wanted to take her.'

'I meant, for that nightcap.'

'Maybe she went to their apartments.'

'She couldn't have gone to Androvich's apartment,' Carella said out loud.

'What was that?'

'There are hotels all over the city, Steve,' Hawes said.

'Yeah,' Carella said. 'Miss Smith, did Barbara ever say anything which would lead you to believe she had *another* apartment?'

'Another one? Why would she need another one? Do you know how much apartments cost in this city?'

'Yes, I do. But did she ever mention anything like that?'

'Not to me, she didn't. Why would she need another apartment?'

'Apparently, Miss Smith, Barbara was seeing a few men and was on ... rather friendly terms with them. An apartment shared with two other girls might have ... well, limited her activities somewhat.'

'Oh, I see what you mean,' Taffy said. She thought about this for a moment. Then she said, 'You're talking about Barbara? Bubbles?'

'Yes.'

Taffy shrugged. 'I never got the idea she was man-crazy. She didn't seem that interested in men.'

'She was ready to run off with one when she disappeared,' Carella said. 'And it's possible she disappeared with a second one.'

'Barbara?' Taffy said. 'Bubbles?'

'Barbara, yes. Bubbles.' Carella paused for a moment. 'I wonder if I could use your phone, Miss Smith?'

'Go right ahead. You can use this one, or the extension in the bedroom. Forgive the mess in there. My roommate is a slob.'

Carella went into the bedroom.

'Marla told me all about you,' Taffy said to Hawes in a whisper.

'She did?'

'Yes. Are you going to call her?'

'Well, I don't know. We've got to wrap up this case first.'

'Oh, sure,' Taffy agreed. 'She's a nice girl. Very sweet.'

'Yes, she seemed nice,' Hawes said. He felt very uncomfortable all at once.

'Do you work nights?' Taffy asked.

'Sometimes, yes.'

'Well, when you're off, why don't you stop by for a cup of coffee?'

'All right, maybe I will.'

'Good,' Taffy said, and she grinned.

Carella came back into the room. 'I just called Androvich's apartment,' he said. 'Thought he might be able to tell us whether or not Barbara was keeping another place.'

'Any luck?'

'He shipped out this morning,' Carella said. 'For Japan.'

Chapter Fifteen

There is a certain look that all big cities take on as five o'clock claims the day. It is a look reserved exclusively for big cities. If you were raised in a small town or a hamlet, you have never seen the look. If you were raised in one of those places that pretend to be huge metropolitan centres but which are in reality only overgrown small towns, you have only seen an imitation of the five o'clock big city look.

The city is a woman, you understand. It could be nothing but a woman. A small town can be the girl next door or an old man creaking in a rocker or a gangly teenager growing out of his dungarees, but the city could be none of these things, the city *is* and can only be a woman. And, like a woman, the city generates love and hate, respect and disesteem, passion and indifference. She is always the same city, always the same woman, but oh the faces she wears, oh the magic guile of this strutting bitch. And if you were born in one of her buildings, and if you know her streets and know her moods, then you love her. Your loving her is not a thing you can control. She has been with you from the start, from the first breath of air you sucked into your lungs, the air mixing cherry blossoms with carbon monoxide, the air of cheap perfume and fresh spring rain, the something in the city air that comes from nothing you can visualize or imagine, the *feel* of city air, the feel of life which you take into your lungs and into your body, this is the city.

And the city is a maze of sidewalks upon which you learned to walk, cracked concrete and sticky asphalt and cobblestones, a hundred thousand corners to turn, a hundred million surprises around each and every one of those corners. This is the city, she grins, she beckons, she cries, her streets are clean sometimes, and sometimes they rustle with fleeing newspapers that rush along the kerbstones in time to the beat of her heart. You look at her, and there are so many things to see, so many things to take into your mind and store there, so many things to remember, a myriad things to pile into a memory treasure chest, and you are in love with everything you see, the city can do no wrong, she is your lady love, and she is yours. You remember every subtle mood that crosses her face, you memorize her eyes, now startled, now tender, now weeping; you memorize her mouth in laughter, her windblown hair, the pulse in her throat. This is no casual love affair. She is as much a part of you as your fingerprints.

You are hooked.

You are hooked because she can change her face, this woman, and change her body, and all that was warm and tender can suddenly become cold and heartless – and still you are in love. You will be in love with her forever, no matter how she dresses, no matter how they change her, no matter who claims her, she is the same city you saw with the innocent eyes of youth, and she is yours.

And at five o'clock, she puts on a different look and you love this look, too; you love everything about her, her rages, her sultry petulance, everything; this is total love that seeks no excuses and no reasons. At five o'clock, her empty streets are suddenly alive with life. She has been puttering in a dusty drawing room all day long, this woman, this city, and now it is five o'clock and suddenly she emerges and you are waiting for her, waiting to clutch her in your arms. There is a jauntiness in her step, and yet it veils a weariness, and together they combine to form an image of past and present merged with a future promise. Dusk sits on the skyline, gently touching the sabre-edged buildings. Starlight is waiting to bathe her streets in silver. The lights of the city, incandescent and fluorescent and neon, are waiting to bracelet her arms and necklace her throat, to hang her with a million gaudy trappings which she does not need. You listen to the hurried purposeful click of her high-heeled pumps and somewhere in the distance there is the growl of a tenor saxophone, far in the distance because this is still five o'clock and the music will not really begin until later, the growl is still deep in the throat. For now, for the moment, there are the cocktail glasses and the muted hum of conversation, the chatter, the light laughter that floats on the air like the sound of shattering glass. And you sit with her, and you watch her eyes, meaningful and deep, and you question her every word, you want to know who she is and what she is, but you will never know. You will love this woman until the day you die, and you will never know her, never come even close to knowing her. Your love is a rare thing bordering on patriotic fervour. For in this city, in this woman, in this big brawling wonderful glittering tender heartless gentle cruel dame of a lady, there is the roar of a nation. If you were born and raised in the city, you cannot think of your country as anything but a giant metropolis. There are no small towns in your nation, there are no waving fields of grain, no mountains, no lakes, no seashores. For you, there is only the city, and she is yours, and love is blind.

Two men in love with the city, Detective Carella and Detective Hawes, joined the throng that rushed along her pavements at five o'clock that afternoon. They did not speak to each other for they were rivals for the same hand, and honourable men do not discuss the woman they both love. They walked into the lobby of the Creo Building and they took the elevator up to the eighteenth floor, and they walked down the deserted corridor to the end of the hall, and then they entered the office of Charles Tudor.

There was no one in the waiting room.

Tudor was locking the door to his inner office as they came in. He turned, still stooping over, the key in the keyhole. He nodded in recognition, finished locking the door, put the keys into his pocket, walked to them with an extended hand and said, 'Gentlemen. Any news?'

Carella took the proffered hand. 'Afraid not, Mr Tudor,' he answered. 'But we'd like to ask you a few more questions.'

'Certainly,' Tudor said. 'You don't mind if we sit here in the waiting room, do you? I've already locked up my private office.'

'This'll be fine,' Carella said.

They sat on the long couch against the wall covered with strippers.

'You said you were in love with Bubbles Caesar, Mr Tudor,' Carella said. 'Did you know that she was seeing at least one other man for certain, and possibly two other men?'

'Barbara?' Tudor asked.

'Yes. Did you know that?'

'No. I didn't.'

'Did you see her very often, Mr Tudor? We're not referring to your business relationship right now.'

'Yes. I saw her quite often.'

'How often?'

'Well, as often as I could.'

'Once a week? Twice a week? More than that? How often, Mr Tudor?'

'I suppose, on the average, I saw her three or four times a week.'

'And what did you do when you saw her, Mr Tudor?'

'Oh, various things.' Tudor gave a small shrug of puzzlement. 'What do people do when they go out? Dinner, dancing, the theatre, a motion picture, a drive in the country. All those things. Whatever we felt like doing.'

'Did you go to bed with her, Mr Tudor?'

'That is my business,' Tudor said flatly. '*And* Barbara's.'

'It might be ours, too, Mr Tudor. Oh, I know, it's a hell of a thing to ask, very personal. We don't like to ask, Mr Tudor. There are a lot of things we don't like to ask, but unfortunately we have to ask those things, whether we like to or not. I'm sure you can understand.'

'No, I'm afraid I cannot,' Tudor said with finality.

'Very well, we'll assume you were intimate with her.'

'You may assume whatever you wish,' Tudor said.

'Where do you live, Mr Tudor?'

'On Blakely Street.'

'Downtown? In The Quarter?'

'Yes.'

'Near Barbara's apartment?'

'Fairly close to it, yes.'

'Did you ever go to Barbara's apartment?'

'No.'

'You never picked her up there?'

'No.'

'But you were seeing her?'

'Yes, of course I was seeing her.'

'And yet you never went to her apartment. Isn't that a little odd?'

'Is it? I despise the housing facilities of most working girls, Detective Carella. When I call on a young lady, I find the curiosity of her roommates unbearable. And so, whenever a young lady shares an apartment with someone else, I prefer to meet her away from the apartment. That is the arrangement I had with Barbara.'

'And apparently an arrangement she preferred. The girls she lived with tell us no man ever came to that apartment to pick her up or take her home. What do you think of that, Mr Tudor?'

Tudor shrugged. 'I am certainly not responsible for Barbara's idiosyncrasies.'

'Certainly not. Did Barbara ever come to your apartment?'

'No.'

'Why not?'

'I live with my father,' Tudor said. 'He's a very old man. Practically ... well, he's very sick. I'm not sure he would have understood Barbara. Or approved of her. And so he never met her.'

'You kept her away from your apartment. Is that right?'

'That is correct.'

'I see.' Carella thought for a moment. He looked at Hawes.

'Where'd you neck, Mr Tudor?' Hawes asked. 'In the back seat of an automobile?'

'That is none of your business,' Tudor said.

'Would you know whether or not Barbara had another apartment?' Hawes asked. 'Besides the one she shared with the two girls?'

'If she had one, I never saw it,' Tudor said.

'You're not married, of course,' Carella said.

'No, I'm not married.'

'Ever married, Mr Tudor?'

'Yes.'

'What's the status now? Separated? Divorced?'

'Divorced. For a long time now, Detective Carella. At least fifteen years.'

'What's your ex-wife's name?'

'Toni Traver. She's an actress. Rather a good one, too.'

'She in this city?'

'I'm sure I don't know. I was divorced from her fifteen years ago. I ran into her in Philadelphia once about eight years ago. I haven't seen her since. Nor do I care to.'

'You paying her alimony, Mr Tudor?'

'She didn't want any. She has money of her own.'

'Does she know about you and Barbara?'

'I don't know. She couldn't care less, believe me.'

'Mmmm,' Carella said. 'And you didn't know about these two other guys Barbara was seeing, right?'

'Right.'

'But surely, if she was seeing them, and if you called for a date or something, she must have said she was busy on that night, no? Didn't you ever ask how come? Didn't you want to know *why* she was busy?'

'I am not a possessive man,' Tudor said.

'But you loved her.'

'Yes. I loved her, and I still love her.'

'Well, how do you feel about it now? Now that you know she was dating two other men, maybe sleeping with both of them, how do you feel about it?'

'I ... naturally, I'm not pleased.'

'No, I didn't think you would be. Did you ever meet a man named Karl Androvich, Mr Tudor?'

'No.'

'How about a man named Mike Chirapadano?'

'No.'

'Ever go to The King and Queen?'

'Yes, of course. I sometimes picked Barbara up at the club.'

'Mike was a drummer in the band there.'

'Really?'

'Yes.' Carella paused. 'He seems to have vanished, Mr Tudor.'

'Really?'

'Yes. At the same time that Barbara did. What do you think of that?'

'I don't know what to think.'

'Think they ran off together?'

'I'm sure I don't know.'

'Do you have a black raincoat and umbrella, Mr Tudor?'

'No, I don't. A what? A black raincoat, did you say?'

'Yes, that's what I said.'

'No, I don't have one.'

'But you do have a raincoat?'

'Yes. A trench coat. It's grey. Or beige. You know, a neutral sort of . . .'

'And the umbrella? Is it a man's umbrella?'

'I don't have an umbrella. I detest umbrellas.'

'Never carry one, right?'

'Never.'

'And you don't know of any other apartment Barbara might have kept, right?'

'I don't know of any, no.'

'Well, thank you very much, Mr Tudor,' Carella said. 'You've been most helpful.'

'Not at all,' Tudor answered.

Outside in the hallway, Carella said, 'He smells, Cotton. Wait for him downstairs and tail him, will you? I'll be back at the squadroom. I want to check on his ex-wife, see if I can get a line on her.'

'What are you thinking of? Jealousy?'

'Who knows? But some torches have been known to burn for more than fifteen years. Why not hers?'

'The way he put it . . .'

'Sure, but every word he spoke could have been a lie.'

'True.'

'Trail him. Get back to me. I'll be waiting for your call.'

'Where do you expect him to lead me?'

'I don't know, Cotton.'

Carella went back to the squadroom. He learned that Toni Traver was a fairly good character actress and that she was at the moment working in a stock playhouse in Sarasota, Florida. Carella talked to her agent who told him that Miss Traver was not accepting alimony from her ex-husband. In fact, the agent said, he and Miss Traver had wedding plans of their own. Carella thanked him and hung up.

At eight p.m. that night, Cotton Hawes called in to report that Tudor had shaken the tail at seven-thirty.

'I'm sorry as hell,' he said.

'Yeah,' Carella answered.

Chapter Sixteen

The clothes turned up the next morning.

They were wrapped in a copy of the *New York Times*. A patrolman in Calm's Point found them in a trash basket. His local precinct called Headquarters because there was a bloodstain on the black raincoat, and Headquarters promptly called the 87th. The clothes were sent to the lab where Grossman inspected them thoroughly.

Besides the raincoat, there was a black flannel suit, a pair of black lisle socks, and a black umbrella.

An examination of the clothing turned up some rather contradictory facts, and all of these were passed on to Carella who studied them and then scratched his head in puzzlement.

To begin with, the bloodstain on the raincoat belonged to the 'O' group, which seemed to tie it in with the hands, and to further tie in with Mike Chirapadano whose service record had listed him as belonging to that blood group. But a careful examination of the black suit had turned up a subsequent small bloodstain on the sleeve. And this bloodstain belonged to the 'B' group. That was the first contradiction.

The second contradiction seemed puzzling all over again. It had to do with three other stains which were found on the black suit. The first of these was of a hair preparation, found on the inside of the collar where the collar apparently brushed against the nape of the neck. The stain was identified as coming from a tonic called Strike. It was allegedly designed for men who had oily scalps and who did not wish to compound the affliction by using an oily hair tonic.

But side by side with this stain was the second stain, and it had been caused by a preparation known as Dram, which was a hair tonic designed to fight dandruff and dry, flaky scalps. It seemed odd that these two scalp conditions could exist in one and the same man. It seemed contradictory that a person with a dry, flaky scalp would also be a person with an oily scalp. Somehow, the two hair preparations did not seem very compatible.

The third stain on the suit jacket was identified as coming from the selfsame Skinglow cosmetic which had been found in the corner of the airline bag, and this led to some confusion as to whether a man or a woman had worn the damn suit. Carella concluded that a man had worn it, but that he had embraced a woman wearing Skinglow. This accounted for that stain, but not for the hair tonic stains which were still puzzling and contradictory.

But there were more contradictions. The human hairs that clung to the fibre of the suit, for example. Some were brown and thin. Others were black and thick and short. And still others were black and thin and very long. The very long black ones presumably were left on the suit by the dame who'd worn the Skinglow. That embrace was shaping up as a very passionate one. But the thin brown hairs? And the thick black short ones? Puzzlement upon puzzlement.

About one thing, there was no confusion. There was a label inside the jacket, and the label clearly read: *Urban-Suburban Clothes.*

Carella looked up the name in the telephone directory, came up with a winner, clipped on his holster, and left the squadroom.

Cotton Hawes was somewhere in the city glued to Charles Tudor, whose trail he had picked up again early in the morning.

Urban-Suburban Clothes was one of those tiny shops which are sandwiched in between two larger shops and which would be missed entirely were it not for the colourful array of offbeat clothes in the narrow window. Carella opened the door and found himself in a long narrow cubicle which had been designed as a coffin for one man and which now held twelve men, all of whom were pawing through ties and feeling the material of sports coats and holding Italian sports shirts up against their chests. He felt an immediate attack of claustrophobia, which he controlled, and then he began trying to determine which of the twelve men in the shop was the owner. It occurred to him that thirteen was an unlucky number, and he debated leaving. He was carrying the bundle of clothes wrapped in brown paper and the bundle was rather bulky and this did not ease the crowded atmosphere of the shop at all. He squeezed past two men who were passing out cold over the off-orange tint of a sports shirt which had no buttons.

'Excuse me,' he said, 'excuse me.' And he executed an off-tackle run around a group of men who were huddled at the tie rack. The ties apparently were made of Indian madras in colours the men were declaring to be simultaneously 'cool', 'wild', and 'crazy'. Carella felt hot, tamed, and very sane.

He kept looking for the owner of the shop, and finally a voice came at his elbow. 'May I help you, sir?' And a body materialized alongside the voice. Carella whirled to face a thin man with a Fu Manchu beard, wearing a tight brown suit over a yellow weskit, and leering like a sex maniac in a nudist camp.

'Yes, yes, you can,' Carella said. 'Are you the owner of this shop?'

'Jerome Jerralds,' the young man said, and he grinned.

'How do you do, Mr Jerralds?' Carella said. 'I'm ...'

'Trouble?' Jerralds said, eyeing the bundle of wrapped clothes. 'One of our garments didn't fit you properly?'

'No, it's ...'

'Did you make the purchase yourself, or was it a gift?'

'No, this ...'

'You didn't buy the garment yourself?'

'No,' Carella said. 'I'm a ...'

'Then it was a gift?'

'No, I'm ...'

'Then how did you get it, sir?'

'The police lab sent the clothes over,' Carella answered.

'The poli – ?' Jerralds started, and his hand went up to stroke the Chinese beard, a cat's-eye ring gleaming on his pinky.

'I'm a cop,' Carella explained.

'Oh?'

'Yeah. I've got a pile of clothes here. I wonder if you can tell me anything about them.'

'Well, I ...'

'I know you're busy, and I won't take much of your time.'

'Well, I ...'

Carella had already unwrapped the package. 'There's a label in the suit,' he said. '*Urban-Suburban Clothes*. This your suit?'

Jerralds studied it. 'Yes, that is our suit.'

'How about the raincoat? It looks like the kind of thing you might sell, but the label's been torn out. Is it your coat?'

'What do you mean, it looks like the kind of thing we might sell?'

'Stylish,' Carella said.

'Oh, I see.'

'With a flair,' Carella said.

'Yes, I see.'

'Important-looking,' Carella said.

'Yes, yes.'

'Cool,' Carella said. 'Wild. Crazy.'

'That's our raincoat, all right,' Jerralds said.

'How about this umbrella?'

'May I see it, please?'

Carella handed him the tagged umbrella.

'No, that's not ours,' Jerralds said. 'We try to offer something different in men's umbrellas. For example, we have one with a handle made from a ram's horn, and another fashioned from a Tibetan candlestick which ...'

'But this one is yours, right?'

'No. Were you interested in ...'

'No, I don't need an umbrella,' Carella said. 'It's stopped raining, you know.'

'Oh, has it?'

'Several days ago.'

'Oh. It gets so crowded in here sometimes ...'

'Yes I can understand. About this suit and this raincoat, can you tell me who bought them?'

'Well, that would be difficult to ...' Jerralds stopped. His hand fluttered to the jacket of the suit, landed on the sleeve, scraped at the stain there. 'Seem to have got something on the sleeve,' he said.

'Blood,' Carella answered.

'Wh – ?'

'Blood. That's a bloodstain. You sell many of these suits, Mr Jerralds?'

'Blood, well it's a popular ... blood? Blood?' He stared at Carella.

'It's a popular number?' Carella said.

'Yes.'

'In this size?'

'What size is it?'

'A forty-two.'

'That's a big size.'

'Yes. The suit was worn by a big man. The raincoat's big, too. Can you remember selling both these items to anyone? There's also a pair of black socks here someplace. Just a second.' He dug up the socks. 'These look familiar?'

'Those are our socks, yes. Imported from Italy. They have no seam, you see, manufactured all in one ...'

'Then the suit, the raincoat and the socks are yours. So the guy is either a steady customer, or else someone who stopped in and made all the purchases at one time. Can you think of anyone? Big guy, size forty-two suit?'

'May I see the suit again, please?'

Carella handed him the jacket.

'This is a very popular number,' Jerralds said, turning the jacket over in his hands. 'I really couldn't estimate how many of them we sell each week. I don't see how I could possibly identify the person who bought it.'

'There wouldn't be any serial numbers on it anywhere?' Carella asked. 'On the label maybe? Or sewn into the suit someplace?'

'No, nothing like that,' Jerralds said. He flipped the suit over and studied both shoulders. 'There's a high padding on this right shoulder,' he said almost to himself. To Carella, he said, 'That's odd because the shoulders are supposed to be unpadded, you see. That's the look we try to achieve. A natural, flowing ...'

'So what does the padding on that right shoulder mean?'

'I don't know, unless ... Oh, wait a minute, wait a minute. Yes, yes, I'll bet this is the suit.'

'Go ahead,' Carella said.

'This gentlemen came in, oh, it must have been shortly after Christmas. A very tall man, very well built. A very handsome man.'

'Yes?'

'He ... well, one leg was slightly shorter than the other. A half-inch, a quarter-inch, something like that. Not serious enough to produce a limp, you understand, but just enough to throw the line of his body slightly out of kilter. I understand there are a great number of men whose ...'

'Yes, but what about this particular man?'

'Nothing special. Except that we had to build up the right shoulder of the jacket, pad it, you know. To compensate for that shorter leg.'

'And this is that jacket?'

'I would think so, yes.'

'Who bought it?'

'I don't know.'

'He wasn't a regular customer of yours?'

'No. He came in off the street. Yes, I remember now. He bought the suit, and the raincoat, and several pairs of socks, and black knit tie. I remember now.'

'But you don't remember his name?'

'No, I'm sorry.'

'Do you keep sales slips?'

'Yes, but ...'

'Do you list a customer's name on the slip?'

'Yes, but . . .'

'But what?'

'This was shortly after Christmas. January. The beginning of January.'

'So?'

'Well, I'd have to go through a pile of records to get to . . .'

'I know,' Carella said.

'We're very busy now,' Jerralds said. 'As you can see . . .'

'Yes, I can see.'

'This is Saturday, one of our busiest days. I'm afraid I couldn't take the time to . . .'

'Mr Jerralds, we're investigating a murder,' Carella said.

'Oh.'

'Do you think you can take the time?'

'Well . . .' Jerralds hesitated. 'Very well, would you come into the back of the store, please?'

He pushed aside a curtain. The back of the store was a small cubbyhole piled high with goods in huge cardboard boxes. A man in jockey shorts was pulling on a pair of pants in front of a full length mirror.

'This doubles as a dressing room,' Jerralds explained. 'Those trousers are just for you, sir,' he said to the half-clad man. 'This way; my desk is over here.'

He led Carella to a small desk set before a dirty, barred window.

'January, January,' he said, 'now where would the January stuff be?'

'Is this supposed to be so tight?' the man in trousers said.

'Tight?' Jerralds asked. 'It doesn't look at all tight, sir.'

'It feels tight to me,' the man said. 'Maybe I'm not used to these pants without pleats. What do you think?' he asked Carella.

'Look okay to me,' Carella said.

'Maybe I'm just not used to it,' the man answered.

'Maybe so.'

'They look wonderful,' Jerralds said. 'That colour is a new one. It's sort of off-green. Green and black, a mixture.'

'I thought it was grey,' the man said, studying the trousers more carefully.

'Well, it looks like grey, and it looks like green, and it also looks like black. That's the beauty of it,' Jerralds said.

'Yeah?' The man looked at the trousers again. 'It's a nice colour,' he said dubiously. He thought for a moment, seeking an escape. 'But they're too tight,' and he began pulling off the trousers. 'Excuse me,' he said, hopping on one leg and crashing into Carella. 'It's a little crowded back here.'

'The January file should be . . .' Jerralds touched one temple with his forefinger and knotted his brow. The finger came down like the finger of doom circling in the air and then dived, tapping a carton which rested several feet from the desk. Jerralds opened the carton and began rummaging among the sales slips.

The man threw the trousers onto the desk and said, 'I like the colour, but they're too tight.' He walked to the carton over which he had draped his own trousers and began pulling them on. 'I can't stand tight pants, can you?' he asked Carella.

'No,' Carella answered.

'I like a lot of room,' the man said.

'No, this is February,' Jerralds said. 'Now where the devil did I put the January slips? Let me think,' and again the finger touched his temple, hesitated there until the light of inspiration crossed his bearded face, and then zoomed like a Stuka to a new target. He opened the second carton and pulled out a sheaf of sales slips.

'Here we are,' he said. 'January. Oh, God, this is going to be awful. We had a clearance sale in January. After Christmas, you know. There are *thousands* of slips here.'

'Well, thanks a lot,' the man said, secure in his own loose trousers now. 'I like a lot of room, you understand.'

'I understand,' Jerralds said as he leafed through the sales slips.

'I'll drop in again sometime. I'm a cab driver, you see. I need a lot of room. After all, I sit on my ass all day long.'

'I understand,' Jerralds said. 'I think it was the second week in January. After the sale. Let me try those first.'

'Well, so long,' the cab driver said. 'Nice meeting you.'

'Take it easy,' Carella answered, and the cabbie pushed through the hanging curtains and into the front of the shop.

'Three shirts at four-fifty per ... no, that's not it. This *is* a job, you know. If you weren't such a nice person, I doubt if I'd ... one pair of swim trunks at ... no ... ties, no ... one raincoat black one suit charcoal, three pair lisle ... here it is, here it is,' Jerralds said. 'I thought so. January tenth. Yes, it was a cash sale.'

'And the man's name?'

'It should be on the top of the slip here. It's a little difficult to read. The carbon isn't too clear.'

'Can you make it out?' Carella asked.

'I'm not sure. Chirapadano, does that sound like a name? Michael Chirapadano?'

Chapter Seventeen

The landlady said, 'Are you here again? Where's your redheaded friend?'

'Working on something,' Carella said. 'I'd like to go through Chira-padano's room again. That okay with you?'

'Why? You got a clue?'

'Maybe.'

'He owes me two months' rent,' the landlady said. 'Come on, I'll take you up.'

They walked upstairs. She cleaned the banister with an oily cloth as they went up. She led Carella to the apartment and was taking out the key when she stopped. Carella had heard the sound, too. His gun was already in his hand. He moved the landlady to one side and was backing off against the opposite wall when she whispered, 'For God's sake, don't break it in. Use my key, for God's sake.'

He took the key from her, inserted it into the lock, and twisted it as quietly as he could. He turned the knob then and shoved against the door. The door would not budge. He heard a frantic scurrying inside the apartment, and he shouted, 'Goddamnit!' and hurled his shoulder against the door, snapping it inward.

A tall man stood in the centre of the room, a bass drum in his hand.

'Hold it, Mike!' Carella shouted, and the man threw the bass drum at him, catching him full in the chest, knocking him backwards and against the landlady who kept shouting, 'I told you not to break it in! Why didn't you use the key!'

The man was on Carella now. He did not say a word. There was a wild gleam in his eyes as he rushed Carella, disregarding the gun in Carella's fist as the landlady screamed her admonitions. He threw a left that caught Carella on the cheek and was drawing back his right when Carella swung the .38 in a side-swiping swing that opened the man's cheek. The man staggered backwards, struggling for balance, tripping over the rim of the bass drum and crashing through the skin. He began crying suddenly, a pitiful series of sobs that erupted from his mouth.

'Now you broke it,' he said. 'Now you went and broke it.'

'Are you Mike Chirapadano?' Carella asked.

'That ain't him,' the landlady said. 'Why'd you break the door in? You cops are all alike! Why didn't you use the key like I told you?'

'I *did* use the damn key,' Carella said angrily. 'All it did was lock the door. The door was already open. You sure this isn't Chirapadano?'

'Of course I'm sure. How could the door have been open? I locked it myself.'

'Our friend here probably used a skeleton key on it. How about that, Mac?' Carella asked.

'Now you broke it,' the man said. 'Now you went and broke it.'

'Broke what?'

'The drum. You broke the damn drum.'

'You're the one who broke it,' Carella said.

'You hit me,' the man said. 'I wouldn't have tripped if you hadn't hit me.'

'Who are you? What's your name? How'd you get in here?'

'You figure it out, big man.'

'Why'd you leave the door unlocked?'

'Who expected anyone to come up here?'

'What do you want here anyway? Who are you?'

'I wanted the drums.'

'Why?'

'To hock them.'

'Mike's drums?'

'Yes.'

'All right, now who are you?'

'What do you care? You broke the bass drum. Now I can't hock it.'

'Did Mike ask you to hock his drums?'

'No.'

'You were stealing them?'

'I was borrowing them.'

'Sure. What's your name?'

'Big man. Has a gun, so he thinks he's a big man.' He touched his bleeding face. 'You cut my cheek.'

'That's right,' Carella said. 'What's your name?'

'Larry Daniels.'

'How do you know Chirapadano?'

'We played in the same band.'

'Where?'

'The King and Queen.'

'You a good friend of his?'

Daniels shrugged.

'What instrument do you play?'

'Trombone.'

'Do you know where Mike is?'

'No.'

'But you knew he wasn't here, didn't you? Otherwise you wouldn't have sneaked up here with your skeleton key and tried to steal his drums. Isn't that right?'

'I wasn't stealing them. I was borrowing them. I was going to give him the pawn ticket when I saw him.'

'Why'd you want to hock the drums?'

'I need some loot.'

'Why don't you hock your trombone?'

'I already hocked the horn.'

'You the junkie Randy Simms was talking about?'

'Who?'

'Simms. Randy Simms. The guy who owns The King and Queen. He said the trombone player on the band was a junkie. That you, Daniels?'

'Okay, that's me. It ain't no crime to be an addict. Check the law. It ain't no crime. And I got no stuff on me, so put that in your pipe and smoke it. You ain't got me on a goddamn thing.'

'Except attempted burglary,' Carella said.

'Burglary, my ass. I was borrowing the drums.'

'How'd you know Mike wouldn't be here?'

'I knew, that's all.'

'Sure. But how? Do you know where he is right this minute?'

'No, I don't know.'

'But you knew he wasn't here.'

'I don't know nothing.'

'A dope fiend,' the landlady said. 'I knew it.'

'Where is he, Daniels?'

'Why do you want him?'

'We want him.'

'Why?'

'Because he owns a suit of clothes that may be connected with a murder. And if you withhold information from us, you can be brought in as an accessory after the fact. Now how about that, Daniels? Where is he?'

'I don't know. That's the truth.'

'When did you see him last?'

'Just before he made it with the dame.'

'What dame?'

'The stripper.'

'Bubbles Caesar?'

'That's her name.'

'When was this, Daniels?'

'I don't remember the date exactly. It was around Valentine's Day. A few days before.'

'The twelfth?'

'I don't remember.'

'Mike didn't show up for work on the night of the twelfth. Was that the day you saw him?'

'Yeah. That's right.'

'When did you see him?'

'In the afternoon sometime.'

'And what did he want?'

'He told me he wouldn't be on the gig that night, and he gave me the key to his pad.'

'Why'd he do that?'

'He said he wanted me to take his drums home for him. So when we quit playing that night, that's what I done. I packed up his drums and took them here.'

'So that's how you got in today. You still have Mike's key.'

'Yeah.'

'And that's how you knew he wouldn't be here. He never did get that key back from you, did he?'

'Yeah, that's right.' Daniels paused. 'I was supposed to call him the next day and we was supposed to meet so I could give him the key. Only I called, and there was no answer. I called all that day, but nobody answered the phone.'

'This was the thirteenth of February?'

'Yeah, the next day.'

'And he had told you he would be with Bubbles Caesar?'

'Well, not directly. But when he give me the key and the telephone number, he made a little joke, you know? He said, "Larry, don't be calling me in the middle of the night because Bubbles and me, we are very deep sleepers." Like that. So I figured he would be making it with Bubbles that night. Listen, I'm beginning to get itchy. I got to get out of here.'

'Relax, Daniels. What was the phone number Mike gave you?'

'I don't remember. Listen, I got to get a shot. I mean, now listen, I ain't kidding around here.'

'What was the number?'

'For Christ's sake, who remembers? This was last month, for Christ's sake. Look, now look, I ain't kidding here. I mean, I got to get out of here. I know the signs, and this is gonna be bad unless I get ...'

'Did you write the number down?'

'What?'

'The number. Did you write it down?'

'I don't know, I don't know,' Daniels said, but he pulled out his wallet and began going through it, muttering all the while, 'I have to get a shot, I have to get fixed, I have to get out of here,' his hands trembling as he riffled through the wallet's compartments. 'Here,' he said at last, 'here it is, here's the number. Let me out of here before I puke.'

Carella took the card.

'You can puke at the station house,' he said.

The telephone number was Economy 8–3165.

At the squadroom, Carella called the telephone company and got an operator who promptly told him she had no record of any such number.

'It may be an unlisted number,' Carella said. 'Would you please check it?'

'If it's an unlisted number, sir, I would have no record of it.'

'Look, this is the police department,' Carella said. 'I know you're not supposed to divulge ...'

'It is not a matter of not divulging the number, sir. It is simply that I would have no record of it. What I'm trying to tell you, sir, is that we do *not* have a list labelled "Unlisted Numbers". Do you understand me, sir?'

'Yes, I understand you,' Carella said. 'But the telephone company has a record of it someplace, doesn't it? Somebody pays the damn bill. Somebody *gets* the bill each month. All I want to know is who gets it?'

'I'm sorry, sir, but I wouldn't know who ...'

'Let me talk to your supervisor,' Carella said.

Charles Tudor had begun walking from his home in The Quarter, and Cotton Hawes walked directly behind him. At a respectable distance, to be sure. It was a wonderful day for walking, a day that whetted the appetite for spring. It was a day for idling along and stopping at each and every store window, a day for admiring the young ladies who had taken off their coats and blossomed earlier than the flowers.

Tudor did not idle, and Tudor did not admire. Tudor walked at a rapid clip, his head ducked, his hands thrust into the pockets of his topcoat, a big man who shouldered aside any passerby who got in his way. Hawes, an equally big man, had a tough time keeping up with him. The sidewalks of The Quarter on that lovely Saturday were cluttered with women pushing baby carriages, young girls strutting with high-tilted breasts, young men wearing faded tight jeans and walking with the lope of male dancers, young men sporting beards and paint-smeared sweat shirts, girls wearing leotards over which were Bermuda shorts, old men carrying canvases decorated with pictures of the ocean, Italian housewives from the neighbourhood carrying shopping bags bulging with long breads, young actresses wearing make-up to rehearsals in the many little theatres that dotted the side streets, kids playing Johnny-on-the-Pony.

Hawes could have done without the display of humanity. If he were to keep up with Tudor, he'd have to ...

He stopped suddenly.

Tudor had gone into a candy store on the corner. Hawes quickened his pace. He didn't know whether or not there was a back entrance to the store, but he had lost Tudor the night before, and he didn't want to lose him again. He walked past the candy store and around the corner. There was only one entrance, and he could see Tudor inside making a purchase. He crossed the street quickly, took up a post in the doorway of a tenement, and waited for Tudor to emerge. When Tudor came out, he was tearing the cellophane top from a package of cigarettes. He did not stop to light the cigarette. He lighted it as he walked along, three matches blowing out before he finally got a stream of smoke.

Doggedly, Hawes plodded along behind him.

'Good afternoon, sir, this is your supervisor; may I help you, sir?'

'Yes,' Carella said. 'This is Detective Carella of the 87th Squad up here in Isola,' he said, pulling his rank. 'We have a telephone number we're trying to trace, and it seems ...'

'Did the call originate from a dial telephone, sir?'

'What call?'

'Because if it did, sir, it would be next to impossible to trace it. A dial telephone utilizes automatic equipment and ...'

'Yes I know that. We're not trying to trace a call, operator, we're trying to ...'

'I'm the supervisor, sir.'

'Yes, I know. We're ...'

'On the other hand, if the call was made from a manual instrument, the possibilities of tracing it would be a little better. Unless it got routed eventually through automatic ...'

'Lady, I'm a cop, and I know about tracing telephone calls, and all I want you to do is look up a number and tell me the party's name and address. That's all I want you to do.'

'I see.'

'Good. The number is Economy 8–3165. Now would you please look that up and give me the information I want?'

'Just one moment, sir.'

Her voice left the line. Carella drummed impatiently on the desk top. Bert Kling, fully recovered, furiously typed up a D.D. report at the adjoining desk.

Tudor was making another stop. Hawes cased the shop from his distant vantage point. It was set between two other shops in a row of tenements, and so the possibility of another entrance was unlikely. If there *was* another entrance, it would not be one accessible to customers of the shop.

Hawes lighted a cigarette and waited for Tudor to make his purchase and come into the street again.

He was in the shop for close to fifteen minutes.

When he came out, he was carrying some white gardenias.

Oh great, Hawes thought, *he's going to see a dame.*

And then he wondered if the dame could be Bubbles Caesar.

'Sir, this is your supervisor.'

'Yes?' Carella said. 'Have you got ...?'

'You understand, sir, that when a person requests an unlisted or un-published telephone number, we ...'

'I'm not a person,' Carella said, 'I'm a cop.' He wrinkled his brow and thought that one over for a second.

'Yes, sir, but I'm referring to the person whose telephone number this is. When that person requests an unpublished number, we make certain that he understands what this means. It means that there will be no record of the listing available, and that no one will be able to get the number from anyone in the telephone company, even upon protest of an emergency condition existing. You understand that, sir?'

'Yes, I do. Lady, I'm a cop investigating a murder. Now will you please ...'

'Oh, I'll give you the information you requested. I certainly will.'

'Then what ...?'

'But I want you to know that an ordinary citizen could not under any circumstances get the same information. I simply wanted to make the telephone company's policy clear.'

'Oh, it's perfectly clear, operator.'

'Supervisor,' she corrected.

'Yes, sure. Now who's that number listed for, and what's the address?'

'The phone is in a building on Canopy Street. The address is 1611.'

'Thank you. And the owner of the phone?'

'No one *owns* our telephones, sir. You realize that our instruments are provided on a rental basis, and that ...'

'Whose name is that phone listed under, oper – supervisor? Would you please ...'

'The listing is for a man named Charles Tudor,' the supervisor said.

'Charles Tudor?' Carella said. 'Now what the hell ...?'

'Sir?' the supervisor asked.

'Thank you,' Carella said, and he hung up. He turned to Kling. 'Bert,' he said, 'get your hat.'

'I don't wear any,' Kling said, so he clipped on his holster instead.

Charles Tudor had gone into 1611 Canopy Street, unlocked the inner vestibule door, and vanished from sight.

Hawes stood in the hallway now and studied the mailboxes. None of them carried a nameplate for Bubbles Caesar or Charles Tudor or Mike Chirapadano or anyone at all with whom Hawes was familiar. Hawes examined the mailboxes again, relying upon one of the most elementary pieces of police knowledge in his second study of the nameplates. For reasons known only to God and psychiatrists, when a person assumes a fictitious name, the assumed name will generally have the same initials as the person's real name. Actually, this isn't a mystery worthy of supernatural or psychiatric secrecy. The simple fact is that a great many people own monogrammed handkerchiefs, or shirts, or suitcases, or dispatch cases, or whatever. And if a man named Benjamin Franklin who has the initials B. F. on his bags and his shirts and his underwear and maybe tattooed on his forehead should suddenly register in a hotel as George Washington, a curious clerk might wonder whether or not Benjy came by his luggage in an illegal manner. Since a man using an assumed name is a man who is not anxious to attract attention, he will do everything possible to make things easier for himself. And so he will use the initials of his real name in choosing an alias.

One of the mailboxes carried a nameplate for a person called Christopher Talley.

It sounded phoney, and it utilized the C. T. initials, and so Hawes made a mental note of the apartment number: 6B.

Then he pressed the bell for apartment 2A, waited for the answering buzz that released the inner door lock, and rapidly climbed the steps to the sixth floor. Outside apartment 6B, he put his ear to the door and listened. Inside the apartment, a man was talking.

'Barbara,' the man said, 'I brought you some more flowers.'

In the police sedan, Carella said, 'I don't get it, Bert. I just don't get it.'

'What's the trouble?' Kling asked.

'No trouble. Only confusion. We find a pair of hands, and the blood group is identified as "O", right?'

'Right.'

'Okay. Mike Chirapadano is in that blood group. He's also a big guy, and he vanished last month, and so that would make him a good prospect for the *victim*, am I right?'

'Right,' Kling said.

'Okay. But when we find the clothes the murderer was wearing, it turns out they belonged to Mike Chirapadano. So it turns out that he's a good prospect for the *murderer*, too.'

'Yeah?' Kling said.

'Yeah. Then we get a line on Bubbles Caesar's hideout, the place she and Chirapadano used, the place we're going to right now ...'

'Yeah?'

'Yeah; and it turns out the phone is listed for Charles Tudor, Bubbles' agent. Now how does that figure?'

'There's 1611 up ahead,' Kling said.

Standing in the hallway, Hawes could hear only the man's voice, and the voice definitely belonged to Charles Tudor. He wondered whether or not he should crash the apartment. Scarcely daring to breathe, trying desperately to hear the girl's replies, he kept his ear glued to the wood of the door, listening.

'Do you like the flowers, Barbara?' Tudor said.

There was a pause. Hawes listened, but could hear no reply.

'I didn't know whether or not you liked gardenias, but we have so many of the others in here. Well, a beautiful woman should have lots of flowers.'

Another pause.

'You *do* like gardenias?' Tudor said. 'Good. You look beautiful today, Barbara. Beautiful. I don't think I've ever seen you looking so beautiful. Did I tell you about the police?'

Hawes listened for the reply. He thought instantly of Marla Phillips' tiny voice, and he wondered if all big girls were naturally endowed with the same voices. He could not hear a word.

'You don't want to hear about the police?' Tudor said. 'Well, they came to see me again yesterday. Asking about you and me. And Mike. And asking whether or not I owned a black raincoat and umbrella. I told them I didn't. That's the truth, Barbara. I really don't own a black raincoat, and I've never liked umbrellas. You didn't know that, did you? Well, there are a lot of things you don't know about me. I'm a very complex person. But we have lots of time. You can learn all about me. You look so lovely. Do you mind my telling you how beautiful you look?'

This time, Hawes heard something.

But the sound had come from behind him, in the hallway.

He whirled, drawing his .38 instantly.

'Put up the gun, Cotton,' Carella whispered.

'Man, you scared the hell out of me!' Hawes whispered back. He peered past Carella, saw Kling standing there behind him.

'Tudor in there?' Carella asked.

'Yeah. He's with the girl.'

'Bubbles?'

'That's right.'

'Okay, let's break it open,' Carella said.

Kling took up a position to the right of the door, Hawes to the left. Carella braced himself and kicked in the lock. The door swung open. They burst into the room with their guns in their hands, and they saw Charles Tudor on his knees at one end of the room. And then they saw what was behind Tudor, and each of the men separately felt identical waves of shock and terror and pity, and Carella knew at once that they would not need their guns.

Chapter Eighteen

The room was filled with flowers. Bouquets of red roses and white roses and yellow roses, smaller bouquets of violets, long-stemmed gladioli, carnations, gardenias, rhododendron leaves in water-filled vases. The room was filled with the aroma of flowers – fresh flowers and dying flowers, flowers that were new, and flowers that had lost their bloom. The room was filled with the overwhelming scent of flowers and the overwhelming stench of something else.

The girl, Bubbles Caesar, lay quite still on the table around which the flowers were massed. Her black hair trailed behind her head, her long body was clad only in a nightgown, her slender hands were crossed over her bosom. A ruby necklace circled her throat. She lay on the table and stared at the ceiling, and she saw nothing, because she was stone cold dead and she'd been that way for a month and her decomposing body stank to high heaven.

Tudor, on his knees, turned to look at the detectives.

'So you found us,' he said quietly.

'Get up, Tudor.'

'You found us,' he repeated. He looked at the dead girl again. 'She's beautiful, isn't she?' he asked of no one. 'I've never known anyone as beautiful as she.'

In the closet, they found the body of a man. He was wearing only his underpants. Both of his hands had been amputated.

The man was Mike Chirapadano.

Oh, he knew that she was dead; he knew that he had killed them both. They stood around him in the squadroom, and they asked their questions in hushed voices because it was all over now and, killer or not, Charles Tudor was a human being, a man who had loved. Not a cheap thief, and not a punk, only a murderer who had loved. But yes, he knew she was dead. Yes, he knew that. Yes, he knew he had killed her, killed them both. He knew.

And yet, as he talked, as he answered the almost whispered questions of the detectives, it seemed he did not know, it seemed he wandered from the cruel reality of murder to another world, a world where Barbara Caesar was still alive and laughing. He crossed the boundary line into this other world with facility, and then recrossed it to reality, and then lost it again until there were no boundaries any more, there was only a man wandering between two alien lands, a native of neither, a stranger to both.

'When they called me from the club,' he said, 'when Randy Simms called me from the club, I didn't know what to think. Barbara was usually very reliable. So I called her apartment, the one she shared with the other girls, and I spoke to one of her roommates, and the roommate told me she hadn't seen her since early that morning. This was the twelfth, February twelfth; I'll remember that day as long as I live, it was the day I killed Barbara.'

'What did you do after you spoke to the roommate, Mr Tudor?'

'I figured perhaps she'd gone to the other apartment, the one on Canopy Street.'

'Were you paying for that apartment, Mr Tudor?'

'Yes. Yes, I was. Yes. But it was *our* apartment, you know. We shared it. We share a lot of things, Barbara and I. We like to do a lot of things together. I have tickets for a show next week. A musical. She likes music. We'll see that together. We do a lot of things together.'

The detectives stood in a silent knot around him. Carella cleared his throat.

'Did you go to the apartment, Mr Tudor? The one on Canopy Street?'

'Yes, I did. I got there sometime around ten o'clock. In the night. It was night-time. And I went right upstairs, and I used my key, and I ... well, she was there. With this man. This man was touching her. In our apartment. Barbara was in *our* apartment with another man.' Tudor shook his head. 'She shouldn't do things like that. She knows I love her. I bought her a ruby necklace for Valentine's Day. Did you see the necklace? It's quite beautiful. She wears it very well.'

'What did you do when you found them, Mr Tudor?'

'I ... I was shocked. I ... I ... I wanted to know. She ... she told me I didn't own her. She told me she was free, she said nobody owned her, not me, not ... not the man she was with and ... and ... and not Karl either, she said, not Karl, I didn't even know who Karl was. She ...

she said she had promised this Karl she'd go away with him, but he didn't own her either, nobody owned her, she said, and … and …'

'Yes, Mr Tudor?'

'I couldn't believe it because … well, I love her. You know that. And she was saying these terrible things, and this man, this Mike, stood there grinning. In his underwear, he was in his underwear, and she had on a nightgown I'd given her, the one *I'd* given her. I … I … I hit him. I kept hitting him, and Barbara laughed, she laughed all the while I was hitting him. I'm a very strong man, I hit him and I kept banging his head against the floor and then Barbara stopped laughing and she said, "You've killed him." I … I …'

'Yes?'

'I took her in my arms, and I kissed her and … and … I … my hands … her throat … she didn't scream … nothing … I simply squeezed and … and she … she … she went limp in my arms. It was his fault I thought, his fault, touching her, he shouldn't have touched her, he had no right to touch the woman I loved and so I … I went into the kitchen looking for a … a knife or something. I found a meat cleaver in one of the drawers and I … I went into the other room and cut off both his hands.' Tudor paused. 'For touching her. I cut off his hands so that he would never touch her again.' His brow wrinkled with the memory. 'There … there was a lot of blood. I … picked up the hands and put them in … in Barbara's overnight bag. Then I dragged his body into the closet and tried to clean up a little. There … there was a lot of blood all over.'

They got the rest of the story from him in bits and pieces. And the story threaded the boundary line, wove between reality and fantasy. And the men in the squadroom listened in something close to embarrassment, and some of them found other things to do, downstairs, away from the big man who sat in the hard-backed chair and told them of the woman he'd loved, the woman he still loved.

He told them he had begun disposing of Chirapadano's body last week. He had started with the hands, and he decided it was best to dispose of them separately. The overnight bag would be safe, he'd thought, because so many people owned similar bags. He had decided to use that for the first hand. But it occurred to him that identification of the body could be made through the finger tips, and so he had sliced those away with a kitchen knife.

'I cut myself,' he said. 'When I was working on the fingertips. Just a small cut, but it bled a lot. My finger.'

'What type blood do you have, Mr Tudor?' Carella asked.

'What? B, I think. Yes, B. Why?'

'That might explain the contradictory stain on the suit, Steve,' Kling said.

'What?' Tudor said. 'The suit? Oh, yes. I don't know why I did that, really. I don't know why. It was just something I had to do, something I … I just *had* to do.'

'What was it you had to do, Mr Tudor?'

'Put on his clothes,' Tudor said. 'The dead man's. I … I put on his suit, and his socks, and I wore his raincoat, and I carried his umbrella. When I went out to … to get rid of the hands.' He shrugged. 'I don't know why. Really, I don't know why.' He paused. 'I threw the clothes away as soon as I realized you knew about them. I went all the way out to Calm's Point, and I threw them in a trash basket.' Tudor looked at the circle of faces around him. 'Will you be keeping me much longer?' he asked suddenly.

'Why, Mr Tudor?'

'Because I want to get back to Barbara,' he told the cops.

They took him downstairs to the detention cells, and then they sat in the curiously silent squadroom.

'There's the answer to the conflicting stuff we found on the suit,' Kling said.

'Yeah.'

'They both wore it. The killer *and* the victim.'

'Yeah.'

'Why do you suppose he put on the dead man's clothes?' Kling shuddered. 'Jesus, this whole damn case ...'

'Maybe he knew,' Carella said.

'Knew what?'

'That he was a victim, too.'

Miscolo came in from the Clerical Office. The men in the squadroom were silent.

'Anybody want some coffee?' he asked.

Nobody wanted any coffee.

"The child Anna
sat on the floor
close to the
wall and played
with her

DOLL

talking to it,
listening...."

This, too is for Dodie and Ray Crane

Chapter One

The child Anna sat on the floor close to the wall and played with her doll, talking to it, listening. She could hear the voices raised in anger coming from her mother's bedroom through the thin separating wall, but she busied herself with the doll and tried not to be frightened. The man in her mother's bedroom was shouting now. She tried not to hear what he was saying. She brought the doll close to her face and kissed its plastic cheek, and then talked to it again, and listened.

In the bedroom next door, her mother was being murdered.

Her mother was called Tinka, a chic and lacquered label concocted by blending her given name, Tina, with her middle name, Karin. Tinka was normally a beautiful woman, no question about it. She'd have been a beautiful woman even if her name were Beulah. Or Bertha. Or perhaps even Brunhilde. The Tinka tag only enhanced her natural good looks, adding an essential gloss, a necessary polish, an air of mystery and adventure.

Tinka Sachs was a fashion model.

She was, no question about it, a very beautiful woman. She possessed a finely sculptured face that was perfectly suited to the demands of her profession, a wide forehead, high pronounced cheekbones, a generous mouth, a patrician nose, slanted green eyes flecked with chips of amber; oh, she was normally a beauty, no question about it. Her body was a model's body, lithe and loose and gently angled, with long slender legs, narrow hips, and a tiny bosom. She walked with a model's insinuating glide, pelvis tilted, crotch cleaving the air, head erect. She laughed with a model's merry shower of musical syllables, painted lips drawing back over capped teeth, amber eyes glowing. She sat with a model's carelessly draped ease, posing even in her own living room, invariably choosing the wall or sofa that best offset her clothes, or her long blonde hair, or her mysterious green eyes flecked with chips of amber; oh, she was normally a beauty.

She was not so beautiful at the moment.

She was not so beautiful because the man who followed her around the room shouting obscenities at her, the man who stalked her from wall to wall and boxed her into the narrow passage circumscribed by the king-sized bed and the marble-topped dresser opposite, the man who closed in on her oblivious to her murmuring, her pleading, her sobbing, the man was grasping a kitchen knife with which he had been slashing her repeatedly for the past three minutes.

The obscenities spilled from the man's mouth in a steady unbroken torrent, the anger having reached a pitch that was unvaried now, neither rising nor falling in volume or intensity. The knife blade swung in a short, tight arc, back and forth, its rhythm as unvaried as that of the words that poured from the man's mouth. Obscenities and blade, like partners in an evil copulation, moved together in perfect rhythm and pitch, enveloping Tinka in alternating splashes of blood and spittle. She kept murmuring the man's name pleadingly, again and again, as the blade ripped into her flesh. But the glittering arc was relentless. The razor-sharp blade, the monotonous flow of obscenities, inexorably forced her bleeding and torn into the far corner of the room, where the back of her head collided with an original Chagall, tilting it slightly askew, the knife moving in again in its brief terrifying arc, the blade slicing parallel bleeding ditches across her small breasts and moving lower across the flat abdomen, her peignoir tearing again with a clinging silky blood-sotted sound as the knife blade plunged deeper with each step closer he took. She said his name once more, she shouted his name, and then she murmured the word 'Please,' and then she fell back against the wall again, knocking the Chagall from its hook so that a riot of framed colour dropped heavily over her shoulder, falling in a lopsided angle past the long blonde hair, and the open red gashes across her throat and naked chest, the tattered blue peignoir, the natural brown of her exposed pubic hair, the blue satin slippers. She fell gasping for breath, spitting blood, headlong over the painting, her forehead colliding with the wide oaken frame, her blonde hair covering the Chagall reds and yellows and violets with a fine misty golden haze, the knife slash across her throat pouring blood onto the canvas, setting her hair afloat in a pool of red that finally overspilled the oaken frame and ran onto the carpet.

Next door, the child Anna clung fiercely to her doll.

She said a reassuring word to it, and then listened in terror as she heard footfalls in the hall outside her closed bedroom door. She kept listening breathlessly until she heard the front door to the apartment open and then close again.

She was still sitting in the bedroom, clutching her doll, when the superintendent came up the next morning to change a faucet washer Mrs Sachs had complained about the day before.

April is the fourth month of the year.

It is important to know that – if you are a cop, you can sometimes get a little confused.

More often than not, your confusion will be compounded of one part exhaustion, one part tedium, and one part disgust. The exhaustion is an ever present condition and one to which you have become slowly accustomed over the years. You know that the department does not recognize Saturdays, Sundays or legal holidays, and so you are even prepared to work on Christmas morning if you have to, especially if someone intent on committing mischief is inconsiderate enough to plan it for that day – witness General George Washington and the unsuspecting Hessians, those drunks. You know that a detective's work schedule does not revolve around a fixed day, and so you have learned to adjust to your odd waking hours and your shorter sleeping time, but you have never been able to adjust to the nagging feeling of exhaustion that is the result of too much crime and too few hours, too few men to pit against it. You are sometimes a drag at home with your wife and children, but that is only because you are tired, boy what a life, all work and no play, wow.

The tedium is another thing again, but it also helps to generate confusion. Crime is the most exciting sport in the world, right? Sure, ask anybody. Then how come it can be so boring when you're a working cop who is typing reports in triplicate and legging it all over the city talking to old ladies in flowered house dresses in apartments smelling of death? How can the routine of detection become something as proscribed as the ritual of a bullfight, never changing, so that even a gun duel in a night-time alley can assume familiar dimensions and be regarded with the same feeling of ennui that accompanies a routine request to the B.C.I.? The boredom is confusing as hell. It clasps hands with the exhaustion and makes you wonder whether this is January or Friday.

The disgust comes into it only if you are a human being. Some cops aren't. But if you are a human being, you are sometimes appalled by what your fellow human beings are capable of doing. You can understand lying because you practise it in a watered-down form as a daily method of smoothing the way, helping the machinery of mankind to function more easily without getting fouled by too much truth-stuff. You can understand stealing because when you were a kid you sometimes swiped pencils from the public school supply closet, and once a toy aeroplane from the five and ten. You can even understand murder because there is a dark and secret place in your own heart where you have hated deeply enough to kill. You can understand all these things, but you are nonetheless disgusted when they are piled upon you in profusion, when you are constantly confronted with liars, thieves and slaughterers, when all human decency seems in a state of suspension for the eight or twelve or thirty-six hours you are in the squadroom or out answering a squeal. Perhaps you could accept an occasional corpse – death is only a part of life, isn't it? It is corpse heaped upon corpse that leads to disgust and further leads to confusion. If you can no longer tell one corpse from another, if you can no longer distinguish one open bleeding head from the next, then how is April any different from October?

It was April.

The torn and lovely woman lay in profile across the bloody face of the Chagall painting. The lab technicians were dusting for latent prints, vacuuming for hairs and traces of fibre, carefully wrapping for transportation the knife found in the corridor just outside the bedroom door, and the dead girl's pocketbook, which seemed to contain everything but money.

Detective Steve Carella made his notes and then walked out of the room and down the hall to where the little girl sat in a very big chair, her feet not touching the floor, her doll sleeping across her lap. The little girl's name was Anna Sachs – one of the patrolmen had told him that the moment Carella arrived. The doll seemed almost as big as she did.

'Hello,' he said to her, and felt the old confusion once again, the exhaustion because he had not been home since Thursday morning, the tedium because he was embarking on another round of routine questioning, and the disgust because the person he was about to question was only a little girl and her mother was dead and mutilated in the room next door. He tried to smile. He was not very good at it. The little girl said nothing. She looked up at him out of very big eyes. Her lashes were long and brown, her mouth drawn in stoic silence beneath a nose she had inherited from her mother. Unblinkingly, she watched him. Unblinkingly, she said nothing.

'Your name is Anna, isn't it?' Carella said.

The child nodded.

'Do you know what my name is?'

'No.'

'Steve.'

The girl nodded again.

'I have a little girl about your age,' Carella said. 'She's a twin. How old *are* you, Anna?'

'Five.'

'That's just how old my daughter is.'

'Mmm,' Anna said. She paused a moment, and then asked, 'Is Mommy killed?'

'Yes,' Carella said. 'Yes, honey, she is.'

'I was afraid to go in and look.'

'It's better you didn't.'

'She got killed last night, didn't she?' Anna asked.

'Yes.'

There was a silence in the room. Outside, Carella could hear the muted sounds of a conversation between the police photographer and the M.E. An April fly buzzed against the bedroom window. He looked into the child's upturned face.

'Were you here last night?' he asked.

'Um-huh.'

'Where?'

'Here. Right here in my room.' She stroked the doll's cheek, and then looked up at Carella and asked, 'What's a twin?'

'When two babies are born at the same time.'

'Oh.'

She continued looking up at him, her eyes tearless, wide, and certain in the small white face. At last she said, 'The man did it.'

'What man?' Carella asked.

'The one who was with her.'

'Who?'

'Mummy. The man who was with her in her room.'

'Who was the man?'

'I don't know.'

'Did you see him?'

'No. I was here playing with Chatterbox when he came in.'

'Is Chatterbox a friend of yours?'

'Chatterbox is my *dolly*,' the child said, and she held up the doll and giggled, and Carella wanted to scoop her into his arms, hold her close, tell her there was no such thing as sharpened steel and sudden death.

'When was this, honey?' he asked. 'Do you know what time it was?'

'I don't know,' she said, and shrugged. 'I only know how to tell twelve o'clock and seven o'clock, that's all.'

'Well . . . was it dark?'

'Yes, it was after supper.'

'This man came in after supper, is that right?'

'Yes.'

'Did your mother know this man?'

'Oh, yes,' Anna said. 'She was laughing and everything when he first came in.'

'Then what happened?'

'I don't know.' Anna shrugged again. 'I was here playing.'

There was another silence.

The first tears welled into her eyes suddenly, leaving the rest of the face untouched; there was no trembling of lip, no crumbling of features, the tears simply overspilled her eyes and ran down her cheeks. She sat as still as a stone, crying soundlessly while Carella stood before her helplessly, a hulking man who suddenly felt weak and ineffective before this silent torrent of grief.

He gave her his handkerchief.

She took it wordlessly and blew her nose, but she did not dry her eyes. Then she handed it back to him and said, 'Thank you,' with the tears still running down her face endlessly, sitting stunned with her small hands folded over the doll's chest.

'He was hitting her,' she said. 'I could hear her crying, but I was afraid to go in. So I . . . I made believe I didn't hear. And then . . . then I *really* didn't hear. I just kept talking with Chatterbox, that was all. That way I couldn't hear what he was doing to her in the other room.'

'All right, honey,' Carella said. He motioned to the patrolman standing in the doorway. When the patrolman joined him, he whispered, 'Is her father around? Has he been notified?'

'Gee, I don't know,' the patrolman said. He turned and shouted, 'Anybody know if the husband's been contacted?'

A Homicide cop standing with one of the lab technicians looked up from his notebook and said, 'He's in Arizona. They been divorced for three years now.'

Lieutenant Peter Byrnes was normally a patient and understanding man, but there were times lately when Bert Kling gave him a severe pain in the ass. And whereas Byrnes, being patient and understanding, could appreciate the reasons for Kling's behaviour, this in no way made Kling any nicer to have around the office. The way Byrnes figured it, psychology was certainly an important factor in police work because it helped you to recognize that there were no longer any villains in the world, there were only disturbed people. Psychology substituted understanding for condemnation. It was a very nice tool to possess, psychology was, until a cheap thief kicked you in the groin one night. It then became somewhat difficult to imagine the thief as a put-upon soul who'd had a shabby childhood. In much the same way, though Byrnes completely understood the trauma that was responsible for Kling's current behaviour, he was finding it more and more difficult to accept Kling as anything but a cop who was going to hell with himself.

'I want to transfer him out,' he told Carella that morning.

'Why?'

'Because he's disrupting the whole damn squadroom, that's why,' Byrnes said. He did not enjoy discussing this, nor would he normally have asked for consultation on any firm decision he had made. His decision, however, was anything but final, that was the damn thing about it. He liked Kling, and yet he no longer liked him. He thought he could be a good cop, but was turning into a bad one. 'I've got enough bad cops around here,' he said aloud.

'Bert isn't a bad cop,' Carella said. He stood before Byrnes's cluttered desk in the corner office and listened to the sounds of early spring on the street outside the building, and he thought of the five-year-old girl named Anna Sachs who had taken his handkerchief while the tears streamed down her face.

'He's a surly shit,' Byrnes said. 'Okay, I know what happened to him, but people have died before, Steve, people have been killed before. And if you're a man you grow up to it, you don't act as if everybody's responsible for it. We didn't have anything to do with his girl friend's death, that's the plain and simple truth, and I personally am sick and tired of being blamed for it.'

'He's not blaming you for it, Peter. He's not blaming any of us.'

'He's blaming the *world*, and that's worse. This morning, he had a big argument with Meyer just because Meyer picked up the phone on his desk. I mean, the goddamn phone was ringing, so instead of crossing the room to his own desk, Meyer picked up the closest phone, which was on Kling's desk, so Kling starts a row. Now you can't have that kind of attitude in a squadroom where men are working together, you can't have it, Steve. I'm going to ask for his transfer.'

'That'd be the worst thing that could happen to him.'

'It'd be the best thing for the squad.'

'I don't think so.'

'Nobody's asking your advice,' Byrnes said flatly.

'Then why the hell did you call me in here?'

'You see what I mean?' Byrnes said. He rose from his desk abruptly and began pacing the floor near the meshed-grill windows. He was a compact man and he moved with an economy that belied the enormous energy in his powerful body. Short for a detective, muscular, with a bullet-shaped head and small blue eyes set in a face seamed with wrinkles, he paced briskly behind his desk and shouted. 'You see the trouble he's causing? Even you and I can't sit down and have a sensible discussion about him without starting to yell. That's *just* what I mean, that's *just* why I want him out of here.'

'You don't throw away a good watch because it's running a little slow,' Carella said.

'Don't give me any goddamn similes,' Byrnes said. 'I'm running a squadroom here, not a clock shop.'

'Metaphors,' Carella corrected.

'What*ever*,' Byrnes said. 'I'm going to call the Chief tomorrow and ask him to transfer Kling out. That's it.'

'Where?'

'What do you mean *where*? What do I care where? Out of here, that's all.'

'But *where*? To another squadroom with a bunch of strange guys, so he can get on *their* nerves even more than he does ours? So he can —'

'Oh, so you admit it.'

'That Bert gets on my nerves? Sure, he does.'

'And the situation isn't improving, Steve, you know that too. It gets worse every day. Look, what the hell am I wasting my breath for? He goes, and that's it.' Byrnes gave a brief emphatic nod, and then sat heavily in his chair again, glaring up at Carella with an almost childish challenge on his face.

Carella sighed. He had been on duty for close to fifty hours now, and he was tired. He had checked in at eight-forty-five Thursday morning, and been out all that day gathering information for the backlog of cases that had been piling up all through the month of March. He had caught six hours' sleep on a cot in the locker room that night, and then been called out at seven on Friday morning by the fire department, who suspected arson in a three-alarm blaze they'd answered on the South Side. He had come back to the squadroom at noon to find four telephone messages on his desk. By the time he had returned all the calls – one was from an assistant M.E. who took a full hour to explain the toxicological analysis of a poison they had found in the stomach contents of a beagle, the seventh such dog similarly poisoned in the past week – the clock on the wall read one-thirty. Carella sent down for a pastrami on rye, a container of milk, and a side of French fries. Before the order arrived, he had to leave the squadroom to answer a burglary squeal on North Eleventh. He did not come back until five-thirty, at which time he turned the phone over to a complaining Kling and went down to the locker room to try to sleep again. At eleven o'clock Friday night, the entire squad, working in flying wedges of three detectives to a team, culminated a two-month period of surveillance by raiding twenty-six known numbers banks in the area, a sanitation project that was not finished until five on Saturday morning. At eight-thirty a.m., Carella answered the Sachs squeal and questioned a crying little girl. It was now ten-thirty a.m., and he was tired, and he wanted to go home, and he didn't want to argue in favour of a man who had become everything the lieutenant said he was, he was just too damn weary. But earlier this morning he had looked down at the body of a woman he had not known at all, had seen her ripped and lacerated flesh, and felt a pain bordering on nausea. Now – weary, bedraggled, unwilling to argue – he could remember the mutilated beauty of Tinka Sachs, and he felt something of what Bert Kling must have known in the Culver Avenue bookshop not four years ago when he'd held the bullet-torn body of Claire Townsend in his arms.

'Let him work with me,' he said.

'What do you mean?'

'On the Sachs case. I've been teaming with Meyer lately. Give me Bert instead.'

'What's the matter, don't you like Meyer?'

'I *love* Meyer, I'm tired, I want to go home to bed, will you please let me have Bert on this case?'

'What'll that accomplish?'

'I don't know.'

'I don't approve of shock therapy,' Byrnes said. 'This Sachs woman was brutally murdered. All you'll do is remind Bert –'

'Therapy, my ass,' Carella said. 'I want to be with him, I want to talk to him, I want to let him know he's still got some people on this goddamn squad who think he's a decent human being worth saving. Now, Pete, I *really* am very very tired and I don't want to argue this any further, I mean it. If you want to send Bert to another squad, that's your business, you're the boss here,

I'm not going to argue with you, that's all. I mean it. Now just make up your mind, okay?'

'Take him,' Byrnes said.

'Thank you,' Carella answered. He went to the door. 'Good night', he said, and walked out.

Chapter Two

Sometimes a case starts like sevens coming out.

The Sachs case started just that way on Monday morning when Steve Carella and Bert Kling arrived at the apartment building on Stafford Place to question the elevator operator.

The elevator operator was close to seventy years old, but he was still in remarkable good health, standing straight and tall, almost as tall as Carella and of the same general build. He had only one eye, however – he was called Cyclops by the superintendent of the building and by just about everyone else he knew – and it was this single fact that seemed to make him a somewhat less than reliable witness. He had lost his eye, he explained, in World War I. It had been bayoneted out of his head by an advancing German in the Ardennes Forest. Cyclops – who up to that time had been called Ernest – had backed away from the blade before it had a chance to pass completely through his eye and into his brain, and then had carefully and passionlessly shot the German three times in the chest, killing him. He did not realize his eye was gone until he got back to the aid station. Until then, he thought the bayonet had only gashed his brow and caused a flow of blood that made it difficult to see. He was proud of his missing eye, and proud of the nickname Cyclops. Cyclops had been a giant, and although Ernest Messner was only six feet tall, he had lost his eye for democracy, which is as good a cause as any for which to lose an eye. He was also very proud of his remaining eye, which he claimed was capable of twenty/twenty vision. His remaining eye was a clear penetrating blue, as sharp as the mind lurking somewhere behind it. He listened intelligently to everything the two detectives asked him, and then he said, 'Sure, I took him up myself.'

'You took a man up to Mrs Sachs's apartment Friday night?' Carella asked.

'That's right.'

'What time was this?'

Cyclops thought for a moment. He wore a black patch over his empty socket, and he might have looked a little like an ageing Hathaway Shirt man in an elevator uniform, except that he was bald. 'Must have been nine or nine-thirty, around then.'

'Did you take the man *down*, too?'

'Nope.'

'What time did you go off?'

'I didn't leave the building until eight o'clock in the morning.'

'You work from when to when, Mr Messner?'

'We've got three shifts in the building,' Cyclops explained. 'The morning shift is eight a.m. to four p.m. The afternoon shift is four p.m. to midnight. And the graveyard shift is midnight to eight a.m.'

'Which shift is yours?' Kling asked.

'The graveyard shift. You just caught me, in fact. I'll be relieved here in ten minutes.'

'If you start work at midnight, what were you doing here at nine p.m. Monday?'

'Fellow who has the shift before mine went home sick. The super called me about eight o'clock, asked if I could come in early. I did him the favour. That was a long night, believe me.'

'It was an even longer night for Tinka Sachs,' Kling said.

'Yeah. Well anyway, I took that fellow up at nine, nine-thirty, and he still hadn't come down by the time I was relieved.'

'At eight in the morning,' Carella said.

'That's right.'

'Is that usual?' Kling asked.

'What do you mean?'

'Did Tinka Sachs usually have men coming here who went up to her apartment at nine, nine-thirty and weren't down by eight the next morning?'

Cyclops blinked with his single eye. 'I don't like to talk about the dead,' he said.

'We're here precisely so you *can* talk about the dead,' Kling answered. 'And about the living who visited the dead. I asked a simple question, and I'd appreciate a simple answer. Was Tinka Sachs in the habit of entertaining men all night long?'

Cyclops blinked again. 'Take it easy, young fellow,' he said. 'You'll scare me right back into my elevator.'

Carella chose to laugh at this point, breaking the tension. Cyclops smiled in appreciation.

'You understand, don't you?' he said to Carella. 'What Mrs Sachs did up there in her apartment was *her* business, not anyone else's.'

'Of course,' Carella said. 'I guess my partner was just wondering why you weren't suspicious. About taking a man up who didn't come down again. That's all.'

'Oh.' Cyclops thought for a moment. Then he said, 'Well, I didn't give it a second thought.'

'Then it *was* usual, is that right?' Kling asked.

'I'm not saying it was usual, and I'm not saying it wasn't. I'm saying if a woman over twenty-one wants to have a man in her apartment, it's not for me to say how long he should stay, all day or all night, it doesn't matter to me, sonny. You got that?'

'I've got it,' Kling said flatly.

'And I don't give a damn what they do up there, either, all day or all night, that's their business if they're old enough to vote. You got that, too?'

'I've got it,' Kling said.

'Fine,' Cyclops answered, and he nodded.

'Actually,' Carella said, 'the man didn't *have* to take the elevator down, did he? He could have gone up to the roof, and crossed over to the next building.'

'Sure,' Cyclops said. 'I'm only saying that neither me nor anybody else working in this building has the right to wonder about what anybody's doing up there or how long they're taking to do it, or whether they choose to leave the building by the front door or the roof or the steps leading to the basement or even by jumping out of the window, it's none of our business. You close that door, you're private. That's my notion.'

'That's a good notion,' Carella said.

'Thank you.'

'You're welcome.'

'What'd the man look like?' Kling asked. 'Do you remember?'

'Yes, I remember,' Cyclops said. He glanced at Kling coldly, and then turned to Carella. 'Have you got a pencil and some paper?'

'Yes,' Carella said. He took a notebook and a slender gold pen from his inside jacket pocket. 'Go ahead.'

'He was a tall man, maybe six-two or six-three. He was blond. His hair was very straight, the kind of hair Sonny Tufts has, do you know him?'

'Sonny *Tufts?*' Carella said.

'That's right, the movie star, him. This fellow didn't look at all like him, but his hair was the same sort of straight blond hair.'

'What colour were his eyes?' Kling asked.

'Didn't see them. He was wearing sunglasses.'

'At night?'

'Lots of people wear sunglasses at night nowadays,' Cyclops said.

'That's true,' Carella said.

'Like masks,' Cyclops added.

'Yes.'

'He was wearing sunglasses, and also he had a very deep tan, as if he's just come back from down south someplace. He had on a light grey raincoat; it was drizzling a little Friday night, do you recall?'

'Yes, that's right,' Carella said. 'Was he carrying an umbrella?'

'No umbrella.'

'Did you notice any of his clothing under the raincoat?'

'His suit was a dark grey, charcoal grey, I could tell that by his trousers. He was wearing a white shirt – it showed up here, in the opening of the coat – and a black tie.'

'What colour were his shoes?'

'Black.'

'Did you notice any scars or other marks on his face or hands?'

'No.'

'Was he wearing any rings?'

'A gold ring with a green stone on the pinky of his right hand – no, wait a minute, it was his left hand.'

'Any other jewellery you might have noticed? Cuff links, tie clasp?'

'No, I didn't see any.'

'Was he wearing a hat?'

'No hat.'

'Was he clean-shaven?'

'What do you mean?'

'Did he have a beard or a moustache?' Kling said.

'No. He was clean-shaven.'

'How old would you say he was?'

'Late thirties, early forties.'

'What about his build? Heavy, medium, or slight?'

'He was a big man. He wasn't fat, but he was a big man, muscular. I guess I'd have to say he was heavy. He had very big hands. I noted the ring on his pinky looked very small for his hand. He was heavy, I'd say, yes, very definitely.'

'Was he carrying anything? Briefcase, suitcase, attaché –'

'Nothing.'

'Did he speak to you?'

'He just gave me the floor number, that's all. Nine, he said. That was all.'

'What sort of voice did he have? Deep, medium, high?'

'Deep.'

'Did you notice any accent or regional dialect?'

'He only said one word. He sounded like anybody else in the city.'

'I'm going to say that word several ways,' Carella said. 'Would you tell me which way sounded most like him?'

'Sure, go ahead.'

'Ny-un,' Carella said.

'Nope.'

'Noin.'

'Nope.'

'Nahn.'

'Nope.'

'Nan.'

'Nope.'

'Nine.'

'That's it. Straight out. No decorations.'

'Okay, good,' Carella said. 'You got anything else, Bert?'

'Nothing else,' Kling said.

'You're a very observant man,' Carella said to Cyclops.

'All I do every day is look at the people I take up and down,' Cyclops answered. He shrugged. 'It makes the job a little more interesting.'

'We appreciate everything you've told us,' Carella said. 'Thank you.'

'Don't mention it.'

Outside the building, Kling said, 'The snotty old bastard.'

'He gave us a lot,' Carella said mildly.

'Yeah.'

'We've really got a good description now.'

'*Too* good, if you ask me.'

'What do you mean?'

'The guy has one eye in his head, and one foot in the grave. So he reels off details even a trained observer would have missed. He might have been making up the whole thing, just to prove he's not a worthless old man.'

'Nobody's worthless,' Carella said mildly. 'Old or otherwise.'

'The humanitarian school of criminal detection,' Kling said.

'What's wrong with humanity?'

'Nothing. It was a human being who slashed Tinka Sachs to ribbons, wasn't it?' Kling asked.

And to this, Carella had no answer.

*   *   *

A good modelling agency serves as a great deal more than a booking office for the girls it represents. It provides an answering service for the busy young girl about town, a baby-sitting service for the working mother, a guidance-and-counselling service for the man-beleaguered model, a *pied-à-terre* for the harried and hurried between-sittings beauty.

Art and Leslie Cutler ran a good modelling agency. They ran it with the precision of a computer and the understanding of an analyst. Their offices were smart and walnut-panelled, a suite of three rooms on Carrington Avenue, near the bridge leading to Calm's Point. The address of the agency was announced over a doorway leading to a flight of carpeted steps. The address plate resembled a Parisian street sign, white enamelled on a blue field, 21 Carrington, with the blue-carpeted steps beyond leading to the second story of the building. At the top of the stairs there was a second blue-and-white enamelled sign, Paris again, except that this one was lettered in lowercase and it read: the cutlers.

Carella and Kling climbed the steps to the second floor, observed the chic nameplate without any noticeable show of appreciation, and walked into a small carpeted entrance foyer in which stood a white desk starkly fashionable against the walnut walls, nothing else. A girl sat behind the desk. She was astonishingly beautiful, exactly the sort of receptionist one would expect in a modelling agency; if she was only the receptionist, my God, what did the *models* look like?

'Yes, gentlemen, may I help you?' she asked. Her voice was Vassar out of finishing school out of country day. She wore eyeglasses with exaggerated black frames that did nothing whatever to hide the dazzling brilliance of her big blue eyes. He makeup was subdued and wickedly innocent, a touch of pale pink on her lips, a blush of rose at her cheeks, the frames of her spectacles serving as liner for her eyes. Her hair was black and her smile was sunshine. Carella answered with a sunshine smile of his own, the one he usually reserved for movie queens he met at the governor's mansion.

'We're from the police,' he said. 'I'm Detective Carella; this is my partner, Detective Kling.'

'Yes?' the girl said. She seemed completely surprised to have policemen in her reception room.

'We'd like to talk to either Mr or Mrs Cutler,' Kling said. 'Are they in?'

'Yes, but what is this in reference to?' the girl asked.

'It's in reference to the murder of Tinka Sachs,' Kling said.

'Oh,' the girl said. 'Oh, yes.' She reached for a button on the executive phone panel, hesitated, shrugged, looked up at them with radiant blue-eyed innocence, and said, 'I suppose you have identification and all that.'

Carella showed her his shield. The girl looked expectantly at Kling. Kling sighed, reached into his pocket, and opened his wallet to where his shield was pinned to the leather.

'We never get detectives up here,' the girl said in explanation, and pressed the button on the panel.

'Yes?' a voice said.

'Mr Cutler, there are two detectives to see you, a Mr King and a Mr Coppola.'

'Kling and Carella,' Carella corrected.

'Kling and Capella,' the girl said.

Carella let it go.

'Ask them to come right in,' Cutler said.

'Yes, sir.' The girl clicked off and looked up at the detectives. 'Won't you go in, please? Through the bull pen and straight back.'

'Through the what?'

'The bull pen. Oh, that's the main office, you'll see it. It's right inside the door there.' The telephone rang. The girl gestured vaguely towards what looked like a solid walnut wall, and then picked up the receiver. 'The Cutlers,' she said. 'One moment, please.' She pressed a button and then said, 'Mrs Cutler, it's Alex Jamison on five-seven, do you want to take it?' She nodded, listened for a moment, and then replaced the receiver. Carella and Kling had just located the walnut knob on the walnut door hidden in the walnut wall. Carella smiled sheepishly at the girl (blue eyes blinked back radiantly) and opened the door.

The bull pen, as the girl had promised, was just behind the reception room. It was a large open area with the same basic walnut-and-white decor, broken by the colour of the drapes and the upholstery fabric on two huge couches against the left-hand window wall. The windows were draped in diaphanous saffron nylon, and the couches were done in a complementary brown, the fabric nubby and coarse in contrast to the nylon. Three girls sat on the couches, their long legs crossed. All of them were reading *Vogue*. One of them had her head inside a portable hair dryer. None of them looked up as the men came into the room. On the right-hand side of the room, a fourth woman sat behind a long white Formica counter, a phone to her ear, busily scribbling on a pad as she listened. The woman was in her early forties, with the unmistakable bones of an ex-model. She glanced up briefly as Carella and Kling hesitated inside the doorway, and then went back to her jottings, ignoring them.

There were three huge charts affixed to the wall behind her. Each chart was divided into two-by-two-inch squares, somewhat like a colourless checkerboard. Running down the extreme left-hand side of each chart was a column of small photographs. Running across the top of each chart was a listing for every working hour of the day. The charts were covered with plexiglass panels, and a black crayon pencil hung on a cord to the right of each one. Alongside the photographs, crayoned onto the charts in the appropriate time slots, was a record and a reminder of any model's sittings for the week, readable at a glance. To the right of the charts, and accessible through an opening in the counter, there was a cubbyhole arrangement of mailboxes, each separate slot marked with similar small photographs.

The wall bearing the door through which Carella and Kling had entered was covered with eight-by-ten black-and-white photos of every model the agency represented, some seventy-five in all. The photos bore no identifying names. A waist-high runner carried black crayon pencils spaced at intervals along the length of the wall. A wide white band under each photograph, plexiglass-covered, served as the writing area for telephone messages. A model entering the room could, in turn, check her eight-by-ten photo for any calls, her photo-marked mailbox for any letters, and her photo-marked slot on one of the three charts for her next assignment. Looking into the room, you somehow got the vague impression that photography played a major part in the business of this agency. You also had the disquieting feeling that you had seen all of these faces a hundred times before, staring down at you from billboards and up at you from magazine covers. Putting an identifying name under any single one of them would have been akin to labelling the Taj Mahal or the Empire State Building. The only naked wall was the one facing them as they entered, and it – like the reception-room wall – seemed to be made of solid walnut, with nary a door in sight.

'I think I see a knob,' Carella whispered, and they stared across the room towards the far wall. The woman behind the counter glanced up as they passed, and then pulled the phone abruptly from her ear with a 'Just a second, Alex,' and said to the two detectives, 'Yes, may I help you?'

'We're looking for Mr Cutler's office,' Carella said.

'Yes?' she said.

'Yes, we're detectives. We're investigating the murder of Tinka Sachs.'

'Oh. Straight ahead,' the woman said. 'I'm Leslie Cutler. I'll join you as soon as I'm off the phone.'

'Thank you,' Carella said. He walked to the walnut wall, Kling following close behind him, and knocked on what he supposed was the door.

'Come in,' a man's voice said.

Art Cutler was a man in his forties with straight blond hair like Sonny Tufts, and with at least six feet four inches of muscle and bone that stood revealed in a dark blue suit as he rose behind his desk, smiling, and extended his hand.

'Come in, gentlemen,' he said. His voice was deep. He kept his hand extended while Carella and Kling crossed to the desk, and then he shook hands with each in turn, his grip firm and strong. 'Sit down, won't you?' he said, and indicated a pair of Saarinen chairs, one at each corner of his desk. 'You're here about Tinka,' he said dolefully.

'Yes,' Carella said.

'Terrible thing. A maniac must have done it, don't you think?'

'I don't know,' Carella said.

'Well, it *must* have been, don't you think?' he said to Kling.

'I don't know,' Kling said.

'That's why we're here, Mr Cutler,' Carella explained. 'To find out what we can about the girl. We're assuming that an agent would know a great deal about the people he repre –'

'Yes, that's true,' Cutler interrupted, 'and especially in Tinka's case.'

'Why especially in her case?'

'Well, we'd handled her career almost from the very beginning.'

'How long would that be, Mr Cutler?'

'Oh, at least ten years. She was only nineteen when we took her on, and she was ... well, let me see, she was thirty in February, no, it'd be almost *eleven* years, that's right.'

'February what?' Kling asked.

'February third,' Cutler replied. 'She'd done a little modelling on the coast before she signed with us, but nothing very impressive. We got her into all the important magazines, *Vogue, Harper's, Mademoiselle*, well, you name them. Do you know what Tinka Sachs was earning?'

'No, what?' Kling said.

'Sixty dollars an hour. Multiply that by an eight- or ten-hour day, an average of six days a week, and you've got somewhere in the vicinity of a hundred and fifty thousand dollars a year.' Cutler paused. 'That's a lot of money. That's more than the president of the United States earns.'

'With none of the headaches,' Kling said.

'Mr Cutler,' Carella said, 'when did you last see Tinka Sachs alive?'

'Late Friday afternoon,' Cutler said.

'Can you give us the circumstances?'

'Well, she had a sitting at five, and she stopped in around seven to pick up her mail and to see if there had been any calls. That's all.'

'Had there?' Kling asked.

'Had there what?'

'Been any calls?'

'I'm sure I don't remember. The receptionist usually posts all calls shortly after they're received. You may have seen our photo wall –'

'Yes,' Kling said.

'Well, our receptionist takes care of that. If you want me to check with her, she may have a record, though I doubt it. Once a call is crayoned onto the wall –'

'What about mail?'

'I don't know if she had any or ... wait a minute, yes, I think she did pick some up. I remember she was leafing through some envelopes when I came out of my office to chat with her.'

'What time did she leave here?' Carella asked.

'About seven-fifteen.'

'For another sitting?'

'No, she was heading home. She has a daughter, you know. A five-year-old.'

'Yes, I know,' Carella said.

'Well, she was going home,' Cutler said.

'Do you know where she lives?' Kling asked.

'Yes.'

'Where?'

'Stafford Place.'

'Have you ever been there?'

'Yes, of course.'

'How long do you suppose it would take to get from this office to her apartment?'

'No more than fifteen minutes.'

'Then Tinka would have been home by seven-thirty ... *if* she went directly home.'

'Yes, I suppose so.'

'Did she say she was going directly home?'

'Yes. No, she said she wanted to pick up some cake, and *then* she was going home.'

'Cake?'

'Yes. There's a shop up the street that's exceptionally good. Many of our mannequins buy cakes and pastry there.'

'Did she say she was expecting someone later on in the evening?' Kling asked.

'No, she didn't say what her plans were.'

'Would your receptionist know if any of those telephone messages related to her plans for the evening?'

'I don't know, we can ask her.'

'Yes, we'd like to,' Carella said.

'What were *your* plans for last Friday night, Mr Cutler?' Kling asked.

'*My* plans?'

'Yes.'

'What do you mean?'

'What time did *you* leave the office?'

'Why would you possibly want to know *that*?' Cutler asked.

'You were the last person to see her alive,' Kling said.

'No, her *murderer* was the last person to see her alive,' Cutler corrected. 'And if I can believe what I read in the newspapers, her *daughter* was the *next*-to-last person to see her alive. So I really can't understand how Tinka's visit to the agency or *my* plans for the evening are in any way germane, or even related, to her death.'

'Perhaps they're not, Mr Cutler,' Carella said, 'but I'm sure you realize we're obliged to investigate every possibility.'

Cutler frowned, including Carella in whatever hostility he had originally reserved for Kling. He hesitated a moment and then grudgingly said, 'My wife and I joined some friends for dinner at *Les Trois Chats*.' He paused and added caustically, 'That's a French restaurant.'

'What time was that?' Kling asked.

'Eight o'clock.'

'Where were you at nine?'

'Still having dinner.'

'And at nine-thirty?'

Cutler sighed and said, 'We didn't leave the restaurant until a little after ten.'

'And then what did you do?'

'Really, is this necessary?' Cutler said, and scowled at the detectives. Neither of them answered. He sighed again and said, 'We walked along Hall Avenue for a while, and then my wife and I left our friends and took a cab home.'

The door opened.

Leslie Cutler breezed into the office, saw the expression on her husband's face, weighed the silence that greeted her entrance, and immediately said, 'What is it?'

'Tell them where we went when we left here Friday night,' Cutler said. 'The gentlemen are intent on playing cops and robbers.'

'You're joking,' Leslie said, and realized at once that they were not. 'We went to dinner with some friends,' she said quickly. 'Marge and Daniel Ronet – she's one of our mannequins. Why?'

'What time did you leave the restaurant, Mrs Cutler?'

'At ten.'

'Was your husband with you all that time?'

'Yes, of course he was.' She turned to Cutler and said, 'Are they allowed to do this? Shouldn't we call Eddie?'

'Who's Eddie?' Kling said.

'Our lawyer.'

'You won't need a lawyer.'

'Are you a new detective?' Cutler asked Kling suddenly.

'What's that supposed to mean?'

'It's supposed to mean your interviewing technique leaves something to be desired.'

'Oh? In what respect? What do you find lacking in my approach, Mr Cutler?'

'Subtlety, to coin a word.'

'That's very funny,' Kling said.

'I'm glad it amuses you.'

'Would it amuse you to know that the elevator operator at 791 Stafford Place gave us an excellent description of the man he took up to Tinka's apartment on the night she was killed? And would it amuse you further to know that the description fits you to a tee? How does *that* hit your funny bone, Mr Cutler?'

'I was nowhere near Tinka's apartment last Friday night.'

'Apparently not. I know you won't mind our contacting the friends you had dinner with, though – just to check.'

'The receptionist will give you their number,' Cutler said coldly.

'Thank you.'

Cutler looked at his watch. 'I have a lunch date,' he said. 'If you gentlemen are finished with your –'

'I wanted to ask your receptionist about those telephone messages,' Carella said. 'And I'd also appreciate any information you can give me about Tinka's friends and acquaintances.'

'My wife will have to help you with that.' Cutler glanced sourly at Kling and said, 'I'm not planning to leave town. Isn't that what you always warn a suspect not to do?'

'Yes, don't leave town,' Kling said.

'Bert,' Carella said casually, 'I think you'd better get back to the squad. Grossman promised to call with a lab report sometime this afternoon. One of us ought to be there to take it.'

'Sure,' Kling said. He went to the door and opened it. 'My partner's a little more subtle than I am,' he said, and left.

Carella, with his work cut out for him, gave a brief sigh, and said, 'Could we talk to your receptionist now, Mrs Cutler?'

Chapter Three

When Carella left the agency at two o'clock that Monday afternoon, he was in possession of little more than he'd had when he first climbed those blue-carpeted steps. The receptionist, radiating wide-eyed helpfulness, could not remember any of the phone messages that had been left for Tinka Sachs on the day of her death. She knew they were all personal calls, and she remembered that some of them were from men, but she could not recall any of the men's names. Neither could she remember the names of the women callers – yes, some of them were women, she said, but she didn't know exactly how many – nor could she remember why *any* of the callers were trying to contact Tinka.

Carella thanked her for her help, and then sat down with Leslie Cutler – who was still fuming over Kling's treatment of her husband – and tried to compile a list of men Tinka knew. He drew another blank here because Leslie informed him at once that Tinka, unlike most of the agency's mannequins (the word 'mannequin' was beginning to rankle a little) kept her private affairs to herself, never allowing a date to pick her up at the agency, and never discussing the men in her life, not even with any of the other mannequins (in fact, the word was beginning to rankle a lot). Carella thought at first that Leslie was suppressing information because of the jackass manner in which Kling had conducted the earlier interview. But as he questioned her more completely, he came to believe that she really knew nothing at all about Tinka's personal matters. Even on the few occasions when she and her husband had been invited to Tinka's home, it had been for a simple dinner for three, with no one else in attendance, and with the child Anna asleep in her own room. Comparatively charmed to pieces by Carella's patience after Kling's earlier display, Leslie offered him the agency flyer on Tinka, the composite that went to all photographers, advertising agency art directors, and prospective clients. He took it, thanked her, and left.

Sitting over a cup of coffee and a hamburger now, in a luncheonette two blocks from the squadroom, Carella took the composite out of its manila envelope and remembered again the way Tinka Sachs had looked the last time he'd seen her. The composite was an eight-by-ten black-and-white presentation consisting of a larger sheet folded in half to form two pages, each printed front and back with photographs of Tinka in various poses.

Carella studied the composite from first page to last:

**TINKA
SACHS**

SIZE 10-12
HEIGHT (S/F) 5′8″
BUST 34
WAIST 23
HIPS 34
HAIR BLONDE
EYES GREEN
SHOE 7-½ AA
GLOVE 7
HAT 22

The Cutlers
21 CARRINGTON ST.

The only thing the composite told him was that Tinka posed fully clothed, modelling neither lingerie nor swimwear, a fact he considered interesting, but hardly pertinent. He put the composite into the manila envelope, finished his coffee, and went back to the squadroom.

Kling was waiting and angry.

'What was the idea, Steve?' he asked immediately.

'Here's a composite on Tinka Sachs,' Carella said. 'We might as well add it to our file.'

'Never mind the composite. How about answering my question?'

'I'd rather not. Did Grossman call?'

'Yes. The only prints they've found in the room so far are the dead girl's. They haven't yet examined the knife, or her pocketbook. Don't try to get me off this, Steve. I'm goddamn good and sore.'

'Bert, I don't want to get into an argument with you. Let's drop it, okay?'

'No.'

'We're going to be working on this case together for what may turn out to be a long time. I don't want to start by –'

'Yes, that's right, and I don't like being ordered back to the squadroom just because someone doesn't like my line of questioning.'

'Nobody ordered you back to the squadroom.'

'Steve, you outrank me, and you told me to come back, and that was *ordering* me back. I want to know why.'

'Because you were behaving like a jerk, okay?'

'I don't think so.'

'Then maybe you ought to step back and take an objective look at yourself.'

'Dammit, it was *you* who said the old man's identification seemed reliable! Okay, so we walk into the office and we're face to face with the man who'd just been *described* to us! What'd you expect me to do? Serve him a cup of tea?'

'No, I expected you to accuse him –'

'Nobody accused him of anything!'

'– of murder and take him right up here to book him,' Carella said sarcastically. '*That's* what I expected.'

'I asked perfectly reasonable questions!'

'You asked questions that were snotty and surly and hostile and amateurish. You treated him like a criminal from go, when you had no reason to. You immediately put him on the defensive instead of disarming him. If I were in his place, I'd have lied to you just out of spite. You made an enemy instead of a friend out of someone who might have been able to help us. That means if I need any further information about Tinka's professional life, I'll have to beg it from a man who now has good reason to hate the police.'

'He fit our description! Anyone would have asked –'

'Why the hell couldn't you ask in a civil manner? And *then* check on those friends he said he was with, and *then* get tough if you had something to work with? What did you accomplish your way? Not a goddamn thing. Okay, you asked me, so I'm telling you. I had work to do up there, and I couldn't afford to waste more time while you threw mud at the walls. *That's* why I sent you back here. Okay? Good. Did you check Cutler's alibi?'

'Yes.'

'*Was* he with those people?'

'Yes.'

'And *did* they leave the restaurant at ten and walk around for a while?'

'Yes.'

'Then Cutler couldn't have been the man Cyclops took up in his elevator.'

'Unless Cyclops got the time wrong.'

'That's a possibility, and I suggest we check it. But the checking should have been done *before* you started hurling accusations around.'

'I didn't accuse anybody of anything!'

'Your entire approach did! Who the hell do you think you are, a Gestapo agent? You can't go marching into a man's office with nothing but an idea and start —'

'I was doing my best!' Kling said. 'If that's not good enough, you can go to hell.'

'It's not good enough,' Carella said, 'and I don't plan to go to hell, either.'

'I'm asking Pete to take me off this,' Kling said.

'He won't.'

'Why not?'

'Because I outrank you, like you said, and *I* want you on it.'

'Then don't ever try that again, I'm warning you. You embarrass me in front of a civilian again and —'

'If you had any sense, you'd have been embarrassed long before I asked you to go.'

'Listen, Carella —'

'Oh, it's *Carella* now, huh?'

'I don't have to take any crap from you, just remember that. I don't care what your badge says. Just remember I don't have to take any crap from you.'

'Or from anybody.'

'Or from anybody, right.'

'I'll remember.'

'See that you do,' Kling said, and he walked through the gate in the slatted railing and out of the squadroom.

Carella clenched his fists, unclenched them again, and then slapped one open hand against the top of his desk.

Detective Meyer Meyer came out of the men's room in the corridor, zipping up his fly. He glanced to his left towards the iron-runged steps and cocked his head, listening to the angry clatter of Kling's descending footfalls. When he came into the squadroom, Carella was leaning over, straightarmed, on his desk. A dead, cold expression was on his face.

'What was all the noise about?' Meyer asked.

'Nothing,' Carella said. He was seething with anger, and the word came out as thin as a razor blade.

'Kling again?' Meyer asked.

'Kling again.'

'Boy,' Meyer said, and shook his head, and said nothing more.

On his way home late that afternoon, Carella stopped at the Sachs apartment, showed his shield to the patrolman still stationed outside her door, and then went into the apartment to search for anything that might give him a line on the men Tinka Sachs had known – correspondence, a memo pad, an address book, anything. The apartment was empty and still. The child Anna Sachs had been taken to the Children's Shelter on Saturday and then released into the custody of Harvey Sadler – who was Tinka's lawyer – to await the arrival of the little girl's father from Arizona. Carella walked through the corridor past Anna's room, the same route the murderer must have taken, glanced in through the open door at the rows of dolls lined up in the bookcase, and then went past the room and into Tinka's spacious bedroom. The bed had been stripped, the blood-stained sheets and blanket sent to the police laboratory. There had been blood stains on the drapes as well, and these too had been taken down and shipped off to Grossman. The windows were bare now, overlooking the rooftops below, the boats moving slowly on the River Dix. Dusk was coming fast, a reminder that it was still only April. Carella flicked on the lights and walked around the chalked outline of Tinka's body on the thick green carpet, the blood soaked into it and dried to an ugly brown. He went to an oval table serving as a desk on the wall opposite the bed, sat in the pedestal chair before it, and began rummaging through the papers scattered over its top. The disorder told him that detectives from Homicide had already been through all this and found nothing they felt worthy of calling to his attention. He sighed and picked up an envelope with an airmal border, turned it over to look at the flap, and saw that it had come from Dennis Sachs – Tinka's ex-husband – in Rainfield, Arizona. Carella took the letter from the envelope, unfolded it, and began reading:

Tuesday, April 6

My darling Tinka —

Here I am in the middle of the desert, writing by the light of a flickering kerosene lamp, and listening to the howl of the wind outside my tent. The others are all asleep already. I have never felt farther away from the city — or from you.

I become more impatient with Oliver's project every day of the week, but perhaps that's because I know what you are trying to do, and everything seems insignificant beside your monumental struggle. Who cares whether or not the Hohokam traversed this desert on their way from Old Mexico? Who cares whether we uncover any of their lodges here? All I know is that I miss you enormously, and respect you,

*and pray for you. My only hope is that your ordeal
will soon be ended, and we can go back to the way
it was in the beginning;· before the nightmare began,
before our love was shattered.
    I will call East again on Saturday. All my
love to Anna...*

                    ... and to you.

                            Dennis

Carella refolded the letter and put it back into the envelope. He had just learned that Dennis Sachs was out in the desert on some sort of project involving the Hohokam, whoever the hell they were, and that apparently he was still carrying the torch for his ex-wife. But beyond that, Carella also learned that Tinka had been going through what Dennis called a 'monumental struggle' and 'ordeal'. What ordeal? Carella wondered. What struggle? And what exactly was the 'nightmare' Dennis mentioned later in his letter? Or was the nightmare the struggle itself, the ordeal, and not something that predated it? Dennis Sachs had been phoned in Arizona this morning by the authorities at the Children's Shelter, and was presumably already on his way East. Whether he yet realized it or not, he would have a great many questions to answer when he arrived.

Carella put the letter in his jacket pocket and began leafing through the other correspondence on the desk. There were bills from the electric company, the telephone company, most of the city's department stores, the Diner's Club, and many of the local merchants. There was a letter from a woman who had done house cleaning for Tinka and was writing to say she could no longer work for her because she and her family were moving back to Jamaica, B.W.I. There was a letter from the editor of one of the fashion magazines, outlining her plans for shooting the new Paris line with Tinka and several other mannequins that summer, and asking whether she would be available or not. Carella read these cursorily, putting them into a small neat pile at one edge of the oval table, and then found Tinka's address book.

There were a great many names, addresses, and telephone numbers in the small red leather book. Some of the people listed were men. Carella studied each name carefully, going through the book several times. Most of the names were run-of-the-mill Georges and Franks and Charlies, while others were a bit more rare like Clyde and Adrian, and still others were pretty exotic like Rion and Dink and Fritz. None of them rang a bell. Carella closed the book, put it into his jacket pocket and then went through the remainder of the papers on the desk. The only other item of interest was a partially completed poem in Tinka's handwriting:

> When I think of what I am
> And of what I might have been,
> I tremble.
> I fear the night.
> Throughout the day,
> I push from dragons conjured in the dark
> Why will they not

He folded the poem carefully and put it into his jacket pocket together with the address book. Then he rose, walked to the door, took a last look into the room, and snapped out the light. He went down the corridor towards the front door. The last pale light of day glanced through Anna's windows into her room, glowing feebly on the faces of her dolls lined up in rows on the bookcase shelves. He went into the room and gently lifted one of the dolls from the top shelf, replaced it, and then recognized another doll as the one Anna had been holding in her lap on Saturday when he'd talked to her. He lifted the doll from the shelf.

The patrolman outside the apartment was startled to see a grown detective rushing by him with a doll under his arm. Carella got into the elevator, hurriedly found what he wanted in Tinka's address book, and debated whether he should call the squad to tell them where he was headed, possibly get Kling to assist him with the arrest. He suddenly remembered that Kling had left the squadroom early. His anger boiled to the surface again. The *hell* with him, he thought, and came out into the street at a trot, running for his car. His thoughts came in a disorderly jumble, one following the next, the brutality of it, the goddamn stalking animal brutality of it, should I try making the collar alone, God that poor kid listening to her mother's murder, maybe I ought to go back to the office first, get Meyer to assist, but suppose my man is getting ready to cut out, why doesn't Kling shape up, oh God, slashed again and again. He started the car. The child's doll was on the seat beside him. He looked again at the name and address in Tinka's book. Well? he thought. Which? Get help or go it alone?

He stepped on the accelerator.

There was an excitement pounding inside him now, coupled with the anger, a high anticipatory clamour that drowned out whatever note of caution whispered automatically in his mind. It did not usually happen this way, there were usually weeks or months of drudgery. The surprise of his windfall, the idea of a sudden culmination to a chase barely begun, unleashed a wild energy inside him, forced his foot onto the gas pedal more firmly. His hands were tight on the wheel. He drove with a recklessness that would have brought a summons to a civilian, weaving in and out of traffic, hitting the horn and the brake, his hands and his feet a part of the machine that hurtled steadily downtown towards the address listed in Tinka's book.

He parked the car, and came out onto the sidewalk, leaving the doll on the front seat. He studied the name plates in the entrance hallway – yes, this was it. He pushed a bell button at random, turned the knob on the locked inside door when the answering buzz sounded. Swiftly he began climbing the steps to the third floor. On the second-floor landing, he drew his service revolver, a .38 Smith & Wesson Police Model 10. The gun had a two-inch barrel that made it virtually impossible to snag on clothing when drawn. It weighed only two ounces and was six and seven-eighths of an inch long, with a blue finish and a checked walnut Magna stock with the familiar S&W monogram. It was capable of firing six shots without reloading.

He reached the third floor and started down the hallway. The mailbox had told him the apartment number was 34. He found it at the end of the hall, and put his ear to the door, listening. He could hear the muted voices of a man and a woman inside the apartment. Kick it in, he thought. You've got enough for an arrest. Kick in the door, and go in shooting if necessary – he's your man. He backed away from the door. He braced himself against the corridor wall opposite the door, lifted his right leg high, pulling back the knee, and then stepped forward and simultaneously unleashed a piston kick, aiming for the lock high on the door.

The wood splintered, the lock ripped from the jamb, the door shot inwards. He followed the opening door into the room, the gun levelled in his right hand. He saw only a big beautiful dark-haired woman sitting on a couch facing the door, her legs crossed, a look of startled surprise on her face. But he had heard a man from outside. Where –?

He turned suddenly. He had abruptly realized that the apartment fanned out on both sides of the entrance door, and that the man could easily be to his right or his left, beyond his field of vision. He turned naturally to the right because he was right-handed, because the gun was in his right hand, and made the mistake that could have cost him his life.

The man was on his left.

Carella heard the sound of his approach too late, reversed his direction, caught a single glimpse of straight blond hair like Sonny Tufts, and then felt something hard and heavy smashing into his face.

Chapter Four

There was no furniture in the small room, save for a wooden chair to the right of the door. There were two windows on the wall facing the door, and these were covered with drawn green shades. The room was perhaps twelve feet wide by fifteen long, with a radiator in the centre of one of the fifteen-foot walls.

Carella blinked his eyes and stared into the semi-darkness.

There were night-time noises outside the windows, and he could see the intermittent flash of neon around the edges of the drawn shades. He wondered what time it was. He started to raise his left hand for a look at his watch, and discovered that it was handcuffed to the radiator. The handcuffs were his own. Whoever had closed the cuff onto his wrist had done so quickly and viciously; the metal was biting sharply into his flesh. The other cuff was clasped shut around the radiator leg. His watch was gone, and he seemed to have been stipped as well of his service revolver, his billet, his cartridges, his wallet and loose change, and even his shoes and socks. The side of his face hurt like hell. He lifted his right hand in exploration and found that his cheek and temple were crusted with dried blood. He looked down again at the radiator leg around which the second cuff was looped. Then he moved to the right of the radiator and looked behind it to see how it was fastened to the wall. If the fittings were loose –

He heard a key being inserted into the door lock. It suddenly occurred to him that he was still alive, and the knowledge filled him with a sense of impending dread rather than elation. *Why* was he still alive? And was someone opening the door right this minute in order to remedy that oversight?

The key turned.

The overhead light snapped on.

A big brunette girl came into the room. She was the same girl who had been sitting on the couch when he'd bravely kicked in the front door. She was carrying a tray in her hands, and he caught the aroma of coffee the moment she entered the room, that and the overriding scent of the heavy perfume the girl was wearing.

'Hello,' she said.

'Hello,' he answered.

'Have a nice sleep?'

'Lovely.'

She was very big, much bigger than she had seemed seated on the couch. She had the bones and body of a showgirl, five feet eight or nine inches tall, with firm full breasts threatening a low-cut peasant blouse, solid thighs sheathed in a tight black skirt that ended just above her knees. Her legs were long and very white, shaped like a dancer's with full calves and slender ankles. She was wearing black slippers, and she closed the door behind her and came into the room silently, the slippers whispering across the floor.

She moved slowly, almost as though she were sleepwalking. There was a current of sensuality about her, emphasized by her dreamlike motion. She seemed to possess an acute awareness of her lush body, and this in turn seemed coupled with the knowledge that whatever she might be – housewife or whore, slattern or saint – men would try to do things to that body, and succeed, repeatedly and without mercy. She was a victim, and she moved with the cautious tread of someone who had been beaten before and now expects attack from any quarter. Her caution, her awareness, the ripeness of her body, the certain knowledge that it was available, the curious look of inevitability the girl wore, all invited further abuses, encouraged fantasies, drew dark imaginings from hidden corners of the mind. Rinsed raven-black hair framed the girl's white face. It was a face hard with knowledge. Smoky Cleopatra makeup shaded her eyes and lashes, hiding the deeper-toned flesh there. Her nose had been fixed once, a long time ago, but it was beginning to fall out of shape so that it looked now as if someone had broken it, and this too added to the victim's look she wore. Her mouth was brightly painted, a whore's mouth, a doll's mouth. It had said every word ever invented. It had done everything a mouth was ever forced to do.

'I brought you some coffee,' she said.

Her voice was almost a whisper. He watched her as she came closer. He had the feeling that she could kill a man as readily as kiss him, and he wondered again why he was still alive.

He noticed for the first time that there was a gun on the tray, alongside the coffee pot. The girl lifted the gun now, and pointed it at his belly, still holding the tray with one hand. 'Back,' she said.

'Why?'

'Don't fuck around with me,' she said. 'Do what I tell you to do when I tell you to do it.'

Carella moved back as far as his cuffed wrist would allow him. The girl crouched, the tight skirt riding up over her thighs, and pushed the tray towards the radiator. Her face was dead serious. The gun was a super .38-calibre Llama automatic. The girl held it steady in her right hand. The thumb safety on the left side of the gun had been thrown. The automatic was ready for firing.

The girl rose and backed away towards the chair near the entrance door, the gun still trained on him. She sat, lowered the gun, and said, 'Go ahead.'

Carella poured coffee from the pot into the single mug on the tray. He took a swallow. The coffee was hot and strong.

'How is it?' the girl asked.

'Fine.'

'I made it myself.'

'Thank you.'

'I'll bring you a wet towel later,' she said. 'So you can wipe off that blood. It looks terrible.'

'It doesn't feel so hot, either,' Carella said.

'Well, who invited you?' the girl asked. She seemed about to smile, and then changed her mind.

'No one, that's true.' He took another sip of coffee. The girl watched him steadily.

'Steve Carella,' she said. 'Is that it?'

'That's right. What's *your* name?'

He asked the question quickly and naturally, but the girl did not step into the trap.

'Detective second/grade,' she said. '87th Squad.' She paused. 'Where's that?'

'Across from the park.'

'What park?'

'Grover Park.'

'Oh, yeah,' she said. 'That's a nice park. That's the nicest park in this whole damn city.'

'Yes,' Carella said.

'I saved your life, you know,' the girl said conversationally.

'Did you?'

'Yeah. *He* wanted to kill you.'

'I'm surprised he didn't.'

'Cheer up, maybe he will.'

'When?'

'You in a hurry?'

'Not particularly.'

The room went silent. Carella took another swallow of coffee. The girl kept staring at him. Outside, he could hear the sounds of traffic.

'What time is it?' he asked.

'About nine. Why? You got a date?'

'I'm wondering how long it'll be before I'm missed, that's all,' Carella said, and watched the girl.

'Don't try to scare me,' she said. 'Nothing scares me.'

'I wasn't trying to scare you.'

The girl scratched her leg idly, and then said, 'There're some questions I have to ask you.'

'I'm not sure I'll answer them.'

'You will,' she said. There was something cold and deadly in her voice. 'I can guarantee that. Sooner or later, you will.'

'Then it'll have to be later.'

'You're not being smart, mister.'

'I'm being very smart.'

'How?'

'I figure I'm alive only because you don't know the answers.'

'Maybe you're alive because I *want* you to be alive,' the girl said.

'Why?'

'I've never had anything like you before,' she said, and for the first time since she'd come into the room, she smiled. The smile was frightening. He could feel the flesh at the back of his neck beginning to crawl. He wet his lips and looked at her, and she returned his gaze steadily, the tiny evil smile lingering on her lips. 'I'm life or death to you,' she said. 'If I tell him to kill you, he will.'

'Not until you know all the answers,' Carella said.

'Oh, we'll get the answers. We'll have plenty of time to get the answers.' The smile dropped from her face. She put one hand inside her blouse and idly scratched her breast, and then looked at him again, and said, 'How'd you get here?'

'I took the subway.'

'That's a lie,' the girl said. There was no rancour in her voice. She accused him matter-of-factly, and then said, 'Your car was downstairs. The registration was in the glove compartment. There was also a sign on the sun visor, something about a law officer on a duty call.'

'All right, I drove here,' Carella said.

'Are you married?'

'Yes.'

'Do you have any children?'

'Two.'

'Girls?'

'A girl and a boy.'

'Then that's who the doll is for,' the girl said.

'What doll?'

'The one that was in the car. On the front seat of the car.'

'Yes,' Carella lied. 'It's for my daughter. Tomorrow's her birthday.'

'He brought it upstairs. It's outside in the living room.' The girl paused. 'Would you like to give your daughter that doll?'

'Yes.'

'Would you like to see her ever again?'

'Yes.'

'Then answer whatever I ask you, without any more lies about the subway or anything.'

'What's my guarantee?'

'Of what?'

'That I'll stay alive.'

'*I'm* your guarantee.'

'Why should I trust you?'

'You have to trust me,' the girl said. 'You're mine.' And again she smiled, and again he could feel the hairs stiffening at the back of his neck.

She got out of the chair. She scratched her belly, and then moved towards him, that same slow and cautious movement, as though she expected someone to strike her and was bracing herself for the blow.

'I haven't got much time,' she said. 'He'll be back soon.'

'Then what?'

The girl shrugged. 'Who knows you're here?' she asked suddenly.

Carella did not answer.

'How'd you get to us?'

Again, he did not answer.

'Did somebody see him leaving Tinka's apartment?'

Carella did not answer.

'How did you know where to come?'

Carella shook his head.

'Did someone identify him? How did you trace him?'

Carella kept watching her. She was standing three feet away from him now, too far to reach, the Llama dangling loosely in her right hand. She raised the gun.

'Do you want me to shoot you?' she asked conversationally.

'No.'

'I'll aim for your balls, would you like that?'

'No.'

'Then answer my questions.'

'You're not going to kill me,' Carella said. He did not take his eyes from the girl's face. The gun was pointed at his groin now, but he did not look at her finger curled inside the trigger guard.

The girl took a step closer. Carella crouched near the radiator, unable to get to his feet, his left hand manacled close to the floor. 'I'll enjoy this,' the girl promised, and struck him suddenly with the butt of the heavy gun, turning the butt up swiftly as her hand lashed out. He felt the numbing shock of metal against bone as the automatic caught him on the jaw and his head jerked back.

'You like?' the girl asked.

He said nothing.

'You *no* like, huh, baby?' She paused. 'How'd you find us?'

Again, he did not answer. She moved past him swiftly, so that he could not turn in time to stop the blow that came from behind him, could not kick out at her as he had planned to do the next time she approached. The butt caught him on the ear, and he felt the cartilage tearing as the metal rasped downwards. He whirled towards her angrily, grasping at her with his right arm as he turned, but she danced out of his reach and around to the front of him again, and again hit him with the automatic, cutting him over the left eye this time. He felt the blood start down his face from the open gash.

'What do you say?' she asked.

'I say go to hell,' Carella said, and the girl swung the gun again. He thought he was ready for her this time. But she was only feinting, and he grabbed out at empty air as she moved swiftly to his right and out of reach. The manacled hand threw him off balance. He fell forward, reaching for support with his free hand, the handcuff biting sharply into his other wrist. The gun butt caught him again just as his hand touched the floor. He felt it colliding with the base of his skull, a two-pound-six-and-a-half-ounce weapon swung with all the force of the girl's substantial body behind it. The pain shot clear to the top of his head. He blinked his eyes against the sudden dizziness. Hold on, he told himself, hold on, and was suddenly nauseous. The vomit came up into his throat, and he brought his right hand to his mouth just as the girl hit him again. He fell back dizzily against the radiator. He blinked up at the girl. Her lips were pulled back taut over her teeth, she was breathing harshly, the gun hand went back again, he was too weak to turn his head aside. The tried to raise his right arm, but it fell limply into his lap.

'Who saw him?' the girl asked.

'No,' he mumbled.

'I'm going to break your nose,' she said. Her voice sounded very far away. He tried to hold the floor for support, but he wasn't sure where the floor was any more. The room was spinning. He looked up at the girl and saw her spinning face and breasts, smelled the heavy cloying perfume and saw the gun in her hand. 'I'm going to break your nose, mister.'

'No.'

'Yes,' she said.

'No.'

He did not see the gun this time. He felt only the excruciating pain of bones splintering. His head rocked back with the blow, colliding with the cast-iron ribs of the radiator. The pain brought him back to raging consciousness. He lifted his right hand to his nose, and the girl hit him again, at the base of the skull again, and again he felt sensibility slipping away from him. He smiled stupidly. She would not let him die, and she would not let him live. She would not allow him to become unconscious, and she would not allow him to regain enough strength to defend himself.

'I'm going to knock out all of your teeth,' the girl said.

He shook his head.

'Who told you where to find us? Was it the elevator operator? Was it that one-eyed bastard?'

He did not answer.

'Do you want to lose all your teeth?'

'No.'

'Then tell me.'

'No.'

'You have to tell me,' she said. 'You *belong* to me.'

'No,' he said.

There was a silence. He knew the gun was coming again. He tried to raise his hand to his mouth, to protect his teeth, but there was no strength in his arm. He sat with his left wrist caught in the fierce biting grip of the handcuff, swollen, throbbing, with blood pouring down his face and from his nose, his nose a throbbing mass of splintered bone, and waited for the girl to knock out his teeth as she had promised, helpless to stop her.

He felt her lips upon him.

She kissed him fiercely and with her mouth open, her tongue searching his lips and his teeth. Then she pulled away from him, and he heard her whisper, 'In the morning, they'll find you dead.'

He lost consciousness again.

On Tuesday morning, they found the automobile at the bottom of a steep cliff some fifty miles across the River Harb, in a sparsely populated area of the adjoining state. Most of the paint had been burned away by what must have been an intensely hot fire, but it was still possible to tell that the car was a green 1961 Pontiac sedan bearing the licence plate RI 7-3461.

The body on the front seat of the car had been incinerated. They knew by what remained of the lower portions that the body had once been a man, but the face and torso had been cooked beyond recognition, the hair and clothing gone, the skin black and charred, the arms drawn up into the typical pugilistic attitude caused by post-mortem contracture of burned muscles, the fingers hooked like claws. A gold wedding band was on the third finger of the skeletal left hand. The fire had eaten away the skin and charred the remaining bones and turned the gold of the ring to a dull black. A .38 Smith & Wesson was caught in the exposed springs of the front seat, together with the metal parts that remained of what had once been a holster.

All of the man's teeth were missing from his mouth.

In the cinders of what they supposed had been his wallet, they found a detective's shield with the identifying number 714-5632.

A call to headquarters across the river informed the investigating police that the shield belonged to a detective second/grade named Stephen Louis Carella.

Chapter Five

Teddy Carella sat in the silence of her living room and watched the lips of Detective Lieutenant Peter Byrnes as he told her that her husband was dead. The scream welled up into her throat, she could feel the muscles there contracting until she thought she would strangle. She brought her hand to her mouth, her eyes closed tight so that she would no longer have to watch the words that formed on the lieutenant's lips, no longer have to see the words that confirmed what she had known was true since the night before when her husband had failed to come home for dinner.

She would not scream, but a thousand screams echoed inside her head. She felt faint. She almost swayed out of the chair, and then she looked up into the lieutenant's face as she felt his supporting arm around her shoulders. She nodded. She tried to smile up at him sympathetically, tried to let him know she realized this was an unpleasant task for him. But the tears were streaming down her face and she wished only that her husband were there to comfort her, and then abruptly she realized that her husband would never be there to comfort her again, the realization circling back upon itself, the silent screams ricochetting inside her.

The lieutenant was talking again.

She watched his lips. She sat stiff and silent in the chair, her hands clasped tightly in her lap, and wondered where the children were, how would she tell the children, and saw the lieutenant's lips as he said his men would do everything possible to uncover the facts of her husband's death. In the meantime, Teddy, if there's anything I can do, anything I can do personally I mean, I think you know how much Steve meant to me, to all of us, if there's anything Harriet or I can do to help in any way, Teddy, I don't have to tell you we'll do anything we can, anything.

She nodded.

There's a possibility this was just an accident, Teddy, though we doubt it, we think he was, we don't think it was an accident, why would he be across the river in the next state, fifty miles from here?

She nodded again. Her vision was blurred by the tears. She could barely see his lips as he spoke.

Teddy, I loved that boy. I would rather have a bullet in my heart than be here in this room today with this, with this information. I'm sorry. Teddy I am sorry.

She sat in the chair as still as a stone.

Detective Meyer Meyer left the squadroom at two p.m. and walked across the street and past the stone wall leading into the park. It was a fine April day, the sky a clear blue, the sun shining overhead, the birds chirping in the newly leaved trees.

He walked deep into the park, and he found an empty bench and sat upon it, crossing his legs, one arm stretched out across the top of the bench, the other hanging loose in his lap. There were young boys and girls holding hands and whispering nonsense, there were children chasing each other and laughing, there were nannies wheeling baby carriages, there were old men reading books as they walked, there was the sound of a city hovering on the air.

There was life.

Meyer Meyer sat on the bench and quietly wept for his friend.

Detective Cotton Hawes went to a movie.

The movie was a western. There was a cattle drive in it, thousands of animals thundering across the screen, men sweating and shouting, horses rearing, bullwhips cracking. There was also an attack on a wagon train, Indians circling, arrows and spears whistling through the air, guns answering, men screaming. There was a fight in a saloon, too, chairs and bottles flying, tables collapsing, women running for cover with their skirts pulled high, fists connecting. Altogether, there was noise and colour and loud music and plenty of action.

When the end titles flashed onto the screen, Hawes rose and walked up the aisle and out into the street.

Dusk was coming.

The city was hushed.

He had not been able to forget that Steve Carella was dead.

Andy Parker, who had hated Steve Carella's guts when he was alive, went to bed with a girl that night. The girl was a prostitute, and he got into her bed and her body by threatening to arrest her if she didn't come across. The girl had been hooking in the neighbourhood for little more than a week. The other working hustlers had taken her aside and pointed out all the Vice Squad bulls and also all the local plainclothes fuzz so that she wouldn't make the mistake of propositioning one of them. But Parker had been on sick leave for two weeks with pharyngitis and had not been included in the girl's original briefing by her colleagues. She had approached what looked like a sloppy drunk in a bar on Ainsley, and before the bartender could catch her eye to warn her, she had given him the familiar 'Wanna have some fun, baby?' line and then had compounded the error by telling Parker it would cost him a fin for a single roll in the hay or twenty-five bucks for all night. Parker had accepted the girl's proposition, and had left the bar with her while the owner of the place frantically signalled his warning. The girl didn't know why the hell he was waving his arms at her. She knew only that she had a John who said he wanted to spend the night with her. She didn't know the John's last name was Law.

She took Parker to a rented room on Culver. Parker was very drunk – he had begun drinking at twelve noon when word of Carella's death reached the squadroom – but he was not drunk enough to forget that he could not arrest this girl until she exposed her 'privates'. He waited until she took off her clothes, and then he showed her his shield and said she could take her choice, a possible three years in the jug, or a pleasant hour or two with a very nice fellow. The girl, who had met very nice fellows like Parker before, all of whom had been Vice Squad cops looking for fleshy handouts, figured this was only a part of her normal overhead, nodded briefly, and spread out on the bed for him.

Parker was very very drunk.

To the girl's great surprise, he seemed more interested in talking than in making love, as the euphemism goes.

'What's the sense of it all, would you tell me?' he said, but did not wait for an answer. 'Son of a bitch like Carella gets cooked in a car by some son of a bitch, what's the sense of it? You know what I see every day of the week, you know what we *all* of us see every day of the week, how do you expect us to stay human, would you tell me? Son of a bitch gets cooked like that, doing his job is all, how do you expect us to stay human? What am I doing here with you, a two-bit whore, is that something for me to be doing? I'm a nice fellow. Don't you know I'm a nice fellow?'

'Sure, you're a nice fellow,' the girl said, bored.

'Garbage every day,' Parker said. 'Filth and garbage, I have the stink in my nose when I go home at night. You know where I live? I live in a garden apartment in Majesta. I've got three and a half rooms, a nice little kitchen, you know, a nice apartment. I've got a hi-fi set and also I belong to the Classics Club, I've got all those books by the big writers, the important writers. I haven't got much time to read them, but I got them all there on a shelf, you should see the books I've got. There are nice people living in that apartment building, not like here, not like what you find in this crumby precinct, how old are you anyway, what are you nineteen, twenty?'

'I'm twenty-one,' the girl said.

'Sure, look at you, the shit of the city.'

'Listen, mister –'

'Shut up, shut up, who the hell's asking you? I'm *paid* to deal with it, all the shit that gets washed into the sewers, that's my job. My neighbours in the building know I'm a detective, they respect me, they look up to me. They don't know that all I do is handle shit all day long until I can't stand the stink of it any more. The kids riding their bikes in the courtyard, they all say, "Good morning, Detective Parker." That's me, a detective. They watch television, you see. I'm one of the good guys. I carry a gun. I'm brave. So look what happens to that son of a bitch Carella. What's the sense?'

'I don't know what you're talking about,' the girl said.

'What's the sense, what's the sense?' Parker said. 'People, boy, I could tell you about people. You wouldn't believe what I could tell you about people.'

'I've been around a little myself,' the girl said drily.

'You can't blame me,' he said suddenly.

'What?'

'You can't blame me. It's not my fault.'

'Sure. Look, mister, I'm a working girl. You want some of this, or not? Because if you –'

'Shut up, you goddamn whore, don't tell me what to do.'

'Nobody's –'

'I can pull you in and make your life miserable, you little slut. I've got the power of life and death over you, don't forget it.'

'Not quite,' the girl said with dignity.

'Not quite, not quite, don't give me any of that crap.'

'You're drunk,' the girl said. 'I don't even think you can –'

'Never mind what I am, I'm not drunk.' He shook his head. 'All right, I'm drunk, what the hell do you care what I am? You think I care what *you* are? You're *nothing* to me, you're *less* than nothing to me.'

'Then what are you doing here?'

'Shut up,' he said. He paused. 'The kids all yell good morning at me,' he said.

He was silent for a long time. His eyes were closed. The girl thought he had fallen asleep. She started to get off the bed, and he caught her arm and pulled her down roughly beside him.

'Stay where you are.'

'Okay,' she said. 'But look, you think we could get this over with? I mean it, mister, I've got a long night ahead of me. I got expenses to meet.'

'Filth,' Parker said. 'Filth and garbage.'

'Okay, already, filth and garbage, do you want it or not?'

'He was a good cop,' Parker said suddenly.

'What?'

'He was a good cop,' he said again, and rolled over quickly and put his head into the pillow.

Chapter Six

At seven-thirty Wednesday morning, the day after the burned wreckage was found in the adjoining state, Bert Kling went back to the apartment building on Stafford Place, hoping to talk again to Ernest Cyclops Messner. The lobby was deserted when he entered the building.

If he had felt alone the day that Claire Townsend was murdered, if he had felt alone the day he held her in his arms in a bookshop demolished by gunfire, suddenly bereft in a world gone cold and senselessly cruel, he now felt something curiously similar and yet enormously different.

Steve Carella was dead.

The last words he had said to the man who had been his friend were angry words. He could not take them back now, he could not call upon a dead man, he could not offer apologies to a corpse. On Monday, he had left the squadroom earlier than he should have, in anger, and sometime that night Carella had met his death. And now there was a new grief within him, a new feeling of helplessness, but it was coupled with an overriding desire to set things right again – for Carella, for Claire, he did not really know. He knew he could not reasonably blame himself for what had happened, but neither could he stop blaming himself. He had to talk to Cyclops again. Perhaps there was something further the man could tell him. Perhaps Carella had contacted him again that Monday night, and uncovered new information that had sent him rushing out to investigate alone.

The elevator doors opened. The operator was not Cyclops.

'I'm looking for Mr Messner,' Kling told the man. 'I'm from the police.'

'He's not here,' the man said.

'He told us he has the graveyard shift.'

'Yeah, well, he's not here.'

'It's only seven-thirty,' Kling said.

'I know what time it is.'

'Well, where is he, can you tell me that?'

'He lives some place here in the city,' the man said, 'but I don't know where.'

'Thank you,' Kling said, and left the building.

It was still too early in the morning for the rush of white-collar workers to subways and buses. The only people in the streets were factory workers hurrying to punch an eight-a.m. timeclock; the only vehicles were delivery trucks and an occasional passenger car. Kling walked swiftly, looking for a telephone booth. It was going to be another beautiful day; the city had been blessed with lovely weather for the past week now. He saw an open drugstore on the next corner, a telephone plaque fastened to the brick wall outside. He went into the store and headed for the directories at the rear.

Ernest Cyclops Messner lived 1117 Gainesborough Avenue in Riverhead, not far from the County Court Building. The shadow of the elevated-train structure fell over the building, and the frequent rumble of trains pulling in and out of the station shattered the silence of the street. But it was a good low-to-middle-income residential area, and Messner's building was the newest on the block. Kling climbed the low flat entrance steps, went into the lobby, and found a listing for E. Messner. He rang the bell under the mailbox, but there was no answering buzz. He tried another bell. A buzz sounded, releasing the lock mechanism on the inner lobby door. He pushed open the door, and began climbing to the seventh floor. It was a little after eight a.m., and the building still seemed asleep.

He was somewhat winded by the time he reached the seventh floor. He paused on the landing for a moment, and then walked into the corridor, looking for apartment 7A. He found it just off the stairwell, and rang the bell.

There was no answer.

He rang the bell again.

He was about to ring it a third time when the door to the apartment alongside opened and a young girl rushed out, looking at her wrist watch and almost colliding with Kling.

'Oh, hi,' she said, surprised. 'Excuse me.'

'That's all right.' He reached for the bell again. The girl had gone past him and was starting down the steps. She turned suddenly.

'Are you looking for Mr Messner?' she asked.

'Yes, I am.'

'He isn't home.'

'How do you know?'

'Well, he doesn't get home until about nine,' she said. 'He works nights, you know.'

'Does he live here alone?'

'Yes, he does. His wife died a few years back. He's lived here a long time, I know him from when I was a little girl.' She looked at her watch again. 'Listen, I'm going to be late. Who *are* you, anyway?'

'I'm from the police,' Kling said.

'Oh, hi.' The girl smiled. 'I'm Marjorie Gorman.'

'Would you know where I can reach him, Marjorie?'

'Did you try his building? He works in a fancy apartment house on –'

'Yes, I just came from there.'

'Wasn't he there?'

'No.'

'That's funny,' Marjorie said. 'Although, come to think of it, we didn't hear him last night, either.'

'What do you mean?'

'The television. The walls are very thin, you know. When he's home, we can hear the television going.'

'Yes, but he works nights.'

'I mean before he leaves. He doesn't go to work until eleven o'clock. He starts at midnight, you know.'

'Yes, I know.'

'Well, that's what I meant. Listen, I really do have to hurry. If you want to talk, you'll have to walk me to the station.'

'Okay,' Kling said, and they started down the steps. 'Are you sure you didn't hear the television going last night?'

'I'm positive.'

'Does he usually have it on?'

'Oh, *con*stantly,' Marjorie said. 'He lives alone, you know, the poor old man. He's got to do *some*thing with his time.'

'Yes, I suppose so.'

'Why did you want to see him?'

She spoke with a pronounced Riverhead accent that somehow marred her clean good looks. She was a tall girl, perhaps nineteen years old, wearing a dark-grey suit and a white blouse, her auburn hair brushed back behind her ears, the lobes decorated with tiny pearl earrings.

'There are some things I want to ask him,' Kling said.

'About the Tinka Sachs murder?'

'Yes.'

'He was telling me about that just recently.'

'When was that?'

'Oh, I don't know. Let me think.' They walked out of the lobby and into the street. Marjorie had long legs, and she walked very swiftly. Kling, in fact, was having trouble keeping up with her. 'What's today, anyway?'

'Wednesday,' Kling said.

'Wednesday, mmm, boy where does the week go? It must have been Monday. That's right. When I got home from the movies Monday night, he was downstairs putting out his garbage. So we talked awhile. He said he was expecting a detective.'

'A detective? Who?'

'What do you mean?'

'Did he say *which* detective he was expecting? Did he mention a name?'

'No, I don't think so. He said he'd talked to some detectives just that morning – that was Monday, right? – and that he'd got a call a few minutes ago saying another detective was coming up to see him.'

'Did he say that exactly? That *another* detective was coming up to see him? A *different* detective?'

'Oh. I don't know if he said just that. I mean, it could have been one of the detectives he'd talked to that morning. I really don't know for sure.'

'Does the name Carella mean anything to you?'

'No.' Marjorie paused. 'Should it?'

'Did Mr Messner use that name when he was talking about the detective who was coming to see him?'

'No, I don't think so. He only said he'd had a call from a detective, that was all. He seemed very proud. He told me they probably wanted him to describe the man again, the one he saw going up to her apartment. The dead girl's. Brrrr, it gives you the creeps, doesn't it?'

'Yes,' Kling said. 'It does.'

They were approaching the elevated station now. They paused at the bottom of the steps.

'This was Monday afternoon, you say?'

'No. Monday night. Monday *night*, I said.'

'What time Monday night?'

'About ten-thirty, I guess. I told you, I was coming home from the movies.'

'Let me get this straight,' Kling said. 'At ten-thirty Monday night, Mr Messner was putting out his garbage, and he told you he had just received a call from a detective who was on his way over? Is that it?'

'That's it.' Marjorie frowned. 'It *was* kind of late, wasn't it? I mean, to be making a business visit. Or do you people work that late?'

'Well, yes, but ...' Kling shook his head.

'Listen, I really have to go,' Marjorie said. 'I'd like to talk to you, but –'

'I'd appreciate a few more minutes of your time, if you can –'

'Yes, but my boss –'

'I'll call him later and explain.'

'Yeah, you don't *know* him,' Marjorie said, and rolled her eyes.

'Can you just tell me whether Mr Messner mentioned anything about this detective the next time you saw him. I mean, *after* the detective was there.'

'Well, I haven't seen him since Monday night.'

'You didn't see him at *all* yesterday?'

'Nope. Well, I usually miss him in the morning, you know, because I'm gone before he gets home. But sometimes I drop in at night, just to say hello, or he'll come in for something, you know, like that. And I told you about the television. We just didn't hear it. My mother commented about it, as a matter of fact. She said Cyclops was probably – that's what we call him, Cyclops, everybody does, he doesn't mind – she said Cyclops was probably out on the town.'

'Does he often go out on the town?'

'Well, I don't think so – but who knows? Maybe he felt like having himself a good time, you know? Listen, I really have to –'

'All right, I won't keep you. Thank you very much, Marjorie. If you'll tell me where you work, I'll be happy to –'

'Oh, the hell with him. I'll tell him what happened, and he can take it or leave it. I'm thinking of quitting, anyway.'

'Well, thank you again.'

'Don't mention it,' Marjorie said, and went up the steps to the platform.

Kling thought for a moment, and then searched in his pocket for a dime. He went into the cafeteria on the corner, found a phone booth, and identified himself to the operator, telling her he wanted the listing for the lobby phone in Tinka's building on Stafford Place. She gave him the number, and he dialled it. A man answered the phone. Kling said, 'I'd like to talk to the superintendent, please.'

'This is the super.'

'This is Detective Kling of the 87th Squad,' Kling said. 'I'm investigating –'

'Who?' the superintendent said.

'Detective Kling. Who's this I'm speaking to?'

'I'm the super of the building. Emmanuel Farber. Manny. Did you say this was a detective?'

'That's right.'

'Boy, when are you guys going to give us some rest here?'

'What do you mean?'

'Don't you have nothing to do but call up here?'

'I haven't called you before, Mr Farber.'

'No, not you, never mind. This phone's being going like sixty.'

'Who called you?'

'Detectives, never mind.'

'Who? Which detectives?'

'The other night.'

'When?'

'Monday. Monday night.'

'A detective called you Monday night?'

'Yeah, wanted to know where he could reach Cyclops. That's one of our elevator operators.'

'Did you tell him?'

'Sure, I did.'

'Who was he? Did he give you his name?'

'Yeah, some Italian fellow.'

Kling was silent for a moment.

'Would the name have been Carella?' he asked.

'That's right.'

'Carella?'

'Yep, that's the one.'

'What time did he call?'

'Oh, I don't know. Sometime in the evening.'

'And he said his name was Carella?'

'That's right, Detective Carella, that's what he said. Why? You know him?'

'Yes,' Kling said. 'I know him.'

'Well, you ask him. He'll tell you.'

'What time in the evening did he call? Was it early or late?'
'What do you mean by early or late?' Farber asked.
'Was it before dinner?'
'No. Oh no, it was after dinner. About ten o'clock, I suppose. Maybe a little later.'
'And what did he say to you?'
'He wanted Cyclops' address, said he had some questions to ask him.'
'About what?'
'About the murder.'
'He said that specifically? He said, "I have some questions to ask Cyclops about the murder?"'
'About the Tinka Sachs murder, is what he actually said.'
'He said, "This is Detective Carella, I want to know –"'
'That's right, this is Detective Carella –'
'"– I want to know Cyclops Messner's address because I have some questions to ask him about the Tinka Sachs murder."'
'No, that's not it exactly.'
'What's wrong with it?' Kling asked.
'He didn't say the name.'
'You just said he *did* say the name. The Tinka Sachs murder. You said –'
'Yes, that's right. That's not what I mean.'
'Look, what –?'
'He didn't say Cyclops' name.'
'I don't understand you.'
'All he said was he wanted the address of the one-eyed elevator operator because he had some questions to ask him about the Tinka Sachs murder. That's what he said.'
'He referred to him as the one-eyed elevator operator?'
'That's right.'
'You mean he didn't know the name?'
'Well, I don't know about that. He didn't know how to *spell* it, though, that's for sure.'
'Excuse me,' the telephone operator said. 'Five cents for the next five minutes, please.'
'Hold on,' Kling said. He reached into his pocket, and found only two quarters. He put one into the coin slot.
'Was that twenty-five cents you deposited, sir?' the operator asked.
'That's right.'
'If you'll let me have your name and address, sir, we'll –'
'No, forget it.'
'– send you a refund in stamps.'
'No, that's all right, operator, thank you. Just give me as much time as the quarter'll buy, okay?'
'Very well, sir.'
'Hello?' Kling said. 'Mr Farber?'
'I'm still here,' Farber said.
'What makes you think this detective couldn't spell Cyclops' name?'
'Well, I gave him the address, you see, and I was about to hang up when he asked me about the spelling. He wanted to know the correct spelling of the name.'

'And what did you say?'

'I said it was Messner, M-E-S-S-N-E-R, Ernest Messner, and I repeated the address for him again, 1117 Gainesborough Avenue in Riverhead.'

'And then what?'

'He said thank you very much and hung up.'

'Sir, was it your impression that he did not know Cyclops' name until you gave it to him?'

'Well, I couldn't say that for sure. All he wanted was the correct spelling.'

'Yes, but he asked for the address of the one-eyed elevator operator, isn't that what you said?'

'That's right.'

'If he knew the name, why didn't he use it?'

'You got me. What's *your* name?' the superintendent asked.

'Kling. Detective Bert Kling.'

'Mine's Farber, Emmanuel Farber, Manny.'

'Yes, I know. You told me.'

'Oh. Okay.'

There was a long silence on the line.

'Was that all, Detective Kling?' Farber said at last. 'I've got to get these lobby floors waxed and I'm –'

'Just a few more questions,' Kling said.

'Well, okay, but could we –?'

'Cyclops had his usual midnight-to-eight-a.m. shift Monday night, is that right?'

'That's right, but –'

'When he came to work, did he mention anything about having seen a detective?'

'He *didn't*,' Farber said.

'He didn't mention a detective at all? He didn't say –'

'No, he didn't come to work.'

'What?'

'He didn't come to work Monday nor yesterday, either,' Farber said. 'I had to get another man to take his place.'

'Did you try to reach him?'

'I waited until twelve-thirty, with the man he was supposed to relieve taking a fit, and finally I called his apartment, three times in fact, and there was no answer. So I phoned one of the other men. Had to run the elevator myself until the man got here. That must've been about two in the morning.'

'Did Cyclops contact you at all any time yesterday?'

'Nope. You think he'd call, wouldn't you?'

'Did he contact you today?'

'Nope.'

'But you're expecting him to report to work tonight, aren't you?'

'Well, he's due at midnight, but I don't know. I hope he shows up.'

'Yes, I hope so, too,' Kling said. 'Thank you very much, Mr Farber. You've been very helpful.'

'Sure thing,' Farber said, and hung up.

Kling sat in the phone booth for several moments, trying to piece together what he had just learned. Someone had called Farber on Monday night at about ten, identifying himself as Detective Carella, and asking for the address of the one-eyed elevator operator. Carella knew the man was named Ernest Messner and nicknamed Cyclops. He would not have referred to him as the one-eyed elevator operator. But more important than that, he would never have called the superintendent at all. Knowing the man's name, allegedly desiring his address, he would have done exactly what Kling had done this morning. He would have consulted the telephone directories and found a listing for Ernest Messner in the Riverhead book, as simple as that, as routine as that. No, the man who had called Farber was not Carella. But he had known Carella's name, and had made good use of it.

At ten-thirty Monday night, Marjorie Gorman had met Cyclops in front of the building and he had told her he was expecting a visit from a detective. That could only mean that 'Detective Carella' had already called Cyclops and told him he would stop by. And now, Cyclops was missing, had indeed been missing since Monday night.

Kling came out of the phone booth, and began walking back towards the building on Gainesborough Avenue.

The landlady of the building did not have a key to Mr Messner's apartment. Mr Messner has his own lock on the door, she said, the same as any of the other tenants in the building, and she certainly did not have a key to Mr Messner's lock, nor to the locks of any of the other tenants. Moreover, she would *not* grant permission to try his skeleton key on the door, and she warned him that if he forced entry into Mr Messner's apartment, she would sue the city. Kling informed her that if she cooperated, she would save him the trouble of going all the way downtown for a search warrant, and she said she didn't *care* about his going all the way downtown, suppose Mr Messner came back and learned she had let the police in there while he was away, *who'd* get the lawsuit then, would he mind telling her?

Kling said he would go downtown for the warrant.

Go ahead then, the landlady told him.

It took an hour to get downtown, twenty minutes to obtain the warrant, and another hour to get back to Riverhead again. His skeleton key would not open Cyclops' door, so he kicked it in.

The apartment was empty.

Chapter Seven

Dennis Sachs seemed to be about forty years old. He was tall and deeply tanned, with massive shoulders and an athlete's easy stance. He opened the door of his room at the Hotel Capistan, and said, 'Detective Kling? Come in, won't you?'

'Thank you,' Kling said. He studied Sachs's face. The eyes were blue, with deep ridges radiating from the edges, starkly white against the bronzed skin. He had a large nose, an almost feminine mouth, a cleft chin. He needed a shave. His hair was brown.

The little girl, Anna, was sitting on a couch at the far end of the large living room. She had a doll across her lap, and she was watching television when Kling came in. She glanced up at him briefly, and then turned her attention back to the screen. A give-away programme was in progress, the M.C. unveiling a huge motor launch to the delighted shrieks of the studio audience. The couch was upholstered in a lush green fabric against which the child's blonde hair shone lustrously. The place was oppressively over-furnished, undoubtedly part of a suite, with two doors leading from the living room to the adjoining bedrooms. A small cooking alcove was tucked discreetly into a corner near the entrance door, a screen drawn across it. The dominant colours of the suite were pale yellows and deep greens, the rugs were thick, the furniture was exquisitely carved. Kling suddenly wondered how much all this was costing Sachs per day, and then tried to remember where he'd picked up the notion that archaeologists were poverty-stricken.

'Sit down,' Sachs said. 'Can I get you a drink?'

'I'm on duty,' Kling said.

'Oh, sorry. Something soft then? A Coke? Seven-Up? I think we've got some in the refrigerator.'

'Thank you, no,' Kling said.

The men sat. From his wing chair, Kling could see through the large windows and out over the park to where the skyscrapers lined the city. The sky behind the buildings was a vibrant blue. Sachs sat facing him, limned with the light flowing through the windows.

'The people at the Children's Shelter told me you got to the city late Monday, Mr Sachs. May I ask where in Arizona you were?'

'Well, part of the time I was in the desert, and the rest of the time I was staying in a little town called Rainfield, have you ever heard of it?'

'No.'

'Yes. Well, I'm not surprised,' Sachs said. 'It's on the edge of the desert. Just a single hotel, a depot, a general store, and that's it.'

'What were you doing in the desert?'

'We're on a dig, I thought you knew that. I'm part of an archaeological team headed by Dr Oliver Tarsmith. We're trying to trace the route of the Hohokam in Arizona.'

'The Hohokam?'

'Yes, That's a Pima Indian word meaning "those who have vanished". The Hohokam were a tribe once living in Arizona, haven't you ever heard of them?'

'No, I'm afraid I haven't.'

'Yes, well. In any case, they seem to have had their origins in Old Mexico. In fact, archaeologists like myself have found copper bells and other objects that definitely link the Hohokam to the Old Mexican civilization. And, of course, we've excavated ball courts – an especially large one at Snaketown – that are definitely Mexican or Mayan in origin. At one site, we found a rubber ball buried in a jar, and it's our belief that it must have been traded through tribes all the way from southern Mexico. That's where the wild rubber grows, you know.'

'No, I didn't know that.'

'Yes, well. The point is that we archaeologists don't know what route the Hohokam travelled from Mexico to Arizona and then to Snaketown. Dr Tarsmith's theory is that their point of entry was the desert just outside Rainfield. We are now excavating for archaeological evidence to support this theory.'

'I see. That sounds like interesting work.'

Sachs shrugged.

'Isn't it?'

'I suppose so.'

'You don't sound very enthusiastic.'

'Well, we haven't had too much luck so far. We've been out there for close to a year, and we've uncovered only the flimsiest sort of evidence, and . . . well, frankly, it's getting a bit tedious. We spend four days a week out on the desert, you see, and then come back into Rainfield late Thursday night. There's nothing much in Rainfield, and the nearest big town is a hundred miles from there. It can get pretty monotonous.'

'Why only *four* days in the desert?'

'Instead of five, do you mean? We usually spend Fridays making out our reports. There's a lot of paperwork involved, and it's easier to do at the hotel.'

'When did you learn of your wife's death, Mr Sachs?'

'Monday morning.'

'You had not been informed up to that time?'

'Well, as it turned out, a telegram was waiting for me in Rainfield. I guess it was delivered to the hotel on Saturday, but I wasn't there to take it.'

'Where were you?'

'In Phoenix.'

'What were you doing there?'

'Drinking, seeing some shows. You can get very sick of Rainfield, you know.'

'Did anyone go with you?'

'No.'

'How did you get to Phoenix?'

'By train.'

'Where did you stay in Phoenix?'

'At the Royal Sands.'

'From when to when?'

'Well, I left Rainfield late Thursday night. I asked Oliver – Dr Tarsmith – if he thought he'd need me on Friday, and he said he wouldn't. I guess he realized I was stretched a little thin. He's a very perceptive man that way.'

'I see. In effect, then, he gave you Friday off.'

'That's right.'

'No reports to write?'

'I took those with me to Phoenix. It's only a matter of organizing one's notes, typing them up, and so on.'

'Did you manage to get them done in Phoenix?'

'Yes, I did.'

'Now, let me understand this, Mr Sachs ...'

'Yes?'

'You left Rainfield sometime late Thursday night ...'

'Yes, I caught the last train out.'

'What time did you arrive in Phoenix?'

'Sometime after midnight. I had called ahead to the Sands for a reservation.'

'I see. When did you leave Phoenix?'

'Mr Kling,' Sachs said suddenly, 'are you just making small talk, or is there some reason for your wanting to know all this?'

'I was simply curious, Mr Sachs. I knew Homicide had sent a wire off to you, and I was wondering why you didn't receive it until Monday morning.'

'Oh. Well, I just explained that. I didn't get back to Rainfield until then.'

'You left Phoenix Monday morning?'

'Yes. I caught a train at about six a.m. I didn't want to miss the jeep.' Sachs paused. 'The expedition's jeep. We usually head out to the desert pretty early, to get some heavy work in before the sun gets too hot.'

'I see. But when you got back to the hotel, you found the telegram.'

'That's right.'

'What did you do then?'

'I immediately called the airport in Phoenix to find out what flights I could get back here.'

'And what did they tell you?'

'There was a TWA flight leaving at eight in the morning, which would get here at four-twenty in the afternoon – there's a two-hour time difference, you know.'

'Yes, I know that. Is that the flight you took?'

'No, I didn't. It was close to six-thirty when I called the airport. I might have been able to make it to Phoenix in time, but it would have been a very tight squeeze, and I'd have had to borrow a car. The trains out of Rainfield aren't that frequent, you see.'

'So what *did* you do?'

'Well, I caught American's eight-thirty flight, instead. Not a through flight; we made a stop at Chicago. I didn't get here until almost five o'clock that night.'

'That was Monday night?'

'Yes, that's right.'

'When did you pick up your daughter?'

'Yesterday morning. Today is Wednesday, isn't it?'

'Yes.'

'You lose track of time when you fly cross-country,' Sachs said.

'I suppose you do.'

The television M.C. was giving away a fourteen-cubic-foot refrigerator with a big, big one-hundred-and-sixty-pound freezer. The studio audience was applauding. Anna sat with her eyes fastened to the screen.

'Mr Sachs, I wonder if we could talk about your wife.'

'Yes, please.'

'The child . . .'

'I think she's absorbed in the programme.' He glanced at her, and then said, 'Would you prefer we discussed it in one of the other rooms?'

'I thought that might be better, yes,' Kling said.

'Yes, you're right. Of course,' Sachs said. He rose and led Kling towards the larger bedroom. His valise, partially unpacked, was open on the stand alongside the bed. 'I'm afraid everything's a mess,' he said. 'It's been hurry up, hurry up from the moment I arrived.'

'I can imagine,' Kling said. He sat in an easy chair near the bed. Sachs sat on the edge of the bed and leaned over intently, waiting for him to begin. 'Mr Sachs, how long had you and your wife been divorced?'

'Three years. And we separated a year before that.'

'The child is how old?'

'Anna? She's five.'

'Is there another child?'

'No.'

'The way you said "Anna," I thought –'

'No, there's only the one child. Anna. That's all.'

'As I understand it, then, you and your wife separated the year after she was born.'

'That's right, yes. Actually, it was fourteen months. She was fourteen months old when we separated.'

'Why was that, Mr Sachs?'

'Why was what?'

'Why did you separate?'

'Well, you know.' Sachs shrugged.

'No, I don't.'

'Well, that's personal. I'm afraid.'

The room was very silent. Kling could hear the M.C. in the living room leading the audience in a round of applause for one of the contestants.

'I can understand that divorce is a personal matter, Mr Sachs, but –'

'Yes, it is.'

'Yes, I understand that.'

'I'd rather not discuss it, Mr Kling. Really, I'd rather not. I don't see how it would help you in solving . . . in solving my wife's murder. Really.'

'I'm afraid *I'll* have to decide what would help us, Mr Sachs.'

'We had a personal problem, let's leave it at that.'

'What sort of a personal problem?'

'I'd rather not say. We simply couldn't live together any longer, that's all.'

'Was there another man involved?'

'Certainly not!'

'Forgive me, but I think you can see how another man might be important in a murder case.'

'I'm sorry. Yes. Of course. Yes, it would be important. But it wasn't anything like that. There was no one else involved. There was simply a . . . a personal problem between the two of us and we . . . we couldn't find a way to resolve it, so . . . so we thought it best to split up. That's all there was to it.'

'What was the personal problem?'

'Nothing that would interest you.'

'Try me.'

'My wife is dead,' Sachs said.

'I know that.'

'Any problem she might have had is certainly –'

'Oh, it was *her* problem then, is that right? Not yours?'

'It was *our* problem,' Sachs said. 'Mr Kling, I'm not going to answer any other questions along these lines. If you insist that I do, you'll have to arrest me, and I'll get a lawyer, and we'll see about it. In the meantime, I'll just have to refuse to cooperate if that's the tack you're going to follow. I'm sorry.'

'All right, Mr Sachs, perhaps you can tell me whether or not you mutually agreed to the divorce.'

'Yes, we did.'

'Whose idea was it? Yours or hers?'

'Mine.'

'Why?'

'I can't answer that.'

'You know, of course, that adultery is the only grounds for divorce in this state.'

'Yes, I know that. There was no adultery involved. Tinka went to Nevada for the divorce.'

'Did you go with her?'

'No. She knew people in Nevada. She's from the West Coast originally. She was born in Los Angeles.'

'Did she take the child with her?'

'No. Anna stayed here with me while she was gone.'

'Have you kept in touch since the divorce, Mr Sachs?'

'Yes.'

'How?'

'Well, I see Anna, you know. We share the child. We agreed to that before the divorce. Stuck out in Arizona there, I didn't have much chance to see her this past year. But usually, I see quite a bit of her. And I talk to Tinka on the phone, I *used* to talk to her on the phone, and I also wrote to her. We kept in touch, yes.'

'Would you have described your relationship as a friendly one?'

'I loved her,' Sachs said flatly.

'I see.'

Again, the room was silent. Sachs turned his head away.

'Do you have any idea who might have killed her?' Kling asked.

'No.'

'None whatever?'

'None whatever.'

'When did you communicate with her last?'

'We wrote to each other almost every week.'

'Did she mention anything that was troubling her?'

'No.'

'Did she mention any of her friends who might have had reason to . . . ?'

'No.'

'When did you write to her last?'

'Last week sometime.'

'Would you remember exactly when?'

'I think it was . . . the fifth or the sixth, I'm not sure.'

'Did you send the letter by air?'

'Yes.'

'Then it should have arrived here before her death.'

'Yes, I imagine it would have.'

'Did she usually save your letters?'

'I don't know. Why?'

'We couldn't find any of them in the apartment.'

'Then I guess she didn't save them.'

'Did *you* save *her* letters?'

'Yes.'

'Mr Sachs, would you know one of your wife's friends who answers this description: Six feet two or three inches tall, heavily built, in his late thirties or early forties, with straight blond hair and –'

'I don't know who Tinka saw after we were divorced. We led separate lives.'

'But you still loved her.'

'Yes.'

'Then why did you divorce her?' Kling asked again, and Sachs did not answer. 'Mr Sachs, this may be very important to us . . .'

'It isn't.'

'Was your wife a dyke?'

'No.'

'Are you a homosexual?'

'No.'

'Mr Sachs, *whatever* it was, believe me, it won't be something new to us. Believe me, Mr Sachs, and please trust me.'

'I'm sorry. It's none of your business. It has nothing to do with anything but Tinka and me.'

'Okay,' Kling said.

'I'm sorry.'

'Think about it. I know you're upset at the moment, but –'

'There's nothing to think about. There are some things I will never discuss with anyone, Mr Kling. I'm sorry, but I owe at least that much to Tinka's memory.'

'I understand,' Kling said, and rose. 'Thank you for your time. I'll leave my card, in case you remember anything that might be helpful to us.'

'All right,' Sachs said.

'When will you be going back to Arizona?'

'I'm not sure. There's so much to be arranged. Tinka's lawyer advised me to stay for a while, at least to the end of the month, until the estate can be settled, and plans made for Anna ... there's so much to do.'

'*Is* there an estate?' Kling asked.

'Yes.'

'A sizeable one?'

'I wouldn't imagine so.'

'I see.' Kling paused, seemed about to say something, and then abruptly extended his hand. 'Thank you again, Mr Sachs,' he said. 'I'll be in touch with you.'

Sachs saw him to the door. Anna, her doll in her lap, was still watching television when he went out.

At the squadroom, Kling sat down with a pencil and pad, and then made a call to the airport, requesting a list of all scheduled flights to and from Phoenix, Arizona. It took him twenty minutes to get all the information, and another ten minutes to type it up in chronological order. He pulled the single sheet from his machine and studied it:

AIRLINE SCHEDULES FROM PHOENIX AND RETURN

EASTBOUND:

Frequency	Airline & Flt.	Departing Phoenix	Arriving Here	Stops		
Exc. Sat.	American #946	12:25 AM	10:45 AM	(Tucson	12:57 AM-	1:35 AM
				(Chicago	6:35 AM-	8:00 AM
Daily	American # 98	7:25 AM	5:28 PM	(Tucson	7:57 AM-	8:25 AM
				(El Paso	9:10 AM-	9:40 AM
				(Dallas	12:00 PM-	12:30 PM
Daily	TWA #146	8:00 AM	4:20 PM	Chicago	12:58 PM-	1:30 PM
Daily	American # 68	8:30 AM	4:53 PM	Chicago	1:27 PM-	2:00 PM
Daily	American # 66	2:00 PM	10:23 PM	Chicago	6:57 PM-	7:30 PM

WESTBOUND:

Frequency	Airline & Flt.	Departing Here	Arriving Phoenix	Stops		
Exc. Sun.	American #965	8:00 AM	11:05 AM	Chicago	9:12 AM-	9:55 AM
Daily	TWA #147	8:30 AM	11:25 AM	Chicago	9:31 AM-	10:15 AM
Daily	American #981	4:00 PM	6:55 PM	Chicago	5:12 PM-	5:45 PM
Daily	TWA #143	4:30 PM	7:40 PM	Chicago	5:41 PM-	6:30 PM
Daily	American # 67	6:00 PM	10:10 PM	(Chicago	7:12 PM-	7:45 PM
				(Tucson	9:08 PM-	9:40 PM

It seemed entirely possible to him that Dennis Sachs could have taken either the twelve-twenty-five flight from Phoenix late Thursday night, or any one of three flights early Friday morning, and still have been here in the city in time to arrive at Tinka's apartment by nine or nine-thirty p.m. He could certainly have killed his wife and caught an early flight back the next morning. Or any one of four flights on Sunday, all of which – because of the time difference – would have put him back in Phoenix that same night and in Rainfield by Monday to pick up the telegram waiting there for him. It was a possibility – remote, but a possibility nonetheless. The brown hair, of course, was a problem. Cyclops had said the man's hair was blond. But a commercial dye or bleach –

One thing at a time, Kling thought. Wearily, he pulled the telephone directory to him and began a methodical check of the two airlines flying to Phoenix. He told them he wanted to know if a man named Dennis Sachs, or any man with the initials D.S., had flown here from Phoenix last Thursday night or Friday morning, and whether or not he had made the return flight any time during the weekend. The airlines were helpful and patient. They checked their flight lists, Something we don't ordinarily do, sir, is this a case involving a missing person? No, Kling said, this is a case involving a murder. Oh, well in that case, sir, but we don't ordinarily do this, sir, even for the police, our flight lists, you see ... Yes, well I appreciate your help, Kling said.

Neither of the airlines had any record of either a Dennis Sachs, or a D.S. taking a trip from or to Phoenix at any time before Monday, April 12th. American Airlines had him listed as a passenger on Flight 68, which had left Phoenix at eight-thirty a.m. Monday morning, and had arrived here at four-fifty-three p.m. that afternoon. American reported that Mr Sachs had not as yet booked return passage.

Kling thanked American and hung up. There was still the possibility that Sachs had flown here and back before Monday, using an assumed name. But there was no way of checking that – and the only man who could make any sort of a positive identification had been missing since Monday night.

The meeting took place in Lieutenant Byrnes's office at five o'clock that afternoon. There were five detectives present in addition to Byrnes himself. Miscolo had brought in coffee for most of the men, but they sipped at it only distractedly, listening intently to Byrnes as he conducted the most unorthodox interrogation any of them had ever attended.

'We're here to talk about Monday afternoon,' Byrnes said. His tone was matter-of-fact, his face expressed no emotion. 'I have the duty chart for Monday, April twelfth, and it shows Kling, Meyer and Carella on from eight to four, with Meyer catching. Is that the way it was?'

The men nodded.

'What time did you get here, Cotton?'

Hawes, leaning against the lieutenant's filing cabinet, the only one of the detectives drinking tea, looked up and said, 'It must've been about five.'

'Was Steve still here?'

'No.'

'What about you, Hal?'

'I got here a little early, Pete,' Willis said. 'I had some calls to make.'

'What time?'

'Four-thirty.'

'Was Steve still here?'

'Yes.'

'Did you talk to him?'

'Yes.'

'What about?'

'He said he was going to a movie with Teddy that night.'

'Anything else?'

'That was about it.'

'I talked to him, too, Pete,' Brown said. He was the only Negro cop in the room. He was sitting in the wooden chair to the right of Byrnes's desk, a coffee container clasped in his huge hands.

'What'd he say to you, Art?'

'He told me he had to make a stop on the way home.'

'Did he say where?'

'No.'

'All right, now let's get this straight. Of the relieving team, only two of you saw him, and he said nothing about where he might have been headed. Is that right?'

'That's right,' Willis said.

'Were you in the office when he left, Meyer?'

'Yes. I was making out a report.'

'Did he say anything to you?'

'He said good night, and he made some joke about bucking for a promotion, you know, because I was hanging around after I'd been relieved.'

'What else?'

'Nothing.'

'Did he say anything to you at any time during the afternoon? About where he might be going later on?'

'Nothing.'

'How about you, Kling?'

'No, he didn't say anything to me, either.'

'Were you here when he left?'

'No.'

'Where were you?'

'I was on my way home.'

'What time did you leave?'

'About three o'clock.'

'Why so early?'

There was a silence in the room.

'Why so early?' Byrnes said again.

'We had a fight.'

'What about?'

'A personal matter.'

'The man is dead,' Byrnes said flatly. 'There are no personal matters any more.'

'He sent me back to the office because he didn't like the way I was behaving during an interview. I got sore.' Kling paused. 'That's what we argued about.'

'So you left here at three o'clock?'

'Yes.'

'Even though you were supposed to be working with Carella on the Tinka Sachs case, is that right?'

'Yes.'

'Did you know where he was going when he left here?'

'No, sir.'

'Did he mention anything about wanting to question anyone, or about wanting to see anyone again?'

'Only the elevator operator. He thought it would be a good idea to check him again.'

'What for?'

'To verify a time he'd given us.'

'Do you think that's where he went?'

'I don't know, sir.'

'Have you talked to this elevator operator?'

'No, sir, I can't locate him.'

'He's been missing since Monday night,' Meyer said. 'According to Bert's report, he was expecting a visit from a man who said he was Carella.'

'Is that right?' Byrnes asked.

'Yes,' Kling said. 'But I don't think it *was* Carella.'

'Why not?'

'It's all in my report, sir.'

'You've read this, Meyer?'

'Yes.'

'What's your impression?'

'I agree with Bert.'

Byrnes moved away from his desk. He walked to the window and stood with his hands clasped behind his back, looking at the street below. 'He found something, that's for sure,' he said, almost to himself. 'He found *something* or *somebody*, and he was killed for it.' He turned abruptly. 'And not a single goddamn one of you knows where he was going. Not even the man who was allegedly working this case with him.' He walked back to his desk. 'Kling, you stay. The rest of you can leave.'

The men shuffled out of the room. Kling stood uncomfortably before the lieutenant's desk. The lieutenant sat in his swivel chair, and turned it so that he was no looking directly at Kling. Kling did not know where he was looking. He eyes seemed unfocused.

'I guess you know that Steve Carella was a good friend of mine,' Byrnes said.

'Yes, sir.'

'A good friend,' Byrnes repeated. He paused for a moment, still looking off somewhere past Kling, his eyes unfocused, and then said, 'Why'd you let him go out alone, Kling?'

'I told you, sir. We had an argument.'

'So you left here at three o'clock, when you knew goddamn well you weren't going to be relieved until four-forty-five. Now what the hell do you call that, Kling?'

Kling did not answer.

'I'm kicking you off this goddamn squad,' Byrnes said. 'I should have done it long ago. I'm asking for your transfer, now get the hell out of here.'

Kling turned and started for the door.

'No, wait a minute,' Byrnes said. He turned directly to Kling now, and there was a terrible look on his face, as though he wanted to cry, but the tears were being checked by intense anger.

'I guess you know, Kling, that I don't have the power to suspend you, I guess you know that. The power rests with the commissioner and his deputies, and they're civilians. But a man can be suspended if he's violated the rules and regulations or if he's committed a crime. The way I look at it, Kling, you've done *both* those things. You violated the rules and regulations by leaving this squadroom and heading home when you were supposed to be on duty, and you committed a crime by allowing Carella to go out there alone and get killed.'

'Lieutenant, I —'

'If I could personally take away your gun and your shield, I'd do it, Kling, believe me. Unfortunately, I can't. But I'm going to call the Chief of Detectives the minute you leave this office. I'm going to tell him I'd like you suspended pending a complete investigation, and I'm going to ask that he recommend that to the commissioner. I'm going to *get* that suspension, Kling, if I have to go to the mayor for it. I'll get departmental charges filed, and a departmental trial, and I'll get you dismissed from the force. I'm *promising* you. Now get the hell out of my sight.'

Kling walked to the door silently, opened it, and stepped into the squadroom. He sat at his desk silently for several moments, staring into space. He heard the buzzer sound on Meyer's phone, heard Meyer lifting the instrument to his ear. 'Yeah?' Meyer said. 'Yeah, Pete. Right. Right. Okay, I'll tell him.' He heard Meyer putting the phone back onto its cradle. Meyer rose and came to his desk. 'That was the lieutenant,' he said. 'He wants me to take over the Tinka Sachs case.'

Chapter Eight

The message went out on the teletype at a little before ten Thursday morning:

> MISSING PERSON WANTED FOR QUESTIONING CONNECTION HOMICIDE
> XXX ERNEST MESSNER ALIAS CYCLOPS MESSNER XXX WHITE MALE AGE
> 68 XXX HEIGHT 6 FEET XXX WEIGHT 170 LBS XXX COMPLETELY BALD
> XXX EYES BLUE LEFT EYE MISSING AND COVERED BY PATCH XXX LAST
> SEEN VICINITY 1117 GAINESBOROUGH AVENUE RIVERHEAD MONDAY
> APRIL 12 TEN THIRTY PM EST XXX CONTACT MISPERBUR OR DET/2G
> MEYER MEYER EIGHT SEVEN SQUAD XXXXXXXXX

A copy of the teletype was pulled off the squadroom machine by Detective Meyer Meyer who wondered why it had been necessary for the detective at the Missing Persons Bureau to insert the word 'completely' before the word 'bald'. Meyer, who was bald himself, suspected that the description was redundant, over-emphatic, and undoubtedly derogatory. It was his under-

standing that a bald person had no hair. None. Count them. None. Why,
then, had the composer of this bulletin (Meyer visualized him as a bushy-
headed man with thick black eyebrows, a black moustache and a full beard)
insisted on inserting the word 'completely', if not to point a deriding finger
at all hairless men everywhere? Indignantly, Meyer went to the squadroom
dictionary, searched through balas, balata, Balaton, Balboa, balbriggan, and
came to:

> **bald** (bôld) adj. **1.** lacking hair on some part of the scalp: *a bald*
> *head or person.* **2.** destitute of some natural growth or covering: *a*
> *bald mountain.* **3.** bare; plain; unadorned: *a bald prose style.* **4.** open;
> undisguised: *a bald lie.* **5.** *Zool.* having white on the head: *bald*
> *eagle.*

Meyer closed the book, reluctantly admitting that whereas it was
impossible to be a little pregnant, it was not equally impossible to be a little
bald. The composer of the bulletin, bushy-haired bastard that he was, had
been right in describing Cyclops as 'completely bald'. If ever Meyer turned
up missing one day, they would describe him in exactly the same way. In the
meantime, his trip to the dictionary had not been a total loss. He would
hereafter look upon himself as a person who lacked hair on his scalp, a person
destitute of some natural growth, bare, plain and unadorned, open and
undisguised, having white on the head. Hereafter, he would be known
zoologically as The Bald Eagle – Nemesis of All Evil, Protector of the
Innocent, Scourge of the Underworld!

'Beware The Bald Eagle!' he said aloud, and Arthur Brown looked up
from his desk in puzzlement. Happily, the telephone rang at that moment.
Meyer picked it up and said, '87th Squad.'

'This is Sam Grossman at the lab. Who'm I talking to?'

'You're talking to The Bald Eagle,' Meyer said.

'Yeah?'

'Yeah.'

'Well, this is The Hairy Ape,' Grossman said. 'What's with you? Spring
fever?'

'Sure, it's such a beautiful day out,' Meyer said, looking through the
window at the rain.

'Is Kling there? I've got something for him on this Tinka Sachs case.'

'I'm handling that one now,' Meyer said.

'Oh? Okay. You feel like doing a little work, or were you planning to fly up
to your aerie?'

'Up *your* aerie, Mac,' Meyer said, and burst out laughing.

'Oh boy, I see I picked the wrong time to call,' Grossman said. 'Okay,
Okay. When you've got a minute later, give me a ring, okay? I'll –'

'The Bald Eagle *never* has a minute later,' Meyer said. 'What've you got
for me?'

'This kitchen knife. The murder weapon. According to the tag, it was
found just outside her bedroom door, guy probably dropped it on his way
out.'

'Okay, what about it?'

'Not much. Only it matches a few other knives in the girl's kitchen, so it's reasonable to assume it belonged to her. What I'm saying is the killer didn't go up there with his own knife, if that's of any use to you.'

'He took the knife from a bunch of other knives in the kitchen, is that it?'

'No, I don't think so. I think the knife was in the bedroom.'

'What would a knife be doing in the bedroom?'

'I think the girl used it to slice some lemons.'

'Yeah?'

'Yeah. There was a pitcher of tea on the dresser. Two lemons, sliced in half, were floating in it. We found lemon-juice stains on the tray, as well as faint scratches left by the knife. We figure she carried the tea, the lemons, and the knife into the bedroom on that tray. Then she sliced the lemons and squeezed them into the tea.'

'Well, that seems like guesswork to me,' Meyer said.

'Not at all. Paul Blaney is doing the medical examination. He says he's found citric-acid stains on the girl's left hand, the hand she'd have held the lemons with while slicing with the right. We've checked, Meyer. She was right-handed.'

'Okay, so she was drinking tea before she got killed,' Meyer said.

'That's right. The glass was on the night table near her bed, covered with her prints.'

'Whose prints were covering the knife?'

'Nobody's,' Grossman said. 'Or I should say *everybody's*. A whole mess of them, all smeared.'

'What about her pocketbook? Kling's report said –'

'Same thing, not a good print on it anywhere. There was no money in it, you know. My guess is that the person who killed her also robbed her.'

'Mmm, yeah,' Meyer said. 'Is that all?'

'That's all. Disappointing, huh?'

'I hoped you might come up with something more.'

'I'm sorry.'

'Sure.'

Grossman was silent for a moment. Then he said, 'Meyer?'

'Yeah?'

'You think Carella's death is linked to this one?'

'I don't know,' Meyer said.

'I liked that fellow,' Grossman said, and hung up.

Harvey Sadler was Tinka Sachs's lawyer and the senior partner in the firm of Sadler, McIntyre and Brooks, with offices uptown on Fisher Street. Meyer arrived there at ten minutes to noon, and discovered that Sadler was just about to leave for the YMCA. Meyer told him he was there to find out whether or not Tinka Sachs had left a will, and Sadler said she had indeed. In fact, they could talk about it on the way to the Y, if Meyer wanted to join him. Meyer said he wanted to, and the two men went downstairs to catch a cab.

Sadler was forty-five years old, with a powerful build and craggy features. He told Meyer he had played offensive back for Dartmouth in 1940, just before he was drafted into the army. He kept in shape nowadays, he said, by playing handball at the Y two afternoons a week, Mondays and Thursdays. At least, he *tried* to keep in shape. Even handball twice a week could not completely compensate for the fact that he sat behind a desk eight hours a day.

Meyer immediately suspected a deliberate barb. He had become over-sensitive about his weight several weeks back when he discovered what his fourteen-year-old son Alan meant by the nickname 'Old Crisco'. A bit of off-duty detective work uncovered the information that 'Old Crisco' was merely high school jargon for 'Old Fat-in-the-Can', a disrespectful term of affection if ever he'd heard one. He would have clobbered the boy, naturally, just to show who was boss, had not his wife Sarah agreed with the little vontz. You *are* getting fat, she told Meyer; you should begin exercising at the police gym. Meyer, whose boyhood had consisted of a series of taunts and jibes from Gentiles in his neighbourhood, never expected to be put down by vipers in his own bosom. He looked narrowly at Sadler now, a soldier in the enemy camp, and suddenly wondered if he was becoming a paranoid Jew. Worse yet, an *obese* paranoid Jew.

His reservations about Sadler and also about himself vanished the moment they entered the locker room of the YMCA, which smelled exactly like the locker room of the YMCA. Convinced that nothing in the world could eliminate suspicion and prejudice as effectively as the aroma of a men's locker room, swept by a joyous wave of camaraderie, Meyer leaned against the lockers while Sadler changed into his handball shorts, and listened to the details of Tinka's will.

'She leaves everything to her ex-husband,' Sadler said. 'That's the way she wanted it.'

'Nothing to her daughter?'

'Only if Dennis predeceased Tinka. In that case, a trust was set up for the child.'

'Did Dennis know this?' Meyer asked.

'I have no idea.'

'Was a copy of the will sent to him?'

'Not by me.'

'How many copies did you send to Tinka?'

'Two. The original was kept in our office safe.'

'Did she *request* two copies?'

'No. But it's our general policy to send two copies of any will to the testator. Most people like to keep one at home for easy reference, and the other in a safe deposit box. At least, that's been our experience.'

'We went over Tinka's apartment pretty thoroughly, Mr Sadler. We didn't find a copy of any will.'

'Then perhaps she *did* send one to her ex-husband. That wouldn't have been at all unusual.'

'Why not?'

'Well, they're on very good terms, you know. And, after all, he *is* the only real beneficiary. I imagine Tinka would have wanted him to know.'

'Mmm,' Meyer said. 'How large an estate is it?'

'Well, there's the painting.'

'What do you mean?'

'The Chagall.'

'I still don't understand.'

'The Chagall painting. Tinka bought it many years ago, when she first

began earning top money as a model. I suppose it's worth somewhere
around fifty thousand dollars today.'

'That's a sizeable amount.'

'Yes,' Sadler said. He was in his shorts now, and he was putting on his
black gloves and exhibiting signs of wanting to get out on the court. Meyer
ignored the signs.

'What about the rest of the estate?' he asked.

'That's it,' Sadler said.

'That's what?'

'The Chagall painting *is* the estate, or at least the substance of it. The rest
consists of household furnishings, some pieces of jewellery, clothing,
personal effects – none of them worth very much.'

'Let me get this straight, Mr Sadler. It's my understanding that Tinka
Sachs was earning somewhere in the vicinity of a hundred and fifty thousand
dollars a year. Are you telling me that all she owned of value at her death was
a Chagall painting valued at fifty thousand dollars?'

'That's right.'

'How do you explain that?'

'I don't know. I wasn't Tinka's financial adviser. I was only her lawyer.'

'As her lawyer, did you ask her to define her estate when she asked you to
draw this will?'

'I did.'

'How did she define it?'

'Essentially as I did a moment ago.'

'When was this, Mr Sadler?'

'The will is dated March twenty-fourth.'

'March twenty-fourth? You mean just last month?'

'That's right.'

'Was there any specific reason for her wanting a will drawn at that
time?'

'I have no idea.'

'I mean, was she worried about her health or anything?'

'She seemed in good health.'

'Did she seem frightened about anything? Did she seem to possess a
foreknowledge of what was going to happen?'

'No, she did not. She seemed very tense, but not frightened.'

'Why was she tense?'

'I don't know.'

'Did you ask her about it?'

'No, I did not. She came to me to have a will drawn. I drew it.'

'Had you ever done any legal work for her prior to the will?'

'Yes. Tinka once owned a house in Mavis County. I handled the papers
when she sold it.'

'When was that?'

'Last October.'

'How much did she get for the sale of the house?'

'Forty-two thousand, five hundred dollars.'

'Was there an existing mortgage?'

'Yes. Fifteen thousand dollars went to pay it off. The remainder went to
Tinka.'

'Twenty . . .' Meyer hesitated, calculating. 'Twenty-seven thousand, five hundred dollars went to Tinka, is that right?'

'Yes.'

'In cash?'

'Yes.'

'Where is it, Mr Sadler?'

'I asked her that when we were preparing the will. I was concerned about estate taxes, and about who would inherit the money she had realized on the sale of the house. But she told me she had used it for personal needs.'

'She had spent it?'

'Yes.' Sadler paused. 'Mr Meyer, I only play here two afternoons a week, and I'm very jealous of my time. I was hoping . . .'

'I won't be much longer, please bear with me. I'm only trying to find out what Tinka did with all this money that came her way. According to you, she didn't have a penny of it when she died.'

'I'm only reporting what she told me. I listed her assets as she defined them for me.'

'Could I see a copy of the will, Mr Sadler?'

'Certainly. But it's in my safe at the office, and I won't be going back there today. If you'd like to come by in the morning . . .'

'I'd hoped to get a look at it before –'

'I assure you that I've faithfully reported everything in the will. As I told you, I was only her lawyer, not her financial adviser.'

'Did she *have* a financial adviser?'

'I don't know.'

'Mr Sadler, did you handle Tinka's divorce for her?'

'No. I began representing her only last year, when she sold the house. I didn't know her before then, and I don't know who handled the divorce.'

'One last question,' Meyer said. 'Is anyone else mentioned as a beneficiary in Tinka's will, other than Dennis or Anna Sachs?'

'They are the only beneficiaries,' Sadler said. 'And Anna only if her father predeceased Tinka.'

'Thank you,' Meyer said.

Back at the squadroom, Meyer checked over the typewritten list of all the personal belongings found in Tinka's apartment. There was no listing for either a will or a bankbook, but someone from Homicide had noted that a key to a safety deposit box had been found among the items on Tinka's workdesk. Meyer called Homicide to ask about the key, and they told him it had been turned over to the Office of the Clerk, and he could pick it up there if he was interested and if he was willing to sign a receipt for it. Meyer was indeed interested, so he went all the way downtown to the Office of the Clerk, where he searched through Tinka's effects, finding a tiny red snap-envelope with the safety deposit box key in it. The name of the bank was printed on the face of the miniature envelope. Meyer signed out the key and then – since he was in the vicinity of the various court buildings, anyway – obtained a court order authorizing him to open the safety deposit box. In the company of a court official, he went uptown again by subway and then ran through a pouring rain, courtesy of the vernal equinox, to the First Northern

National Bank on the corner of Phillips and Third, a few blocks from where
Tinka had lived.

A bank clerk removed the metal box from a tier of similar boxes, asked
Meyer if he wished to examine the contents in private, and then led him and
the court official to a small room containing a desk, a chair, and a chained
ballpoint pen. Meyer opened the box.

There were two documents in the box. The first was a letter from an art
dealer, giving an appraisal of the Chagall painting. The letter stated simply
that the painting had been examined, that it was undoubtedly a genuine
Chagall, and that it could be sold at current market prices for anywhere
between forty-five and fifty thousand dollars.

The second document was Tinka's will. It was stapled inside a lawyer's
blueback, the firm name Sadler, McIntyre and Brooks printed on the
bottom of the binder, together with the address, 80 Fisher Street.
Typewritten and centred on the page was the legend LAST WILL AND
TESTAMENT OF TINKA SACHS. Meyer opened the will and began reading:

LAST WILL AND TESTAMENT
of
TINKA SACHS

    I, Tinka Sachs, a resident of this city,
county, and state, hereby revoke all wills and
codicils by me at any time heretofore made and
do hereby make, publish and declare this as and
for my Last Will and Testament.

    FIRST: I give, devise and bequeath to my
former husband, DENNIS R. SACHS, if he shall
survive me, and, if he shall not survive me, to
my trustee, hereinafter named, all of my
property and all of my household and personal
effects including without limitation, clothing,
furniture and furnishings, books, jewelry, art
objects, and paintings.

    SECOND: If my former husband Dennis shall
not survive me, I give, devise and bequeath my
said estate to my Trustee hereinafter named, IN
TRUST NEVERTHELESS, for the following uses and
purposes:

    (1) My Trustee shall hold, invest and
re-invest the principal of said trust and shall
collect the income therefrom until my daughter,
ANNA SACHS, shall attain the age of twenty-one
(21) years, or sooner die.

(2) My Trustee shall, from time to time; distribute to my daughter ANNA before she has attained the age of twenty-one (21) so much of the net income (and the net income of any year not so distributed shall be accumulated and shall, after the end of such year, be deemed principal for purposes of this trust) and so much of the principal of this trust as my Trustee may in his sole and unreviewable discretion determine for any purposes deemed advisable or convenient by said Trustee, provided, however, that no principal or income in excess of an aggregate amount of Five Thousand Dollars ($5,000) in any one year shall be used for the support of the child unless the death of the child's father, DENNIS R. SACHS, shall have left her financially unable to support herself. The decision of my Trustee with respect to the dates of distribution and the sums to be distributed shall be final.

(3) If my daughter, ANNA, shall die before attaining the age of twenty-one (21) years, my Trustee shall pay over the then principal of the trust fund and any accumulated income to the issue of my daughter, ANNA, then living, in equal shares, and if there be no such issue then to those persons who would inherit from me had I died intestate immediately after the death of ANNA.

THIRD: I nominate, constitute and appoint my former husband, DENNIS R. SACHS, Executor of this my Last Will and Testament. If my said former husband shall predecease me or shall fail to qualify or cease to act as Executor, then I appoint my agent and friend, ARTHUR G. CUTLER, in his place as successor or substitute executor and, if my former husband shall predecease me, as TRUSTEE of the trust created hereby. If my said friend and agent shall fail to qualify or cease to act as Executor or Trustee, then I appoint his wife, LESLIE CUTLER, in his place as successor or substitute executor and/or

The rest of the will was boilerplate. Meyer scanned it quickly, and then
turned to the last page where Tinka had signed her name below the words
'IN WITNESS WHEREOF, I sign, seal, publish and declare this as my Last Will
and Testament' and where, below that, Harvey Sadler, William McIntyre
and Nelson Brooks had signed as attesting witnesses. The will was dated
March twenty-fourth.

The only thing Sadler had forgotten to mention – or perhaps Meyer
hadn't asked him about it – was that Art Cutler had been named trustee in
the event of Dennis Sachs's death.

Meyer wondered if it meant anything.

And then he calculated how much money Tinka had earned in eleven
years at a hundred and fifty thousand dollars a year, and wondered again why
her only possession of any real value was the Chagall painting she had
drenched with blood on the night of her death.

Something stank.

Chapter Nine

He had checked and rechecked his own findings against the laboratory's
reports on the burned wreckage, and at first only one thing seemed clear to
Paul Blaney. Wherever Steve Carella had been burned to death, it had not
been inside that automobile. The condition of the corpse was unspeakably
horrible; it made Blaney queasy just to look at it. In his years as medical
examiner, Blaney had worked on cases of thaermic trauma ranging from the
simplest burns to cases of serious and fatal exposure to flame, light, and
electric energy – but these were the worst fourth-degree burns he had ever
seen. The body had undoubtedly been cooked for hours: The face was
unrecognizable, all of the features gone, the skin black and tight, the single
remaining cornea opaque, the teeth undoubtedly loosened and then lost in
the fire; the skin on the torso was brittle and split; the hair had been burned
away, the flesh completely gone in many places, showing dark red-brown
skeletal muscles and charred brittle bones. Blaney's internal examination
revealed pale, cooked involuntary muscles, dull and shrunken viscera. Had
the body been reduced to its present condition inside that car, the fire would
have had to rage for hours. The lab's report indicated that the automobile,
ignited by an explosion of gasoline, had burned with extreme intensity, but
only briefly. It was Blaney's contention that the body had been burned
elsewhere, and then put into the automobile to simulate death there by
explosion and subsequent fire.

Blaney was not paid to speculate on criminal motivation, but he wondered now why someone had gone to all this trouble, especially when the car fire would undoubtedly have been hot enough to eliminate adequately and for ever any intended victim. Being a methodical man, he continued to probe. His careful and prolonged investigation had nothing to do with the fact that the body belonged to a policeman, or even to a policeman he had known. The corpse on the table was not to him a person called Steve Carella; it was instead a pathological puzzle.

He did not solve that puzzle until late Friday afternoon.

Bert Kling was alone in the squadroom when the telephone rang. He lifted the receiver.

'Detective Kling, 87th Squad,' he said.

'Bert, this is Paul Blaney.'

'Hello, Paul, how are you?'

'Fine, thanks. Who's handling the Carella case?'

'Meyer's in charge. Why?'

'Can I talk to him?'

'Not here right now.'

'I think this is important,' Blaney said. 'Do you know where I can reach him?'

'I'm sorry, I don't know where he is.'

'If I give it to you, will you make sure he gets it sometime tonight?'

'Sure,' Kling said.

'I've been doing the autopsy,' Blaney said. 'I'm sorry I couldn't get back to you people sooner, but a lot of things were bothering me about this, and I wanted to be careful. I didn't want to make any statements that might put you on the wrong track, do you follow?'

'Yes, sure,' Kling said.

'Well, if you're ready, I'd like to trace this for you step by step. And I'd like to say at the onset that I'm absolutely convinced of what I'm about to say. I mean, I know how important this is, and I wouldn't dare commit myself on guesswork alone – not in a case of this nature.'

'I've got a pencil,' Kling said. 'Go ahead.'

'To begin with, the comparative conditions of vehicle and cadaver indicated to me that the body had been incinerated elsewhere for a prolonged period of time, and only later removed to the automobile where it was found. I now have further evidence from the lab to support this theory. I sent them some recovered fragments of foreign materials that were embedded in the burned flesh. The fragments proved to be tiny pieces of wood charcoal. It seems certain now that the body was consumed in a *wood* fire, and not a gasoline fire such as would have occurred in the automobile. It's my opinion that the victim was thrust headfirst into a fireplace.'

'What makes you think so?'

'The upper half of the body was severely burned, whereas most of the pelvic region and all of the lower extremities are virtually untouched. I think the upper half of the body was pushed into the fireplace and kept there for many hours, possibly throughout the night. Moreover, I think the man was murdered *before* he was thrown into the fire.'

'Before?'

'Yes, I examined the air passages for possible inhaled soot, and the blood for carboxyhaemoglobin. The presence of either would have indicated that the victim was alive during the fire. I found neither.'

'Then how *was* he killed?' Kling asked.

'That would involve guesswork,' Blaney said. 'There's evidence of extradural haemorrhage, and there are also several fractures of the skull vault. But these may only be post-mortem fractures resulting from charring, and I wouldn't feel safe in saying the victim was murdered by a blow to the head. Let's simply say he was dead before he was incinerated, and leave it at that.'

'Then why was he thrown into the fire?' Kling asked.

'To obliterate the body beyond recognition.'

'Go on.'

'The teeth, as you know, were missing from the head, making dental identification impossible. At first I thought the fire had loosened them, but upon further examination, I found bone fragments in the upper gum. I now firmly believe that the teeth were knocked out of the mouth before the body was incinerated, and I believe this was done to further prevent identification.'

'What are you saying, Blaney?'

'May I go on? I don't want any confusion about this later.'

'Please,' Kling said.

'There was no hair on the burned torso. Chest hair, underarm hair, and even the upper region of pubic hair had been singed away by the fire. Neither was there any hair on the scalp, which would have been both reasonable and obvious had the body been thrust into a fireplace head first, as I surmise it was. But upon examination, I was able to find surviving hair roots in the subcutaneous fat below the dermis on the torso and arms, even though the shaft and epithelial sheath had been destroyed. In other words, though the fire had consumed whatever hair had once existed on the torso and arms, there was nonetheless evidence that hair *had been growing* there. I could find no such evidence on the victim's scalp.'

'What do you mean?'

'I mean that the man who was found in that automobile was bald to begin with.'

'What?'

'Yes, nor was this particularly surprising. The atrophied internal viscera, the distended aorta of the heart, the abundant fatty marrow, large medullary cavities, and dense compact osseous tissue all indicated a person well on in years. Moreover, it was my initial belief that only one eye had survived the extreme heat – the right eye – and that it had been rendered opaque whereas the left eye had been entirely consumed by the flames. I have now carefully examined that left socket and it is my conclusion that there had not been an eye in it for many many years. The optic nerve and tract simply do not exist, and there is scar tissue present which indicates removal of the eye long before –'

'Cyclops!' Kling said. 'Oh my God, it's Cyclops!'

'Whoever it is,' Blaney said, 'it is *not* Steve Carella.'

He lay naked on the floor near the radiator.

He could hear rain lashing against the window panes, but the room was warm and he felt no discomfort. Yesterday, the girl had loosened the handcuff a bit, so that it no longer was clamped so tightly on his wrist. His nose was still swollen, but the throbbing pain was gone now, and the girl had washed his cuts and promised to shave him as soon as they were healed.

He was hungry.

He knew that the girl would come with food the moment it grew dark; she always did. There was one meal a day, always at dusk, and the girl brought it to him on a tray and then watched him while he ate, talking to him. Two days ago, she had showed him the newspapers, and he had read them with a peculiar feeling of unreality. The picture in the newspapers had been taken when he was still a patrolman. He looked very young and very innocent. The headline said he was dead.

He listened for the sound of her heels now. He could hear nothing in the other room; the apartment was silent. He wondered if she had gone, and felt a momentary pang. He glanced again at the waning light around the edges of the window shades. The rain drummed steadily against the glass. There was the sound of traffic below, tyres hushed on rainswept streets. In the room, the gloom of dusk spread into the corners. Neon suddenly blinked against the drawn shades. He waited, listening, but there was no sound.

He must have dozed again. He was awakened by the sound of the key being inserted in the door lock. He sat upright, his left hand extended behind him and manacled to the radiator, and watched as the girl came into the room. She was wearing a short silk dressing gown belted tightly at the waist. The gown was a bright red, and she wore black high-heeled pumps that added several inches to her height. She closed the door behind her, and put the tray down just inside the door.

'Hello, doll,' she whispered.

She did not turn on the overhead light. She went to one of the windows instead and raised the shade. Green neon rainsnakes slithered along the glass pane. The floor was washed with melting green, and then the neon blinked out and the room was dark again. He could hear the girl's breathing. The sign outside flashed again. The girl stood near the window in the red gown, the green neon behind her limning her long legs. The sign went out.

'Are you hungry, doll?' she whispered, and walked to him swiftly and kissed him on the cheek. She laughed deep in her throat, then moved away from him and went to the door. The Llama rested on the tray alongside the coffeepot. A sandwich was on a paper plate to the right of the gun.

'Do I still need this?' she asked, hefting the gun and pointing it at him.

Carella did not answer.

'I guess not,' the girl said, and laughed again, that same low throaty laugh that was somehow not at all mirthful.

'Why am I alive?' he said. He was very hungry, and he could smell the coffee deep and strong in his nostrils, but he had learned not to ask for his food. He had asked for it last night, and the girl had deliberately postponed feeding him talking to him for more than an hour before she reluctantly brought the tray to him.

'You're not alive,' the girl said. 'You're dead. I showed you the papers, didn't I? You're dead.'

'Why didn't you really kill me?'

'You're too valuable.'

'How do you figure that?'

'You know who killed Tinka.'

'Then you're better off with me dead.'

'No.' The girl shook her head. 'No, doll. We want to know how you found out.'

'What difference does it make?'

'Oh, a lot of difference,' the girl said. 'He's very concerned about it, really he is. He's getting very impatient. He figures he made a mistake some place, you see, and he wants to know what it was. Because if *you* found out, chances are somebody else will sooner or later. Unless you tell us what it was, you see. Then we can make sure nobody else finds out. Ever.'

'There's nothing to tell you.'

'There's plenty to tell,' the girl said. She smiled. 'You'll tell us. Are you hungry?'

'Yes.'

'Tch,' the girl said.

'Who was that in the burned car?'

'The elevator operator. Messner.' The girl smiled again. 'It was my idea. Two birds with one stone.'

'What do you mean?'

'Well, I thought it would be a good idea to get rid of Messner just in case he was the one who led you to us. Insurance. And I also figured that if everybody thought you were dead, that'd give us more time to work on you.'

'If Messner was my source, why do you have to work on me?'

'Well, there are a lot of unanswered questions,' the girl said. 'Gee, that coffee smells good, doesn't it?'

'Yes,' Carella said.

'Are you cold?'

'No.'

'I can get you a blanket if you're cold.'

'I'm fine, thanks.'

'I thought, with the rain, you might be a little chilly.'

'No.'

'You look good naked,' the girl said.

'Thank you.'

'I'll feed you, don't worry,' she said.

'I know you will.'

'But about those questions, they're really bothering him, you know. He's liable to get bugged completely and just decide the hell with the whole thing. I mean, I like having you and all, but I don't know if I'll be able to control him much longer. If you don't cooperate, I mean.'

'Messner was my source,' Carella said. 'He gave me the description.'

'Then it's a good thing we killed him, isn't it?'

'I suppose so.'

'Of course, that still doesn't answer those questions I was talking about.'

'What questions?'

'For example, how did you get the name? Messner may have given you a description, but where did you get the name? Or the address, for that matter?'

'They were in Tinka's address book. Both the name *and* the address.'

'Was the description there, too?'

'I don't know what you mean.'

'You know what I mean, doll. Unless Tinka had a *description* in that book of hers, how could you match a name to what Messner had told you?' Carella was silent. The girl smiled again. 'I'm *sure* she didn't have descriptions of people in her address book, did she?'

'No.'

'Good, I'm glad you're telling the truth. Because we found the address book in your pocket the night you came busting in here, and we know damn well there're no descriptions of people in it. You hungry?'

'Yes, I'm very hungry,' Carella said.

'I'll feed you, don't worry,' she said again. She paused. 'How'd you know the name and address?'

'Just luck. I was checking each and every name in the book. A process of elimination, that's all.'

'That's another lie,' the girl said. 'I wish you wouldn't lie to me.' She lifted the gun from the tray. She held the gun loosely in one hand, picked up the tray with the other, and then said, 'Back off.'

Carella moved as far back as the handcuff would allow. The girl walked to him, crouched, and put the tray on the floor.

'I'm not wearing anything under this robe,' she said.

'I can see that.'

'I thought you could,' the girl said, grinning, and then rose swiftly and backed towards the door. She sat in the chair and crossed her legs, the short robe riding up on her thighs. 'Go ahead,' she said, and indicated the tray with a wave of the gun.

Carella poured himself a cup of coffee. He took a quick swallow, and then picked up the sandwich and bit into it.

'Good?' the girl asked, watching.

'Yes.'

'I made it myself. You have to admit I take good care of you.'

'Sure,' Carella said.

'I'm going to take even better care of you,' she said. 'Why'd you lie to me? Do you think it's nice to lie to me?'

'I didn't lie.'

'You said you reached us by luck, a process of elimination. That means you didn't know who or what to expect when you got here, right? You were just looking for someone in Tinka's book who would fit Messner's description.'

'That's right.'

'Then why'd you kick the door in? Why'd you have a gun in your hand? See what I mean? You knew who he was *before* you got here. You knew he was the one. How?'

'I told you. It was just luck.'

'Ahh, gee, I wish you wouldn't lie. Are you finished there?'

'Not yet.'

'Let me know when.'

'All right.'

'I have things to do.'

'All right.'

'To *you*,' the girl said.

Carella chewed on the sandwich. He washed it down with a gulp of coffee.
He did not look at the girl. She was jiggling her foot now, the gun hand
resting in her lap.

'Are you afraid?' she asked.

'Of what?'

'Of what I might do to you.'

'No. Should I be?'

'I might break your nose all over again, who knows?'

'That's true, you might.'

'Or I might even keep my promise to knock out all your teeth.' The girl
smiled. '*That* was my idea, too, you know, knocking out Messner's teeth.
You people can make identifications from dental charts, can't you?'

'Yes.'

'That's what I thought. That's what I told him. *He* thought it was a good
idea, too.'

'You're just *full* of good ideas.'

'Yeah, I have a lot of good ideas,' the girl said. 'You're not scared,
huh?'

'No.'

'I would be, if I were you. Really, I would be.'

'The worst you can do is kill me,' Carella said. 'And since I'm already
dead, what difference will it make?'

'I like a man with a sense of humour,' the girl said, but she did not smile. 'I
can do worse than kill you.'

'What can you do?'

'I can corrupt you.'

'I'm incorruptible,' Carella said, and smiled.

'Nobody's incorruptible,' she said. 'I'm going to make you *beg* to tell us
what you know. Really. I'm warning you.'

'I've told you everything I know.'

'Uh-uh,' the girl said, shaking her head. 'Are you finished there?'

'Yes.'

'Shove the tray away from you.'

Carella slid the tray across the floor. The girl went to it, stooped again, and
picked it up. She walked back to the chair and sat. She crossed her legs. She
began jiggling her foot.

'What's your wife's name?' she asked.

'Teddy.'

'That's a nice name. But you'll forget it soon enough.'

'I don't think so,' Carella said evenly.

'You'll forget her name, and you'll forget her, too.'

He shook his head.

'I promise,' the girl said. 'In a week's time, you won't even remember
your *own* name.'

The room was silent. The girl sat quite still except for the jiggling of her
foot. The green neon splashed the floor, and then blinked out. There were
seconds of darkness, and then the light came on again. She was standing
now. She had left the gun on the seat of the chair and moved to the centre of

the room. The neon went out. When it flashed on again, she had moved closer to where he was manacled to the radiator.

'What would you like me to do to you?' she asked.

'Nothing.'

'What would you like to do to me?'

'Nothing,' he said.

'No?' she smiled. 'Look, doll.'

She loosened the sash at her waist. The robe parted over her breasts and naked belly. Neon washed the length of her body with green, and then blinked off. In the intermittent flashes, he saw the girl moving – as though in a silent movie – towards the light switch near the door, the open robe flapping loose around her. She snapped on the overhead light, and then walked slowly back to the centre of the room and stood under the bulb. She held the front of the robe open, the long pale white sheath of her body exposed, the red silk covering her back and her arms, her fingernails tipped with red as glowing as the silk.

'What do you think?' she asked. Carella did not answer. 'You want some of it?'

'No,' he said.

'You're lying.'

'I'm telling you the absolute truth,' he said.

'I could make you forget her in a minute,' the girl said. 'I know things you never dreamed of. You want it?'

'No.'

'Just try and get it,' she said, and closed the robe and tightened the sash around her waist. 'I don't like it when you lie to me.'

'I'm not lying.'

'You're naked, mister, don't tell *me* you're not lying.' She burst out laughing and walked to the door, opening it, and then turned to face him again. Her voice was very low, her face serious. 'Listen to me, doll,' she said. 'You are *mine*, do you understand that? I can do whatever I want with you, don't you forget it. I'm promising you right here and now that in a week's time you'll be crawling on your hands and knees to me, you'll be licking my feet, you'll be *begging* for the opportunity to tell me what you know. And once you tell me, I'm going to throw you away, doll, I'm going to throw you broken and cracked in the gutter, doll, and you're going to wish, believe me, you are just going to *wish* it was you they found dead in that car, believe me.' She paused. 'Think about it,' she said, and turned out the light and went out of the room.

He heard the key turning in the lock.

He was suddenly very frightened.

Chapter Ten

The car had been found at the bottom of a steep embankment off Route 407. The road was winding and narrow, a rarely used branch connecting the towns of Middlebarth and York, both of which were serviced by wider, straighter highways. 407 was an oiled road, potholed and frost-heaved, used almost entirely by teenagers searching for a night-time necking spot. The shoulders were muddy and soft, except for one place where the road widened and ran into the approach to what had once been a gravel pit. It was at the bottom of this pit that the burned vehicle and its more seriously burned passenger had been discovered.

There was only one house on Route 407, five and half miles from the gravel pit. The house was built of native stone and timber, a rustic affair with a screened back porch overlooking a lake reportedly containing bass. The house was surrounded by white birch and flowering forsythia. Two dogwoods flanked the entrance driveway, their buds ready to burst. The rain had stopped but a fine mist hung over the lake, visible from the turn in the driveway. A huge oak dripped clinging raindrops onto the ground. The countryside was still. The falling drops clattered noisily.

Detectives Hal Willis and Arthur Brown parked the car at the top of the driveway, and walked past the dripping oak to the front door of the house. The door was painted green with a huge brass doorknob centred in its lower panel and a brass knocker centred in the top panel. A locked padlock still hung in a hinge hasp and staple fastened to the door. But the hasp staple had been pried loose of the jamb, and there were deep gouges in the wood where a heavy tool had been used for the job. Willis opened the door, and they went into the house.

There was the smell of contained woodsmoke, and the stench of something else. Brown's face contorted. Gagging, he pulled a handkerchief from his back pocket and covered his nose and mouth. Willis had backed away towards the door again, turning his face to the outside air. Brown took a quick look at the large stone fireplace at the far end of the room, and then caught Willis by the elbow and led him outside.

'Any question in your mind?' Willis asked.

'None,' Brown said. 'That's the smell of burned flesh.'

'We got any masks in the car?'

'I don't know. Let's check the trunk.'

They walked back to the car. Willis took the keys from the ignition and leisurely unlocked the trunk. Brown began searching.

'Everything in here but the kitchen sink,' he said. 'What the hell's this thing?'

'That's mine,' Willis said.

'Well, what is it?'

'It's a hat, what do you think it is?'

'It doesn't look like any hat I've ever seen,' Brown said.

'I wore it on a plant couple of weeks ago.'

'What were you supposed to be?'

'A foreman.'

'Of what?'

'A chicken market.'

'That's *some* hat, man,' Brown said, and chuckled.

'That's a good hat,' Willis said. 'Don't make fun of my hat. All the ladies who came in to buy chickens said it was a darling hat.'

'Oh, no question,' Brown said. 'It's a cunning hat.'

'Any masks in there?'

'Here's *one*. That's all I see.'

'The canister with it?'

'Yeah, it's all here.'

'Who's going in?' Willis said.

'I'll take it,' Brown said.

'Sure, and then I'll have the NAACP down on my head.'

'We'll just have to chance that,' Brown said, returning Willis' smile. 'We'll just have to chance it, Hal.' He pulled the mask out of its carrier, found the small tin of antidim compound, scooped some onto the provided cloth, and wiped it onto the eyepieces. He seated the facepiece on his chin, moved the canister and head harness into place with an upward, backward sweep of his hands, and then smoothed the edges of the mask around his face.

'Is it fogging?' Willis said.

'No, it's okay.'

Brown closed the outlet valve with two fingers and exhaled, clearing the mask. 'Okay,' he said, and began walking towards the house. He was a huge man, six feet four inches tall and weighing two hundred and twenty pounds, with enormous shoulders and chest, long arms, big hands. His skin was very dark, almost black, his hair was kinky and cut close to his scalp, his nostrils were large, his lips were thick. He looked like a Negro, which is what he was, take him or leave him. He did not at all resemble the white man's pretty concept of what a Negro *should* look like, the image touted in a new wave of magazine and television ads. He looked like himself. His wife Caroline liked the way he looked, and his daughter Connie liked the way he looked, and – more important – *he* liked the way he looked, although he didn't look so great at the moment with a mask covering his face and hoses running to the canister resting at the back of his neck. He walked into the house and paused just inside the door. There were parallel marks on the floor beginning at the jamb and running vertically across the room. He stooped to look at the marks more closely. They were black and evenly spaced, and he recognized them immediately as scuff marks. He rose and followed the marks to the fireplace, where they ended. He did not touch anything in or near the open mouth of the hearth; he would leave that for the lab boys. But he was convinced now that a man wearing shoes, if nothing else, had been dragged across the room from the door to the fireplace. According to what they'd learned yesterday,

Ernest Messner had been incinerated in a wood-burning fire. Well, there
had certainly been a wood-burning fire in this room, and the stink he and
Willis had encountered when entering was sure as hell the stink of burned
human flesh. And now there were heel marks leading from the door to the
fireplace. Circumstantially, Brown needed nothing more.

The only question was whether the person cooked in this particular
fireplace was Ernest Messner or somebody else.

He couldn't answer that one, and anyway his eyepieces were beginning to
fog. He went outside, took off the mask, and suggested to Willis that they
drive into either Middlebarth or York to talk to some real estate agents about
who owned the house with the smelly fireplace.

Elaine Hinds was a small, compact redhead with blue eyes and long
fingernails. Her preference ran to small men, and she was charmed to
distraction by Hal Willis, who was the shortest detective on the squad. She
sat in a swivel chair behind her desk in the office of Hinds Real Estate in
Middlebarth, and crossed her legs, and smiled, and accepted Willis's match
to her cigarette, and graciously murmured, 'Thank you,' and then tried to
remember what question he had just asked her. She uncrossed her legs,
crossed them again, and then said, 'Yes, the house on 407.'

'Yes, do you know who owns it?' Willis asked. He was not unaware of the
effect he seemed to be having on Miss Elaine Hinds, and he suspected he
would never hear the end of it from Brown. But he was also a little puzzled.
He had for many years been the victim of what he called the Mutt and Jeff
phenomenon, a curious psychological and physiological reversal that made
him irresistibly attractive to very big girls. He had never dated a girl who was
shorter than five-nine in heels. One of his girl friends was five-eleven in her
stockinged feet, and she was hopelessly in love with him. So he could not
now understand why tiny little Elaine Hinds seemed so interested in a man
who was only five feet eight inches tall, with the slight build of a dancer and
the hands of a Black Jack dealer. He had, of course, served with the Marines
and was an expert at judo, but Miss Hinds had no way of knowing that he
was a giant among men, capable of breaking a man's back by the mere flick of
an eyeball – well, almost. What then had caused her immediate attraction?
Being a conscientious cop, he sincerely hoped it would not impede the
progress of the investigation. In the meantime, he couldn't help noticing
that she had very good legs and she kept crossing and uncrossing them like
an undecided virgin.

'The people who own that house,' she said, uncrossing her legs, 'are Mr
and Mrs Jerome Brandt, would you like some coffee or something? I have
some going in the other room.'

'No, thank you,' Willis said. 'How long have –'

'Mr Brown?'

'No, thank you.'

'How long have the Brandts been living there?'

'Well, they haven't. Not really.'

'I don't think I understand,' Willis said.

Elaine Hinds crossed her legs, and leaned close to Willis, as though about
to reveal something terribly intimate. 'They bought it to use as a summer
place,' she said. 'Mavis County is a marvellous resort area, you know, with

many many lakes and streams and with the ocean not too far from any point in the county. We're supposed to have less rainfall per annum than –'

'When did they buy it, Miss Hinds?'

'Last year. I expect they'll open the house after Memorial Day, but it's been closed all winter.'

'Which explains the broken hasp on the front door,' Brown said.

'Has it been broken?' Elaine said. 'Oh, dear,' and she uncrossed her legs.

'Miss Hinds, would you say that many people in the area knew the house was empty?'

'Yes, I'd say it was common knowledge, do you enjoy police work?'

'Yes, I do,' Willis said.

'It must be terribly exciting.'

'Sometimes the suspense is unbearable,' Brown said.

'I'll just *bet* it is,' Elaine said.

'It's my understanding,' Willis said, glancing sharply at Brown, 'that 407 is a pretty isolated road, and hardly ever used. Is that correct?'

'Oh, yes,' Elaine said. 'Route 126 is a much better connection between Middlebarth and York, and of course the new highway runs past both towns. As a matter of fact, most people in the area *avoid* 407. It's not a very good road, have you been on it?'

'Yes. Then, actually anyone living around here would have known the house was empty, and would also have known the road going by it wasn't travelled too often. Would you say that?'

'Oh, yes, Mr Willis, I definitely *would* say that,' Elaine said.

Willis looked a little startled. He glanced at Brown, and then cleared his throat. 'Miss Hinds, what sort of people are the Brandts? Do you know them?'

'Yes, I sold the house to them. Jerry's an executive at IBM.'

'And his wife?'

'Maxine's a woman of about fifty, three or four years younger than Jerry. A lovely person.'

'Respectable people, would you say?'

'Oh, yes, *entirely* respectable,' Elaine said. 'My goodness, of *course* they are.'

'Would you know if either of them were up here Monday night?'

'I don't know. I imagine they would have called if they were coming. I keep the keys to the house here in the office, you see. I have to arrange for maintenance, and it's necessary –'

'But they didn't call to say they were coming up?'

'No, they didn't.' Elaine paused. 'Does this have anything to do with the auto wreck on 407?'

'Yes, Miss Hinds, it does.'

'Well, how could Jerry or Maxine be even *remotely* connected with that?'

'You don't think they could?'

'Of course not. I haven't seen them for quite some time now, but we did work closely together when I was handling the deal for them last October. Believe me, you couldn't find a sweeter couple. That's unusual, especially with people who have their kind of money.'

'Are they wealthy, would you say?'

'The house cost forty-two thousand five hundred dollars. They paid for it in cash.'

'Who'd they buy it from?' Willis asked.

'Well, you probably wouldn't know her, but I'll bet your wife would.'

'I'm not married,' Willis said.

'Oh? *Aren't* you?'

'Who'd they buy it from?' Brown asked.

'A fashion model named Tinka Sachs. Do you know her?'

If they had lacked, before this, proof positive that the man in the wrecked automobile was really Ernest Messner, they now possessed the single piece of information that tied together the series of happenings and eliminated the possibility of reasonable chance or coincidence:

1. Tinka Sachs had been murdered in an apartment on Stafford Place on Friday, April ninth.
2. Ernest Messner was the elevator operator on duty there the night of her murder.
3. Ernest Messner had taken a man up to her apartment and had later given a good description of him.
4. Ernest Messner had vanished on Monday night, April twelfth.
5. An incinerated body was found the next day in a wrecked auto on Route 407, the connecting road between Middlebarth and York, in Mavis County.
6. The medical examiner had stated his belief that the body in the automobile had been incinerated in a wood fire elsewhere and only later placed in the automobile.
7. There was only one house on Route 407, five and a half miles from where the wrecked auto was found in the gravel pit.
8. There had been a recent wood fire in the fireplace of that house, and the premises smelled of burned flesh. There were also heel marks on the floor, indicating that someone had been dragged to the fireplace.
9. The house had once been owned by Tinka Sachs, and was sold only last October to its new owners.

It was now reasonable to assume that Tinka's murderer knew he had been identified, and had moved with frightening dispatch to remove the man who'd seen him. It was also reasonable to assume that Tinka's murderer knew of the empty house in Mavis County and had transported Messner's body there for the sole purpose of incinerating it beyond recognition, the further implication being that the murderer had known Tinka at least as far back as last October when she'd still owned the house. There were still a few unanswered questions, of course, but they were small things and nothing that would trouble any hard-working police force anywhere. The cops of the 87th wondered, for example, who had killed Tinka Sachs, and who had killed Ernest Messner, and who had taken Carella's shield and gun from him and wrecked his auto, and whether Carella was still alive, and where?

It's the small things in life that can get you down.

Those airline schedules kept bothering Kling.

He knew he had been taken off the case, but he could not stop thinking about those airline schedules, or the possibility that Dennis Sachs had flown from Phoenix and back sometime between Thursday night and Monday morning. From his apartment that night, he called Information and asked for the name and number of the hotel in Rainfield, Arizona. The local operator connected him with Phoenix Information, who said the only hotel listing they had in Rainfield was for the Major Powell on Main Street, was this the hotel Kling wanted? Kling said it was, and they asked if they should place the call. He knew that if he was eventually suspended, he would lose his gun, his shield and his salary until the case was decided, so he asked the operator how much the call would cost, and she said it would cost two dollars and ten cents for the first three minutes, and sixty-five cents for each additional minute. Kling told her to go ahead and place the call, station to station.

The man who answered the phone identified himself as Walter Blount, manager of the hotel.

'This is Detective Bert Kling,' Kling said. 'We've had a murder here, and I'd like to ask you some questions, if I may. I'm calling long distance.'

'Go right ahead, Mr Kling,' Blount said.

'To begin with, do you know Dennis Sachs?'

'Yes, I do. He's a guest here, part of Dr Tarsmith's expedition.'

'Were you on duty a week ago last Thursday night, April eighth?'

'I'm on duty *all* the time,' Blount said.

'Do you know what time Mr Sachs came in from the desert?'

'Well, I couldn't rightly say. They usually come in at about seven, eight o'clock, something like that.'

'Would you say they came in at about that time on April eighth?'

'I would say so, yes.'

'Did you see Mr Sachs leaving the hotel at any time that night?'

'Yes, he left, oh, ten-thirty or so, walked over to the railroad station.'

'Was he carrying a suitcase?'

'He was.'

'Did he mention where he was going?'

'The Royal Sands in Phoenix, I'd reckon. He asked us to make a reservation for him there, so I guess that's where he was going, don't you think?'

'Did you make the reservation for him personally, Mr Blount?'

'Yes, sir, I did. Single with a bath, Thursday night to Sunday morning. The rates —'

'What time did Mr Sachs return on Monday morning?'

'About six a.m. Had a telegram waiting for him here, his wife got killed. Well, I guess you know that, I guess that's what this is all about. He called the airport right away, and then got back on the train for Phoenix, hardly unpacked at all.'

'Mr Blount, Dennis Sachs told me that he spoke to his ex-wife on the telephone at least once a week. Would you know if that was true?'

'Oh, sure, he was always calling back east.'

'How often, would you say?'

'At least once a week, that's right. Even more than that, I'd say.'

'How much more?'

'Well ... in the past two months or so, he'd call her three, maybe four times a week, something like that. He spent a hell of a lot of time making calls back east, ran up a pretty big phone bill here.'

'Calling his wife, you mean.'

'Well, not only her.'

'Who else?'

'I don't know who the other party was.'

'But he *did* make calls to other numbers here in the city?'

'Well, *one* other number.'

'Would you happen to know that number off-hand, Mr Blount?'

'No, but I've got a record of it on our bills. It's not his wife's number because I've got that one memorized by heart, he's called it regular ever since he first came here a year ago. This other one is new to me.'

'When did he start calling it?'

'Back in February, I reckon.'

'How often?'

'Once a week, usually.'

'May I have the number please?'

'Sure, just let me look it up for you.'

Kling waited. The line crackled. His hand on the receiver was sweating.

'Hello?' Blount said.

'Hello?'

'The number is SE – I think that stands for Sequoia – SE 3-1402.'

'Thank you,' Kling said.

'Not at all,' Blount answered.

Kling hung up, waited patiently for a moment with his hand on the receiver, lifted it again, heard the dial tone, and instantly dialled SE 3-1402. The phone rang insistently. He counted each separate ring, four, five, six, and suddenly there was an answering voice.

'Dr Levi's wire,' the woman said.

'This is Detective Kling of the 87th Squad here in the city,' Kling said. 'Is this an answering service?'

'Yes, sir, it is.'

'Whose phone did you say this was?'

'Dr Levi's.'

'And the first name?'

'Jason.'

'Do you know where I can reach him?'

'I'm sorry, sir, he's away for the weekend. He won't be back until Monday morning.' The woman paused. 'Is this in respect to a police matter, or are you calling for a medical appointment?'

'A police matter,' Kling said.

'Well, the doctor's office hours begin at ten Monday morning. If you'd care to call him then, I'm sure –'

'What's his home number?' Kling asked.

'Calling him there won't help you. He really is away for the weekend.'

'Do you know where?'

'No, I'm sorry.'

'Well, let me have his number, anyway,' Kling said.

'I'm not supposed to give out the doctor's home number. I'll try it for you, if you like. If the doctor's there – which I know he isn't – I'll ask him to call you back. May I have your number, please?'

'Yes, it's Roxbury 2, that's RO 2, 7641.'

'Thank you.'

'Will you please call me in any event, to let me know if you reached him or not?'

'Yes, sir, I will.'

'Thank you.'

'What did you say your name was?'

'Kling, Detective Bert Kling.'

'Yes, sir, thank you,' she said, and hung up.

Kling waited by the phone.

In five minutes' time, the woman called back. She said she had tried the doctor's home number and – as she'd known would be the case all along – there was no answer. She gave him the doctor's office schedule and told him he could try again on Monday, and then she hung up.

It was going to be a long weekend.

Teddy Carella sat in the living room alone for a long while after Lieutenant Byrnes left, her hands folded in her lap, staring into the shadows of the room and hearing nothing but the murmur of her own thoughts.

We now know, the lieutenant had said, that the man we found in the automobile definitely wasn't Steve. He's a man named Ernest Messner, and there is no question about it, Teddy, so I want you to know that. But I also want you to know this doesn't mean Steve is still alive. We just don't know anything about that yet, although we're working on it. The only thing it *does* indicate is that at least he's not for certain dead.

The lieutenant paused. She watched his face. He looked back at her curiously, wanting to be sure she understood everything he had told her. She nodded.

I knew this yesterday, the lieutenant said, but I wasn't sure, and I didn't want to raise your hopes until I had checked it out thoroughly. The medical examiner's office gave this top priority, Teddy. They still haven't finished the autopsy on the Sachs case because, well, you know, when we thought this was Steve, well, we put a lot of pressure on them. Anyway, it isn't. It isn't Steve, I mean. We've got Paul Blaney's word for that, and he's an excellent man, and we've also got the corroboration – what? Corroboration, did you get it? the corroboration of the chief medical examiner as well. So now I'm sure, so I'm telling you. And about the other, we're working on it, as you know, and as soon as we've got anything, I'll tell you that, too. So that's about all, Teddy. We're doing our best.

She had thanked him and offered him coffee, which he refused politely, he was expected home, he had to run, he hoped she would forgive him. She had shown him to the door, and then walked past the playroom, where Fanny was watching television, and then past the room where the twins were sound asleep and then into the living room. She turned out the lights and went to sit near the old piano Carella had bought in a secondhand store downtown, paying sixteen dollars for it and arranging to have it delivered by a furniture man in the precinct. He had always wanted to play the piano, he told her, and was going to start lessons – you're never too old to learn, right, sweetheart?

The lieutenant's news soared within her, but she was fearful of it, suspicious: Was it only a temporary gift that would be taken back? Should she tell the children, and then risk another reversal and a second revelation that their father was dead? 'What does that mean?' April had asked. 'Does dead mean he's never coming back?' And Mark had turned to his sister and angrily shouted, 'Shut up, you stupid dope!' and had run to his room where his mother could not see his tears.

They deserved hope.

They had the right to know there was hope.

She rose and went into the kitchen and scribbled a note on the telephone pad, and then tore off the sheet of paper and carried it out to Fanny. Fanny looked up when she approached, expecting more bad news, the lieutenant brought nothing but bad news nowadays. Teddy handed her the sheet of paper, and Fanny looked at it:

Wake the children.
Tell them their father
may still be alive.

Fanny looked up quickly.

'Thank God,' she whispered, and rushed out of the room.

Chapter Eleven

The patrolman came up to the squadroom on Monday morning, and waited outside the slatted rail divider until Meyer signalled him in. Then he opened the gate and walked over to Meyer's desk.

'I don't think you know me,' he said. 'I'm Patrolman Angieri.'

'I think I've seen you around,' Meyer said.

'I feel funny bringing this up because maybe you already know it. My wife said I should tell you, anyway.'

'What is it?'

'I only been here at this precinct for six months, this is my first precinct, I'm a new cop.'

'Um-huh,' Meyer said.

'If you already know this, just skip it, okay? My wife says maybe you don't know it, and maybe it's important.'

'Well, what is it?' Meyer asked patiently.

'Carella.'

'What about Carella?'

'Like I told you, I'm new in the precinct, and I don't know all the detectives by name, but I recognized him later from his picture in the paper, though it was a picture from when he was a patrolman. Anyway, it was him.'

'What do you mean? I don't think I'm with you, Angieri.'

'Carrying the doll,' Angieri said.

'I still don't get you.'

'I was on duty in the hall, you know? Outside the apartment. I'm talking about the Tinka Sachs murder.'

Meyer leaned forward suddenly. 'Yeah, go ahead,' he said.

'Well, he come up there last Monday night, it must've been five-thirty, six o'clock, and he flashed the tin, and went inside the apartment. When he come out, he was in a hell of a hurry, and he was carrying a doll.'

'Are you telling me Carella was at the Sachs apartment last Monday night?'

'That's right.'

'Are you sure?'

'Positive.' Angieri paused. 'You *didn't* know this, huh? My wife was right.' He paused again. 'She's *always* right.'

'What did you say about a doll?'

'A doll, you know? Like kids play with? Girls? A big doll. With blonde hair, you know? A *doll*.'

'Carella came out of the apartment carrying a child's doll?'

'That's right.'

'Last Monday night?'

'That's right.'

'Did he say anything to you?'

'Nothing.'

'A doll,' Meyer said, puzzled.

It was nine a.m. when Meyer arrived at the Sachs apartment on Stafford Place. He spoke briefly to the superintendent of the building, a man named Manny Farber, and then took the elevator up to the fourth floor. There was no longer a patrolman on duty in the hallway. He went down the corridor and let himself into the apartment, using Tinka's own key, which had been lent to the investigating precinct by the Office of the Clerk.

The apartment was still.

He could tell at once that death had been here. There are different silences in an empty apartment, and if you are a working policeman, you do not scoff at poetic fallacy. An apartment vacated for the summer has a silence unlike one that is empty only for the day, with its occupants expected back that night. And an apartment that has known the touch of death possesses a silence unique and readily identifiable to anyone who has ever stared down at a corpse. Meyer knew the silence of death, and understood it, though he could not have told you what accounted for it. The disconnected humless electrical appliances; the unused, undripping water taps; the unringing telephone; the stopped unticking clocks; the sealed windows shutting out all street noises; these were all a part of it, but they only contributed to the whole and were not its sum and substance. The real silence was something only felt, and had nothing to do with the absence of sound. It touched something deep within him the moment he stepped through the door. It seemed to be carried on the air itself, a shuddering reminder that death had passed this way, and that some of its frightening grandeur was still locked inside these rooms. He paused with his hand on the doorknob, and then sighed and closed the door behind him and went into the apartment.

Sunlight glanced through closed windows, dust beams silently hovered on the unmoving air. He walked softly, as though reluctant to stir whatever ghostly remnants still were here. When he passed the child's room he looked through the open door and saw the dolls lined up in the bookcase beneath the windows, row upon row of dolls, each dressed differently, each staring back at him with unblinking glass eyes, pink cheeks glowing, mute red mouths frozen on the edge of articulation, painted lips parted over even plastic teeth, nylon hair in black, and red, and blonde, and the palest silver.

He was starting into the room when he heard a key turning in the front door.

The sound startled him. It cracked into the silent apartment like a crash of thunder. He heard the tumblers falling, the sudden click of the knob being turned. He moved into the child's room just as the front door opened. His eyes swept the room – bookcases, bed, closet, toy chest. He could hear heavy footsteps in the corridor, approaching the room. He threw open the closet door, drew his gun. The footsteps were closer. He eased the door towards him, leaving it open just a crack. Holding his breath, he waited in the darkness.

The man who came into the room was perhaps six feet two inches tall, with massive shoulders and a narrow waist. He paused just inside the doorway, as though sensing the presence of another person, seemed almost to be sniffing the air for a telltale scent. Then, visibly shrugging away his own correct intuition, he dismissed the idea and went quickly to the bookcases. He stopped in front of them and began lifting dolls from the shelves, seemingly at random, bundling them into his arms. He gathered up seven or eight of them, rose, turned towards the door, and was on his way out when Meyer kicked open the closet door.

The man turned, startled, his eyes opening wide. Foolishly, he clung to the dolls in his arms, first looking at Meyer's face, and then at the Colt .38 in Meyer's hand, and then up at Meyer's face again.

'Who are you?' he asked.

'Good question,' Meyer said. 'Put those dolls down, hurry up, on the bed there.'

'What . . . ?'

'Do as I say, mister!'

The man walked to the bed. He wet his lips, looked at Meyer, frowned, and then dropped the dolls.

'Get over against the wall,' Meyer said.

'Listen, what the hell . . . ?'

'Spread your legs, bend over, lean against the wall with your palms flat. Hurry up!'

'All right, take it easy.' The man leaned against the wall. Meyer quickly and carefully frisked him – chest, pockets, waist, the insides of his legs. Then he backed away from the man and said, 'Turn around, keep your hands up.'

The man turned, his hands high. He wet his lips again, and again looked at the gun in Meyer's hand.

'What are you doing here?' Meyer asked.

'What are *you* doing here?'

'I'm a police officer. Answer my –'

'Oh. Oh, okay,' the man said.

'What's okay about it?'

'I'm Dennis Sachs.'

'Who?'

'Dennis –'

'Tinka's husband?'

'Well, her ex-husband.'

'Where's your wallet?'

'Right here in my –'

'Don't reach for it! Bend over against the wall again, go ahead.'

The man did as Meyer ordered. Meyer felt for the wallet and found it in his right hip pocket. He opened it to the driver's licence. The name on the licence was Dennis Robert Sachs. Meyer handed it back to him.

'All right, put your hands down. What are you doing here?'

'My daughter wanted some of her dolls,' Sachs said. 'I came back to get them.'

'How'd you get in?'

'I have a key. I used to live here, you know.'

'It was my understanding you and your wife were divorced.'

'That's right.'

'And you still have a key?'

'Yes.'

'Did she know this?'

'Yes, of course.'

'And that's all you wanted here, huh? Just the dolls.'

'Yes.'

'Any doll in particular?'

'No.'

'Your daughter didn't specify any particular doll?'

'No, she simply said she'd like some of her dolls, and she asked if I'd come get them for her.'

'How about *your* preference?'

'*My* preference?'

'Yes. Did *you* have any particular doll in mind?'

'Me?'

'That's right, Mr Sachs. You.'

'No. What do you mean? Are you talking about *dolls*?'

'That's right, that's what I'm talking about.'

'Well, what would I want with any *specific* doll?'

'That's what *I'd* like to know.'

'I don't think I understand you.'

'Then forget it.'

Sachs frowned and glanced at the dolls on the bed. He hesitated, then shrugged and said, 'Well, is it all right to take them?'

'I'm afraid not.'

'Why not? They belong to my daughter.'

'We want to look them over, Mr Sachs.'

'For what?'

'I don't know for what. For *anything*.'

Sachs looked at the dolls again, and then he turned to Meyer and stared at him silently. 'I guess you know this has been a pretty bewildering conversation,' he said at last.

'Yeah, well, that's the way mysteries are,' Meyer answered. 'I've got work to do, Mr Sachs. If you have no further business here, I'd appreciate it if you left.'

Sachs nodded and said nothing. He looked at the dolls once again, and then walked out of the room, and down the corridor, and out of the apartment. Meyer waited, listening. The moment he heard the door close behind Sachs, he sprinted down the corridor, stopped just inside the door, counted swiftly to ten, and eased the door open no more than an inch. Peering out into the hallway, he could see Sachs waiting for the elevator. He looked angry as hell. When the elevator did not arrive, he pushed at the button repeatedly and then began pacing. He glanced once at Tinka's supposedly closed door, and then turned back to the elevator again. When it finally arrived, he said to the operator, 'What took you so long?' and stepped into the car.

Meyer came out of the apartment immediately, closed the door behind him, and ran for the service steps. He took the steps down at a gallop, pausing only for an instant at the fire door leading to the lobby, and then opening the door a crack. He could see the elevator operator standing near the building's entrance, his arms folded across his chest. Meyer came out into the lobby quickly, glanced back once at the open elevator doors, and then ran past the elevator and into the street. He spotted Sachs turning the corner up the block, and broke into a run after him. He paused again before turning the corner. When he sidled around it, he saw Sachs getting into a taxi. There was no time for Meyer to go to his own parked car. He hailed another cab and said to the driver, just like a cop, 'Follow that taxi,' sourly reminding himself that he would have to turn in a chit for the fare, even though he knew Petty Cash would probably never reimburse him. The taxi driver turned for a quick look at Meyer, just to see who was pulling all this cloak and dagger nonsense, and then silently began following Sachs's cab.

'You a cop?' he asked at last.

'Yeah,' Meyer said.

'Who's that up ahead?'

'The Boston Strangler,' Meyer said.

'Yeah?'

'Would I kid you?'

'You going to pay for this ride, or is it like taking apples from a pushcart?'

'I'm going to pay for it,' Meyer said. 'Just don't lose him, okay?'

It was almost ten o'clock, and the streets were thronged with traffic. The lead taxi moved steadily uptown and then crosstown, with Meyer's driver skilfully following. The city was a bedlam of noise – honking horns, grinding gears, squealing tyres, shouting drivers and pedestrians. Meyer leaned forward and kept his eye on the taxi ahead, oblivious to the sounds around him.

'He's pulling up, I think,' the driver said.

'Good. Stop about six car lengths behind him.' The taxi meter read eighty-five cents. Meyer took a dollar bill from his wallet, and handed it to the driver the moment he pulled over the kerb. Sachs had already gotten out of his cab and was walking into an apartment building in the middle of the block.

'Is this all the city tips?' the driver asked. 'Fifteen cents on an eighty-five-cent ride?'

'The city, my ass,' Meyer said, and leaped out of the cab. He ran up the street, and came into the building's entrance alcove just as the inner glass door closed behind Sachs. Meyer swung back his left arm and swiftly ran his hand over every bell in the row on the wall. Then, while waiting for an answering buzz, he put his face close to the glass door, shaded his eyes against the reflective glare, and peered inside. Sachs was nowhere in sight; the elevators were apparently around a corner of the lobby. A half-dozen answering buzzes sounded at once, releasing the lock mechanism on the door. Meyer pushed it open, and ran into the lobby. The floor indicator over the single elevator was moving, three, four, five – and stopped. Meyer nodded and walked out to the entrance alcove again, bending to look at the bells there. There were six apartments on the fifth floor. He was studying the names under the bells when a voice behind him said, 'I think you're looking for Dr Jason Levi.'

Meyer looked up, startled.

The man standing behind him was Bert Kling.

Dr Jason Levi's private office was painted an antiseptic white, and the only decoration on its wall was a large, easily readable calendar. His desk was functional and unadorned, made of grey steel, its top cluttered with medical journals and books, X-ray photographs, pharmaceutical samples, tongue depressors, prescription pads. There was a no-nonsense look about the doctor as well, the plain face topped with leonine white hair, the thick-lensed spectacles, the large cleaving nose, the thin-lipped mouth. He sat behind his desk and looked first at the detectives and then at Dennis Sachs, and waited for someone to speak.

'We want to know what you're doing here, Mr Sachs,' Meyer said.

'I'm a patient,' Sachs said.

'Is that true, Dr Levi?'

Levi hesitated. Then he shook his massive head. 'No,' he said. 'That is not true.'

'Shall we start again?' Meyer asked.

'I have nothing to say,' Sachs answered.

'Why'd you find it necessary to call Dr Levi from Arizona once a week?' Kling asked.

'Who said I did?'

'Mr Walter Blount, manager of the Major Powell Hotel in Rainfield.'

'He was lying.'

'Why would he lie?'

'I don't *know* why,' Sachs said. 'Go ask *him*.'

'No, we'll do it the easy way,' Kling said. 'Dr Levi, *did* Mr Sachs call you from Arizona once a week?'

'Yes,' Levi said.

'We seem to have a slight difference of opinion here,' Meyer said.

'Why'd he call you?' Kling asked.

'Don't answer that, Doctor!'

'Dennis, what are we trying to hide? She's dead.'

'You're a doctor, you don't have to tell them anything. You're like a priest. They can't force you to —'

'Dennis, she is dead.'

'Did your calls have something to do with your wife?' Kling asked.

'No,' Sachs said.

'Yes,' Levi said.

'Was *Tinka* your patient, Doctor, is that it?'

'Yes.'

'Dr Levi, I *forbid* you to tell these men anything more about —'

'She was my patient,' Levi said. 'I began treating her at the beginning of the year.'

'In January?'

'Yes. January fifth. More than three months ago.'

'Doctor, I swear on my dead wife that if you go ahead with this, I'm going to ask the AMA to —'

'Nonsense!' Levi said fiercely. 'Your wife is dead! If we can help them find her killer —'

'You're not helping them with anything! All you're doing is dragging her memory through the muck of a criminal investigation.'

'Mr Sachs,' Meyer said, 'whether you know it or not, her memory is already in the muck of a criminal investigation.'

'Why did she come to you, Doctor?' Kling asked. 'What was wrong with her?'

'She said she had made a New Year's resolution, said she had decided once and for all to seek medical assistance. It was quite pathetic, really. She was so helpless, and so beautiful, and so alone.'

'I *couldn't* stay with her any longer!' Sachs said. 'I'm not made of iron! I couldn't handle it. That's why we got the divorce. It wasn't my fault, what happened to her.'

'No one is blaming you for anything,' Levi said. 'Her illness went back a long time, long before she met you.'

'What was this illness, Doctor?' Meyer asked.

'Don't tell them!'

'Dennis, I *have* to —'

'You *don't* have to! Leave it the way it is. Let her live in everyone's memory as a beautiful exciting woman instead of —'

Dennis cut himself off.

'Instead of what?' Meyer asked.

The room went silent.

'Instead of what?' he said again.

Levi sighed and shook his head.

'Instead of a drug addict.'

Chapter Twelve

In the silence of the squadroom later that day, they read Dr Jason Levi's casebook:

January 5

The patient's name is Tina Karin Sachs. She is divorced, has a daughter aged five. She lives in the city and leads an active professional life, which is one of the reasons she was reluctant to seek assistance before now. She stated, however, that she had made a New Year's resolution, and that she is determined to break the habit. She has been a narcotics user since the time she was seventeen, and is now addicted to heroin.

I explained to her that the methods of withdrawal which I had thus far found most satisfactory were those employing either morphine or methadone, both of which had proved to be adequate substitutes for whatever drugs or combinations of drugs my patients had previously been using. I told her, too, that I personally preferred the morphine method.

She asked if there would be much pain involved. Apparently she had once tried cold-turkey withdrawal and had found the attempt too painful to bear. I told her that she would experience withdrawal symptoms – nausea, vomiting, diarrhoea, lacrimation, dilation of pupils, rhinorrhoea, yawning, gooseflesh, sneezing, sweating – with either method. With morphine, the withdrawal would be more severe, but she could expect relative comfort after a week or so. With methadone, the withdrawal would be easier, but she might still feel somewhat tremulous for as long as a month afterwards.

She said she wanted to think it over, and would call me when she had decided.

January 12

I had not expected to see or hear from Tinka Sachs again, but she arrived here today and asked my receptionist if I could spare ten minutes. I said I could, and she was shown into my private office, where we talked for more than forty-five minutes.

She said she had not yet decided what she should do, and wanted to discuss it further with me. She is, as she had previously explained, a fashion model. She receives top fees for her modelling and was now afraid that treatment might entail either pain or sickness which would cause her to lose employment, thereby endangering her career. I told her that her addiction to heroin had made her virtually careerless anyway, since she was spending much of her income on the purchase of drugs. She did not particularly enjoy this observation, and quickly rejoindered that she thoroughly relished all the fringe benefits of modelling – the fame, the recognition, and so on. I asked her if she really enjoyed anything but heroin, or really thought of anything but heroin, and she became greatly agitated and seemed about to leave the office.

Instead, she told me that I didn't know what it was like, and she hoped I understood she had been using narcotics since she was seventeen, when she'd first tried marijuana at a beach party in Malibu. She had continued smoking marijuana for almost a year, never tempted to try any of 'the real shit' until a photographer offered her a sniff of heroin shortly after she'd begun modelling. He also tried to rape her afterwards, a side effect that nearly caused her to abandon her beginning career as a model. Her near-rape, however, did not dissuade her from using marijuana or from sniffing heroin every now and then, until someone warned her that inhaling the drug could damage her nose. Since her nose was part of her face, and her face was part of what she hoped would become her fortune, she promptly stopped the sniffing process.

The first time she tried injecting the drug was with a confirmed addict, male, in a North Hollywood apartment. Unfortunately, the police broke in on them, and they were both arrested. She was nineteen years old at the time, and was luckily released with a suspended sentence. She came to this city the following month, determined never to fool with drugs again, hoping to put three thousand miles between herself and her former acquaintances. But she discovered, almost immediately upon arrival, that the drug was as readily obtainable here as it was in Los Angeles. Moreover, she began her association with the Cutler Agency several weeks after she got here, and found herself in possession of more money than she would ever need to support both herself *and* a narcotics habit. She began injecting the drug under her skin, into the soft tissue of her body. Shortly afterwards, she abandoned the subcutaneous route and began shooting heroin directly into her veins. She has been using it intravenously ever since, has for all intents and purposes been hopelessly hooked since she first began skin-popping. How, then, could I expect to cure her? How could she wake up each morning without knowing that a supply of narcotics was available, in fact accessible? I explained that hers was the common fear of all addicts about to undergo treatment, a reassurance she accepted without noticeable enthusiasm.

I'll think about it, she said again, and again left. I frankly do not believe she will ever return again.

January 20

Tinka Sachs began treatment today.

She has chosen the morphine method (even though she understands the symptoms will be more severe) because she does not want to endanger her career by a prolonged withdrawal, a curious concern for someone who has been endangering her career ever since it started. I had previously explained that I wanted to hospitalize her for several months, but she flatly refused hospitalization of any kind, and stated that the deal was off if that was part of the treatment. I told her that I could not guarantee lasting results unless she allowed me to hospitalize her, but she said we would have to hope for the best because she wasn't going to admit herself to any damn hospital. I finally extracted from her an agreement to stay at home under a nurse's care at least during the first several days of withdrawal, when the symptoms would be most severe. I warned her against making any illegal purchases and against associating with any know addicts or pushers. Our schedule is a rigid one. To start, she will receive ¼ grain of morphine four times daily – twenty minutes before each meal. The doses will be administered hypodermically, and the morphine will be dissolved in thiamine hydrochloride.

It is my hope that withdrawal will be complete within two weeks.

January 21

I have prescribed Thorazine for Tinka's nausea, and belladonna and pectin for her diarrhoea. The symptoms are severe. She could not sleep at all last night. I have instructed the nurse staying at her apartment to administer three grains of Nembutal tonight before Tinka retires, with further instructions to repeat 1½ grains if she does not sleep through the night.

Tinka has taken excellent care of her body, a factor on our side. She is quite beautiful and I have no doubt she is a superior model, though I am at a loss to explain how photographers can have missed her obvious addiction. How did she keep from 'nodding' before the cameras? She has scrupulously avoided marking either her lower legs or her arms, but the insides of her thighs (she told me she does not model either lingerie or bathing suits) are covered with hit marks.

Morphine continues at ¼ grain four times daily.

January 22

I have reduced the morphine injections to ¼ grain twice daily, alternating with ⅛ grain twice daily. Symptoms are still severe. She has cancelled all of her sittings, telling the agency she is menstruating and suffering cramps, a complaint they have apparently heard from their models before. She shows no desire to eat. I have begun prescribing vitamins.

January 23

The symptoms are abating. We are now administering ⅛ grain four times daily.

January 24

Treatment continuing with ⅛ grain four times daily. The nurse will be discharged tomorrow, and Tinka will begin coming to my office for her injections, a procedure I am heartily against. But it is either that or losing her entirely, and I must go along.

January 25

Started one grain codeine twice daily, alternating with ⅛ grain morphine twice daily. Tinka came to my office at eight-thirty, before breakfast, for her first injection. She came again at twelve-thirty, and at six-thirty. I administered the last injection at her home at eleven-thirty. She seems exceptionally restless, and I have prescribed ½ grain of phenobarbital daily to combat this.

January 26

Tinka Sachs did not come to the office today. I called her apartment
several times, but no one answered the telephone. I did not dare call the
modelling agency lest they suspect she is undergoing treatment. At three
o'clock, I spoke to her daughter's governess. She had just picked the child up
at the playschool she attends. She said she did not know where Mrs Sachs
was, and suggested that I try the agency. I called again at midnight. Tinka
was still not home. The governess said I had awakened her. Apparently, she
saw nothing unusual about her employer's absence. The working arrangement calls for her to meet the child after school and to spend as much time
with her as is necessary. She said that Mrs Sachs is often gone the entire
night, in which case she is supposed to take the child to school in the
morning, and then call for her again at two-thirty. Mrs Sachs was once gone
for three days, she said.

I am worried.

February 4

Tinka returned to the office again today, apologizing profusely, and
explaining that she had been called out of town on an assignment; they were
shooting some new tweed fashions and wanted a woodland background. I
accused her of lying, and she finally admitted that she had not been out of
town at all, but had instead spent the past week in the apartment of a friend
from California. After further questioning, she conceded that her California
friend is a drug addict, is in fact the man with whom she was arrested when
she was nineteen years old. He arrived in the city last September, with very
little money, and no place to live. She staked him for a while, and allowed
him to live in her Mavis County house until she sold it in October. She then
helped him to find an apartment on South Fourth, and she still sees him
occasionally.

It was obvious that she had begun taking heroin again.

She expressed remorse, and said that she is more than ever determined to
break the habit. When I asked if her friend expects to remain in the city, she
said that he does, but that he has a companion with him, and no longer needs
any old acquaintance to help him pursue his course of addiction.

I extracted a promise from Tinka that she would never see this man again,
nor try to contact him.

We begin treatment again tomorrow morning. This time I insisted that a
nurse remain with her for at least two weeks.

We will be starting from scratch.

February 9

We have made excellent progress in the past five days. The morphine
injections have been reduced to $\frac{1}{8}$ grain four times daily, and tomorrow we
begin alternating with codeine.

Tinka talked about her relationship with her husband for the first time
today, in connection with her resolve to break the habit. He is, apparently,
an archaeologist working with an expedition somewhere in Arizona. She is
in frequent touch with him, and in fact called him yesterday to say she had
begun treatment and was hopeful of a cure. It is her desire, she said, to begin
a new life with him once the withdrawal is complete. She knows he still loves

her, knows that had it not been for her habit they would never have parted.

She said he did not learn of her addiction until almost a year after the child was born. This was all the more remarkable since the baby – fed during pregnancy by the bloodstream of her mother, metabolically dependent on heroin – was quite naturally an addict herself from the moment she was born. Dennis, and the family pediatrician as well, assumed she was a colicky baby, crying half the night through, vomiting, constantly fretting. Only Tinka knew that the infant was experiencing all the symptoms of cold-turkey withdrawal. She was tempted more than once to give the child a secret fix, but she restrained from doing so, and the baby survived the torment of force withdrawal only to face the subsequent storm of separation and divorce.

Tinka was able to explain the hypodermic needle Dennis found a month later by saying she was allergic to certain dyes in the nylon dresses she was modelling and that her doctor had prescribed an antihistamine in an attempt to reduce the allergic reaction. But she could not explain the large sums of money that seemed to be vanishing from their joint bank account, nor could she explain his ultimate discovery of three glassine bags of a white powder secreted at the back of her dresser drawer. She finally confessed that she was a drug addict, that she had been a drug addict for close to seven years and saw nothing wrong with it so long as she was capable of supporting the habit. He goddamn well knew she was earning most of the money in his household, anyway, so what the fuck did he want from her?

He cracked her across the face and told her they would go to see a doctor in the morning.

In the morning, Tinka was gone.

She did not return to the apartment until three weeks later, dishevelled and bedraggled, at which time she told Dennis she had been on a party with three coloured musicians from a club downtown, all of them addicts. She could not remember what they had done together. Dennis had meanwhile consulted a doctor, and he told Tinka that drug addiction was by no means incurable, that there were ways of treating it, that success was almost certain if the patient – Don't make me laugh, Tinka said. I'm hooked through the bag and back, and what's more I like it, now what the hell do you think about that? Get off my back, you're worse than the monkey!

He asked for the divorce six months later.

During that time, he tried desperately to reach this person he had taken for a wife, this stranger who was nonetheless the mother of his child, this driven animal whose entire life seemed bounded by the need for heroin. Their expenses were overwhelming. She could not let her career vanish because without her career she could hardly afford the enormous amounts of heroin she required. So she dressed the part of the famous model, and lived in a lavishly appointed apartment, and rode around town in hired limousines, and ate at the best restaurants, and was seen at all the important functions – while within her the clamour for heroin raged unabated. She worked slavishly, part of her income going towards maintaining the legend that was a necessary adjunct of her profession, the remainder going towards the purchase of drugs for herself and her friends.

There were always friends.

She would vanish for weeks at a time, lured by a keening song she alone heard, compelled to seek other addicts, craving the approval of people like herself, the comradeship of the dream society, the anonymity of the shooting gallery where scars were not stigmata and addiction was not a curse.

He would have left her sooner but the child presented a serious problem. He knew he could not trust Anna alone with her mother, but how could he take her with him on archaeological expeditions around the world? He realized that if Tinka's addiction were allowed to enter the divorce proceedings, he would be granted immediate custody of the child. But Tinka's career would automatically be ruined, and who knew what later untold hurt the attendant publicity could bring to Anna? He promised Tinka that he would not introduce the matter of her addiction if she would allow him to hire a responsible governess for the child. Tinka readily agreed. Except for her occasional binges, she considered herself to be a devoted and exemplary mother. If a governess would make Dennis happy and keep this sordid matter of addiction out of the proceedings, she was more than willing to go along with the idea. The arrangements were made.

Dennis, presumably in love with his wife, presumably concerned about his daughter's welfare, was nonetheless content to abandon one to eternal drug addiction, and the other to the vagaries and unpredictabilities of living with a confirmed junkie. Tinka, for her part, was glad to see him leave. He had become a puritanical goad, and she wondered why she'd ever married him in the first place. She supposed it had had something to do with the romantic notion of one day kicking the habit and starting a new life.

Which is what you're doing now, I told her.

Yes, she said, and her eyes were shining.

February 12

Tinka is no longer dependent on morphine, and we have reduced the codeine intake to one grain twice daily, alternating with ½ grain twice daily.

February 13

I received a long-distance call from Dennis Sachs today. He simply wanted to know how his wife was coming along and said that if I didn't mind he would call once a week – it would have to be either Friday or Saturday since he'd be in the desert the rest of the time – to check on her progress. I told him that the prognosis was excellent, and I expressed the hope that withdrawal would be complete by the twentieth of the month.

February 14

Have reduced the codeine to ½ grain twice daily, and have introduced thiamine twice daily.

February 15

Last night, Tinka slipped out of the apartment while her nurse was dozing. She has not returned, and I do not know where she is.

February 20

Have been unable to locate Tinka.

March 1

Have called the apartment repeatedly. The governess continues to care for Anna – but there has been no word from Tinka.

March 8

In desperation, I called the Cutler Agency today to ask if they have any knowledge of Tinka's whereabouts. They asked me to identify myself, and I said I was a doctor treating her for a skin allergy (Tinka's own lie!) They said she had gone to the Virgin Islands on a modelling assignment and would not be back until the twentieth of March. I thanked them and hung up.

March 22

Tinka came back to my office today.

The assignment had come up suddenly, she said, and she had taken it, forgetting to tell me about it.

I told her I thought she was lying.

All right, she said. She had seized upon the opportunity as a way to get away from me and the treatment. She did not know why, but she had suddenly been filled with panic. She knew that in several days, a week at most, she would be off even the thiamine – and then what would there be? How could she possibly get through a day without a shot of *something*?

Art Cutler had called and proposed the St Thomas assignment, and the idea of sun and sand had appealed to her immensely. By coincidence, her friend from California called that same night, and when she told him where she was going he said that he'd pack a bag and meet her down there.

I asked her exactly what her connection is with this 'friend from California', who now seems responsible for two lapses in her treatment. What lapse? she asked, and then swore she had not touched anything while she was away. This friend was simply *that*, a good friend.

But you told me he is an addict, I said.

Yes, he's an addict, she answered. But he didn't even *suggest* drugs while we were away. As a matter of fact, I think I've kicked it completely. That's really the only reason I came here, to tell you that it's not necessary to continue treatment any longer. I haven't had anything, heroin or morphine or *anything*, all the while I was away. I'm cured.

You're lying, I said.

All right, she said. If I wanted the truth, it was her California friend who'd kept her out of prison those many years ago. He had told the arresting officers that he was a pusher, a noble and dangerous admission to make, and that he had forced a shot on Tinka. She had got off with the suspended sentence while he'd gone to prison; so naturally she was indebted to him. Besides, she saw no reason why she shouldn't spend some time with him on a modelling assignment, instead of running around with a lot of faggot designers and photographers, not to mention the Lesbian editor of the magazine. Who the hell did I think I was, her keeper?

I asked if this 'friend from California' had suddenly struck it rich.

What do you mean? she said.

Well, isn't it true that he was in need of money and a place to stay when he first came to the city?

Yes, that's true.

Then how can he afford to support a drug habit and also manage to take a vacation in the Virgin Islands? I asked.

She admitted that she paid for the trip. If the man had saved her from a prison sentence, what was so wrong about paying his fare and his hotel bill? I would not let it go.

Finally, she told me the complete story. She had been sending him money over the years, not because he asked her for it, but simply because she felt she owed something to him. His lie had enabled her to come here and start a new life. The least she could do was send him a little money every now and then. Yes, she had been supporting him ever since he arrived here. Yes, yes, it was she who'd invited him along on the trip; there had been no coincidental phone call from him that night. Moreover, she had not only paid for *his* plane fare and hotel bill, but also for that of his companion, whom she described as 'an extremely lovely young woman.'

And no heroin all that while, right?

Tears, anger, defence.

Yes, there had been heroin! There had been enough heroin to sink the island, and she had paid for every drop of it. There had been heroin morning, noon, and night. It was amazing that she had been able to face the cameras at all, she had blamed her drowsiness on the sun. That needle had been stuck in her thigh constantly, like a glittering glass cock! Yes, there had been heroin, and she had loved every minute of it! What the hell did I want from her?

I want to cure you, I said.

March 23

She accused me today of trying to kill her. She said that I have been trying to kill her since the first day we met, that I know she is not strong enough to withstand the pains of withdrawal, and that the treatment will eventually result in her death.

Her lawyer has been preparing a will, she said, and she would sign it tomorrow. She would begin treatment after that, but she knew it would lead to her ultimate death.

March 24

Tinka signed her will today.

She brought me a fragment of a poem she wrote last night:

> *When I think of what I am*
> *And of what I might have been,*
> *I tremble.*
> *I fear the night.*
> *Throughout the day,*
> *I rush from dragons conjured in the dark.*
> *Why will they not*

I asked her why she hadn't finished the poem. She said she couldn't finish it until she knew the outcome herself. What outcome do you want? I asked her.

I want to be cured, she said.

You *will* be cured, I told her.

March 25

We began treatment once more.

March 27

Dennis Sachs called from Arizona again to enquire about his wife. I told him she had suffered a relapse but that she had begun treatment anew, and that we were hoping for complete withdrawal by April 15th at the very latest. He asked if there was anything he could do for Tinka. I told him that the only person who could do anything for Tinka was Tinka.

March 28

Treatment continues.
¼ grain morphine twice daily.
⅛ grain morphine twice daily.

March 30

⅛ grain morphine four times daily.
Prognosis good.

March 31

⅛ grain morphine twice daily.
One grain codeine twice daily.

April 1

Tinka confessed today that she has begun buying heroin on the sly, smuggling it in, and has been taking it whenever the nurse isn't watching. I flew into a rage. She shouted 'April Fool!' and began laughing.
I think there is a chance this time.

April 2

One grain codeine four times daily.

April 3

One grain codeine twice daily.
½ grain codeine twice daily.

April 4

½ grain codeine four times daily.

April 5

½ grain codeine twice daily, thiamine twice daily.

April 6

Thiamine four times daily. Nurse was discharged today.

April 7

Thiamine three times daily.
We are going to make it!

April 8
Thiamine twice daily.

April 9
She told me today that she is certain the habit is almost kicked. This is my feeling as well. The weaning from hypodermics is virtually complete. There is only the promise of a new and rewarding life ahead.

That was where the doctor's casebook ended because that was when Tinka Sachs was murdered.

Meyer glanced up to see if Kling had finished the page. Kling nodded, and Meyer closed the book.

'He took two lives from her,' Meyer said. 'The one she was ending, and the one she was beginning.'

That afternoon Paul Blaney earned his salary for the second time in four days. He called to say he had completed the post-mortem examination of Tinka Sachs and had discovered a multitude of scars on both upper front thighs. It seemed positive that the scars had been caused by repeated intravenous injections, and it was Blaney's opinion that the dead girl had been a drug addict.

Chapter Thirteen

She had handcuffed both hands behind his back during one of his periods of unconsciousness, and then had used a leather belt to lash his feet together. He lay naked on the floor now and waited for her arrival, trying to tell himself he did not need her, and knowing that he needed her desperately.

It was very warm in the room, but he was shivering. His skin was beginning to itch but he could not scratch himself because his hands were manacled behind his back. He could smell his own body odours – he had not been bathed or shaved in three days – but he did not care about his smell or his beard, he only cared that she was not here yet, what was keeping her?

He lay in the darkness and tried not to count the minutes.

The girl was naked when she came into the room. She did not put on the light. There was the familiar tray in her hands, but it did not carry food any more. The Llama was on the left-hand side of the tray. Alongside the gun were a small cardboard box, a book of matches, a spoon with its handle bent back towards the bowl, and a glassine envelope.

'Hello, doll,' she said. 'Did you miss me?'

Carella did not answer.

'Have you been waiting for me?' the girl asked. 'What's the matter, don't you feel like talking?' She laughed her mirthless laugh. 'Don't worry, baby,' she said. 'I'm going to fix you.'

She put the tray down on the chair near the door, and then walked to him.

'I think I'll play with you awhile,' she said. 'Would you like me to play with you?'

Carella did not answer.

'Well, if you're not even going to talk to me, I guess I'll just have to leave. After all, I know when I'm not –'

'No, don't go,' Carella said.

'Do you want me to stay?'

'Yes.'

'Say it.'

'I want you to stay.'

'That's better. What would you like, baby? Would you like me to play with you a little?'

'No.'

'Don't you like being played with?'

'No.'

'What do you like, baby?'

He did not answer.

'Well, you have to tell me,' she said, 'or I just won't give it to you.'

'I don't know,' he said.

'You don't know what you like?'

'Yes.'

'Do you like the way I look without any clothes on?'

'Yes, you look all right.'

'But that doesn't interest you, does it?'

'No.'

'What *does* interest you?'

Again, he did not answer.

'Well, you *must* know what interests you. Don't you know?'

'No, I don't know.'

'Tch,' the girl said, and rose and began walking towards the door.

'Where are you going?' he asked quickly.

'Just to put some water in the spoon, doll,' she said soothingly. 'Don't worry. I'll be back.'

She took the spoon from the tray and walked out of the room, leaving the door open. He could hear the water tap running in the kitchen. Hurry up, he thought, and then thought, No, I don't need you, leave me alone, goddamn you, leave me alone!

'Here I am,' she said. She took the tray off the seat of the chair and then sat and picked up the glassine envelope. She emptied its contents into the spoon, and then struck a match and held it under the blackened bowl. 'Got to cook it up,' she said. 'Got to cook it up for my baby. You getting itchy for it, baby? Don't worry, I'll take care of you. What's your wife's name?'

'Teddy,' he said.

'Oh my,' she said, 'you still remember. That's a shame.' She blew out the match. She opened the small box on the tray, and removed the hypodermic syringe and needle from it. She affixed the needle to the syringe, and depressed the plunger to squeeze any air out of the cylindrical glass tube. From the same cardboard box, which was the original container in which the syringe had been marketed, she took a piece of absorbent cotton, which she placed over the milky white liquid in the bowl of the spoon. Using the cotton as a filter, knowing that even the tiniest piece of solid matter would clog the tiny opening in the hypodermic needle, she drew the liquid up into the syringe, and then smiled and said. 'There we are, all ready for my doll.'

'I don't want it,' Carella said suddenly.

'Oh, honey, please don't lie to me,' she said calmly. 'I *know* you want it, what's your wife's name?'

'Teddy.'

'Teddy, tch, tch, well, well,' she said. From the cardboard box, she took a loop of string, and then walked to Carella and put the syringe on the floor beside him. She looped the piece of string around his arm, just above the elbow joint.

'What's your wife's name?' she asked.

'Teddy.'

'You want this, doll?'

'No.'

'Oooh, it's very good,' she said. 'We had some this afternoon, it was very good stuff. Aren't you just aching all over for it, what's your wife's name?'

'Teddy.'

'Has she got tits like mine?'

Carella did not answer.

'Oh, but that doesn't interest you, does it? All that interests you is what's right here in this syringe, isn't that right?'

'No.'

'This is a very high-class shooting gallery, baby. No eyedroppers here, oh no. Everything veddy veddy high-tone. Though I don't know how we're going to keep ourselves in junk now that little Sweetass is gone. He shouldn't have killed her, he really shouldn't have.'

'Then why did he?'

'I'll ask the questions, doll. Do you remember your wife's name?'

'Yes.'

'What is it?'

'Teddy.'

'Then I guess I'll go. I can make good use of this myself.' She picked up the syringe. 'Shall I go?'

'Do what you want to do.'

'If I leave this room,' the girl said, 'I won't come back until tomorrow morning. That'll be a long long night, baby. You think you can last the night without a fix?' She paused. 'Do you want this or not?'

'Leave me alone,' he said.

'No. No, no, we can't leave you alone. In a little while, baby, you are going to tell us everything you know, you are going to tell us exactly how you found us, you are going to tell us because if you don't we'll leave you here to drown in your own vomit. Now what's you wife's name?'

'Teddy.'

'No.'

'Yes. Her name is Teddy.'

'How can I give you this if your memory's so good?'

'Then don't give it to me.'

'Okay,' the girl said, and walked towards the door. 'Goodnight, doll. I'll see you in the morning.'

'Wait.'

'Yes?' The girl turned. There was no expression on her face.

'You forgot your tourniquet,' Carella said.

'So I did,' the girl answered. She walked back to him and removed the string from his arm. 'Play it cool,' she said. 'Go ahead. See how far you get by playing it cool. Tomorrow morning you'll be rolling all over the floor when I come in.' She kissed him swiftly on the mouth. She sighed deeply. 'Ahh,' she said, 'why do you force me to be mean to you?'

She went back to the door and busied herself with putting the string and cotton back into the box, straightening the book of matches and the spoon, aligning the syringe with the other items.

'Well, goodnight,' she said, and walked out of the room, locking the door behind her.

Detective Sergeant Tony Kreisler of the Los Angeles Police Department did not return Meyer's call until nine o'clock that Monday night, which meant it was six o'clock on the Coast.

'You've had me busy all day long,' Kreisler said. 'It's tough to dig in the files for these ancient ones.'

'Did you come up with anything?' Meyer asked.

'I'll tell you the truth, if this hadn't been a homicide you're working on, I'd have given up long ago, said the hell with it.'

'What've you got for me?' Meyer asked patiently.

'This goes back twelve, thirteen years. You really think there's a connection?'

'It's all we've got to go on,' Meyer said. 'We figured it was worth a chance.'

'Besides, the city paid for the long-distance call, right?' Kreisler said, and began laughing.

'That's right,' Meyer said, and bided his time, and hoped that *Kreisler's* city was paying for *his* call, too.

'Well, anyway,' Kreisler said, when his laughter had subsided, 'you were right about that arrest. We picked them up on a violation of Section 11500 of the Health and Safety Code. The girl's name wasn't Sachs then, we've got her listed as Tina Karin Grady, you suppose that's the same party?'

'Probably her maiden name,' Meyer said.

'That's what I figure. They were holed up in an apartment in North Hollywood with more than twenty-five caps of H, something better than an eighth of an ounce, not that it makes any difference out here. Out here, there's no minimum quantity constituting a violation. Any amount that can be analysed as a narcotic is admissible in court. It's different with you guys, I know that.'

'That's right,' Meyer said.

'Anyway, the guy was a mainliner, hit marks all over his arms. The Grady girl looked like sweet young meat, it was tough to figure what she was doing with a creep like him. She claimed she didn't know he was an addict, claimed he'd invited her up to the apartment, got her drunk, and then forced a shot on her. There were no previous marks on her body, just that one hit mark in the crook of her el —'

'What a minute,' Meyer said.

'Yeah, what's the matter?'

'The *girl* claimed he'd forced the shot on her?'

'That's right. Said he got her drunk.'

'It wasn't the *man* who alibied her?'

'What do you mean?'

'Did the man claim he was a pusher and that he'd forced a fix on the girl?'

Kreisler began laughing again. 'Just catch a junkie who's willing to take a fall as a pusher. Are you kidding?'

'The girl told her doctor that the man alibied her.'

'Absolute lie,' Kreisler said. '*She* was the one who did all the talking, convinced the judge she was innocent, got off with a suspended sentence.'

'And the man?'

'Convicted, served his time at Soledad, minimum of two, maximum of ten.'

'Then *that's* why she kept sending him money. Not because she was indebted to him, but only because she felt guilty as hell.'

'She deserved a break,' Kreisler said. 'What the hell, she was a nineteen-year-old kid. How do you know? Maybe he *did* force a blast on her.'

'I doubt it. She'd been sniffing the stuff regularly and using pot since she was seventeen.'

'Yeah, well, we didn't know that.'

'What was the man's name?' Meyer asked.

'Fritz Schmidt.'

'Fritz? Is that a nickname?'

'No, that's his square handle. Fritz Schmidt.'

'What's the last you've got on him?'

'He was paroled in four. Parole Office gave him a clean bill of health, haven't had any trouble from him since.'

'Do you know if he's still in California?'

'Couldn't tell you.'

'Okay, thanks a lot,' Meyer said.

'Don't mention it,' Kreisler said, and hung up.

There were no listings for Fritz Schmidt in any of the city's telephone directories. But according to Dr Levi's casebook, Tinka's 'friend from California' had only arrived here in September. Hardly expecting any positive results, Meyer dialled the Information operator, identified himself as a working detective, and aksed if she had anything for a Mr Fritz Schmidt in her new listings.

Two minutes later, Meyer and Kling clipped on their holsters and left the squadroom.

The girl came back into the room at nine-twenty-five. She was fully clothed. The Llama was in her right hand. She closed the door gently behind her, but did not bother to switch on the overhead light. She watched Carella silently for several moments, the neon blinking around the edges of the drawn shade across the room. Then she said, 'You're shivering, baby.'

Carella did not answer.

'How tall are you?' she asked.

'Six-two.'

'We'll get some clothes to fit you.'

'Why the sudden concern?' Carella asked. He was sweating profusely, and shivering at the same time, wanting to tear his hands free of the cuffs, wanting to kick out with his lashed feet, helpless to do either, feeling desperately ill and knowing the only thing that would cure him.

'No concern at all, baby,' she said. 'We're dressing you because we've got to take you away from here.'

'Where are you taking me?'

'Away.'

'Where?'

'Don't worry,' she said. 'We'll give you a nice big fix first.'

He felt suddenly exhilarated. He tried to keep the joy from showing on his face, tried not to smile, hoping against hope that she wasn't just teasing him again. He lay shivering on the floor, and the girl laughed and said, 'My, it's rough when a little jolt is overdue, isn't it?'

Carella said nothing.

'Do you know what an overdose of heroin is?' she asked suddenly.

The shivering stopped for just a moment, and then began again more violently. Her words seemed to echo in the room, do you know what an overdose of heroin is, overdose, heroin, do you, do you?

'Do you?' the girl persisted.

'Yes.'

'It won't hurt you,' she said. 'It'll *kill* you, but it won't hurt you.' She laughed again. 'Think of it, baby. How many addicts would you say there are in this city? Twenty thousand, twenty-one thousand, what's your guess?'

'I don't know,' Carella said.

'Let's make it twenty thousand, okay? I like round numbers. Twenty thousand junkies out there, all hustling around and wondering where their next shot is coming from, and here we are about to give you a fix that'd take care of seven or eight of them for a week. How about that? That's real generosity, baby.'

'Thanks,' Carella said. 'What do you think,' he started, and stopped because his teeth were chattering. He waited. He took a deep breath and tried again. 'What do you think you'll . . . you'll accomplish by killing me?'

'Silence,' the girl said.

'How?'

'You're the only one in the world who knows who we are or where we are. Once you're dead, silence.'

'No.'

'Ah, *yes*, baby.'

'I'm telling you no. They'll find you.'

'Uh-uh.'

'Yes.'

'How?'

'The same way I did.'

'Uh-uh. Impossible.'

'If *I* uncovered your mistake –'

'There *was* no mistake, baby.' The girl paused. 'There was only a little girl playing with her doll.'

The room was silent.

'We've got the doll, honey. We found it in your car, remember? It's a very nice doll. Very expensive, I'll bet.'

'It's a present for my daughter,' Carella said. 'I told you –'

'You weren't going to give your daughter a *used* doll for a present, were you? No, honey.' The girl smiled. 'I happened to look under the doll's dress a few minutes ago. Baby, it's all over for you, believe me.' She turned and opened the door. 'Fritz,' she yelled to the other room, 'come in here and give me a hand.'

The mailbox downstairs told them Fritz Schmidt was in apartment 34. They took the steps up two at a time, drawing their revolvers when they were on the third floor, and then scanning the numerals on each door as they moved down the corridor. Meyer put his ear to the door at the end of the hall. He could hear nothing. He moved away from the door, and then nodded to Kling. Kling stepped back several feet, bracing himself, his legs widespread. There was no wall opposite the end door, nothing to use as a launching support for a flat-footed kick at the latch. Meyer used Kling's body as the support he needed, raising his knee high as Kling shoved him out and forwards. Meyer's foot connected. The lock sprang and the door swung wide. He followed it into the apartment, gun in hand, Kling not three feet behind him. They fanned out the moment they were inside the room, Kling to the right, Meyer to the left.

A man came running out of the room to the right of the large living room. He was a tall man with straight blond hair and huge shoulders. He looked at the detectives and then thrust one hand inside his jacket and down towards his belt. Neither Meyer nor Kling waited to find out what he was reaching for. They opened fire simultaneously. The bullets caught the man in his enormous chest and flung him back against the wall, which he clung to for just a moment before falling headlong to the floor. A second person appeared in the doorway. The second person was a girl, and she was very big, and she held a pistol in her right hand. A look of panic was riding her face, but it was curiously coupled with a fixed smile, as though she'd been expecting them all along and was ready for them, was in fact welcoming their arrival.

'Watch it, she's loaded!' Meyer yelled, but the girl swung around swiftly, pointing the gun into the other room instead, aiming it at the floor. In the split second it took her to turn and extend her arm, Kling saw the man lying trussed near the radiator. The man was turned away from the door, but Kling knew instinctively it was Carella.

He fired automatically and without hesitation, the first time he had ever shot a human being in the back, placing the shot high between the girl's shoulders. The Llama in her hand went off at almost the same instant, but the impact of Kling's slug sent her falling halfway across the room, her own bullet going wild. She struggled to rise as Kling ran into the room. She turned the gun on Carella again, but Kling's foot struck her extended hand, kicking the gun up as the second shot exploded. The girl would not let go. Her fingers were still tight around the stock of the gun. She swung it back a third time and shouted, 'Let me *kill* him, you bastard!' and tightened her finger on the trigger.

Kling fired again.

His bullet entered her forehead just above the right eye. The Llama went off as she fell backwards, the bullet spanging against the metal of the radiator and then ricocheting across the room and tearing through the drawn window shade and shattering the glass behind it.

Meyer was at his side.

'Easy,' he said.

Kling had not cried since that time almost four years ago when Claire was killed, but he stood in the centre of the neon-washed room now with the dead and bleeding girl against the wall and Carella naked and shivering near the radiator, and he allowed the hand holding the pistol to drop limply to his side, and then he began sobbing, deep bitter sobs that racked his body.

Meyer put his arm around Kling's shoulders.

'Easy,' he said again. 'It's all over.'

'The doll,' Carella whispered. 'Get the doll.'

Chapter Fourteen

The doll measured thirty inches from the top of her blonde head to the bottoms of her black patent-leather shoes. She wore white bobby socks, a ruffled white voile dress with a white underslip, a black velveteen bodice, and a ruffled lace bib and collar. What appeared at first to be a simulated gold brooch was centred just below the collar.

The doll's trade name was Chatterbox.

There were two D-size flashlight batteries and one 9-volt transistor battery in a recess in the doll's plastic belly. The recess was covered with a flesh-coloured plastic top that was kept in place by a simple plastic twist-lock. Immediately above the battery box, there was a flesh-coloured, open plastic grid that concealed the miniature electronic device in the doll's chest. It was this device after which the doll had been named by its creators. The device was a tiny recorder.

The brooch below the doll's collar was a knob that activated the recording mechanism. To record, a child simply turned the decorative knob counter-clockwise, waited for a single beep signal, and began talking until the beep sounded again, at which time the knob had to be turned once more to its centre position. In order to play back what had just been recorded, the child had only to turn the knob clockwise. The recorded message would continue to play back over and over again until the knob was once more returned to the centre position.

When the detectives turned the brooch-knob clockwise, they heard three recorded voices. One of them belonged to Anna Sachs. It was clear and distinct because the doll had been in Anna's lap when she'd recorded her message on the night of her mother's murder. The message was one of reassurance. She kept saying over and over again to the doll lying across her lap, 'Don't be frightened, Chatterbox, please don't be frightened. It's nothing, Chatterbox, don't be frightened,' over and over again.

The second voice was less distinct because it had been recorded through the thin wall separating the child's bedroom from her mother's. Subsequent tests by the police laboratory showed the recording mechanism to be extremely sensitive for a device of its size, capable of picking up shouted words at a distance of twenty-five feet. Even so, the second voice would not have been picked up at all had Anna not been sitting very close to the thin dividing wall. And, of course, especially towards the end, the words next door had been screamed.

From beep to beep, the recording lasted only a minute and a half. Throughout the length of the recording, Anna talked reassuringly to her doll. 'Don't be frightened, Chatterbox, please don't be frightened. It's nothing, Chatterbox, don't be frightened.' Behind the child's voice, a running counterpoint of horror, was the voice of Tinka Sachs, her mother. Her words were almost inaudible at first. The presented only a vague murmur of faraway terror, the sound of someone repeatedly moaning, the pitiable rise and fall of a voice imploring – but all without words because the sound had been muffled by the wall between the rooms. And then, as Tinka became more and more desperate, as her killer followed her unmercifully around the room with a knife blade, her voice became louder, the words became more distinct. 'Don't! Please don't!' always behind the child's soothing voice in the foreground, 'Don't be frightened, Chatterbox, please don't be frightened,' and her mother shrieking, 'Don't! Please don't! Please,' the voices intermingling, 'I'm bleeding, please, it's nothing, Chatterbox, don't be frightened, Fritz, stop, please, Fritz, stop, stop, oh please, it's nothing, Chatterbox, don't be frightened.'

The third voice sounded like a man's. It was nothing more than a rumble on the recording. Only once did a word come through clearly, and that was the word 'Slut!' interspersed between the child's reassurances to her doll, and Tinka's weakening cries for mercy.

In the end, Tinka shouted the man's name once again, 'Fritz!' and then her voice seemed to fade. The next word she uttered could have been a muted 'please,' but it was indistinct and drowned out by Anna's 'Don't cry, Chatterbox, try not to cry.'

The detectives listened to the doll in silence, and then watched while the ambulance attendants carried Carella out on one stretcher and the still-breathing Schmidt out on another.

'The girl's dead,' the medical examiner said.

'I know,' Meyer answered.

'Who shot her?' one of the Homicide cops asked.

'I did,' Kling answered.

'I'll need the circumstances.'

'Stay with him,' Meyer said to Kling. 'I'll get to the hospital. Maybe that son of a bitch wants to make a statement before he dies.'

```
          I didn't intend to kill her.
          She was happy as hell when I came in,
     laughing and joking because she thought she was
     off the junk at last.
          I told her she was crazy, she would never
     kick it.
          I had not had a shot since three o'clock
     that afternoon, I was going out of my head.   I
     told her I wanted money for a fix, and she said
```

she couldn't give me money any more, she said she
wanted nothing more to do with me or Pat, that's
the name of the girl I'm living with. She had no
right to hold out on me like that, not when I was
so sick. She could see I was ready to climb the
walls, so she sat there sipping her goddamn iced
<u>tea</u>, and telling me she was not going to keep me
supplied any more, she was not going to spend
half her income keeping me in shit. I told her
she owed it to me. I spent four years in Soledad
because of her, the little bitch, she owed it to
me! She told me to leave her alone. She told
me to get out and leave her alone. She said she
was finished with me and my kind. She said she
had kicked it, did I understand, she had kicked
it!

    Am I going to die?

    I

    I picked

    I picked the knife up from the tray.

    I didn't intend to kill her, it was just I
needed a fix, couldn't she see that? For
Christ's sake, the times we used to have
together. I stabbed her, I don't know how many
times.

    Am I going to die?

    The painting fell off the wall, I remember
that.

    I took all the bills out of her pocketbook
on the dresser, there was forty dollars in tens.
I ran out of the bedroom and dropped the knife
someplace in the hall, I guess, I don't even
remember. I realized I couldn't take the
elevator down, that much I knew, so I went up to
the roof and crossed over to the next building
and got down to the street that way. I bought
twenty caps with the forty dollars. Pat and me
got very high afterwards, very high.

    I didn't know Tina's kid was in the
apartment until tonight, when Pat accidentally
tipped to that goddamn talking doll.

    If I'd known she was there, I might have
killed her, too. I don't know.

Fritz Schmidt never got to sign his dictated confession because he died seven minutes after the police stenographer began typing it.

The lieutenant stood by while the two Homicide cops questioned Kling. They had advised him not to make a statement before Byrnes arrived, and now that he was here they went about their routine task with despatch. Kling could not seem to stop crying. The two Homicide cops were plainly embarrassed as they questioned him, a grown man, a cop no less, crying that way. Byrnes watched Kling's face, and said nothing.

The two Homicide cops were called Carpenter and Calhoun. They looked very much alike. Byrnes had never met any Homicide cops who did not look exactly alike. He supposed it was a trademark of their unique speciality. Watching them, he found it difficult to remember who was Carpenter and who was Calhoun. Even their voices sounded alike.

'Let's start with your name, rank, and shield number,' Carpenter said.

'Bertram Kling, detective/third, 74-579.'

'Squad?' Calhoun said.

'The Eight-Seven.' He was still sobbing. The tears rolled down his face endlessly.

'Technically, you just committed a homicide, Kling.'

'It's excusable homicide,' Calhoun said.

'Justifiable,' Carpenter corrected.

'Excusable,' Calhoun repeated. 'Penal Law 1054.'

'Wrong,' Carpenter said. 'Justifiable, P.L. 1055. "Homicide is justifiable when committed by a public officer in arresting a person who has committed a felony and is fleeing from justice." *Just*ifiable.'

'Was the broad committing a felony?' Calhoun asked.

'Yes,' Kling said. He nodded. He tried to wipe the tears from his eyes. 'Yes. Yes, she was.' The tears would not stop.

'Explain it.'

'She was ... she was ready to shoot Carella. She was trying to kill him.'

'Did you fire a warning shot?'

'No. Her back was turned to me and she was ... she was levelling the gun at Carella, so I fired the minute I came into the room. I caught her between the shoulders, I think. With my first shot.'

'Then what?'

Kling wiped the back of his hand across his eyes. 'Then she ... she started to fire again, and I kicked out at her hand, and the slug went wild. When she ... when she got ready to fire the third time, I ... I ...'

'You killed her,' Carpenter said flatly.

'Justifiable,' Calhoun said.

'Absolutely,' Carpenter agreed.

'I said so all along,' Calhoun said.

'She'd already committed a felony by abducting a police officer, what the hell. And then she fired two shots at him. If that ain't a felony, I'll eat all the law books in this crumby state.'

'You got nothing to worry about.'

'Except the Grand Jury. This has to go to the Grand Jury, Kling, same as if you were an ordinary citizen.'

'You still got nothing to worry about,' Calhoun said.

'She was going to kill him,' Kling said blankly. His tears suddenly stopped. He stared at the two Homicide cops as though seeing them for the first time. 'Not again,' he said. 'I couldn't let it happen again.'

Neither Carpenter nor Calhoun knew what the hell Kling was talking about. Byrnes knew, but he didn't particularly feel like explaining. He simply went to Kling and said, 'Forget those departmental charges I mentioned. Go home and get some rest.'

The two Homicide cops didn't know what the hell *Byrnes* was talking about, either. They looked at each other, shrugged, and chalked it all up to the eccentricities of the 87th.

'Well,' Carpenter said. 'I guess that's that.'

'I guess that's that,' Calhoun said. Then, because Kling seemed to have finally gotten control of himself, he ventured a small joke. 'Stay out of jail, huh?' he said.

Neither Byrnes nor Kling even smiled.

Calhoun and Carpenter cleared their throats and walked out without saying good-night.

She sat in the darkness of the hospital room and watched her sedated husband, waiting for him to open his eyes, barely able to believe that he was alive, praying now that he would be well again soon.

The doctors had promised to begin treatment at once. They had explained to her that it was difficult to fix the length of time necessary for anyone to become an addict, primarily because heroin procured illegally varied in its degree of adulteration. But Carella had told them he'd received his first injection sometime late Friday night, which meant he had been on the drug for slightly more than three days. In their opinion, a person psychologically prepared for addiction could undoubtedly become a habitual user in that short a time, if he was using pure heroin of normal strength. But they were working on the assumption that Carella had never used drugs before and had been injected only with narcotics acquired illegally and therefore greatly adulterated. If this was the case, anywhere between two and three weeks would have been necessary to transform him into a confirmed addict. At any rate, they would begin withdrawal (if so strong a word was applicable at all) immediately, and they had no doubt that the cure (and again they apologized for using so strong a word) would be permanent. They had explained that there was none of the addict's usual psychological dependence evident in Carella's case, and then had gone on at great length about personality disturbances, and tolerance levels, and physical dependence – and then one of the doctors suddenly and quietly asked whether or not Carella had ever expressed a prior interest in experimenting with drugs.

Teddy had emphatically shaken her head.

Well, fine then, they said. We're sure everything will work out fine. We're confident of that, Mrs Carella, as for his nose, we'll have to make a more thorough examination in the morning. We don't know when he sustained the injury, you see, or whether or not the broken bones have already knitted. In any case, we should be able to reset it, though it may involve an operation. Please be assured we'll do everything in our power. Would you like to see him now?

She sat in the darkness.

When at last he opened his eyes, he seemed surprised to see her. He smiled and then said, 'Teddy.'

She returned the smile. She touched his face tentatively.

'Teddy,' he said again, and then – because the room was dark and because she could not see his mouth too clearly – he said something which she was sure she misunderstood.

'That's your name,' he said. 'I didn't forget.'

EIGHTY MILLION EYES

"The man
was sitting
on a bench
in the
reception
room when Miles Vollner
came back from lunch that
Wednesday afternoon...."

This is for Judy and Fred Underhill

Chapter One

The man was sitting on a bench in the reception room when Miles Vollner came back from lunch that Wednesday afternoon. Vollner glanced at him, and then looked quizzically at his receptionist. The girl shrugged slightly and went back to her typing. The moment Vollner was inside his private office, he buzzed her.

'Who's that waiting outside?' he asked.

'I don't know, sir,' the receptionist said.

'What do you mean, you don't know?'

'He wouldn't give me his name, sir.'

'Did you ask him?'

'Yes, I did.'

'What did he say?'

'Sir, he's sitting right here,' the receptionist said, her voice lowering to a whisper. 'I'd rather not –'

'What's the matter with you?' Vollner said. 'This is *my* office, not *his*. What did he say when you asked him his name?'

'He – he told me to go to hell, sir.'

'What?'

'Yes, sir.'

'I'll be right out,' Vollner said.

He did not go right out because his attention was caught by a letter on his desk, the afternoon mail having been placed there some five minutes ago by his secretary. He opened the letter, read it quickly, and then smiled because it was a large order from a retailer in the Midwest, a firm Vollner had been trying to get as a customer for the past six months. The company Vollner headed was small but growing. It specialized in audio-visual components, with its factory across the River Harb in the next state, and its business and administrative office here on Shepherd Street in the city. Fourteen people worked in the business office – ten men and four women. Two hundred and six people worked in the plant. It was Vollner's hope and expectation that both office and factory staffs would have to be doubled within the next year, and perhaps trebled the year after that. The large order from the Midwest retailer confirmed his beliefs, and pleased him enormously. But then he remembered the man sitting outside, and the smile dropped from his face. Sighing, he went to the door, opened it, and walked down the corridor to the reception room.

The man was still sitting there.

He could not have been older than twenty-three or twenty-four, a sinewy man with a pale narrow face and hooded brown eyes. He was clean-shaven and well dressed, wearing a grey topcoat open over a darker grey suit. A pearl-grey fedora was on top of his head. He sat on the bench with his arms folded across his chest, his legs outstretched, seemingly quite at ease. Vollner went to the bench and stood in front of him.

'Can I help you?' he said.

'Nope.'

'What do you want here?'

'That's none of your business,' the man said.

'I'm sorry,' Vollner answered, 'but it is my business. I happen to own this company.'

'Yeah?' He looked around the reception room, and smiled. 'Nice place you've got.'

The receptionist, behind her desk, had stopped typing and was watching the byplay. Vollner could feel her presence behind him.

'Unless you can tell me what you want here,' he said, 'I'm afraid I'll have to ask you to leave.'

The man was still smiling. 'Well,' he said, 'I'm not about to tell you what I want here, and I'm not about to leave, either.'

For a moment, Vollner was speechless. He glance at the receptionist, and then turned back to the man. 'In that case,' he said, 'I'll have to call the police.'

'You call the police, and you'll be very sorry.'

'We'll see about that,' Vollner said. He walked to the receptionist's desk and said, 'Miss Di Santo, will you get me the police, please?'

The man rose from the bench. He was taller than he had seemed while sitting, perhaps six feet two or three inches, with wide shoulders and enormous hands. He moved towards the desk and, still smiling, said, 'Miss Di Santo, I wouldn't pick up that phone if I was you.'

Miss Di Santo wet her lips and looked at Vollner.

'Call the police,' Vollner said.

'Miss Di Santo, if you so much as put your hand on that telephone, I'll break your arm. I promise that.'

Miss Di Santo hesitated. She looked again to Vollner, who frowned and then said, 'Never mind, Miss Di Santo,' and without saying another word, walked to the entrance door and out into the corridor and towards the elevator. His anger kept building inside him all the way down to the lobby floor. He debated calling the police from a pay phone, and then decided he would do better to find a patrolman on the beat and bring him back upstairs personally. It was two o'clock, and the city streets were thronged with afternoon shoppers. He found a patrolman on the corner of Shepherd and Seventh, directing traffic. Vollner stepped out into the middle of the intersection and said, 'Officer, I'd –'

'Hold it a minute, mister,' the patrolman said. He blew his whistle and waved at the oncoming automobiles. Then he turned back to Vollner and said, 'Now, what is it?'

'There's a man up in my office, won't tell us what his business is.'

'Yeah?' the patrolman said.

'Yes. He threatened me and my receptionist, and he won't leave.'

'Yeah?' The patrolman kept looking at Vollner curiously, as though only half-believing him.

'Yes. I'd like you to come up and help me get him out of there.'
'You would, huh?'
'Yes.'
'And who's gonna handle the traffic on this corner?' the patrolman said.
'This man is threatening us,' Vollner said. 'Surely that's more important than –'
'This is one of the biggest intersections in the city right here, and you want me to leave it.'
'Aren't you supposed to –'
'Mister, don't bug me, huh?' the patrolman said, and blew his whistle, and raised his hand, and then turned and signalled to the cars on his right.
'What's your shield number?' Vollner said.
'Don't bother reporting me,' the patrolman answered. 'This is my post, and I'm not supposed to leave it. You want a cop, go use the telephone.'
'Thanks,' Vollner said tightly. 'Thanks a lot.'
'Don't mention it,' the patrolman said breezily, and looked up at the traffic light, and then blew his whistle again. Vollner walked back to the kerb and was about to enter the cigar store on the corner, when he spotted a second policeman. Still fuming, he walked to him rapidly and said, 'There's a man up in my office who refuses to leave and who is threatening my staff. Now just what the hell do you propose to do about it?'
The patrolman was startled by Vollner's outburst. He was a new cop and a young cop, and he blinked his eyes and then immediately said, 'Where's your office, sir? I'll go back there with you.'
'This way,' Vollner said, and they began walking towards the building. The patrolman introduced himself as Ronnie Fairchild. He seemed brisk and efficient until they entered the lobby, where he began to have his first qualms.
'Is the man armed?' he asked.
'I don't think so,' Vollner said.
'Because if he is, maybe I ought to get some help.'
'I think you can handle it,' Vollner said
'You think so?' Fairchild said dubiously, but Vollner had already led him into the elevator. They got out of the car on the tenth floor, and again Fairchild hesitated. 'Maybe I ought to call this in,' he said. 'After all ...'
'By the time you call it in, the man may *kill* someone,' Vollner suggested.
'Yeah, I suppose so,' Fairchild said hesitantly, thinking that if he *didn't* call this in and ask for help, the person who got killed might very well be himself. He paused outside the door to Vollner's office. 'In there, huh?' he said.
'That's right.'
'Well, okay, let's go.'
They entered the office. Vollner walked directly to the man, who had taken his seat on the bench again, and said, 'Here he is, officer.'
Fairchild pulled back his shoulders. He walked to the bench. 'All right, what's the trouble here?' he asked.
'No trouble, officer.'
'This man tells me you won't leave his office.'
'That's right. I came here to see a girl.'

'Oh,' Fairchild said, ready to leave at once now that he knew this was only a case of romance. 'If that's all ...'

'What girl?' Vollner said.

'Cindy.'

'Get Cindy out here,' Vollner said to his receptionist, and she rose immediately and hurried down the corridor. 'Why didn't you tell me you were a friend of Cindy's?'

'You didn't ask me,' the man said.

'Listen, if this is just a private matter —'

'No, wait a minute,' Vollner said, putting his hand on Fairchild's arm. 'Cindy'll be out here in a minute.'

'That's good,' the man said. 'Cindy's the one I want to see.'

'Who are you?' Vollner asked.

'Well, who are *you*?'

'I'm Miles Vollner. Look, young man —'

'Nice meeting you, Mr Vollner,' the man said, and smiled again.

'What's your name?'

'I don't think I'd like to tell you that.'

'Officer, ask him what his name is.'

'What's your name, mister?' Fairchild said, and at that moment the receptionist came back, followed by a tall blonde girl wearing a blue dress and high-heeled pumps. She stopped just alongside the receptionist's desk and said, 'Did you want me, Mr Vollner?'

'Yes, Cindy. There's a friend of yours here to see you.'

Cindy looked around the reception room. She was a strikingly pretty girl of twenty-two, full-breasted and wide-hipped, her blonde hair cut casually close to her head, her eyes a cornflower blue that echoed the colour of her dress. She studied Fairchild and then the man in grey. Puzzled, she turned again to Vollner.

'A friend of *mine*?' she asked.

'This man says he came here to see you.'

'Me?'

'He says he's a friend of yours.'

Cindy looked at the man once more, and then shrugged. 'I don't know you,' she said.

'No, huh?'

'No.'

'That's too bad.'

'Listen, what is this?' Fairchild said.

'You're *going* to know me, baby,' the man said.

Cindy looked at him coldly, and said, 'I doubt that very much,' and turned and started to walk away. The man came off the bench immediately, catching her by the arm.

'Just a second,' he said.

'Let go of me.'

'Honey, I'm *never* gonna let go of you.'

'Leave that girl alone,' Fairchild said.

'We don't need fuzz around here,' the man answered. 'Get lost.'

Fairchild took a step towards him, raising his club. The man whirled suddenly, planting his left fist in Fairchild's stomach. As Fairchild doubled over, the man unleashed a vicious uppercut that caught him on the point of his jaw and sent him staggering back towards the wall. Groggily, Fairchild reached for his gun. The man kicked him in the groin, and he fell to the floor groaning. The man kicked him again, twice in the head, and then repeatedly in the chest. The receptionist was screaming now. Cindy was running down the corridor, shouting for help. Vollner stood with his fists clenched, waiting for the man to turn and attack him next.

Instead, the man only smiled and said, 'Tell Cindy I'll be seeing her,' and walked out of the office.

Vollner immediately went to the phone. Men and women were coming out of their private offices all up and down the corridor now. The receptionist was still screaming. Quickly, Vollner dialled the police and was connected with the 87th Precinct.

Sergeant Murchison took the call and advised Vollner that he'd send a patrolman there immediately and that a detective would stop by either later that day or early tomorrow morning.

Vollner thanked him and hung up. His hand was trembling, and his receptionist was still screaming.

In another part of the 87th Precinct, on a side street off Culver Avenue, in the midst of a slum as rank as a cesspool, there stood an innocuous-looking brick building that had once served as a furniture loft. It was now magnanimously called a television studio. The Stan Gifford Show originated from this building each and every Wednesday night of the year, except during the summer hiatus.

It was a little incongruous to see dozens of ivy-league, narrow-tied advertising and television men trotting through a slum almost every day of the week in an attempt to put together Gifford's weekly comedy hour. The neighbourhood citizens watched the procession of creators with a jaundiced eye; the show had been on the air for three solid years, and they had grown used to seeing these aliens in their midst. There had never been any trouble between the midtown masterminds and the uptown residents, and there probably never would be – a slum has enough troubles without picking on a network. Besides, most of the people in the neighbourhood liked the Stan Gifford Show, and would rush indoors the moment it took to the air. If all these nuts were required to put together the show every week, who were they to complain? It was a good show, and it was free.

The good show, and the free one, had been rehearsing since the previous Friday in the loft of North Eleventh, and it was now 3:45 p.m. on Wednesday afternoon, which meant that in exactly four hours and fifteen minutes, a telop would flash in homes across the continent announcing the Stan Gifford Show to follow, and then there would be a station break with commercial, and then the introductory theme music, and then organized bedlam would once again burst forth from approximately twenty million television sets. The network, gratuitously giving itself the edge in selling prime time to potential sponsors, estimated that in each viewing home there were at least two people, which meant that every Wednesday night at 8:00 p.m., eighty million eyes would draw a bead on the smiling coutenance of Stan Gifford as he waved from the screen and said, 'Back for more, huh?' In the hands of a lesser personality, this opening remark – even when delivered with a smile – might have caused many viewers to switch to another channel or even turn off the set completely. But Stan Gifford was charming, intelligent, and born with an intuitive sense of comedy. He knew what was funny and what was not, and he could even turn a bad joke into a good one simply by acknowledging its failure with a deadpan nod and slightly contrite look at his adoring fans. He exuded an ease that seemed totally unrehearsed, a calm that could only be natural.

'Where the hell is Art Wetherley?' he shouted frantically at his assistant director.

'Here just a minute ago, Mr Gifford,' the A.D. shouted back, and then instantly yelled for quiet on the set. The moment quiet was achieved, he broke the silence by shouting, 'Art Wetherley! Front and centre, on the double!'

Wetherley, a diminutive gag writer who had been taking a smoke on one of the fire escapes, came into the studio, walked over to Gifford and said, 'What's up, Stan?'

Gifford was a tall man, with a pronounced widow's peak – he was actually beginning to bald, but he preferred to think of his receding hairline as a pronounced widow's peak – penetrating brown eyes, and a generous mouth. When he smiled, his eyes crinkled up from coast to coast, and he looked like a youthful, beardless Santa Claus about to deliver a bundle of goodies to needy waifs. He was not smiling now, and Wetherley had seen the unsmiling Gifford often enough to know that his solemn countenance meant trouble.

'Is this supposed to be a joke?' Gifford asked. He asked the question politely and quietly, but there was enough menace in his voice to blow up the entire city.

Wetherley, who could be as polite as anyone in television when he wanted to, quietly said, 'Which one is that, Stan?'

'This mother-in-law line,' Gifford said. 'I thought mother-in-law jokes went out with nuclear fission.'

'I wish *my* mother-in-law had gone out with nuclear fission,' Wetherley said, and then instantly realized this was not a time for adding one bad joke to another. 'We can cut the line,' he said quickly.

'I don't want it cut. I want a substitute for it.'

'That's what I meant.'

'Then why didn't you say what you meant?' Gifford looked across the studio at the wall clock, which was busily ticking off minutes to air time. 'You'd better hurry,' he said. 'Stay away from mother-in-law, and stay away from Liz Taylor, and stay away from the astronauts.'

'Gee,' Wetherley said, deadpan, 'what does that leave?'

'Some people actually think you're funny, you know that?' Gifford said, and he turned his broad back on Wetherley and walked away.

The assistant director, who had been standing near one of the booms throughout the entire conversation, sighed heavily and said, 'Boy, I hope he calms down.'

'*I* hope he drops dead,' Wetherley answered.

Steve Carella watched as his wife poured coffee into his cup. 'You're beautiful,' he said, but her head was bent over the coffeepot, and she could not see his lips. He reached out suddenly and cupped her chin with his hand,

and she lifted her head curiously, a faint half smile on her mouth. He said again, 'Teddy, you're beautiful,' and this time she watched his lips, and this time she saw the words on his mouth, and understood them and nodded in acknowledgment. And then, as if his voice had thundered into her silent world, as if she had been waiting patiently all day long to unleash a torrent of words, she began moving her fingers rapidly in the deaf-mute alphabet.

He watched her hands as they told him of the day's events. Behind the hands, her face formed a backdrop, the intense brown eyes adding meaning to each silent word she delivered, the head of black hair cocking suddenly to one side to emphasize a point, the mouth sometimes moving into a pout, or a grimace, or a sudden radiant smile. He watched her hands and her face, interpolating a word or a grunt every now and then, sometimes stopping her when she formed a sentence too quickly, and marvelling all the while at the intense concentration in her eyes, the wonderful animation she brought to the telling of the simplest story. When in turn she listened, her eyes watched intently, as if afraid of missing a syllable, her face mirroring whatever was being said. Because she never heard the intonations or subtleties of any voice, her imagination supplied emotional content that sometimes was not there at all. She could be moved to tears or laughter by a single innocuous sentence; she was like a child listening to a fairy tale, her mind supplying every fantastic unspoken detail. As they did the dishes together, their conversation was a curious blend of household plans and petty larceny, problems with the butcher and the lineup, a dress marked down to twelve ninety-five and a suspect's .38-calibre pistol. Carella kept his voice very low. Volume meant nothing to Teddy, and he knew the twins were asleep in the other room. There was a hushed warmth to that kitchen, as if it gently echoed a city that was curling up for the night.

In ten minutes' time, in twenty million homes, forty million people would turn eighty million eyes on a smiling Stan Gifford who would look out at the world and say, 'Back for more, huh?'

Carella, who did not ordinarily enjoy watching television, had to admit that he was one of those forty million hopeless unwashed addicts who turned to Gifford's channel every Wednesday night. Unconsciously, he kept one eye on the clock as he dried the dishes. For whatever perverse reasons, he derived great pleasure from Gifford's taunting opening statement, and he would have felt cheated if he had tuned in too late to hear it. His reaction to Gifford surprised even himself. He found most television a bore, an attitude undoubtedly contracted from Teddy, who derived little if any pleasure from watching the home screen. She was perfectly capable of reading the lips of a performer when the director chose to show him in a close shot. But whenever an actor turned his back or moved into a long shot, she lost the thread of the story and began asking Carella questions. Trying to watch her moving hands and the screen at the same time was an impossible task. Her frustration led to his entanglement which in turn led to further frustration, so he decided the hell with it.

Except for Stan Gifford.

At three minutes to eight that Wednesday night, Carella turned on the television set, and then made himself comfortable in an easy chair. Teddy opened a book and began reading. He watched the final moments of the show immediately preceding Gifford's (a fat lady won a refrigerator) and then read the telop stating STAN GIFFORD IS NEXT, and then watched the station break and commercial (a very handsome, dark-haired man was making love to a cigarette with each ecstatic puff he took), and then there was a slight electronic pause, and Gifford's theme music started.

'Okay if I turn this light a little lower?' Carella asked. Teddy, her nose buried in her book, did not see him speak. He touched her hand gently, and she looked up. 'Okay to dim this light?' he asked again, and she nodded just as Gifford's face filled the screen.

The smile broke like thunder over Mandalay.

'Back for more, huh?' Gifford said, and Carella burst out laughing and then turned down the lights. The single lamp behind Teddy's chair cast a warm glow over the room. Directly opposite it the colder light of the electronic tube threw a bluish rectangle on the floor directly beneath it. Gifford walked to a table, sat, and immediately went into a monologue, his customary manner of opening the show.

'I was talking to Julius the other day,' he said immediately, and the line, for some curious reason, brought a laugh from the studio audience as well as from Carella. 'He's got a persecution complex, I'll swear to it. An absolute paranoiac.' Another laugh. 'I said to him, "Look, Julie —" I call him Julie because, after all, we've known each other for a long time, some people say I'm almost like a son to him. "Look, Julie," I said to him, "what are you getting all upset about? So a lousy soothsayer stops you on the way to the forum and gives you a lot of baloney about the ides of March, why do you let this upset you, huh? Julie baby, the people *love* you." Well, he turned to me and said, "Brutus, I know you think I'm being foolish, but ...'

And that's the way it went. For ten solid minutes, Gifford held the stage alone, pausing only to garner his laughs, or to deliver his contrite look when a joke fell flat. At the end of the ten minutes he introduced his dance ensemble, who held the stage for another five minutes. He then paraded his first guest, a buxom Hollywood blonde who sang a torch song and did a skit with him, and before anyone at home realized it, the first half of the show was over. Station break, commercial. Carella got a bottle of beer from the refrigerator, and settled down to enjoy the remaining half hour.

Gifford came on to introduce a group of folk singers who sang *Greensleeves* and *Scarlet Ribbons*, a most colourful combination. He walked onto the stage again as soon as they were finished, and then went to work in earnest. His next guest was a male Hollywood personality. The male Hollywood personality seemed to be somewhat at a loss because he could neither sing nor dance nor, according to some critics, even act. But Gifford engaged him in some very high-priced banter for a few minutes, and then personally began a commercial about triple-roasted coffee while the Hollywood visitor went off to change his costume for a promised skit. Gifford finished the commercial and then motioned to someone standing just off camera. A stagehand carried a chair into viewing range. Gifford thanked him with a small bow, and then placed the chair in the centre of the enormous, empty stage.

He had been on camera for perhaps five minutes now, a relatively short time, and when he sat in the chair and heaved a weary sigh, everyone was a little surprised. He kept sitting in the chair, saying nothing, doing nothing.

There was no music behind him. He was simply a man sitting in a chair in the middle of an empty stage, but Carella felt himself beginning to smile because he knew Gifford was about to do one of his pantomimes. He touched Teddy's arm, and she looked up from her book. 'The pantomime,' he said, and she nodded, put down her book, and turned her eyes towards the screen.

Gifford continued doing nothing. He simply sat there and looked out at the audience. But he seemed to be watching something in the very far distance. The stage was silent as Gifford kept watching this something in the distance, a something that seemed to be getting closer and closer. Then, suddenly, Gifford got out of the chair, pulled it aside, and watched the something as it roared past him. He wiped his brow, faced his chair in another direction, and sat again. Now he leaned forward. It was coming from the other direction. Closer it came, closer, and again Gifford got up, pulled his chair aside at the last possible moment, and watched the imaginary thing speed past him. He sat again, facing another direction.

Carella burst into laughter as Gifford spotted it coming at him once more. This time, he got out of the chair with a determined and fierce look on his face. He held the chair in front of him like a lion tamer, defying the something to attack. But again at the last moment he pulled out of the way to let the something roar past. It was now on his left. He turned, whipping the chair around. The camera came in for a tight shot of his perplexed and completely helpless face.

Another look crossed that face.

The camera eye was in tight for the closeup, and it caught the sudden faintness that flashed across the puzzled features. Gifford seemed to sway for an instant, and then he put one hand to his eyes, as if he weren't seeing too clearly, as if the something rushing from the left had taken on real dimensions all at once. He squeezed his eyes shut tightly, and then shook his head, and then staggered back several paces and dropped the chair, just as the something streaked by him.

It was all part of the act, of course. Everyone knew that. But somehow, Gifford's pantomime had taken on a reality that transcended humour. Somehow, there was real confusion in his eyes as he watched the nameless something begin another charge. The camera stayed on him in a tight closeup. Gifford looked directly into the camera, and there was a pathetically pleading look on his face, and suddenly contact was made again, suddenly the audience began laughing. This was the same sweet and gentle man being pursued by a persistent nemesis. This was comedy again.

Carella did not laugh.

Gifford reached down for the chair. The close shot on one camera yielded to a long shot on another camera. His fingers closed around the chair. He righted it, and then sat in it weakly, his head drooping, and again the audience howled, but Carella was leaning forward now, watching Gifford with a deadly cold impersonal fixed stare.

Gifford clutched his abdomen, as if struck there by the invisible juggernaut. He seemed suddenly dizzy, and his face went pale, and he seemed in danger of falling out of the chair. And then, all at once, for eighty million eyes to see, he became violently ill. The camera was caught unaware for a moment. It lingered on his helpless sickness an instant longer, and then suddenly cut away.

Carella stared at the screen numbly as the orchestra struck up a sprightly tune.

Chapter Two

There were two squad cars and an ambulance parked in the middle of the street when Detective Meyer pulled up in front of the loft. Five patrolmen were standing before the single entrance to the building, trying valiantly to keep back the crowd of reporters, photographers, and just plain sightseers who thronged the sidewalk. The newspapermen were making most of the noise, shouting some choice Anglo-Saxon phrases at the policemen who had heard it all already and who refused to budge an inch. Meyer got out of the car and looked for Patrolman Genero, who had called the squadroom not five minutes before. He spotted him almost at once, and then elbowed his way through the crowd, squeezing past an old lady who had thrown a bathrobe over her nightgown, 'I beg your pardon, ma'am,' and then shoving aside a fat man smoking a cigar, 'Would you mind getting the hell out of my way?' and finally reaching Genero, who looked pale and tired as he stood guarding the entrance doorway.

'Boy, am I glad to see you!' Genero said.

'I'm glad to see you, too,' Meyer answered. 'Did you let anyone get by?'

'Only Gifford's doctor and the people from the hospital.'

'Who do I talk to in there?'

'The producer of the show. His name's David Krantz. Meyer, it's bedlam in there. You'd think God dropped dead.'

'Maybe he did,' Meyer said patiently, and he entered the building.

The promised bedlam started almost at once. There were people on the iron-runged stairways, and people in the corridor, and they all seemed to be talking at once, and they all seemed to be saying exactly the same thing. Meyer cornered a bright-eyed young man wearing thick-lensed spectacles and said, 'Where do I find David Krantz?'

'Who wants to know?' the young man answered.

'Police,' Meyer said wearily.

'Oh. Oh! He's upstairs. Third floor.'

'Thanks,' Meyer said. He began climbing the steps. On the third floor, he stopped a girl in a black leotard and said, 'I'm looking for David Krantz.'

'Straight ahead,' the girl answered. 'The man with the moustache.'

The man with the moustache was in the centre of a circle of people standing under a bank of hanging lights. At least five other girls in black leotards, a dozen or so more in red spangled dresses, and a variety of men in suits, sweaters, and work clothes were standing in small clusters around the wide expanse of the studio floor. The floor itself was covered with the debris of television production: cables, cameras, hanging mikes, booms, dollies, cue cards, crawls, props and painted scenery. Beyond the girls, and beyond the knot of men surrounding the man with the moustache, Meyer could see a hospital intern in white talking to a tall man in a business suit. He debated looking at the body first, decided it would be best to talk to the head man, and broke into the circle.

'Mr Krantz?'

Krantz turned with an economy and swiftness of movement that was a little startling. 'Yes, what is it?' he said, snapping the words like a whip. He was dressed smartly, quietly, neatly. His moustache was narrow and thin. He gave an immediate impression of wastelessness in a vast wasteland.

Meyer, who was pretty quick on the draw himself, immediately flipped open his wallet to his shield. 'Detective Meyer, 87th Squad,' he said. 'I understand you're the producer.'

'That's right,' Krantz answered. 'What now?'

'What do you mean what now, Mr Krantz?'

'I mean what are the police doing here?'

'Just a routine check,' Meyer said.

'For a man who died of an obvious heart attack?'

'Well, I didn't know you were a doctor, Mr Krantz.'

'I'm not. But any fool —'

'Mr Krantz, it's very hot in here, and I've been working all day, and I'm tired, you know? Don't start bugging me right off the bat. From what I understand —'

'Here we go,' Krantz said to the circle of people around him.

'Here we go *where*?' Meyer said.

'If a maiden lady dies of old age in her own bed, every cop in the city is convinced it's homicide.'

'Oh? Who told you that, Mr Krantz?'

'I used to produce a half-hour mystery show. I'm familiar with the routine.'

'And what's the routine?'

'Look, Detective Meyer, what do you want from me?'

'I want you to cut it out, first of all. I'm trying to ask some pretty simple questions about what seems to be an accidental —'

'*Seems*? See what I mean?' he said to the crowd.

'Yeah, *seems*, Mr Krantz. And you're making it pretty difficult. Now if you'd like me to get a subpoena for your arrest, we can talk it over at the station house. It's up to you.'

'Now you're kidding, Detective Meyer. You've got no grounds for arresting me.'

'Try Section 1851 of the Penal Law,' Meyer said flatly. ' "*Resisting public officer in the discharge of his duty*: A person who, in any case or under any circumstances not otherwise specially provided for, wilfully resists, delays, or obstructs a public officer in dis —" '

'All right, all right,' Krantz said. 'You've made your point.'

'Then get rid of your yes-men, and let's talk.'

The crowd disappeared without a word. In the distance, Meyer could see the tall man arguing violently with the intern in white. He turned his full attention to Krantz and said, 'I thought the show had a studio audience.'

'It does.'

'Well, where are they?'

'We put them all upstairs. Your patrolman said to hold them.'

'I want one of your people to take all their names and tell them to go home.'

'Can't the police take –'

'I've got a mad house in the street outside, and only five men to take care of it. Would you mind helping me, Mr Krantz? I didn't want him dead any more than you did.'

'All right, I'll take care of it.'

'Thanks. Now, what happened?'

'He died of a heart attack.'

'How do you know? Had he ever had one before this?'

'Not that I know of, but –'

'Then let's leave that open for the time being, okay? What time was it when he collapsed?'

'I can get that for you. Somebody was probably keeping a timetable. Hold it a second. George! Hey, George!'

A man wearing a cardigan sweater and talking to one of the dancers turned abruptly at the sound of his name. He peered around owlishly for a moment, obviously annoyed, trying to locate the person who'd called him. Krantz raised his hand in signal, and the man picked up a battery-powered megaphone from the seat of the chair beside him and, still annoyed, walked towards the two men.

'This is George Cooper, our assistant director,' Krantz said. 'Detective Meyer.'

Cooper extended his hand cautiously. Meyer realized at once that the scowl on Cooper's face was a perpetual one, a mixed look of terrible inconvenience and unspeakable injury, as if he were a man trying to think in the midst of a revolution.

'How do you do?' he said.

'Mr Meyer wants to know what time Stan collapsed.'

'What do you mean?' Cooper said, making the sentence sound like a challenge to a duel. 'It was after the folk singers went off.'

'Yes, but what time? Did anybody keep a record?'

'I can run the tape,' Cooper said grudgingly. 'Do you want me to do that?'

'Please,' Meyer said.

'What happened?' Cooper asked. 'Is it a heart attack?'

'We don't –'

'What else could it be?' Krantz interrupted.

'Well, I'll run the tape,' Cooper said. 'You going to be around?'

'I'll be here,' Meyer assured him.

Cooper nodded once, briefly, and walked away scowling.

'Who's that arguing with the intern over there?' Meyer asked.

'Carl Nelson,' Krantz replied. 'Stan's doctor.'

'Was he here all night?'

'No. I reached him at home and told him to come over here in a hurry. That was after I'd called the ambulance.'

'Get him over here, will you?'

'Sure,' Krantz said. He raised his arm and shouted, 'Carl? Have you got a minute?'

Nelson broke away from the intern, turned back to hurl a last word at him, and then walked briskly to where Meyer and Krantz were waiting. He was broad as well as tall, with thick black hair greying at the temples. There was a serious expression on his face as he approached, and a high colour in his cheeks. His lips were pressed firmly together, as if he had made a secret decision and was now ready to defend it against all comers.

'That idiot wants to move the body,' he said immediately. 'I told him I'd report him to the AMA if he did. What do you want, Dave?'

'This is Detective Meyer. Dr Nelson.'

Nelson shook hands briefly and firmly. 'Are you getting the medical examiner to perform an autopsy?' he asked.

'Do you think I should, Dr Nelson?'

'Didn't you see the way Stan died?'

'No. How did he die?'

'It was a heart attack, wasn't it?' Krantz said.

'Don't be ridiculous. Stan's heart was in excellent condition. When I arrived here at about nine o'clock, he was experiencing a wide range of symptoms. Laboured respiration, rapid pulse, nausea, vomiting. We tried a stomach pump, but that didn't help at all. He went into convulsion at about nine-fifteen. The third convulsion killed him at nine-thirty.'

'What are you suggesting, Dr Nelson?'

'I'm suggesting he was poisoned,' Nelson said flatly.

In the phone booth on the third-floor landing, Meyer deposited his dime and then dialled the home number of Lieutenant Peter Byrnes. The booth was hot and smelly. He waited while the phone rang on the other end. Byrnes himself answered, his voice sounding fuzzy with sleep.

'Pete, this is Meyer.'

'What time is it?' Byrnes asked.

'I don't know. Ten-thirty, eleven o'clock.'

'I must have dozed off. Harriet went to a movie. What's the matter?'

'Pete, I'm investigating this Stan Gifford thing, and I thought I ought to –'

'What Stan Gifford thing?'

'The television guy. He dropped dead tonight, and –'

'What television guy?'

'He's a big comic.'

'Yeah?'

'Yeah. Anyway, his doctor thinks we ought to have an autopsy done right away. Because he had a convulsion, and –'

'Strychnine?' Byrnes asked immediately.

'I doubt it. He was vomiting before he went into convulsion.'

'Arsenic?'

'Could be. Anyway, I think the autopsy's a good idea.'

'Go ahead, ask the M.E. to do it.'

'Also, I'm going to need some help on this. I've got some more questions to ask here, and I thought we might get somebody over to the hospital right away. To be there when the body arrives, you see? Get a little action from them.'

'That's a good idea.'

'Yeah, well, Cotton's out on a plant, and Bert was just answering a squeal when I left the office. Could you call Steve for me?'

'Sure.'

'Okay, that's all. I'll ring you later if it's not too late.'

'What time did you say it was?'

Meyer looked at his watch. 'Ten-forty-five.'

'I must have dozed off,' Byrnes said wonderingly, and then hung up.

George Cooper was waiting for Meyer when he came out of the booth. The same look was on his face, as if he had swallowed something thoroughly distasteful and was allowing his anger to feed his nausea.

'I ran that tape,' he said.

'Okay.'

'I timed the second half with a stop watch. What do you want to know?'

'When he collapsed.'

Cooper looked sourly at the pad in his hand and said, 'The folk singers went off at eight-thirty-seven. Stan came on immediately afterwards. He was on camera with that Hollywood ham for two minutes and twelve seconds. When the guest went off to change, Stan did the coffee commercial. He ran a little over the paid-for minute, actually a minute and forty seconds. He started his pantomime at eight-forty-one prime fifty-two. He was two minutes and fifty-five seconds into it when he collapsed. That means he was on camera for a total time of seven minutes and seventeen seconds. He collapsed at eight-forty-four prime seventeen.'

'Thanks,' Meyer said. 'I appreciate your help.' He started walking towards the door leading to the studio floor. Cooper stepped into his path. His eyes met Meyer's, and he stared into them searchingly.

'Somebody poisoned him, huh?' he said.

'What makes you think that, Mr Cooper?'

'They're all talking about it out there.'

'That doesn't necessarily make it true, does it?'

'Dr Nelson says you'll be asking for an autopsy.'

'That's right.'

'Then you *do* think he was poisoned.'

Meyer shrugged. 'I don't think anything yet, Mr Cooper.'

'Listen,' Cooper said, and his voice dropped to a whisper. 'Listen, I . . . I don't want to get anybody in trouble but . . . before the show tonight, when we were rehearsing –' He stopped abruptly. He glanced into the studio. A man in a sports jacket was approaching the hallway, reaching for the package of cigarettes in his pocket.

'Go ahead, Mr Cooper,' Meyer said.

'Skip it,' Cooper answered and walked away quickly. The man in the sports jacket came into the hallway. He nodded briefly to Meyer, put the cigarette into his mouth, leaned against a wall, and struck a match. Meyer took out a cigarette of his own, and then said, 'Excuse me. Do you have a light?'

'Sure,' the man said. He was a small man, with piercing blue eyes and crew-cut hair that gave his face a sharp triangular shape. He struck a match for Meyer, shook it out, and then leaned back against the wall again.

'Thanks,' Meyer said.

'Don't mention it.'

Meyer walked to where Krantz was standing with Nelson and the hospital intern. The intern was plainly confused. He had answered an emergency call, and now no one seemed to know what they wanted him to do with the body. He turned to Meyer pleadingly, hoping for someone who would forcefully take command of the situation.

'You can move the body,' Meyer said. 'Take it to the morgue for autopsy. Tell your man one of our detectives'll be down there soon. Carella's his name.'

The intern left quickly, before anybody could change his mind. Meyer glanced casually towards the corridor, where the man in the sports jacket was still leaning against the wall, smoking.

'Who's that in the hallway?' he asked.

'Art Wetherley,' Krantz answered. 'One of our writers.'

'Was he here tonight?'

'Sure,' Krantz said.

'All right, who else is connected with the show?'

'Where do you want me to start?'

'I want to know who was here tonight, that's all.'

'Why?'

'Oh, Mr Krantz, *please*. Gifford could have died from the noise alone in this place, but there's a possibility he was poisoned. Now who was here tonight?'

'All right, *I* was here. And my secretary. And my associate producer and his secretary. And the unit manager and his secretary. And the –'

'Does everybody have a secretary?'

'Not everybody.'

'Let me hear the rest.'

Krantz folded his arms, and then began reciting by rote. 'The director, and the assistant director. The two Hollywood stars, and the folk singers. Two scenic designers, a costume designer, the booking agent, the choral director, the chorus – seventeen people in it – the orchestra conductor, two arrangers, thirty-three musicians, five writers, four librarians and copyists, the music contractor, the dance accompanist, the choreographer, six dancers, the rehearsal pianist, the lighting director, the audio man, two stage managers, twenty-nine engineers, twenty-seven electricians and stage-hands, three network policemen, thirty-five pages, three makeup men, a hair stylist, nine wardrobe people, four sponsors' men, and six guests.' Krantz nodded in quiet triumph. 'That's who was here tonight.'

'What were you trying to do?' Meyer asked. 'Start World War III?'

Paul Blaney, the assistant medical examiner, had never performed an autopsy on a celebrity before. The tag on the corpse's wrist told him, as if he had not already been told by Carella and Meyer, who were waiting outside in the corridor, that the man lying on the stainless-steel table was Stan Gifford, the television comedian. Blaney shrugged. A corpse was a corpse, and he was only thankful that this one hadn't been mangled in an automobile accident. He never watched television, anyway. Violence upset him.

He picked up his scalpel.

He didn't like the idea of two detectives waiting outside while he worked. The next thing he knew, they'd be coming into the autopsy room with him and giving their opinions on the proper way to hold a forceps. Besides, he rather resented the notion that a corpse, simply because it was a celebrity corpse, was entitled to preferential treatment – like calling a man in the middle of the goddamn night to make an examination. Oh, sure, Meyer had patiently explained that this was an unusual case and likely to attract a great deal of publicity. And yes, the symptoms certainly seemed to indicate poisoning of some sort, but still Blaney didn't like it.

It smacked of pressure. A man should be allowed to remove a liver or a set of kidneys in a calm, unhurried way. Not with anxious policemen breathing down his neck. The usual routine was to perform the autopsy, prepare the report, and then send it on to the investigating team of detectives. If a homicide was indicated, it was sometimes necessary to prepare additional reports, which Blaney did whenever he felt like it, more often not. These were sent to Homicide North or South, the chief of police, the commander of the detective division, the district commander, and the technical police laboratory. Sometimes, and only when Blaney was feeling in a particularly generous mood, he would call the investigating precinct detective and give him a verbal necropsy report over the phone. But he had never had cops waiting in the corridor before. He didn't like the idea. He didn't like it at all.

Viciously, he made his incision.

In the corridor outside, Meyer sat on a bench alongside one green-tinted wall and watched Carella, who paced back and forth before him like an expectant father. Patiently, Meyer turned his head in a slow cycle, following Carella's movement to the end of the short corridor and back again. He was almost as tall as Carella, but more heavily built, so that he seemed squat and burly, especially when he was sitting.

'How'd Mrs Gifford take it?' Carella asked.

'Nobody likes the idea of an autopsy,' Meyer said. 'But I drove out to her house, and told her why we were going ahead, and she agreed it seemed necessary.'

'What kind of a woman?'

'Why?'

'If someone poisoned him . . .'

'She's about thirty-eight or thirty-nine, tall, attractive, I guess. It was a little hard to tell. Her mascara was running all over her face.' Meyer paused. 'Besides, she wasn't at the studio, if that means anything.'

'Who *was* at the studio?' Carella asked.

'I had Genero take down all their names before they were released.' Meyer paused. 'I'll tell you the truth, Steve, I hope this autopsy comes up with a natural cause of death.'

'How many people were in the studio?' Carella said.

'Well, I think we can safely discount the studio audience, don't you?'

'I guess so. How many were in the studio audience?'

'Five hundred and sixty.'

'All right, let's safely discount them.'

'So that leaves everyone who was connected with the show, and present tonight.'

'And how many is that?' Carella asked. 'A couple of dozen?'

'Two hundred and twelve people,' Meyer said.

The door to the autopsy room opened, and Paul Blaney stepped into the corridor, pulling off a rubber glove the way he had seen doctors do in the movies. He looked at Meyer and Carella sourly, greatly resenting their presence, and then said, 'Well, what is it you'd like to know?'

'Cause of death,' Meyer said.

'Acute poisoning,' Blaney answered flatly.

'Which poison?'

'Did the man have a history of cardiac ailments?'

'Not according to his doctor.'

'Mmmmm,' Blaney said.

'Well?' Carella said.

'That's very funny because ... well, the poison was strophanthin. I recovered it in the small intestine, and I automatically assumed –'

'What's strophanthin?'

'It's a drug similar to digitalis, but more powerful.'

'Why'd you ask about a possible cardiac ailment?'

'Well, both drugs are used therapeutically in the treatment of cardiac cases. Digitalis by infusion, usually, and strophanthin intravenously or intramuscularly. The normal dose is very small.'

'Of strophanthin, do you mean?'

'Yes.'

'Is it ever given by pill or capsule?'

'I doubt it. It may have been produced as a pill years ago, but it's been replaced by other drugs today. As a matter of fact, I don't know any doctors who'd normally prescribe it.'

'What do you mean?'

'Well, whenever there's a rhythmical disturbance or a structural lesion, digitalis is the more commonly prescribed stimulant. But strophanthin . . .' Blaney shook his head.

'Why not strophanthin?'

'I'm not saying it's *never* used, don't misunderstand me. I'm saying it's *rarely* used. A hospital pharmacy may get a call for it once in five years. A doctor would prescribe it only if he wanted immediate results. It acts much faster than digitalis.' Blaney paused. 'Are you sure this man didn't have a cardiac history?'

'Positive.' Carella hesitated a moment and then said, 'Well, what form *does* it come in today?'

'An ampule, usually.'

'Liquid?'

'Yes, ready for injection. You've seen ampules of penicillin, haven't you? Similar to that.'

'Does it come in powder form?'

'It could, yes.'

'What kind of powder?'

'A white crystalline. But I doubt if any pharmacy, even a hospital pharmacy, would stock the powder. Oh, you might find one or two, but it's very rare.'

'What's the lethal dose?' Carella asked.

'Anything over a milligram is considered dangerous. That's one one-thousand of a gram. Compare that to the fatal dose of digitalis, which is about two and a half grams, and you'll understand what I mean about power.'

'How large a dose did Gifford have?'

'I couldn't say exactly. Most of it, of course, had already been absorbed, or he wouldn't have died. It's not easy to recover strophanthin from the organs, you know. It's very rapidly absorbed, and very easily destroyed. Do you want me to guess?'

'Please,' Meyer said.

'Judging from the results of my quantitative analysis, I'd say he ingested at least two full grains.'

'Is that a lot?' Meyer asked.

'It's about a hundred and thirty times the lethal dose.'

'What!'

'Symptoms would have been immediate,' Blaney said. 'Nausea, vomiting, eventual convulsion.'

The corridor was silent for several moments. Then Carella said, 'What do you mean by immediate?'

Blaney looked surprised. 'Immediate,' he answered. 'What else does immediate mean but immediate? Assuming the poison was injected –'

'He was out there for maybe ten minutes,' Carella said, 'with the camera on him every second. He certainly didn't –'

'It was exactly seven minutes and seventeen seconds,' Meyer corrected.

'Whatever it was, he didn't take an injection of strophanthin.'

Blaney shrugged. 'Then maybe the poison was administered orally.'

'How?'

'Well . . .' Blaney hesitated. 'I suppose he could have broken open one of the ampules and swallowed the contents.'

'He didn't. He was on camera. You said the dose was enough to bring on immediate symptoms.'

'Perhaps not so immediate if the drug was taken orally. We really don't know very much about the oral dose. In tests with rabbits, *forty* times the normal intramuscular dose and *eighty* times the normal intravenous dose proved fatal when taken by mouth. Rabbits aren't humans.'

'But you said Gifford probably had *a hundred and thirty* times the normal dose.'

'That's my estimate.'

'How long would that have taken to bring on symptoms?'

'Minutes.'

'How many minutes?'

'Five minutes perhaps, I couldn't say exactly.'

'And he was on camera for more than seven minutes. So the poison must have got into him just before he came on.'

'I would say so, yes.'

'What about this ampule?' Meyer said. 'Could it have been dumped into something he drank?'

'Yes, it could have.'

'Any other way he could have taken the drug?'

'Well,' Blaney said, 'if he'd got hold of the drug in powder form somehow, I suppose two grains could have been placed in a gelatin capsule.'

'What's a gelatin capsule?' Meyer asked.

'You've seen them,' Blaney said. 'Vitamins, tranquillizers, stimulants . . . many pharmaceuticals are packed in gelatin capsules.'

'Let's get back to "immediate" again,' Carella said.

'Are we still –'

'How long does it take for a gelatin capsule to dissolve in the body?'

'I have no idea. Several minutes, I would imagine. Why?'

'Well, the capsule would have had to dissolve before any poison could be released, isn't that right?'

'Yes, of course.'

'So immediate doesn't always mean immediate, does it? In this case, immediately means after the capsule dissolves.'

'I just told you it would have dissolved within minutes.'

'How *many* minutes?' Carella asked.

'I don't know. You'll have to check that with the lab.'

'We will,' Carella said.

Chapter Three

The man assigned to investigate the somewhat odd incident in Miles Vollner's office was Detective Bert Kling. Early Thursday morning, while Carella and Meyer were still asleep, Kling took the subway down to the precinct, stopped at the squadroom to see if there were any messages for him on the bulletin board, and then bused over to Shepherd Street. Vollner's office was on the tenth floor. The lettering on the frosted-glass door disclosed that the name of the firm was VOLLNER AUDIO-VISUAL COMPONENTS, unimaginative but certainly explicit. Kling opened the door and stepped into the reception room. The girl behind the reception desk was a small brunette, her hair cut in bangs across her forehead. She looked up as Kling walked in, smiled, and said, 'Yes, sir, may I help you?'

'I'm from the police,' Kling said. 'I understand there was some trouble here yesterday.'

'Oh, *yes*,' the girl said, 'there *certainly was!*'

'Is Mr Vollner in yet?'

'No, he isn't,' the girl said. 'Was he expecting you?'

'Well, not exactly. The desk sergeant –'

'Oh, he doesn't usually come in until about ten o'clock,' the girl said. 'It's not even nine-thirty yet.'

'I see,' Kling said. 'Well, I have some other stops to make, so maybe I can catch him later on in the –'

'Cindy's here, though,' the girl said.

'Cindy?'

'Yes. She's the one he came to see.'

'What do you mean?'

'The one he *said* he came to see, anyway.'

'The assailant, do you mean?'

'Yes. He said he was a friend of Cindy's.'

'Oh. Well, look, do you think I could talk to her? Until Mr Vollner gets here?'

'Sure, I don't see why not,' the girl said, and pressed a button in the base of her phone. Into the receiver, she said, 'Cindy, there's a detective here to talk about yesterday. Can you see him? Okay, sure.' She replaced the receiver. 'In a few minutes, Mr ...' She let the sentence hang.

'Kling.'

'Mr Kling. She's got someone in the office with her.' The girl paused. 'She interviews applicants for jobs out at the plant, you see.'

'Oh. Is she in charge of hiring?'

'No, our personnel director does all the hiring.'

'Then why does she interview –'

'Cindy is assistant to the company psychologist.'

'Oh.'

'Yes, she interviews all the applicants, you know, and later our psychologist tests them. To see if they'd be happy working out at the plant. I mean, they have to put together these tiny transistor things, you know, there's a lot of pressure doing work like that.'

'I'll bet there is,' Kling said.

'Sure, there is. So they come here, and first she talks to them for a few minutes, to try to find out what their background is, you know, and then if they pass the first interview, our psychologist gives them a battery of psychological tests later on. Cindy's work is very important. She majored in psychology at college, you know. Our personnel director won't even consider a man if Cindy and our psychologist say he's not suited for the work.'

'Sort of like picking a submarine crew,' Kling said.

'What? Oh, yes, I guess it is,' the girl said, and smiled. She turned as a man came down the corridor. He seemed pleased and even inspired by his first interview with the company's assistant psychologist. He smiled at the receptionist, and then he smiled at Kling and went to the entrance door, and then turned and smiled at them both again, and went out.

'I think she's free now,' the receptionist said. 'Just let me check.' She lifted the phone again, pressed the button, and waited. 'Cindy, is it all right to send him in now? Okay.' She replaced the receiver. 'Go right in,' she said. 'It's number fourteen, the fifth door on the left.'

'Thank you,' Kling said.

'Not at all,' the girl answered.

He nodded and walked past her desk and into the corridor. The doors on the left-hand side started with the number eight and then progressed arithmetically down the corridor. The number thirteen was missing from the row. In its place, and immediately following twelve, was fourteen. Kling wondered if the company's assistant psychologist was superstitious, and then knocked on the door.

'Come in,' the girl's voice said.

He opened the door.

The girl was standing near the window, her back to him. One hand held a telephone receiver to her ear, the blonde hair pushed away from it. She was wearing a dark skirt and a white blouse. The jacket that matched the skirt was draped over the back of her chair. She was very tall, and she had a good figure and a good voice. 'No, John,' she said, 'I didn't think a Rorschach was indicated. Well, if you say so. I'll call you back later, I've got someone with me. Right. G'bye.' She turned to put the phone back onto its cradle, and then looked up at Kling.

They recognized each other immediately.

'What the hell are *you* doing here?' Cindy said.

'So you're Cindy,' Kling said. 'Cynthia Forrest. I'll be damned.'

'Why'd they send *you*? Aren't there any other cops in that precinct of yours?'

'I'm the boss's son. I told you that a long time ago.'

'You told me a lot of things a long time ago. Now go tell your captain I'd prefer talking to another –'

'My lieutenant.'

'*Whatever* he is. I mean, *really*, Mr Kling, I think there's such a thing as adding insult to injury. The way you treated me when my father was killed –'

'I think there was a great deal of misunderstanding all around at that time, Miss Forrest.'

'Yes, and mostly on your part.'

'We were under pressure. There was a sniper loose in the city –'

'Mr Kling, *most* people are under pressure *most* of the time. It was my understanding that policemen are civil servants, and that –'

'We are, that's true.'

'Yes, well, you were anything *but* civil. I have a long memory, Mr Kling.'

'So do I. Your father's name was Anthony Forrest, he was the first victim of those sniper killings. Your mother –'

'Look, Mr Kling –'

'Your mother's name is Clarice, and you've got –'

'Clara.'

'Clara, right, and you've got a younger brother named John.'

'Jeff.'

'Jeff, right. You were majoring in education at the time of the shootings –'

'I switched to psychology in my junior year.'

'Downtown at Ramsey University. You were nineteen years old –'

'Almost twenty.'

'– and that was close to three years ago, which makes you twenty-two.'

'I'll be twenty-two next month.'

'I see you graduated.'

'Yes, I have,' Cindy said curtly. 'Now, if you'll excuse me, Mr Kling –'

'I've been assigned to investigate this complaint, Miss Forrest. Something of this nature is relatively small potatoes in our fair city, so I can positively guarantee the lieutenant won't put another man on it simply because you don't happen to like my face.'

'Among *other* things.'

'Yes, well, that's too bad. Would you like to tell me what happened here yesterday?'

'I would like to tell you nothing.'

'Don't you want us to find the man who came up here?'

'I do.'

'Then –'

'Mr Kling, let me put this as flatly as I can. I don't like you. I didn't like you the last time I saw you, and I *still* don't like you. I'm afraid I'm just one of those people who never change their minds.'

'Bad failing for a psychologist.'

'I'm not a psychologist *yet*. I'm going for my master's at night.'

'The girl outside told me you're assistant to the company –'

'Yes, I am. But I haven't yet taken my boards.'

'Are you allowed to practise?'

'According to the law in this state – I thought you just *might* be familiar with it, Mr Kling – no one can be licensed to –'

'No, I'm not.'

'Obviously. No one can be licensed to practise psychology until he has a master's degree *and* a Ph.D., *and* has passed the state boards. I'm not practising. All I do is conduct interviews and sometimes administer tests.'

'Well, I'm relieved to hear that,' Kling said.

'What the hell is that supposed to mean?'

'Nothing,' Kling said, and shrugged.

'Look, Mr Kling, if you stay here a minute longer, we're going to pick up right where we left off. And as I recall it, the last time I saw you, I told you to drop dead.'

'That's right.'

'So why don't you?'

'Can't,' Kling said. 'This is my case.' he smiled pleasantly, sat in the chair beside her desk, made himself comfortable and very sweetly said, 'Do you want to tell me what happened here yesterday, Miss Forrest?'

When Carella got to the squadroom at ten-thirty that morning, Meyer was already there, and a note on his desk told him that a man named Charles Mercer at the police laboratory had called at 7:45 a.m.

'Did you call him back?' Carella asked.

'I just got in a minute ago.'

'Let's hope he came up with something,' Carella said, and dialled the lab. He asked for Charles Mercer and was told that Mercer had worked the graveyard shift and had gone home at eight o'clock.

'Who's this?' Carella asked.

'Danny Di Tore.'

'Would you know anything about the tests Mercer ran for us? On some gelatin capsules?'

'Yeah, sure,' Di Tore said. 'Just a minute. That was some job you gave Charlie, you know?'

'What'd he find out?'

'Well, to begin with, he had to use a lot of different capsules. They come in different thicknesses, you know. Like all the manufacturers don't make them the same.'

'Pick up the extension, will you, Meyer?' Carella said, and then into the phone, 'Go ahead, Di Tore.'

'And also, there's a lot of things that can affect the dissolving speed. Like if a man just ate, his stomach is full and the capsule won't dissolve as fast. If the stomach's empty, you get a speedier dissolving rate.'

'Yeah, go ahead.'

'It's even possible for one of these capsules to pass right through the system without dissolving at all. That happens with older people sometimes.'

'But Mercer ran the tests,' Carella said.

'Yeah, sure. He mixed a batch of five-percent-solution hydrochloric acid, with a little pepsin. To stimulate the gastric juices, you know? He poured that into a lot of separate containers and then dropped the capsules in.'

'What'd he come up with?'

'Well, let me tell you what he did. He used different brands, you see, and also different sizes. They come in different sizes, you know, the higher the number, the smaller the size. Like a four is smaller than a three, don't ask me.'

'And what's he find out?'

'They dissolve at different rates of speed, ten minutes, four minutes, eight minutes, twelve minutes. The highest was fifteen minutes, the lowest three minutes. That's a lot of help, huh?'

'Well, it's not exactly what I –'

'But most of them took an average of about six minutes to dissolve. That gives you something to fool around with.'

'Six minutes, huh?'

'Yeah.'

'Okay. Thanks a lot, Di Tore. And thank Mercer, will you?'

'Don't mention it. It kept him awake.'

Carella replaced the phone on its cradle and turned to Meyer.

'So what do you think?'

'What am I, a straight man? What *else* can I think? Whether Gifford drank it, or swallowed it, it had to be just before he went on.'

'Had to be. The poison works within minutes, and the capsule takes approximately six minutes to dissolve. He was on for seven.'

'Seven minutes and seventeen seconds,' Meyer corrected.

'You think he took it knowingly?'

'Suicide?'

'Could be.'

'In front of forty million people?'

'Why not? There's nothing an actor likes better than a spectacular exit.'

'Well, maybe,' Meyer said, but he didn't sound convinced.

'We'd better find out who was with him just before he went on.'

'That should be very simple,' Meyer said. 'Only two hundred and twelve people were there last night.'

'Let's call your Mr Krantz. Maybe he'll be able to help us.'

Carella dialled Krantz's office and asked to talk to him. The switchboard connected him with a receptionist, who in turn connected him with Krantz's secretary, who told him that Krantz was out, would he care to leave a message? Carella asked her to wait a moment, and then covered the mouthpiece.

'Are we going out to see Gifford's wife?' he asked Meyer.

'I think we'd better,' Meyer said.

'Please tell Mr Krantz that he can reach me at Mr Gifford's home, will you?' Carella said, and then he thanked her and hung up.

*   *   *

Larksview was perhaps a half hour outside the city, an exclusive suburb that miraculously managed to provide its homeowners with something more than the conventional sixty-by-a-hundred plots. In a time of encroaching land development, it was pleasant and reassuring to enter a community of wide rolling lawns, of majestic houses set far back from quiet winding roads. Detective Meyer had made the trip to Larksview the night before, when he felt it necessary to explain to Melanie Gifford why the police wanted to do an autopsy, even though her permission was not needed. But now, patiently and uncomplainingly, he made the drive again, seeing the community in daylight for the first time, somehow soothed by its well-ordered, gentle terrain. Carella had been speculating wildly from the moment they left the city, but he was silent now as they pulled up in front of a pair of stone pillars set on either side of a white gravel driveway. A half-dozen men with cameras and another half-dozen with pads and pencils were shouting at the two Larksview patrolmen who stood blocking the drive. Meyer rolled down the window on his side of the car and shouted, 'Break it up here! We want to get through.'

One of the patrolmen moved away from the knot of newspapermen and walked over to the car. 'Who are *you*, Mac?' he said to Meyer, and Meyer showed him his shield.

'87th Precinct, huh?' the patrolman said. 'You handling this case?'

'That's right,' Meyer said.

'Then why don't you send some of your boys out on this driveway detail?'

'What's the matter?' Carella said, leaning over. 'Can't you handle a couple of reporters?'

'A couple? You shoulda seen this ten minutes ago. The crowd's beginning to thin out a little now.'

'Can we get through?' Meyer asked.

'Yeah, sure, go ahead. Just run right over them. We'll sweep up later.'

Meyer honked the horn, and then stepped on the gas pedal. The newspapermen pulled aside hastily, cursing at the sedan as its tyres crunched over the gravel.

'Nice fellas,' Meyer said. 'You'd think they'd leave the poor woman alone.'

'The way *we're* doing, huh?' Carella said.

'This is different.'

The house was a huge Georgian Colonial, with white clapboard siding and pale-green shutters. Either side of the door was heavily planted with big old shrubs that stretched beyond the boundaries of the house to form a screen of privacy for the back acres. The gravel driveway swung past the front door and then turned upon itself to head for the road again, detouring into a small parking area to the left of the house before completing its full cycle. Meyer drove the car into the parking space, pulled up the emergency brake, and got out. Carella came around from the other side of the car, and together they walked over the noisy gravel to the front door. A shining brass bell pull was set in the jamb. Carella took the knob and yanked it. The detectives waited. Carella pulled the knob again. Again, they waited.

'The Giffords have help, don't they?' Carella said, puzzled.

'If you were making half a million dollars a year, wouldn't you have help?'

'I don't know,' Carella said. '*You're* making fifty-five hundred a year, and Sarah doesn't have help.'

'We don't want to seem ostentatious,' Meyer said. 'If we hired a housekeeper, the commissioner might begin asking me about all that graft I've been taking.'

'You too, huh?'

'Sure. Cleared a cool hundred thousand in slot machines alone last year.'

'My game's white slavery,' Carella said. 'I figure to make –'

The door opened.

The woman who stood there was small and Irish and frightened. She peered out into the sunshine and then said, in a very small voice, with a faint brogue, 'Yes, what is it, please?'

'Police department,' Carella said. 'We'd like to talk to Mrs Gifford.'

'Oh.' The woman looked more distressed than ever. 'Oh, yes,' she said. 'Yes, come in. She's out back with the dogs. I'll see if I can find her. Police, did you say?'

'That's right, ma'am,' Carella said. 'If she's out back, couldn't we just go around and look for her?'

'Oh,' the woman said. 'I don't know.'

'You *are* the housekeeper?'

'Yes, sir, I am.'

'Well, *may* we walk around back?'

'All right, but –'

'Do the dogs bite?' Meyer asked cautiously.

'No, they're very gentle. Besides, Mrs Gifford is with them.'

'Thank you,' Carella said. They turned away from the door and began walking on the flagstone path leading to the rear of the house. A woman appeared almost the moment they turned the corner of the building. She was coming out of a small copse of birch trees set at the far end of the lawn, a tall blonde woman wearing a tweed skirt, loafers, and a blue cardigan sweater, looking down at the ground as two golden retrievers ran ahead of her. The dogs saw the detectives almost immediately and began barking. The woman raised her head and her eyes curiously, and then hesitated a moment, her stride breaking.

'That's Melanie Gifford,' Meyer whispered.

The dogs were bounding across the lawn in enormous leaps. Meyer watched their approach uneasily. Carella, who was a city boy himself, and unused to seeing jungle beasts racing across open stretches of ground, was certain they would leap at his jugular. He was, in fact, almost tempted to draw his pistol when the dogs stopped some three feet away and began barking in furious unison.

'Shhh!' Meyer said, and he stamped his foot on the ground. The dogs, to Carella's immense surprise, turned tail and ran yelping back to their mistress, who walked directly towards the detectives now, her head high, her manner openly demanding.

'Yes?' she said. 'What is it?'

'Mrs Gifford?' Carella asked.

'Yes?' The voice was imperious. Now that she was closer, Carella studied her face. The features were delicately formed, the eyes grey and penetrating, the brows slightly arched, the mouth full. She wore no lipstick. Grief seemed to lurk in the corners of those eyes, and on that mouth; grief sat uninvited and omnipresent on her face, robbing it of beauty. 'Yes?' she said again, impatiently.

'We're detectives, Mrs Gifford,' Meyer said. 'I was here last night. Don't you remember?'

She studied him for several seconds, as if in disbelief. The goldens were still barking, courageous now that they were behind her skirts. 'Yes, of course,' she said at last, and then added, 'Hush, boys,' to the dogs, who immediately fell silent.

'We'd like to ask you some questions, Mrs Gifford,' Carella said. 'I know this is a trying time for you, but –'

'That's quite all right,' she answered. 'Would you like to go inside?'

'Wherever you say.'

'If you don't mind, may we stay out here? The house . . . I can't seem to . . . it's open out here, and fresh. After what happened . . .'

Carella, watching her, had the sudden notion she was acting. A slight frown creased his forehead. But immediately, she said, 'That sounds terribly phony and dramatic, doesn't it? I'm sorry. You must forgive me.'

'We understand, Mrs Gifford.'

'Do you really?' she asked. A faint sad smile touched her unpainted mouth. 'Shall we sit on the terrace? It won't be too cool, will it?'

'The terrace will be fine,' Carella said.

They walked across the lawn to where a wide flagstone terrace adjoined the rear doors of the house, open to the woods alive with autumn colour. There were white wrought-iron chairs and a glass-topped table on the terrace. Melanie pulled a low white stool from beneath the table and sat. The detectives pulled up chairs opposite her, sitting higher than Melanie, looking down at her. She turned her face up pathetically, and again Carella had the feeling that this, too, was carefully staged, that she had deliberately placed herself in a lower chair so that she would appear small and defenceless. On impulse, he said, 'Are you an actress, Mrs Gifford?'

Melanie looked surprised. The grey eyes opened wide for a moment, and then she smiled the same wan smile and said, 'I used to be. Before Stan and I were married.'

'How long ago were you married, Mrs Gifford?'

'Six years.'

'Do you have any children?'

'No.'

Carella nodded. 'Mrs Gifford,' he said, 'we're primarily interested in learning about your husband's behaviour in the past few weeks. Did he seem despondent, or overworked, or troubled by anything?'

'No, I don't think so.'

'Was he the type of man who confided things to you?'

'Yes, we were very close.'

'And he never mentioned anything that was troubling him?'

'No. He seemed very pleased with the way things were going.'

'What things, Mrs Gifford?'

'The show, the new stature he'd achieved in television. He'd been a night-club comic before the show went on the air, you know.'

'I didn't know that.'

'Yes. Stan started in vaudeville many years ago, and then drifted into night-club work. He was working in Vegas, as a matter of fact, when they approached him to do the television show.'

'And it's been on the air how many years now?'

'Three years.'

'How old was your husband, Mrs Gifford?'

'Forty-eight.'

'And how old are you?'

'Thirty-seven.'

'Was this your first marriage?'

'Yes.'

'Your husband's?'

'Yes.'

'I see. Would you say you were happily married, Mrs Gifford?'

'Yes. Extremely happy.'

'Mrs Gifford,' Carella said flatly, 'do you think your husband committed suicide?'

Without hesitation, Melanie said, 'No.'

'You know he was poisoned, of course?'

'Yes.'

'If you don't think he killed himself, you must think –'

'I think he was murdered. Yes.'

'Who do you think murdered him, Mrs Gifford?'

'I think –'

'Excuse me, ma'am,' the voice said from the opened French doors leading to the terrace. Melanie turned. Her housekeeper stood there apologetically. 'It's Dr Nelson, ma'am.'

'On the telephone?' Melanie said, rising.

'No ma'am. He's here.'

'Oh.' Melanie frowned. 'Well, ask him to join us, won't you?' She sat immediately. 'Again,' she said.

'What?'

'He was here last night. Came over directly from the show. He's terribly worried about my health. He gave me a sedative and then called twice this morning.' She folded her arms across her knees, a slender graceful woman who somehow made the motion seem awkward. Carella watched her in silence for several moments. The terrace was still. On the lawn, one of the golden retrievers began barking at a laggard autumn bird.

'You were about to say, Mrs Gifford?'

Melanie looked up. Her thoughts seemed to be elsewhere.

'We were discussing your husband's alleged murder.'

'Yes. I was about to say I think Carl Nelson killed him.'

Chapter Four

Dr Carl Nelson came onto the terrace not two minutes after Melanie had spoken his name, going first to her and kissing her on the cheek, and then shaking hands with Meyer, whom he had met the night before. He was promptly introduced to Carella, and he acknowledged the introduction with a firm handclasp and a repetition of the name, 'Detective Carella,' with a slight nod and a smile, as if he wished to imprint it on his memory. He turned immediately to Melanie then, and said, 'How are you, Mel?'

'I'm fine, Carl,' she said. 'I told you that last night.'

'Did you sleep well?'

'Yes.'

'This has been very upsetting,' Nelson said. 'I'm sure you gentlemen can understand.'

Carella nodded. He was busy watching the effect Nelson seemed to be having on Melanie. She had visibly withdrawn from him the moment he stepped onto the terrace, folding her arms across her chest, hugging herself as though threatened by a strong wind. The pose was assuredly a theatrical one, but it seemed genuine nonetheless. If she was not actually frightened of this tall man with the deep voice and the penetrating brown eyes, she certainly appeared suspicious of him; and the suspicion seemingly forced her to turn inward, to flee into icy passivity.

'Was the autopsy conducted?' Nelson asked Meyer.

'Yes, sir.'

'May I ask what the results were? Or are they classified?'

'Mr Gifford was killed by a large dose of strophanthin,' Carella said.

'Strophanthin?' Nelson looked honestly surprised. 'That's rather unusual, isn't it?'

'Are you familiar with the drug, Dr Nelson?'

'Yes, of course. That is, I know of it. I don't think I've ever prescribed it, however. It's rarely used, you know.'

'Dr Nelson, Mr Gifford wasn't a cardiac patient, was he?'

'No. I believe I told that to Detective Meyer last night. Certainly not.'

'He wasn't taking digitalis or any of the related glucosides?'

'No, sir.'

'What *was* he taking?'

'What do you mean?'

'Was he taking any drugs?'

Nelson shrugged. 'No. Not that I know of.'

'Well, you're his personal physician. If anyone *would* know, it'd be you, isn't that so?'

'That's right. No, Stan wasn't taking any drugs. Unless you want to count headache tablets and vitamin pills.'

'What kind of headache tablets?'

'An empirin-codeine compound.'

'And the vitamins?'

'B-complex with vitamin C.'

'How long had he been taking the vitamins?'

'Oh, several months. He was feeling a little tired, run-down, you know. I suggested he try them.'

'You prescribed them?'

'*Prescribed* them? No.' Nelson shook his head. 'He was taking a brand called PlexCin, Mr Carella. It can be purchased at any drugstore without a prescription. But I *suggested* it to him, yes.'

'You suggested this specific brand?'

'Yes. It's manufactured by a reputable firm, and I've found it to be completely relia –'

'Dr Nelson, how are these vitamins packaged?'

'In a capsule. Most vitamins are.'

'How large a capsule?'

'An O capsule, I would say. Perhaps a double O.'

'Dr Nelson, would you happen to know whether or not Mr Gifford was in the habit of taking his vitamins during the show?'

'Why no, I . . .' Nelson paused. He looked at Carella and then turned to Melanie, and then looked at Carella again. 'You certainly don't think. . . .' Nelson shrugged. 'But then, I suppose anything's possible.'

'What were *you* thinking, Dr Nelson?'

'That perhaps someone substituted strophanthin for the vitamins?'

'Would that be possible?'

'I don't see why not,' Nelson said. 'The PlexCin capsule is an opaque gelatin that comes apart in two halves. I suppose someone could conceivably have opened the capsule, removed the vitamins, and replaced them with strophanthin.' He shrugged again. 'But that would seem an awfully long way to go to. . . .' He stopped.

'To what, Dr Nelson?'

'Well . . . to murder someone, I suppose.'

The terrace was silent again.

'Did he take these vitamin capsules every day?' Carella asked.

'Yes,' Nelson answered.

'Would you know *when* he took them yesterday?'

'No, I –'

'*I* know when,' Melanie said.

Carella turned to her. She was still sitting on the low stool, still hugging herself, still looking chilled and lost and forlorn.

'When?' Carella asked.

'He took one after breakfast yesterday morning.' Melanie paused. 'I met him for lunch in town yesterday afternoon. He took another capsule then.'

'What time was that?'

'Immediately after lunch. About two o'clock.'

Carella sighed.

'What is it, Mr Carella?' Melanie asked.

'I think my partner is beginning to hate clocks,' Meyer said.

'What do you mean?'

'You see, Mrs Gifford, it takes six minutes for a gelatin capsule to dissolve, releasing whatever's inside it. And strophanthin acts immediately.'

'Then the capsule he took at lunch couldn't have contained any poison.'

'That's right, Mrs Gifford. He took it at two o'clock, and he didn't collapse until about eight-forty-four. That's a time span of almost seven hours. No, the poison *had* to be taken while he was at the studio.'

Nelson looked thoughtful for a moment. 'Then wouldn't it be wise to question –' he began, and stopped speaking abruptly because the telephone inside was ringing furiously, shattering the afternoon stillness.

David Krantz was matter-of-fact, businesslike, and brief. His voice fairly crackled over the telephone wire.

'You called me?' he asked.

'Yes.'

'How's Melanie?'

'She seems fine.'

'You didn't waste any time getting over there, did you?'

'We try to do our little jobs,' Carella said drily, remembering Meyer's description of his encounter with Krantz, and wondering whether everybody in television had such a naturally nasty tone of voice.

'What is it you want?' Krantz said. 'This phone hasn't stopped ringing all morning. Every newspaper in town, every magazine, every *cretin* in this city wants to know exactly what happened last night! How do *I* know what happened?'

'You were there, weren't you?'

'I was up in the sponsor's booth. I only saw it on the monitor. What do you want from me? I'm very busy.'

'I want to know exactly where Stan Gifford was last night before he went on camera for the last time.'

'How do I know where he was? I just told you I was up in the sponsor's booth.'

'Where does he usually go when he's off camera, Mr Krantz?'

'That depends on how much time he has.'

'Suppose he had the time it took for some folk singers to sing two songs?'

'Then I imagine he went to his dressing room.'

'Can you check that for me?'

'Whom would you like me to check it with? Stan's dead.'

'Look, Mr Krantz, are you trying to tell me that in your well-functioning, smoothly oiled organization, *nobody* has any idea where Stan Gifford was while those singers were on camera?'

'I didn't say that.'

'What did you say? I'm sure I misunderstood you.'

'I said *I* didn't know. I was up in the sponsor's booth. I went up there about fifteen minutes before air time.'

'All right, Mr Krantz, thank you. You've successfully presented your alibi. I assume that Gifford did not come up to the sponsor's booth at any time during the show?'

'Exactly.'

'Then you couldn't have poisoned him, isn't that your point?'
'I wasn't trying to establish an alibi for myself. I simply –'
'Mr Krantz, who *would* know where Gifford was? Would somebody know? Would *anybody* in your organization know?'
'I'll check on it. Can you call me later?'
'I'd rather stop by. Will you be in your office all day?'
'Yes, but –'
'There are some further questions I'd like to ask you.'
'About what?'
'About Gifford.'
'Am I a suspect in this damn thing?'
'Did I say that, Mr Krantz?'
'No, I said it. Am I?'
'Yes, Mr Krantz, you are,' Carella said, and hung up.

On the way back to the city, Meyer was peculiarly silent. Carella, who had spelled him at the wheel, glanced at him and said, 'Do you want to hit Krantz now or after lunch?'
'After lunch,' Meyer said.
'You seem tired. What's the matter?'
'I think I'm coming down with something. My head feels stuffy.'
'All that clean, fresh suburban air,' Carella said.
'No, I must be getting a cold.'
'I can see Krantz alone,' Carella said. 'Why don't you go on home?'
'No, it's nothing serious.'
'I mean it. I can handle –'
'Stop it already,' Meyer said. 'You'll make me *meshugah*. You sound just like my mother used to. You'll be asking me if I got a clean handkerchief next.'
'You got a clean handkerchief?' Carella asked, and Meyer burst out laughing. In the middle of the laugh, he suddenly sneezed. He reached into his back pocket, hesitated, and turned to Carella.
'You see that?' he said. 'I *haven't* got a clean handkerchief.'
'My mother taught me to use my sleeve,' Carella said.
'All right, may I use your sleeve?' Meyer said.
'What'd you think of our esteemed medical man?'
'Is there any Kleenex in this rattletrap?'
'Try the glove compartment. What'd you think of Dr Nelson?'
Meyer reached into the glove compartment, found a box of tissues, and blew his nose resoundingly. He sniffed again, said, 'Ahhhhhh,' and then immediately said, 'I have a thing about doctors, anyway, but this one I *particularly* dislike.'
'How come?'
'He looks like a smart movie villain,' Meyer said.
'Which means we can safely eliminate him as a suspect, right?'
'There's a better reason than that for eliminating him. He was home during the show last night.' Meyer paused. 'On the other hand, he's a doctor, and would have access to a rare drug like strophanthin.'
'But he was the one who suggested an autopsy, remember?'
'Right. Another good reason to forget all about him. If you just poisoned

somebody, you're not going to tell the cops to look for poison, are you?'

'A smart movie villain might do just that.'

'Sure, but then a smart movie cop would instantly know the smart movie villain was trying to pull a swiftie.'

'Melanie Wistful seems to think he did it,' Carella said.

'Melanie Mournful, you mean. Yeah. I wonder why?'

'We'll have to ask her.'

'I wanted to, but Carl Heavy wouldn't quit the scene.'

'We'll call her later. Make a note.'

'Yes, sir,' Meyer said. He was silent for a moment, and then he said, 'This case stinks.'

'Give me a good old-fashioned hatchet murder any day.'

'Poison is a woman's weapon as a rule, isn't it?' Meyer asked.

'Sure,' Carella said. 'Look at history. Look at all the famous poisoners. Look at Neill Cream and Carlyle Harris. Look at Roland B. Molineux. Look at Henri Landru, look at . . .'

'All right, already, I get it,' Meyer said.

Lieutenant Peter Byrnes read Kling's report that Thursday afternoon, and then buzzed the squadroom and asked him to come in. When he arrived, Byrnes offered him a chair (which Kling accepted) and a cigar (which Kling declined) and then lighted his own cigar and blew out a wreath of smoke and said, 'What's this "severe distaste for my personality" business?'

Kling shrugged. 'She doesn't like me, Pete. I can't say I blame her. I was going through a bad time. Well, what am I telling you for?'

'Mmm,' Byrnes said. 'You think there's anything to this prison possibility?'

'I doubt it. It was a chance, though, so I figured we had nothing to lose.' He looked at his watch. 'She ought to be down at the BCI right this minute, looking through their pictures.'

'Maybe she'll come up with something.'

'Maybe. As a follow-up, I called some of the families of Redfield's other victims. I haven't finished them all yet, still a few more to go. But the ones I reached said there'd been no incidents, no threats, nothing like that. I was careful about it, Pete, don't worry. I told them we were making a routine follow-up. I didn't want to alarm them.'

'Yeah, good,' Byrnes said. 'But you don't feel there's a revenge thing working here, is that it?'

'Well, if there is, it'd have to be somebody Redfield knew before we caught him, or somebody he met in stir. Either way, why should anybody risk his own neck for a dead man?'

'Yeah,' Byrnes said. He puffed meditatively on his cigar, and then glanced at the report again. 'Four teeth knocked out, and three broken ribs,' he said. 'Tough customer.'

'Well, Fairchild's a new cop.'

'I know that. Still, this man doesn't seem to have much respect for the law, does he?'

'To put it mildly,' Kling said, smiling.

'Your report says he grabbed the Forrest girl by the arm.'

'That's right.'

(DO NOT FOLD OR ROLL THIS REPORT)

POLICE DEPARTMENT	COMPLAINT REPORT COPY	DETECTIVE SQUAD 87th
CRIME CLASSIFICTION Assault		PRECINCT 87th
		COMPLAINT NUMBER 306B-41-11
		DATE OF THIS REPORT 10/14

NAME OF COMPLAINANT SURNAME	FIRST NAME AND INITIALS	ADDRESS OF COMPLAINANT
Vollner	Miles S.	1116 Shepherd Street
DATE AND TIME OF OCCURRENCE October 13	2 P.M.	PLACE OF OCCURRENCE Same as above
DATE AND TIME REPORTED BY THE COMPLAINANT 10/13	2:30 P.M.	DETECTIVE ASSIGNED Bertram Kling

DETAILS:

INTERROGATION OF MILES VOLLNER AND CYNTHIA FORREST:

Miles Vollner is president of Vollner Audio-Visual Components at 1116 Shepherd Street. He states that xxxxxx he returned from lunch at about one forty-five p.m. on Wednesday, October xxxx 13th to find a man sitting in his reception room. The man refused to give his name or state his business, and thereafter threatned Mr. Vollner's receptionist (Janice Di Santo) when Vollner asked her to call the police. Vollner promptly went down to the street and enlisted the air of Patrolman Ronald Fairchild, shield number 36-104, 87th Precinct, who accompanied him back to the office. When xxxx confronted by Fairchild, xxxxxx the man stated that he had come there to see a girl, and when asked which girl, he said, "Cindy." (Cindy is the nickname for Miss Cynthia Forrest, who is assistant to the company psychologist.)

Vollner sent for Miss Forrest who looked at the man and claimed she did not know him. When she attempted to leave, the man grabbed ger by the arm, at which point Fairchild warned him to leave her alone, moving toward him and rasing his club. The man attacked Fairchild, kicking him repeatedl in the head and chest after he fell to the floor. Fairchild xx was later sent to Buena Vista Hospital. Four teeth xxxx had been kicked out of his mouth, and he had suffered three broken ribs. Vollner states he hd never before seen the man, and Miss Forrest states so, too.

Miss Forrest is the daughter of the deceased Anthony Forrest (DD Reports 201A - 46 - 01 through 201A - 46 - 31) first victim of the sniper killings two years xxxxx six months ago. Check of records show that Lewis Redfield was tried and convicted first degree murder, sentenced to death in the electric chair, executed at Castleview Penitentiary last March. There seems to be no connection between this case and the sniper murders, but have arranged for Miss Forrest to look at mug shots of any prisoners serving time at Castleview (during Redfield's imprisonment there) and subsequently released. Doubt if this will come up with a make since Redfield was in the death house for entire length of term before execution, althought he may have had some contact with general prison population and arranged for harrassment of Miss Forrest and other survivors of his victims.

Miss Forrest's previous contact with me on sniper case has left severe distaste for my personality. If subsequent investigation is indicated, I respectfully submit that case be truned over to someone else on the squad.

Bertram Kling

Detective 3rd/Grade Bertram Kling

'I don't like it, Bert. If this guy can be so casual about beating up a cop, what'll he do if he gets that girl alone sometime?'

'Well, that's the thing.'

'I think we ought to get him.'

'Sure, but who is he?'

'Maybe we'll get a make downtown. From those mug shots.'

'She promised to call in later, as soon as she's had a look.'

'Maybe we'll be lucky.'

'Maybe.'

'If we're not, I think we ought to smoke out this guy. I don't like cops getting beat up, that's to begin with. And I don't like the idea of this guy maybe waiting to jump on that girl. He knocked out four of Fairchild's teeth and broke three of his ribs. Who knows what he'd do to a helpless little girl?'

'She's about five-seven, Pete. Actually, that's pretty big. For a girl, I mean.'

'Still. If we're not careful here, we may wind up with a homicide on our hands.'

'Well, that's projecting a little further than I think we have to, Pete.'

'Maybe, maybe not. I think we ought to smoke him out.'

'How?'

'Well, I'm not sure yet. What are you working on right now?'

'Those liquor-store holdups. And also an assault.'

'When was the last holdup?'

'Three nights ago.'

'What's your plan?'

'He seems to be hitting them in a line, Pete, straight up Culver Avenue. I thought I'd plant myself in the next store up the line.'

'You think he's going to hit again so soon?'

'They've been spaced about two weeks apart so far.'

'Then there's no hurry, right?'

'Well, he may change the timetable.'

'He may change the pattern, too. In which case you'll be sitting in the wrong store.'

'That's true. I just thought –'

'Let it wait. What's the assault?'

'Victim is a guy named Vinny Marino, he's a small-time pusher, lives on Ainsley Avenue. About a week ago, two guys pulled up in a car and got out with baseball bats. They broke both his legs. The neighbourhood rumble is that he was fooling around with one of their wives. That's why they went for his legs, you see, so he wouldn't be able to chase around any more. It's only coincidental that he's a pusher.'

'For my part, they could have killed him,' Byrnes said. He took his handkerchief from his back pocket, blew his nose, and then said, 'Mr Marino's case can wait, too. I want you to stay with this one, Bert.'

'I think we'd do better with another man. I doubt if I'll be able to get any co-operation at all from her.'

'Who can I spare?' Byrnes asked. 'Willis and Brown are on that knife murder, Hawes is on a plant of his own, Meyer and Carella are on this damn television thing, Andy Parker –'

'Well, maybe I can switch with one of them.'

'I don't like cases to change hands once they've been started.'

'I'll do whatever you say, Pete, but –'

'I'd appreciate it,' Byrnes said.

'Yes, sir.'

'You can follow up the vendetta possibility if you like, but I agree with you. It'll probably turn out to be a dead end.'

'I know. I just felt –'

'Sure, it was worth a try. See where it goes. Contact the rest of those survivors, and listen to what the Forrest girl has to say when she calls later on. But I wouldn't bank on anything along those lines, if I were you.' Byrnes paused, puffed on his cigar, and then said, 'She claims she doesn't know him, huh?'

'That's right.'

'I thought maybe he was an old boy friend.'

'No.'

'Rejected, you know, that kind of crap.'

'No, not according to her.'

'Maybe he just wants to get in her pants.'

'Maybe.'

'Is she good-looking?'

'She's attractive, yes. She's not a raving beauty, but I guess she's attractive.'

'Then maybe that's it.'

'Maybe, but why would he go after her in this way?'

'Maybe he doesn't *know* any other way. He sounds like a hood, and hoods take what they want. He doesn't know from candy or flowers. He sees a pretty girl he wants, so he goes after her – even if it means beating her up to get her. That's my guess.'

'Maybe.'

'And that's in our favour. Look what happened to Fairchild when he got in this guy's way. He knocked out his teeth and broke his ribs. *Whatever* he wants from this girl – and it's my guess all he wants is her tail – he's not going to let anybody stop him from getting it, law or otherwise. That's where you come in.'

'What do you mean?'

'That's how we smoke him out. I don't want to do anything that'll put this girl in danger. I want this punk to make his move against *you*, Bert.'

'Me?'

'You. He knows where she works, and chances are he knows where she lives, and I'll bet my life he's watching her every minute of the day. Okay, let's give him something to watch.'

'Me?' Kling said again.

'You, that's right. Stay with that girl day and night. Let's –'

'Day and *night*?'

'Well, within reason. Let's get this guy so goddamn sore at you that he comes after you and tries to do exactly what he did to Fairchild.'

Kling smiled. 'Gee,' he said, 'suppose he succeeds?'

'Fairchild is a new cop,' Byrnes said. 'You told me so yourself.'

'Okay, Pete, but you're forgetting something, aren't you?'

'What's that?'

'The girl doesn't like me. She's not going to take kindly to the idea of spending time with me.'

'Ask her if she'd rather get raped some night in the elevator after this guy has knocked out her teeth and broken some of her ribs. Ask her that.'

Kling smiled again. 'She might prefer it.'

'I doubt it.'

'Pete, she hates me. She *really* ...'

Byrnes smiled. 'Win her over, boy,' he said. 'Just win her over, that's all.'

David Krantz worked for a company named Major Broadcasting Associates, which had its offices downtown on Jefferson Street, Major Broadcasting, or MBA as it was familiarly called in the industry, devoted itself primarily to the making of filmed television programmes, but every now and then it ventured into the production of a live show. The Stan Gifford Show was – or at least had been – one of the three shows they presented live from the city each week. A fourth live show was produced bi-monthly on the Coast. MBA was undoubtedly the giant of the television business, and since success always breeds contempt, it had been given various nicknames by disgruntled and ungrateful industry wags. These ranged from mild jibes like Money Banks Anonymous, through gentle epithets like Mighty Bloody Assholes, to genuinely artistic creations like Master Bullshit Artists. Whatever you called the company, and however you sliced it, it was important and vast and accounted for more than sixty per cent of the nation's television fare each week.

The building on Jefferson Street was owned by MBA, and featured floor after floor of wood-panelled offices, ravishing secretaries and receptionists exported from the Coast, and solemn-looking young men in dark suits and ties, white shirts, and black shoes and socks. David Krantz was a solemn-looking man wearing the company uniform, but he wasn't as young as he used to be. His secretary showed Meyer and Carella into the office, and then closed the door gently behind them. 'I've met Mr Meyer,' Krantz said, a trace of sarcasm in his voice, 'but I believe you and I have only had the pleasure on the telephone, Mr Caretta.'

'Carella.'

'Carella, forgive me. Sit down, won't you. I'm expecting a call on the tieline, so if I have to interrupt our chat, I know you'll understand.'

'Certainly,' Carella said.

Krantz smoothed his moustache. 'Well, what is it you want to know?'

'First, did you find out where Gifford went while he was off camera?'

'I haven't been able to locate George Cooper. He's our A.D., he's the man who'd know.'

'What's an A.D.?' Carella asked.

'Assistant director,' Meyer said. 'I talked to him last night, Steve. He's the one who timed that tape for me.'

'Oh.'

'I tried to reach him at home,' Krantz said, 'but no one answered the phone. I'll try it again, if you like.'

'Where does he live?' Carella asked.

'Downtown, in The Quarter. It's his responsibility to see that everyone's in on cue. I'm sure he would know just where Stan went while the folk singers were on. Shall I have my secretary try him again?'

'Please,' Carella said.

Krantz buzzed for his secretary. In keeping with company policy, she was a tall and beautiful redhead wearing a tight green sweater and skirt. She listened attentively as Krantz told her to try Cooper's number again, and then said, 'We're ready on that call to the Coast now, Mr Krantz.'

'Thank you,' Krantz said. 'Excuse me,' he said to Carella and Meyer, and then he lifted the receiver. 'Hello, Krantz here. Hello, Frank, what is it? *Who*? The *writer*? What do you *mean*, the writer? The *writer* doesn't like the changes that were made? Who the hell asked him for his opinion? Well, I *know* he wrote the script, what difference does that make? Just a second now, start from the beginning, will you? Who made the changes? Well, he's a perfectly capable producer, why should the writer have any complaints? He says *what*? He says it's his script, and he resents a half-assed producer tampering with it? Listen, who *is* this fellow, anyway? Who? I never heard of him. What's he done before? The *Saturday Review* says what? Well, what the hell's some literary intelligentsia magazine got to do with the people who watch television? What do I care if he's a novelist, can he write television scripts? Who hired him, anyway? Was this cleared here, or was it a Coast decision? Don't give me any of that crap, Frank, novelists are a dime a dozen. Yeah, even *good* novelists. It's the guy who can write a decent television script that's hard to find. You say he *can* write a decent television script? Then what's the problem? Oh, I see. He doesn't like the changes that were made. Well, what changes *were* made, Frank, can you tell me that? I see, um-huh, the prostitute was rewritten as a nun, um-huh, I see, and she doesn't die at the end, she performs a miracle instead, um-huh, well, how about the hero? Not a truck driver any more, huh? Oh, I see, he's a football coach now, I get it. Um-huh, works at the college nearby the church, um-huh. Is it still set in London? Oh, I see. I see, yes, you want to shoot it at UCLA, sure, that makes sense, a lot closer to the studio. Well, gee, Frank, off the top of my head, I'd say the revisions have made it a much better script, I don't know what the hell the writer's getting excited about. Explain to him that the changes are really minor and that large stretches of his original dialogue and scenes are intact, just the way he wrote them. Tell him we've had pressure from the network, and that this necessitated a few minor – no, use the word "transitional" – a few transitional changes that were made by a competent producer because there simply wasn't time for lengthy consultations about revisions. Tell him we have the highest regard for his work, and that we're well aware of what the *Saturday Review* said about him, but explain that we're all in the same goddamn ratrace, and what else can we do when we're pressured by networks and sponsors and deadlines? Ask him to be reasonable, Frank. I think he'll understand. Fine. Listen, what did the pregnant raisin tell the police? Well, go ahead, guess. Nope. Nope. She said, "I was graped!"' Krantz burst out laughing. 'Okay, Frank, I'll talk to you. Right. So long.'

He hung up. The door to his office opened a second afterwards, and the pretty redhead paused in the doorframe and said, 'I still can't reach Mr Cooper.'

'Keep trying him,' Krantz said, and the girl went out. 'I'm sorry about the interruption, gentlemen. Shall we continue?'

'Yes,' Carella said. 'Can you tell me who was in that booth with you last night?'

'You want the names?'

'I'd appreciate them.'

'I anticipated you,' Krantz said. 'I had my secretary type up a list right after you called this morning.'

'That was very thoughtful of you,' Carella said.

'In this business, I try to anticipate *everything*.'

'It's a pity you couldn't have anticipated Gifford's death,' Carella said.

'Yeah, well, that was unforeseen,' Krantz said absolutely straight-faced, shaking his head solemnly. 'I'll have my secretary bring in that list.' He pushed a button on his phone. 'She used to work for our head of production out at the studio. Did you ever see tits like that before?'

'Never,' Carella said.

'They're remarkable,' Krantz said.

The girl came into the office. 'Yes, sir?'

'Bring in that list you typed for me, would you? How're you doing with Mr Cooper?'

'I'll try him again, sir.'

'Thank you.'

'Yes, sir,' she said and went out.

'Remarkable,' Krantz said.

'While she's getting that list,' Carella said, 'why don't you fill us in, Mr Krantz?'

'Sure. Gladine was in the booth with me, she's usually there to take any notes I might –'

'Gladine?'

'My secretary. The tits,' Krantz said. He gestured with his hands.

'Oh. Sure.'

'My associate producer was up there, too. Dan Hollis is his name, he's been with MBA for close to fifteen years.'

'Who was minding the store?' Meyer asked.

'What do you mean?'

'If you and your associate were in the sponsor's booth –'

'Oh. Well, our unit manager was down on the floor, and our director was in the control booth, of course, and our assistant director was making sure everyone –'

'I see, okay,' Meyer said. 'Who else was in the sponsor's booth with you?'

'The others were guests. Two of them were sponsors' representatives; one was a Hollywood director who's shooting a feature for the studio and who thought Gifford might be right for a part; and the other two were –'

The door opened.

'Here's that list, sir,' Gladine said. 'We're trying Mr Cooper now.'

'Thank you, Gladine.'

'Yes, sir,' she said and walked out. Krantz handed the typewritten list to Carella. Carella looked at the list, and then passed it to Meyer.

'Mr and Mrs Feldensehr, who are they?' Meyer asked.

'Friends of Carter Bentley, our unit manager. He invited them in to watch the show.'

'That's all then, huh? You and your secretary, your associate Dan Hollis ... Who's this Nathan Crabb?'

'The Hollywood director. I told you, he –'

'Yes, fine, and Mr and Mrs Feldensehr, and are these last two the sponsor's men?'

'That's right.'

'Eight people in all,' Carella said. 'And five of them were guests.'

'That's right.'

'You told us there were *six* guests, Mr Krantz.'

'No, I said five.'

'Mr Krantz,' Meyer said, 'last night you told me there were *six*.'

'I must have meant Gladine.'

'Your secretary?' Carella said.

'Yes. I must have included her as one of the guests.'

'That's a little unusual, isn't it, Mr Krantz? Including an employee of the company as a guest?'

'Well ...'

There was a long silence.

'Yes?' Carella said.

'Well ...'

There was another silence.

'We may be investigating a homicide here, Mr Krantz,' Meyer said softly. 'I don't think it's advisable to hide anything from us at this point, do you?'

'Well, I ... I suppose I can trust you gentlemen to be discreet.'

'Certainly,' Carella said.

'Nathan Crabb? The director? The one who was here to look at Stan, see if he was right for –'

'Yes?'

'He had a girl with him, the girl he's grooming for his next picture. I deliberately left her name off the list.'

'Why?'

'Well, Crabb is a married man with two children. I didn't think it wise to include the girl's name.'

'I see.'

'I can have it added to the list, if you like.'

'Yes, we'd like that,' Carella said.

'What time did you go up to the sponsor's booth?' Meyer asked suddenly.

'Fifteen minutes before the show started,' Krantz said.

'At seven-forty-five?'

'That's right. And I stayed there right until the moment Stan got sick.'

'Who was there when you arrived?'

'Everyone but Crabb and the girl.'

'What time did they get there?'

'About five minutes later. Ten to eight – around then.'

The door to Krantz's office opened suddenly. Gladine smiled and said, 'We've reached Mr Cooper, sir. He's on oh-three.'

'Thank you, Gladine.'

'Yes, sir,' she said, and went out.

Krantz picked up the phone. 'Hello,' he said, 'Krantz here. Hello, George, I have some policemen in my office, they're investigating Stan's death. They wanted to ask you some questions about his exact whereabouts during the show last night. Well, hold on, I'll let you talk to one of them. His name's Capella.'

'Carella.'

'Carella, I'm sorry. Here he is, George.'

Krantz handed the phone to Carella. 'Hello, Mr Cooper,' Carella said. 'Are you at home now? Do you expect to be there for a while? Well, I was wondering if my partner and I might stop by. As soon as we leave here. Fine. Would you let me have the address, please?' He took a ballpoint pen from his inside jacket pocket, and began writing the address on an MBA memo slip. 'Fine,' he said again. 'Thank you, Mr Cooper, we'll see you in a half hour or so. Goodbye.' He handed the phone back to Krantz, who replaced it on the cradle.

'Is there anything else I can do for you?' Krantz asked.

'Yes,' Meyer said. 'You can ask your secretary to get us the addresses and phone numbers of everyone who was in the sponsor's booth when you went up there last night.'

'Why? Are you going to check to see that I *really* went up there fifteen minutes before the show?'

'And *remained* there until Gifford collapsed, right?'

'Right,' Krantz said. He shrugged. 'Go ahead, check it. I'm telling the exact truth. I have nothing to hide.'

'We're sure you haven't,' Carella said pleasantly. 'Have her call us with the information, will you?' He extended his hand, thanked Krantz for his time, and then walked out past Gladine's desk, Meyer following him. When they got to the elevator, Meyer said, 'Re*mark*able!'

The Quarter was all the way downtown, jammed into a minuscule portion of the city, its streets as crowded as a bazaar. Jewellery shops, galleries, bookstores, sidewalk cafés, expresso joints, pizzerias, paintings on the kerb, bars, basement theatres, art movie houses, all combined to give The Quarter the flavour, if not the productivity, of a real avant-garde community. George Cooper lived on the second floor of a small apartment building on a tiny, twisting street. The fire escapes were hung with flowerpots and brightly coloured serapes, the doorways were painted pastel oranges and greens, the brass was polished, the whole street had been conceived and executed by the people who dwelt in it, as quaintly phony as a blind con man.

They knocked on Cooper's door and waited. He answered it with the same scowling expression Meyer had come to love the night before.

'Mr Cooper?' Meyer said. 'You remember me, don't you?'

'Yes, come in,' Cooper said. He scowled at Meyer, whom he knew, and then impartially scowled at Carella, who was a stranger.

'This is Detective Carella.'

Cooper nodded and led them into the apartment. The living room was sparsely furnished, a narrow black couch against one wall, two black Bertoia chairs against another, the decorating scheme obviously planned to minimize the furnishings and emphasize the modern paintings that hung facing

each other on the remaining two walls. The detectives sat on the couch.
Cooper sat in one of the chairs opposite them.

'What we'd like to know, Mr Cooper, is where Stan Gifford went last
night while those folk singers were on,' Carella said.

'He went to his dressing room,' Cooper answered without hesitation.

'How do you know that?'

'Because that's where I went to cue him later on.'

'I see. Was he alone in the dressing room?'

'No,' Cooper said.

'Who was with him?'

'Art Wetherley. And Maria Vallejo.'

'Wetherley's a writer,' Meyer explained to Carella. 'Who's Maria – what's
her name?'

'Vallejo. She's our wardrobe mistress.'

'And they were both with Mr Gifford when you went to call him?'

'Yes.'

'Would you know how long they were with him?'

'No.'

'How long did *you* stay in the dressing room, Mr Cooper?'

'I knocked on the door, and Stan said, "Come in," and I opened the door,
poked my head inside and said, "Two minutes, Stan," and he said, "Okay,"
and I waited until he came out.'

'Did he come out immediately?'

'Well, almost immediately. A few seconds. You can't kid around on
television. Everything's timed to the second, you know. Stan knew that.
Whenever he was cued, he came.'

'Then you really didn't spend any time at all in the dressing room, did
you, Mr Cooper?'

'No. I didn't even go inside. As I told you, I just poked my head in.'

'Were they talking when you looked in?'

'I think so, yes.'

'They weren't arguing or anything, were they?'

'No, but....' Cooper shook his head.

'What is it, Mr Cooper?'

'Nothing. Would you fellows like a drink?'

'Thanks, no,' Meyer said. 'You're sure you didn't hear anyone arguing?'

'No.'

'No raised voices?'

'No.' Cooper rose. 'If you don't mind, I'll have one. It's not too early to
have one, is it?'

'No, go ahead,' Carella said.

Cooper walked into the other room. They heard him pouring his drink,
and then he came back into the living room with a short glass containing ice
cubes and a healthy triple shot of whisky. 'I hate to drink so damn early in
the afternoon,' he said. 'I was on the wagon for a year, you know. How old do
you think I am?'

'I don't know,' Carella said.

'Twenty-eight. I look older than that, don't I?'

'No, I wouldn't say so,' Carella said.

'I used to drink a lot,' Cooper explained, and then took a swallow from the glass. The scowl seemed to vanish from his face at once. 'I've cut down.'

'When Mr Gifford left the dressing room,' Meyer said, 'you were with him, right?'

'Yes.'

'Did you meet anyone between the dressing room and the stage?'

'Not that I remember. Why?'

'Would you remember if you'd met anyone?'

'I think so, yes.'

'Then the last people who were with Gifford were Art Wetherley, Maria Vallejo, and you. In fact, Mr Cooper, if we want to be absolutely accurate, the very *last* person was *you*.'

'I suppose so. No, wait a minute. I think he said a word to one of the cameramen, just before he went on. Something about coming in for the close shot. Yes, I'm sure he did.'

'Did Mr Gifford eat anything in your presence?'

'No.'

'Drink anything?'

'No.'

'Put anything into his mouth at all?'

'No.'

'Was he eating or drinking anything when you went into the dressing room?'

'I didn't *go* in, I only *looked* in. I think maybe there were some coffee containers around. I'm not sure.'

'They were drinking coffee?'

'I told you, I'm not sure.'

Carella nodded and then looked at Meyer and then looked at Cooper, and then very slowly and calmly said, 'What is it you want to tell us, Mr Cooper?'

Cooper shrugged. 'Anything you want to know.'

'Yes, but specifically.'

'I don't want to get anybody in trouble.'

'What is it, Mr Cooper?'

'Well ... well, Stan had a fight with Art Wetherley yesterday. Just before the show. Not a fight, an argument. Words. And ... I said something about I wished Stan would calm down before we went on the air, and Art ... Look, I don't want to get him in trouble. He's a nice guy, and I wouldn't even mention this, but the papers said Stan was poisoned and ... well, I don't know.'

'What did he say, Mr Cooper?'

'He said he wished Stan would drop dead.'

Carella was silent for a moment. He rose then and said, 'Can you tell us where Mr Wetherley lives, please?'

Cooper told them where Wetherley lived, but it didn't matter very much because Wetherley was out when they got there. They checked downstairs with his landlady, who said she had seen him leaving the building early that morning, no he didn't have any luggage with him, why in the world would he be carrying luggage at ten o'clock in the morning? Carella and Meyer told the landlady that perhaps he would be carrying luggage if he planned to leave the city, and the landlady told them he never left the city on Thursday because that was when MBA ran the tape of the show from the night before so the writers could see which jokes had got the laughs and which hadn't, and that was very important in Mr Wetherley's line of work. Carella and Meyer explained that perhaps, after what had happened last night, the tape might not be run today. But the landlady said it didn't matter what had happened last night, they'd probably get a replacement for the show, and then Mr Wetherley would have to write for it, anyway, so it was very important that he see the tape today and know where the audience laughed and where it didn't. They thanked her, and then called MBA, who told them the tape was not being shown today and no, Wetherley was not there.

They had coffee and crullers in a diner near Wetherley's apartment, debated putting out a Pickup-and-Hold on him, and decided that would be a little drastic on the basis of hearsay, assuming Cooper was telling the truth to begin with – which he might not have been. They were knowledgeable and hip cops and they knew all about this television ratrace where people slit each others' throats and stabbed each other in the back. It was, after all, quite possible that Cooper was lying. It was, in fact, quite possible that *everybody* was lying. So they called the squadroom and asked Bob O'Brien to put what amounted to a telephone surveillance on Wetherley's apartment, calling him every half hour, and warning him to stay right in that apartment where he was, in case he happened to answer the phone. O'Brien had nothing else to do but call Wetherley's apartment every half hour, being involved in trying to solve three seemingly related Grover Park muggings, so he was naturally very happy to comply with Carella's wishes. The two detectives discussed how large a tip they should leave the waitress, settled on a trifle more than fifteen per cent because she was fast and had good legs, and then went out into the street again.

The late afternoon air was crisp and sharp, the city vibrated with a shimmering clarity that caused buildings to leap out from the sky. The streets seemed longer, stretching endlessly to a distant horizon that was almost visible. The land marks both men had grown up with, the familiar sights that gave the city perspective and reality, seemed to surround them intimately now, seemed closer and more intricately detailed. You could reach out to touch them, you could see the sculptured stone eye of a gargoyle twelve storeys above the street. The people, too, the citizens who gave a city its tempo and its pace, walked with their topcoats open, no longer faceless, contagiously enjoying the rare autumn day, filling their lungs with air that seemed so suddenly sweet. Carella and Meyer crossed the avenue idly, both men smiling. They walked together with the city between them like a beautiful young girl, sharing her silently, somewhat awed in her radiant presence.

For a little while at least, they forgot they were investigating what looked like a murder.

Chapter Five

As Kling had anticipated, Cindy Forrest was not overwhelmed by the prospect of having to spend even an infinitesimal amount of time with him. She reluctantly admitted, however, that such a course might be less repulsive than the possibility of spending an equal amount of time in a hospital. It was decided that Kling would pick her up at the office at noon Friday, take her to lunch, and then walk her back again. He reminded her that he was a city employee and that there was no such thing as an expense account for taking citizens to lunch while trying to protect them, a subtlety Cindy looked upon as simply another index to Kling's personality. Not only was he obnoxious, but he was apparently cheap as well.

Thursday's beautiful weather had turned foreboding and blustery by Friday noon. The sky above was a solemn grey, the streets seemed dimmer, the people less animated. He picked her up at the office, and they walked in silence to a restaurant some six blocks distant. She was wearing high heels, but the top of her head still came only level with his chin. They were both blonde, both hatless. Kling walked with his hands in his coat pockets. Cindy kept her arms crossed over her middle, her hands tucked under them. When they reached the restaurant, Kling forgot to hold open the door for her, but only the faintest flick of Cindy's blue eyes showed that this was exactly what she expected from a man like him. Too late, he allowed her to precede him into the restaurant.

'I hope you like Italian food,' he said.

'Yes, I do,' she answered, 'but you might have asked *first*.'

'I'm sorry, but I have a few other things on my mind besides worrying about which restaurant you might like.'

'I'm sure you're a very busy man,' Cindy said.

'I am.'

'Yes, I'm sure.'

The owner of the restaurant, a short Neapolitan woman with masses of thick black hair framing her round and pretty face, mistook them for lovers and showed them to a secluded table at the rear of the place. Kling remembered to help Cindy off with her coat (she mumbled a polite thank you) and then further remembered to hold out her chair for her (she acknowledged this with a brief nod). The waiter took their order and they sat facing each other without a word to say.

The silence lengthened.

'Well, I can see this is going to be perfectly charming,' Cindy said. 'Lunch with you for the next God knows how long.'

'There are things I'd prefer doing myself, Miss Forrest,' Kling said. 'But, as you pointed out yesterday, I am only a civil servant. I do what I'm told to do.'

'Does Carella still work up there?' Cindy asked.

'Yes.'

'I'd much rather be having lunch with him.'

'Well, those are the breaks,' Kling said. 'Besides, he's married.'

'I know he is.'

'In fact, he's got two kids.'

'I know.'

'Mmm. Well, I'm sure he'd have loved this choice assignment, but unfortunately he's involved with a poisoning at the moment.'

'Who got poisoned?'

'Stan Gifford.'

'Oh? Is he working on that? I was reading about it in the paper just yesterday.'

'Yes, it's his case.'

'He must be a good detective. I mean, to get such an important case.'

'Yes, he's very good,' Kling said.

The table went silent again. Kling glanced over his shoulder towards the door, where a thickset man in a black overcoat was just entering.

'Is that your friend?' he asked.

'No. And he's *not* my friend.'

'The lieutenant thought he might have been one of your ex-boy friends.'

'No.'

'Or someone you'd met someplace.'

'No.'

'You're sure you didn't recognize any of those mug shots yesterday?'

'I'm positive. I don't know who the man is, and I can't imagine what he wants from me.'

'Well, the lieutenant has some ideas about that, too.'

'What were his ideas?'

'Well, I'd rather not discuss them.'

'Why not?'

'Because ... well, I'd just rather not.'

'Is it the lieutenant's notion that this man wants to lay me?' Cindy asked.

'What?'

'I said is it the –'

'Yes, something like that,' Kling answered, and then cleared his throat.

'I wouldn't be surprised,' Cindy said.

The waiter arrived at that moment, sparing Kling the necessity of further comment. Cindy had ordered the antipasto to start, a supposed speciality of the house. Kling had ordered a cup of minestrone. He carefully waited for her to begin eating before he picked up his spoon.

'How is it?' he asked her.

'Very good.' She paused. 'How's the soup?'

'Fine.'

They ate in silence for several moments.

'What *is* the plan exactly?' Cindy asked.

'The lieutenant thinks your admirer is something of a hothead, a reasonable assumption, I would say. He's hoping we'll be seen together, and he's hoping our man will take a crack at me.'

'In which case?'

'In which case I will crack him back and carry him off to jail.'

'My hero,' Cindy said drily, and attacked an anchovy on her plate.

'I'm supposed to spend as much time with you as I can,' Kling said, and paused. 'I guess we'll be having dinner together tonight.'

'What?'

'Yes,' Kling said.

'Look, Mr Kling —'

'It's not *my* idea, Miss Forrest.'

'Suppose I've made other plans?'

'Have you?'

'No, but —'

'Then there's no problem.'

'I don't usually go out for dinner, Mr Kling, unless someone is escorting me.'

'I'll be escorting you.'

'That's not what I meant. I'm a working girl. I can't afford —'

'Well, I'm sorry about the financial arrangements, but as I explained —'

'Yes, well, you just tell your lieutenant I can't afford a long, leisurely dinner every night, that's all. I earn a hundred and two dollars a week after taxes, Mr Kling. I pay my own college tuition and the rent on my own apartment —'

'Well, this shouldn't take too long. If our man spots us, he may make his play fairly soon. In the meantime, we'll just have to go along with it. Have you seen the new Hitchcock movie?'

'What?'

'The new —'

'No, I haven't.'

'I thought we'd go see it after dinner.'

'Why?'

'Got to stay together.' Kling paused. 'I could suggest a long walk as an alternative, but it might be pretty chilly by tonight.'

'I could suggest your going home after dinner,' Cindy said. 'As an alternative, you understand. Because to tell the truth, Mr Kling, I'm pretty damned tired by the end of a working day. In fact, on Tuesdays, Wednesdays, and Thursdays, I barely have time to grab a hamburger before I run over to the school. I'm not a rah-rah party girl. I think you ought to understand that.'

'Lieutenant's orders,' Kling said.

'Yeah, well, tell *him* to go see the new Hitchcock movie. I'll have dinner with you, if you insist, but right after that I'm going to bed.' Cindy paused. 'And I'm *not* suggesting that as an alternative.'

'I didn't think you were.'

'Just so we know where we stand.'

'I know exactly where we stand,' Kling said. 'There are a lot of people in this city, Miss Forrest, and one of them is the guy who's after you. I don't know how long it'll take to smoke him out, I don't know when or where he'll spot us. But I *do* know he's not going to see us together if you're safe and cosy in your little bed and I'm safe and cosy in mine.' Kling took a deep breath. 'So what we're going to do, Miss Forrest, is have dinner together tonight, and then see the Hitchcock movie. And then we'll go for coffee and something afterwards, and then I'll take you home. Tomorrow's Saturday, so we can plan on a nice long day together. Sunday, too. On Monday –'

'Oh, God,' Cindy said.

'You said it,' Kling answered. 'Cheer up, here comes your lasagna.'

Because a white man punched a Negro in a bar on Culver Avenue just about the time Cindy Forrest was putting her first forkful of lasagna into her mouth, five detectives of the 87th Precinct were pressed into emergency duty to quell what looked like the beginnings of a full-scale riot. Two of those detectives were Meyer and Carella, the theory being that Stan Gifford was already dead and gone whereas the Culver Avenue fist fight could possibly lead to a good many more corpses before nightfall if something were not done about it immediately.

There was, of course, nothing that could be done about it immediately. A riot will either start or not start, and all too often the presence of policemen will only help to enflame a gathering crowd, defeating the reason for their being there in the first place. The patrolmen and detectives of the 87th could only play a waiting game, calming citizens wherever they could, spotting people they knew in the crowd and talking good sense to them, assuring them that *both* men involved in the fight had been arrested, and not only the Negro. There were some who could be placated, and others who could not. The cops roamed the streets like instant father images, trying to bind the wounds of a century of speaking belated words of peace, by patting a shoulder tolerantly, by asking to be accepted as friends. Too many of the cops were not friends and the people knew goddamn well they weren't. Too many of the cops were angry men with angry notions of their own about Negroes and Puerto Ricans, inborn prejudices that neither example nor reprimand could change. It was touch and go for a long while on that windy October afternoon.

By four o'clock, the crowds began to disperse. The patrolmen were left behind in double strength, but the detectives were relieved to resume their investigations. Meyer and Carella went downtown to see Maria Vallejo.

Her street was in one of the city's better neighbourhoods, a block of old brownstones with clean-swept stoops and curtained front doors. They entered the tiny lobby with its polished brass mailboxes and bell buttons, found a listing for Maria in apartment twenty-two, and rang the bell. The answering buzz was long and insistent; it continued noisily behind them as they climbed the carpeted steps to the second floor. They rang the bell outside the door with its polished brass 2s. It opened almost immediately.

Maria was small and dark and bursting with energy. She was perhaps thirty-two, with thick dark hair pulled tightly to the back of her head, flashing brown eyes, a generous mouth, and a nose that had been turned up by a plastic surgeon. She wore a white blouse and black tapered slacks. A pair of large gold hoop earrings adorned her ears, but she wore no other jewellery. She opened the door as though she were expecting party guests and then looked out at the detectives in undisguised puzzlement.

'Yes?' she said. 'What is it?' She spoke without a trace of accent. If Carella had been forced to make a regional guess based on her speech, he'd have chosen Boston or one of its suburbs.

'We're from the police,' he said, flashing his buzzer. 'We're investigating the death of Stan Gifford.'

'Oh, sure,' she said. 'Come on in.'

They followed her into the apartment. The apartment was furnished in brimming good taste, cluttered with objects picked up in the city's better antique and junk shops. The shelves and walls were covered with ancient nutcrackers and old theatre posters and a French puppet, and watercolour sketches for costumes and stage sets, and several enamelled army medals, and black silk fan, and pieces of driftwood. The living room was small, with wide curtained windows overlooking the street, luminous with the glow of the afternoon sun. It was furnished with a sofa and chair covered in deep-green velvet, a bentwood rocker, a low needle-point footstool, and a marble-topped table on which lay several copies of *Paris Match*.

'Do sit down,' Maria said. 'Can I get you a drink? Oh, you're not allowed, are you? Some coffee?'

'I can use a cup,' Carella said.

'It's on the stove. I'll just pour it. I always keep a pot on the stove. I guess I drink a million cups of coffee a day.' She went into the small kitchen. They could see her standing at a round, glass-topped table over which hung a Tiffany lampshade, pouring the coffee from an enamelled hand-painted pot. She carried the cups, spoons, sugar, and cream into the living room on a small teakwood tray, shoved aside the copies of the French magazine to make room for it, and then served the detectives. She went to sit in the bentwood rocker then, sipping at her coffee, rocking idly back and forth.

'I bought this when Kennedy was killed,' she said. 'Do you like it? It keeps falling apart. What did you want to know about Stan?'

'We understand you were in his dressing room with him Wednesday night just before he went on, Miss Vallejo. Is that right?'

'That's right,' she said.

'Were you alone with him?'

'No, there were several people in the room.'

'Who?'

'Gee, I don't remember offhand. I think Art was there, yes . . . and maybe one other person.'

'George Cooper?'

'Yes, that's right. Say, how did *you* know?'

Carella smiled. 'But Mr Cooper didn't come into the room, did he?'

'Oh, sure he did.'

'What I mean is, he simply knocked on the door and called Mr Gifford, isn't that right?'

'No, he came in,' Maria said. 'He was there quite a while.'

'How much time would you say Mr Cooper spent in the dressing room?'

'Oh, maybe five minutes.'

'You remember that clearly, do you?'

'Oh, yes. He was there, all right.'

'What else do you remember, Miss Vallejo? What happened in that dressing room Wednesday night?'

'Oh, nothing. We were just talking. Stan was relaxing while those singers were on, and I just sort of drifted in to have a smoke and chat, that's all.'

'What did you chat about?'

'I don't remember.' She shrugged. 'It was just small talk. The monitor was going and those nuts were singing in the background, so we were just making small talk, that's all.'

'Did Mr Gifford eat anything? Or drink anything?'

'Gee, no. No, he didn't. We were just talking.'

'No coffee? Nothing like that?'

'No. No, I'm sorry.'

'Did he take a vitamin pill? Would you happen to have noticed that?'

'Gee, no, I didn't notice.'

'Or *any* kind of a pill?'

'No, we were just talking, that's all.'

'Did you like Mr Gifford?'

'Well ...'

Maria hesitated. She got out of the rocker and walked to a coffee table near the couch. She put down her cup, and then walked back to the rocker again, and then shrugged.

'Did you like him, Miss Vallejo?'

'I don't like to talk about the dead,' she said.

'We were talking about him just fine until a minute ago.'

'I don't like to speak *ill* of the dead,' she corrected.

'Then you didn't like him?'

'Well, he was a little demanding, that's all.'

'Demanding how?'

'I'm the show's wardrobe mistress, you know.'

'Yes, we know.'

'I've got eight people working under me. That's a big staff. I'm responsible for all of them, and it's not easy to costume that show each week, believe me. Well, I ... I don't think Stan made the job any easier, that's all. He ... well ... well, really, he didn't *know* very much about costumes, and he pretended he did, and ... well, he got on my nerves sometimes, that's all.'

'I see,' Carella said.

'But you went into his dressing room to chat, anyway,' Meyer said through his nose, and then sniffed.

'Well, there wasn't a feud between us or anything like that. It's just that every once in a while, we yelled at each other a little, that's all. Because he didn't know a damn thing about costumes, and I happen to know a great deal about costumes, that's all. But that didn't stop me from going into his dressing room to chat a little. I don't see anything so terribly wrong about going into his dressing room to chat a little.'

'No one said anything was wrong, Miss Vallejo.'

'I mean, I know a man's been murdered and all, but that's no reason to start examining every tiny little word that was said, or every little thing that was done. People *do* argue, you know.'

'Yes, we know.'

Maria paused. She stopped rocking, and she turned her head towards the curtained windows streaming sunlight and very softly said, 'Oh, what's the use? I guess they've already told you Stan and I hated each other's guts.' She shrugged her shoulders hopelessly. 'I think he was going to fire me. I heard he wouldn't put up with me any longer.'

'Who told you that?'

'David. He said – David Krantz, our producer – he said Stan was about to give me the axe. That's why I went to his dressing room Wednesday night. To ask him about it, to try to ... well, the job pays well. Personalities shouldn't enter into a person's work. I didn't want to lose the job, that's all.'

'*Did* you discuss the job with him?'

'I started to, but then Art came in, and right after that George, so I didn't get a chance.' She paused again. 'I guess it's academic now, isn't it?'

'I guess so.'

Meyer blew his nose noisily, put his tissue away, and then casually said, 'Are you very well known in the field, Miss Vallejo?'

'Oh, yes, sure.'

'So even if Mr Gifford *had* fired you, you could always get another job. Isn't that so?'

'Well ... word gets around pretty fast in this business. It's not good to get fired from *any* job, I'm sure you know that. And in television ... I would have preferred to resign, that's all. So I wanted to clear it up, you see, which is why I went to his dressing room. To clear it up. If it was true he was going to let me go, I wanted the opportunity of leaving the job of my own volition, that's all.'

'But you never got a chance to discuss it.'

'No. I told you. Art walked in.'

'Well, thank you, Miss Vallejo,' Carella said, rising. 'That was very good coffee.'

'Listen ...'

She had come out of the bentwood rocker now, the rocker still moving back and forth, and she stood in the centre of the room with the sun blazing on the curtains behind her. She worried her lip for a moment, and then said, 'Listen, I didn't have anything to do with this.'

Meyer and Carella said nothing.

'I didn't like Stan, and maybe he was going to fire me, but I'm not nuts, you know. I'm a little temperamental maybe, but I'm not nuts. We didn't get along, that's all. That's no reason to kill a man. I mean, a lot of people on the show didn't get along with Stan. He was a difficult man, that's all, and the star. We blew our stacks every now and then, that's all. But I didn't kill him. I ... I wouldn't know how to begin hurting someone.'

The detectives kept staring at her. Maria gave a small shrug.

'That's all,' she said.

The afternoon was dying by the time they reached the street again. Carella glanced at his watch and said, 'Let's call Bob, see if he had any luck with our friend Wetherley.'

'You call,' Meyer said. 'I feel miserable.'

'You'd better get to bed,' Carella said.

'You know what Fanny Brice said is the best cure for a cold, don't you?' Meyer asked.

'No, what?'

'Put a hot Jew on your chest.'

'Better take some aspirin, too,' Carella advised.

They went into the nearest drugstore, and Carella called the squadroom. O'Brien told him he had tried Wetherley's number three times that afternoon, but no one had answered the phone. Carella thanked him, hung up, and went out to the car, where Meyer was blowing his nose and looking very sick indeed. By the time they got back to the squadroom, O'Brien had called the number a fourth time, again without luck. Carella told Meyer to get the hell home, but Meyer insisted on typing up at least one of the reports on the people they'd talked to in the past two days. He left the squadroom some twenty minutes before Carella. Carella finished the reports in time to greet his relief, Andy Parker, who was a half hour late as usual. He tried Wetherley's number once more, and then told Parker to keep trying it all night long, and to call him at home if he reached Wetherley. Parker assured him that he would, but Carella wasn't at all sure he'd keep the promise.

He got home to his house in Riverhead at seven-fifteen. The twins met him at the door, almost knocking him over in their headlong rush to greet him. He picked up one under each arm, and was swinging them towards the kitchen when the telephone rang.

He put down the children and went to the phone.

'Hello?' he said.

'Bet you thought I wouldn't, huh?' the voice said.

'Who's this?'

'Andy Parker. I just called Wetherley. He told me he got home about ten minutes ago. I advised him to stick around until you got there.'

'Oh,' Carella said. 'Thanks.'

He hung up and turned towards the kitchen, where Teddy was standing in the doorway. He looked at her silently for several moments, and she stared back at him, and then he shrugged and said simply, 'I guess I can eat before I leave.'

Teddy sighed almost imperceptibly, but Mark, the eldest of the twins by five minutes, was watching the byplay with curious intensity. He made a vaguely resigned gesture with one hand and said, 'There he goes.' And April, thinking it was a game, threw herself into Carella's arms, squeezed the breath out of him, and squealed, 'There he goes, there he goes, there he goes!'

Art Wetherley was waiting for him when he got there. He led Carella through the apartment and into a studio overlooking the park. The studio contained a desk upon which sat a typewriter, an ash tray, a ream of blank paper and what looked like another ream of typewritten sheets covered with pencilled hen scratches. There were several industry award plaques on the wall, and a low bookcase beneath them. Wetherley gestured to one of the two chairs in the room, and Carella sat in it. He seemed extremely calm, eminently at ease, but the ash tray on his desk was full of cigarettes, and he lighted another one now.

'I'm not used to getting phone calls from the police,' he said at once.

'Well, we were here –'

'Especially when they tell me to stay where I am, not to leave the apartment.'

'Andy Parker isn't the most tactful –'

'I mean, I didn't know this was a dictatorship,' Wetherley said.

'It isn't, Mr Wetherley,' Carella said gently. 'We're investigating a murder, however, and we were here yesterday, but –'

'I was staying with a friend.'

'What friend?'

'A girl I know. I felt pretty shook up Wednesday night after this . . . thing happened, so I went over to her apartment. I've been there the past two days.' Wetherley paused. 'There's no law against that, is there?'

'Certainly not,' Carella smiled. 'I'm sorry if we inconvenienced you, but we did want to ask you some questions.'

Wetherley seemed slightly mollified. 'Well, all right,' he said. 'But there was no need, really, to warn me not to leave the apartment.'

'I apologize for that, Mr Wetherley.'

'Well, all right,' Wetherley said.

'I wonder if you could tell me what happened in Stan Gifford's dressing room Wednesday night. Just before he left it.'

'I don't remember in detail.'

'Well, tell me what you *do* remember.'

Wetherley thought for a moment, crushed out his cigarette, lighted a new one, and then said, 'Maria was there when I came in. She was arguing with Stan about something. At least . . .'

'Arguing?'

'Yes. I could hear them shouting at each other before I knocked on the door.'

'Go ahead.'

'The atmosphere was a little strained after I went in, and Maria didn't say very much all the while I was there. But Stan and I were joking, mostly about the folk singers. He hated folk singers, but this particular group is hot right now, and he was talked into hiring them.'

'So you were making jokes about them?'

'Yes. While we watched the act on the monitor.'

'I see. In a friendly manner, would you say?'

'Oh, yes.'

'Then what happened?'

'Well . . . then George came in. George Cooper, the show's A.D.'

'He came into the room?'

'Yes.'

'How long did he stay?'

'Oh, three or four minutes, I guess.'

'I see. But *he* didn't argue with Gifford, did he?'

'No.'

'Just Maria?'

'Yes. Before I got there, you understand.'

'Yes, I understand. And what about you?' Carella asked.

'Me?'

'Yes. What about your argument with Gifford before the show went on the air?'

'Argument? Who said there was an argument?'

'Wasn't there one?'

'Certainly not.'

Carella took a deep breath. 'Mr Wetherley, didn't you say you wished Stan Gifford would drop dead?'

'No, sir.'

'You did *not* say that?'

'No, sir, I did not. Stan and I got along very well.' Wetherley paused. 'A lot of people on the show *didn't* get along with him, you understand. But I never had any trouble.'

'*Who* didn't get along with him, Mr Wetherley?'

'Well, Maria, for one, I just told you that. And David Krantz didn't particularly like him. He was always saying within earshot of Stan, that all actors are cattle, and that comedians are only funny actors. And George Cooper didn't exactly enjoy his role of . . . well, handyman, almost. Keeping everyone quiet on the set, and running for coffee, and bringing Stan his pills, and making sure everybody –'

'Bringing Stan his *what?*'

'His pills,' Wetherley said. 'Stan was a nervous guy, you know. I guess he was on tranquillizers. Anyway, George was the chief errand boy and bottle washer, hopping whenever Stan snapped his fingers.'

'Did George bring him a pill Wednesday night?'

'When?' Wetherley asked.

'Wednesday night. When he came to the dressing room.'

Wetherley concentrated for a moment, and then said, 'Now that you mention it, I think he did.'

'You're sure about that?'

'Yes, sir. I'm positive.'

'And did Stan *take* the pill from him?'

'Yes, sir.'

'And did he swallow it?'

'Yes, sir.'

Carella rose suddenly. 'Would you mind coming along with me, Mr Wetherley?' he asked.

'Come along? Where?'

'Uptown. There are a few things we'd like to get straight.'

The few things Carella wanted to get straight were the conflicting stories of the last three people to have been with Gifford before he went on camera. He figured that the best way to do this was in the squadroom, where the police would have the psychological advantage in the question-and-answer game. There was nothing terribly sinister about the green globes hanging outside the station house, or about the high desk in the muster room or the sign advising all visitors to stop at the desk, or even the white sign announcing DETECTIVE DIVISION in bold black letters, and pointing towards the iron-runged steps leading upstairs. There was certainly nothing menacing about the steps themselves or the narrow corridor they opened onto, or the various rooms in that corridor with their neatly lettered signs, INTERROGATION, LAVATORY, CLERICAL. The slatted-wood railing that divided the corridor from the squadroom was innocuous-looking, and the squad-room itself – in spite of the fire-mesh grids over the windows – looked like any business office in the city, with desks, and filing cabinets and ringing telephones, and a water cooler, and bulletin boards, and men working in shirt sleeves. But Art Wetherley, Maria Vallejo, and George Cooper were visibly rattled by their surroundings, and they became more rattled when they were taken into separate rooms for their interrogations. Bob O'Brien, a big cop with a sweet and innocently boyish look, questioned Cooper in the lieutenant's office. Steve Carella questioned Maria in the Clerical Office, kicking out Alf Miscolo, who was busy typing up his records and complained bitterly. Meyer Meyer, suffering from a cold, and not ready to take any nonsense, questioned Art Wetherley at the table in the barely furnished Interrogation Room. The three detectives had decided beforehand what questions they would ask, and what their approach would be. In separate rooms, with different suspects, they went through a familiar routine.

'You said you weren't drinking coffee, Miss Vallejo,' Carella said. 'Mr Cooper tells us there were coffee containers in that room. Were there or weren't there?'
'No. I don't remember. I know *I* didn't have any coffee.'
'Did Art Wetherley?'
'No. I didn't see him drink anything.'
'Did George Cooper hand Gifford a pill?'
'No.'
'Were you arguing with Gifford before Art Wetherley came in?'
'No.'

'Let's go over this one more time, Mr Cooper.' O'Brien said. 'You say you only knocked on the door and poked your head into the room, is that right?'
'That's right.'
'You were there only a few seconds.'
'Yes. Look, I –'
'Did you give Stan Gifford a pill?'
'A pill? No! No, I didn't!'
'But there were coffee containers in the room, huh?'
'Yes. Look, I didn't give him anything! What are you trying . . . ?'
'Did you hear Art Wetherley say he wished Gifford would drop dead?'
'Yes!'

'All right, Wetherley,' Meyer said, 'when did Cooper give him that pill?'
'As soon as he came into the room.'
'And Gifford washed it down with what?'
'With the coffee we were drinking.'
'You were all drinking coffee, huh?'
'Yes.'
'*Who* was?'
'Maria, and Stan, and I was, too.'

'Then why'd you go to that room, Maria, if not to argue?'
'I went to . . . to talk to him. I thought we could –'
'But you *were* arguing, weren't you?'
'No. I swear to God, I wasn't –'

'Then why are you lying about the coffee? Were you drinking coffee, or weren't you?'

'No. No coffee. Please, I ...'

'Now hold it, hold it, Mr Cooper. You were either in that room or not in it. You either gave him a pill or you –'

'I didn't, I'm telling you.'

'Did you *ever* give him pills?'

'No.'

'He was taking tranquillizers, wasn't he?'

'I don't know what he was taking. I never brought him anything.'

'Never?'

'Once maybe, or twice. An aspirin. If he had a headache.'

'But never a tranquillizer?'

'No.'

'How about a vitamin capsule?'

'He handed him the pill,' Wetherley said.

'What kind of a pill?'

'I don't know.'

'Think!'

'I'm thinking. A small pill.'

'What colour?'

'White.'

'A tablet, you mean? Like an aspirin? Like that?'

'Yes. Yes, I think so. I don't remember.'

'Well, you saw it, didn't you?'

'Yes, but ...'

They put it all together afterwards in the squadroom. They left the three suspects in the lieutenant's office with a patrolman watching over them and sat around Carella's desk and compared their answers. They were not particularly pleased with the results, but neither were they surprised by them. They had all been cops for a good many years, and nothing human beings perpetrated against each other ever surprised them. They were perhaps a little saddened by what they discovered each and every time, but never surprised. They were used to dealing with facts, and they accepted the facts in the Stan Gifford case with grim resolution.

The facts were simple and disappointing.

They decided after comparing results that all three of their suspects were lying.

Maria Vallejo *had* been arguing with Gifford, and she *had* been drinking coffee, but she denied both allegations because she realized how incriminating these seemingly isolated circumstances might seem. She recognized quite correctly that someone could have poisoned Gifford by dropping something into his coffee. If she admitted there had been coffee in the dressing room, that indeed she and Gifford had been drinking coffee together, and if she then further admitted they'd been arguing, could she not have been the one who slipped the lethal dose into the sponsor's brew? So Maria had lied in her teeth, but had graciously refused to incriminate anyone else while she was lying. It was enough for her to fabricate her own way out of what seemed like a horrible trap.

Art Wetherley had indeed wished his employer would drop dead, and he had wished it out loud, and he had wished it in the presence of someone else. And that night, lo and behold, Stan Gifford *did* collapse, on camera, for millions to see. Art Wetherley, like a child who'd made a fervent wish, was startled to realize it had come true. Not only was he startled; he was frightened. He immediately remembered what he'd said to George Cooper before the show, and he was certain Cooper would remember it, too. His fear reached new dimensions when he recalled that he had been one of the last few people to spend time with Gifford while he was alive, and that his proximity to Gifford in an obvious poisoning case, coupled with his chance remark during rehearsal, could easily serve to pin a thoroughly specious murder rap on him. When a detective called and warned him not to leave the apartment, Wetherley was certain he'd been picked as the patsy of the year, an award that did not come gold-plated like an Emmy. In desperation, he had tried to discredit Cooper's statement by turning the tables and presenting Cooper as a suspect himself. He had seen Cooper bringing aspirins to Gifford at least a few times in the past three years. He decided to elaborate on what he'd seen, inventing a pill that had never changed hands on the night Gifford died, senselessly incriminating Cooper. But a frightened man doesn't care who takes the blame, so long as it's not himself.

In much the same way, Cooper came to the sudden realization that not only was he one of the last people to be with Gifford, he was *the* last person. Even though he had spent several minutes with Gifford in the dressing room, he thought it was safer to say he had only poked his head into it. And whereas Gifford hadn't stopped to talk to a soul before he went on camera, Cooper thought it was wiser to add a mystery cameraman. Then, to clinch his own escape from what seemed like a definitely compromising position, he remembered Wetherley's earlier outburst and promptly paraded it before the investigating cops, even though he knew the expression was one that was uttered a hundred times a day during any television rehearsal.

Liars all.

But murderers none.

The detectives were convinced, after a gruelling three-hour session, that these assorted liars were now babbling all in the cleansing catharsis of truth. Yes, we lied, they all separately admitted, but now we speak the truth, the shining truth. We did not kill Stan Gifford. We wouldn't know strohoosis from a hole in the wall. Besides, we are kind gentle people; look at us. Liars, yes, but murderers, no. We did not kill. That is the truth.

We did not kill.

The detectives believed them.

They had heard enough lies in their professional lives to know that truth has a shattering ring that can topple skyscrapers. They sent the three home without apologizing for any inconvenience. Bob O'Brien yawned, stretched, asked Carella if he needed him any more, put on his hat, and left. Meyer and Carella sat in the lonely squadroom and faced each other across the desk. It was five minutes to midnight. When the telephone rang, it momentarily startled them. Meyer lifted it from the cradle.

'Meyer, 87th Squad,' he said. 'Oh, hi, George.' To Carella, he whispered,

'It's Temple. I had him out checking Krantz's alibi.' Into the phone again, he said, 'What'd you get? Right. Uh-huh. Right. Okay, thanks.' He hung up. 'He finally got to the last person on Krantz's list, that Hollywood director. He'd been to the theatre, just got back to the hotel. His little bimbo was with him.' Meyer wiggled his eyebrows.

Carella looked at him wearily. 'What'd Temple get?'

'He says they all confirmed Krantz's story. He got to the sponsor's booth a good fifteen minutes before the show went on, and he was there right up to the time Gifford got sick.'

'Mmm,' Carella said.

They stared at each other glumly. Midnight had come and gone; it was another day. Meyer sniffed noisily. Carella yawned and then washed his hand over his face.

'What do you think?' he said.

'I don't know. What do *you* think?'

'I don't know.'

The men were silent.

'Maybe he *did* kill himself,' Carella said.

'Maybe.'

'Oh, man, I'm exhausted,' Carella said.

Meyer sniffed.

Chapter Six

He had followed them to the restaurant and the movie theatre, and now he stood in the doorway across from her house, waiting for her to come home. It was a cold night, and he stood huddled deep in the shadows, his coat collar pulled high on the back of his neck, and his hands thrust into his coat pockets, his hat low on his forehead.

It was ten minutes past twelve, and they had left the movie theatre at eleven-forty-five, but he knew they would be coming straight home. He had been watching the girl long enough now to know a few things about her, and one of those things was that she didn't sleep around much. Last month sometime, she had shacked up with a guy on Banning Street, just for the night, and the next morning after she left the apartment he had gone up to the guy and had worked him over with a pair of brass knuckles, leaving him crying like a baby on the kitchen floor. He had warned the guy against calling the police, and he had also told him he should never go near Cindy Forrest again, never try to see her again, never even try to call her again. The guy had held his broken mouth together with one bloody hand, and nodded his head, and begged not to be hit again – that was one guy who wouldn't be bothering *her* any more. So he knew she didn't sleep around too much, and besides he knew she wouldn't be going anyplace but straight home with this blond guy because this blond guy was a cop.

He had got the fuzz smell from him almost the minute he first saw him, early this afternoon when he came to the office to take her to lunch. He knew the look of fuzz and the smell of fuzz, and he realized right off that the very smart bulls of this wonderful city were setting a trap for him and that he was supposed to fall right into it – here I am, fuzz, take me.

Like fun.

He had stayed far away from the restaurant where they had lunch, getting the fuzz stink sharp and clear in his nostrils and knowing something was up, but not knowing what kind of a trap was being set for him, and wanting to make damn sure before he made another move. The blond guy walked like a cop, that was an unmistakable cop walk. And also he had a sneaky way of making the scene, his head turned in one direction while he was really casing the opposite direction, a very nice fuzz trick that known criminals sometimes utilized, but that mostly cops from here to Detroit and back again were very familiar with. Well, he had known cops all across this fine little country of America, he had busted more cops' heads than he could count on all his fingers and toes. He wouldn't mind busting another, just for the fun of it, but not until he knew what the trap was. The one thing he wasn't going to do was walk into a trap.

In the wintertime, or like now when it was getting kind of chilly and a guy had to wear a coat, you could always tell when he was heeled because if he was wearing a shoulder harness, the button between the top one and the third one was always left unbuttoned. If he was wearing the holster clipped to his belt, then a button was left undone just above the waist, so the right hand could reach in and draw – that was the first concrete tipoff that Blondie was a cop. He was a cop, and he wore his gun clipped to his belt. Watching him from outside the plate-glass window of the second restaurant later that day, there had been the flash of Blondie's tin when he went to pay his check, opening his wallet, with the shield catching light for just a second. That was the second concrete fact, and a smart man don't need more than one or two facts to piece together a story, not when the fuzz smell is all over the place to begin with.

The only thing he didn't know now was what the trap was, and whether or not he should accommodate Blondie by walking into it and maybe beating him up. He thought it would be better to work on the girl, though. It was time the girl learned what she could do and couldn't do, there was no sense putting it off. The girl had to know that she couldn't go sleeping around with no guys on Banning Street, or for that matter anyplace in the city. And she also had to know she couldn't play along with the cops on whatever trap they were cooking up. She had to know it now, and once and for all, because he wasn't planning on staying in the shadows for long. The girl had to know she was *his* meat and his *alone*.

He guessed he'd beat her up tonight.

He looked at his watch again. It was fifteen minutes past twelve, and he began to wonder what was keeping them. Maybe he should have stuck with them when they came out of the movie house, instead of rushing right over here. Still, if Blondie –

A car was turning into the street.

He pulled back into the shadows and waited. The car came up the street slowly. Come on, Blondie, he thought, you ain't being followed, there's no reason to drive slow. He grinned in the darkness. The car pulled to the kerb.

Blondie got out and walked around to the other side, holding open the door for the girl, and then walking her up the front steps. The building was a grey, four-storey job, and the girl lived on the top floor rear. The name on the bell read C. FORREST, that was the first thing he'd found out about her, almost two months ago. A little while after that, he'd broken open the lock on her mailbox and found two letters addressed to Miss Cynthia Forrest – it was a good thing she wasn't married, because if she was, her husband would have been in for one hell of a time – and another letter addressed to Miss Cindy Forrest, this one from a guy over in Thailand, serving with the Peace Corps. The guy was lucky he was over in Thailand, or he'd have had a visitor requesting him to stop writing letters to little Sweetpants.

Blondie was unlocking the inner vestibule door for her now. The girl said good night – he could hear her voice clear across the street – and Blondie gave her the keys and said something with his back turned, and which couldn't be heard. Then the door closed behind her, and Blondie came down the steps, walking with a funny fuzz walk, like a boxer moving towards the ring where a pushover sparring partner was waiting, and keeping his head ducked, though this was a cop trick and those eyes were most likely flashing up and down the street in either direction even though the head was ducked and didn't seem to be turning. Blondie got into the car – the engine was still running – put it into gear, and drove off.

He waited.

In five minutes' time, the car pulled around the corner again and drifted slowly past the grey building.

He almost burst out laughing. What did Blondie think he was playing around with, an amateur? He waited until the car rounded the corner again, and then he waited for at least another fifteen minutes, until he was sure Blondie wasn't coming back.

He crossed the street rapidly then, and walked around the corner and into the building directly behind the girl's. He went straight through the building, opening the door at the rear of the ground floor and stepping out into the back yard. He climbed the clothesline pole near the fence separating the yard from the one behind it, leaped over the fence, and dropped to his knees. Looking up, he could see a light burning in the girl's window on the fourth floor. He walked towards the rear of the building, cautiously but easily, jumping up for the fire-escape ladder, pulling it down, and then swinging up onto it and beginning to climb. He went by each window with great care, especially the other lighted one on the second floor, flitting past it like a shadow and continuing on up to the third floor, and then stepping onto the fourth-floor fire escape, *her* fire escape.

There was a wooden cheese box resting on the iron slats of the fire escape floor, the dried twigs of dead flowers stuck into the stiff earth it contained. The fire escape was outside her bedroom. He peered around the edge of the window, but the room was empty. He glanced to his right and saw that the tiny bathroom window was lighted; the girl was in the bathroom. He debated going right into the bedroom while she was occupied down the hall, but decided against it. He wanted to wait until she was in bed. He wanted to scare her real good.

The only light in the room came from a lamp on the night table near the girl's bed. The bed was clearly visible from where he crouched outside on the fire escape. There was a single chair on this side of the bed, he would have to avoid that in the dark. He wanted his surprise to be complete; he didn't want to go stumbling over no furniture and waking her up before it was time. The window was open just a trifle at the top, probably to let in some air, she'd probably opened it when she came into the apartment. He didn't know whether or not she'd close and lock it before going to bed, maybe she would. This was a pretty decent neighbourhood, though, without any incidents lately – he'd checked on that because he was afraid some cheap punk might burst into the girl's apartment and complicate things for him – so maybe she slept with the window open just a little, at the top, the way it was now. While she was in the bathroom, he studied the simple lock on the sash and decided it wouldn't be a problem, anyway, even if she locked it.

The bathroom light went out suddenly.

He flattened himself against the brick wall of the building. The girl was humming when she came into the room. The humming trailed off abruptly, she was turning on the radio. It came on very loud, for Christ's sake, she was going to wake up the whole damn building! She kept twisting the dial until she found the station she wanted, sweet music, lots of violins and muted trumpets, and then she lowered the volume. He waited. In a moment, she came to the window and pulled down the shade. Good, he thought, she didn't lock the window. He waited a moment longer, and then flattened himself onto the fire escape so that he could peer into the room beneath the lower edge of the shade, where the girl had left a good two-inch gap between it and the window sill.

The girl was still dressed. She was wearing the tan dress she had worn to dinner with Blondie, but when she turned away and began walking towards the closet, he saw that she had already lowered the zipper at the back. The dress was spread in a wide V, the white elastic line of her brassiere crossing her back, the zipper lowered to a point just above the beginning curve of her buttocks. The radio was playing a song she knew, and she began humming along with it again as she opened the closet door and took her nightgown from a hook. She closed the door and then walked to the bed, sitting on the side facing the window and lifting her dress up over her thighs to unhook first one garter and then the other. She took off her shoes and rolled down her stockings, and then walked to the closet to put the shoes away and to put the stockings into some kind of a bag hanging on the inside doorknob. She closed the door again, and then took off her dress, standing just outside the closet and not moving towards the bed again. In her bra and half slip, she walked over to the other side of the room, where he couldn't see her any more, almost as if the lousy little bitch knew he was watching her! She was still humming. His hands were wet. He dried them on the sleeves of his coat and waited.

She came back so suddenly that she startled him. She had taken off her underwear, and she walked swiftly to the bed, naked, to pick up her nightgown. Jesus, she was beautiful! Jesus, he hadn't realized how goddamn beautiful she really was. He watched her as she bent slightly to pull the gown over her head, straightened, and then let it fall down over her breasts and her tilted hips. She yawned. She looked at her watch and then went across the room again, out of sight, and came back to the bed carrying a paperback book. She got into the bed, her legs parting, opening, as she swung up onto it, and then pulled the blanket up over her knees, and fluffed the pillow, and scratched her jaw, and opened the book. She yawned. She looked at her watch again, seemed to change her mind about reading the book, put it down on the night table, and yawned again.

A moment later, she turned out the light.

The first thing she heard was the voice.

It said 'Cindy,' and for the briefest tick of time she thought she was dreaming because the voice was just a whisper. And then she heard it again, 'Cindy,' hovering somewhere just above her face, and her eyes popped wide, and she tried to sit up but something pressed her fiercely back against the pillow. She opened her mouth to scream, but a hand clamped over her lips. She stared over the edge of the thick fingers into the darkness, trying to see. 'Be quiet, Cindy,' the voice said. 'Just be quiet now.'

His grip on her mouth was hard and tight. He was straddling her now, his knees on the bed, his legs tight against her pinioned arms, sitting on her abdomen, one arm flung across her chest, holding her to the pillow.

'Can you hear me?' he asked.

She nodded. His hand stayed tight on her mouth, hurting her. She wanted to bite his hand, but she could not free her mouth. His weight upon her was unbearable. She tried to move, but she was helplessly caught in the vice of his knees, the tight band of his arm thrown across her chest.

'Listen to me,' he said, 'I'm going to beat the shit out of you.'

She believed him instantly; terror rocketed into her skull. Her eyes were growing accustomed to the darkness. She could dimly see his grinning face hovering above her. His fingers smelled of tobacco. He kept his right hand clamped over her mouth, his left arm thrown across her chest, lower now, so that the hand was gripping her breast. He kept working his hand as he talked to her, grasping her through the thin nylon gown, squeezing her nipple as his voice continued in a slow lazy monotone, 'Do you know why I'm going to beat you, Cindy?'

She tried to shake her head, but his hand was so tight against her mouth that she could not move. She knew she would begin to cry within the next few moments. She was trembling beneath his weight. His hand was cruel on her breast. Each time he tightened it on her nipple, she winced with pain.

'I don't like you to go out with cops,' he said. 'I don't like you to go out with *anybody*, but cops especially.'

She could see his face clearly now. He was the same man who had come to the office, the same man who had beaten up the policeman. She remembered the way he had kicked the policeman when he was on the floor, and she began trembling more violently. She heard him laugh.

'I'm going to take my hand off your mouth now,' he said, 'because we have to talk. But if you scream, I'll kill you. Do you understand me?'

She tried to nod. His hand was relaxing. He was slowly lifting it from her mouth, cupped, as though cautiously peering under it to see if he had captured a fly. She debated screaming, and knew at once that if she did he would keep his promise and kill her. He shifted his body to the left, relaxing his grip across her chest, lifting his arms, freeing her breast. He rested his hands palms downwards on his thighs, his legs bent under him, his knees still holding her arms tightly against her side, most of his weight still on her abdomen. Her breast was throbbing with pain. A trickle of sweat rolled down towards her belly and she thought for a moment it was blood, had he made her bleed somehow? A new wave of fear caused her to begin trembling again. She was ashamed of herself for being so frightened, but the fear was something uncontrollable, a raw animal panic that shrieked silently of pain and possible death.

'You'll get rid of him tomorrow,' he whispered. He sat straddling her with his huge hands relaxed on his own thighs.

'Who?' she said. 'Who do you –'

'The cop. You'll get rid of him tomorrow.'

'All right.' She nodded in the darkness. 'All right,' she said again.

'You'll call his precinct – what precinct is it?'

'The eight . . . the 87th, I think.'

'You'll call him.'

'Yes. Yes, I will.'

'You'll tell him you don't need a police escort no more. You'll tell him everything is all right now.'

'Yes, all right,' she said. 'Yes, I will.'

'You'll tell him you patched things up with your boy friend.'

'My . . .' She paused. Her heart was beating wildly, she was sure he could feel her heart beating in panic. 'My *boy* friend?'

'Me,' he said, and grinned.

'I . . . I don't even know you,' she said.

'I'm your boy friend.'

She shook her head.

'I'm your lover.'

She kept shaking her head.

'Yes.'

'I don't *know* you,' she said, and suddenly she began weeping. 'What do you want from me? Please, won't you go? Won't you please leave me alone? I don't even know you. Please, please.'

'Beg,' he said, and grinned.

'Please, please, please . . .'

'You're going to tell him to stop coming around.'

'Yes, I *am*. I *said* I would.'

'Promise.'

'I promise.'

'You'll keep the promise,' he said flatly.

'Yes, I will. I told you –'

He slapped her suddenly and fiercely, his right hand abruptly leaving his thigh and coming up viciously towards her face. She blinked her eyes an instant before his open palm collided with her cheek. She pulled back rigidly, her neck muscles taut, her eyes wide, her teeth clamped together.

'You'll keep the promise,' he said, 'because this is a sample of what you'll get if you don't.'

And then he began beating her.

She did not know where she was at first. She tried to open her eyes, but something was wrong with them, she could not seem to open her eyes. Something rough was against her cheek, her head was twisted at a curious angle. She felt a hundred separate throbbing areas of hurt, but none of them seemed connected with her head or her body, each seemed to pulse with a solitary intensity of its own. Her left eye trembled open. Light knifed into the narrow crack of opening eyelid, she could open it no further. Light flickered into the tentative opening, flashes of light pulsated as the flesh over her eye quivered.

She was lying with her cheek pressed to the rug.

She kept trying to open her left eye, catching fitful glimpses of grey carpet as the eye opened and closed spasmodically, still not knowing where she was, possessing a sure knowledge that something terrible had happened to her, but not remembering what it was as yet. She lay quite still on the floor, feeling each throbbing knot of pain, arms, legs, thighs, breasts, nose, the separate pains combining to form a recognizable mass of flesh that was her body, a whole and unified body that had been severely beaten.

And then, of course, she remembered instantly what had happened.

Her first reaction was one of whimpering terror. She drew up her shoulders, trying to pull her head deeper into them. Her left hand came limply towards her face, the fingers fluttering, as though weakly trying to fend off any further blows.

'Please,' she said.

The word whispered into the room. She waited for him to strike her again, every part of her body tensed for another savage blow, and when none came, she lay trembling lest she was mistaken, fearful that he was only pretending to be gone while silently waiting to attack again.

Her eye kept flickering open and shut.

She rolled over onto her back and tried to open the other eye, but again only a crack of winking light came through the trembling lid. The ceiling seemed so very far away. Sobbing, she brought her hand to her nose, thinking it was running, wiping it with the back of her hand, and then realizing that blood was pouring from her nostrils.

'Oh,' she said. 'Oh, my God.'

She lay on her back, sobbing in anguish. At last, she tried to rise. She made it to her knees, and then fell to the floor again, sprawled on her face. The police, she thought, I must call the police. And then she remembered why he had beaten her. He did not want the police. Get rid of the police, he had said. She got to her knees again. Her gown was torn down the front. Her breasts were splotched with purple bruises. The nipple of her right breast looked as raw as an open wound. Her throat, the torn gown, the sloping tops of her breasts were covered with blood from her nose. She cupped her hand under it, and then tried to stop the flow by holding a torn shred of nylon under the nostrils, struggling to her feet and moving unsteadily towards her dressing table, where she knew she'd left her house keys, Kling had returned her house keys, she had left them on the dresser, she would put them at the back of her neck, they would stop the blood, groping for the dresser top, a severe pain on the side of her chest, had he kicked her the way he'd kicked that policeman, get rid of the police, oh my God, oh God, oh God dear God.

She could not believe what she saw in the mirror.

The image that stared back at her was grotesque and frightening, hideous beyond belief. Her eyes were puffed and swollen, the pupils invisible, only a narrow slit showing on the bursting surface of each discoloured bulge. Her face was covered with blood and bruises, a swollen mass of purple lumps, her blonde hair was matted with blood, there were welts on her arms, and thighs, and legs.

She felt suddenly dizzy. She clutched the top of the dressing table to steady herself, taking her hand away from her nose momentarily, watching the falling drops of blood spatter onto the white surface. A wave of nausea came and passed. She stood with her hand pressed to the top of the table, leaning on her extended arm, her head bent, refusing to look into the mirror again. She must not call the police. If she called the police, he would come back and do this to her again. He had told her to get rid of the police, she would call Kling in the morning and tell him everything was all right now, she and her boy friend had patched it up. In utter helplessness, she began crying again, her shoulders heaving, her nose dripping blood, her knees shaking as she clung to the dressing table for support.

Gasping for breath, she stood suddenly erect and opened her mouth wide, sucking in great gulps of air, her hand widespread over her belly like an open fan. Her fingers touched something wet and sticky, and she looked down sharply, expecting more blood, expecting to find herself soaked in blood that seeped from a hundred secret wounds.

She raised her hand slowly towards her swollen eyes.

She fainted when she realized the wet and sticky substance on her belly was semen.

Bert Kling kicked down the door of her apartment at ten-thirty the next morning. He had begun trying to reach her at nine, wanting to work out the details of their day together. He had let the phone ring seven times, and then decided he'd dialled the wrong number. He hung up, and tried it again. This time, he let it ring for a total of ten times, just in case she was a heavy sleeper. There was no answer. At nine-thirty, hoping she had gone down for breakfast and returned to the apartment by now, he called once again. There was still no answer. He called at five-minute intervals until ten o'clock, and then clipped on his gun and went down to his car. It took him a half hour to drive from Riverhead to Cindy's apartment on Glazebrook Street. He climbed the steps to the fourth floor, knocked on her door, called her name, and then kicked it open.

He phoned for an ambulance immediately.

She regained consciousness briefly before the ambulance arrived. When she recognized him, she mumbled, 'No, please, get out of here, he'll know,' and then passed out again.

Outside Cindy's open bedroom window, Kling discovered a visible heel print on one of the iron slats of the fire escape, just below the sill. And very close to that, wedged between two of the slats, he found a small fragment of something that looked like wadded earth. There was the possibility, however small, that the fragment had been dislodged from the shoe of Cindy's attacker. He scooped it into a manilla envelope and marked it for transportation to Detective-Lieutenant Sam Grossman at the police laboratory.

Chapter Seven

Every time Kling went downtown to the lab on High Street, he felt the way he had when he was eleven years old and his parents gave him a Gilbert Chemistry Set for Christmas. The lab covered almost half the first-floor area of the Headquarters building, and although Kling realized it was undoubtedly a most mundane place to Grossman and his cohorts, to him it was a wonderland of scientific marvel. To him, there was truth and justice in the orderly arrangement of cameras and filters, spotlights and enlargers, condensers and projectors. There was an aura of worlds unknown in the silent array of microscopes, common and stereoscopic, comparison and polarizing. There was magic in the quartz lamp with its ultraviolet light, there was poetry in the beakers and crucibles, the flasks and tripods, the burettes and pipettes, the test tubes and Bunsen burners. The police lab was *Mechanics Illustrated* come to life, with balance scales and drafting tools, tape measures and micrometers, scalpels and microtomes, emery wheels and vices. And hovering over it all was the aroma of a thousand chemicals, hitting the nostrils like a waft of exotic perfume caught in the single sail of an Arabian bark.

He loved it, and he wandered into it like a small boy each time, often forgetting that he had come there to discuss the facts of violence or death.

Sam Grossman never forgot the facts of violence or death. He was a tall man, big-boned, with the hands and face of a New England farmer. His eyes were blue and guileless behind thick-rimmed eyeglasses. He spoke softly and with a gentility and warmth reminiscent of an era long past, even though his voice carried the clipped stamp of a man who dealt continually with cold scientific fact. Taking off his glasses in the police lab that Monday morning, he wiped the lenses with a corner of his white lab coat, put them back on the bridge of his nose, and said, 'You gave us an interesting one this time, Bert.'

'How so?'

'Your man was a walking catalogue. We found traces of everything but the kitchen sink in that fragment.'

'Anything I can use?'

'Well, that depends. Come on back here.'

The men walked the length of the lab, moving between two long white counters bearing test tubes of different chemicals, some bubbling, all reminding Kling of a Frankenstein movie.

'Here's what we were able to isolate from that fragment. Seven different identifiable materials, all embedded in, or clinging to, or covering the basic material, which in itself is a combination of three materials. I think you were

right about him having carried it on his shoe. Any other way, he couldn't
have picked up such a collection of junk.'

'You think it was caught on his heel?'

'Probably wedged near the rear of the shoe, where the sole joins the heel.
Impossible to tell, of course. We're just guessing. It seems likely, though,
considering the garbage he managed to accumulate.'

'What kind of garbage?'

'Here,' Grossman said.

Each minute particle or particles of 'garbage' had been isolated and
mounted on separate microscope slides, all of them labelled for identification. The slides were arranged vertically in a rack on the counter top, and
Grossman ticked off each one with his forefinger as he explained.

'The basic compostion is made up of the materials on these first three
slides, blended to form a sort of mastic to which the other elements
undoubtedly clung.'

'And what are those three materials?' Kling asked.

'Suet, sawdust, and blood,' Grossman replied.

'Human blood?'

'No. We ran the Uhlenhuth precipitin reaction test on it. It's definitely
not human.'

'That's good.'

'Well, yes,' Grossman said, 'because it gives us something to play with.
Where would we be most likely to find a combination of sawdust, suet, and
animal blood?'

'A butcher shop?' Kling asked.

'That's our guess. And our fourth slide lends support to the possibility.'
Grossman tapped the slide with his finger. 'It's an animal hair. We weren't
certain at first because the granulation resembled that of a human hair. But
the medullary index – the relation between the diameter of the medulla and
the diameter of the whole hair – was zero point five. Narrower than that
would have indicated it was human. It's definitely animal.'

'What kind of an animal?' Kling asked.

'We can't tell for certain. Either bovine or equine. Considering the other
indications, the hair probably came from an animal one would expect to find
in a butcher shop, most likely a steer.'

'I see,' Kling said. He paused. 'But . . .' He paused again. 'They're *stripped*
by the time they get to a butcher shop, aren't they?'

'What do you mean?'

'Well, the hide's been taken off by that time.'

'So?'

'Well, you just wouldn't find a hair from a steer's hide in a butcher shop,
that's all.'

'I see what you mean. A slaughterhouse would be a better guess, wouldn't
it?'

'Sure,' Kling said. He thought for a moment. 'There're some slaughterhouses here in the city, aren't there?'

'I'm not sure. I think all the slaughtering's done across the river, in the
next state.'

'Well, at least this gives us something to look into.'

'We found a few other things as well,' Grossman said.

'Like what?'

'Fish scales.'

'What?'

'Fish scales, or at least a single particle of a fish scale.'

'In a slaughterhouse?'

'It doesn't sound likely, does it?'

'No. I'm beginning to like your butcher shop idea again.'

'You are, huh?'

'Sure. A combined butcher shop and fish market, why not?'

'What about the animal hair?'

'A dog maybe?' Kling suggested.

'We don't think so.'

'Well, how would a guy pick up a fish scale in a slaughterhouse?'

'He didn't have to,' Grossman said. 'He could have picked it up wherever he went walking. He could have picked it up anyplace in the city.'

'That narrows it down a lot,' Kling said.

'You've got to visualize this as a lump composed of suet, blood –'

'Yeah, and sawdust –'

'Right, that got stuck to his shoe. And you've go to visualize him walking around and having additional little pieces of garbage picked up by this sticky wad of glopis –'

'Sticky wad of *what*?'

'Glopis. That's an old Yiddish expression.'

'Glopis?'

'Glopis.'

'And the animal hair was stuck to the glopis, right?'

'Right.'

'And also the fish scale?'

'Right.'

'And what else?'

'These aren't in any particular order, you understand. I mean, it's impossible to get a progressive sequence of where he might have been. We simply –'

'I understand,' Kling said.

'Okay, we found a small dot of putty, a splinter of creosoted wood, and some metal filings which we identified as copper.'

'Go on.'

'We also found a tiny piece of peanut.'

'Peanut,' Kling said blankly.

'That's right. And to wrap it all up, the entire sticky suet mess of glopis was soaked with gasoline. Your friend stepped into a lot.'

Kling took a pen from his jacket pocket. Repeating the items out loud, and getting confirmation from Grossman as he went along, he jotted them into his notebook:

1- Suet
2- Sawdust
3- Blood (Animal)
4- Hair (Animal)
5- Fish Scale
6- Putty
7- Wood Splinter (creosoted)
8- Metal Filings (copper)
9- Peanut
10- Gasoline

'That's it, huh?'

'That's it,' Grossman said.

'Thanks. You just ruined my day.'

The drawing from the police artist was waiting for Kling when he got back to the squadroom. There were five artists working for the department, and this particular pencil sketch had been made by Detective Victor Haldeman, who had studied at the Art Students League in New York and later at the Art Institute in Chicago before joining the force. Each of the five artists, before being assigned to this special duty, had held other jobs in the department: two of them had been patrolmen in Isola, and the remaining three had been detectives in Calm's Point, Riverhead, and Majesta respectively. The Bureau of Criminal Identification was located at Headquarters on High Street, several floors above the police lab. But the men assigned to the artists' section of the bureau worked in a studio annex at 600 Jessup Street.

Their record was an impressive one. Working solely from verbal descriptions supplied by witnesses who were sometimes agitated and distraught, they had in the past year been responsible for twenty-eight positive identifications and arrests. So far this year, they had made sixty-eight drawings of described suspects, from which fourteen arrests had resulted. In each case, the apprehended suspect bore a remarkable resemblance to the sketch made from his description. Detective Haldeman had talked to all of the people who had been present when Vollner's office was invaded Wednesday afternoon, listening to descriptions of face, hair, eyes, nose, mouth from Miles Vollner, Cindy Forrest, Grace Di Santo, and Ronnie Fairchild, the patrolman who was still hospitalized. The composite drawing he made took three and a half hours to complete. It was delivered to Kling in a manilla envelope that Monday morning. The drawing itself was protected by a celluloid sleeve into which it had been inserted. There was no note with the drawing, and the drawing was unsigned. Kling took it out of the envelope and studied it.

Andy Parker, who was strolling past Kling's desk on his way to the toilet, stopped and looked at the drawing.

'Who's that?'

'Suspect,' Kling said.

'No kidding? I thought maybe it was Cary Grant.'

'You know what you ought to do, Andy?' Kling asked, not looking up at him as he put the drawing back into the manilla envelope.

'What?' Parker asked.

'You should join the police force. I understand they're looking for comical cops.'

'Ha!' Parker said, and went out to the toilet where he hoped to occupy himself for the next half hour with a copy of *Life* Magazine.

Forty miles away from the precinct that Monday morning, twenty-five miles outside the city limits, Detectives Meyer and Carella drove through the autumn countryside on their way to Larksview and the home of Mrs Stan Gifford.

They had spent all day Saturday and part of Sunday questioning a goodly percentage of the 212 people who were present in the studio loft that night. They did not consider any of them possible suspects in a murder case. As a matter of fact, they were trying hard to find something substantial upon which to hang a verdict of suicide. Their line of questioning followed a single simple direction: They wanted to know whether anyone connected with the show had, at any time before or during the show, seen Stan Gifford put anything into his mouth. The answers did nothing to substantiate a theory of suicide. Most of the people connected with the show were too busy to notice who was putting what into his mouth; some of the staff hadn't come across Gifford at all during the day; and those who *had* spent any time with him had definitely not seen anything go into his mouth. A chat with David Krantz revealed that Gifford was in the habit of forestalling dinner until after the show each Wednesday, eating a heavy lunch to carry him through the day. This completely destroyed the theory that perhaps Gifford had eaten again after meeting his wife. But it provided a new possibility for speculation, and it was this possibility that took Meyer and Carella to Larksview once more.

Meyer was miserable. His nose was stuffed, his throat was sore, his eyes were puffed and swollen. He had been taking a commercial cold preparation over the weekend, but it hadn't helped him at all. He kept blowing his nose, and then talking through it, and then blowing it again. He made a thoroughly delightful partner and companion.

Happily, the reporters and photographers had forsaken the Gifford house now that the story had been pushed off the front page and onto the pages reserved for armchair detection. Meyer and Carella drove to the small parking area, walked to the front door, and once again pulled the brass knob set into the jamb. The housekeeper opened the door, peeked out cautiously, and then said, 'Oh, it's you again.'

'Is Mrs Gifford home?' Carella asked.

'I'll see,' she said, and closed the door in their faces. They waited on the front stoop. The woods surrounding the house rattled their autumn colours with each fresh gust of wind. In a few moments, the housekeeper returned.

'Mrs Gifford is having coffee in the dining room,' she said. 'You may join her, if you wish.'

'Thank you,' Carella said, and they followed her into the house. A huge winding staircase started just inside the entrance hall, thickly carpeted, swinging to the upper story of the house. French doors opened onto the living room, and through that and beyond it was a small dining room with a bay window overlooking the back yard. Melanie Gifford sat alone at the table, wearing a quilted robe over a long pink nylon nightgown, the laced edges of the gown showing where the robe ended. Her blonde hair was uncombed, and hung loosely about her face. As before, she wore no makeup, but she seemed more rested now, and infinitely more at ease.

'I was just having breakfast,' she said. 'I'm afraid I'm a late sleeper. Won't you have something?'

Meyer took the chair opposite her, and Carella sat beside her at the table. She poured coffee for both men and then offered them the English muffins and marmalade, which they declined.

'Mrs Gifford,' Carella said, 'when we were here last time, you said something about your husband's physician, Carl Nelson.'

'Yes,' Melanie said. 'Do you take sugar?'

'Thank you.' Carella spooned a teaspoonful into his coffee, and then passed the sugar bowl to Meyer. 'You said you thought he'd murdered –'

'Cream?'

'Thank you – your husband. Now what made you say that, Mrs Gifford?'

'I believed it.'

'Do you still believe it?'

'No.'

'Why not?'

'Because I see now that it would have been impossible. I didn't know the nature of the poison at the time.'

'Its speed, do you mean?'

'Yes. Its speed.'

'And you mean it would have been impossible because Dr Nelson was at home during the show, and not at the studio, is that right?'

'Yes.'

'But what made you suspect him in the first place?'

'I tried to think of who could have had access to poison, and I thought of Carl.'

'So did we,' Carella said.

'I imagine you would have,' Melanie answered. 'These muffins are very good. Won't you have some?'

'No, thank you. But even if he did have access, Mrs Gifford, why would he have wanted to kill your husband?'

'I have no idea.'

'Didn't the two men get along?'

'You know doctors,' Melanie said. 'They all have God complexes.' She paused, and then added, 'In any universe, there can only be one God.'

'And in Stan Gifford's universe, *he* was God.'

Melanie sipped at her coffee and said, 'If an actor hasn't got his ego, then he hasn't got anything.'

'Are you saying the two egos came into conflict occasionally, Mrs Gifford?'

'Yes.'

'But not in any serious way, surely.'

'I don't know what men consider serious. I know that Stan and Carl occasionally argued. So when Stan was killed, as I told you, I tried to figure out who could have got his hands on any poison, and I thought of Carl.'

'This was before you knew the poison was strophanthin.'

'Yes. Once I found out what the poison was, and knowing Carl was home that night, I realized –'

'But if you didn't know the poison was strophanthin, then it could have been anything, any poison, isn't that right?'

'Yes. But –'

'And you also must have known that a great many poisons can be purchased in drugstores, usually in compounds of one sort or another. Like arsenic or cyanide . . .'

'Yes, I suppose I knew that.'

'But you still automatically assumed Dr Nelson had killed your husband.'

'I was in shock at the time. I didn't know what to think.'

'I see,' Carella said. He picked up his cup and took a long deliberate swallow. 'Mrs Gifford, you said your husband took a vitamin capsule after lunch last Wednesday.'

'That's right.'

'Did he have that capsule with him, or did you bring it to him when you went into the city?'

'He had it with him.'

'Was he in the habit of taking vitamin capsules with him?'

'Yes,' Melanie said. 'He was supposed to take one after every meal. Stan was a very conscientious man. When he knew he was going into the city, he carried the vitamins with him, in a small pillbox.'

'Did he take only one capsule to the city last Wednesday? Or *two*?'

'One,' Melanie said.

'How do you know?'

'Because there were two on the breakfast table that morning. He swallowed one with his orange juice, and he put the other in the pillbox, and then put it in his pocket.'

'And you saw him take that second capsule after lunch?'

'Yes. He took it out of the pillbox and put it on the table the moment we were seated. That's what he usually did – so he wouldn't forget to take it.'

'And to your knowledge, he did not have any other capsules with him. That was the only capsule he took after leaving this house last Wednesday.'

'That's right.'

'Who put those capsules on the breakfast table, Mrs Gifford?'

'My housekeeper.' Melanie looked suddenly annoyed. 'I'm not sure I understand all this,' she said. 'If he took the capsule at lunch, I don't see how it could possibly –'

'We're only trying to find out for sure whether or not there were only two capsules, Mrs Gifford.'

'I just told you.'

'We'd like to be sure. We know the capsule he took at lunch couldn't possibly have killed him. But if there was a third capsule –'

'There were only two,' Melanie said. 'He knew he was coming home for dinner after the show, the way he did every Wednesday night. There was no need for him to carry more than –'

'More than the one he took at lunch.'

'Yes.'

'Mrs Gifford, do you know whether or not your husband had any insurance on his life?'

'Yes, of course he did.'

'Would you know in what amount?'

'A hundred thousand dollars.'

'And the company?'

'Municipal Life.'

'Who's the beneficiary, Mrs Gifford?'

'I am,' Melanie replied.

'I see,' Carella said.

There was brief silence. Melanie put down her coffee cup. Her eyes met Carella's levelly. Quietly, she said, 'I'm sure you didn't mean to suggest, Detective Carella –'

'Mrs Gifford, this is all routine –'

'– that I might have had anything to do with the death of –'

'– questioning. I don't know *who* had anything to do with your husband's death.'

'*I* didn't.'

'I hope not.'

'Because, you see, Detective Carella, a hundred thousand dollars in insurance money would hardly come anywhere near the kind of income my husband earned as a performer. I'm sure you know that he recently signed a two-million dollar contract with the network. And I can *assure* you he's always been more than generous to me. Or perhaps you'd like to come upstairs and take a look at the furs in my closet or the jewels on my dresser.'

'I don't think that'll be necessary, Mrs Gifford.'

'I'm sure it won't. But you might also like to consider the fact that Stan's insurance policy carried the usual suicide clause.'

'I'm not sure I follow you, Mrs Gifford.'

'I'm saying, Detective Carella, that unless you can find a murderer – unless you can *prove* there was foul play involved in my husband's death – his insurance company will conclude he was a suicide. In which case, I'll receive only the premiums already paid in, and not a penny more.'

'I see.'

'Yes, I hope you do.'

'Would you know whether or not your husband left a will, Mrs Gifford?' Meyer asked.

'Yes, he did.'

'Are you also a beneficiary in his will?'

'I don't know.'

'You never discussed it with him?'

'Never. I know there's a will, but I don't know what its terms are.'

'Who *would* know, Mrs Gifford?'

'His lawyer, I imagine.'

'And the lawyer's name?'

'Salvatore Di Palma.'

'In the city?'

'Yes.'

'You won't mind if we call him?'

'Why should I?' Melanie paused again, and again stared at Carella. 'I don't mind telling you,' she said, 'that you're beginning to give me a severe pain in the ass.'

'I'm sorry.'

'Does part of your "routine questioning" involve badgering a man's widow?'

'I'm sorry, Mrs Gifford,' Carella said. 'We're only trying to investigate every possibility.'

'Then how about investigating the possibility that I led a full and happy life with Stan? When we met, I was working in summer stock in Pennsylvania, earning sixty dollars a week. I've had everything I ever wanted from the moment we were married, but I'd gladly give all of it – the furs, the jewels, the house, even the clothes on my back – if that'd bring Stan to life again.'

'We're only –'

'Yes, you're only investigating every possibility, I know. Be human,' she said. 'You're dealing with people, not ciphers.'

The detectives were silent. Melanie sighed.

'Did you still want to see my housekeeper?'

'Please,' Meyer said.

Melanie lifted the small bell near her right hand, and gave it a rapid shake. The housekeeper, as though alert and waiting for the tiny sound, came into the dining room immediately.

'These gentlemen would like to ask you some questions, Maureen,' Melanie said. 'If you don't mind, gentlemen, I'll leave you alone. I'm late for an appointment now, and I'd like to get dressed.'

'Thank you for your time, Mrs Gifford,' Carella said.

'Not at all,' Melanie said, and walked out of the room.

Maureen stood by the table, uncertainly picking at her apron. Meyer glanced at Carella, who nodded. Meyer cleared his throat, and said, 'Maureen, on the day Mr Gifford died, did you set the breakfast table for him?'

'For him and for Mrs Gifford, yes, sir.'

'Do you always set the table?'

'Except on Thursdays and every other Sunday, which are my days off. Yes, sir, I always set the table.'

'Did you put Mr Gifford's vitamin capsules on the table that morning?' Meyer asked.

'Yes, sir. Right alongside his plate, same as usual.'

'How many vitamin capsules?'

'Two.'

'Not three?'

'I said two,' Maureen said.

'Was anyone in the room when you put the capsules on the table?'

'No, sir.'

'Who came down to breakfast first? Mr Gifford or Mrs Gifford?'

'Mrs Gifford came in just as I was leaving.'

'And then Mr Gifford?'

'Yes. I heard him come down about five minutes later.'

'Do these vitamin capsules come in a jar?'

'A small bottle, sir.'

'Could we see that bottle, please?'

'I keep it in the kitchen,' Maureen paused. 'You'll have to wait while I get it.'

She went out of the room. Carella waited until he could no longer hear her footfalls, and then asked, 'What are you thinking?'

'I don't know. But if Melanie Gifford was alone in the room with those two capsules, she could have switched one of them, no?'

'The one he was taking to lunch, huh?'

'Yeah.'

'Only one thing wrong with that theory,' Carella said.

'Yeah, I know. He had lunch seven hours before he collapsed.' Meyer sighed and shook his head. 'We're *still* stuck with that lousy six minutes. It's driving me nuts.'

'Besides, it doesn't look as though Melanie had any reason to do in her own dear Godlike husband.'

'Yeah,' Meyer said. 'It's just I get the feeling she's too cooperative, you know? Her and the good doctor both. So very damn helpful. He right away diagnoses poison and insists we do an autopsy. She immediately points to him as a suspect, then changes her mind when she finds out about the poison. And both of them conveniently away from the studio on the night Gifford died.' Meyer nodded his head, a thoughtful expression on his face. 'Maybe that six minutes is *supposed* to drive us nuts.'

'How do you mean?'

'Maybe we were *supposed* to find out which poison killed him. I mean, we'd naturally do an autopsy anyway, right? And we'd find out it was strophanthin, and we'd also find out how fast strophanthin works.'

'Yeah, go ahead.'

'So we'd automatically rule out anybody who wasn't near Gifford before he died.'

'That's almost the entire city, Meyer.'

'No, you know what I mean. We'd rule out Krantz, who says he was in the sponsor's booth, and we'd rule out Melanie, who was here, and Nelson, who was at his own house.'

'That still needs checking,' Carella said.

'Why? Krantz said that was where he reached him after Gifford collapsed.'

'That doesn't mean Nelson was there all night. I want to ask him about that. In fact, I'd like to stop at his office as soon as we get back to the city.'

'Okay, but do you get my point?'

'I think so. Given a dead end to work with, knowing how much poison Gifford had swallowed, and knowing how fast it worked, we'd come to the only logical conclusion: suicide. Is that what you mean?'

'Right,' Meyer said.

'Only one thing wrong with your theory, friend.'

'Yeah, what?'

'The facts. It *was* strophanthin. It *does* work instantly. You can speculate all you want, but the facts remain the same.'

'Facts, facts,' Meyer said. 'All I know –'

'Facts,' Carella insisted.

'Suppose Melanie did switch that lunch capsule? We still haven't checked Gifford's will. She may be in it for a healthy chunk.'

'All right, suppose she did. He'd have dropped dead on his way to the studio.'

'Or suppose Krantz got to him *before* he went up to the sponsor's booth?'

'Then Gifford would have shown symptoms of poisoning before the show even went on the air.'

'Arrrggh, facts,' Meyer said, and Maureen came back into the room.

'I asked Mrs Gifford if it was all right,' she said. She handed the bottle of vitamin capsules to Carella. 'You can do whatever you like with them.'

'We'd like to take them with us, if that's all right.'

'Mrs Gifford said whatever you like.'

'We'll give you a receipt,' Meyer said. He looked at the bottle of vitamins in Carella's hand. The capsules were jammed into the bottle, each one opaque, and coloured purple and black. Meyer stared at them sourly. 'You're looking for a third capsule,' he said to Carella. 'There're a *hundred* of them in that bottle.'

He blew his nose then, and began making out a receipt for the vitamins.

Chapter Eight

Dr Carl Nelson's office was on Hall Avenue in a white apartment building with a green awning that stretched to the kerb. Carella and Meyer got there at one o'clock, took the elevator up to the fifth floor, and then announced themselves to a brunette nurse, who said the doctor had a patient with him at the moment, but she'd tell him they were here, wouldn't they please have a seat?

They had a seat.

In ten minutes' time, an elderly lady with a bandage over one eye came out of the doctor's private office. She smiled at the two detectives, either soliciting sympathy for her wound, or offering sympathy for whatever had brought them to see a doctor. Carl Nelson came out of his office with his hand extended.

'How are you?' he said. 'Come in, come in. Any news?'

'Well, not really, doctor,' Carella said. 'We simply wanted to ask you a few questions.'

'Happy to help in any way I can,' Nelson said. He turned to his nurse and asked, 'When's my next appointment, Rhoda?'

'Two o'clock, doctor.'

'No calls except emergencies until then, please,' Nelson said, and he led the detectives inside. He sat immediately at his desk, offered Carella and Meyer chairs, and then folded his hands before him in a professionally relaxed, patiently expectant way.

'Are you a general practitioner, Dr Nelson?' Meyer asked.

'Yes, I am.' Nelson smiled. 'That's a nasty cold you've got there, Detective Meyer. I hope you're taking something for it.'

'I'm taking *everything* for it,' Meyer said.

'There're a lot of viruses going around,' Nelson said.

'Yes,' Meyer agreed.

'Dr Nelson,' Carella said, 'I wonder if you'd mind telling us a little about yourself.'

'Not at all,' Nelson said. 'What would you like to know?'

'Well, whatever you feel is pertinent.'

'About what? My life? My work? My aspirations?'

'Any of it, or all of it,' Carella said pleasantly.

Nelson smiled. 'Well. . . .' He paused, thinking. 'I'm forty-three years old, a native of this city, attended Haworth University here. I was graduated with a B.S. in January of 1944, and got drafted just in time for the assault on Cassino.'

'How old were you at the time, Dr Nelson?'

'Twenty-two.'

'Was this Army?'

'Yes. The Medical Corps.'

'Were you an officer or an enlisted man?'

'I was a corporal. I was attached to a field hospital in Castelforte. Are you familiar with the country?'

'Vaguely,' Carella said.

'There was some fierce fighting,' Nelson said briefly. He sighed, dismissing the entire subject. 'I was discharged in May of 1946. I began medical school that fall.'

'What school was that, Dr Nelson?'

'Georgetown University. In Washington, D.C.'

'And then you came back here to begin practice, is that it?'

'Yes. I opened my own office in 1952.'

'This same office?'

'No, my first office was uptown. In Riverhead.'

'How long have you been at this location, doctor?'

'Since 1961.'

'Are you married?'

'No.'

'Have you ever been married?'

'Yes. I was divorced seven years ago.'

'Is your former wife alive?'

'Yes.'

'Living in this city?'

'No. She lives in San Diego with her new husband. He's an architect there.'

'Do you have any children?'

'No.'

'You said something about your aspirations, doctor. I wonder ...'

'Oh.' Nelson smiled. 'I hope to start a small rest home one day. For elderly people.'

'Where?'

'Most likely in Riverhead, where I began practice.'

'Now, Dr Nelson,' Carella said, 'it's our understanding that you were at home last Wednesday night when Mr Krantz called to tell you what had happened. Is that correct?'

'Yes, that's correct.'

'Were you home all night, Dr Nelson?'

'Yes, I went home directly from here.'

'And what time did you leave here?'

'My usual evening hours are from five o'clock to eight o'clock. I left here last Wednesday night at about ten minutes past eight.'

'Can anyone verify that?'

'Yes, Rhoda left with me. Miss Barnaby, my nurse; you just met her. We both left at the same time. You can ask her if you like.'

'Where did you go when you left the office?'

'Home. I already said I went directly home.'

'Where do you live, Dr Nelson?'

'On South Fourteenth.'

'South Fourteenth, mmm, so it should have taken you, oh, fifteen minutes at the most to get from here to your house, is that right?'

'That's right. I got home at about eight-thirty.'

'Was anyone there?'

'Just my housekeeper. Mrs Irene Janlewski. She was preparing my dinner when the call came from the studio. Actually, I didn't need the call.'

'Why not?'

'I'd seen Stan collapse.'

'What do you mean, Dr Nelson?'

'I was watching the show. I turned it on the moment I got home.'

'At about eight-thirty, is that right?'

'Yes, that's about when I got home.'

'What was happening when you turned on the show?' Meyer asked.

'Happening?'

'Yes, on the screen,' Meyer said. He had taken out his black notebook and a pencil and seemed to be taking notes as Nelson spoke. Actually, he was studying the page opposite the one on which he was writing. On that page, in his own hand, was the information George Cooper had given him last Wednesday night at the studio. The folk singers had gone off at eight-thirty-seven, and Gifford had come on immediately afterwards, staying on camera with his Hollywood guest for two minutes and twelve seconds. When the guest went off to change . . .

'Stan was doing a commercial when I turned the set on,' Nelson said. 'A coffee commercial.'

'That would have been at about eight-forty,' Meyer said.

'Yes, I suppose so.'

'Actually, it would have been exactly eight-thirty-nine and twelve seconds,' Meyer said, just to be ornery.

'What?' Nelson asked.

'Which means you didn't turn the set on the moment you got into the house. Not if you got home at eight-thirty.'

'Well, I suppose I talked with Mrs Janlewski for a few minutes, asked if there were any calls, settled a few household problems, you know.'

'Yes,' Meyer said. 'The important thing, in any case, is that you were watching Gifford when he got sick.'

'Yes, I was.'

'Which was at exactly eight-forty-four and seventeen seconds,' Meyer said, feeling a wild sense of giddy power.

'Yes,' Nelson agreed. 'I suppose so.'

'What did you think when you saw him collapse?'

'I didn't know what to think. I rushed to the closet for my hat and coat, and was starting out when the telephone rang.'

'Who was it?'

'David Krantz.'

'And he told you that Gifford was sick, is that right?'

'Right.'

'Which you already knew.'

'Yes, I already knew it.'

'But when you saw Gifford collapse, you didn't know *what* was wrong with him.'

'No, I didn't.'

'Later on, Dr Nelson, when I spoke to you at the studio, you seemed certain he'd been poisoned.'

'That's true. But that –'

'It was you, in fact, who suggested that we have an autopsy performed.'

'That's correct. When I got to the studio, the symptoms were unmistakable. A first-year med student could have diagnosed acute poisoning.'

'You didn't know what *kind* of poison, of course.'

'How could I?'

'Dr Nelson,' Carella said, 'did you ever argue with Stan Gifford?'

'Yes. All friends argue every now and then. It's only acquaintances who never have any differences of opinion.'

'What did you argue about?'

'I'm sure I don't remember. Everything. Stan was an alert and well-informed person, with a great many opinions on most things that would concern a thinking man.'

'I see. And so you argued about them.'

'We *discussed* them, might be a better way of putting it.'

'You discussed a wide variety of things, is that right?'

'Yes.'

'But you did not *argue* about these things?'

'Yes, we argued, too.'

'About matters of general concern.'

'Yes.'

'Never about anything specific. Never about anything you might consider personal.'

'We argued about personal matters, yes.'

'Like what?'

'Well, I can't remember any off-hand. But I know we argued about personal matters from time to time.'

'Try to remember, Dr Nelson,' Carella said.

'Has Melanie told you?' Nelson asked suddenly. 'Is that what this is about?'

'Told us what, Dr Nelson?'

'Are you looking for confirmation, is that it? I can assure you the entire incident was idiotic. Stan was drunk, otherwise he wouldn't have lost his temper that way.'

'Tell us about it,' Meyer said calmly.

'There'd been a party at his house, and I was dancing with Melanie. Stan had been drinking heavily, and he ... well, he behaved somewhat ridiculously.'

'How did he behave?'

'He accused me of trying to steal his wife, and he ... he tried to strike me.'

'What did *you* do, Dr Nelson?'

'I defended myself, naturally.'

'How? Did you hit him back?'

'No. I simply held up my hands – to ward off his blows, you understand. He was very drunk, really incapable of inflicting any harm.'

'When *was* this party, Dr Nelson?'

'Just after Labor Day. In fact, a week before the show went on the air again. After the summer break, you know. It was a sort of celebration.'

'And Stan Gifford thought you were trying to steal his wife, is that right?'

'Yes.'

'Merely because you were dancing with her.'

'Yes.'

'Had you been dancing with her a lot?'

'No. I think that was the second time all evening.'

'Then his attack was really unfounded, wasn't it?'

'He was drunk.'

'And that's why you feel he attacked you, because he was drunk?'

'And because David Krantz provoked him.'

'David Krantz? Was he at the party, too?'

'Yes, most of the people involved with the show were there.'

'I see. How did Mr Krantz provoke him?'

'Oh, you know the stupid jokes some people make.'

'No, what sort of jokes, Dr Nelson?'

'About our dancing together, you know. David Krantz is a barbarian. It's my considered opinion that he's oversexed and attributes evil thoughts to everyone else in the world, as compensation.'

'I see. Then you feel it was Krantz who gave Gifford the idea that you were trying to steal his wife?'

'Yes.'

'Why would he do that?'

'He hated Stan. He hates all actors, for that matter. He calls them *cattle*, that's supposed to *endear* them to him, you know.'

'How did Gifford feel about *him*?'

'I think the feelings were mutual.'

'Gifford hated Krantz, too, is that what you mean?'

'Yes.'

'Then why did he take Krantz seriously that night?'

'What do you mean?'

'At the party. When Krantz said you were trying to steal Mrs Gifford.'

'Oh. I don't know. He was drunk. I guess a man will listen to anyone when he's drunk.'

'Um-huh,' Carella said. He was silent for a moment. Then he asked, 'But in spite of this incident, you remained his personal physician, is that right?'

'Oh, of *course*. Stan apologized to me the very next day.'

'And you continued to be friends?'

'Yes, certainly. I don't even know why Melanie brought this up. I don't see what bearing –'

'She didn't,' Meyer said.

'Oh. Well, who told you about it then? Was it Krantz? I wouldn't put it past him. He's a goddamn troublemaker.'

'No one told us, actually,' Meyer said. 'This is the first we've heard of the incident.'

'Oh,' Nelson paused. 'Well, it doesn't matter. I'd rather you heard it from me than from someone else who was at the party.'

'That's very sensible of you, Dr Nelson. You're being most cooperative.' Carella paused. 'If it's all right with you, we'll simply verify with your nurse that you left here with her at about ten minutes past eight last Wednesday night. And we'll –'

'Yes, you certainly may verify it with her.'

'And we'd also like to call your housekeeper – with your permission, of course – to verify that you arrive home at about eight-thirty, as you say, and remained there until after Krantz's phone call.'

'Certainly. My nurse will give you my home number.'

'Thank you, Dr Nelson. You've been very cooperative,' Carella said, and they went out to talk to Miss Barnaby, who told them the doctor had arrived at the office at four-forty-five last Wednesday afternoon and had not left until office hours were over, at ten minutes past eight. She was absolutely certain about this because she and the doctor had left at the same time. She gave them the doctor's home number so that they could speak to Mrs Janlewski, the housekeeper, and they thanked her politely and went downstairs and then out of the building.

'He's very cooperative,' Carella said.

'Yes, he's very very cooperative,' Meyer agreed.

'Let's put a tail on him,' Carella said.

'I've got a better idea,' Meyer said. 'Let's put a tail on him and Krantz *both.*'

'Good idea.'

'You agree?'

'Sure.'

'You think one them did it?'

'I think you did it,' Carella said, and suddenly slipped his handcuffs from his belt and snapped one of them onto Meyer's wrist. 'Come along now, no tricks,' he said.

'You know what a guy needs like a hole in the head when he's got a bad cold?' Meyer said.

'What?'

'A partner who plays jokes.'

'I'm not playing jokes, mister,' Carella said, his eyes narrowing. 'I happen to know that Stan Gifford took out a seven-million-dollar insurance policy on his life, payable to your wife Sarah as beneficiary in the event that he died on any Wednesday between eight-thirty and nine thirty p.m. during the month of October. I further happen to know –'

'Oh, boy,' Meyer said, 'start up with *goyim.*'

Back at the squadroom, they made two telephone calls.

The first was to the Municipal Life, where they learned that Stanley Gifford's insurance policy had been written only a year and a half ago, and contained a clause that read, 'Death within two years from the date of issue of this policy, from suicide while sane or insane, shall limit the company's liability hereunder to the amount of the premiums actually paid hereon.'

The second was to Mr Salvatore Di Palma, Gifford's lawyer, who promptly confirmed that Melanie Gifford had not been familiar with the terms of her husband's will.

'Why do you want to know?' he asked.

'We're investigating his murder,' Carella said.

'There's nothing in Stan's will that would have caused Melanie to even *consider* murder,' Di Palma said.

'Why do you say that?'

'Because I know what's in the will.'

'Can you tell us?'

'I would not regard it as appropriate for me to reveal the contents of the will to any person until it has first been read to Mr Gifford's widow.'

'We're investigating a murder,' Carella said.

'Look, take my word for it,' Di Palma said. 'There's nothing here to indicate –'

'You mean he doesn't leave her anything?'

'Did I say that?'

'No, *I* said it,' Carella said. 'Does he, or doesn't he?'

'You're twisting my arm,' Di Palma said, and then chuckled. He liked talking to Italians. They were the only civilized people in the world.

'Come on,' Carella said, 'help a working man.'

'Okay, but you didn't hear it from me,' Di Palma said, still chuckling. 'Stan came in early last month, asked me to revise his will.'

'Why?'

'He didn't say. The will now leaves his house and his personal property to Mrs Adelaide Garfein, that's his mother, she's a widow in Poughkeepsie, New York.'

'Go ahead.'

'It leaves one-third of the remainder of his estate to the American Guild of Variety Artists, one-third to the Academy of Television Arts and Sciences, and one-third to the Damon Runyon Cancer Fund.'

'And Melanie?'

'Zero,' Di Palma said. 'That's what the change was all about. He cut her out of it completely.'

'Thank you very much.'

'For what?' Di Palma said, and chuckled again. 'I didn't tell you anything, did I?'

'You didn't say a word,' Carella said. 'Thanks again.'

'Don't mention it,' Di Palma said, and hung up.

'So?' Meyer asked.

'He left her nothing,' Carella said. 'Changed the will early last month.'

'Nothing?'

'Nothing.' Carella paused. 'That's pretty funny, don't you think? I mean, here's this sweet woman who had led a full and happy life with her husband, and who wants to take us upstairs to show us all her furs and jewellery and such – and just last month he cuts her out of his will. That's pretty funny, I think.'

'Yeah, especially since just last month he also took a sock at our doctor friend and accused him of trying to steal his wife.'

'Yeah, that's a very funny coincidence,' Carella said.

'Maybe he really *believed* Nelson was trying to steal his wife.'

'Maybe so.'

'Mmm,' Meyer said. He thought for a moment and then said, 'But she still looks clean, Steve. She doesn't get a cent either way.'

'Unless we find a murderer, in which case it's no longer suicide, in which case she collects a hundred G's from the insurance company.'

'Yeah, but that *still* leaves her out. Because if she's the one who did it, she wouldn't plan it to look like a *suicide*, would she?'

'What do you mean?'

'This thing looks exactly like a suicide. Listen, for all I know, it *is* one.'

'So?'

'So if you're hoping to get a hundred thousand dollars on an insurance policy that has a suicide clause, you're sure as hell not going to plan a murder that looks like a suicide, right?'

'Right.'

'So?' Meyer said.

'So Melanie Gifford looks clean.'

'Yeah.'

'Guess what I found out?' Carella said.

'What?'

'Gifford's real name is Garfein.'

'Yeah?'

'Yeah.'

'So what? *My* real name is Rock Hudson.'

Chapter Nine

Considering the number of *human* killings that took place daily in the five separate sections of the city, Kling was surprised to discover that the city could boast of only one slaughterhouse. Apparently the guiding fathers and the Butchers Union (who gave him the information) were averse to killing animals within the city limits. The single slaughtering-house was on Boswell Avenue in Calm's Point, and it specialized in the slaughtering of lambs. Most of the city's killing, as Grossman had surmised, was done in four separate slaughterhouses across the river, in the next state. Since Calm's Point was closest, Kling hit the one on Boswell Avenue first. He was armed with the list he had compiled at the lab earlier that day, together with the drawing he had received from the BCI. He didn't know exactly what he was looking for, or exactly what he hoped to discover. He had never been inside a slaughterhouse before.

After visiting the one in Calm's Point, he never wanted to step inside another one as long as he lived. Unfortunately, there were four more to check across the river.

He was used to blood; a cop gets used to blood. He was used to the sight of human beings bleeding in a hundred different ways from a thousand different wounds, he was used to all that. He had been witness to sudden attacks with razor blades or knives, pistols or shotguns, had seen the body case torn or punctured, the blood beginning to flow or spurt. He had seen them dead and bleeding, and he had seen them alive and in the midst of attack – bleeding. But he had never seen an animal killed before, and the sight made him want to retch. He could barely concentrate on what the head butcher was telling him. The bleating of the lambs rang in his ears, the stench of blood filled the air. The head butcher looked at the drawing Kling extended, leaving a bloody thumbprint on the celluloid sleeve, and shook his head. Behind him the animals shrieked.

The air outside was cold, it drilled the nostrils. He sucked breath after breath into his lungs, deeply savouring each cleansing rush. He did not want to go across that river, but he went. Forsaking lunch, because he knew he would not be able to keep it down, he hit two more slaughterhouses in succession and – finding nothing – grimly prepared to visit the next two on his list.

There is an intuitive feel to detection, and the closest thing to sudden truth – outside of fiction – is the dawning of awareness of a cop when he is about to make a fresh discovery. The moment Kling drove onto the dock he knew he would hit pay dirt. The knowledge was sudden and fierce. He stepped out of the police sedan with a faint vague smile on his face, looking up at the huge white sign across the top of the building, facing the river, PURLEY BROTHERS, INC. He stood in the centre of the open dock, an area the size of a baseball diamond, and took his time surveying the location, while all the while the rising knowledge clamoured within him, this is it, this is it, this is it.

One side of the dock was open to the waterfront. Beyond the two marine gasoline pumps at the water's edge, Kling could see across the river to where the towers of the city were silhoutted against the grey October sky. His eye lingered on the near distance for a moment, and then he swung his head to the right, where a half-dozen fishing boats were tied up, fishermen dumping their nets and their baskets, leaping onto the dock and then sitting with their booted legs hanging over its edge while they scraped and cleaned their fish and transferred them to fresh baskets lined with newspapers. The grin on his face widened because he knew for certain now that this was pay dirt, that everything would fall into place here on this dock.

He turned his attention back to the slaughterhouse that formed almost one complete side of the rectangular dock area. Gulls shrieked in the air over the river where waste material poured from an open pipe. Railroad tracks fed the rear of the brick building, a siding that ran from the yards some five hundred feet back from the dock. He walked to the tracks and began following them to the building.

They led directly to the animal pens, empty now, alongside of which were the metal entrance doors to the slaughterhouse. He knew what he would find on the floor inside; he had seen the floors of three such places already.

The manager was a man named Joe Brady, and he was more than delighted to help Kling. He took him into a small, glass-partitioned office overlooking the killing floor (Kling sat with his back to the glass) and then accepted the drawing Kling handed to him, and pondered it for several moments, and then asked, 'What is he, a nigger?'

'No,' Kling said. 'He's a white man.'

'You said he attacked a girl, didn't you?'

'Yes, that's right.'

'And he ain't a nigger?' Brady shook his head.

'You can see from the drawing that he's white,' Kling said. An annoyed tone had crept into his voice. Brady did not seem to notice.

'Well, it's hard to tell from a drawing,' he said. 'I mean, the way the shading is done here, look, right here, you see what I mean? That could be a nigger.'

'Mr Brady,' Kling said flatly, 'I do not like that word.'

'What word?' Brady asked.

'Nigger.'

'Oh, come on,' Brady said, 'don't get on your high horse. We got a half a dozen niggers working here, they're all nice guys, what the hell's the matter with you?'

'The word offends me,' Kling said. 'Cut it out.'

Brady abruptly handed back the drawing. 'I've never seen this guy in my life,' he said. 'If you're finished here, I got to get back to work.'

'He doesn't work here?'

'No.'

'Are all of your employees full-time men?'

'All of them.'

'No part-time workers, maybe somebody who worked here for just a few days –'

'I know everybody who works here,' Brady said. 'That guy don't work here.'

'Is he someone who might possibly make deliveries here?'

'What kind of deliveries?'

'I don't know. Maybe –'

'The only thing we get delivered here is animals.'

'I'm sure you get other things delivered here, Mr Brady.'

'Nothing,' Brady said, and he rose from behind his desk. 'I got to get back to work.'

'Sit down, Mr Brady,' Kling said. His voice was harsh.

Surprised, Brady looked at him with rising eyebrows, ready to *really* take offence.

'I said sit down. Now go ahead.'

'Listen, mister –' Brady started.

'No, you listen, mister,' Kling said. 'I'm investigating an assault, and I have good reason to believe this man' – he tapped the drawing – 'was somewhere around here last Friday. Now, I don't like your goddamn attitude, Mr Brady, and if you'd like the inconvenience of answering some questions uptown at the station house instead of here in your nice cosy office overlooking all that killing out there, that's just fine with me. So why don't you get your hat and we'll just take a little ride, okay?'

'What for?' Brady said.

Kling did not answer. He sat grimly on the side of the desk opposite Brady and studied him coldly. Brady looked deep into his eyes.

'The only thing we get delivered here is animals,' he said again.

'Then how'd the paper cups get here?'

'Huh?'

'On the water cooler,' Kling said. 'Don't brush me off, Mr Brady, I'm goddamn good and sore.'

'Okay, okay,' Brady said.

'Okay! Who delivers stuff here?'

'A lot of people. But I know most of them, and I don't recognize that picture.'

'Are there any deliveries made that you would not ordinarily see?'

'What do you mean?'

'Does anything come into this building that you personally would not check?'

'I check anything that goes in or out. What do you mean? You mean *personal* things, too?'

'Personal things?'

'Things that have nothing to do with the business?'

'What'd you have in mind, Mr Brady?'

'Well, some of the guys order lunch from the diner across the dock. They got guys working there who bring the lunch over. Of coffee sometimes. I got my own little hot plate here in the office, so I don't have to send out for coffee, and also I bring my lunch from home. So I don't usually get to see the guys who make the deliveries.'

'Thank you,' Kling said, and rose.

Brady could not resist a parting shot. 'Anyway,' he said, 'most of them delivery guys are niggers.'

The air outside was clean, blowing fresh and wet off the river. Kling sighted the diner on the opposite end of the dock rectangle and quickly began walking towards it. It was set in a row of shops that slowly came into sharper focus as he moved closer to them. The two shops flanking the diner were occupied by a plumber and a glazier.

He took out his notebook and consulted it: suet, sawdust, blood, animal hair, fish scale, putty, wood splinter, metal filings, peanut, and gasoline. The only item he could not account for was the peanut, but maybe he'd find one in the diner. He was hopeful, in fact, of finding something more than just a peanut inside. He was hopeful of finding the man who had stopped at the slaughterhouse and stepped into the suet, blood and sawdust to which the animal hair had later clung when he crossed the pens outside. He was hopeful of finding the man who had walked along the creosoted railroad tracks, picking up a wood splinter in the sticky mess on his heel. He was hopeful of finding the man who had stopped on the edge of the dock where the fishermen were cleaning fish, and later walked through a small puddle of gasoline near the marine pumps, and then into the glazier's where he had acquired the dot of putty, and the plumber's where the copper filings had been added to the rest of the glopis. He was hopeful of finding the man who had beaten Cindy senseless, and the possibility seemed strong that this man made deliveries for the diner. Who else could wander so easily in and out of so many places? Kling unbuttoned his coat and reassuringly touched the butt of his revolver. Briskly, he walked to the door of the diner and entered.

The smell of greasy food assailed his nostrils. He had not eaten since breakfast, and the aroma combined with his slaughterhouse memories to bring on a feeling of nausea. He took a seat at the counter and ordered a cup of coffee, wanting to look over the personnel before he showed his drawing to anyone. There were two men behind the counter, one white and one coloured. Neither looked anything at all like the drawing. Behind a passthrough into the kitchen, he caught a glimpse of another white man as he put down a hamburger for pickup. He was not the suspect, either. Two Negro delivery boys in white jackets were sitting in a booth near the cash register, where a baldheaded white man sat poking his teeth with a matchstick. Kling assumed he had seen every employee in the place, with the possible exception of the short-order cook. He finished his coffee, went to the cash register, showed his shield to the baldheaded man and said, 'I'd like to talk to the manager, please.'

'I'm the manager and the owner both,' the baldheaded man said. 'Myron Krepps, how do you do?'

'I'm Detective Kling. I wonder if you would take a look at this picture and tell me if you know the man.'

'I'd be more than happy to,' Krepps said. 'Did he do something?'

'Yes,' Kling said.

'May I ask what it is he done?'

'Well, that's not important,' Kling said. He took the drawing from its envelope and handed it to Krepps. Krepps cocked his head to one side and studied it.

'Does he work here?' Kling asked.

'Nope,' Krepps said.

'Has he ever worked here?'

'Nope,' Krepps said.

'Have you ever seen him in the diner?'

Krepps paused. 'Is this something serious?'

'Yes,' Kling said, and then immediately asked, 'Why?' He could not have said what instinct provoked him into pressing the issue, unless it was the slight hesitation in Krepps's voice as he asked his question.

'How serious?' Krepps said.

'He beat up a young girl,' Kling said.

'Oh.'

'Is that serious enough?'

'That's pretty serious,' Krepps admitted.

'Serious enough for you to tell me who he is?'

'I thought it was a minor thing,' Krepps said. 'For minor things, who needs to be a good citizen?'

'Do you know this man, Mr Krepps?'

'Yes, I seen him around.'

'Have you seen him here in the diner?'

'Yes.'

'How often?'

'When he makes his rounds.'

'What do you mean?'

'He goes to all the places on the dock here.'

'Doing what?'

'I wouldn't get him in trouble for what he does,' Krepps said. 'As far as I'm concerned, it's no crime what he does. The city is unrealistic, that's all.'

'What is it that he does, Mr Krepps?'

'It's only that you say he beat up a young girl. That's serious. For that, I don't have to protect him.'

'Why does he come here, Mr Krepps? Why does he go to all the places on the dock?'

'He collects for the numbers,' Krepps said. 'Whoever wants to play the numbers, they give him their bets when he comes around.'

'What's his name?'

'They call him Cookie.'

'Cookie what?'

'I don't know his last name. Just Cookie. He comes to collect for the numbers.'

'Do you sell peanuts, Mr Krepps?'

'What? Peanuts?'

'Yes.'

'No, I don't sell peanuts. I carry some chocolates and some Life Savers and some chewing-gum, but no peanuts. Why? You like peanuts?'

'Is there any place on the dock where I can get some?'

'Not on the dock,' Krepps said.

'Where then?'

'Up the street. There's a bar. You can get peanuts there.'

'Thank you,' Kling said. 'You've been very helpful.'

'Good, I'm glad,' Krepps said. 'Now, please, would you mind paying for the coffee you drank?'

The front plate-glass window of the bar was painted a dull green. Bold white letters spelled out the name, BUDDY'S, arranged in a somewhat sloppy semicircle in the centre of the glass. Kling walked into the bar and directly to the phone booth some five feet beyond the single entrance door. He took a dime from his pocket, put it in the slot, and dialled his own home phone. While the phone rang unanswered on the other end, he simulated a lively conversation and simultaneously cased the bar. He did not recognize Cindy's attacker among any of the men sitting at the bar itself or in the booths. He hung up, fished his dime from the return chute, and walked up to the bar. The bartender looked at him curiously. He was either a college kid who had wandered into the waterfront area by accident – or else he was a cop. Kling settled the speculation at once by producing his shield.

'Detective Bert Kling,' he said. '87th Squad.'

The bartender studied the shield with an unwavering eye – he was used to bulls wandering in and out of his fine establishment – and then asked in a very polite, prep-school voice, 'What is it that you wish, Detective Kling?'

Kling did not answer at once. Instead, he scooped a handful of peanuts from the bowl on the bar top, put several into his mouth, and began chewing noisily. The proper thing to do, he supposed, was to inquire about some violation or other, garbage cans left outside, serving alcohol to minors, any damn thing to throw the bartender off base. The next thing to do was have the lieutenant assign another man or men to a stakeout of the bar, and simply pick up Cookie the next time he wandered in. That was the proper procedure, and Kling debated using it as he munched on his peanuts and stared silently at the bartender. The only trouble with picking up Cookie, of course, was that Cindy Forrest had been frightened half to death by him. How could you persuade a girl who'd been beaten senseless that it was in her own interest to identify the man who had attacked her? Kling kept munching his peanuts. The bartender kept watching him.

'Would you like a beer or something, Detective Kling?' he asked.

'You the owner?'

'I'm Buddy. You want a beer?'

'Uh-uh,' Kling said, chewing. 'On duty.'

'Well, was there something on your mind?' Buddy asked.

Kling nodded. He had made his decision. He began baiting his trap. 'Cookie been in today?'

'Cookie who?'

'You get a lot of people named Cookie in here?'

'I don't get *anybody* named Cookie in here,' Buddy said.

'Yeah, you do,' Kling said, and nodded. He scooped up another handful of peanuts. 'Don't you know him?'

'No.'

'That's a shame.' Kling began munching peanuts again. Buddy continued watching him. 'You're sure you don't know him?'

'Never heard of him.'

'That's too bad,' Kling said. 'We want him. We want him real bad.'

'What for?'

'He beat up a girl.'

'Yeah?'

'Yeah. Sent her to the hospital.'

'No kidding?'

'That's right,' Kling said. 'We've been searching the whole damn city for him.' He paused, and then took a wild gamble. 'Couldn't find him at the address we had in the Lousy File, but we happen to know he comes in here a lot.'

'How do you happen to know that?'

Kling smiled. 'We've got ways.'

'Mmm,' Buddy said noncommittally.

'We'll get him,' Kling said, and again he took a wild gamble. 'The girl identified his picture. Soon as we pick him up, goodbye, Charlie.'

'He's got a record, huh?'

'No,' Kling answered. 'No record.'

Buddy leaned forward slightly, ready to pounce. 'No record, huh?'

'Nope.'

'Then how'd you get his picture for the girl to identify?' Buddy said, and suddenly smiled.

'He's in the numbers racket,' Kling said. Idly, he popped another peanut into his mouth.

'So?'

'We've got a file on them.'

'On who?'

'On half the guys involved with numbers in this city.'

'Yeah?' Buddy said. His eyes had narrowed to a squint. It was plain to see that he did not trust Kling and was searching for a flaw in what he was being told.

'Sure,' Kling said. 'Addresses, pictures, even prints of some of them.'

'Yeah?' Buddy said again.

'Yeah.'

'What for?'

'Waiting for them to step out of line.'

'What do you mean?'

'I mean something bigger than numbers. Something we can lock them up for and throw away the key.'

'Oh.' Buddy nodded. He was convinced. This, he understood. The devious ways of cops, he understood. Kling tried to keep his face blank. He picked up another handful of peanuts.

'Cookie's finally stepped over the line. Once we get him, the girl takes another look, and bingo! First-degree assault.'

'He used a weapon?'

'Nope, his hands. But he tried to kill her nonetheless.'

Buddy shrugged.

'We'll get him, all right,' Kling said. 'We know who he is, so it's just a matter of time.'

'Yeah, well.' Buddy shrugged.

'All we have to do is find him, that's all. The rest is easy.'

'Yeah, well, sometimes finding a person can be extremely difficult,' Buddy said, reactivating his prep-school voice.

'I'm going to give you a word of warning, friend,' Kling said.

'What's that?'

'Keep your mouth shut about my being in here.'

'Who would I tell?'

'I don't know *who* you'd tell, but it better be *nobody*.'

'Why would I want to obstruct justice?' Buddy said, an offended look coming onto his face. 'If this Cookie person beat up a girl, why then good luck to you in finding him.'

'I appreciate your sentiments.'

'Sure.' Buddy paused, and glanced down at the peanut bowl. 'You going to eat *all* of those, or what?'

'Remember what I told you,' Kling said, hoping he wasn't overdoing it. 'Keep your mouth shut. If this leaks, and we trace it back to you ...'

'Nothing leaks around here but the beer tap,' Buddy answered, and moved away when someone at the other end of the bar signalled him. Kling sat a moment longer, and then rose, put another handful of peanuts into his mouth, and walked out.

On the pavement outside, he permitted himself a smile.

The item appered in both afternoon newspapers later that day.

It was small and hardly noticeable, buried as it was in a morass of print on the fourth page of both papers. Its headline was brief but eye-catching:

Witnesses to Beating Balk

Two witnesses to the brutal beating of Patrolman Ronald Fairchild last Wednesday, October 11, refused today to identify a photograph of the alleged attacker.

The picture was taken from a police file of "numbers racketeers" and had been shown previously to another victim of the same suspect. Miss Cynthia Forrest, recuperating from a bad beating at Elizabeth Rushmore Hospital here, positively identified the photograph and agreed to testify against the known suspect when he is apprehended.

Patrolman Critical

Detective-Lieutenant Peter

Byrnes, whose 87th Squad is investigating both assaults, commented today, "The apathy of these other witnesses is appalling. Patrolman Fairchild has been in coma and on the critical list at Buena Vista Hospital ever since he was admitted last week. If this man dies, we are dealing with a homicide here. Were it not for decent people like Miss Forrest, this city would never get to prosecute a criminal case."

Byrnes read the article in the privacy of his corner office, and then looked up at Kling, who was standing on the other side of his desk, beaming with the pride of authorship.

'Is Fairchild really on the critical list?' he asked.

'Nope,' Kling answered.

'Suppose our man checks?'

'Let him check. I've alerted Buena Vista.'

Byrnes nodded and looked at the article again. He put it aside then, and said, 'You made me sound like a jerk.'

Chapter Ten

Meyer and Carella were in the squadroom when Kling came out of the lieutenant's office.

'How you doing?' Carella asked him.

'So-so. We were just looking over the cheese.'

'What cheese?'

'Ah-ha,' Kling said mysteriously, and left.

'When did the lab say they'd call back on those vitamin capsules?' Carella asked.

'Sometime today,' Meyer answered.

'*When* today? It's past five already.'

'Don't jump on me,' Meyer said, and rose from his desk to walk to the water cooler. The telephone rang. Carella lifted it from the cradle.

'87th Squad, Carella,' he said.

'Steve, this is Bob O'Brien.'

'Yeah, what's up, Bob?'

'How long do you want me to stick with this Nelson guy?'

'Where are you?'

'Outside his house. I tailed him from his office to the hospital and then here.'

'What hospital?'

'General Presbyterian.'

'What was he doing there?'

'Search me. Most doctors are connected with hospitals, aren't they?'

'I guess so. When did he leave his office?'

'This afternoon, after visiting hours.'

'What time was that?'

'A little after two.'

'And he went directly to the hospital?'

'Yeah. He drives a little red MG.'

'What time did he leave the hospital?'

'About a half hour ago.'

'And went straight home?'

'Right. You think he's bedded down for the night?'

'I don't know. Call me in an hour or so, will you?'

'Right. Where'll you be? Home?'

'No, we'll be here a while yet.'

'Okay,' O'Brien said, and hung up. Meyer came back to his desk with a paper cup full of water. He propped it against his telephone, and then opened his desk drawer and took out a long cardboard strip of brightly coloured capsules.

'What's that?' Carella asked.

'For my cold,' Meyer said, and popped one of the capsules out of its cellophane wrapping. He put it into his mouth and washed it down with water. The phone rang again. Meyer picked it up.

'87th Squad, Meyer.'

'Meyer, this is Andy Parker. I'm still with Krantz, just checking in. He's in a cocktail lounge with a girl has boobs like watermelons.'

'What size, would you say?' Meyer asked.

'Huh? How the hell do I know?'

'Okay, just stick with him. Call in again later, will you?'

'I'm tired,' Parker said.

'So am I.'

'Yeah, but I'm *really* tired,' Parker said, and hung up.

Meyer replaced the phone on its cradle. 'Parker,' he said. 'Krantz is out drinking.'

'That's nice,' Carella said. 'You want to send out for some food?'

'With this cold, I'm not very hungry,' Meyer said.

'With this case, I'm not very hungry,' Carella said.

'There should be mathematics.'

'What do you mean?'

'To a case. There should be the laws of mathematics. I don't like cases that defy addition and subtraction.'

'What the hell was Bert grinning about when he left?'

'I don't know. He grins a lot,' Meyer said, and shrugged. 'I like two and two to make four. I like suicide to be suicide.'

'You think this is suicide?'

'No. That's what I mean. I don't like suicide to be murder. I like mathematics.'

'I failed geometry in high school,' Carella said.

'Yeah?'

'Yeah.'

'Our facts are right,' Meyer said, 'and the facts add up to suicide. But I don't like the feel.'

'The feel is wrong,' Carella agreed.

'That's right, the feel is wrong. The feel is murder.'

The telephone rang. Meyer picked it up. '87th Squad, Meyer,' he said. 'You again? What now?' He listened. 'Yeah? Yeah? Well, I don't know, we'll check it. Okay, stick with it. Right.' He hung up.

'Who?' Carella said.

'Bob O'Brien. He says a blue Thunderbird just pulled up to Nelson's house, and a blonde woman got out. He wanted to know if Melanie Gifford drives a blue Thunderbird.'

'I don't know what the hell she drives, do you?'

'No.'

'Motor Vehicle Bureau's closed, isn't it?'

'We can get them on the night line.'

'I think we'd better.'

Meyer shrugged. 'Nelson is a friend of the family. It's perfectly reasonable for her to be visiting him.'

'Yeah, I know,' Carella said. 'What's the number there?'

'Here you go,' Meyer said, and flipped open his telephone pad. 'Of course, there was that business at Gifford's party.'

'The argument, you mean?' Carella said, dialling.

'Yeah, when Gifford took a sock at the doctor.'

'Yeah.' Carella nodded. 'It's ringing.'

'But Gifford was drunk.'

'Yeah. Hello,' Carella said into the phone. 'Steve Carella, Detective/Second, 87th Squad. Checking automobile registration for Mrs Melanie Gifford, Larksview. Right, I'll wait. What? No, that's Gifford, with a G. Right.' He covered the mouthpiece. 'Doesn't Bob know what she looks like?' he asked.

'How would he?'

'That's right. This goddamn case is making me dizzy.' He glanced down at the cardboard strip of capsules on Meyer's desk. 'What's that stuff you're taking, anyway?'

'It's supposed to be good,' Meyer said. 'Better than all that other crap I've been using.'

Carella looked up at the wall clock.

'Anyway, I only have to take them twice a day,' Meyer said.

'Hello,' Carella said into the phone. 'Yes, go ahead. Blue thunderbird convertible, 1964. Right, thank you.' He hung up. 'You heard?'

'I heard.'

'That's pretty interesting, huh?'

'That's *very* interesting.'

'What do you suppose old Melanie Wistful wants with our doctor friend?'

'Maybe she's got a cold, too,' Meyer said.

'Maybe so.' Carella sighed. 'Why only twice?'

'Huh?'

'Why do you only have to take them twice a day?'

Five minutes later, Carella was placing a call to Detective-Lieutenant Sam Grossman at his home in Majesta.

Bob O'Brien was standing across the street from Nelson's brownstone on South Fourteenth when Meyer and Carella arrived. The red MG was parked in front of the doorway, and behind that was Melanie Gifford's blue Thunderbird. Meyer and Carella walked up to where he stood with his shoulders hunched and his hands in his pockets. He recognized them immediately, but only nodded in greeting.

'Getting pretty chilly,' he said.

'Mmm. She still in there?'

'Yep. The way I figure it, he's got the whole building. Ground floor is the entry, first floor must be the kitchen, dining and living room area, and the top floor's the bedrooms.'

'How the hell'd you figure that?' Meyer asked.

'Ground-floor light went on when the woman arrived – is she Mrs Gifford?'

'She is.'

'Mmm-huh,' O'Brien said, 'and out again immediately afterwards. The lights on the first floor were on until just a little while ago. An older woman came out at about seven. I figured she's either the cook or the housekeeper or both.'

'So they're alone in there, huh?'

'Yeah. Light went on upstairs just about ten minutes after the old lady left. See that small window? I figured that's the john, don't you?'

'Yeah, must be.'

'That went on first, and then off, and then the light in the big window went on. That's a bedroom, sure as hell.'

'What do you suppose they're doing in there?' Meyer asked.

'I know what *I'd* be doing in there,' O'Brien said.

'Why don't you go home?' Carella said.

'You don't need me?'

'No. Go on, we'll see you tomorrow.'

'You going in?'

'Yeah.'

'You sure you won't need me to take pictures?'

'Ha ha,' Meyer said, and then followed Carella, who had already begun crossing the street. They paused on the front step. Carella found the doorbell and rang it. There was no answer. He rang it again. Meyer stepped back off the stoop. The lights on the first floor went on.

'He's coming down,' Meyer whispered.

'Let him come down,' Carella said. 'Second murderer.'

'Huh?'

'Macbeth, Act III, scene 3.'

'Boy,' Meyer said, and the entry lights went on. The front door opened a moment later.

'Dr Nelson?' Carella said.

'Yes?' The doctor seemed surprised, but not particularly annoyed. He was wearing a black silk robe, and his feet were encased in slippers.

'I wonder if we might come in,' Carella said.

'Well, I was just getting ready for bed.'

'This won't take a moment.'

'Well . . .'

'You're alone, aren't you, doctor?'

'Yes, of course,' Nelson said.

'May we come in?'

'Well . . . well, yes. I suppose so. But I *am* tired, and I hope –'

'We'll be as brief as we possibly can,' Carella said, and he walked into the house. There was a couch in the entry, a small table before it. A mirror was on the wall opposite the door; a shelf for mail was fastened to the wall below it. Nelson did not invite them upstairs. He put his hands in the pockets of his robe, and made it clear from his stance that he did not intend moving farther into the house than the entry hall.

'I've got a cold,' Meyer said.

Nelson's eyebrows went up just a trifle.

'I've been trying everything,' Meyer continued. 'I just started on some new stuff. I hope it works.'

Nelson frowned. 'Excuse me, Detective Meyer,' he said, 'but did you come here to discuss your –'

Carella reached into his jacket pocket. When he extended his hand to Nelson, there was a purple-and-black gelatin capsule on the palm.

'Do you know what this is, Dr Nelson?' he asked.

'It looks like a vitamin capsule,' Nelson answered.

'It is, to be specific, a PlexCin capsule, the combination of Vitamin C and B-complex that Stan Gifford was using.'

'Oh, yes,' Nelson said, nodding.

'In fact, to be more specific, it is a capsule taken from the bottle of vitamins Gifford kept in his home.'

'Yes?' Nelson said. He seemed extremely puzzled. He seemed to be wondering exactly where Carella was leading.

'We sent the bottle of capsules to Lieutenant Grossman at the lab this afternoon,' Carella said. 'No poison in any of them. Only vitamins.'

'But I've got a cold,' Meyer said.

Nelson frowned.

'And Detective Meyer's cold led us to call Lieutenant Grossman again, just for the fun of it. He agreed to meet us at the lab, Dr Nelson. We've been down there for the past few hours. Sam – that's Lieutenant Grossman – had some interesting things to tell us, and we wanted your ideas. We want to be as specific about this as possible, you see, since there are a great many specifics in the Gifford case. Isn't that right?'

'Yes, I suppose so.'

'The specific poison, for example, and the specific dose, and the specific speed of the poison, and the specific dissolving rate of a gelatin capsule, isn't that right?'

'Yes, that's right,' Nelson said.

'You're an attending physician at General Presbyterian, aren't you, Dr Nelson?'

'Yes, I am.'

'We spoke to the pharmacist there just a little while ago. He tells us they stock strophantin in its crystalline powder form, oh, maybe three or four grains of it. The rest is in ampules, and even that isn't kept in any great amount.'

'That's very interesting. But what –'

'Open the capsule, Dr Nelson.'

'What?'

'The vitamin capsule. Open it. It comes apart. Go ahead. The size is a double-O, Dr Nelson. You know that, don't you?'

'I would assume it was either an O or a double-O.'

'But let's be specific. This specific capsule that contains the vitamins Gifford habitually took is a double-O.'

'All right then, it's a double-O.'

'Open it.'

Nelson sat on the couch, put the capsule on the low table, and carefully pulled one part from the other. A sifting of powder fell onto the table top.

'That's the vitamin compound, Dr Nelson. The same stuff that's in every one of those capsules in Gifford's bottle. Harmless. In fact, to be specific, beneficial. Isn't that right?'

'That's right.'

'Take another look at the capsule,' Nelson looked. 'No, Dr Nelson, *inside* the capsule. Do you see anything?'

'Why ... there ... there appears to be another capsule inside it.'

'Why, yes!' Carella said. 'Upon my soul, there *does* appear to be another capsule inside it. As a matter of fact, Dr Nelson, it is a number *three* gelatin capsule, which, as you see, fits very easily into the large double-O capsule. We made this sample at the lab.' He lifted the larger capsule from the table and then shook out the rest of its vitamin contents. The smaller capsule fell onto the table top. Using his forefinger, Carella pushed the smaller capsule away from the small mound of vitamins and said, 'The third capsule, Dr Nelson.'

'I don't know what you mean.'

'We were looking for a third capsule, you see. Since the one Gifford took at lunch couldn't possibly have killed him. Now, Dr Nelson, if this smaller capsule were loaded with two grains of stophanthin and placed inside the larger capsule, *that* could have killed him, don't you think?'

'Certainly, but it would have –'

'Yes, Dr Nelson?'

'Well, it seems to me that ... that the smaller capsule would have dissolved very rapidly, too. I mean –'

'You mean, don't you, Dr Nelson, that if the outside capsule took six minutes to dissolve, the inside capsule might take, oh, let's say another three or four or five or however many minutes to dissolve. Is that what you mean?'

'Yes.'

'So that it doesn't really change anything, does it? The poison still would have had to be taken just before Gifford went on.'

'Yes, I would imagine so.'

'But I have a cold,' Meyer said.

'Yes, and he's taking some capsules of his own,' Carella said, smiling. 'Only has to take two a day because the drug is released slowly over a period of twelve hours. They're called time-release capsules, Dr Nelson. I'm sure you're familiar with them.' Nelson seemed as if he were about to rise, and Carella instantly said, 'Stay where you are, Dr Nelson, we're not finished.'

Meyer smiled and said, 'Of course, my capsules were produced commercially. I imagine it would be impossible to duplicate a time-release capsule without manufacturing facilities, wouldn't it, Dr Nelson?'

'I would imagine so.'

'Well, to be specific,' Carella said, 'Lieutenant Sam Grossman said it *was* impossible to duplicate such a capsule. But he remembered experiments from way back in his Army days, Dr Nelson, when some of the doctors in his outfit were playing around with what is called enteric coating. Did the doctors in your outfit try it, too? Are you familiar with the expression "enteric coating", Dr Nelson?'

'Of course I am,' Nelson said, and he rose, and Carella leaned across the table and put his hands on the doctor's shoulders and slammed him down onto the couch again.

'Enteric coating,' Carella said, 'as it specifically applies to this small *inside* capsule, Dr Nelson, means that if the capsule had been immersed for exactly thirty seconds in a one per cent solution of formaldehyde, and then allowed to dry –'

'What is all this? Why are you –'

'– and then held for two weeks to allow the formaldehyde to act upon the gelatin, hardening it, then the –'

'I don't know what you mean!'

'I mean that a capsule treated in just that way would *not* dissolve in normal gastric juices for at least *three* hours, Dr Nelson, by which time it would have left the stomach. And after that, it would dissolve in the small intestine within a period of *five* hours. So you see, Dr Nelson, we're not working with six minutes any more. Only the outside capsule would have dissolved that quickly. We're working with anywhere from three to eight *hours*. We're working with a soft outer shell and a hard inner nucleus containing two full grains of poison. To be specific, Dr Nelson, we are working with the capsule Gifford undoubtedly took at lunch on the day he was murdered.'

Nelson shook his head. 'I don't know what you're talking about,' he said. 'I had nothing to do with any of this.'

'Ahhh, Dr Nelson,' Carella said. 'Did we forget to mention that the pharmacy at General Presbyterian has a record of all drugs ordered by its physicians? The record shows you have been personally withdrawing small quantities of strophanthin from the pharmacy over the past month. There is no evidence that you were administering the drug to any of your patients at the hospital during that period of time.' Carella paused. 'We know exactly *how* you did it, Dr Nelson. Now would you like to tell us *why*?'

Nelson was silent.

'Then perhaps Mrs Gifford would,' Carella said. He walked to the stairwell at the far end of the entry. 'Mrs Gifford,' he called, 'would you please put on your clothes and come downstairs?'

Elizabeth Rushmore Hospital was on the southern rim of the city, a complex of tall white buildings that faced the River Dix. From the hospital windows, one could watch the river traffic, could see in the distance the smokestacks puffing up black clouds, could follow the spidery strands of the three bridges that connected the island to Sands Spit, Calm's Point, and Majesta.

A cold wind was blowing off the water. He had called the hospital earlier that afternoon and learned that evening visiting hours ended at eight o'clock. It was now seven-forty-five, and he stood on the river's edge with his coat collar raised, and looked up at the lighted hospital windows and once again went over his plan.

He had thought at first that the whole thing was a cheap cop trick. He had listened attentively while Buddy told him about the visit of the blond cop, the same son of a bitch; Buddy said his name was Kling, Detective Bert Kling. Holding the phone receiver to his ear, he had listened, and his hand had begun sweating on the black plastic. But he had told himself all along that it was only a crumby trick, did they think he was going to fall for such a cheap stunt?

Still, they had known his name; Kling had asked for Cookie. How could they have known his name unless there really *was* a file someplace listing guys who were involved with numbers? And hadn't Kling mentioned something about not being able to locate him at the address they had for him in the file? If anything sounded legit, that sure as hell did. He had moved two years ago, so maybe the file went back before then. And besides, he hadn't been home for the past few days, so even if the file was a *recent* one, well then they wouldn't have been able to locate him at his address because he simply hadn't been there. So maybe there was some truth in it, who the hell knew?

But a picture? Where would they have gotten a picture of him? Well, that was maybe possible. If the cops really did have such a file, then maybe they also had a picture. He knew goddamn well that they took pictures all the time, mostly trying to get a line on guys in narcotics, but maybe they did it for numbers, too. He had seen laundry trucks or furniture vans parked in the same spot on a street all day long, and had known – together with everybody else in the neighbourhood – that it was cops taking pictures. So maybe it was possible they had a picture of him, too. And maybe that little bitch had really pointed him out, maybe so, it was a possibility. But it still smelled a little, there were still too many unanswered questions.

Most of the questions were answered for him when he read the story in the afternoon paper. He'd almost missed it because he had started from the back of the paper, where the racing results were, and then had only turned to the front afterwards, sort of killing time. The story confirmed that there *was* a file on numbers racketeers, for one thing, though he was pretty sure about that even before he'd seen the paper. It also explained why Fairchild couldn't make the identification, too. You can't be expected to look at a picture of somebody when you're laying in the hospital with a coma. He didn't think he'd hit the bastard that hard, but maybe he didn't know his own strength. Just to check he'd called Buena Vista as soon as he'd read the story and asked how Patrolman Fairchild was doing. They told him he was still in coma and on the critical list, so that part of it was true. And, of course, if those jerks in the office where Cindy worked were too scared to identify the picture, well then Fairchild's condition explained why Cindy was the only person the cops could bank on.

The word 'homicide' had scared him. If that son of a bitch *did* die, and if the cops picked him up and Cindy said, yes, that's the man, well, that was it, pal. He thought he'd really made it clear to her, but maybe she was tougher than he thought. For some strange reason, the idea excited him, the idea of her not having been frightened by the beating, of her still having the guts to identify his picture and promise to testify. He could remember being excited when he read the story, and the same excitement overtook him now as he looked up at the hospital windows and went over his plan.

Visiting hours ended at eight o'clock, which meant he had exactly ten minutes to get into the building. He wondered suddenly if they would let him in so close to the deadline, and he immediately began walking towards the front entrance. A wide slanting concrete canopy covered the revolving entrance doors. The hospital was new, an imposing edifice of aluminium and glass and concrete. He pushed through the revolving doors and walked immediately to the desk on the right of the entrance lobby. A woman in white – he supposed she was a nurse – looked up as he approached.

'Miss Cynthia Forrest?' he said.

'Room seven-twenty,' the woman said, and immediately looked at her watch. 'Visiting hours are over in a few minutes, you know,' she said.

'Yes, I know, thanks,' he answered, and smiled, and walked swiftly to the elevator bank. There was only one other civilian waiting for an elevator; the rest were all hospital people in white uniforms. He wondered abruptly if there would be a cop on duty outside her door. Well, if there is, he thought, I just call it off, that's all. The elevator doors opened. He stepped in with the other people, pushed the button for the seventh floor, noticed that one of the nurses reached for the same button after he had pushed it, and then withdrew quietly to the rear of the elevator. The doors closed.

'If you ask me,' a nurse was saying, 'it's psoriasis. Dr Kirsch said it's blood poisoning, but did you see that man's leg? You can't tell me that's from blood poisoning.'

'Well, they're going to test him tomorrow,' another nurse said.

'In the meantime, he's got a fever of a hundred and two.'

'That's from the swollen leg. The leg's all infected, you know.'

'Psoriasis,' the first nurse said, '*that's* what it is,' and the doors opened. Both nurses stepped out. The doors closed again. The elevator was silent. He looked at his watch. It was five minutes to eight. The elevator stopped again at the fourth floor, and again at the fifth. On the seventh floor, he got off the elevator with the nurse who had earlier reached for the same button. He hesitated in the corridor for a moment. There was a wide-open area directly in front of the elevators. Beyond that was a large room with a bank of windows, the sunroom, he supposed. To the right and left of the elevators were glass doors leading to the patients' rooms beyond. A nurse sat at a desk some three feet before the doors on the left. He walked swiftly to the desk and said, 'Which way is seven-twenty?'

The nurse barely looked up. 'Straight through,' she said. 'You've only got a few minutes.'

'Yes, I know, thanks,' he said, and pushed open the glass door. The room just inside the partition was 700, and the one beyond that was 702, so he assumed 720 was somewhere at the end of the hall. He looked at his watch. It was almost eight o'clock. He hastily scanned the doors in the corridor, walking rapidly, finding the one marked MEN halfway down the hall. Pushing open the door, he walked immediately to one of the stalls, entered it, and locked it behind him.

In less than a minute, he heard a loudspeaker announcing that visiting hours were now over. He smiled, lowered the toilet seat, sat, lighted a cigarette, and began his long wait.

He did not come out of the men's room until midnight. By that time, he had listened to a variety of patients and doctors as they discussed an endless variety of ills and ailments, both subjectively and objectively. He listened to each of them quietly and with some amusement because they helped to pass the time. He had reasoned that he could not make his move until the hospital turned out the lights in all the rooms. He didn't know what time taps was in this crumby place, but he supposed it would be around ten or ten-thirty. He had decided to wait until midnight, just to be sure. He figured that all of the visiting doctors would be gone by that time, and so he knew he had to be careful when he came out into the corridor. He didn't want anyone to stop him or even to see him on the way to Cindy's room.

It was a shame he would have to kill the little bitch.

She could have really been something.

There was a guy who came back to pee a total of seventeen times between eight o'clock and midnight. He knew because the guy was evidently having some kind of kidney trouble, and every time he came into the john he would walk over to the urinals – the sound of his shuffling slippers carrying into the locked stall – and then he would begin cursing out loud while he peed, 'Oh, you son of a bitch! Oh, what did I do to deserve such pain and misery?' and like that. One time, while he was peeing, some other guy yelled out from the stall alongside, 'For God's sake, Mandel, keep your sickness to yourself.'

And then the guy standing at the urinals had yelled back, 'It should happen to *you*, Liebowitz! It should *rot*, and fall off of you, and be washed down the drain into the river, may God hear my plea!'

He had almost burst out laughing, but instead he lighted another cigarette and looked at his watch again, and wondered what time they'd be putting all these sick jerks to bed, and wondered what Cindy would be wearing. He could still remember her undressing that night he'd beat her up, the quick flash of her nudity – he stopped his thoughts. He could not think that way. He had to kill her tonight, there was no sense thinking about – and yet maybe *while* he was doing it, maybe it would be like last time, maybe with her belly smooth and hard beneath him, maybe like last time maybe he could.

The men's room was silent at midnight.

He unlocked the stall and came out into the room and then walked past the sinks to the door and opened it just a bit and looked out into the corridor. The floors were some kind of hard polished asphalt tile, and you could hear the clicking of high heels on it for a mile, which was good. He listened as a nurse went swiftly down the corridor, her heels clicking away, and then he listened until everything was quiet again. Quickly, he stepped out into the hall. He began walking towards the end of the corridor, the steadily mounting door numbers flashing by on left and right, 709, 710, 711 ... 714, 715, 716 ...

He was passing the door to room 717 on his left, when it opened and a nurse stepped into the corridor. He was too startled to speak at first. He stopped dead, breathless, debating whether he should hit her. And then, from somewhere, he heard a voice saying, 'Good evening, nurse,' and he hardly recognized the voice as his own because it sounded so cultured and pleasant and matter-of-fact. The nurse looked at him for just a moment longer, and then smiled and said, 'Good evening, doctor,' and continued walking down the corridor. He did not turn to look back at her. He continued walking until he came to room 720. Hoping it was a private room, he opened the door, stepped inside quickly, closed the door immediately, and leaned against it, listening. He could hear nothing in the corridor outside. Satisfied, he turned into the room.

The only light in the room came from the windows at the far end, just beyond the bed. He could see the silhouette of her body beneath the blankets, the curved hip limned by the dim light coming from the window. The blanket was pulled high over her shoulders and the back of her neck, but he could see the short blonde hair illuminated by the dim glow of moonlight from the windows. He was getting excited again, the way he had that night he beat her up. He reminded himself why he was here – this girl could send him to the electric chair. If Fairchild died, this girl was all they needed to convict him. He took a deep breath and moved towards the bed.

In the near-darkness, he reached for her throat, seized it between his huge hands and then whispered, 'Cindy,' because he wanted her to be awake and looking straight up into his face when he crushed the life out of her. His hands tightened.

She sat erect suddenly. Two fists flew up between his own hands, up and outward, breaking the grip. His eyes opened wide.

'Surprise!' Bert Kling said, and punched him in the mouth.

Chapter Eleven

Detectives are not poets; there is no iambic pentameter in a broken head.

If Meyer were William Shakespeare, he might have indeed belived that 'Love is a smoke raised with the fume of sighs,' but he wasn't William Shakespeare. If Steve Carella were Henry Wadsworth Longfellow, he would have known that 'Love is every busy with his shuttle,' but alas, you know, he wasn't Henry Wadsworth Longfellow – though he did have an Uncle Henry who lived in Red Bank, New Jersey. As a matter of fact, if either of the two men were Buckingham or Ovid or Byron, they might have respectively realized that 'love is the salt of life', and 'the perpetual source of fears and anxieties,' and 'a capricious power' – but they weren't poets, they were only working cops.

Even as working cops, they might have appreciated Homer's comment (from the motion picture of the same name) which, translated into English subtitles by Nikos Konstantin, went something like this: '*Who love too much, hate in the like extreme.*'

But they had neither seen the picture nor read the book, what the hell can you expect from flatfoots?

Oh, they could tell you tales of love, all right. Boy, the tales of love they could tell. They had heard tales of love from a hundred and one people, or maybe even more. And don't think they didn't know what love was all about, oh, they knew what it was all about, all right. Love was sweet and pure and marvellous, love was magnificent. Hadn't they loved their mothers and their fathers and their aunts and uncles and such? Hadn't they kissed a girl for the first time when they were thirteen or fourteen or something, wasn't that love? Oh boy, it sure was. And weren't they both happily married men who loved their wives and their children? Listen, it wouldn't pay to tell them about love because they knew all about it, yes, sir.

'We love each other,' Nelson said.

'We love each other,' Melanie said.

The pair sat in the 2.00 a.m. silence of the squadroom and dictated their confessions to police stenographers, sitting at separate desks, their hands still stained with the ink that had been used to fingerprint them. Meyer and Carella listened unemotionally, silently, patiently – they had heard it all before. Neither Nelson nor Melanie seemed to realize that they would be taken from the precinct by police van at 9.00 a.m., brought downtown for arraignment, and put into separate cells. They had been seeing each other secretly for more than a year, they said, but they did not yet seem to realize they would not see each other again until they were brought to trial – and then perhaps never after.

Carella and Meyer listened silently as their tale of love unfolded.

'You can't legislate against love,' Nelson said, transforming another man's comment, but making his meaning clear enough. 'This thing between Melanie and me just happened. Neither of us wanted it, and neither of us asked for it. It just happened.'

'It just happened,' Melanie said at the desk nearby. 'I remember exactly when. We were sitting outside the studio in Carl's car one night, waiting for Stan to take off his makeup so the three of us could go to dinner together. Carl's hand touched mine, and the next thing we knew we were kissing. We fell in love shortly afterwards. I guess we fell in love.'

'We fell in love,' Nelson said. 'We tried to stop ourselves. We knew it wasn't right. But when we saw we couldn't stop, we went to Stan and told him about it, and asked him for a divorce. This was immediately after the incident at his party, when he tried to hit me. Last month, September. We told him we were in love and that Melanie wanted a divorce. He flatly refused.'

'I think he'd known about us all along,' Melanie said. 'If you say he revised his will, then that's why he must have done it. He must have known that Carl and I were having an affair. He was a very sensitive man, my husband. He must have known that something was wrong long before we told him about it.'

'The idea to kill him was mine,' Nelson said.

'I agreed to it readily,' Melanie said.

'I began drawing strophanthin from the hospital pharmacy last month. I know the pharmacist there, I often stop in when I'm short of something or other, something I need in my bag or at my office. I'll stop in and say, "Hi, Charlie, I need some penicillin," and of course he'll give it to me because he knows me. I did the same thing with the strophanthin. I never discussed why I needed it. I assumed he thought it was for my private practice, outside the hospital. At any rate, he never questioned me about it, why should he?'

'Carl prepared the capsule,' Melanie said. 'At the breakfast table that Wednesday, after Stan had taken his morning vitamins, I switched the remaining capsule for the one containing the poison. At lunch, I watched while he washed it down with water. We knew it would take somewhere between three and eight hours for the capsule to dissolve, but we didn't know exactly how long. We didn't necessarily expect him to die on camera, but it didn't matter, you see. We'd be nowhere near when it happened, and that was all that mattered. We'd be completely out of it.'

'And yet,' Nelson said, 'we realized that I would be a prime suspect. After all, I am a physician, and I do have access to drugs. We planned for this possibility by making certain that *I* was the one who suggested foul play, *I* was the one who demanded an autopsy.'

'We also figured,' Melanie said, 'that it would be a good idea if I said I suspected Carl. Then, once you found out what kind of poison had been used – how fast it worked, I mean – and once you knew Carl had been home all during the show, well then you'd automatically drop him as a suspect. That was what we figured.'

'We love each other,' Nelson said.

'We love each other,' Melanie said.

They sat still and silent after they had finished talking. The police stenographers showed them transcripts of what they had separately said, and they signed multiple copies, and then Alf Miscolo came out of the Clerical Office, handcuffed the pair, and led them downstairs to the detention cells.

'One for us, one for the lieutenant, and one for Homicide,' Carella told his stenographer. The stenographer merely nodded. He, too, had heard it all already. There was nothing you could tell him about love or homicide. He put on his hat, dropped the requested number of signed confessions on the desk nearest the railing, and went out of the squadroom. As he walked down the corridor, he could hear muted voices behind the closed door of the Interrogation Room.

'Why'd you beat her up?' Kling asked.

'I didn't beat up nobody,' Cookie said. 'I love that girl.'

'You *what?*'

'I love her, you deaf? I loved her from the first minute I ever seen her.'

'When was that?'

'The end of the summer. August. It was on the Stem. I just made a collection in a candy store on the corner there, and I was passing this Pokerino place in the middle of the block, and I thought maybe I'd stop in, kill some time, you know? The guy outside was giving his spiel, and I was standing there listening to him, so many games for a quarter, or whatever the hell it was. I looked in and there was this girl in a dark-green dress, leaning over one of the tables and rolling the balls, I think she had something like three queens, I'm not sure.'

'All right, what happened then?'

'I went in.'

'Go ahead.'

'What do you want from me?'

'I want to know why you beat her up.'

'I didn't beat her up, I told you that!'

'Who'd you think was in that bed tonight, you son of a bitch?'

'I didn't *know* who was in it. Leave me alone. You got nothing on me, you think I'm some snot-nosed kid?'

'Yeah, I think you're some snot-nosed kid,' Kling said. 'What happened that first night you saw her?'

'Nothing. There was a guy with her, a young guy, one of these advertising types. I kept watching her, that's all. She didn't know I was watching her, she didn't even know I existed. Then I followed them when they left, and found out where she lived, and after that I kept following her wherever she went. That's all.'

'That's *not* all.'

'I'm telling you that's all.'

'Okay, play it your way,' Kling said. 'Be a wise guy. We'll throw everything but the goddamn kitchen sink at you.'

'I'm telling you I never laid a finger on her. I went up to her office to let her know, that's all.'

'Let her know what?'

'That she was my girl. That, you know, she wasn't supposed to go out with nobody else or see nobody, that she was *mine*, you dig? That's the only reason I went up there, to let her know. I didn't expect all that kind of goddamn trouble. All I wanted to do was tell her what I expected from her, that's all.'

John 'Cookie' Cacciatore lowered his head. The brim of the hat hid his eyes from Kling's gaze.

'If you'd all have minded your own business, everything would have been all right.'

The squadroom was silent.

'I love that girl,' he said.

And then, in a mumble, 'You lousy bastard, you almost killed me tonight.'

Morning always comes.

In the morning, Detective Bert Kling went to Elizabeth Rushmore Hospital and asked to see Cynthia Forrest. He knew this was not the normal visiting time, but he explained that he was a working detective, and asked that an allowance be made. Since everyone in the hospital knew that he was the cop who'd captured a hoodlum on the seventh floor the night before, there was really no need to explain. Permission was granted at once.

Cindy was sitting up in bed.

She turned her head towards the door as Kling came in, and then her hand went unconsciously to her short blonde hair, fluffing it.

'Hi,' he said.

'Hello.'

'How do you feel?'

'All right.' She touched her eyes gingerly. 'Has the swelling gone down?'

'Yes.'

'But they're still discoloured, aren't they?'

'Yes, they are. You look all right, though.'

'Thank you.' Cindy paused. 'Did ... did he hurt you last night?'

'No.'

'You're sure.'

'Yes, I'm sure.'

'He's a vicious person.'

'I know he is.'

'Will he go to jail?'

'To prison, yes. Even without your testimony. He assaulted a police officer.' Kling smiled. 'Tried to strangle me, in fact. That's attempted murder.'

'I'm ... I'm very frightened of that man,' Cindy said.

'Yes, I can imagine.'

'But....' She swallowed. 'But if it'll help the case, I'll ... I'd be willing to testify. If it'll help, I mean.'

'I don't know,' Kling said. 'The D.A.'s office'll have to let us know about that.'

'All right,' Cindy said, and was silent. Sunlight streamed through the windows, catching her blonde hair. She lowered her eyes. Her hand picked nervously at the blankets. 'The only thing I'm afraid of is ... is when he gets out. Eventually, I mean. When he gets out.'

'Well, we'll see that you have police protection,' Kling said.

'Mmm,' Cindy said. She did not seem convinced.

'I mean ... I'll *personally* volunteer for the job,' Kling said, and hesitated. Cindy raised her eyes to meet his. 'That's ... very kind of you,' she said slowly.

'Well ...' he answered and shrugged.

The room was silent.

'You could have got hurt last night,' Cindy said.

'No. No, there wasn't a chance.'

'You could have,' she insisted.

'No, really.'

'Yes,' she said.

'We're not going to start arguing again, are we?'

'No,' she said, and laughed, and then winced and touched her face. 'Oh, God,' she said, 'it still hurts.'

'But only when you laugh, right?'

'Yes,' she said, and laughed again.

'When do you think you'll be out of here?' Kling asked.

'I don't know. Tomorrow, I suppose. Or the day after.'

'Because I thought ...'

'Yes?'

'Well ...'

'What is it, Detective Kling?'

'I know you're a working girl ...'

'Yes?'

'And that you don't normally eat out.'

'That's right, I don't,' Cindy said.

'Unless you're escorted.'

Cindy waited.

'I thought . . .'

She waited.

'I thought you'd like to have dinner with me sometime. When you're out of hospital, I mean.' He shrugged. 'I mean, *I'd* pay for it,' Kling said, and lapsed into silence.

Cindy did not answer for several moments. Then she smiled and said simply, 'I'd love to,' and paused, and immediately said, 'When?'

"She came in like a lady, that
April. The poet may have been
right, but there
really wasn't
a trace of
cruelty about
her this year."

THE
HECKLER

This is for my father-in-law Harry Melnick –
who inspired it

Chapter One

She came in like a lady, that April.

The poet may have been right, but there really wasn't a trace of cruelty about her this year. She was a delicate thing who walked into the city with the wide-eyed innocence of a maiden, and you wanted to hold her in your arms because she seemed alone and frightened in this geometric maze of strangers, intimidated by the streets and the buildings, shyly touching you with the pale-grey eyes of a lady who'd materialized somehow from the cold marrow of March.

She wandered mist-shrouded through the city, a city that had become suddenly green in exuberant welcome. She wandered alone, reaching into people the way she always does, but not with cruelty. She touched wellsprings deep inside, so that people for a little while, sensing her approach, feeling her come close again, turned a soft vulnerable pulsing interior to her, turned it outward to face the harsh angles of the city's streets and buildings, held out tenderness to be touched by tenderness, but only for a little while.

And for that little while, April would linger on the walks of Grover Park, linger like white mist on a mountain meadow, linger on the paths and in the budding trees, spreading a delicate perfume on the air. And along the lake and near the statue of Daniel Webster below Twelfth Street, the cornelian cherry shrubs would burst into early bloom. And further west, uptown, facing Grover Avenue and the building which housed the men of the 87th Precinct, the bright yellow blossoms of forsythias would spread along the park's retaining wall in golden-banked fury while the Japanese quince waited for a warmer spring, waited for April's true and warm and rare and lovely smile.

For Detective Meyer Meyer, April was a Gentile.

Sue him; she was a Gentile. Perhaps for Detective Steve Carella April was a Jewess.

Which is to say that, for both of them, April was a strange and exotic creature, tempting, a bit unreal, warm, seductive, shrouded with mystery. She crossed the avenue from Grover Park with the delicate step of a lady racing across a field in yellow taffeta, and she entered the squadroom in her insinuating perfume and rustling petticoats, and she turned the minds of men to mush.

Steve Carella looked up from the filing cabinets and remembered a time when he was thirteen and experiencing his first kiss. It had been an April night, long, long ago.

Meyer Meyer glanced through the grilled windows at the new leaves in the park across the street and tried to listen patiently to the man who sat in the hard-backed chair alongside his desk, but he lost the battle to spring, and he sat idly wondering how it felt to be seventeen.

The man who sat opposite Meyer Meyer was named Dave Raskin, and he owned a dress business. He also owned about two hundred and ten pounds of flesh which was loosely distributed over a six-foot-two-inch frame garbed at the moment in a pale blue tropical suit. He was a good-looking man in a rough-hewn way, with a high forehead and greying hair which was receding above the temples, a nose with the blunt chopping edge of a machete, an orator's mouth, and a chin which would have been completely at home on a Roman balcony in 1933. He was smoking a foul-smelling cigar and blowing the smoke in Meyer's direction. Every now and then Meyer waved his hand in front of his face, clearing the air, but Raskin didn't quite appreciate the subtlety. He kept sucking on the soggy end of his cigar and blowing smoke in Meyer's direction. It was hard to appreciate April and feel like seventeen while swallowing all that smoke and listening to Raskin at the same time.

'So Marcia said to me, you work right in his own precinct, Meyer's,' Raskin said. 'So what are you afraid of? You grew up with his father, he was a boyhood friend of yours, so you should be afraid to go see him? What is he now, a detective? This is to be afraid of?' Raskin shrugged. 'That's what Marcia said to me.'

'I see,' Meyer said, and he waved his hand to clear the air of smoke.

'You want a cigar?' Raskin asked.

'No. No, thank you.'

'Good cigars. My son-in-law sent them to me from Nassau. He took my daughter there on their honeymoon. A good boy. A periodontist. You know what that is?'

'Yes,' Meyer said, and again he waved his hand.

'So it's true what Marcia said. I did grow up with your father, Max, God rest his soul. So why should I be afraid to come here to see his son, Meyer? I was at the *briss*, would you believe it? When you were circumcised, *you*, I was there, *me*. So I should be afraid now to come to you with a little problem, when I knew your father we were kids together? I should be afraid? You sure you don't want a cigar?'

'I'm sure.'

'Very good cigars. My son-in-law sent them to me from Nassau.'

'Thank you, no Mr Raskin.'

'Dave, Dave. Please. Dave.'

'Dave, what seems to be the trouble? I mean, why *did* you come here? To the squadroom.'

'I got a heckler.'

'What?'

'A heckler.'

'What do you mean?'

'A pest.'

'I don't think I understand.'

'I've been getting phone calls,' Raskin said. 'Two, three times a week. I pick up the phone and a voice asks, "Mr Raskin?" and I say, "Yes?" and the voice yells, "*If you're not out of that loft by April thirtieth, I'm going to kill you!*" And then whoever it is hangs up.'

'Is this a man or a woman?' Meyer asked.

'A man.'

'And that's all he says?'

'That's all he says.'

'What's so important about this loft?'

'Who knows? It's a crumby little loft on Culver Avenue, it's got rats the size of crocodiles, you should see them. I use it to store dresses there. Also I got some girls there, they do pressing for me.'

'Then you wouldn't say it was a desirable location?'

'Desirable for other rats, maybe. But not so you should call a man and threaten him.'

'I see. Well, do you know anyone who might want you dead?'

'Me? Don't be ridiculous,' Raskin said. 'I'm well liked by everybody.'

'I understand that,' Meyer said, 'but is there perhaps a crank or a nut among any of your friends who might just possibly have the foolish notion that it might be nice to see you dead?'

'Impossible.'

'I see.'

'I'm a respected man. I go to temple every week. I got a good wife and a pretty daughter and a son-in-law he's a periodontist. I got two retail stores here in the city, and I got three stores in farmers' markets out in Pennsylvania, and I got the loft right here in this neighbourhood, on Culver Avenue. I'm a respected man, Meyer.'

'Of course,' Meyer said understandingly. 'Well, tell me, Dave, could one of your friends be playing a little joke on you, maybe?'

'A joke? I don't think so. My friends, you should pardon the expression, are all pretty solemn bastards. I'll tell you the truth, Meyer, no attempt to butter you up. When your dear father Max Meyer died, God rest his soul, when your dear father and my dear friend Max Meyer passed away, this world lost a very great funny man. That is the truth, Meyer. This was a hilarious person, always with a laugh on his lips, always with a little joke. This was a very funny man.'

'Yes, oh yes,' Meyer said, and he hoped his lack of enthusiasm did not show. It had been his dear father, that very funny man Max Meyer who – in retaliation for being presented with a change-of-life baby – had decided to name his new son Meyer Meyer, the given name to match the surname. This was very funny indeed, the gasser of all time. When Max announced the name at the *briss* those thirty-seven years ago, perhaps all the guests, including Dave Raskin, had split a gut or two laughing. For Meyer Meyer, who had to grow up with the name, the humour wasn't quite that convulsive. Patiently he carried the name like an albatross. Patiently he suffered the gibes and the jokes, suffered the assaults of people who decided they didn't like his face simply because they didn't like his name. He wore patience as his armour and carried it as his standard. *Omnia Meyer in tres partes divisa est:* Meyer and Meyer and Patience. Add them all together, and you got a Detective 2nd/Grade who worked out of the 87th Squad, a tenacious cop who never let go of anything, who doggedly and patiently worried a case to its conclusion, who used patience the way some men used glibness or good looks.

So the odd name hadn't injured him after all. Oh yes, it hadn't been too pleasant, but he'd survived and he was a good cop and a good man. He had grown to adult size and was apparently unscarred. Unless one chose to make the intellectual observation that Meyer Meyer was completely bald and that the baldness could have been the result of thirty-seven years of sublimation. But who the hell wants to get intellectual in a detective squadroom?

Patient now, having learned over the years that hating his father wasn't going to change his name, having in fact felt a definite loss when his father died, the loss all sons feel when they are finally presented with the shoes they've wanted to fill for so long, forgetting the malice he had borne, patiently reconstructing a new image of the father as a kind and gentle man, but eliminating all humour from that image, patiently Meyer listened to Raskin tell about the comedian who'd been his father, but he did not believe a word of it.

'So it isn't a man trying to be funny, believe me,' Raskin said. 'If it was that, do you think I'd have come up here? I got nothing better to do with my time, maybe?'

'Then what *do* you think, Dave? That this man is really going to kill you if you don't get out of the loft?'

'Kill me? Who said that?' It seemed to Meyer in that moment that Dave Raskin turned a shade paler. '*Kill* me? *Me?*'

'Didn't he say he was going to kill you?'

'Well yes, but –'

'And didn't you just tell me you didn't think this was a joke?'

'Well yes, but –'

'Then apparently you believe he *is* going to kill you unless you vacate the loft. Otherwise you wouldn't be here. Isn't that correct?'

'No, that's not correct!' Raskin said with some indignation. 'By you, maybe, that is correct, but not by me. By me, it is not correct at all. Dave Raskin didn't come up here he thinks somebody's going to kill him.'

'Then why did you come up, Dave?'

'Because this heckler, this pest, this shmuck who's calling me up two, three times a week, he's scaring the girls who work for me. I got three Puerto Rican girls they do pressing for me in the Culver Avenue loft. So every time this bedbug calls, if I don't happen to be there, he yells at the girls, "*Tell that son of a bitch Raskin I'm going to kill him unless he gets out of that loft!*" Crazy, huh? But he's got the girls scared stiff, they can't do any work!'

'Well, what do you want me to do?' Meyer asked.

'Find out who he is. Get him to stop calling me. He's threatening me, can't you see that?'

'I see it, all right. But I don't think there's enough here to add up to extortion, and I can't – This guy hasn't made any *real* attempts on your life, has he?'

'What are you gonna do?' RAskin asked. 'Wait until he kills me? Is that what? And then you'll make a nice funeral for me?'

'But you said you didn't think he was serious.'

'To kill me, I don't think so. But *suppose*, Meyer. Just suppose. Listen, there are crazy people all over, you know that, don't you?'

'Yes, certainly.'

'So suppose this crazy nut comes after me with a shotgun or a butcher knife or something? I get to be one of those cases in the newspaper where I went to the police and they told me to go home and don't worry.'

'Dave –'

'"Dave, Dave!" Don't "Dave" me. I remember you when you was in diapers. I come here and tell you a man said he's going to kill me. Over and over again, he's said it. So this is attempted murder, no?'

'No, this is not attempted murder.'

'And not extortion, either? Then what is it?'

'Disorderly conduct,' Meyer said. 'He's used offensive, disorderly, threatening, abusive, or insulting language.' Meyer paused and thought for a moment. 'Gee, I don't know, maybe we have got extortion. He *is* trying to get you out of that loft by threatening you.'

'Sure. So go pick him up,' Raskin said.

'Who?' Meyer asked.

'The person who's making the calls.'

'Well, we don't know who he is, do we?'

'That's simple,' Raskin said. 'Just trace the next call.'

'Impossible to do in this city,' Meyer said. 'All our telephone equipment is automatic.'

'So what do we do?'

'I don't know,' Meyer said. 'Does he call at any specific time?'

'So far, all the calls have come in the afternoon, late. Just about closing time, between four and five.'

'Well, look,' Meyer said, 'maybe I'll stop by, this afternoon or tomorrow. To listen in on the calls, if any come. Where's the loft?'

'Twelve thirteen Culver Avenue,'' Raskin said. 'You can't miss it. It's right upstairs over the bank.'

In the streets, the kids were yelling 'April Fool!' as the punch line to their first-of-April jokes. And they chased each other into Grover Park the way kids will always chase each other, leaping the stone walls and cavorting along the path and ducking behind trees and bushes.

'Watch out, Frankie! There's a tiger on that rock!' and then he shouted 'April Fool!'

And then dashing off again to duck behind another rock or another tree, the punch line old and clichéd by this time, but delighting them nonetheless each time it was shouted.

'Over your head, Johnny! An eagle! *April Fool!'*

Running over the close-cropped grass and then one of the boys ducking into the trees again, and his voice coming from somewhere in the woods, a voice tinged with shock and and awe, reaching out for the path.

'Frankie! There's a dead guy in here!'

And this time no one shouted 'April Fool!'

Chapter Two

The gentleman they found in Grover Park had been dressed for the approaching summer. Or perhaps *undressed* for it, depending on how you chose to view the situation. No matter how you chose to view it, he was wearing only a pair of black shoes and a pair of white socks, and that's about as close to being naked as you can come in the streets of any big city. Not that this gentleman was overly worried about arousing the ire of the law. This gentleman was dead.

He had, in fact, if a summary glance at the wounds in his chest meant anything, been killed by a shot gun at fairly close range. He lay on his back under the trees and a small knot of experts in death surrounded the body and made faces indicative of disgust and empathy and boredom and indifference, but mostly of pain. Steve Carella was one of the policemen who looked down at the body of the naked man. Carella's eyes were squinted almost shut even though there was no sunshine under the canopy of the trees. There was a sour look on Carella's face, a look of disapproval and anger laced with discomfort. He looked at the man and he thought *Nobody should die in April*, and he noted automatically the shotgun wounds on the man's chest and, just as automatically, he noticed that there was a single large entrance wound and several zones of small satellite perforations produced by pellets which scattered from the main charge. The large entrance wound told him that the gun had been fired anywhere from one to three yards away from the victim. Up to a yard's distance, the shotgun would have produced a wound with a lot of tattooing, burning, and blackening. And beyond three yards, the shot would have dispersed, and formed constellationlike patterns on the victim's skin. Knowing this, and not knowing much more than this at the moment, Carella's mind made the associations unconsciously and unemotionally while another part of him looked down at this person who had once been a man and who was now a ludicrously naked, loosely jointed pile of fleshy, angular rubbish – no longer a man; simply something soft and spongy, but not a man. Life had been robbed from this mass of flesh, and now there was nothing but death housed in the skin case. Carella wiped a hand across his mouth even though he was not sweating.

It was cool in the copse of trees where the policemen worked. Flashbulbs popped around the dead man. A powdered chalk line was sprayed onto the ground, outlining the body. The laboratory technicians searched the bushes for footprints. The men stood about in uneasy clusters, discussing the world's heavyweight champion fight, the pennant race, the nice weather they'd had this past week, anything but death which stared up at them from the ground. And then they finished their work, all the work they could do for the time being. They hoisted the corpse onto a stretcher and carried it to the path, and then out of the park and over to the kerb where an ambulance was waiting. They slid the corpse into the back of the meat wagon, and took it to General Hospital where the autopsy would be performed. Carella thought for a moment about the stainless-steel autopsy table which was laced with troughs like a carving board's, troughs to catch the blood – the table slightly tilted – and channel it towards the basin at the far end, he thought of that goddam unemotionally sterile stainless-steel table, and he thought of scalpels and he tightened his fists in anger and again he thought *Nobody should die in April*, and he walked out to the police sedan parked at the kerb and drove back to the precinct house. He could not find a parking space closer than two blocks away. He parked the car on Grover Avenue and walked back to the building facing the park.

Somehow the mottled stone front of the ancient building seemed to blend with April. The grey assumed a softer tone when juxtaposed to the vibrant blue sky beyond it. The hanging green globes captured something of the blue, and the white numerals '87' on each globe picked up a touch of the clouds that hung fat and lazy in the early spring sky. The similarity ended the moment Carella climbed the low flat steps of the front stoop and passed into the muster room. High-ceilinged, bare except for the muster desk and Sergeant Dave Murchison who sat behind it, the room resembled nothing more than the cheerless, featureless face of an iceberg. Carella nodded to the sergeant and followed the pointing white wooden hand which told him – in case he didn't know after all these years – where to find the DETECTIVE DIVISION. Where to find it was upstairs. He mounted the iron-runged steps, noticing for the first time what a clatter his shoes made against the metal, turned left into the upstairs corridor, passed two benches flanking the hallway, and was passing the men's lavatory when he almost collided with Miscolo who came out of the room zipping up his fly.

'Hey, you're just the man I want to see,' Miscolo said.

'Uh-oh,' Carella answered.

'Come on, come on, stop making faces. Come into the office a minute, will you?'

The office he referred to was the Clerical Office, labelled with a hand-lettered sign in the corridor, a cubbyhole just outside the slatted, wooden railing which divided the corridor from the detective squadroom. Alf Miscolo was in charge of the Clerical Office, and he ran it with all the hard-fisted, clearheaded mercilessness of an Arabian stablekeeper. His horses, unfortunately, were usually a handful of patrolmen who had pulled twenty-fours' duty as records clerks. But if Miscolo had been given, let us say, a hundred men with whom to run his clerical office, all crime in that fair city would have been eliminated in the space of two days. In conjunction with the police laboratory downtown on High Street, and the Bureau of Criminal Identification, Miscolo's dossier on criminals would have made it absolutely impossible to commit a crime without risking immediate capture and incarceration. Or so Miscolo fantasied.

The Clerical Office, at the moment, was empty. Its green filing cabinets lined the right-hand wall of the room, facing the two desks opposite it. At the far end of the room, a single huge window, covered on the outside with wire mesh and the grime of a decade, was opened to the fragrance of April.

'What a day, hah?' Miscolo said. He wagged his head in appreciation.

'All right, what's on your mind?' Carella said.

'Two things.'

'Shoot.'

'First, May Reardon.'

'What about her?'

'Well, you know, Stevie, Mike Reardon worked here for a long time before he got killed. And I liked Mike. I mean, Everybody did. You did, too.'

'I did,' Carella admitted.

'And he left May and two kids. That ain't no picnic, Stevie. So she makes the precincts beds, but what the hell does that give her? Enough to feed two kids? Stevie, this is a tough pull. You got a wife, you got kids. God forbid, suppose something should happen to you, you want Teddy living on what precinct beds get her? Do you?'

'No,' Carella said. 'What do you want?'

'I thought we could all chip in. The guys on the squad, and the patrolmen, too. Just a little something more each week to boost that bed money. What do you say, Stevie?'

'Count me in.'

'Will you talk to the other bulls?'

'Now, listen –'

'I'll talk to the patrolmen. What do you say?'

'I'm a lousy salesman, Miscolo.'

'Aw, this ain't like selling nothing, Stevie. This is giving that little girl a break. Did you ever see that little girl, Stevie? She's so goddam Irish, you want to cry.'

'Why?'

'I don't know. Irish girls make me want to cry.' He shrugged. He was not a handsome man. His nose was massive, and his eyebrows were bushy, and there was a thickness about his neck which created the impression of head sitting directly on shoulders. He was not a handsome man. And yet, in that moment, as he said what he had to say about Irish girls, as he shrugged boyishly afterwards, there was an enormous appeal to the man. He realized in an instant that Carella was staring at him, and he turned away in embarrassment and said, 'What the hell do I know why? Maybe the first girl I laid was Irish – how do I know?'

'Maybe,' Carella said.

'So, will you talk to the other bulls or not?'

'I'll talk to them,' Carella said.

'Okay. To get something done around here, you got to go around pulling teeth.'

'What was the second thing?'

'Huh?'

'The second thing. You said there were two –'

'Yeah, that's right, I did.' Miscolo frowned. 'I can't think of the other thing right now. It'll come to me.'

'That's it, then?'

'Yeah. You just come up from the street?'

Carella nodded.

'How's it look out there?'

'Same as always,' Carella said. He sat for just a moment longer and then waved at Miscolo and went out of the office into the corridor. He pushed through the gate in the railing, threw his Panama at the hat rack, missed, and was heading to pick it up when Berk Kling stooped for it.

'Thanks,' Carella said. He began taking off his jacket as he walked to Meyer's desk.

'What was it?' Meyer asked.

'Looks like a homicide,' Carella answered.

'Man or woman?'

'Man.'

'Who?'

'No identification,' Carella said. 'He got shot at close range with a shotgun, that's my guess. All he was wearing was shoes and socks.' Carella shrugged. 'I better make out a report. I didn't see anybody from Homicide there, Meyer. Suppose they've given up on us?'

'Who knows? They only like to make noise, anyway. They know the stiff officially belongs to whichever precinct is lucky enough to find it.'

'Well, this one belongs to us,' Carella said, wheeling over a typing cart.

'They doing an autopsy?' Meyer asked.

'Yeah.'

'When do you suppose we'll have the report?'

'I don't know. What's today?'

Meyer shrugged. 'Bert! What's today?'

'April first,' Kling said, 'Steve, some dame phoned about –'

'Yeah, but what *day*?' Meyer asked.

'Wednesday,' Kling said. 'Steve, this dame called about an hour ago, something about a dry-cleaning store and a counterfeit bill. You know anything about it?'

'Yeah, I'll call her back later,' Carella said.

'So when do you think we'll have the report?' Meyer asked again.

'Tomorrow, I suppose. Unless the M.E.'s office got an unusually large number of stiffs today.'

Andy Parker, who was sitting by the water cooler with his feet up on the desk, threw down a movie magazine and said, 'You know who I'd like to get in the hay?'

'Anybody,' Carella answered, and he began typing up his report.

'Wise guy,' Parker said. 'I been looking over these movie stars, and there is only one girl in this whole magazine who'd be worth my time.' He turned to Kling who was reading a paper-backed book. 'You know who, Bert?'

'Quiet, I'm trying to read,' Kling said.

'I wish some of you buys would try to *work*,' Meyer said. 'This goddam squadroom is beginning to resemble a country club.'

'I *am* working,' Kling said.

'Yeah, I can see that.'

'These are stories about the deductive method.'

'The what?'

'Of detection. Haven't you ever heard of Sherlock Holmes?'

'Everybody's heard of Sherlock Holmes,' Parker said. 'You want to know which of these broads –'

'I'm reading a very good story,' Kling said. 'You ever read it, Meyer?'
'What's it called?'
'"The Redhead League,"' Kling said.
'No,' Meyer answered. 'I don't read mysteries. They only make me feel stupid.'

The autopsy report did not arrive at the squadroom until Friday afternoon, April 3. And, as if by black magic, a call from the assistant medical examiner came at the exact moment the manila envelope bearing the report was placed on Carella's desk.
'Eighty-seventh Squad, Carella,' he said.
'Steve, Paul Blaney.'
'Hello, Paul,' Carella said.
'Did that necropsy report get there yet?'
'I'm not sure. A man with hospital pallor just dumped an envelope on my desk. It may be it. Want to hang on a second?'
'Sure,' Blaney said.
Carella opened the envelope and pulled out the report. 'Yeah, this is it,' he said into the phone.
'Good. I'm calling to apologize. We just had a full house, Steve, and first things came first. Yours was the shotgun murder, wasn't it?'
'Yeah.'
'I hate shotgun wounds,' Blaney said. 'Shotgun woulds really look like gun wounds, have you ever noticed that? Especially when they're fird at close range.'
'Well, a forty-five doesn't leave a very pretty hole, either,' Carella said.
'Or a thirty-eight, for that matter. But there's something more lethal about a shotgun, I don't know. Did you see the size of the hole in your customer?'
'I did,' Carella said.
'It's worse in contact wounds, of course. I've seen cases where guys have stuck the barrel of a shotgun into their mouths and then pulled the trigger. Man, that is not nice to look at. Believe me.'
'I believe you.'
'All the goddam explosive force of the gases, you know. In contact wounds.' Blaney paused, and for a moment Carella could visualize the man's violet eyes, eyes which seemed somehow suited to the dispassionate dismemberment of corpses, neuter eyes that performed tasks requiring neuter emotions. 'Well, this wasn't a contact wound, but whoever did the shooting was standing pretty close. You know how a shotgun cartridge works, don't you? I mean, about the wad of coarse felt that holds the powder charge at the base of the cartridge?'
'Yes.'
'Well, the goddam cartridge wad was driven into the track together with the pellets.'
'What track? What do you mean, track?'
'Of the cartridge,' Blaney said. 'The track. The path of the pellets. Into the guy's chest. Into his body. The track.'
'Oh.'
'Yeah,' Blaney said, 'and the goddam felt wad had followed the pellets into

the guy's chest. So you can imagine the force of the blast, and how close the killer was standing.'

'Any idea what gauge shotgun was used?'

'You'll have to get that from the lab,' Blaney said. 'I sent over everything I dug out of the guy, and I also sent over the shoes and socks. I'm sorry about being so late on the report, Steve. I'll make it up to you next time.'

'Okay, thanks, Paul.'

'Looks like another nice day, doesn't it?'

'Yeah.'

'Okay, Steve, I won't keep you. So long.'

'So long,' Carella said. He put the phone back into its cradle, and then picked up the report from the Medical Examiner's office. It did not make very pleasant reading.

Chapter Three

Three of the men in the poker game were getting slightly p.o.'d. It wasn't so much that they minded losing – the *hell* they didn't mind! – it was simply that losing to the fourth man, the man with the hearing aid, was somehow degrading. Perhaps it was the cheerlessness with which he played. Or perhaps it was the air of inevitability he wore on his handsome features, a look which told them he would ultimately triumph, no matter what skill they brought to the game, no matter how often fortune smiled upon them.

Chuck, the burliest of the four men, looked at his cards sourly and then glanced across the table to where the deaf man sat. The deaf man was wearing grey flannel slacks and a navy-blue blazer over a white dress shirt open at the throat. He looked as if he had just got off a yacht someplace. He looked as if he were waiting for a butler to serve him a goddam Martini. He also looked like a man who was sitting with four cards to a high straight.

The game was five-card stud. Two of the players had dropped out on the third card, leaving only the deaf man and Chuck in the game. Looking across at the deaf man's hand, Chuck saw the three exposed cards: a jack of spades, a queen of clubs and a king of diamonds. He was reasonably certain that the hole card was either a ten or an ace, more probably a ten.

Chuck's reasoning, to himself, seemed sound. He was sitting with a pair of aces and a six of clubs exposed. His hold card was a third ace. His three-of-a-kind had the deaf man's possible straight beat. If the deaf man's hole card was a ten, he was sitting with a four-card straight, both ends of which were open. The chances of filling it seemed pretty slim. If his hole card was the ace, his straight was open on only one end, and the chances of filling it were narrower. Besides, there was always the possibility that Chuck would catch either a full house or four-of-a-kind on that last card. His bet seemed like a safe one.

'Aces bet a hundred,' he said.

'Raise a hundred,' the deaf man answered, and Chuck had his first tremor of anxiety.

'On what?' he asked. 'All I see is three cards to a straight.'

'If you looked more closely, you'd see a winning hand.'

Chuck nodded briefly, not in agreement with the deaf man, but with an inner conviction of his own. 'Raise *you* a hundred,' he said.

'That's fair,' the deaf man said. 'And once again.'

Chuck studied the deaf man's hand once more. Three cards to a straight showing. The fourth card to the straight obviously in the hole. Whether it was open on one end or both, it still needed a fifth card.

'*And* a hundred,' Chuck said.

'Be careful now,' the deaf man advised. 'I'll just call.'

He put his chips into the pot. Chuck dealt the next card. It was the ten of hearts.

'There's your goddam straight,' he said.

He dealt his own card. The four of diamonds.

'Aces still bet,' the deaf man said.

'I check,' Chuck said.

'I'll bet a hundred,' the deaf man said, and Chuck's face fell.

'Yeah,' he answered. 'I'll see you.'

The deaf man turned over the hole card. Sure enough, it was the ace.

'Straight to the ace,' he said. 'I think that beats your three aces.'

'How'd you know I had three aces?' Chuck asked, watching the deaf man pull in his winnings.

'Only from the force of your betting. I don't think you'd have bet so heavily with two pair. So I assumed you already had your third ace.'

'And you raised three aces? On the strength of a *possible* straight?'

'On the strength of percentages, Chuck,' the deaf man said, stacking his chips into a neat pile. 'On the strength of percentages.'

'Some percentages,' Chuck said. 'Luck, that's all. Dumb luck.'

'No, not quite. I was sitting with four cards to a one-ended straight: the jack, queen, king and ace. In order to make my straight, I needed a ten – any ten. And this was the only possible way of improving my hand to beat your three aces. I had to catch that ten. If *not*, if for example I simply paired one of my cards, I couldn't possibly beat you. Am I right? So what were my chances of completing the straight? My chances against making it were nine to one, Chuck.'

'Well, those seem like pretty damn steep odds to me.'

'Do they? consider the fact that no tens had appeared at any time during the game. Of course, either you – or our friends before they dropped out – could have been holding tens in the hole. But I knew you had an ace in the hole, and I took a chance on our friends.'

'The odds were still too steep. You should have dropped out.'

'But then I'd have lost, wouldn't I? And your own odds against improving your hand were even steeper.'

'How could they be? I had you beat to begin with! I had three aces!'

'Yes, but how could you improve them? In one of two ways. Either by catching a fourth ace or by catching another six to give you a full house. I knew you *couldn't* catch the fourth ace because I was sitting with it in the hole. In any case, the odds on catching it, even if I *hadn't* been holding it, would have been thirty-nine to one. Considerably higher than nine to one, don't you think?'

'What about the possibility of a full house? I could have caught that other six.'

'True, you could have. The odds against it, though, were fourteen and two-thirds to one. Which, again, is higher than the nine to one odds I was bucking. And, weighted against this was the fact that our two friends were both showing sixes when they dropped out. This means there was only one six left in the deck, and it further means that the odds on catching that last six were essentially the same as they'd be for catching the fourth ace – thirty-nine to one. Get it, Chuck? My odds were nine to one. Yours were thirty-nine to one.'

'You're forgetting something, aren't you?'

'I never forget anything,' the deaf man said.

'You're forgetting that *neither* of us could have improved our hands. And if neither of us improved, I'd have won. Three aces beats an incompleted straight.'

'That's true. But it's not something I forgot. It was simply a calculated risk. Remember, Chuck, that your pair of aces didn't turn up until the fourth card had been dealt. If your first two exposed cards had been aces, I'd have dropped out immediately. Up to that point, we were both on equal footing more or less. You had an ace and a six showing on the board. I had an ace in the hole, and a king and queen showing on the board. My hand seemed just about as strong as yours. I suspected you had a pair of aces but, considering my own ace in the hole, I thought you might be bluffing a strong bet on a pair of sixes. And *any* pair I caught would have beat those. I think I played the hand correctly.'

'I think it was luck,' Chuck maintained.

'Perhaps.' The deaf man smiled. 'But *I* won, didn't I'

'Sure. And since you won, you can come on real strong about how you figured it all out beforehand.'

'But I did, Chuck.'

'You only *say* you did. If you'd have lost, it'd be a different story. You'd have been making excuses all over the lot to explain away your mistakes.'

'Hardly,' the deaf man said. 'I am not a person who admits to mistakes. The word *mistake* isn't even in my vocabulary.'

'No? Then what do you call it?'

'Deviation. Truth is a constant, Chuck. It is only the observation of truth which is a variable. The magnitude of error depends on the difference between the unchanging truth and the faithfulness of the observation. And so error can only be defined as deviation, not mistake.'

'Bullshit,' Chuck said, and the other men around the table laughed.

'Precisely,' the deaf man said, laughing along with them. 'Bullshit. Error is simply the amount of bullshit attached to any true observation. Do you want to deal, Rafe?'

The tall thin man on Chuck's left raised his gold-rimmed spectacles and wiped the tears from his eyes. He took the cards and began shuffling them.

'One thing I've got to say is this is gonna be the godamnedest caper there ever was.' He shoved the deck at Chuck. 'You want to cut?'

'What's the use?' Chuck said petulantly. 'Run them.'

The man sitting opposite Rafe said, 'What's the game?' He put the question tentatively because he was a newcomer to the group, and not yet too sure of his standing. Nor was he yet too certain as to exactly who his predecessor had been or why he'd been dropped from the quartet. He possessed only one quality which could be considered useful to the group, and he had stopped considering that a quality some ten years ago. This quality was the making of bombs. Bombs, that is. You know, bombs. The old man sitting at the table with the other three had been quite adept at fashioning lethal exploding devices. He had lent his talents at one time to a certain foreign power and had spent a good many years in prison regretting this peccadillo, but his early political affiliations had not been questioned by the deaf man when he'd been hired. The deaf man was content to know he could still put together a bomb if called upon to do so. He was particularly interested in learning that the old man could put together incendiary bombs as well as the exploding garden variety. His versatility seemed to please the deaf man immensely. Pop couldn't have cared less either way. All he knew was that he was being hired to do a job – and as far as he could tell, the only qualifications he possessed for that job was his ability to make bombs.

He could not have known, not at this stage of the game, that his second qualification was his age. Pop was sixty-three years old, and that was just young enough, just old enough; that was perfect.

'This is seven-card stud,' Rafe told him. 'Deuces wild.'

'I don't like these bastardized versions of poker,' the deaf man said. 'They throw off the percentages.'

'Good,' Chuck said. Maybe we'll stand a chance of winning. You play poker as if you're out to slit your mother's throat.'

'I play poker as if I'm out to win,' the deaf man said. 'Isn't that the right way to play?'

Rafe began laughing again, his blue eyes misting behind their gold-rimmed eyeglasses. He dealt the cards, said, 'King bets,' and put the deck down on the table.

'Twenty-five,' the old man said hesitantly.

'Call,' Chuck said.

'I'll see you,' Rafe said.

The deaf man studied his cards. He was holding a six in the hole, together with a jack. His exposed card was a five. He glanced around the table quickly, and just as quickly pulled his cards together.

'I fold,' he said.

He sat just a moment longer and then rose suddenly, a tall good-looking man in his late thirties who moved with the economy and grace of a natural athlete. His hair was blond and cut close to his skull. His eyes were a dark blue. They flicked now to the street outside, through the plate-glass window of the store front and the inverted legend:

CHELSEA POPS, INC.

The street side of the store was quiet. An old woman struggled past with a full shopping bag and then moved out of sight. Behind the store, at the back of it, all was chaos. Bulldozers, steam shovels, construction crews swarmed over the vast levelled lot.

'You'd better make this the last hand,' the deaf man said. 'We've got lots of work to do.'

Rafe nodded. Chuck raised the pot, and the old man dropped out.
'Want to come with me a minute?' the deaf man asked him.
'Sure,' he said.
He pushed back his chair and followed the deaf man to the door leading down to the cellar. The cellar was cool and moist. The smell of fresh earth clung to the walls. The deaf man walked to a long table and opened a box there. He pulled out a grey garment and said, 'You'll be wearing this tonight, Pop. While we work. Want to try it on.'
Pop took the garment and fingered it as if he were making a purchase in a men's clothing store. His fingers stopped suddenly, and his eyes widened.
'I can't wear that,' he said.
'Why not?' the deaf man asked.
'I won't put it on. Not me.'
'Why not?'
'There's blood on it,' Pop said.
For a moment, for a brief moment in the still, earth-smelling coolness of the basement, it seemed as if the deaf man would lose his temper, as if he would flare into sudden undisciplined anger at the old man's rebellion. And then he smiled suddenly, radiantly.
'All right,' he said. 'I'll get a new one for you.'
He took the grey garment from the old man and put it back into the box.

Chapter Four

A picture of the unidentified dead man ran in three of the afternoon tabloids on Thursday, April 9. The papers hit the stands at about twelve noon, one of them carrying it on the front page, the other relegating it to page four, but all of them running the shrieking headline DO YOU KNOW THIS MAN? The man in the photo seemed to have his eyes closed, and a police artist had sketched a pair of swimming trunks over his exposed genitalia. If anything, the black shoes and white socks looked even more ludicrous now that they were accompanied by the trunks.
DO YOU KNOW THIS MAN? the reader read and then looked at this picture of an old duffer who'd undoubtedly been snapped sleeping at a public beach, one of those fellows whose soles are tender and who wears shoes while traversing the sand, some sort of publicity stunt probably, and then the reader saw the copy under the picture, and the copy under the picture informed one and all that this old duffer was not asleep, that he was deader than a mackerel and that the smear on his chest was not a printer's smudge but a bona fide shotgun wound which had been carelessly left there by a man with urticaria of the trigger finger.
The papers hit the stands at about twelve noon.
At twelve-fifteen, Cliff Savage showed up in the muster room of the 87th Precinct. Spotlessly dressed, a tan Panama shoved onto the back of his head, a white handkershief peeking from the breast pocket of a brown dupioni silk

suit, Savage sauntered up to the desk and said, 'My name's Savage. I'm a reporter.' He threw the picture of the unidentified man onto the desk. 'Who's handling this case?'

Sergeant Dave Murchison looked at the photo, grunted, looked at Savage, grunted again, and then said, 'What did you say your name was?'

'Cliff Savage.'

'And what newspaper are you from?'

Savage sighed and pulled a press card from his wallet. He put the card onto the desk top, alongside the newspaper photo of the dead man. Murchison looked at it, grunted, and said, 'Steve Carella's on the case. How come your name sounds familiar, Mac'

'Beats me,' Savage said. 'I'd like to see Carella. He in?'

'I'll check.'

'Don't bother. I'll just go straight up,' Savage said.

'The hell you will, mister. You just hold your horses. That press card don't give you the run of the station house.' Murchison picked up one of the wires protruding from the switchboard and plugged it in. He waited a moment, and then said, 'Steve, this is Dave downstairs. A guy named Cliff Savage is here, says he's a reporter, wants to – What? Okay.' Murchison pulled out the wire. 'Says you should go drop dead, Mr Savage.'

'He said that?'

'Word for word.'

'What the hell kind of attitude is that?' Savage wanted to know.

'I gather he don't like you too much, is what I gather,' Murchison said.

'Can you plug in and let me talk to him?'

'Steve wouldn't like that, Mr Savage.'

'Then get me Lieutenant Byrnes.'

'The lieutenant ain't in today.'

'Who's catching up there?'

'Steve.'

Savage frowned, picked up the press card and, without another word, walked out of the muster room. He walked down the low flat steps onto the sidewalk and then he turned right and walked two blocks in the April sunshine to a candy store on Grover Avenue. He made change at the counter, walked to the telephone booth at the rear of the shop, dug a small black address book from his back pocket, and searched for an 87TH PRECINCT listing. There was none. He looked up BYRNES, PETER and found a number for the precinct, FRederick 7-8024. He put his dime into the slot and dialed it.

'Eighty-seventh Precinct, Sergeant Murchison,' a voice on the other end said.

'You ran a picture of a dead man in the newspaper today,' Savage said.

'Yeah? What about it?'

'I know who he is. I'd like to talk to the detective handling the case.'

'One moment sir,' Murchison said.

Savage nodded, grinned, and then waited. In a moment, another voice came onto the line.

'Eighty-seventh Squad, Detective Carella.'

'Are you the cop in charge of the case involving the man they found in the park?'

'That's right,' Carella said. 'Who's this, please?'

'Are you the cop who sent the pictures out to the newspapers?'

'That's right. Sir, the desk sergeant tells me –'

'Why didn't you send one to my paper, Carella?'

'Wha –' There was a long pause on the line. 'Is that you, Savage?'

'Yeah, this is me.'

'Didn't you get my message?'

'It would be inconvenient for me to drop dead at the moment.'

'Look, Savage, I'm not a polite feuder. I'm not interested in mixing clever talk with you. You almost got my wife killed once, you son of a bitch, and if you ever show your face around here I'll throw you out the window. Does that make it clear?'

'The Commissioner might like to know why every other paper in the city –'

'The hell with you and the Commissioner both! Goodbye, Savage,' Carella said, and he hung up.

Savage held the dead receiver in his hand for just a moment, then he slammed it onto the hook and stormed out of the booth.

The Puerto Rican girl's name was Margarita. She had been in the city for only six months, and she didn't speak English too well. She enjoyed working for Mr Raskin because he was a nice, cheerful man who did not shout too much. It was important to Margarita that the person for whom she worked did not shout. Margarita reported for work at nine o'clock each morning. The Culver Avenue loft was only five blocks from her house, and she enjoyed the walk to and from work each day. Once she got to the loft, she went into the bathroom and changed from her street clothes to a smock which she wore while pressing. Since she lived so close to the loft, someone had once suggested to her that she wear the smock to work rather than changing after she got there. But Margarita felt that the smock was not suitable attire for the street. And so every morning she put on a sweater and a skirt and then changed to the smock after she got to the loft. She never wore anything under the smock. She pressed dresses all day long, and it got very hot in that loft and she didn't want the bother of panties and brassiere.

She was a very well-formed girl, Margarita, and as she hefted that steam iron her breasts frolicked beneath the loose smock in time to the accompanying jiggle of her buttocks. Which was another thing she liked about Mr Raskin. Mr Raskin never came up behind her and pinched her. She had worked for another man before him, and he was always pinching her. Mr Raskin was a very cheerful man who kept his hands to himself and who didn't mind the girls telling jokes in Spanish every now and then. So long as they got the work done.

There were two other girls besides Margarita, but Margarita was the unofficial foreman of the group. Each morning, when all the girls had had their second cup of coffee and changed into their smocks and fixed their makeup, Margarita would roll over the dollies with the cartons of dresses which Mr Raskin had bought in wholesale lots, and she would turn them over to the girls who would press out all the wrinkles. Margarita would work right alongside them, that iron flashing over the creased skirts and bodices, those breasts jutting and bouncing. Then she would have a consultation with Mr Raskin about pricing the dresses, and then she and the girls would mark each of the dresses and that evening Mr Raskin would take them to the retail stores or to the farmers' markets, depending on which outlets needed merchandise. It was a very smooth-running operation. Sometimes, when she discussed prices with Mr Raskin, he would try to see into the low front of her dress because he knew she wore nothing underneath, but she didn't mind him looking because he never touched. He was a gentleman, and she liked working for him. As far as Margarita was concerned, David Raskin was the nicest man in the entire world.

Which is why she couldn't understand the threatening calls.

Why would anyone in the world want to threaten Mr Raskin? And especially over so stupid a thing as a dirty loft? No, Margarita could not understand it, and each time the caller phoned, she would feel frightened for her boss, and she would say a silent prayer in Spanish.

She was not frightened on the afternoon of Thursday, April 9 when the delivery man entered the loft.

'Anybody here?' he called from the door at the opposite end.

'Jus' a mini',' Margarita said, and she put down her steam iron and then ran the length of the loft to the entrance doorway, forgetting that she was wearing nothing beneath the smock, and puzzled by the goggle-eyed expression on the delivery man's face when she reached him.

The delivery man took a handkerchief from his back pocket and wiped his forehead with it.

'You know something?' he said breathlessly.

Margarita smiled. 'What?'

'You ought to be in burlesque, sister. I mean it. Burlesque is crying for you.'

'What ees thees bul-esk?'

'Oh, sister. Oh, sister.' The delivery man sighed and rolled his eyes. 'Look, where do you want these cartons?' he asked, his eyes swinging back to the low-cut front of the smock. 'I've got about fourteen cartons of stuff downstairs, so tell me where you want it, and it's yours.'

'Oh, I don' know,' Margarita said. 'my boss, he is no here ri' now.'

'I only want to know where you want it dumped, sister.'

'What ees it, anyways?' Margarita asked.

'Don't know, sister, I only work for the trucking company. Come on, choose a spot. Go down to the other end of the loft again, and then run down this way and choose a spot as you come, okay?'

Margarita giggled. 'Why I got to run for?' she asked, knowing full well what he was referring to. 'You put them inside here, near the door, okay?'

'Okay, sister.' The delivery man winked. 'Sssssss,' he said, as if he were a steam radiator. He wiggled his eyebrows, rolled his eyes and then went downstairs. He came up a few moments later with another man, carrying a heavy carton between them. Together they began setting it down just inside the door. The first man gestured with his eyebrows toward Margarita who was stooping to pick up a hanger. The second man almost crushed his fingers as they put down the carton. It took them an hour and a half, what with the various distractions provided by Margarita, to carry thirteen of the cartons upstairs. They were carrying the fourteenth and final carton into the loft when Dave Raskin arrived.

'So what's all this?' he asked.

'Who are you?' the delivery man said. 'Mr Minsky?' He winked at Raskin. Raskin didn't get the joke, so he didn't wink back. Margarita had gone back to her pressing and was throwing herself into her work with wild abandon. The second delivery man was leaning against one of the cartons and wishing he had a better seat and a box of popcorn.

'Who is Mr Minsky?' Raskin said. 'Who, in fact, are *you*? And what is all these boxes, would you mind telling me?'

'Are you David Raskin?'

'I am he.'

'Darask Frocks, Inc.?'

'Yes?'

'Then these are yours, mister.'

'*What* is mine?'

'Search me. We're only truckers, mister. What does it say on the cartons?'

Raskin studied the bold black lettering on the side of one of the cartons. 'It says "Sandhurst Paper Company, New Bedford, Massachusetts"!' Raskin scratched his head. 'I don't know any Sandhurst Paper Company in New Bedford, Massachusetts. What is this?'

The delivery men were in no hurry to leave. Margarita at the table was pressing up a storm, and it was a delightful storm indeed.

'Why don't you open one of the cartons?' the first man suggested.

The second man nodded in vague abstraction and said, 'Sure, why don't you?'

'Will that be all right?' Raskin asked.

'Sure. It's addressed to you, so open it.'

'Sure,' the second man said.

Raskin began struggling with the carton. The two delivery men sat on the edge of his desk and watched Margarita's monumental bout with the steam iron. Finally, Raskin managed to pry loose two of the staples holding the carton closed. He tore the cardboard flap open, ripped the opening still larger and reached into the carton where he found a horde of smaller boxes resembling shoe boxes. He pulled one of these out, placed it on his desk top, and then lifted the lid.

The box was full of envelopes.

'Envelopes?' Raskin said.

'That's what they are,' the first man said.

'That's what they are, all right,' the second man said.

'Envelopes? But who ordered . . . ?' and Raskin suddenly stopped talking. He pulled one of the envelopes from the box and turned it over so that he could read the printing on the flap. It read:

> David Raskin
> The Vacant Loft, Inc.
> 30 April Avenue
> Isola

'Is that a new store you're opening?' the first man asked.

'Take these back,' Raskin said. 'I didn't order them.'

'Hey, we can't do that, mister. You already opened —'

'Take them back,' Raskin said, and he pulled the telephone to him.

'Who you calling?' the second man said. 'The manufacturer?'

'No,' Raskin answered. 'The police.'

Teddy Carella was in a robe when her husband came home from work that night. He kissed her as he crossed the threshold of the big monstrous house they lived in, and didn't truly realize she was so attired until they'd gone into the kitchen together. Then, surprised because the house was so still at six-thirty in the evening, surprised that Teddy was wearing high-heeled bedroom slippers with the robe – her *silk* robe, at that – he asked first, 'Where are the children?'

Teddy's hands moved in silent answer. *Asleep.*

'And Fanny?' he asked.

Her fingers moved again. *Thursday.*

'Oh yeah, her day off,' and suddenly it was all very clear to him. He did not acknowledge that he'd tipped to her plans or her preparations. He pretended he did not see the bottle of white wine resting on its side in the refrigerator when she opened the door to take out the melon. He pretended that he did not notice the exaggerated female way in which Teddy moved this evening, or the fact that she was wearing a subtly penetrating perfume, or that she had made up her eyes, startlingly wide and brown in her oval face, but that her lips carried not a trace of lipstick, her lips seemed more than anxious to be kissed – he pretended he noticed none of these things.

He went into the bathroom to wash, and then he took of his holster and gun and put them into the top drawer of their dresser, and then he put on a tee shirt and threw his soiled white shirt into the hamper, and then he came downstairs. Teddy had set the table outdoors on the patio. A cool breeze rustled through the grape arbour, crossed the patio, lifted the skirt of her robe to reveal the long lissome curve of her leg. She did not move to flatten the skirt.

'Guess who I ran into today?' Carella said, and then realized that Teddy's back was to him, and that she could not hear him. He tapped her gently and she turned, her eyes moving instantly to his lips.

'Guess who I ran into today?' he repeated, and her eyes followed each muscular contraction and relaxation of his mouth so that – though she was born a deaf-mute – she could almost hear each separate word as it rolled from his tongue. She raised her eyebrows in question. There were times when she used sign language to convey her thoughts to her husband; other times, when there was no real necessity for a formal language between them, when the simple cocking of an eye or nuance of mouth, sometimes a glint, sometimes the rarest of subtle expressions served to tell him what she was thinking. He loved her most during those times, he supposed. Her face was a beautiful thing, oval and pale, with large brown eyes and a full sensuous mouth. Black hair curled wildly about her head, echoing the colour of her eyes, setting the theme for the rest of the woman who was Teddy Carella, a theme of savagery which sprang through the blatant curve of her breast and the ripe swelling of hip and thigh and splendid calf, narrow ankles, narrow waist, a woman with the body of a barbarian and the gentle tenderness of a slave. And never was she more lovely than when her face explained something to him, never more lovely than when her eyes 'spoke.' She raised her eyebrows in question now, and fastened her eyes to his mouth again, waiting.

'Cliff Savage,' he said.

She tilted her head to one side, puzzled. She shrugged. Then she shook her head.

'Savage. The reporter. Remember?'

And then she remembered all at once, and the light broke over her face and her hands moved quickly, bursting with questions. *What did he want? My God, how many years has it been? Do you remember what that fool did? We weren't even married then, Steve. Do you remember? We were so young.*

'One at a time, will you?' Carella said. 'He was beefing because I'd sent that I.D. photo to every newspaper but his.' Carella chuckled. 'I thought that'd get a rise out of the bastard. And it did. Man, was he steaming! Do you know something, honey? I don't think he even realizes what he did. He doesn't even know he could have got you killed.'

Carella shook his head.

What Savage had done, actually, was run a story in his newspaper several years back, a story which had strongly hinted that a detective named Steve Carella had confided to his fiancée, a girl named Theodora Franklin, some suspicions he had about a series of cop killings. In addition, Savage had also listed Teddy's address in the newspaper, and he could not have fingered her more effectively than if he'd led the killer to her apartment in person. The news story had indeed smoked out the killer. It had also damn near got Teddy killed.

Do you remember? she said with her hands again, and an expression of total sadness crossed her face and Carella remembered what she had said to him not a moment ago, *We were so young,* and he wondered what she'd really meant and suddenly he took her into his arms.

She came to him desperately, as if she had been waiting for his arms all day long. She clung to him, and he was not surprised to find her hot tears on the side of his neck.

'Hey, what's the matter?' he said. Weeping, she kept her face buried against the side of his neck so that she could not 'hear' him. He twisted his right hand in her hair and pulled back her head. 'What's the matter?'

She shook her head.

'Tired of your humdrum existence?' he asked.

She did not answer.

'Bored by the four walls?'

Still she would not answer.

'Long for a life of romantic adventure?' Carella paused. 'What's the matter, honey? Look, your eyes are running all over your face, and after you spent so much time making them up.'

Teddy sat bolt upright in his lap, an expression of shocked outrage on her face. Her black brows swooped down. Her right hand darted up in front of his face. Rapidly the fingers spelled out their message.

My eyes!

'Well, honey –'

Then you did notice! And you probably noticed everything else, too! The –

'Honey, what are you getting all –?'

Shut up! Get away from me!

She tried to get off his lap, but his hands slid up under the robe, and though she struggled to free herself, his hands were strong úpon her and at last she relaxed in his arms, and his hands roamed beneath the loose gown, touching her belly and her smooth flanks, stroking her gently as he spoke, his lips moving beneath her listening fingers.

'So sometimes you feel like an old matron,' he said. 'Sometimes you roam this big shell of a house in your dirty dungarees and you wipe runny noses all day long and keep cigarette butts out of the twins' mouths, and wonder when the hell your adventuresome husband is coming home. And sometimes you long for it to be the way it used to be, Teddy, before we were married, when every time was like the first time and the last time rolled into one, when my eyes went up like butane every time I saw you, when it was young, Teddy, when it was new and shining and young.'

She stared at her husband in solemn wonder because there were times when he seemed to be such an insensitive lout, times when he seemed to be only the uncouth slob who told dirty jokes in a detective squadroom and who brought all of his grubbiness home with him, times when she felt alone in her silent world without even the comfort of the person who had been to her the one shining spark in her life, and then suddenly – suddenly there he was again, the person she had known all along, her Steve, the person who knew the things she was feeling, who had felt them himself, and who could talk about them until, until . . .

'And you want it to be that way again, honey, that wild crazy young flying way that was for kids, Teddy, but we're not kids, anymore. So you dressed yourself up for me tonight. It's Fanny's day off, so you rushed the kids into their beds, and you put on your black shorty nightgown – I saw it when the wind caught your robe – and your good silk robe and your fancy high-heeled slippers, and you put that shadow all round your eyes, and you left your lips naked and Teddy, Teddy baby, I love you anywhich way you are, in a potato sack, or digging in the back yard, or right after you had the babies and they rolled you in on the maternity table, or taking a bath, or cooking, or swimming, dressed, naked, reading, weeping, baby, baby I love you and it only gets better all the time and I'll be goddamned if I'm going to cater to your silly back-to-seventeen movement and get all excited because you're in a nightgown and high-heeled pumps, especially, especially when I've been planning on *exactly* this all day long, all goddam day long! Take your fingers off my mouth, I want to kiss you.'

He kissed her, and he didn't ask her afterward whether or not there was any of that flying jazz they had known as kids, or whether or not the world went up in neon, and whether or not Mongolian gongs and bugles went off – he didn't ask her. Instead he slipped the robe from her shoulders, lowered it to her waist, kissed the full rich globes of her breasts, felt her trembling beneath his fingers, and carried her to the new grass lining the patio. And then he held her to him naked, and he didn't ask her anything, and she didn't say anything, and whereas neither of them flew and whereas there was no flash of neon and no crashing of gongs or bleating of bugles, he had the distinct impression that the sky was crumbling and that he was about to fall of the edge of the earth. And, from the way she clung to him so desperately, he knew she was experiencing the same odd sensation.

Chapter Five

The squadroom was jammed to capacity on that Friday, April 10. Sometimes it just happened that way. There were days when the man who was catching barely had anyone to talk to. Everybody else on the team was out preventing crime or collecting graft or some damn thing. But on that Friday, April 10, that old squadroom was just the most bustling old place on Grover Avenue. Detectives, patrolmen, the lieutenant, the captain, messengers from downtown, citizens making complaints – everybody seemed to be in the room that morning. Telephones rang and typewriters clattered and the place had the air of a thriving, if small, business concern.

At the desk closest to the grilled windows that faced the street, Meyer Meyer was on the telephone talking to Dave Murchison, the desk sergeant.

'That's right, Dave,' he said. 'Sandhurst Paper Company in New Bedford, Massachusetts. What? How the hell do I know where New Bedford is? Right next to Old Bedford and Middle Bedford, I guess. That's the way it usually works, isn't it?' He paused. 'Right. Buzz me when you've got them.' He hung up to find Andy Parker standing alongside the desk.

'There's also,' Parker said, 'East Bedford and West Bedford.'

'And Bedford Centre,' Kling put in.

'You guys got nothing to do but clown around?' Meyer asked. 'Come on, look alert. Suppose the Chief of Detectives should walk in here?'

'He can't,' Parker said. 'He's downtown running the lineup. He wouldn't come visit no grubby squadroom like this. Downtown, they give him a microphone and a bunch of bulls who have to laugh at his crumby jokes every morning.'

'Except Fridays, Saturdays and Sundays,' Kling said. 'Today is Friday.'

'That's right,' Meyer said. 'So you see, he just *might* walk in here and find you with your thumb up your behind.'

'The fact is,' Parker said, 'I only come in here to see if there was any messages for me. Because maybe you didn't notice, but I'm dressed for a plant, and in exactly –' he shoved back his cuff and looked at his wrist watch, 'in exactly forty-five minutes, I'll be leaving you gentlmen to take my position in the candy store.'

'What are you supposed –'

'So don't make no cracks about my working or not working. I go on at ten-thirty, and that's that.'

'Yeah, but what are you supposed to be dressed *as*?' Meyer asked.

In truth, the question was not put in jest. For whereas Andy Parker may have felt he'd donned a costume for his candy store plant, the fact was that he looked much the same as he always looked. Which was to say, he looked like a slob. There are people, you know, who always look like slobs. There's simply nothing to be done about it. This tendency towards sloppiness first exhibits itself when the subject is still a child. Dress him for a birthday party and five minutes later he will look as if he'd been run over by a steamroller. Nor will he look that way because he's run through a mud puddle or anything. Oh, no. He will simply look that way because he has within him, inside his beating little heart, the makings of a true slob. It is not good to discourage slobs. They will become slobs anyway.

Andy Parker was a true slob. Five minutes after he'd shaved, he looked as if he needed a shave again. Ten minutes after he'd tucked his shirttail into his trousers, the shirttail was hanging out again. Fifteen minutes after he'd shined his shoes, his shoes were scuffed again. Listen, that was the way he was. Did this necessarily make him a bad cop? Absolutely not. His being a bad cop had nothing whatever to do with his being a slob. He *was* a slob, and he *was* a bad cop – but the two phenomena were not at all related.

In any case, Lieutenant Byrnes had planted Andy Parker in a candy store on North Eleventh with the idea of getting him to smell out the alleged pushers who were peddling their lovely little packets of junk in that spot. Andy Parker was supposed to look like a junkie. It hardly seems necessary to explain, in this communications-enlightened day and age, that a junkie is not a man who buys and sells scrap iron. A junkie is a person who buys junk. Junk is dope. A junkie in short, is a drug addict – as if you didn't know. Now, Parker had seen a great many junkies throughout his career and it could be assumed that he knew what a junkie looked like. But if the casual observer took his 'costume' as an indication, that observer would be forced to conclude that a junkie looked like Andy Parker. For although Meyer Meyer was studying him quite closely, Andy Parker seemed to be dressed the way he always dressed. Which was like a slob.

'Don't tell me what you're supposed to be,' Meyer said. 'Let me guess.' Meyer wrinkled his brow. 'A floorwalker in a department stores. Am I right?'

'That's what he's supposed to be,' Kling said. 'Only, Andy, you forgot a carnation in your lapel.'

'Come on, don't kid me,' Parker said seriously.

'Then what could he be?' Meyer said. 'Just a minute, I've got it! An usher at a fancy wedding!'

'Come on, come on,' Parker said, just as Lieutenant Byrnes pushed his way through the slatted-rail divider and into the office.

'Mark my words,' he said, 'this precinct is going to have the biggest traffic problem in the city as soon as that damn shopping centre is finished. I just drove through there and even the *workmen's* cars are causing a bottleneck. You can imagine what it's going to be like when all those stores are finished.' Byrnes shook his head and said to Parker, 'I thought you were supposed to be in that candy store.'

'Ten-thirty,' Parker said.

'Won't kill you to get there a little early,' Byrnes said.

'I already established that I'm a late sleeper.'

'You established that the minute you began working for this squad,' Byrnes said.

'Huh?'

'I'm telling you, Frick's gonna have to detail six squad cars to that shopping centre,' Byrnes said, dismissing Parker's puzzled look. 'Did you see the big sign they've got up, listing all the stores? There's gonna be a bakery, and a movie house, and a supermarket, and a bank, and a delicatessen, and a department store, and –'

'That's why he's the lieutenant around here,' Meyer said. 'Because he's so observant.'

'The hell with you,' Byrnes said, grinning, and he went into his office to the left of the divider. He paused at the door and said, 'Steve in yet?'

'Not yet,' Meyer said.

'Who's catching?'

'I am,' Kling answered.

'Let me know when Steve gets in, will you?'

'Yes, sir.'

The telephone on Meyer's desk rang. He picked up the receiver quickly. 'Eighty-seventh Squad, Meyer. Oh yes, Dave, put it right through.' He covered the mouthpiece and said to Kling, 'My New Bedford call,' and then waited.

'Detective Meyer?' a voice asked.

'Yes?'

'I have your party on the line. One moment, please.'

Meyer waited.

'Go ahead, please,' the operator said.

'Hello?' Meyer said.

A static-filled voice on the other end said, 'Sandhurst Paper Company, good morning.'

'Good morning,' Meyer said. 'This is Detective Meyer of the Eighty-seventh Detective Squad down in –'

'Good morning, Detective Meyer.'

'Good morning. I'm trying to trace an order that was placed for –'

'One moment please, I'll give you our Order Department.'

Meyer waited. In the promised moment, a man's voice came onto the line.

'Order Department, good morning.'

'Good morning, this is Detective Meyer of the Eighty seventh Squad, in –'

'Good morning, Detective Meyer.'

'Good morning. I wonder if you can help me. A man named David Raskin here in Isola received several cartons of envelopes and stationery from your company, but he did not place an order for this material. I wonder if you could tell me who *did*.'

'What was his name again, sir?'

'David Raskin.'

'And the address?'

'Darask Frocks, Inc., Twelve thirteen Culver Avenue here in the city.'

'And when was the order delivered, sir?'

'Just yesterday.'

'One moment, please.'

Meyer waited. While he waited, Steve Carella came into the squadroom. Meyer covered the mouthpiece and said, 'Steve, the loot wants to see you.'

'Right. Did the lab call?'

'Nope.'

'Any luck on the photo so far?'

'Not a peep. Give it time. It only ran yester – Hello?'

'Detective Breyer?' the voice on the phone said.

'Yes?'

'That order *was* placed by Mr Raskin.'

'When was this, please?'

'Ten days ago. It usually takes us a week to ten days to fill an order.'

'Then that would be on April first, is that right?'

'March thirty-first, to be exact, sir.'

'Was it a mail order?'

'No, sir. Mr Raskin called personally.'

'He called and ordered the material, is that right?'

'Yes, sir, he did.'

'What did he sound like?'

'Sir?'

'What kind of a voice did he have?'

'A very nice voice, I think. It's difficult to remember.'

'Is there anything you *do* remember about him?'

'Well, not really. We handle a great many orders each day, you understand, and –'

'I understand. Well, thank you very much for –'

'There *was* one thing.'

'What was that, sir?'

'He asked me to talk a little louder, Mr Raskin did. During the conversation. He said, 'Excuse me, but would you talk a little louder? I'm slightly deaf, you know.''

'I see,' Meyer said, shrugging. 'Well, thanks again.'

The telephone on the desk nearest Meyer's rang. Andy Parker, who was doing nothing but killing time, picked up the receiver.

'Eighty-seventh Squad, Detective Parker,' he said.

'Carella there?' the voice on the other end asked.

'Yeah, just a second. Who's this?'

'Peter Kronig at the lab.'

'Just a second, Kronig.' Parker put down the phone and bellowed, 'Steve, for you!' He looked around the squadroom.

'Where the hell's Carella? He was here a minute ago.'

'He went in to see the loot,' Kling said.

Parker picked up the phone again. 'Kronig, he's in with the lieutenant. You want him to call back, or you want to give it to me?'

'This is just a report on those shoes and socks the mortuary sent over. You got a pencil?'

'Yeah, just a second,' Parker said sourly. He hadn't hoped to become involved in any work this morning before heading for his candy store, and he silently vowed never to pick up a ringing telephone again unless it was absolutely necessary. He sat on the edge of the desk and reached over for a pad and pencil. He wiped one finger across his nose, said, 'Okay, Kronig, shoot,' into the telephone and leaned over the desk with the pencil poised over the pad and the receiver propped against his ear.

'The socks can be had anywhere, Parker. Just a blend of sixty per cent dacron and forty per cent cotton. We could have narrowed it down to four or five trade names, but there didn't seem much sense to doing that. You can pick the damn things up in the five and ten, if you like.'

'Okay,' Parker said. 'That it?' On the pad he wrote simply, 'Socks – no make.'

'No, there're the shoes,' Kronig said. 'We may have run into a bit of luck there, though we can't figure out how it ties with the morgue's description of the body.'

'Let me have it,' Parker said.

'The shoes are simple black shoes, no perforation on the top, quarter or heel. No decorations anywhere. We checked them through and found out they're manufactured by the American T.H. Shoe Company in Pittsburgh. This is a pretty big outfit, Parker, and they put out a huge line of men's shoes and women's play shoes, casual stuff, you know?'

'Yeah,' Parker said, and still he wrote nothing on the pad. 'So what about this particular pair of shoes?'

'Well, this outfit makes shoes for the U.S. Navy. Just a single model. A plain black shoe.'

'Yeah,' Parker said.

'You got it?'

'I got it. This is the shoe, right?'

'Right. So how does that check out against the morgue's description?'

'What do you mean?'

'They said the guy was sixty-five years old! You know any sixty-five-year-old sailors?'

Parker thought for a minute. 'I'll bet there are some sixty-five-year-old admirals,' he said. 'They're sailors, ain't they?'

'I never thought of that,' Kronig said. 'Well, anyway, that's it. They make the shoe for the Navy, and it can only be purchased from Navy ship's services. Eight ninety-five the pair. Think an admiral would wear such a cheap shoe?'

'I don't know any admirals,' Parker said. 'Also, this is Carella's headache, not mine. I'll pass it on to him. Thanks for calling.'

'Don't mention it,' Kronig said, and he hung up.

'Do admirals wear shoes that cost only eight ninety-five?' Parker asked no one.

'*I* wear shoes that cost more than that,' Meyer said, 'and I'm only a cop.'

'I read someplace that J. Edgar Hoover doesn't like cops to be called cops,' Kling said.

'Yeah? I wonder why that is?' Parker scratched his head. 'We're cops, ain't we? If we ain't cops, what are we then?'

Captain Frick pushed his way through the gate in the railing and said, 'Frankie Hernandez here?'

'He's in the john, Captain,' Meyer said. 'You want him?'

'Yeah, yeah,' Frick said. There was a pained and harried expression on his face, as if something dreadful had happened and he didn't quite know how to cope with it. If the truth were known, of course, there weren't very many things that Captain Frick could cope with. He was, technically, in charge of the entire precinct, although his actual command very rarely extended beyond the uniformed force. In any case, he hardly ever offered any advice to Lieutenant Byrnes who ran the detective squad quite capably and effectively. Frick was not a very bright man, and his approach to police work was perhaps comparable to the approach of an old woman toward a will to be settled. He allowed the actual settling to be handled by those better qualified to handle it, and then he reaped the rewards. And yet, all the while it was being handled for him, he fretted and fussed like a hen sitting on a laggard egg.

He fretted and fussed now while he waited for Frankie Hernandez to come out of the men's room. He would have followed him into the room but Frick firmly believed that police business should be conducted in dignified surroundings. So he paced back and forth just inside the railing, one eye on the closed men's room door, waiting for the appearance of the detective. When Hernandez did come out of the room, he went to him immediately.

'Frankie, I've got a problem,' he said.

'What is it, Captain Frick?' Hernandez asked. He was drying his hands on his handkerchief. He had, in fact, been heading for the Clerical Office to tell Miscolo there were no more paper towels in the bathroom when Frick intercepted him.

'There's a boy who keeps getting into trouble, a nice kid, but he keeps swiping things from the fruit carts, little things, nothing to get upset about, except he's done it maybe seven, eight times already, he's a Puerto Rican kid, Frankie, and I think you know him, and I think we can save both him and the law a lot of headaches if somebody talks to him right now, which is why I'm coming to you, I'm sure you know the kid, his name is Juan Boridoz, would you talk to him please, Frankie, before he gets himself in trouble? His mother was in her yesterday afternoon and she seems like a nice hard-working lady, and she doesn't deserve a kid who'll wind up in the courts. He's only twelve, Frankie, so we can still catch him. Will you talk to him?'

'Sure, I will,' Hernandez said.

'You know the kid?'

Hermandez smiled. 'No,' he said, 'but I'll find him.' It was a common assumption among the men of the 87th that Frankie Hernandez knew every single person of Spanish or Puerto Rican descent in the precinct territory. He had, it was true, been born and raised in the precinct, and he *did* know a great many of the residents therein. But there was more to the assumption of the other men than a simple recognition of his birthplace. Frankie Hernandez was a sort of liaison between the cops and the Puerto Ricans in the precinct. The other cops came to him when they wanted advice or information. Similarly, the people came to him whenever they needed protection, either from criminal elements or from the law. There were people on both sides of the fence who hated Frankie Hernandez. Some men in the department hated him because he was Puerto Rican and, despite department edicts about the prevalence of brotherhood among the man in blue, these men simply felt a Puerto Rican had no right being a cop and certainly no right being a detective. Some people in the streets hated him because he had flatly refused to square any raps for them, raps ranging from speeding tickets to disorderly conduct, or sometimes assault, and on several occasions burglary. Hernandez wanted no part of it. he let it be known quickly and plainly that, old neighbourhood ties be damned, he was a cop and his job was enforcing the law.

For the most part, Frankie Hernandez was a highly respected man. He had come out of the streets in one of the city's hottest delinquency areas, carrying the albatross of 'cultural conflict' about his youthful neck, breaking through the 'language barrier' (only Spanish was spoken in his home when he was a child) and emerging from the squalour of the slums to become a Marine hero during the Second World War, and later a patrolman ironically assigned to the streets which had bred him. He was now a Detective 3rd/Grade. It had been a long hard pull, and the battle still hadn't been won – not for Frankie Hernandez, it hadn't. Frankie Hernandez, you see, was fighting for a cause. Frankie Hernandez was trying to prove to the world at large that the Puerto Rican guy could also be the *good* guy.

'So will you talk to him, Frankie?' Frick asked again.

'Sure I will. This afternoon some time. Okay?'

Frick's mouth widened into a grateful smile. 'Thanks, Frankie,' he said, and he clapped him on the shoulder and went hurrying off down the corridor to his office downstairs. Hernandez opened the door to the Clerical Office and said, 'Miscolo, we're out of towels in the bathroom.'

'Okay, I'll get some,' Miscolo said, without looking up from his typing. Then, as an afterthought, he wheeled from the machine and said, 'Hey, Frankie, did Steve mention about May Reardon?'

'Yeah.'

'You in?'

'I'm in.'

'Good, good. I'll get a fresh roll of towels later.'

Hernandez went into the squadroom. He was just about to sit at his desk when the telephone rang. He sighed and picked it up.

Behind the closed door marked LT. PETER BYRNES, Steve Carella watched his superior officer and wished this were not quite as apainful for Byrnes as it seemed to be. The lieutenant clearly had no stomach for what he was doing or saying, and his reluctance to carry out an obviously unpleasant task showed in his face and in the set of his body and also in the clenching of his hands.

'Look,' Byrnes said, 'don't you think I hate that son of a bitch as much as you do?'

'I know, Pete,' Carella said. 'I'll do whatever –'

'You think I enjoyed that call I got from Detective Lieutenant Abernathy yesterday afternoon? Right after you left, Steve, the phone buzzes and it's a patrolman in the Public Relations Office downtown on High Street, and he asks me to hold on a moment for a call from Lieutenant Abernathy. So Abernathy gets on the phone and he wants to know if a man named Steve Carella works for me, and did I know that this man had sent out photos to all the newspapers except one and that if the police department was to expect co-operation from the press in the future, it would have to show equal consideration to *all* of the city's newspapers. So he demanded that I give this Carella a reprimand and that a copy of the photo go out to Cliff Savage's paper immediately, together with a note from Carella apologizing for his oversight. Abernathy wants to see a copy of the note, Steve.'

'Okay,' Carella said.

'You know I hate that son of a bitch Savage.'

'I know,' Carella said. 'I should have sent him the picture. Kid stuff never gets anybody anyplace.'

'You sore at me?'

'What the hell for? The order came from upstairs, didn't it?'

'Yeah.' Byrnes shook his bullet-shaped head and pulled a sour face. 'Just write a little note, Steve. Sorry I overlooked your paper, something like that. The day we have to kiss Savage's ass is the day I turn in my buzzer.'

'Okay,' Carella said. 'I'll get on it right away.'

'Yeah,' Byrnes said. 'You get any make on that picture yet?'

'Not yet,' Carella said, and he opened the door. 'Anything else, Pete?'

'No, no, go ahead. Get back to work. Go ahead.'

Carella went out into the squadroom. Hernandez came over to him and said, 'There was a call for you while you were with the loot, Steve.'

'Oh?' Carella said.

'Yeah. Some guy saw the picture of the stiff in the papers. Said he recognized him.'

Chapter Six

The man who had phoned the 87th to identify the photograph of the stiff was named Christopher Random. He was a man in his early sixties, and he had only four teeth in his mouth, two upper front and two lower front. He had told Detective Hernandez that he could be found in a bar called Journey's End, and it was there indeed that Carella and Hernandez found him at eleven-thirty that morning.

Journey's End may have been just that for a good many of the bar's customers. They were all wearing wrinkled and soiled grey suits. They were all wearing caps. They were all past fifty, and they all had the veined noses and fogged eyes of the habitual drinker.

Christopher Random had that nose and those eyes, and in addition he had only those four teeth, so that he looked like a remarkable specimen of something preserved in alcohol. Carella asked the bartender which of the men in the grey wrinkled suits was Random, and the bartender pointed him out and then he and Hernandez went to the end of the bar and Carella flashed the tin at Random, who blinked, nodded and casually threw off the shot of whisky which rested on the bar before him.

"Mr Random?' Carella said.

'That's me,' Random said. 'Christopher Random, scourge of the Orient.'

'What makes you say that?' Carella asked.

'I beg your pardon? Say what?'

'Scourge of the Orient.'

'Oh.' Random thought for a few moments. 'No reason,' he said, shrugging. 'Just an expression.'

'You called the precinct, sir, to say you knew who that dead man was, is that right?'

'That is right, sir,' Random said. 'What is your name, sir?'

'Carella. And this is Detective Hernandez.'

'Nice to meet you two gentlemen,' Random said. 'Would either of you care for a little refreshment, or are you not allowed to imbibe while wearing the blue?' He paused. 'That's just an expression,' he said.

'We're not allowed to drink on duty,' Carella said.

'That is a shame,' Random said. 'Sir, that is a crying shame. Barkeep, I would like another whisky, please. Now then, about that photograph?'

'Yes, sir, what about it?' Carella said. 'Who was he?'

'I don't know.'

'But I thought –'

'That is to say, I don't know what his name is. Or, to be more precise, I don't know what his full name is. I do know his first name.'

'And what's that?' Hernandez asked.

'Johnny.'

'But Johnny what, you don't know?'

'That is correct, sir. Johnny what, I do not know. Or even Johnny Who.' Random smiled. 'That's just an expression,' he said. 'Ahh, here's my whisky now. Drink hearty, lads, this stuff here puts hair on your clavicle it does, arghhhhh!' He smacked his lips, set the glass down again and asked, 'Where were we?'

'Johnny.'

'Yes, sir. Johnny.'

'What about him? How do you happen to know him?'

'I met him in a bar, sir.'

'Where?'

'On The Stem, I believe.'

'The Stem and where?'

'North Eighteenth?'

'Are you asking us or telling us?' Carella said.

'I don't know the street exactly,' Random said, 'but I do know the name of the bar, it is called, sir, the Two Circles, does that help you?'

'Maybe,' Carella said. 'When did this meeting take place?'

'Let me think,' Random said. His brow wrinkled. He sucked spit in around his four teeth and made horrible noises with his mouth. 'I think better with a bit of refreshment before me,' he said subtly.

'Bartender, another whisky,' Carella said.

'Why, thank you, sir, that's good of you,' Random said. 'I think I met him a few nights before the beginning of the month. March twenty-ninth or thirtieth, something like that. It was a Saturday night, I remember.'

Carella flipped open his wallet and pulled a small celluloid calendar from one of the compartments. 'Saturday was the twenty-eighth,' he said. 'Was that the date?'

'If it was the last Saturday in March, yes, sir.'

'There were no Saturdays in March after that one,' Carella said, smiling.

'Then that, sir, was the date, yes, sir. Ahhh, here's my whisky now. Drink hearty, lads, this stuff puts hair on your clavicle it does, arghhhhh!' He smacked his lips, set the glass down again and asked, 'Where were we?'

'Johnny,' Hernandez said. 'Met him in a bar called the Two Circles up on The Stem on Saturday night, March twenty-eighth. Go on.'

'Did you write all that down, sir?' Random asked.

'I did.'

'Remarkable.'

'How old would you say the man was?' Carella asked. 'This fellow Johnny.'

'In his sixties, I would say.'

'In good health, would you say?'

Random shrugged. 'I don't know. I'm not a physician, you understand.'

'I know. But was he coughing or anything? Did he look pale or run-down? Did he have any tics or nervous mannerisms? Did he –'

'He seemed to be in perfectly good health,' Random said, 'as far as I could tell. You understand, I didn't ask him to take off his clothes so I could give him a physical examination, you understand, sir. I am saying only that, on the surface, looking at him with my naked eye, and without the benefit of a medical education, I would say this fellow Johnny was as fit as a fiddle.' Random paused. 'That's just an expression,' he said.

'Okay,' Carella said, 'he told you his first name was Johnny. Did he mention his last name?'

'No, sir, he did not. Sir, with all due respect to the Police Department, any extended conversation makes me exceedingly thirsty. I do wish I could . . .'

'Bartender, another whisky,' Hernandez said. 'He didn't give you his last name, correct?'

'Correct.'

'What did he say?'

'He said he was on his way to work.'

'Work? What kind of work?'

'He didn't say.'

'But this was the nighttime, wasn't it?'

'That is correct, sir. It was a Saturday night.'

'And he said he was going to work?'

'Yes, sir, that is exactly what he said.'

'But he didn't say what kind of work?'

'No, sir,' Random said. 'Of course, he was wearing the uniform.'

'Uniform?' Carella said.

'Uniform?' Hernandez echoed.

'Was it a sailor's uniform?' Carella asked. 'Was he a sailor, Mr Random?'

'Ahhhh,' Random said, 'here's my whisky now. Drink hearty, lads, this stuff here puts hair on your clavicle, it does, arghhhhh!' He smacked his lips, set the glass down again and asked, 'Where were we?'

'The uniform. Was it a sailor's uniform?'

'A sailor's uniform? On a man well into his sixties? Now, sirs, that's pretty silly, if you ask me.'

'Well, what kind of a uniform was it?'

'It was grey,' Random said.

'Go on.'

'It could have been a postman's uniform,' Random said.

'*Was* it?'

'I don't know. Or a bus driver's.'

'Well, which was it? A postman's or a bus driver's?'

'I don't know. To tell you the truth, I wasn't feeling too well that night, you understand. I was having a little trouble with my eyes, you understand. Focusing, you understand. So all I can remember is that it was a grey uniform, with a uniform cap and all.'

'It wasn't a chauffeur's uniform, was it?'

'No, sir, it was grey. *Grey*. No black. No, not a chauffeur's uniform.' Random paused. 'But he *was* working for somebody. I remember that. So I guess that would let out the post office, wouldn't it? Unless he was talking about his foreman, that's a possibility, isn't it?'

'He mentioned his employer's name?' Carella asked.

'Well, no, not exactly,' Random said. 'Only indirectly.'

'What did he say?'

'He said he had to get to work or the deaf man would be angry. That's what he said.'

'The who?' Carella asked. 'The *dead* man?'

'No, no, the *deaf* man. Deaf. You know. Hard of hearing. Deaf. Of course, that may have been just an expression.'

'You're sure that's what he said?' Carella asked.

'Yes, sir.'

'Anything else about this deaf man?'

'No, sir.'

'Or about where he was going to work?'

'No, sir. Not a word.'

'You're sure you're remembering this correctly, Mr Random?' Hernandez asked.

'Of course I remember it,' Random said. 'Why shouldn't I?'

'Well, you said you were a little out of focus.'

'Yes, but –'

'What you meant was that you'd had a little too much to drink, isn't that right?' Hernandez asked.

'Well, yes, but –'

'What you meant was that you had a couple of sheets to the wind, isn't that right?' Hernandez asked.

'That's just an expression,' Carella said quickly. '*Were* you kind of loaded, Mr Random?'

'I suppose so,' Random said philosophically.

'But in spite of that, you do remember what happened?'

'I do, sir,' Random said.

'What do you think?' Hernandez asked.

Carella nodded. 'I believe him.'

The man was wearing a chauffeur's uniform. He stood in the doorway of the haberdashery, and he looked around at the fedoras and derbies and caps and Homburgs, and he held his own hat in his hands and stared into the shop, waiting. One of the salesmen spotted him and walked over instantly.

'Yes, sir,' he said. 'May I help you?'

'Mr Lombardo, please?' the chauffeur said.

'Just a moment. He's in the back. I'll get him for you.'

The salesman went into the back of the store and returned a moment later with Mr Lombardo, the owner. Lombardo wore a dark grey suit and a beautiful white shirt with a grey foulard necktie. A cat's-eye ring glistened on his pinky.

'Yes, sir?' he said to the chauffeur. 'May I help you?'

'Mr Lombardo?' the chauffeur said.

'Yes?' Mr Lombardo frowned. Perhaps he already knew what was coming.

'The car's waiting, sir,' the chauffeur said.

'You don't say?'

'Yes, sir.'

'*What* car, may I ask?'

'The car you ordered, sir.' The chauffeur looked puzzled. 'I'm from Carey Cadillac, sir.' He nodded his head, as if that simple statement explained everything.

'Carey Cadillac?' The chauffeur kept nodding. 'The car? It's outside? Waiting?'

He nodded again, studied Lombardo's scowl, and desperately plunged ahead. 'You said twelve noon, sir, and it's twelve noon now. So I'm ready and waiting, sir.' He tried a grin which evaporated the moment he saw Lombardo's scowl deepen. Finally, completely routed, he returned to his original statement, delivering it with cold hauteur. 'The car's waiting, sir.'

'I didn't order any car,' Lombardo said calmly.

'But you did, sir. James Lombardo, Lombardo's Haberdashery, eight thirty-seven —'

'I did not order any automobile!' Lombardo said, his voice rising.

'It's that lunatic again, Mr Lombardo,' the salesman said.

'I know it!'

'Call the police, Mr Lombardo,' the salesman advised. 'This has gone too far. Those telephone threats and all these —'

'You're right,' Lombardo said. 'This has gone far enough.' And he started for the telephone.

'Hey, what about the car?' the chauffeur wanted to know.

'I didn't order it,' Lombardo said, dialing. 'some madman has been trying to get me to vacate my store. This is just another one of his stunts.'

'Well, look —'

'I did not order it!' Lombardo shouted. Into the telphone he said, 'Operator? Get me the police.'

The chauffeur shrugged, stared at Lombardo for a moment, and then put on his cap and went out of the haberdashery. The black Cadillac was parked at the kerb, but he didn't go directly to it. Instead, he went to the plate-glass front of the store next door to the haberdashery. And, longingly, he studied the sapphires and rubies and emeralds and diamonds which were spread on black velvet in the window.

Sighing, he went back to the car and drove away.

Chapter Seven

The deaf man and Rafe had been sitting in the ferry-house waiting-room for close to a half hour, watching the people who came and went, watching especially the number of policemen patrolling the docks or hanging around the waiting-room, or coming on and off the ferry itself. A huge clock was at one end of the pale green room, and the deaf man looked up at the clock occasionally, and occasionally he studied the ferry schedule in his hands. The inside of the schedule looked like this:

ISOLA TO MAJESTA Daylight Saving Time Schedule symbols should be checked carefully against "REFERENCES" in center of tables.		REFERENCES	MAJESTA TO ISOLA Daylight Saving Time Schedule symbols should be checked carefully against "REFERENCES" in center of tables.	
Lve Isola	Arr Majesta		Lve Majesta	Arr Isola
12:15AM	12:45AM	A—Will run on Saturdays only.	1:00AM	1:30AM
A12:45	1:15		A 1:45	2:15
1:45	2:15	B—Will run on Sundays only.	2:30	3:00
A 2:15	2:45		A 3:15	3:45
3:15	3:45	C—Will run on Saturdays and Sundays only.	B 4:45	5:15
B 3:45	4:15		C 5:00	5:30
C 4:15	4:45		6:45	7:15
6:05	6:35	D—Will run on weekdays only.	8:15	8:45
D 7:30	8:00		D 8:30	9:00
D 8:00	8:30	E—Will run only on May 30, July 4, and September 7.	D 8:45	9:15
9:05	9:35		10:00	10:30
11:00	11:30		11:45	12:15PM
12:30PM	1:00PM	Authorised and distributed by the River Harb Ferry Company, not responsible for errors, all times subject to change without notice, all fares ten cents additional if tickets are purchased on boat.	1:30PM	2:00
2:15	2:45		3:00	3:30
4:05	4:35		5:00	5:30
5:45	6:15		D 5:30	6:00
6:05	6:35		6:30	7:00
E 7:15	7:45		8:00	8:30
8:45	9:15		9:30	10:00
9:15	9:45		10:00	10:30
9:45	10:15		10:20	10:50
11:00	11:30		11:35	12:05AM

The deaf man studied the timetable, made a mental note and then walked to the nearest ticket booth.

'Good morning,'' he said to the ticket seller in his gentle voice, smiling.

'Morning,' the ticket seller said, not looking up. The ticket seller seemed to be counting something. All ticket sellers always seem to be counting something no matter when you approach their windows. They are either counting money, or new tickets, or cancelled tickets, or stamps, or schedules, or sometimes they are counting their big toes, but they are always counting something, and they are always too busy with what they are counting to look up at you. This one was no exception. The deaf man was smiling his most powerful smile and talking in his most persuasively gentle voice, but the ticket seller went right on counting whatever it was he was counting, and he didn't look up once during the entire conversation.

'Does your ferry carry trucks?' the deaf man asked.

'Depends on how big.'

'Well, I wasn't thinking of a trailer truck,' the deaf man said, gently, his blue eyes twinkling.

'Well, what kind of a truck *were* you thinking of?'

'An ice-cream truck.'

'Ice-cream truck, huh? You mean like Good Humour? Like that?'

'Yes. Not Good Humour, but a truck of that size. That's exactly what I meant.'

'We carry 'em.'

'What was that? I'm sorry, I'm a little deaf.'

'I said we carry 'em. Ice-cream trucks.'

'Do I need a ticket in advance, or can I buy it on the ferry?'

'You buy it on the ferry.'

'Would you mind looking at this ferry schedule, please?' the deaf man said, and he shoved the schedule under the barred window. The ticket seller did not look up. His eyes shifted toward the schedule, but he continued counting, and he would not look up at the deaf man.

'What about it?'

'It say's effective April 13. That's next Monday.'

'That's right. What about it? We still got some old schedules over there, if you want them.'

'No, no, this is just what I want. But will these arrivals and departures be in effect for a while?'

'Absolutely. Don't put out a new schedule until June sometime. And even that'll be the same, actually, except it makes people feel better when they see new dates on a timetable.'

'Then these times will be in effect throughout April and May, is that right?'

'June, too,' the ticket seller said. '*And* July, for that matter. *And* August. Schedule don't change again until we go off daylight-saving time. That's in September sometime.'

'I see, thank you. And I can buy a ticket for the truck after I have boarded the ferry with it, is that also correct?'

'Yep, that's right.'

'Should I get here very far in advance, or can you usually accommodate all the vehicles that want passage?'

'We got room for twenty-five cars. Seldom get more'n a dozen. Plenty of room aboard the old tub. Not many people want to go to Majesta. Sure, it's nice and quiet there, but it ain't exactly anybody's idea of city life, if you know what I mean.'

'Well, thank you very much,' the deaf man said. 'What time does the next ferry leave?'

The ticket seller did not stop counting, nor did he look up at the clock or down at his wrist watch. He simply said, 'Eleven o'clock.'

'Thank you,' the deaf man said. He walked away from the window, nodded pleasantly at a uniformed cop standing near the newspaper stand, and strode rapidly to where Rafe was sitting on the bench. He sat beside him unobtrusively.

'I'll be going over to Majesta,' he said. 'You have some phone calls to make, don't you?'

'Yes, I do,' Rafe said, nodding. The sight of the uniformed cop made him somewhat anxious. He did not like policemen. He had spent five years in prison because of policemen.

'I just checked the schedule,' the deaf man told him. 'We'll plan on catching the 5.45 p.m. boat on the evening of the caper. The one after that is at 6.05. That gives us a twenty-minute leeway, should anything go wrong.'

'Do you think anything will go wrong?' Rafe asked. He was a tall thin man with a mild manner, a manner accentuated by the gold-rimmed eyeglasses and sandy-blond hair.

'No,' the deaf man said confidently. 'Nothing will go wrong.'

'How can you be sure?'

'I can be sure because I have studied the probabilities. And I can be sure because I know exactly what we are dealing with.'

'And what's that?'

'An outmoded police force,' the deaf man said.

'They weren't so outmoded when they sent me to jail,' Rafe said quietly, glumly.

'Examine the Police Department, if you will,' the deaf man said. 'There are approximately thirty thousand cops in this sprawling metropolis. And this figure includes all of them, inspectors, deputy inspectors, detectives, patrolmen, veterinarians, policewomen, everything. The total police force numbers thirty thousand. That's it.'

'So?'

'So there are approximately ten million people in this city. And it is the task of those thirty thousand policemen to see that those ten million people do not commit various criminal acts against each other. If we divide the number of potential law-breakers by the number of policemen, we can say – roughly – that each cop is responsible for the conduct of about three hundred thirty-three people, am I right?'

Rafe did some laborious long division. 'Yes, that's about right.'

'Now, obviously, one cop – even assuming he is armed with the most modern weapons – couldn't possibly control three hundred thirty-three people should they, for example, decide to commit three hundred thirty-three crimes in three hundred thirty-three places at the same time. It would be physically impossible for one cop to prevent all of those crimes because he couldn't possibly be in two places at the same time, one of the basic laws of physics. But, of course, there are a vast number of policemen who, in combination, can be brought into action against a multitude of simultaneous criminal explosions. But even these men, in combination, could not cope with, if you will, ten million people committing ten million crimes simultaneously. Despite the permutations.'

'I don't understand you,' Rafe said.

'Permutations,' the deaf man said. 'The number of possible ways – well, let's take a deck of cards. You'll be more at ease with cards than with policemen. There are fifty-two cards in the deck. If we want to know how many possible ways there are of arranging those fifty-two cards, we start with the simple permutation, written this way.' He took a slip of paper from his pocket and quickly jotted:

$$^{52}P_{52}$$

'I still don't understand,' Rafe said.

'That's simply the mathematical way of writing the permutations of 52. We call *all* the arrangements we can make by selecting all the numbers of a group 'simple permutations.' The equation becomes . . .' And he wrote:

$$^{52}P_{52} = 52!$$

'That tells us how many possible ways there are of arranging a deck of 52 cards.'

'What's the exclamation point for?' Rafe asked.

'It's not an exclamation point. There are no interjections in mathematics. It simply indicates that the number must be multiplied by every whole number below it until we get to 1. For example, the number four followed by that symbol simply means 4 times 3 times 2 times 1.'

'So how many ways *can* you arrange a deck of cards?'

'52! ways – or 52 times 51 times 50 times 49 times – well, all the way down until you reach the figure 1. It would take all day to multiply it out. But at the risk of making you nervous again, let's go back to something of more concern to us, policemen. And, specifically, the detectives of the Eighty-seventh Squad. There are normally sixteen men on the squad. But when we pull our job, two will be on vacation and two will be in Washington taking an FBI course.'

'That leaves twelve,' Rafe said.

'Right. Let's try to figure how many possible combinations those twelve men can arrange themselves into, shall we? The equation would be this.' He wrote:

$$^{12}P_{12} = 12!$$

'Which means,' he went on, '12 times 11 times 10, and so on. Let's see what that come to.' Quickly, he began multiplying figures on his sheet of paper. 'Well, here you are,' he said. 'All the possible combinations for twelve men, 12 times 11 times 10 down through 1, is 479,001,600. It sounds staggering, doesn't it?'

'It sure does. Even *one* cop sounds staggering to me,' Rafe said.

'Of course, detectives usually work in pairs, and not in teams of twelve or eight or six or what have you. And this would automatically limit the number of possible combinations. Besides, we need not concern ourselves with the permutations of those twelve men. We need only to abstract a theory about law enforcement and crime prevention. It seems to me, Rafe, that the police operate on their own limited theory of probability. Obviously with their inadequate force of thirty thousand, they cannot possibly hope to be everywhere at once. This is a damned big city and a great many people in it are practising criminals. So the police operate against percentages. They figure in this fashion, more or less: A certain number of criminals must escape detection *for the moment* because we can't possibly hope to be where they are when a crime is being committed or because we can't successfully investigate every crime even after it's been committed; however, *in the long run*, we will one day catch a previously undetected criminal because we will be in the right place at the right time or because the situation for a successful investigation will present itself. '*In the long run*' – those are the key words in probability.'

'I think I'd better go make my phone calls,' Rafe said. 'Besides, your ferry's coming in.'

'Just a moment, Rafe. "*In the long run.*" Remember those words. If you flipped a penny five times in succession, the first five flips might come up tails. If you stopped flipping right there, you might come to the conclusion that a penny will come up tails one hundred per cent of the times it is flipped. Deviation, remember? The difference between observation and reality. Actually, the longer you kept flipping that penny, the closer you would come to the truth. Which is, of course, that it will turn up heads fifty per cent of the time and tails the remaining fifty per cent. So the cops are playing the long run. They've got this rather cute, quaint, antiquated, friendly, bumbling law enforcement machine and *in the long run*, through a combination of choice and chance, they will make their arrests and maintain order – primarily because the percentages are on their side. Most citizens, you see, are law-abiding. But tell me something, Rafe.'

'What?' Rafe asked.

'What happens when someone comes along and screws up the percentages? What happens when the police are forced to cope with something the like of which they've never encountered before? What happens when they're pushed into dealing with the *short* run?'

'I don't know,' Rafe said. 'What happens?'

'We'll walk off with two and a half million bucks,' the deaf man said. 'That's what.'

The real estate agent in Majesta was quite taken with his caller. The man was tall and good-looking, with pleasant blue eyes and a manner reminiscent of the Old South. At the same time, the man knew what he wanted and he wasted no time in stating his needs.

'A small house with a garage,' the deaf man said. 'It needn't be close to the ferry, and I shall only need it for a few weeks. The garage must be large enough to hold two cars: a sedan and a small truck.'

'I see, sir,' the agent said. 'And the house? How large a house will it be?'

'It should accommodate four adults,' the deaf man said. He grinned pleasantly. 'My colleagues and I are working on a screenplay which will be shot in the city streets this summer. We want two weeks of uninterrupted work, no telephones, no visitors. That's why we thought of Majesta.'

'I see,' the agent said. 'You're a screen writer then, is that right?'

'That's right.'

'Well, I knew you were *something* right off the bat. I could tell.'

'Well, thank you,' the deaf man said.

'Sure. And I think I've got just the house for you.' He paused. 'What movie company do you work for?'

'An independent outfit,' the deaf man said quickly.

'You write anything else besides movie scripts?

'Oh yes, a great many things.'

'Would I know your name?' the agent asked.

'Perhaps.'

'Well, what is it? I'll need it for our records, anyway.'

'Thomas Wolfe,' the deaf man said.

'Oh, sure,' the agent said, smiling. 'Sure. I think I even read a few of your books. Sure.'

Sitting in the phone booth, Rafe put a small tick mark alongside the tenth number on his list. There were fifteen numbers after that one, and all of the exchanges were for locations on the south side of the city, or – to be more precise – on the south side of the territory under the command of the Eighty-seventh Precinct. David Raskin's phone number was among those on the list. So was James Lombardo's. Dave Raskin ran a dress loft. Jim Lombardo ran a haberdashery. The two men had nothing at all in common. Unless one wished to comment on the fact that Dave's loft was over a bank and Jim's hat store was next door to a jewellery concern. Otherwise, there was no similarity.

Of the twenty-five numbers on the list, six belonged to clothing stores, eight belonged to restaurants, one belonged to Raskin, one belonged to Lombardo, three belonged to candy shops, two belonged to leather goods stores, one belonged to a travel agency, two belonged to shoe stores, and the last belonged to a tie shop.

Very innocent-looking concerns.

But Dave Raskin's loft was over a bank. And Jim Lombardo's hat shop was next door to a jewellery concern. Thirteen more of the stores on that list were next door to banks. Six were next door to rather fancy jewellery shops. One was next door to a firm which made money loans. Another was next door to a firm which sold silverware. The twenty-fourth store on the list was a Chinese restaurant which was located on the second floor of a building which housed a quaint little shop on the ground floor; the shop had close to five hundred thousand dollars' worth of Oriental jade in the window. And the twenty-fifty store was next door to a company which dealt in foreign exchange and which kept huge sums of cold cash in its safe.

Rafe dialed the eleventh number on his list and waited for the phone to be picked up on the other end. When the voice came on, he asked, 'Mr Carmichael?'

'Yes?' the man said.

'Get out of that store, Mr Carmichael!' Rafe shouted.

'Get out before the thirieth, or I'll kill you!'

Chapter Eight

'Car twenty-three, car twenty-three, signal thirteen, signal thirteen.'
   'This is twenty-three.'
   'Signal thirteen, seven three five Gramercy Street, repeat seven three five Gramercy Street, complainant Sergei Rosnakoff, stink bomb in incinerator, signal thirteen. Car thirty-six, car thirty-six, signal eleven, signal –'
   'This is thirty-six. Go ahead.'
   'This is twenty-three, what was that address again?'
   'Hold it, thirty-six. I gave it to you twice, twenty-three. What the –'
   'This is thirty-six, thirty-six, over.'
   'That's seven three five Gramercy. You got that, twenty-three?'
   'Seven three five Gramercy, Roger.'
   'Car thirty-six, car thirty-six, come in car . . .'

CENTRAL COMPLAINT DESK REPORT

TIME	DATE	RECEIVED BY
9:12 AM	APR 13	PTL. JACOBS
CITY SECTION	PRECINCT	DESK OFFICER
BETHTOWN	HQ COMMAND	SGT EDWARDS

ADDRESS __735 GRAMERCY STREET__ FLOOR __GROUND__
NAME OF COMPLAINANT __SERGEI ROSNAKOFF__
CRIME REPORTED __DISORDERLY CONDUCT (?)__
DETAILS __STINK BOMB IN INCINERATOR. BUILDING SUPER SMELT SOMETHING STRANGE, SAYS SOMEBODY THREW A STINK BOMB DOWN THE INCINERATOR. DISPATCHED TO BETHTOWN MOTOR PATROL.__

DISPATCHER NO. __12__ TIME __9:15 AM__

C.B.D. 16

POLICE DEPARTMENT

Case Report

For. *Captain Charles Hendricks*

CLASSIFICATION *Investigation of Complaint*

Officer Assigned *Patrolman Ralph Allen* Shield No. *35-416*

Place of Occurrence *735 Gramercy Street*

Date of Occurrence *April 13*   Time of Occurrence *9:00 AM*

Date Reported *April 13*   Time Reported *9:12 AM*

BRIEF OUTLINE OF CRIME

Super of the building said somebody threw a stink bomb into the garbage incinerator. Investigated claim, found what caused smell, but it was no stink bomb. Removed same from incinerator room.

WITNESSES (Name, Address, and Nature of Testimony)

Sergei Ronakoff
735 Gramercy Street

      Super of the bldg, man who made the complaint

EVIDENCE (Quantity, Form, and Relationship to Crime)

Burnt clothing and tobacco pouch.

IF DELIVERY URGENT BUT PICKUP & HOLD CONTACT
RIVERHEAD PCT (*(*(* 98TH PCT 98TH XXXXXXXX
XXXXXXXXXX
INFORMATION REQUEST HQ COMMAND GENERAL REQUEST
ALL PCTS ALL PCTS ALL PCTS XXXXXXXXX PRECINCTS
GEN RQUEST INFORMATION XXXXXXX MAN'S UNIFORM
GREY BRASS BUTTONS TOBACCO POUCH FOUND REMAINS
BURNT CHARRED BETHTOWN APT BLDG INCINERATOR XXX
SUSPECT POSS POWDER BURNS ON CLOTH XXXXX INFO OR
ASSIST UNSOLVED SHOOTING CASES CONTACT HQ XXX
HQ COMMAND DET LT DOUGHETY DOUGHERTY DOUGHERTY
XXXXXXXX
        X   XXXXX   XXXX   XXX
APRIL 13 GENERAL ALARM ALL PCTS BE ON LOOKOUT
WOMAN BLONDE AGE 24   5 FEET 4 INCHES 110 LBS
EXTREMELY ATTRACTIVE LAST SEEN WEARING BLUE S

EVIDENCE TAG

PRECINCT	ARREST NO.
102nd	—
DATE	AIDED NO.
4/13	—
	CHARGE
	—

NAME OF COMPLAINANT

Sergei Romakoff

ADDRESS OF COMPLAINANT

735 Gramercy St

NAME: INJURED DECEASED

ADDRESS

PR. CLK. VOUCHER NO

3412

PCT. VOUCHER NO.

102-451

NAME OF DEFENDANT
ADDRESS OF DEFENDANT
NATURE AND DESCRIPTION OF EVIDENCE
Burnt material found in incinerator
ARRESTING OFFICER *Ptl. Ralph Allora*
TIME AND PLACE COURT EXAMINATION

Pr Cts Sn

POLICE DEPARTMENT

Police Headquarters Command

89 High Street, Isola

BY MESSENGER

BY MESSENGER

TO:

Detective Stephen Louis Carella
87th Detective Squad
87th Precinct
711 Grover Avenue
Isola

Enclosed herewith is laboratory report received on the charred scraps
of uniform garment taken from Bethtown incinerator, and forwarded as
per your request received at 3:07 P.M. this afternoon.

Please note that report is preliminary and incomplete concerning matchbook discovered in pocket of uniform coat, but laboratory tests should
be complete by tomorrow Tuesday April 14 and suggest you contact Lieutenant Samuel Grossman at that time should you desire further information your case.

Sincerely,

Albert N. Dougherty

Det/Lt. Albert N. Dougherty
Headquarters Command

AD/rl
cc: Lt. Samuel Grossman

POLICE LABORATORY

89 High Street

Isola

LABORATORY REPORT

FR. CLK. VOUCHER NO. _____ 9402 _____ PCT. VOUCHER NO. _ 202-451 _

LABORATORY REPORT NO. _ L-9034 _ TECHNICIAN _ Peter Kronig _

DATE RECEIVED _ 4/13 _ DATE THIS REPORT _ 4/13 _

NATURE OF EVIDENCE: Burnt material and tobacco pouch found in
incinerator of apratment building.

CONCLUSIONS:

1) Material is 60% nylon, 40% wool, apparently a men's
man's garment, grey in color, with brass buttons,
no labels or ident tags, no mfg name on buttons.
Suggest that garment is uniform of some type.

2) For most part, garment burnt and charred by incinerator fire but
indication in powder burn under too similar shotgun markings portion below left breast pocket. metal staple in pocket ashes indicates possible presence of matchbook, tests to be concluded.

3) Tobacco pouch remaining mostly ashes, leather and rubber, smoldering
rubber caused smell precipitating complaint. Tobacco scraps prvsent
in untouched portion of pouch mixture tradename Smoker's Pipe, Moralo
Moralco Tobacco, North Carolina, nationally distributed, soft pack
and in tin.

4) Hair oil or other grease stain portion of garment which seems to
be lapel, but would run prove negative for compo or make.

REMARKS: Should staple prove to have come from match folder, report on same
will follow.

Chapter Nine

Lieutenant Sam Grossman was one of those rare and vanishing individuals who take extreme pride in their work. As one of these, he was not the type of man who would wait for someone to call for information once that information was available. He had worked all day Monday on the matchbook remains which had been found with the charred uniform material in the incinerator. He was in receipt of a carbon copy of Doughtery's letter, and so he knew that Steve Carella was interested in the case. But even if the interested party hadn't been someone Grossman knew and liked, even if it had been an obscure patrolman pounding a beat on Majesta, Grossman's attitude would have remained the same. He was now in possession of information which could prove extremely valuable to the man investigating the case. He'd be damned if he was going to wait for that man to call him.

Nor had Grossman come into possession of this possibly valuable information through a stroke of luck, or even through the performance of a few simple laboratory tests. There are, you know, some laboratory tests which are extremely simple and which require no patience or perseverance. The reconstruction of burnt paper, unfortunately, does not fall into this category.

To begin with, the matchbook found with the material was contained by what the lab assumed to be the breast pocket of the jacket. The presence of the matchbook would not have been suspected at all had not one of Grossman's capable assistants noticed the glint of metal among the commingled ashes. Upon study, the metal turned out to be a tiny staple of the kind that holds matches to an outside cover. And once the presence of the remains of a matchbook had been determined, the real work lay just around the corner.

There were possibly four or five methods which could have been used to reconstruct the burnt matchbook, all of which required the patience of Job, the steadiness of Gibraltar, and the perseverance of Senator McCarthy. The method best suited to this particular document was discussed by Grossman and his assistants and, when they'd agreed on the proper approach, they rolled up their sleeves and got to work.

The first thing they did was to prepare a hot solution of one per cent gelatine in water. They then placed this solution in a flat developing pan. Then, with his assistant holding a glass plate as close to the ash as he could get, Grossman delicately and gingerly fanned the ash out onto the plate. No one breathed. Inching the plate toward the gelatine solution, the men slowly submerged it so that the solution just covered the surface of the plate. The ash had now been moistened, and the difficult and painstaking job of flattening it without destroying it remained to be done. Finally another glass plate was pressed into place above the first one, and both were squeezed together to dispel any air bubbles. The plates sandwiching the ash were then put into a printing frame and the suspect matchbook was photographed on an orthochromatic plate and printed on compression paper.

Simple.

It took five hours.

At the end of that time the men went home.

On Tuesday morning Sam Grossman called Steve Carella..

'Hello, Steve,' he said. 'I hate to barge in, but I've got a report on that match folder, and I couldn't see any good reason for waiting for you to call me. You don't mind, do you?'

'Not at all, Sam. How've you been?'

'Fine, thanks. I'm sorry that report on the uniform wasn't more helpful, Steve.'

'It was a pretty good one.'

'Not really. What the hell good is a report on a uniform if we can't tell you what kind of a uniform it was? Who cares whether it was nylon or wool or horse manure? You want to know whether it belonged to a bus driver or a mail-man or whatever, am I right?'

'That's right, Sam. But some of that other stuff in the report —'

'Side effects and not really important. The folder may be something else again, though.'

'Something good?'

'Considering what we had to work with, I think we did an amazing job.'

'What have you got, Sam?'

'Well, to begin with, your suspect is twenty-three years old and probably a college graduate.'

'Huh?'

'He has, at some time during the past year, smoked a marijuana cigarette and gone to bed with a blonde between the ages of nineteen and twenty-two.'

'What!' Carella said, astonished.

'Yes,' Grossman said. 'And from this match folder ash, we were able to determine that our suspect served in the U.S. Cavalry as a gunner in a tank during the Korean War. In addition to that —'

'You got all this from that burnt matchbook?' Carella asked, and Grossman began laughing. The dawn broke slowly. Carella, holding the phone close to his violated ear, began to grin. 'You bastard,' he said. 'I believed you for a minute there. What *did* you get from the matchbook?'

'The name of a hotel,' Grossman said.

'Here? This city?'

'Yep.'

'Shoot.'

'The Hotel Albion. It's on Jefferson and South Third.'

'Thank you, Sam.'

'Don't thank me yet. You can probably pick up these matches in any cigar store in the city.'

'Or maybe not, Sam. Maybe they're private hotel stock. The Albion, the Albion. That's not one of those big chain jobs like Hilton runs, is it?'

'No. It's a small quiet place right on Jefferson.'

'That's what I thought. So maybe this *is* a break. In any case, I'll check it out. Thanks again, Sam.'

'Right. How's Teddy?'

'Fine.'

'And the twins?'

'Growing.'

'Good. I'll be talking to you,' Grossman said, and he hung up.

Carella looked at the hotel name he'd jotted onto the pad on his desk. He nodded, pulled the phone to him, and dialed the number of his home in Riverhead.

'Hello?' a sprightly voice answered.

'Fanny, this is Steve,' he said. 'Is Teddy still there, or did I miss her?'

'She's upstairs taking a bath. What is it, Steve? I was just feeding the twins.'

'Fanny, I'm supposed to meet Teddy at three o'clock outside Bannerman's and I thought I'd be able to make it, but it doesn't look that way now. Would you just tell her I'll meet her for dinner at six at the Green Door? Have you got that? Six o'clock at –'

'I heard it the first time. Your son is screaming his head off at me, would you mind if I – Oh, holy mother of God!'

'What's the matter?'

'He's just thrown his spoon at April and hit her right in the eye with it! I don't know why I stay on in this madhouse. It seems to me –'

'Aw, you love us, you old bag,' Carella said.

'An old bag is what I'll be before the year is out. Me who used to provoke street whistles not two months ago.'

'Will you give her my message, dearie?' Carella asked, imitating her thick Irish brogue.

'Yes, I'll give her your message, dearie. And will you take a message from me, dearie?'

'What is it, dearie?'

'In the future, don't be calling at twelve noon because that is the time your darling little twins are being fed. And I've got my hands full enough with *two* Carellas not to have third come bothering me. Is that clear, sir?'

'Yes, dearie.'

'All right, I'll give your wife the message. Poor darling, she's been rushing about like a mad fool so that she'd meet you on time, and now you call with –'

'Goodbye, dearie,' Carella said. 'Go take the spoon out of April's eye.'

He hung up, smiling, wondering how he and Teddy had ever managed to run a household without Fanny. Of course, he told himself, before Fanny there hadn't been the twins, either. In fact, had the twins not been born, Fanny would not have been hired as a two-week postnatal nurse. And then when they'd moved into the new house, the monster which was on the market for back taxes, and Fanny's two weeks were up – well, it was difficult to say exactly what had prompted her to stay on at practically no salary, unless it was the fact that she had come to think of the Carellas as her own. Whatever her motive, and Carella never thought too much about motive except when he was working on a case, he was damned grateful for her existence. He sometimes had qualms that his children would grow up speaking with an Irish brogue since, by necessity, it was her speech they imitated and not the nonexistent speech of their mother. And only last week, he was nearly shocked out of his skin when young Mark said, 'Damn it, dearie, I don't want to go to bed yet.' But all in all, things were working out fine.

Carella stood up, opened the top drawer of his desk, took his gun and holster from it, and clipped it to the right side of his belt. He took his jacket from where it was draped over the back of his chair, put it on, and then tore the top page from the pad and stuck the sheet into his pocket.

"I probably won't be back for the rest of the day,' he told Parker.

'Where you going?' Parker asked. 'A movie?'

'No, a burlesque,' Carella said. 'I dig naked broads.'

'Ha!' Parker said.

They're tearing down the whole damn city, Meyer thought as he passed the building site of the new shopping centre on Grover Avenue and the huge sign announcing that the work was being done by the Uhrbinger Construction Company. In truth, his observations was slightly in error since what they were doing was not tearing down the whole damn city but building up a major portion of it. As Lieutenant Byrnes had reported so accurately, the new shopping centre would be a self-contained commercial operation with a large parking lot and with a conglomeration of services designed to lure housewives from everywhere in the city. The new stores were set in a low modern building which clashed violently with the surrounding grimy fingers of the slum tenements but which nonetheless presented an open area of clean space where the city dweller felt as if he could once again breathe while picking up his package of Wheaties or while cashing a twenty-dollar bill at the bank. Of course, entering the bank or the supermarket was still some weeks away from reality. The sites of these enterprises still crawled with workmen in overalls and sweat-stained shirts, so that perhaps Meyer's observation was not too far from the truth after all. The men rushing about with wooden beams and copper pipes *did* seem to be a demolition crew rather than a construction gang.

He sighed heavily, wondering how he would ever adjust to this new image of a neighbourhood he had come to know quite well over the years. It was odd, he thought, but a person very rarely looked at the neighbourhood where he spent his entire working day, until they began to make changes there. And then, quite suddenly, the old way, the old buildings, the old streets seemed to become very dear and the new way seemed to be an encroachment upon something private and familiar.

What the hell's the matter with you? he thought. *You like slums?*

Yeah, I like slums.

Besides, the 87th Precinct isn't a slum. Part of it is a slum, yes. But you couldn't call the apartment houses lining Silvermine Road a slum. And some of the shops on The Stem were actually pretty fancy. And Smoke Rise, along the river, was as elegant as anything you were likely to find anywhere. So, all right, I'm rationalizing. For the most part, this is probably the crumbiest neighbourhood in the city, and we've undoubtedly got the highest crime rate and our fire department is probably the busiest in the world, but I guess I like it here. I've never asked for a transfer and God knows there have been times when I was pretty damned disgusted, and yet I've never asked for a transfer, so I guess I really like it here.

Which, again, answers your question.

Yeah, I like slums.

I like slums because they are alive. I hate them because they breed crime and violence and filth – but I like them because they are alive.

It was twelve noon, and Meyer Meyer walked the streets of this slum that was alive, passing the construction site on Grover Avenue and then cutting up Thirteenth and walking north. The neighbourhood was a rich amalgam of colour, the colour of flesh tones ranging from the purest white through the myriad shades of tan and brown and into the deepest brown, a brown bordering on black. Colour, too, in the April finery of the precinct citizens, and colour in the shop windows, bolts of blue silk and pink taffeta, and colour on the sidewalk stands, the rich scarlet of ripe apples, and the subtle sunshine of bananas, and the purple bruise of grapes. And colour, too, in the language of the streets, the profanity interlaced with the pseudo-musical jargon, the English of the underprivileged, and the bastardized Spanish, the Jewish peddler shouting his wares with a heavy Yiddish accent, the woman on the street corner wailing psalms to the indifferent blue sky of April. And all of it alive, all of it bursting with the juice of life, all of it raw and primitive somehow, stripped of all the nonsense of twentieth century ritual, that's what he meant by alive, this is what Meyer Meyer meant. For perhaps it was uncouth and uncivilized, but there was no question here of which fork to pick up first at the dinner table, and no question here of the proper way to introduce a duchess to a marquis, no question here of the little civilities, the little courtesies that separate us from the barbarians and at the same time steal from us our humanity. The precinct was as basic as life itself – and as rich.

And so he walked the streets there without fear even though he knew that violence could erupt around him at any moment. And he walked with a spring to his step, and he breathed deeply of air which stank of exhaust fumes but which was, nonetheless, the head air of April, and he felt very glad to be alive.

The loft which David Raskin occupied was directly over a bank.

Mercantile Trust was the name of the bank. The name was engraved on two bronze plaques, one of which decorated either side of the huge bronze bank doors which were open to admit the noonday traffic. A sign stuck to one of the open doors advised any interested party that the bank was changing quarters on April thirtieth and would be ready for business at its new location on May first. Meyer passed the bank, and the sign, and then climbed the steps to David Raskin's loft. A thumb-smeared sign hanging to the left of a huge fireproof door advised Meyer Meyer that he had located

DARASK FROCKS, INC
*Women's Garments Of
Distinction*

Meyer did not knock. He went into the loft, stared down at the front of Margarita's low-cut smock for a second or two, asked for David Raskin and was ushered to the back of the loft where Raskin himself, standing in his undershirt and sweating profusely, was working with the girls pressing dresses. Raskin seemed to be in excellent high spirits.

'Hallo, hallo, Meyer!' he shouted. 'What a day for pressing dresses, hah? A beautiful April day, what a day! It's nice out, hah, Meyer?'

'Beautiful,' Meyer replied.

'April, that's the only time of the year. April is just right for everything, and I mean *everything*, Meyer, even an old man like me could say it, *everything*, Meyer!'

'You seem very happy today,' Meyer said.

'Yes, yes, I'm happy like a little lark. You know why? I'll tell you why. To begin with, my crazyman hasn't called since Friday. Already this is Tuesday, and thank God nothing has come for me, no stationery, nothing, and no telephone calls, either.' Raskin beamed. 'So I'm happy. My girls aren't frightened, and I'm not pestered by this *meshugenuh* heckler. Also, I'm making money like a crazy thief.'

'Good,' Meyer said. 'Maybe he's given up the game, huh? Figured he wasn't getting enough of a rise out of you, maybe.' Meyer shrugged. 'I am glad to hear there've been no incidents since Friday, Dave. And of course I'm glad to hear your business is going so well.'

'It couldn't be better. I got six dozen summer dresses yesterday for – guess what? Guess how much?'

'I don't know. How much?'

'A dollar each dress! Can you imagine something like that? These beautiful little summer things, sleeveless you know, and a little tight across the backside, I'll sell them like hot cakes, they'll come running all the way from Bethtown to buy these, I can sell them for four dollars each and they'll snap them up! I'm telling you, Meyer, I'll make a fortune. You saw the bank downstairs when you were coming in?'

'Yes,' Meyer said, grinning.

'Okay. Right under where we're standing, right here under my feet, they got their vault. And into this vault, Meyer, I'm going to place thousands and thousands of dollars!'

'You'd better do it in a hurry,' Meyer said, 'because the bank is moving at the end of the month.'

'Slow or in a hurry,' Raskin said chuckling, 'I'll do it. I'll be known as the sultan of sexy garments, the lama of ladies' coats and dresses, the monarch of maternity clothes, the king of Culver Avenue! Me, David Raskin! If I keep buying dresses at a dollar each – *oi gevalt*, what a steal! – a dollar apiece and selling them for four dollars, Meyer, I could build my *own* bank! I won't need already the vault downstairs! Meyer, I'll be a millionaire! Can't you see me now? I'll only –'

The telephone rang. Raskin walked to it, still talking to Meyer, not breaking his conversational stride.

'– drive a Cadillac car, nothing else, and I'll wear silk underwear and in Miami Beach I'll be known as –'

He picked up the receiver.

'Hello – the biggest tipper on Collins Aven –'

'You son of a bitch!' the voice said. 'Get out of that loft before the thirtieth, or I'll kill you!'

Chapter Ten

The Hotel Albion was on Jefferson Avenue near South Third Street. A narrow green canopy stretched from the hotel entrance to the street, and a doorman wearing a green uniform and watching the girls strut by in their April cottons, sprang to attention as Carella approached, promptly pulled open one of the brass-bound doors for him, and damn near threw a salute.

'Thank you,' Carella said.

'You're-welcome-sir!' the doorman shouted smartly.

Carella raised his eyebrows appreciatively, went into the lobby, and felt immediately that he had left the city somewhere far behind him. The lobby was small and quiet. Rich dark woods dominated the ceilings and the walls. A thick Persian carpet covered the floor. The furniture was upholstered in vibrant red-and-green velvet, and a huge cut-glass chandelier dominated the ceiling. He felt that he was no longer in the United States, felt somehow that Venice must look like this, rich and vibrant and somehow decadent, somehow out of place with the bustling twentieth century, a city misplaced in time. He had never been to Venice, never indeed been outside of America except during the war, and yet he knew instinctively that this hotel would have fit into that waterlogged city with uninhibited ease. He took off his hat and walked to the main desk. There was no one behind it. The hotel, in fact, seemed to be deserted, as if news of an impending atom bomb blast had sent everyone creaking downstairs to the wine cellar. A bell rested on the counter. He reached out with one hand and tapped it. The bell tinkled in the small lobby, cushioned by the velvet chairs and the Persian rug and the thick draperies on the windows, muffled by the overwhelming soddenness of the surrounding materials.

Carella heard the shuffle of soft-soled slippers over steps. He looked up. A small thin man was coming down from the first floor. He walked with a slight stoop, a man in his sixties wearing a green eye shade and a brown cardigan sweater which had been knitted for him by a maternal aunt in New Hampshire. He looked like that Yankee-type fellow who plays the small-town hotel clerk in all the movies, or the small-town postmaster, or the one the convertible pulls alongside to ask directions of, that guy, you know the one. He looked exactly like him. For a moment, listening to his creaky tread on the steps, watching him come into the cloistered silence of the lobby, Carella had the feeling that he was in a movie himself, that he would speak a line which had been written for him by some Hollywood mastermind and would be answered in turn with another scripted line.

'Hello, young feller,' the Yankee-type said. 'Can I be of some assistance?'

'I'm from the police,' Carella said. He reached into his back pocket, pulled out his wallet, and opened it to where his shield was pinned to the leather.

'Um-hum,' the Yankee said, nodding. 'What can I do for you?'

'I don't believe I caught your name, sir,' Carella said and knew instantly that the man would reply, 'Didn't throw it, young feller,' and almost winced before the words left the old-timer's mouth.

'Didn't throw it, young feller,' the Yankee said. 'But it's Pitt. Roger Pitt.'

'How do you do, Mr Pitt. My name is Detective Carella. We found the remains of a –'

'Carella, did you say?'

'Yes.'

'Carella?'

'Yes.'

'How d'do?' Pitt said.

'Fine, thank you. We found the remains of a uniform in an incinerator, sir, and we also found a matchbook from your hotel, the Hotel Albion, and there's the possibility that this uniform might tie in with a case we are investigating, and so I wondered –'

'*You* investigating the case?'

'Yes, sir.'

'You a detective?'

'Yes, sir.'

'Well, what was it you wanted to know?'

'To begin with, do you know anyone named Johnny?'

'Johnny what?'

'We don't know. But he might have been the person who was wearing this uniform.'

'Johnny, huh?'

'Yes. Johnny.'

'Sure.'

The lobby was silent.

'You know him?' Carella asked.

'Sure.'

'What's his last name?'

'Don't know.'

'But . . .'

'Lotte's feller,' Pitt said.

'Lotte?'

'Lotte Constantine. Lives right upstairs. He's been by here a lot, Johnny.'

'I see. And this Lotte Constantine is his girl friend, is that right?'

'That's right,' Pitt said.

'How old a man would you say this Johnny was?'

'Was?' Pitt asked quickly, his eyes narrowing. 'In his sixties, I guess.'

Carella reached into his inside jacket pocket. He pulled out a photograph encased in lucite. He put it face up on the counter. It was the photo of the dead man which had run in the metropolitan dailies.

'Is that the man you're thinking of?' Carella asked.

Pitt studied the photo. 'Course,' he said, 'I never seen him in a bathing suit. Or asleep.'

'But is that him?'

'It could be. This ain't a very good picture, is it?'

'Perhaps not.'

'I mean, it looks like Johnny, and yet it don't. There seems to be something missing.'

'There is,' Carella said.

'What's that?'

'Life. The man in that picture is dead.'

'Oh.' Pitt seemed to wash his hands of the matter quite suddenly. 'Look, maybe you better ask Lotte. I mean, she'd know better than me.'

'Where can I reach her?'

'She's right upstairs. I'll give her a ring, and maybe she'll come on down to the lobby.'

'No, that's all right, I'll go up. I wouldn't want —'

'Won't take a second to buzz her,' Pitt said. He went to the switchboard and plugged in one of the rubber snakes there. Holding the earpiece to his right ear, he waited a moment and then said, 'Lotte? This is Roger downstairs. There's a feller here asking questions about Johnny. Yes, that's right, *your* Johnny. Well, I thought maybe you wouldn't mind talking to him. Well, he's from the police, Lotte. Now, Lotte, there's no need to go getting upset. No, he seems to be a very nice young feller. Okay, I'll tell him.'

Pitt put down the headset, pulled out the plug, and said, 'She'll be right down. She got a little upset when she heard you was a cop.'

'Everybody gets upset when they hear that,' Carella said, smiling.

He leaned against the counter and waited for the arrival of Miss Lotte Constantine. If there was one thing he disliked, he supposed it was interrogating old people. Actually, there were a great many things he disliked, and a great many people would testify to the fact that Steve Carella was, on occasion, a goddamned crab. So it was an understatement to say, 'If there was *one* thing he disliked.' But, among his other dislikes, interrogating oldsters took high priority, and interrogating old *women* particularly annoyed him. He had no idea why he disliked old women unless it had something to do with the fact that they were no longer young. In any case, he found talking to them trying to his patience, and he was not now looking forward to meeting Miss Lotte Constantine, the girl friend of a man who had been in his sixties.

He watched a luscious redhead in a very tight skirt as she navigated her way down the carpet-covered steps from the first floor. Because the skirt was so tight, the girl had lifted it above her knees, and she walked downstairs with her head slightly bent, watching the steps, a hank of red hair falling over one eye.

'Here she is now,' Pitt said, and Carella turned to look into the lobby, saw no one there, and then looked up the steps beyond the redhead, still seeing no one, and then the redhead was swivelling over to the desk with a lubricated hip and thigh movement that made him seasick, and she extended a hand tipped with scarlet claws and she said in the sexiest voice since Mae West was a girl, 'Hello, I'm Lotte Constantine.'

Carella swallowed hard and said, 'You? Are? Miss Constantine?'

The girl smiled. Her lips moved back from her teeth like tinted clouds pulling aside to let the sunshine through. A dimple appeared in either cheek. Her green eyes flashed. 'Yes,' she said. 'And you are . . .?'

'Detective Carella,' he said, struggling to regain some of his composure.

He had expected a woman in her late fifties and when he'd been confronted with a *zaftig* redhead who'd seemed, at a distance, to be in her early thirties, he'd been flabbergasted, to say the least. At close range, however, he realized this girl was no older than twenty-three, bursting all over the place with youth and vitality and abundant flesh that threatened every stitch of clothing she wore. So he automatically thought of the old man who had been Johnny Something-or-other, and then he automatically thought of *Middle of the Night*, and Oh my, he thought, oh my, oh my.

'Could we sit down and talk a little, Miss Constantine?' he asked.

'Certainly,' she said. She smiled shyly, as if she were unused to sitting with strange men. Her lashes fluttered. She sucked in a deep breath and Carella turned away, pretending to look for a chair.

'We can sit over there,' Lotte said, and she began leading the way. Carella walked behind her. Married man and all, he had to admit this girl had the plumpest, most inviting bottom he had seen in a dog's age. He was tempted to pinch her, but he restrained himself. I'm much too young for her, he thought, and he grinned.

'Why are you smiling?' the girl asked, sitting and crossing her legs.

'I was only thinking you're a lot younger than I imagined you would be.'

'What did you imagine?'

'Truthfully?'

'Of course,' Lotte said.

'A woman in her fifties.'

'Why?'

'Well . . .' Carella shrugged. He took the picture from his pocket again. 'Know this man?'

She glanced at the picture and nodded immediately. 'Yes,' she said. 'What's happened to him?' She did not blench or gasp or wince or blush or grimace. She simply said, 'Yes,' and then, matter-of-factly and just as quickly, said, 'What's happened to him?'

'He's dead,' Carella said.

She nodded. She said nothing. Then she gave a tiny shrug of her shoulders, and then she nodded again.

'Who was he?' Carella asked.

'Johnny.'

'Johnny who?'

'Smith.'

Carella stared at her.

'Yes, Smith,' she said. 'John Smith.'

'And who are you? Pocahontas?'

'I don't think that's funny. He told me his name was John Smith. Why shouldn't I believe him?'

'Why shouldn't you indeed? How long had you known him, Miss Constantine?'

'Since January.'

'When did you see him last?'

'Last month sometime.'

'Can you remember when last month?'

'The end of the month.'

'Were you and he very serious?'

Lotte shrugged. 'I don't know,' she said wistfully. 'What's serious?'

'Were you . . . more than just friends, Miss Constantine?'

'Yes,' she said abruptly. She nodded, as if lost in thought, as if alone in the silent lobby that reminded Carella of Venice. 'Yes.' She nodded again. 'Yes, we were more than just friends.' She lifted her eyes and then tossed her head and brushed a long strand of red hair away from her forehead. Defiantly she said, 'We were lovers.'

'All right,' Carella said. 'Any idea who'd want him dead, Miss Constantine?'

'No.' She paused. 'How – how did he die?'

'I was wondering when you'd get to that.'

Lotte Constantine looked Carella straight in the eye. 'What the hell are you?' she asked. 'A tough cop?'

Carella did not answer.

'Do I *have* to want to know how he died?' she said. 'Isn't it enough that he's dead?.

'Most people would be curious,' Carella said.

'I'm not *most* people,' she answered. 'I'm me. Lotte Constantine. You're a great one, aren't you? A regular little IBM machine, aren't you? Punch-punch, put in the card and out comes the right answer. You come here telling me Johnny is dead, and then you start asking a lot of fool questions and then you tell me what the reaction of *most* people would be, well the hell with you, Detective Whatever-your-name-is, *most* twenty-two-year-old girls wouldn't fall in love with a man who's sixty-six years old, yes, sixty-six, don't look so goddamned surprised, that's how old Johnny was, so don't go telling me what *most* people would do, you can take *most* people and drown them, for all care.'

'He was shot at close range with a shotgun,' Carella said, and he did not take his eyes from her face. Nothing crossed that face. No expression, not the slightest nuance of emotion.

'All right,' she said, 'he was shot at close range with a shotgun. Who did it?'

'We don't know.'

'*I* didn't.'

'Nobody said you did.'

'Then what the hell are you doing here?'

'We're only trying to make a positive identification, Miss Constantine.'

'Well, you've made it. Your dead man is John Smith.'

'Would you say that name was a great deal of help, Miss Constantine?'

'What the hell do you want from me? It was *his* name, not mine.'

'And he never told you his real name?'

'He said his name was John Smith.'

'And you believed him?'

'Yes.'

'Suppose he'd told you his name was John Doe?'

'Mister, I'd have believed him if he told me his name was Joseph Stalin. Now how about that?'

'That's how it was, huh?' Carella asked.

'That's how it was.'

'What'd he do for a living?' Carella asked.

'Retired. He was getting social security.'
'And the uniform?'
'What uniform?' Lotte Constantine asked with wide open eyes.
'The uniform. The one somebody stripped off of him and dumped into an incinerator.'
'I don't know what you're talking about.'
'You never saw him in a uniform?'
'Never.'
'Did he have any job? Besides the retirement money. Did he run an elevator or anything?'
'No. I gave him –' Lotte stopped suddenly.
'Yes?'
'Nothing.'
'You gave him money? Is that what you were about to say?'
'Yes.'
'Where did he live, Miss Constantine?'
'I . . . I don't know.'
'What do you mean, you –'
'I don't know where he lived. He . . . he came here a lot.'
'To stay?'
'Sometimes.'
'For how long?'
'The . . . the longest he ever stayed was . . . was for two weeks.'
'Pitt know about this?'
Lotte shrugged. 'I don't know. What difference does it make? I'm a good customer. I've been living in this hotel ever since I came to the city four years ago. What difference would it make if an old man –' She caught herself, stopped speaking, and returned Carella's level gaze. 'Stop staring at me as if I was Lolita or something. I loved him.'
'And he never mentioned a uniform, is that right? Or a job?'
'He mentioned a deal.'
'What kind of a deal?' Carella asked, leaning forward.
The girl uncrossed her legs. 'He didn't say.'
'But he did mention a deal?'
'Yes.'
'When was this?'
'The last time I saw him.'
'What did he say?'
'Only that he had a deal cooking with the deaf man.'
They were sitting in velvet chairs around a small coffee table in an ornate lobby which suddenly went as still as death.
'The deaf man?' Carella said.
'Yes.'
He sucked in a deep breath.
'Who's the deaf man?'
'I don't know.'
'But Johnny had some kind of a deal with him, right?'
'Yes. That's what he said. He said he had a deal with the deaf man, and that he'd be very rich soon. He was going – we were going to get married.'
'The deaf man,' Carella said aloud. He sighed heavily. 'Where can I reach

you if I need you, Miss Constantine?'
'Either here or at The Harem Club.'
'What do you do there?'
'I'm a cigarette girl. I sell cigarettes. That's where I met Johnny. At the club.'
'He bought cigarettes from you?'
'No. He smokes – he *smoked* – a pipe. I sold him pipe tobacco.'
'Smoker's Pipe?' Carella asked. 'Was that the brand?'
'Why . . . why, yes. How –'
'Here's my card, Miss Constantine,' Carella said. 'If you should think of anything else that might help me, give me a call, won't you?'
'Like what?'
'What do you mean?'
'Like what do you want me to call you about? How do I know what'll help you?'
'Well, any further information about this deaf man would –'
'I don't know anything else about him.'
'Or anything Johnny might have said regarding this deal of hi –'
'I told you everything he said.'
Carella shrugged.
'You want your card back?' Lotte Constantine asked.

That night, the deaf man celebrated.
Perhaps things were going well at the ice-cream store behind the construction site. Or perhaps he was simply anticipating what would begin happening the next day. Perhaps, like a good general, he was drinking a symbolic toast on the eve of battle.
The symbolic toast, in this case, was the taking of a nineteen-year-old girl whose attributes were surely not mental.
But the deaf man, you see, was an economical man and a man who never lost sight of his goals. He was not interested, that evening, in a discussion of mathematics. Nor was he interested in learning about the ambitions or tribulations or strivings for independence or strugglings for realization of self of any member of the opposite sex. He was interested in making love, pure and simple. He had been casing his love partner in much the same way he'd have cased the site of a future robbery. He had been casing her for two weeks, attracted by her obvious beauty at first – the girl was a brunette with luminous brown eyes and a full pouting mouth; her breasts, even in the waitress uniform she wore, were large and inviting; her legs beneath the hem of the white garment were splendidly curved to a trim ankle – and attracted, too, by the smooth-skinned freshness of her youth.
Casually, the deaf man struck up a conversation with her. The girl, as he'd suspected, would not qualify for a teaching position at Harvard. Their first conversation, as he later recalled it, went something like this. He had ordered a chocolate eclair for dessert.
The girl said, 'I see you have a sweet tooth.'
'Yes, indeed,' the deaf man said.
She had cocked one eyebrow coquettishly. 'Well, sweets for the sweet,' she answered, and swivelled away from the table.
Slowly, he had engaged her in further conversations, strengthening his

opinion of her potential. When he finally asked her out, he was certain she would accept immediately – and she did.

That evening, the fourteenth of April, he had dazzled her with his brilliance at dinner. She sat in wide-eyed wonder, contributing little to the conversation, fascinated with his speech. They walked under a star-scattered sky later, guided imperceptibly by the deaf man to an apartment on Franklin Street. When the deaf man suggested that they go up for a drink, the girl demurred slightly, and he felt a quickening of passion; this would not be a pushover; there would be a struggle and a chase to whet his appetite.

They did not talk much in the apartment. They sat on the modern couch in the sunken living-room and the girl took off her shoes and pulled her knees up under her, and the deaf man poured two large snifters of brandy, and they sat rolling the glasses in their hands, the girl peeking over the edge of her glass the way she had seen movie stars do, the deaf man drinking the brandy slowly, savouring the taste of the lip-tingling alcohol, anticipating what he would do to this girl, anticipating his pleasure with a slow cruelty that began mounting inside him, a carefully controlled cruelty – control, he reminded himself, control.

By midnight, the girl was totally witless.

Chapter Eleven

Well, the fifteenth was the middle of the month, and a hell of a month it was shaping up to be so far.

All things considered, and not even taking into account the petty daily crimes which bugged every man working the squad, April so far – despite the lovely weather – was beginning to assume the characteristics of a persistent migraine. And no man on the squad had a bigger headache than Meyer Meyer.

Meyer, it seemed, had become the man officially assigned to the Heckler Case. That it was now a bona fide 'case,' there seemed to be no doubt. What had started with David Raskin as a simple series of threatening phone calls and foolish pranks had somehow mushroomed into something with the proportions of an epidemic. Slowly, bit by bit, the complaints had come in until the list of shop or restaurant owners reporting threatening calls and acts of harassment had grown to a total of twenty-two. Some of the complainants were truly terrified by the threats; others were simply annoyed by the disruption of their business. Meyer, taking the calls, became more and more convinced that one man, or one group of men, was responsible for the heckling. In any case, the *modus operandi* seemed identical.

But what he couldn't understand was what the hell was so important about April thirtieth?

Or why these particular shops had been chosen? A haberdashery, a Chinese restaurant, a tie store, a leather goods shop, a candy shop – what was so important about these particular locations?

Meyer simply couldn't figure it.

Nor was Steve Carella much better off with his case, the case of the almost-naked dead man found in Grover Park. Why, he wondered, had anyone wanted old John Smith dead? Or, for that matter, why would the dead man have taken an assumed name? And such a phoney one at that? John Smith! My God! How many hotel and motel registers in the United States carried that pseudonym daily? And who was this deaf guy? And why had twenty-two-year-old Lotte Constantine wanted to invest time and money in sixty-six-year-old John Smith? (The obvious alias rankled every time he thought of it.) The deaf man. Who? And he pulled a face at the ironies of fate. The one person who meant everything in the world to him was a deaf mute, his wife Teddy. And now his adversary was someone known only as the deaf man. The juxtaposition was irony with a knife-edge, but Carella was not amused. He was only puzzled. Truly and honestly puzzled.

And when it's going bad, you might expect the people who are causing you trouble to let up for a while, mightn't you? When two stalwart and intelligent detectives were struggling with two separate nuts which seemed un-crackable and which caused both men a considerable loss of sleep, when these two intrepid protectors of the innocent, these indefatigable investigators, these supporters of law and order, when these two darned nice fellows were trying their utmost to get out from under two miserable cases, wouldn't it have been decent and only cricket to leave them alone, to allow them a respite from their torments? Friends, wouldn't it have been the decent thing to do? Cop lovers of the world, wouldn't it have been the only nice way, the only good way, the only fair way?

Sure.

On April 15, which was a balmy spring day blowing fresh breezes off the River Harb to the north, the harassment began anew.

It began with a difference, however.

It seemed to be concentrated against Dave Raskin, as if all armies had suddenly massed on poor Raskin's frontiers and were pressing forward with their spring invasion. If you looked at this sudden offensive one way, you could assume the enemy was doing his best to plague Raskin and the cops. But if you looked at it another way, you could think of the concentrated attack as a guide, a signpost, a singling-out of the one store among twenty-five, a divine hand pointing, a divine voice saying, 'Look and ye shall see; knock and it shall be opened unto ye.'

Meyer Meyer looked, but he didn't see at first. Later on, when he knocked, it was truly opened unto him. And he didn't for a moment suspect that this was what was desired of him, that the sudden spring offensive against Dave Raskin's loft was designed to alert a police department which, with all due respect to those stalwarts, seemed to be somewhat asleep. You can play percentages only if your opponents are playing some sort of percentages themselves. Whatever the deaf man's plan, it wouldn't work if the cops didn't at least *suspect* what he was up to. And so the tanks rolled into high gear, churning through the spring mud, and the dive bombers warmed up on the airfields and took off into the chill early morning air and from across the city, the big guns began thundering against poor Dave Raskin's loft.

At ten o'clock on the morning of April 15, four hundred and thirty folding chairs were delivered to Raskin.

They were piled on the floor, and against the wall, and on the tables, and in the hallway, and down the steps, and some of them even overflowed onto the sidewalk. David Raskin insisted that he had not ordered any folding chairs, but the truck driver was a persistent man who told Raskin he always delivered what he was supposed to deliver and if Raskin had a beef he could call the chair company and discuss it with them. David Raskin called both the chair company and the 87th Squad, and then he paced the floor of his loft waiting for the chair people to come pick up the chairs again and waiting for Meyer Meyer to do something. There was, naturally, nothing Meyer Meyer could do except call the chair company who confirmed the fact that David Raskin had ordered the chairs sometime last week for delivery that day which, again naturally, David Raskin had not done.

So Meyer Meyer ran his hand over his bald head and cursed in pig Latin, a trick he had learned as a boy because his mother had not allowed swearing in her house. And David Raskin paced the floor of his loft and cursed in very loud English which, fortunately, his Puerto Rican girls did not understand too well.

At twelve-thirty on the nose, the caterers arrived.

The caterers arrived and with them they brought enough food to feed the entire Russian Army together with a few Yugoslavian partisans, or so it seemed. Actually they brought only enough food to feed the four hundred and thirty lunch guests who were to occupy the four hundred and thirty folding chairs. They brought little bottles containing Martinis and Manhattans, and they brought celery and olives and carrot sticks, and they brought onion soup, and they brought roast beef and turkey and candied sweet potatoes and asparagus tips au gratin and coffee, tea or milk, and orange sherbet and chocolate layer cake and little mints and – man, David Raskin positively flipped! The caterers insisted that he had called them and ordered this veritable feast and Raskin told them he didn't know four hundred and thirty people in the entire world, let alone four hundred and thirty people he would care to invite for lunch, and the caterers said he had ordered the stuff, they had prepared all the food, what the hell were they supposed to do with it all, this wasn't folding chairs which you could return, this was food, food, FOOD, especially cooked and prepared for the occasion, who was going to pay the bill?

'The man who ordered this *megillah!*' Raskin shouted.

'*You* ordered it!' the caterers shouted back.

'I ordered nothing! Get it out of here! Get it out! Out! Out! Out!'

There were fourteen musicians in the orchestra, and they were all carrying their instruments, instruments like trombones and saxophones, and a bass drum, and a bass fiddle, and trumpets, and even a French horn or two. And they were also carrying music stands and they wanted to know where they should set up, and Raskin told the leader – a small man with a Hitler moustache and a personality to match – that he could go set up in the River Dix, just get the hell out of his loft, he did not order any damned orchestra! To which the man with the Hitler moustache said. 'You came down to the union personally and left a twenty-dollar deposit when you hired the band!'

'*Me!*' Raskin shouted. 'I came down to the *firshtunkenuh* union? I don't even know where your dirty union *is*, I came down? Get out of here with those drums!' and that was when the men returned to pick up the chairs, and the way Raskin finally got everybody out of the place was by calling Meyer again, who rushed over and tried to settle things as best he could.

That was on the fifteenth, and a jolly Wednesday that was, by George.

On Monday the twentieth, only four items arrived, and they were obviously a mistake.

The four items were:

2 PICKS

2 SHOVELS

David Raskin mopped his feverish brow.

'I didn't order these,' he said.

The delivery boy shrugged and consulted the order slip. 'Two picks and two shovels. Says so right here.'

Patiently, Raskin said, 'I didn't order them. You see, there's a crazy man who –'

'Two picks and two shovels,' the delivery boy said firmly. 'Deliver to the loft at twelve-thirteen Culver Avenue. See? Says so right here. Can you read that, mister?'

'I can read it, but I didn't order –'

'Deliver to the loft at twelve thirteen Culver Avenue after Darask Frocks, Inc. has vacated the premises. Oh.' The delivery boy's voice dropped as he continued reading. 'Call FRederick 7-3458 before delivery. Oh.'

'I got news for you,' Raskin said. 'That's my phone number, but I ain't never vacating these premises. So forget this delivery.'

'They've alread been paid for,' the delivery boy said.

And suddenly, David Raskin felt extremely shrewd. Suddenly, David Raskin was confronted with the single clue which would split this mystery wide open, suddenly David Raskin was presented with that opportunity which comes to all men but once in a lifetime, the chance to solve something, the chance to be a hero.

'Tell me,' he said casually, though his heart was pounding, '*who ordered the picks and shovels?*'

The delivery boy looked at his slip. 'Here's the name of the man right here,' he said.

'What is it? What is it?' Raskin asked excitedly.

'L. Sordo,' the delivery boy replied.

Now, whereas Meyer Meyer, by his own admission, had *not* read 'The Redheaded League,' he *had* read a book by a gentleman known as Ernest Hemingway, and the title of that beautiful volume was *For Whom the Bell Tolls*, which is about a lovely guerilla girl laid in Spain. There is a memorable character called El Sordo in the book and, as any half-wit knows, *el sordo* in Spanish means 'the deaf one' or, because of the masculine *o* ending, 'the deaf man.'

It seemed obvious to Meyer at this point that someone with a hearing deficiency was the person responsible for the various threats everyone had been receiving. The gentleman at the Sandhurst Paper Company in New Bedford, Massachusetts, had told Meyer not too long ago that the person who'd ordered the envelopes had said, 'Excuse me, but would you talk a little louder? I'm slightly deaf, you know.'

And now someone had ordered two picks and two shovels to be delivered *after* Darask Frocks, Inc. vacated the loft, but those picks and shovels had obviously been delivered by mistake *before* Raskin got out, and the man who'd ordered those tools was a man who called himself L. Sordo. So not only was there a strong possibility that this was the same man who'd ordered the Massachusetts envelopes but there was a sneaking suspicion on Meyer's part that this fellow wanted to be known, he wanted to be sure he was given credit for his handywork, wanted to be certain his byline appeared on everything he created, El Sordo, The Deaf Man.

And sitting not three feet away from Meyer Meyer at his own desk was Detective Steve Carella who was fairly convinced that a person who'd used the alias of John Smith had had something cooking with someone known only as the deaf man, and that if he could get some sort of a lead onto this deaf man fellow, he would be a lot closer toward solving the case.

The trouble was, of course, that Meyer Meyer was working on a series of threatening phone calls and harassments and Steve Carella was working on a shotgun homicide and neither man saw fit to discuss his respective case with his colleague. That was the way things were going that April. In a squadroom where everyone generally was willing to discuss anything and everything involving police work, toilet training, marital technique and pennant races, nobody seemed too talkative that April. Even Bert Kling, who managed to finish his volume of Sherlock Holmes stories between phone conversations with his fiancée, failed to discuss any of the yarns with Meyer Meyer. That's the way things were going that April.

Well, on Monday of the following week, the advertisement appeared in the two morning dailies which carried classified advertisements. The ad read:

WANTED

Redheads! Redheads! Redheads! To model women's dresses in swank Culver Avenue showroom. No experience necessary. Apply 12 noon. Darask Frocks, Inc. 1213 Culver Avenue, Mr Raskin. Redheads! Redheads! Redheads!

And man, the redheads came out of the sewers that day! No one in the world would have believed there were so many redheads in the entire city. Rome is supposed to be the city of redheads, but at twelve noon on April 27 there were dozens, hundreds, thousands of redheads of every conceivable size, shape, and hue standing in a disorderly line in front of Dave Raskin's loft, trailing past the open doors of the bank going around the corner. There were fat redheads and skinny redheads, tall ones and short ones, busty ones and flat-chested ones, hippy ones and straight ones, flaming redheads and auburn redheads, natural orange redheads and bleached scarlet redheads, and each and every one of them wanted to see Dave Raskin about this job of modelling women's dresses in the swank Culver Avenue showroom. The line sailed clear around the block and past the bank and into the open doorway alongside the bank and up the steps and into the loft where Dave

Raskin frantically tried to explain he was not hiring any damn models that day.

And all of a sudden, the dawn broke.

All of a sudden, Meyer Meyer tipped to what was afoot.

Just the way he was supposed to.

Chapter Twelve

He slammed the phone down angrily and said, 'Raskin again! The heckler sent him thousands of redheads! I'm telling you, Bert, this is driving me nuts. All of a sudden, he's concentrating on poor Dave. What does he want from the guy? What's he after?'

Kling, working hard at his desk, looked up and said, 'What's a four-letter word for walking sticks?'

'Huh?'

'The puzzle,' Kling said, tapping the newspaper on his desk.

'Is that all you've got to do with your time?'

'What's a four-letter –'

'There are no four-letter words in my vocabulary.'

'Come on. 'Walking sticks. A four-letter word.'

'Legs,' Meyer answered. 'So what could that crazy nut want from Raskin? Why does he want him out of that loft?'

'You think it *could* be?'

'Could be what? What are you talk –'

'Legs.'

'I don't know. Don't bother me. Why did he stop calling all the other guys? Twenty-three stores by the last count, and all of a sudden silence except for Raskin. What does he want from him? His money? But who keeps money in a loft? Where people keep money is in –'

Meyer stopped talking. A look of shocked recognition had crossed his face. His eyes had opened wide, and his mouth had dropped open in surprise. The word caught in his throat, refusing to budge.

'What's a four-letter word that means a slope or acclivity?' Kling asked.

'A bank,' Meyer said breathlessly, pushing the word out of his mouth.

'Yeah, that's right. Like the bank of a riv –'

'A bank,' Meyer said again, his mouth still hanging open, a dazed and glassy look in his eyes.

'I heard you the –'

'A bank!' he said. 'The bank! The bank under the loft! The bank, Bert! The goddamned bank!'

'Huh? What?'

'That's why he wants Raskin out! He wants to chop through that loft floor and come through the ceiling of the bank vault! That's what those picks and shovels were for! But they were delivered too early by mistake! He's going to rob that bank, but he's got to do it before the thirtieth of April because the bank is moving then! *That's* why all the pressure on Raskin! Oh man, how could I have –'

'Yeah, that was a good story,' Kling said, not looking up from his paper.

'*What* was a good story?' Meyer asked, confused.

'"The Redhead League,"' Kling said.

Meyer shrugged. 'Come on,' he said. 'I want to talk to the lieutenant.' He grabbed Kling's wrist and dragged him across the room. He almost forgot to knock on Byrne's door.

The squadroom was empty when Carella entered it not five minutes later. He looked around, yelled 'Anybody home?' and went to his desk. 'Hey, where is everybody?' he yelled again.

The door to Byrne's office opened briefly. Meyer's bald head appeared. 'In here, Steve,' he said, and then closed the door again instantly.

Ever since he had learned the dead man's alias – the patently transparent 'John Smith' – he had been going through the files of known criminals in an attempt to locate the man's real name. He had found nothing even resembling the dead man. It was now the twenty-eighth of April and he seemed no closer to identifying his man – much less solving his case – than he'd been on the day the body was discovered in the park. He supposed that set some sort of record for inept detection but, by God, he was really trying, and nothing seemed to jell. He had considered the possibility that the shapely Lotte Constantine had done in the old man herself, and he had assigned Bert Kling to a surveillance of the girl while he himself had tried to get a line on her. From what he could gather, the girl was perfectly clean. She had come to the city from Indiana some four years back. She had held a series of unrelated jobs before landing the job as a cigarette girl in the Harem Club two years back. She had never been in trouble with the police. Her employer at the Harem described her as 'a lovely, quiet girl.' Her affection for the dead 'John Smith' had apparently been very real. Her co-workers at the club informed Kling that since she'd met the man who called himself 'Johnny,' she had not dated another man, even though men at the club were constantly asking her. Bert Kling, reporting on the girl's movements, stated that she generally slept late, went to dancing school on Mondays, Wednesdays and Fridays, dramatics classes on Tuesdays and Thursdays, and reported for work daily at the Harem at 8.00 p.m. where she donned her abbreviated costume and black net stockings, not removing them until three in the morning, at which time she went directly home. Kling had been tailing her since April eighteenth and this was the twenty-eighth. In one of his reports, Bert Kling wrote, '*She has a lovely behind, this girl, and I don't mind tailing her. But, Steve, I think she's clean. I think I'm wasting my time.*'

Carella was inclined to agree, but he decided to maintain the surveillance for at least a few more days.

But now, considering the seeming innocence of this girl, considering the fact that she and 'John Smith' really did seem to be in love with each other, it occurred to him that the man might possibly have been telling her the truth. In fact, Carella could find no really good reason for assuming the man had lied. And, in thinking about the situation, Carella realized that he had fallen into the trap of accepting the nearest and easiest conclusion without bothering to search for the more elusive but perhaps more rewarding answer. And, as frequently happened in such cases, the *real* truth was as close to hand as was the *apparent* truth. In this case, it was even closer.

John Smith was an obvious alias.

That was the apparent truth.

The girl Lotte Constantine had told Carella that John Smith was retired and living on his social security cheques. Carella pulled the Isola telephone directory to him and looked up 'UNITED STATES GOVERNMENT' and, under that, 'SOCIAL SECURITY ADMIN.' The small type advised Carella to 'See US Govt Health Educ & Welfare Dept of,' so he looked up 'HEALTH EDUC & WELFARE DEPT OF' on the same page but slightly to the left, and under that he found:

> Social Security Admin –
>   Bur of Old Age & Survivors Ins –
>   For Info Call The Office Nearest Your Home –
>   Isola Dist Offices –

And beneath that were four listings for offices in Isola, none of which were near his home (which happened to be in Riverhead) but one of which was fairly close to the squadroom of the 87th Precinct, from whence he was making the phone call. Carella asked Murchison for an outside line, and he dialled the number. He identified himself, told the switchboard operator what information he was seeking, and was promptly connected to a woman with a kindly voice who said her name was Mary Goodery. Carella could not have invented a better name to have gone with that gentle voice. He told Mary Goodery what he wanted, and Mary Goodery asked him to wait.

When she came back onto the line, she said, 'Yes, indeed, we do have records for a Mr John Smith.'

'You do?' Carella said, amazed because he was certain the thing could not be as simple as all that.

'Yes, sir, we do.'

'This John Smith is how old, please?'

'Just one moment sir,' Mary Goodery said, and she studied her record card, and then her voice came back to the telephone, 'Sixty-six in March. He has been receiving Federal social security benefits for more than a year now.'

'Would you know if he was also working? I mean, in addition to receiving his cheques?'

'I wouldn't know, sir. You understand, don't you, that anyone who earns more than one hundred dollars a month – that's twelve hundred dollars for the year – is automatically disqualified for social security benefits?'

'No, I didn't know that.'

'Yes,' Miss Goodery said.

'I see. But you wouldn't know whether or not he was holding down a job which paid him less than a hundred a month, would you?'

'I have no record of that, sir, no.'

'Thank you, Miss Goodery.'

'Not at all,' she said, and she hung up.

Carella put the receiver back into the cradle and sat staring reflectively through the open window.

'Oh, my God!' he said suddenly, and he pulled the phone to him, got an outside line, and dialled rapidly.

'Social Security Administration,' a voice said.

'Would you get me Miss Goodery, please?' Carella said.

'Just a moment, sir.'

Carella waited, wondering how he'd ever got to be a detective, wondering how it happened that a *klutz* like him could manage to stay alive in a job which sometimes required quick thinking, wondering how . . .

'Miss Goodery,' that good woman said.

'This is Detective Carella again,' he admitted. 'I forget to ask you something.'

'Yes?'

'Do you – do you have an address listed for John Smith?' Carella said, and he winced at his own stupidity.

'An address? Why, yes, I'm sure we do. If you'll just wait while I get his folder again.'

'Certainly,' Carella said, and he leaned back to wait.

In a few moments, Mary Goodery came back with the address for an apartment building on Franklin Street.

Fanny got her idea that afternoon at lunch, and she moved on it as soon as she had discussed it with Teddy. 'Discussed' is perhaps the wrong word. For, whereas Teddy was perfectly capable of having a discussion, the conversation which took place at the kitchen table that afternoon was not a discussion but a monologue.

The twins had alread been fed and put in for their nap. Fanny had made a batch of scrambled eggs and onions for herself and Teddy, and the two women sat at the kitchen table now, eating in silence, the strong aroma of onions and eggs and hot coffee filling the large kitchen. Both women wore slacks, Teddy's form-fitting and trim over a youthful body, Fanny's form-fitting over a body which was thick and solid and which had served its mistress well for more than fifty years. Teddy was shovelling a forkful of eggs into her mouth when Fanny said, out of the blue, 'Why would they first strip the uniform off him and then throw it into an incinerator?'

Teddy looked up inquisitively.

'I'm talking about Steve's case,' Fanny said.

Teddy nodded.

'Obviously, that uniform is pretty damned important, wouldn't you say? Otherwise, why bother to take it off the man? Whoever killed him left his shoes and socks on, isn't that right? Navy socks, mind you, but apparently the Navy part didn't mean a damn or they'd have taken the shoes off him, too. But they did take the uniform off. That they did. Now why? I'll tell you why. Because that uniform probably had some kind of a marking on it, something that would have told any interested party something very important about the man who was wearing it. And maybe something about why he was killed. So what kind of a uniform could it be?'

Teddy shrugged and continued eating her eggs.

'Did you ever see a man in his sixties delivering mail, or driving a bus? I never did,' Fanny said. 'But I *have* seen men in their sixties working as bank guards, or night watchmen, or elevator operators. And didn't Steve say this John Smith was on his way to *work* the night Random met him in the bar?

Isn't that what Steve said? Sure, it is. So why hasn't Steve thought of it before this? That man was a night watchman, or I'll eat my hat. And for some reason, that uniform would identify the place where he was a watchman, and whoever killed the man doesn't want that spot to be identified. Now that's what I'm betting, Teddy, and I'm going to tell Steve the minute he gets here.' Fanny nodded emphatically. 'In fact, I'm going to call and tell him right now.'

She went to the telephone and dialled FRederick 7-8024.

'Eighty-seventh Precinct, Sergeant Murchison.'

'This is Fanny Knowles. May I talk to Steve, please?'

'Fanny *who?*' Murchison said.

'Fanny Knowles, you dumb Irishman!' Fanny shouted. 'Fanny Knowles who lives with the Carellas and who's only called that run-down station house a hundred times already in the past year and spoken to yourself, you big jerk sitting on your fat butt! Fanny Knowles, now get me Steve Carella, would you please, dearie?'

'One of these days, Fanny . . .'

'Yes, dearie?' she said sweetly.

'Never mind. I can't get you Steve because he's gone out, said he wouldn't be back until late this afternoon, if at all. Had an appointment on Franklin Street he wanted to check, and said it might take a bit of time.'

'That's too bad,' Fanny said. 'I had an idea for him. About the case he's working on.'

'Well,' Murchison said with saccharine solicitude, 'he'll just have to struggle along without your assistance, I guess. Was there any other cop you want to offer help to today? We got a whole squadroom of them upstairs.'

'Go to the devil,' Fanny said, and she hung up.

The whole squadroom of cops was really *none* of them at the moment. Carella had gone out to look up the address given him by Mary Goodery. Parker was still on his candy store plant, Hernandez was out interrogating a burglary victim, and Meyer and Kling were in the lieutenant's office. The squadroom was empty and stone silent. Anyone could have walked up there and marched out with all the typewriters and electric fans.

In Byrne's office, Meyer was divulging his sudden brainstorm, his eyes aglow. Byrnes sat behind his desk, his fingers before him in a small cathedral. Kling leaned against the wall and listened sceptically.

'It's *obvious* that's what he's trying to pull,' Meyer said. 'I'm surprised I didn't see it before this.'

'It's too obvious,' Kling said dryly.

'What do you mean?' Meyer answered, annoyed. 'Don't start telling me —'

'Let him talk, Meyer,' Byrnes said.

'All I know is that a guy who's going to rob a bank isn't going to point a finger at it. He's not going to say, "That is it, fellas, so please be waiting for me when I bust in, okay?" It's just too damn obvious.'

'Then why were those shovels sent to the loft?'

'To let us *think* he was going to break into that bank,' Kling said. 'Aren't you forgetting something? He's been calling a bunch of *other* stores, too.'

'Restaurants, clothing stores, a tie —'

'So what's Raskin's place? The Taj Mahal?' Kling said. 'Raskin runs a wholesale dress business. What the hell does that matter? It's not Raskin's place he's calling attention to. It's the bank downstairs! Okay, how many of those other places are over banks, or next door to them?'

'I never thought of that,' Meyer said. 'Where's that list of stores?'

'On your desk,' Kling said.

Meyer ran out of the room. Kling shook his head and said, 'It looks like a smoke screen to me, sir. I may be wrong, but it smells to high heaven. The man couldn't be that stupid or that egotistical. He's pointed an obvious finger at Raskin's loft, right over the bank, and he's even had some picks and shovels delivered there, supposedly by accident. And the redheads today. It's just too obvious.'

'What about the redheads?' Meyer asked, coming back into the room with his list. He went directly to the phone, got an outside line and began dialling.

'The A. Conan Doyle story,' Kling said. '"The Redheaded League."'

'Stop *hocking* me with your damn mysteries,' Meyer said. 'We're trying – Hello?' He said into the phone. 'Mr Lombardo? James Lombardo? This is Detective Meyer of the Eighty-seventh Squad. Listen, could you please tell me what's next door to you? What? Oh, a lingerie shop. Well, thank y – What? *What's* on the other side? Oh, I see. Thank you, Mr Lombardo. No, nothing yet. Thank you.' He replaced the phone on its cradle.

'Well?' Byrne said.

'A lingerie shop on one side of him, and a jewellery shop on the other.'

'Jewellery,' Kling said.

'Yeah.' Meyer looked at his list again. 'Let me try another one of these.'

'Sure,' Kling said. '"The Redheaded League." The son of a bitch is referring us to his source.'

'What do you mean, Bert?' Byrnes asked. Meyer, standing alongside him, was dialling again.

'You know the story, don't you? These men run an ad in a London paper, advertising for redheads to fill a vacancy in the League. The idea is that the League will pay this man I-forget-how-many pounds a week for copying words from the encyclopedia, but the copying job must be done in the League's offices. Well, this redheaded man applies for the position and gets it, and every day he trots out to the office and copies words.'

'It sounds implausible to me,' Meyer said. Into the phone, he said, 'Let me talk to Mr Chen, please.'

'Not implausible at all,' Kling said. Meyer suddenly began talking again, so he shifted his attention to Byrnes. 'The reason they want the redhead out of his shop, you see, is because they're digging a tunnel to the bank across the way. Finally, when they're ready to rob the bank, the man loses his job. He contacts Holmes to see if he can't do something about his being fired, and of course Sherlock figures out exactly what's going on.'

'How the hell does he do that?' Meyer asked, hanging up. 'That was the Chinese restaurant. It's over an antique shop. Rare jade mostly. I'm gonna call one more place.' Rapidly, he began dialling again.

'So what's happened here?' Kling asked Byrnes. 'This guy called God knows how many stores which are alongside banks and jewellery shops and –'

'We're not sure on *all* of them yet,' Meyer said, waiting for someone to pick up the phone on the other end.

'We're pretty sure,' Kling said. 'He calls all these guys and he hopes one of them'll call the cops, or all of them. He wants them to call the cops. Why? Because there're twenty-three stores so far, and who knows how many others who didn't bother to call us. Then he directs attention to Raskin's loft because he wants us to think he's going to hit *that* bank. And today he takes out an ad for *redheads*, making sure we don't miss the significance of the Sherlock Holmes story. He draws a direct parallel. He wants us to tip, wants us to figure out he's going to rob the bank under Raskin's loft. Okay, why?'

Into the phone, Meyer said, 'Thank you very much, Mr Goldfarb. yes, thank you.' He hung up. 'The travel agency,' he said. 'It's next door to a bank.'

'Sure,' Kling said. 'So you know why he's doing this?'

'Why?' Byrnes asked.

'Because he's not going to hit that bank under the loft at all. He's going to hit one of the other twenty-three. The rest are just his smoke screen.'

'Which one is he gonna hit?' Meyer asked.

Kling shrugged. 'That's the big question, Meyer.'

'What do we do, Pete?'

'What's today?' Byrnes asked.

'The twenty-eighth.'

'And his deadline is the thirtieth?'

'Yes.'

'That gives us two days. I imagine we can put some men on.'

'What do you mean?'

'We'll cover those shops. I'll have to get help from some of the other squads. One man to a shop. You say there are twenty-three of them?'

'So far.'

'That's a hell of a lot of men to be throwing out of action,' Byrnes said. He shook his head. 'I'd better call Headquarters on this. I'm going to need more help than the squads can give. We can't put so many detectives out of action.'

'Why not patrolmen?' Kling said.

'They'd never catch him. He'd spot the uniforms.'

'Put them on special duty. Plainclothes. It's only for two days.'

'That's a good idea,' Byrnes said. 'I'll talk to Captain Frick.' He reached for the phone. 'There's only one thing that puzzles me,' he said.

'What's that?'

'If none of these shopowners move – if none of them yield to his threat to get out by the thirtieth – how in hell will he pull this job?'

The men stared at each other blankly.

They had just asked the two-and-a-half-million-dollar question.

And none of them knew the answer.

Chapter Thirteen

The four men sat on the hillside overlooking the ice-cream factory. The factory was surrounded by a cyclone fence and within that fence there were at least thirty white ice-cream trucks lined up in three identical rows. Two smokestacks jutted up into the April sky, and a huge sign straddled the stacks:

PICK-PAK ICE CREAM
The Big Lick on a Stick

The four men looked like a group of congenial buddies who had been out for a late afternoon stroll, who'd discovered this grassy hillock overlooking the ice-cream plant, and who'd decided to sit and rest their weary feet. There was certainly nothing sinister-looking about any of the men. If they'd showed up at Central Casting for parts in a grade-B gangster film, each and every one of them would have been turned down. And yet three of the four men had police records, and two of the men were, at that very moment, carrying guns. And even though their conversation was carried on in low and gentle tones, accompanied by sincere facial expressions, these men were discussing the future commission of a crime.

The deaf man was the tallest and handsomest of the four. He sat looking out over the rows of white trucks, a strand of grass beneath his teeth.

'That's where we get it,' he said.

Chuck, sitting next to him, fished for a cigarette in the pocket of his jacket, pulling out a single cigarette while leaving the package inside the pocket. He took out a book of matches, lifted the cover, bent one match over from the rest so that it was close to the striking surface, closed the cover, and then struck the match, all with one hand, the match flaming but still attached to the folder.

'Plenty trucks,' he said, and he blew out a stream of smoke.

'We only need one, Chuck,' the deaf man said.

'That's for sure. When do we grab it?'

'Tomorrow.'

'The day before, huh?'

'The *night* before,' the deaf man corrected.

'What time?'

'I figured along about midnight. Rafe's been casing the lot for a week. Rafe, do you want to fill us in?'

Rafe adjusted his gold-rimmed glasses, let out a sigh and ran a busy hand through his straw-blonde hair. He seemed reluctant to speak. It almost seemed as if speaking pained him physically.

'There's a simple padlock on the gate,' he said, his voice very low, as if he had learned at an early age that people who speak softly are generally listened to. 'I can open it with a bobby pin.'

'He's speaking figuratively,' the deaf man said. He grinned. 'Aren't you, Rafe?'

'Sure, not a bobby pin, but this is a snap, believe me. Also, there's no watchman in the yard. So once we're in, we're in.'

'Are the ignition keys left in the trucks?' Chuck asked.

'No. We'll have to cross the wires.'

'No possibility of getting duplicates made?'

'I don't see how.'

'That might be worth thinking about,' Chuck said, turning to the deaf man. 'I mean, we can't keep the thing running all the time, can we? And if the law shows, who wants to be fooling around with wires under the dash?'

'Once we get the truck away from here, I can rig a switch that works without an ignition key,' Rafe said. 'Don't worry about that.'

'I'm not worried, I'm only thinking ahead. This isn't a penny-ante thing we're involved in here, Rafe.'

'Nobody said it was.'

'Okay. Is the fence wired?'

'No.'

'Are you sure?'

'Positive. Apparently they're not too concerned about the trucks. There's an alarm for the plant, and there's also a watchman who –'

'Oh-oh,' Chuck said.

'No, no, nothing to worry about,' the deaf man assured him quickly. 'He never comes out into the yard, and we won't make our play until he's up on the top floor of the building.'

'How do we know when that is?' Chuck asked.

'It's at eleven p.m.,' Rafe said. 'He begins making his rounds at that time. Takes the elevator up to the sixth floor and then starts down on foot. We'll start working on the fence at eleven. We'll grab the truck when he reaches the top floor.'

'And how will we know when he reaches the top floor?'

'You can see his flashlight as he walks around. It lights up the whole damn floor. Okay?'

'Sounds good so far. We grab the truck and we're out before he gets a chance to come all the way downstairs again, right?'

'Right.'

'Then what?' Chuck asked.

'We drive the truck to the store.'

'Think that's smart?'

'Why not? It says Chelsea Pops, Inc. right on our window, doesn't it?'

'Sure. But it says Pick-Pak Ice Cream on the side of the truck.'

'The truck'll be in the back yard. Nobody's going to go looking there. Besides, Pop can keep away any visitors while we work on it.'

Pop, who had not uttered a word thus far, cleared his throat and said, 'Sure, I can do that. Its Rafe and Chuck who'll be taking the truck, is that right?'

'That's right, Pop,' the deaf man said.

'And they'll drive it to the store where you and I'll be waiting, is that right?'

'That's right, Pop.'

'Will I be dressed, or what?'

'Yes, of course,' the deaf man said. 'Your job is to keep any unwanted visitors away.'

'Okay.' The old man put a hand up to shade his eyes and squinted at the rows of white trucks in the lot below. 'Is that tin covering the trucks?' he asked.

'It's a porcelainized metal of some sort,' Rafe answered. 'Why?'

'Will we have any trouble getting the new signs on it?'

'I don't think so. We've got an electric drill and carborundum bits. Those things can drill through *steel*.'

'Mmm, that's good,' the old man said, nodding.

'What about the license plate?' Chuck asked, sucking in on his cigarette.

'What about it?' the deaf man said.

'We're grabbing the truck the night before the job, aren't we?' he asked. He was truly an ugly man with the squat solidity of a gorilla, huge shoulders and long, dangling arms, massive hands, a square short-snouted head. And yet he spoke quietly, almost gently.

'Yes, the night before the job,' the deaf man said.

'So they'll be looking for it, won't they? What I mean is, the watchman'll call the cops either as soon as he hears that truck taking off, or as soon as he realizes it's gone, depending on how much on the ball he is. Next thing you know a whole description is going out, you know how the cops work, don't you? So next thing you know, the license plate is being flashed to every squad car in the city. So where does that leave us? So that's what I meant when I asked about the plate.'

'Naturally, the plate will be changed.'

'But when? It's a long haul from here to the store. If that watchman is on the ball, the license plate number can be on the air in five minutes. I'll be driving this truck, you know.'

'So what's your idea?'

'I say we change the plate right here in the lot, even before we start the truck. That's what I say.'

'All right.'

'Fine. And it can't be an ordinary plate, you know. You look at those trucks down there, you'll see they're not carrying ordinary plates. That's a special kind of commercial plate. We'll have to scout around for some between now and the thirtieth.'

'We will,' the deaf man said.

'The other thing that bothers me is working in the open in the back yard, when we get to the store. You know what I mean? Even if the license plate isn't flashed, every cop in the city'll be looking for a Pick-Pak Ice Cream truck. So there we are drilling holes into the side of one. That doesn't smell so hot to me.'

'What do you suggest?'

'Can't we build some kind of a temporary screen?'

'I'm afraid a screen would attract attract attention.'

'Well, I don't like working in the back yard. This is too big a thing to take a risk like that.'

'Could we take the truck to Majesta?' the old man asked. 'Work on it there?'

'That would really be dangerous. A half-hour ferry ride? No, that would be out of the question.'

'Why don't we rent a private garage somewhere near here?' Rafe said. 'We can drive to it as soon as we have the truck, make our changes, and then go over to the store. Once the changes are made, we're safe.'

'I think that would be best,' the deaf man said. 'I'll contact some real estate agents tomorrow. This is a fairly rural section, so perhaps we'll have some luck. If not, we're simply going to have to chance working in the open.'

'If we can't get a garage near here, I'd rather drive it to some dark street and do the job there instead of in that back yard.'

'Let's not cross our bridges,' the deaf man said. 'It's agreed that I'll try to find a garage in this neighbourhood tomorrow. Let's leave it at that for now.'

'Okay,' Chuck said.

'But we'll be taking the truck tomorrow, right?' the old man asked. He paused. 'I don't like to ask too many questions, but I did get in this sort of late, and . . .'

'That's all right. yes. We take the truck tomorrow night.'

'And the big job?'

'The next day, of course. April thirtieth.'

The old man nodded. 'Who'll be driving on the day of the big job?'

'Rafe.'

'Who'll be with him?'

'I will,' the deaf man said.

'Have you got uniforms?'

'I've ordered them. I'm to pick them up tomorrow.'

'Where will Chuck and I be?' Pop asked.

'After you deliver your packages?' the deaf man said, and he grinned.

'Yes.'

'You'll go immediately to the house in Majesta. You should be finished by one o'clock or so. I expect you'll both catch the two-fifteen boat. Or, at worst, the four-oh-five.'

'And you and Rafe? Which boat will you be on with the truck?'

'We're trying for the five-forty-five. If not, we'll catch the six-oh-five.'

'And when's the one after that?'

'Seven-fifteen,' Rafe said.

'We don't have to worry about any boat beyond the six-oh-five,' the deaf man said. 'We're starting the job at five o'clock, and it shouldn't take more than ten minutes to do the remaining work. Another ten minutes to load the cartons, and another ten to get to the ferry.'

'With the loot,' Pop said.

'I should hope so,' the deaf man said, smiling.

'And when do we leave Majesta?'

'As soon as things begin to cool. We can work that out while we're there. We'll leave one at a time. Last man takes the car. The ice-cream truck stays behind, in the garage.'

'You think of everything, don't you?' Chuck said, and there was a tinge of bitterness to his voice.

'I try to,' the deaf man said flatly. 'I find it's just as simple to think of everything as *not* to. And a hell of a lot safer.'

'I hope you've thought of everything,' Chuck said.

'I have, believe me.' He looked at his watch. 'We'd better get back to the store,' he said. 'I want to get to work again. We've got a lot to do before Thursday.'

'Look, I hate to sound too cautious,' the old man said.

'What is it?'

'I'm going to have to take another look at those maps you drew. I mean, I've got to know exactly where to plant those things.'

'Certainly,' the deaf man said, and he reached into his inside jacket pocket. 'I thought I had them with me,' he said. 'I guess I left them at the Franklin Street apartment. I'll stop by for them.'

'Think that's safe?' Chuck asked, a worried look on his ugly features. 'Going back to that apartment?'

'I think so, yes,' the deaf man said. 'As a matter of fact, I was there again just last night, entertaining a lady friend.' He stared at Chuck defiantly. 'I'll meet you back at the store. You can begin working again as soon as it's dark. Pop, you take up your usual post. We have to be finished by Thursday, remember that.'

The building on Franklin Street was an elegant dwelling which, some twenty years ago, had been among the most aristocratic apartment houses. Time and the vagaries of the taste makers, a fickleness which shifted the desirability of neighbourhoods from the south side to the north side with the swiftness of summer lightning, had combined to render Franklin Street no longer as desirable as the buildings to the south. The local joke now was that no one went to the north side unless it was to take a steamer to Europe, and the bromide was not very far from the truth. But the buildings on Franklin Street had not succumbed to the shoddy encroachments of the slums as had some of the buildings within the territory of the 87th Precinct, buildings which had once been princely and which had slowly been strangled by the octopus of poverty. The buildings on Franklin Street still had doormen and elevator operators. There were no profanities scrawled on the walls of the entrance foyers. The rents in these now-unfashionable buildings were still very fashionably high.

Which led Carella to wonder how a man like John Smith, who had been existing on his social security cheques, could afford to live in a joint like 457 Franklin Street. Carella stood on the sidewalk underneath the green canopy and looked into the entrance foyer. A doorman standing just inside the glass entrance doors stared out at him, opened one of the doors in anticipation, and came out onto the sidewalk.

'Help you, sir?' he asked.

'Yes. I'm trying to locate one of your tenants, a man named John Smith.'

'Yes, sir, he's one of our tenants,' the doorman said. 'But he ain't around right now. In fact, I ain't seen him for quite some time.'

'For how long?'

'Oh, since last month some time.'

'Mmm. How long has he been living here, would you know?'

'Just a few months, sir.'

'When did he move in, would you say?'

The doorman studied Carella narrowly. 'Are you a friend of his?' he asked.

'No, I'm a cop.' He flashed the buzzer.

'Oh.'

'Yes. When did he move in, can you tell me that?'

'The end of February, I think it was.'

'And the last night you saw him was in March, that right?'

'That's right.'

'Was he living alone?'

'I don't know. He was here quite a lot.'

'But alone?'

'What?'

'Alone? Was he here alone?'

'Well, I just told you –'

'There were visitors?'

'Yes.'

'Living with smith?'

'Maybe. It don't matter to the building, you know. Long as the tenant don't disturb tenants, its his apartment, after all. So long as he don't play the radio late or make noise or do anything against –' The doorman's eyebrows went up quizzically. 'The *law?*' he asked. 'Is Mr Smith in some kind of trouble?'

'Well, I wouldn't worry about it, if I were you. I'd like to take a look at the apartment. Think you can let me in?'

'I'd have to check that with the building manager. And he won't be here until this afternoon.'

'Call him,' Carella said.

'Well, I –'

'It's very important,' Carella said. He smiled. 'Call him, won't you?'

The doorman seemed dubious for a moment. Then he smiled back to Carella and said, 'Sure, I'll call him.'

Carella followed him into the building. The lobby had been redecorated recently, the furniture looking shining and new and unused. The doorman went into a small office, made his call and returned to Carella, still smiling. 'Miracles will never cease,' he said. 'The old bastard said okay. Only things is we ain't got a pass key or anything. I mean, he said if you can get in, okay, he don't want any trouble with the police. But everybody buys their own locks, and we don't have keys to none of the apartments.'

'Well, just take me up, and I'll try some of my keys, okay?' Carella said.

'You carry skeleton keys, huh?' the doorman said, grinning knowingly.

Carella winked slyly. Together they took the elevator up to the sixth floor, and then walked down the corridor to apartment 6C.

'There it is,' the doorman said. 'Nice apartment. Seven rooms. Very nice. It has this sunken living-room.'

'Skeleton keys, how about that!' the doorman said, still grinning. The doorman watched him as he began trying the keys in the lock. There were, in addition to his own house keys, perhaps half a dozen skeleton keys hanging from the ring. He tried them all. Not one of them turned the lock.

'No good?' the doorman asked.

'Not very,' Carella said, shaking his head. 'How many floors to this building?'

'Nine.'

'Fire escapes?'

'Sure.'

'Think you can take me up to the roof?'

'You going to come down the fire escape?' the doorman asked.

'I'm going to try,' Carella said. 'Maybe Smith left his window open.'

'Man, you guys sure work for your money, don't you?' the doorman said admiringly.

Carella winked slyly and stepped into the elevator. He got off at the ninth floor and walked the flight to the roof, opening the fire door and stepping out onto the asphalt. He could see the city spread out around him as he crossed the roof, the sharp, vertical rectangles of the apartment buildings slit with open windows, the water tanks atop each roof nesting like shining dark birds, the blue sky beyond and the tracery of the bridges that connected Isola to the other parts of the city, the solid heavy lines of the old bridges, and the more delicate soaring lines of the newer bridges, and far below him the sound of street traffic and the hum of a city rushing with life, kids flying kites from neighbouring rooftops, a man down the street swinging his long bamboo pole at his pigeons, the pigeons fluttering into the air in a sudden explosion of grey, beating wings, the April sun covering the asphalt of the roof with yellow warmth.

He walked to the edge of the roof and glanced down the nine stories to the interior courtyard below. Gripping the ladder tightly, he swung over the tiled parapet and began working his way down to the fire escape on the ninth floor. He did not glance into the windows. He didn't want any women screaming for a cop. He kept working his way downward, not looking to the right or the left, going down the ladder hand over hand, and then marching across the fire escape, and onto the next ladder until he reached the sixth floor. He squatted outside apartment 6C and looked through the window. The apartment was empty. He tried the window.

It was locked.

'Damn it,' he said, and he moved along the fire escape to the second window. He was beginning to feel like a burglar, and he wished he had a small hand drill with which to bore into the wood and a hunk of wire to slip into the hole to lift the window catch. He was beginning to feel like an ill-equipped thief until he tried the second window and lo and begorrah, the goddam window was unlocked. He looked into the apartment again, and then slowly slid the window up and climbed over the sill.

The place was silent.

He dropped onto the thick rug and hastily scanned an apartment done in expensive good taste, sleek modern furniture set low against muted wall tones. His eyes touched each piece of furniture, lighted on the Danish desk in one corner of the living-room. He went to it instantly and pulled down the drop-leaf front. He had hoped to find some letters or an address book or something which could give him a further lead onto the people Smith had known, and especially the identity of the deaf man. But there was nothing of value. He closed the desk and oriented himself, figuring the kitchen to be that way, off the dining-room, and the bedrooms to be that way, at the other end of the living-room. He walked through the living-room, his shoes whispering against the thick rug, and through the open arch and into the first of three bedrooms flanking a Spartan white corridor.

There was a faint trace of perfume in the bedroom.

The bed was neatly made, a black nightgown folded at its foot. Carella picked up the gown and looked for a label. It had come from one of the most expensive stores in the city. He sniffed it, smelled the same perfume that was in the air, and then dropped it onto the bed again, wondering if the gown belonged to Lotte Constantine, wondering too if she'd been lying when she said she didn't know where John Smith had lived. He shrugged, snapped on a lamp resting on one of the night tables and pulled open the top drawer of the table.

The first thing he saw was a series of crude drawings, either maps or floor plans, none of them labelled, all of them having several things in common. To begin with, each of the maps or floor plans (it was difficult to tell exactly what they were supposed to represent) was marked with X's scattered onto the face of the drawing. There was no clue anywhere on any of the drawings as to just what the X's were supposed to represent. The maps had something else in common. Each of them had a name scrawled onto the right-hand corner. There were six maps in all.

The name on three of the maps was: CHUCK.

The remaining three maps had first carried one name, and that name was: JOHNNY. But the name had been crossed off all three, and another name written in its place: POP.

Johnny, Carella thought. *John Smith?*

The second thing in the drawer was a portion of a blueprint, neat and professional. He unfolded it and studied it for a moment:

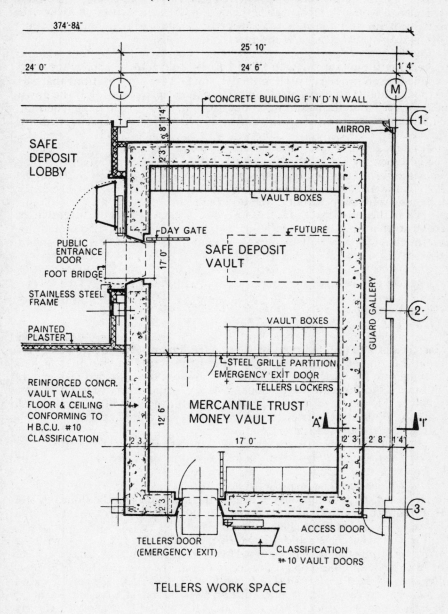

374'-8¼"

25' 10"

24' 0"   24' 6"   1' 4"

L   M

CONCRETE BUILDING F'N'D'N WALL

MIRROR

SAFE
DEPOSIT
LOBBY

VAULT BOXES

DAY GATE   FUTURE

SAFE DEPOSIT
VAULT

PUBLIC
ENTRANCE
DOOR

FOOT BRIDGE

STAINLESS STEEL
FRAME

PAINTED
PLASTER

VAULT BOXES

STEEL GRILLE PARTITION
EMERGENCY EXIT DOOR
TELLERS LOCKERS

REINFORCED CONCR.
VAULT WALLS,
FLOOR & CEILING
CONFORMING TO
H.B.C.U. #10
CLASSIFICATION

MERCANTILE TRUST
MONEY VAULT

'A'   'I'

17' 0"   12' 3" 2' 8" 1' 4"

GUARD GALLERY

ACCESS DOOR

TELLERS' DOOR
(EMERGENCY EXIT)

CLASSIFICATION
10 VAULT DOORS

TELLERS WORK SPACE

He was folding the blueprint when the telephone rang, startling him. He hesitated a moment, debating whether or not he should answer it. He put the blueprint down on the night table, wiped his hand across his sweating upper lip, and then picked up the receiver.

'Hello,' he said.

'This is Joey,' the voice on the other end told him.

'Yes?'

'Joey, the doorman. The guy who took you upstairs.'

'Oh, yes,' Carella said.

'I see you got in.'

'Yes.'

'Listen, I didn't know what to do. So I figured I'd call and tell you.'

'Tell me what?'

'Mr Smith. John Smith, you know?'

'What about him?'

'He's on his way upstairs,' the doorman said.

'What?' Carella said, and at that instand he heard a key being turned in the front door.

Chapter Fourteen

Carella stood in the bedroom with the telephone receiver in one hand, the blueprint on the night table before him, the sound of the turning lock clicking into his mind. He put down the phone at once, turned off the light and moved to the right of the door, his hand going instantly to his service revolver. He flattened himself against the wall, the gun in his right hand, waiting. He heard the front door open, and then close again.

The apartment was silent for a moment.

Then he heard the cushioned sound of footsteps against the rug.

Did I leave that living-room window open? he wondered.

The footsteps hesitated, and then stopped.

Did I leave the desk open? he wondered.

He heard the footsteps again, heard a board squeak in the flooring, and then heard the sound of another door opening. A fine sheen of sweat covered his face now, clung to his chest beneath his shirt. The ·38 Police Special was slippery in his fist. He could hear his own heart leaping in his chest with the erratic rhythm of an African bongo. He heard the door closing again, a closet he imagined, and then footsteps once more, and he wondered *Does he know I'm here? Does he know? DOES HE KNOW?* And then he heard a sound which was not familiar to him, a clicking metallic sound, as of metal grating against metal, an unfamiliar sound and yet a sound which was curiously familiar, and then the floor board squeaked again, and the cushioned footsteps came closer to the open arch at the end of the living-room, and hesitated, and stopped.

Carella waited.

The footsteps retreated.

He heard another click, and then a twenty-second spell of dead silence; and then music erupted into the apartment, loud and raucous, and Carella instantly knew this man in the apartment was armed and would begin shooting within the next few moments, hoping to use the music as cover. He did not intend to give his opponent the opportunity of being the one to start the festivities. He hefted the gun in his right hand, sucked in a deep breath, and stepped into the arch.

The man turned from the hi-fi unit alongside the wall.

In a split second, Carella saw the hearing-aid in the man's right ear, and then the shotgun the man was holding, and suddenly it was too late, suddenly the shotgun exploded into sound.

Carella whirled away from the blast. He could hear the whistling pellets as they screamed across the confined space of the apartment, and then felt them lash into his shoulder like a hundred angry wasps, and he thought only, *Oh God, not again!* and fired a shot at the tall blonde man who was already sprinting across the apartment. His shoulder felt suddenly numb. He tried to lift the hand with the gun and quickly found he couldn't and just as quickly shifted the gun to his left hand and triggered off another shot, high and wide, as the deaf man raised the shotgun and swung the stock at Carella's head. A single barrel, Carella thought in the split second before the stock collided with the side of his head, a single barrel, no time to reload, and a sudden flashing explosion of rocketing yellow pain, slam the stock again, suns revolving, a universe slam the stock, Oh God, oh God! and tears sprang into his eyes because the pain was so fierce, the pain of his shoulder and the awful pain of the heavy wooden stock of the shotgun crashing into – Oh God, oh mother oh God oh God . . .

When Carella was carried to the hospital later that day, the doctors there knew that he was still alive, but most of them were unwilling to venture a guess as to how long he would remain that way. He had lost a lost of blood on the floor of that apartment. He had not been discovered lying there unconscious until some three hours after he'd been repeatedly clobbered with the rather unbending stock of the shotgun. It was the doorman of the building, Joey, who had discovered him at six o'clock that evening. Lieutenant Byrnes, interrogating the doorman in the presence of a police stenographer, got the following information:

BYRNES: What made you go up there, anyway?

JOEY: Well, like I told you, he'd been up there a very long time. And I had already seen Mr Smith come downstairs again. So I –

BYRNES: Can you describe this Mr Smith?

JOEY: Sure. He's around my height, maybe six-one, six-two, and I guess he weighs around a hun' eighty, a hun' ninety pounds. He's got blonde hair and blue eyes, and he wears this hearing-aid in his right ear. He's a little deaf. He came downstairs carrying something wrapped in a newspaper.

BYRNES: Carrying what?

JOEY: I don't know. Something long. Maybe a fishing-rod or something like that.

BYRNES: Maybe a rifle? Or a shotgun?

JOEY: Maybe. I didn't see what was under the paper.
BYRNES: What time did he come down?
JOEY: Around three, three-thirty, I guess.
BYRNES: And when did you remember that Detective Carella was still in the apartment?
JOEY: That's hard to say, exactly. I had gone over to the candy store where there's this cute little blonde, she works behind the counter. And I was shooting the breeze with her while I had an egg cream, and then I guess I went back to the building, and I wondered if Car – What's his name?
BYRNES: Carella.
JOEY: He's Italian?
BYRNES: Yes.
JOEY: How about that? I'm Italian, too. A *paisan*, huh? How about that?
BYRNES: That's amazing.
JOEY: How about that? So I wondered if he was still up there, and I buzzed the apartment. No answer. Then – I don't know – I guess I was curious, I mean, Mr Smith having come down already and all that, so I hopped in the elevator and went up to the sixth floor and knocked on the door. There was no answer and the door was locked.
BYRNES: What'd you do then?
JOEY: I remembered that Car – What's his name?
BYRNES: Carella, Carella.
JOEY: Yeah, Carella, how about that? I remembered he'd gone up on the roof, so I figured I'd go take a look up there, which I done. Then, while I was up there, I figured I might as well go down the fire escape and take a peek into 6C, which I also done. And that was when I seen him laying on the floor.
BYRNES: What'd you do?
JOEY: I opened the window, and I went into the apartment. Man, I never seen so much blood in my life. I thought he was dead. I thought the poor bas – Are you taking down *everything* I'm saying?
STENO: What?
BYRNES: Yes, he's taking down everything you say.
JOEY: Then cut out that word, huh? Bastard, I mean. That don't look nice.
BYRNES: What did you think when you found Carella?
JOEY: I thought he was dead. All that blood. Also, his head looked caved in.
BYRNES: What did you do?
  (No answer)
  I said what did you do then?
JOEY: I passed out cold.

As it turned out, not only had Joey passed out cold, but he had later revived and been sick all over the thick living-room rug, and had only then managed to pull himself to a telephone to call the police. The police had got to the apartment ten minutes after Joey had made the call. By this time, the living-room rug had sopped up a goodly amount of Carella's blood, and he looked dead. Lying there pale and unmoving, he looked dead. The first patrolman to see him almost tagged the body D.O.A. The second patrolman felt for a pulse, found a feeble one, and instantly called in for a meat wagon. The interne who admitted Carella to the Emergency Section of the Rhodes

Clinic estimated that he would be dead within the hour. The other doctors refused to commit themselves in this day and age of scientific miracles. Instead, they began pumping plasma into him and treating him for multiple concussion and extreme shock. Somebody in the front office put his name on the critical list, and somebody else called his wife. Fanny Knowles took the call. She said, 'Oh, sweet loving mother of Jesus!' Both she and Teddy arrived at the hospital not a half-hour later. Lieutenant Byrnes was already there waiting. At 1 a.m. on April 29, Lieutenant Byrnes sent both Teddy and Fanny home. Steve Carella was still on the critical list. At 8 a.m., Lieutenant Byrnes called Frankie Hernandez at home.

'Frankie,' he said, 'did I wake you?'

'Huh? Wha'? Who's this?'

'This is me. Pete.'

'Pete who? Oh, oh, OH! Hello, Lieutenant. Whattsa matter? Something wrong?'

'You awake?'

'Is he dead?' Hernandez asked.

'What?'

'Steve. Is he all right?'

'He's still in coma. They won't know for a while yet.'

'Oh, man, I was just having a dream,' Hernandez said. 'I dreamt he was dead. I dreamt he was laying face down on the sidewalk in a puddle of blood, and I went over to him, crying for him, saying "Steve, Steve, Steve" again and again, and then I rolled him over, and Pete, it wasn't Steve's face looking up at me, it was my own. Oh man, that gave me the creeps. I hope he pulls through this.

'Yeah.'

Both men were silent for several seconds. Then Byrnes said, 'You awake?'

'Yes. What is it?'

'I wouldn't cut in on what's supposed to be your day off, Frankie. I know you were up all last night . . .'

'What is it, Pete?'

'I want you to check out the apartment where Steve got it. I wouldn't ask you ordinarily, Frankie, but I'm in one hell of a bind here. You know, we've got these damn stores under surveillance because Meyer and Kling've got me convinced this nut's gonna hit one of them. Well, Captain Frick let me have the patrolmen I needed, but he reserved the right to pull them if he needs them anyplace else. So I had to work out some kind of a system where a team of detectives would be on the prowl ready to relieve any of these cops if something else came up. I couldn't pull Parker out of the candy store, and I couldn't get those two men back from Washington where they're taking that damn FBI course, so I had to pull two men off vacation, and I've got these two teams cruising around now, Meyer and Kling, and this other pair, ready to either relieve or assist, whichever is necessary. I'm practically running the squad singlehanded, Frankie. Steve's in the hospital, and I'm going out of my mind worrying about him, that guy is like a son to me, Frankie. I'd check this out myself, believe me, but I got to go down to City Hall this afternoon to make arrangements for that damn ball game tomorrow – of all times the Governor's got to come down to throw out the ball, and the damn ball park has to be in my precinct, so that'll mean – I don't know where I'm gonna get all the men, Frankie. I just don't know.'

He paused.

There was another long silence.

'His face is all smashed in,' Byrnes said at last. 'Did you see him, Frankie?'

'I didn't get a chance to go over there yet, Pete. I had –'

'All smashed in,' Byrnes said.

The silence came back. Byrnes sighed.

'You can see what a bind I'm in. I've got to ask you to do me the favour, Frankie.'

'Whatever you say, Pete.'

'Would you check that apartment? The lab's already been through it, but I want one of my own boys to go over it thoroughly. Will you?'

'Sure. What's the address?'

'Four fifty-seven Franklin Street.'

'I'll just have some breakfast and get dressed, Pete. Then I'll go right over.'

'Thanks. Will you phone in later?'

'I'll keep in touch.'

'Okay, fine. Frankie, you know, you've been on the case with Steve, you know what his thinking on it has been, so I thought . . .'

'I don't mind at all, Pete.'

'Good. Call me later.'

'Right,' Hernandez said, and he hung up.

Hernandez did not, in truth, mind being called on his day off. To begin with, he knew that all policemen are on duty twenty-four hours a day every day of the year, and he further knew that Lieutenant Byrnes knew this. And knowing this, Byrnes did not have to ask Hernandez for a favour, all he had to do was say, 'Get in here, I need you.' But he *had* asked Hernandez if he'd mind, he had put it to him as a matter of choice, and Hernandez appreciated this immensely. Too, he had never heard the lieutenant sound quite so upset in all the time he'd been working for him. He had seen Peter Byrnes on the edge of total collapse, after three days without sleep, the man's eyes shot with red, weariness in his mouth and his posture and his hands. He had heard his voice rapping out orders hoarsely, had seen his fingers trembling as he lifted a cup of coffee, had indeed known him at times when panic seemed but a hairsbreadth away. But he had never heard Byrnes the way he sounded this morning. Never.

There was something of weariness in his voice, yes, and something of panic, yes, and something of despair, but these elements did not combine to form the whole; the whole had been something else again, the whole had been something frightening which transmitted itself across the copper telephone wires and burst from the receiver on the other end with a bone-chilling sentience of its own. The whole had been as if – as if Byrnes were staring into the eyes of death, as if Byrnes were choking on the stench of death in his nostrils, as if Byrnes had a foreknowledge of what would happen to Steve Carella, a foreknowledge so strong that it leaped telephone wires and made the blood run suddenly cold.

In his tenement flat, with the sounds of the city coming alive outside his window, Frankie Hernandez suddenly felt the presence of death. He shuddered and went quickly into the bathroom to shower and shave.

Joey, the doorman, recognized him as a policeman instantly.

'You come about my *paisan*, huh?' Joey asked.

'Who's your *paisan*?' Hernandez asked.

'Carella. The cop who got his block knocked off upstairs.'

'Yes, that's who I've come about.'

'Hey, you ain't Italian, are you?' Joey asked.

'No.'

'What are you, Spanish or something?'

'Puerto Rican,' Hernandez answered, and he was instantly ready to take offence. His eyes met Joey's, searched them quickly and thoroughly. No, there would be no insult.

'You want to go up to the apartment? Hey, I don't even know your name,' Joey said.

'Detective Hernandez.'

'That's a pretty common Spanish name, ain't it?'

'Pretty common,' Hernandez said as they went into the building.

'The reason I know is I studied Spanish in high school,' Joey said. 'That was my language there. *Habla usted español?*'

'*Si, un poquito,*' Hernandez answered, lying. He did not speak Spanish only slightly. He spoke it as well as any native of Madrid – no, that was false. In Madrid, the Spanish was pure, and a *c* or a *z* before certain vowels took a *th* sound. In Puerto Rico, the sound became an *s*. The word for 'five,' for example – spelled *cinco* in both Spain and Latin America – was pronounced *theen-koh* in spain and *seen-koh* in Puerto Rico. But he spoke the language like a native when he wanted to. He did not very often want to.

'I know Spanish proverbs,' Joey said. 'You know any Spanish proverbs?'

'Some,' Hernandez said as they walked toward the elevator.

'Three years of high-school Spanish, and all I can do is quote proverbs,' Joey said. 'What a drag, huh? Here, listen. *No hay rosas sin espinas.* How about that one? You know what that one means?'

'Yes,' Hernandez said, grinning.

'Sure. There ain't no roses without thorns. Here's another one, a very famous one. *No se ganó Zamora en una hora.* Is that right?'

'That's right,' Hernandez said. 'Your pronunciation is very good.'

'Rome was not built in a day,' Joey translated. 'Man, that one kills me. I'll bet I know more Spanish proverbs than half the people in Spain. Here's the elevators. So the guy who said he was John Smith wasn't John Smith, is that right?'

'That's right,' Hernandez said.

'So now the only real question is which of those two guys was John Smith? The blonde guy with the hearing-aid? Or the old duffer who used to come to the apartment and whose picture your lieutenent showed to me. That's the question, huh?'

'The old man *was* John Smith,' Hernandez said. 'And whatever the blonde's name is, he's wanted for criminal assault.'

'Or maybe murder if my *paisan* dies, huh?'

Hernandez did not answer.

'God forbid,' Joey said quickly. 'Come on, I'll take you up. The door's open. There was guys here all last night taking pictures and sprinkling powder all over the joint. When they cleared out, they left the door open.

You think Carella's gonna be all right?'
'I hope so.'
'Me, too,' Joey said, and he sighed and set the elevator in motion.
'How often was the old man here?' Hernandez asked.
'That's hard to say. You'd see him on and off, you know.'
'Was he a hardy man?'
'Healthy, you mean?'
'Yes.'
'Yeah, he seemed pretty healthy to me,' Joey said. 'Here's the sixth floor.'
They stepped out into the corridor.
'But the apartment was rented by the blonde one, is that right? The deaf man? He was the one who called himself John Smith?'
'Yeah, that's right.'
'Why the hell would he use the old man's name unless he was hiding from something? And even then . . .' Hernandez shook his head and walked down the hall to apartment 6C.
'You gonna need me?' Joey asked.
'No, go on.'
''Cause our elevator operator is sick, you know. So I got to run the elevator and also take care of the door. So if you don't mind . . .'
'No, go right ahead,' Hernandez answered. He went into the apartment, impressed at once by the expensive modern furniture, overwhelmed at once by the total absence of sound, the silence that pervades every empty apartment like an old couple living in a back room. He walked swiftly to the arch between the living-room and the bedroom corridor. The rug there was stained with dried blood. Carella's. Hernandez wet his lips and walked back into the living-room. He tabulated the units in the room which would warrant a thorough search: the drop-leaf desk, the hi-fi and liquor cabinet, the bookcases, and – that was *it* for the living-room.

He took off his jacket and threw it over one of the easy chairs. Then he pulled down his tie, rolled up his sleeves, crossed to the windows and opened them, and began working on the desk. He searched the desk from top to bottom and found nothing worth a second glance.

He shrugged, straightened up, and was walking toward the hi-fi unit when he noticed that something had fallen from his inside jacket pocket when he'd tossed it over the back of the chair. He walked across the room and stooped at the base of the chair, picking up the photograph encased in lucite, the photo of the dead man who had been identified as John Smith. He scooped his jacket from the back of the chair and was putting the picture into the pocket again when the front door opened suddenly.

Hernandez raised his eyes.

There, standing in the doorway, was the man whose picture he'd been looking at a moment before, the dead man named John Smith.

Chapter Fifteen

'Who are you?' the man in the doorway said. 'What do you want here?'

He was wearing a sailor's uniform, and he took a step into the room as Hernandez's hand dropped the photograph and reached for the Police Special holstered at his side. The sailor's eyes widened.

'What?' he started, and he turned toward the door again.

'Hold it!' Hernandez snapped.

The sailor stopped. Cautiously, he turned to face the ·38.

'Wh – what's the gun for?' he asked.

'Who are you?' Hernandez asked.

'John Smith,' the sailor replied.

Hernandez moved closer to him. The voice had been young, and the man's body was trim and youthful in the tight-fitting Navy blues. Hernandez blinked, and then realized he was not looking at a reincarnation of the dead man they'd found in Grover Park, but he was damn well looking at a spitting image of him, some forty years younger.

'Where's my father?' Smith said.

'John Smith your father?'

'Yes. Where is he?'

Hernandez didn't want to answer that question, not just yet he didn't. 'What made you think you'd find him here?' he asked.

'This is the address he gave me,' the young John Smith said. 'Who are *you*?'

'When did he give you the address?'

'We've been writing to each other. I was down in Guantánamo Bay on a shakedown cruise,' Smith said. His eyes narrowed. 'You a cop or something?'

'That's what I am.'

'I knew it. I can smell fuzz a mile away. Is the old man in some trouble?'

'When did you hear from him last?'

'I don't know. Beginning of the month, I guess. What's he done?'

'He hasn't done anything.'

'Than what are you doing here?'

'Your father's dead,' Hernandez said flatly.

Smith backed up against the wall as if Hernandez had hit him. He simply recoiled from Hernandez's words, inching backward until he collided with the wall, and then he leaned against the wall, and he stared into the room, without seeing Hernandez, simply stared into the room blankly, and said, 'How?'

'Murdered,' Hernandez said.

'Who?'

'We don't know.'

The room was silent.

'Who'd want to kill him?' Smith asked the silence.

'Maybe you can tell us,' Hernandez said. 'What was his last letter about?'

'I don't know, I don't remember,' Smith said. He seemed dazed. He kept leaning against the wall, his head tilted back against the plaster, looking up at the ceiling.

'Try,' Hernandez said gently. He holstered the ·38 and walked to the bar unit. He poured a stiff hooker of brandy and carried it to Smith. 'Here. Drink this.'

'I don't drink.'

'Take it.'

Smith took the glass, sniffed it, and tried to hand it back. Hernandez forced it to his mouth. Smith drank, almost gagging. He coughed and pushed the glass away from him.

'I'm all right,' he said.

'Sit down.'

'I'm all right.'

'*Sit down!*'

Smith nodded and went to one of the modern easy chairs, sinking into it. He stretched out his long legs. He did not look at Hernandez. He kept studying the tips of his highly polished shoes.

'The letter,' Hernandez said. 'What did it say?'

'I don't know. It was a long time ago.'

'Did he mention a girl named Lotte Constantine?'

'No. Who's she?'

'Did he mention anyone called the deaf man?'

'No.' Smith looked up. 'The *what*?'

'Never mind. What *did* he say in the letter?'

'I don't know. I think he started off by thanking me for the shoes. Yeah, that's right.'

'What shoes?'

'I got a pair of shoes for him from ship's service. I'm on a destroyer, we were just commissioned last month up in Boston. So my father sent me his shoe size and I picked up a pair for him in the ship's store. They're good shoes, and I get them for something like nine bucks, he couldn't come anywhere near that price on the outside.' Smith paused. 'There's nothing dishonest about that.'

'Nobody said there was.'

'Well, there ain't. I paid money for the shoes. It ain't as if I was cheating the government. Besides, it's all one and the same. Before he got his job, his only income came from the goverment, anyway. So it's six of one and half a dozen of —'

'What job?' Hernandez asked quickly.

'Huh? Oh, I don't know. In his last letter, he was telling me about some job he got.'

'What kind of job?'

'As a night watchman.'

Hernandez leaned closer to Smith. 'Where?'

'I don't know.'

'Didn't he say where?'

'No.'

'He *must* have said where!'

'He didn't. He said he was working as a night watchman, but that the job would be finished on May first, and after that he could afford to retire. That's all he said.'

'What did he mean?'

'I don't know. My father always had big ideas.' Smith paused. 'None of them ever paid off.'

'Afford to retire,' Hernandez said, almost to himself. 'On what? On a night watchman's salary?'

'He only just got the job,' Smith said. 'He couldn't have meant that. It was probably something else. One of his get-rich-quick schemes.'

'But he said he'd only be working until May first, is that right?'

'Yeah.'

'He didn't give the name of the firm? He didn't say where he was working?'

'No, I told you.' Smith paused. 'Why'd anyone want to kill him? He never hurt a soul in his life.'

And suddenly he began weeping.

The costume rental shop was in downtown Isola on Detavoner Avenue. There were three dummies in the front window. One was dressed as a clown, another was dressed as a pirate, and the third and last was dressed as a World War I pilot. The window was grimy, and the dummies were dusty, and the costumes looked moth-eaten, too. The owner of the shop was a jovial man named Douglas McDouglas who'd once wanted to be an actor and who had settled for the next best thing to it. Now, rather than creating fantasies on stage, he helped others to create fantasies by renting the costumes they needed for amateur plays, masquerade parties and the like. He was no competition for the bigger, theatre rental shops nor did he wish to be. He was simply a man who was happy doing the kind of work he did.

The deaf man entered the shop, and Douglas McDouglas recognized him at once.

'Hello there, Mr Smith,' he said. 'How's every little thing?'

'Just fine,' the deaf man answered. 'And how are things with you?'

'Couldn't be better,' McDouglas answered, and he burst into contagious laughter. He was a fat man, and the layers of flesh under his vest rippled when he laughed. He put his hands on his belly as if to control the pulsating flesh, and said, 'Are you here for the costumes?'

'I am,' the deaf man said.

'They're ready,' McDouglas said. 'Nice and clean. Just got them back from the cleaners day before yesterday. What kind of play is this one, Mr Smith?'

'It's not a play,' the deaf man said. 'It's a movie.'

'With ice-cream men in it, huh?'

'Yes.'

'And night watchmen, too, huh?'

'What do you mean?'

'The two night watchmen uniforms. The one you got 'way back, and the one you came in for near the beginning of the month. Ain't they for the movie, too?'

'Yes, I suppose so,' the deaf man said.

'Will you be returning them all together?'

'Yes,' he lied. He had no intention of returning any of the costumes.

'What's the movie called?' McDouglas asked.

The deaf man smiled. 'The Great Bank Robbery,' he answered.

McDouglas burst into laughter again. 'A comedy?'

'More like a tragedy,' the deaf man said.

'You filming it her in Isola?' ·

'Yes.'

'Soon?'

'We start shooting tomorrow.'

'Sounds exciting.'

'I think it will be. Would you get me the costumes, please? I don't want to rush you, but . . .'

'Sure thing,' McDouglas said, and he went into the back of the shop.

The Great Bank Robbery, the deaf man thought, and he grinned. I wonder what you would say, fat boy, if you really knew. I wonder what you will think when you hear the news over your radio. Will you feel like an accessory before the fact? And will you rush to the police with a description of 'John Smith,' the man who rented these costumes? But then, John Smith is dead, isn't he?

And you don't know that, Mr McDouglas, do you?

You don't know that John Smith, garrulous old John Smith, was shot to death while wearing a costume hired from this very shop, now do you? Garrulous old John Smith who, we discovered, was dropping just a few hints too many about what is going to take place tomorrow. A dangerous man to have about, that John Smith. And he remained talkative even after we'd warned him, and so Good-bye, Mr Smith, it was lovely having you in our friendly little group, but speech is silver, Mr Smith, and silence, ahhh, silence is golden, and so we commit you to eternal silence, BAM!

The deaf man grinned.

And then, of course, it was necessary to dispose of the costume. It would not have been necessary were you not such an organized man, Mr McDouglas. But stamped into the lining of each of your costumes is the name of your shop, and we couldn't have run the risk of the police stripping down a corpse and then coming here to ask you questions about it, now could we, Mr McDouglas? No, no, it was far better the way we did it. Strip the uniform from the body, cart it to Grover Park, and leave it there as naked as the jaybirds.

Again, the deaf man grinned.

I'm really terribly sorry to report, Mr McDouglas, that your lovely night watchman's uniform was burned to ashes in an incinerator. But that was the only way, you see. We shall do the same thing with these costumes. The police may get to you eventually, Mr McDouglas, but we certainly don't want them reaching you any sooner than they ordinarily might.

And when they get to you, you will of course describe me.

The deaf man grinned.

But is my hair really blonde, Mr McDouglas? Or is it bleached especially for this jolly little caper? And am I *really* hard of hearing? Or is the button in my ear a further device to confuse identification? Those are the questions the police must ask themselves, Mr McDouglas.

I somehow feel they'll have themselves a merry little chase.

'Here we are,' McDouglas said, coming from the back of the shop. 'How do you like them?'

The deaf man studied the white uniforms.

'Very nice, Mr McDouglas,' he said. 'How much is that?'

'Pay me when you bring them back,' McDouglas said.

The deaf man smiled graciously. 'Thank you.'

'I've been in this business twenty-five years,' McDouglas said, 'and I've never been stuck with a bum cheque, and I've never yet had anybody steal a costume from me. And in all that time, I never once took a deposit and the people always paid for the costumes when they brought them back.' McDouglas rapped his knuckles on the wooden counter. 'I've never been robbed yet.'

'Well,' the deaf man said, grinning, 'there's always a first time,' and McDouglas burst out laughing. The deaf man continued watching him, grinning.

When his laughter subsided, McDouglas said, 'Who's directing this movie of yours?'

'I am.'

'That must be hard. Directing a movie.'

'Not if you plan everything beforehand,' the deaf man answered.

That night, they put the first part of their plan into action.

At 11.01, a moment after the night watchman at the Pick-Pak Ice Cream Company entered the elevator which would take him to the top floor of the building, Rafe ran a bony hand through his straw-blonde hair, adjusted his gold-rimmed eyeglasses and, without uttering a sound, promptly picked the lock on the front gate. Chuck, burly and apelike, pushed the gate back far enough for both men to enter. He rolled it closed again and they both walked to the nearest truck. Chuck got to work on the front license plate and Rafe got to work on the rear one.

At 11.03 they looked up to the top floor of the factory and saw the night watchman's flashlight illuminating the blank windows like a flitting soul behind a dead man's eyes.

By 11.05 the transfer of plates had been effectively accomplished, Chuck opened the hood of the truck and climbed in behind the wheel. Rafe found the ignition wires and crossed them. Chuck backed the truck out, Rafe climbed in beside him. He did not bother to close the gate again. The time was 11.07.

It took them fifteen minutes to drive crosstown to the rented store near the new shopping centre. Pop and the deaf man were waiting in the back yard when the truck pulled in. The deaf man was wearing dark-grey slacks and a grey sports jacket. His black loafers were highly polished. They glowed even in the dim light from the street lamp.

Pop was wearing the uniform of a night watchman, the second uniform rented by the deaf man in McDouglas's shop.

The time was 11.23.

'Everything go all right?' the deaf man asked.

'Fine,' Chuck said.

'Then let's get the signs on. Pop, you can take up your post now.'

The old man walked out to the sidewalk near the front of the shop. The other men went into the store and came out carrying a drill and bit, an extension cord, a flashlight, two huge metal signs reading 'Chelsea Pops' and a box of nuts and bolts. Chuck began drilling holes into the side of the truck. Rafe and the deaf man began fastening on the first sign as soon as Chuck was finished.

The time was 11.41.

At 11.45, the patrolman appeared. His name was Dick Genero, and he ambled along the sidewalk nonchalantly, not expecting trouble and not looking for it. He could see a light flashing behind the store rented by that ice cream company, but the truck was effectively screened from the street by the building itself. On the sidewalk, he saw a man in uniform. At first, he thought it was another cop. Then he realized it was only a night watchman.

'Hello,' he said to the man.

'Hello,' Pop replied.

'Nice night, huh?' Genero asked.

'Beautiful.'

Genero glanced toward the light in the back yard. 'Working back there?' he asked.

'Yeah,' Pop replied. 'The ice-cream people.'

'That what I figured,' Genero said. 'Couldn't be the shopping-centre people. They're all finished with their construction, aren't they?'

'Sure,' Pop said.

'You a new man?'

Pop hesitated. 'How do you mean?'

'Used to be another fellow here,' Genero said. 'When they were first building the centre.'

'Oh, yeah,' Pop said.

'What was his name?' Genero asked.

For a moment, Pop felt as if he'd walked into a trap. He didn't know the name of the man who'd preceded him. He wondered not if this cop knew the name and was testing him, or if he was just asking a simple question to make conversation.

'Freddie, wasn't it?' Pop said.

'I forget,' Genero replied. He glanced over at the centre. 'They sure put these things up fast, don't they?'

'They sure do,' Pop answered, relieved. He did not look toward the back yard. He did not want this stupid cop to think anything unusual was happening back there.

'The supermarket opened yesterday,' Genero said, 'And the drugstore, too. Bank's moving in tomorrow afternoon, be ready for business on the first. It's amazing the way they work things nowadays.'

'It sure is,' Pop said.

'A bank is all I need on my beat,' Genero said. 'Another headache to worry about.' He studied Pop for a moment, and then asked, 'You going to be here steady?'

'No,' Pop answered. 'I'm just on temporary.'

'Until all the stores are in, huh?'

'That's right.'

'Too bad,' Genero said, grinning. 'You'da made my job easier.'

The light behind the ice-cream store went out suddenly. Genero looked toward the back yard.

'Guess they're finished,' he said.

'I wish *I* was,' Pop answered. 'I'll be here all night long.'

Genero chuckled. 'Well, keep an eye on the bank for me, will you?' he said. He clapped the old man on the shoulder. 'I'll be seeing you.'

Whistling, he walked up the street past the ice-cream store, turned the corner, and moved out of sight.

The time was 12.00 midnight.

The truck behind the store now belonged to Chelsea Pops, Inc.

The three men who'd fastened the new signs into place went back into the store, and down into the basement, and then into the tunnel they'd dug across the back yard.

The tunnel was no makeshift job. They had, after all, been working on it for a very long time. It was high and wide, and shored up with thick wooden beams which braced the ceiling and the walls. It had been necessary to make a sturdy tunnel because men and equipment had been working above-ground all the while the tunnel was being dug. The deaf man had been certain they were deep enough to avoid any cave-ins, but he'd made the tunnel exceptionally strong anyway.

'I don't want anyone dropping in on us,' he had punned intentionally, and then grinned with the other men and got back to work.

The construction work aboveground, the legitimate work that went into the building of the shopping centre, had really been an excellent cover for the daylight digging of the tunnel. With all that noise and confusion on the surface, no one even once imagined that some of the noise was coming from *below* the ground. During the night, of course, the men had to exercise a little more caution. But even then, they'd been protected by their phoney night watchman.

The interesting part of the job, the deaf man thought, was that their construction of the tunnel had kept pace with the legitimate construction of the bank. The construction aboveground was open to all viewers. Painstakingly, the deaf man had watched while the vault was being built, had watched while the all-important wiring box for the alarm system had been imbedded in the concrete floor of the vault and then covered with another three-foot layer of concrete. The alarm, he knew, would be of the very latest variety. But he also knew there wasn't an alarm system in the world which Rafe could not render useless provided he could get at the wiring box.

The men had proceeded to get at the wiring box. As the shell of the bank took form and shape around the impregnable vault, the tunnel drove relentlessly across the back yard and then under the vault itself, and finally into the concrete until the underside of the vault was exposed. A web of steel had been crisscrossed into the vault floor between layers of concrete. The steel was almost impregnable, the rods constructed of laminated layers of metal, the grain of one layer running contrary to the grain of the next. A common hacksaw would have broken on those laminated steel rods in the first thirty seconds of sawing. And the crisscrossing web made the task of forcible entry even more difficult since it limited the work space. Set an inch apart from each other, crossed like a fisherman's net, each laminated rod of steel became a separate challenge defying entry. And beyond the mat, embedded in the second layer of concrete, was the wiring box for the alarm system. Assuredly, the vault was almost impregnable.

Well, almost is not quite.

The men had a long time to work. They used acid on the steel, drop by drop, eating away each separate rod, day by day, working slowly and surely, keeping pace with the shell of the bank as it grew higher over their heads. By the twenty-sixth of April they had cut a hole with a three-foot diameter into the mat. They had then proceeded to chip away at the concrete until they reached the wiring box. Rafe had unscrewed the bottom of the box and studied the system carefully. As he'd suspected, the system was the most modern kind, a combination of the open- and closed circuit systems.

In an open-circuit alarm system, the cheapest kind, the alarm sounds when the current is closed. The closed-circuit system operates on a different electrical principle. There is always a weak current running through the wiring and if the wires are cut, the alarm will sound when that current is broken.

The combination system works both ways. The alarm will sound if the current is broken, and the alarm will also sound when contact is established.

Anyone with a pair of shears can knock out the open-circuit system. All he has to do is cut the wires. The closed-contact system is a little more difficult to silence because it requires a cross-contacting of the wires. Rafe knew how to knock out both systems, and he also knew how to take care of the combination system – but that would have to wait until the evening of the thirtieth. It was the deaf man's contention that the alarm system would be tested when the money was put into the new vault. And when it was tested, he wanted it to sound off loud and clear. So the cover was screwed back onto the wiring box – the box was left exactly the way it had been found – and the men ignored it for now, hacking away at the concrete floor until they were some four inches from the inside of the vault. Four inches of concrete would hold anyone standing on it, the deaf man figured. But at the same time, four inches of concrete could be eliminated in ten minutes with the use of a power drill.

The belly of the vault was open.

When the alarm was set on the day the bank opened, no one in the world would be able to tell that the vault, for all practical purposes, had already been broken into. The belly of the vault was open.

And so was its mouth. And its mouth was waiting for the more than two million dollars which would be transferred from the Mercantile Trust Company under Dave Raskin's loft to the new bank at three o'clock tomorrow afternoon.

Tonight, as the men chipped away at the concrete floor, the deaf man grinned securely. Pop was outside and waiting to turn away any curious eyes. Authority loved other authority, and a night watchman, in the eyes of the police, somehow became an automatic honourary member of the force.

'Let's play some poker later,' the deaf man said, almost cheerfully, secure in the knowledge that not a single living soul knew they were under the ground looking up at the ripped-out guts of an impregnable bank vault. Not a damn living soul can guess where we are at this moment, he thought, and he clapped Chuck on the shoulder in a sudden gesture of camaraderie.

He was wrong.

There *was* a living soul who could have made a pretty good guess as to where they were at that moment.

But he was lying flat on his back in a hospital room, and he was deep in coma.

His name was Steve Carella.

Chapter Sixteen

It was Thursday, the last day of April.

Not one cop working out of the 87th was happy to get up that morning. Not one cop would be any happier by the time night fell.

To begin with, no cop liked the idea of another cop getting shot. It was sort of hard luck, you know? Sort of hoodoo. It was something like walking under a ladder, or stepping on a crack in the sidewalk, or writing a book with thirteen chapters. Nobody liked it. They were superstitious, yes. But more than that, they were human. And, whereas during the course of the working day they were able to pretend that their profession was compounded mainly of pleasant interviews with interesting people, delightful phone conversations with lovely debutantes, fascinating puzzles which required stimulating brainwork, bracing legwork in and around the most exciting city in the world, fraternal camaraderie with some of the nicest colleagues to be found anywhere, and the knowledge that one was part of a spirited and glorious team dedicated to law enforcement and the protection of the citizens of these United States – whereas every cop fed himself this crap from time to time, there was the persistently throbbing, though constantly submerged, knowledge that this wonderful, exciting, spirited, bracing, fraternal job could get a guy killed if he didn't watch his step.

The squadroom was inordinately silent on that last Thursday in April.

Because coupled with the knowledge that Steve Carella lay in coma in a hospital bed was the somewhat guilty relief usually experienced by a combat soldier when his buddy takes a sniper's bullet. The men of the 87th were sorry as hell that Steve Carella had been shot. But they were also glad it had been he and not they. The squadroom was silent with sorrow and guilt.

The hospital was silent, too.

A light drizzle had begun at 11 a.m., grey and persistent, moistening the streets but not washing them, staining the hospital windows, dissolving the panes of glass, covering the floors with the projection of the rain pattern, giant amoebalike shapes that gnawed at the antiseptic corridors.

Teddy Carella sat on a bench in the corridor and watched the rain pattern oozing along the floor. She did not want the shifting, magnified globules of water to reach her husband's room. In her fantasy, the projected image of the darting raindrops was the image of death itself, stealthily crawling across the floor, stopping at the very edge of the window's shadow, just short of the door to Steve's room. She could visualize the drops spreading farther and farther across the corridor, devouring the floor, battering at the door, knocking it down, and then sliding across the room to envelop the bed, to engulf her husband in gelatinelike death, to smother him in shadow.

She shuddered the thought aside.

There was a tiny bird against a white sky. The bird hung motionless. There was no wind, no sound, only the bird hanging against a white sky, emptiness.

And suddenly there was the rushing sound of a great wind gathering somewhere far in the distance, far across the sky, across the huge, deserted, barren plain, gathering in volume, and suddenly the dust swarmed across the barren plain, dust lifting into the sky, and the noise of the wind grew and grew and the bird hanging motionless was swept farther upward and began to drop like a stone, falling, falling, as the wind darkened the sky, rushing, the wind heaving into the sky, overwhelming the sky until it turned to grey and then seemed to invert itself, involuting, turning to a deep black while the roar of the wind carried the bird down, descending yellow beak, black devouring eyes.

He stood alone on the plain, his hair whipped by the wind, his clothing flapping wildly about his body, and he raised his fists impotently to the angry descending bird, and he screamed into the wind, screamed into the wind, and his words came back into his face and he felt the beak of the bird knifing into his shoulder with fire, felt the talons ripping, tearing, felt flame lashing his body, and still he screamed into the towering rush of black wind against his frail body, his impotent fists, screaming, screaming.

'What's he saying?' Lieutenant Byrnes asked.

'I don't know,' Hernandez answered.

'Listen. He's trying to say something.'

'Ubba,' Carella said. He twisted his head on the pillow. 'Ubba,' he mumbled.

'It's nothing,' Hernandez said. 'He's delirious.'

'Ubba,' Carella said. 'Ubba cruxtion.'

'He's trying to say something,' Byrnes insisted.

'Ubba crusha,' Carella said.

And then he screamed wordlessly.

The two men, Chuck and Pop, had started work at twelve noon. They had synchronized their watches when leaving the store, and had made plans to meet at the ferry slip at four-oh-five. A revised estimate of the time it would take to accomplish their jobs had caused them to realize they could never catch the two-fifteen boat. So, the four-oh-five it was. And, if either one of them did not appear at that time, the other was to proceed to Majesta without him.

Their jobs, actually, were not too difficult – but they were time-consuming. Each of them carried a large suitcase, and each of the suitcases carried a total of twelve bombs. Six of the bombs were explosive; six were incendiary. Pop had made all of the bombs, and he was rather proud of his handiwork. It had been a long time since he'd practised his craft, and he was pleased to note that he hadn't lost his touch. His bombs were really quite simple and could be expected to wreak quite a bit of havoc. Naturally, neither he nor Chuck wanted to be anywhere around when the bombs went off, and so each of the bombs carried a time fuse. The explosive bombs made use of simple alarm clocks and batteries and a system of wiring set to detonate several sticks of dynamite. The incendiary bombs were slightly more complicated and for those Pop had to rig a chemical time fuse.

The deaf man had specified that he wanted the explosions and the fires to start sometime between 4 and 4.30 p.m. He wanted both explosions *and* fires to be violent, and he wanted Pop to make sure the fires would not be extinguished before 5.45 p.m. Pop had set each of the exploding machines for 4.15. The incendiary bombs were another thing again; a chemical time fuse could not be set with the same accuracy as an alarm clock unless a great deal of experimentation were done beforehand.

Pop had done a great deal of experimentation.

He knew that concentrated sulphuric acid when dropped into a mixture of potassium chlorate and powdered sugar would immediately start a raging fire. For the purposes of his time fuse, he needed something which would keep the sulphuric acid away from the mixture until such time as the fire was desired. This was no small task. He began experimenting with cork. And he discovered through a series of long tests, that cork would char when exposed to the acid, and that it would take four hours for the acid to eat through ·025 inches of cork or, in other words, a slice of cork which was one fortieth of an inch thick.

Pop prepared his bombs.

He filled a shoe box with oil-soaked rags. Into the centre of the box, he set a small cardboard container filled with a mixture of potassium chlorate and powdered sugar, sealed so that the mixture would not spill out. Into the top surface of the small container, he cut a hole which would accommodate the neck of a small bottle. The bottle would be filled with a 70 per cent solution of sulphuric acid, sealed with a cork cap which was one-fortieth of an inch thick, and then stuck into the hole in the top of the container at twelve noon, when the men left to do their work. In approximately four hours' time, the acid would have eaten through the cork and begun to drip onto the mixture in the container. A violent fire would ensue, aided and assisted by the oil-soaked rags. In other words, the fires would begin at approximately four o'clock – *approximately* because it was difficult to cut a slice of cork exactly one-fortieth of an inch thick and even a slight variation would, because the rate of char remained constant, start the conflagration either slightly earlier or slightly later. In any case, Pop estimated, the fires would start at *about* four o'clock, give or take a few minutes either way, and the deaf man seemed more than pleased with the estimate.

At twelve noon, Chuck and Pop stuck the bottles of sulphuric acid into the holes cut in the cardboard containers, the thin slices of cork being the only thing between the acid and the mixture. Then they sealed the shoe boxes, packed their suitcases, and trotted off to disrupt a city.

By one-thirty, when the ball game started, Chuck had set three incendiary bombs and one exploding bomb in the baseball stadium near the River

Harb. He had set two of the incendiaries in the grandstand, and the third in the bleachers. The explosive had been left just inside the main entrance arch, in a trash basket there. The deaf man had figured that the game would break sometime around four-thirty. The bomb was set for four-fifteen, and he hoped its explosion would cause a bit of confusion among the departing spectators – especially since there would be three fires in the stadium by that time. To ensure that the fires would still be roaring by the time the bomb exploded, he had instructed Chuck to cut the hoses of every fire extinguisher he saw anywhere in the stadium, and Chuck had done that and was now anxious to get away before anyone spotted him.

There were eight bombs left in Chuck's valise. He consulted his two remaining maps, each marked with his name in the right-hand corner, and began moving quickly toward his remaining destinations. The first of these was a motion picture theatre on The Stem. He paid for a ticket at the box office, climbed instantly to the balcony, and consulted his map again. Two X's on the map indicated where he was to place his explosives, directly over the balcony's supporting columns and close to the projection booth where there was the attendant possibility of the explosion causing a fire and a stench when it hit the film. The main purpose of the blasts, of course, was to knock down the balcony, but the deaf man was not a person to turn aside residuals. In the corridor outside the balcony, Chuck glanced around hastily, and then slashed the hoses on the extinguishers. Rapidly, he left the theatre. A glance at his watch told him it was two-fifteen. He would damn well have to hurry if he wanted to catch that four-oh-five boat.

He was now in possession of six remaining Bombs.

The deaf man wanted three of them to be placed in Union Station: an incendiary in the baggage room, an explosive on the track of the incoming Chicago Express (due at four-ten), and another explosive on the counter of the circular information booth.

The remaining three bombs could be placed by Chuck at his discretion – provided, of course, they were all deposited at different locations on the south side of the precinct. The deaf man had suggested leaving an incendiary in a subway car, and an explosive in the open-air market on Chament Avenue, but the final decisions were being left to Chuck, dependent on time and circumstance.

'Suppose I put them where there aren't any people?' Chuck had asked.

'That would be foolish,' the deaf man said.

'I mean, look, this is supposed to be a bank heist.'

'Yes.'

'So why do we have to put these things where – where a lot of people'll get hurt?'

'Where would you like to put them? In an empty lot?'

'Well, no, but –'

'I've never heard of confusion in a vacuum,' the deaf man had replied.

'Still – damn it, suppose we get caught? You're fooling around with – with *murder* here, do you realize that? Murder!'

'So!'

'So look, I know there are guys who'd slit their own grandmother's throat for a nickel, but –'

'I'm not one of them,' the deaf man had answered coldly. 'There happens to be two and a half million dollars at stake here.' He had paused. 'Do you want out, Chuck?'

Chuck had not wanted out. Now, as he headed for Union Station, the suitcase was noticeably and happily lighter. He was itching to get the job over and done with. He didn't want to be anywhere south of the Mercantile Trust Company after four o'clock. If everything went according to the deaf man's plan, that part of the precinct would be an absolute madhouse along about then, and Chuck wanted no part of chaos.

The oil refinery was set on the River Dix, at the southern tip of the island of Isola. Pop walked up to the main gate and reached into his pocket for the identification badge the deaf man had given him. He flashed the badge casually at the guard, and the guard nodded, and Pop walked through the gate, stopped once to consult the X's on his map, and then walked directly to the tool shed behind the administration building. The tool shed, besides being stocked with the usual number of saws and hammers and screw-drivers, contained a few dozen cans of paint, turpentine, and varnish. Pop opened the door of the shed and put one of his explosive bombs in a cardboard carton of trash just inside the door. Then he closed the door and began walking toward the paymaster's shack near the first of the huge oil tanks.

By one-forty-five he had set four bombs in the refinery. He walked through the main gate, waved good-bye to the guard, hailed a cab and headed for a plant some thirty blocks distant, a plant which faced south toward the River Dix, its chimneys belching smoke to the city's sky twenty-four hours a day.

The sign across the top of that plant read EASTERN ELECTRIC.

It produced electric power for 70 per cent of the homes and businesses on the south side of the 87th Precinct.

At 3.00 p.m., they closed the doors of the old Mercantile Trust for the last time.

Mr Wesley Gannley, manager of the bank, watched with some sadness as his employees left for the new bank in the completed shopping centre. Then he went back into the vault where the guards were carrying the bank's stock – two million, three hundred fifty-three thousand, four hundred twenty dollars and seventy-four cents in American currency – to the waiting armoured truck outside.

Mr Gannley thought it was nice that so much money was being taken to the new bank. Usually, his bank had some eight hundred thousand dollars on hand, an amount which was swelled every Friday, payroll day, to perhaps a million and a quarter. There were a great many firms, however which paid their employees every two weeks, and still others which had monthly bonus programmes. In any case, April 30 was the end of the month, and tomorrow was a Friday, May 1, and so the bank was holding, besides its usual deposits and money on hand, an unusually large amount of payroll money, and this pleased Mr Gannley immensely. It seemed fitting that a spanking-new bank should open shop with a great deal of cold cash.

He stepped out onto the side walk as the bank guards transferred that cold cash to the truck. From the grime-stained window of his loft upstairs, Dave

Raskin watched the transaction with mild interest, and then took a huge puff
on his soggy cigar and turned back to studying the front of Margarita's
smock.

By 3.30 p.m., the $2,353,420.74 was safe and snug in the new vault of the
new bank in the new shopping centre. Mr Gannley's employees were busily
making themselves at home in their new quarters, and all seemed right with
the world.

At 4.00 p.m., the deaf man began making his phone calls.

He made the calls from the telephone in the ice-cream store behind the
new bank. Rafe was waiting in the drugstore across the street from the bank,
watching the bank's front door. He would report back to the deaf man as
soon as everyone had left the bank. In the meantime, the deaf man had his
own work to do.

The typewritten list beside the telephone had one hundred names on it.
The names were those of stores, offices, movie theatres, shops, restaurants,
utilities, and even private citizens on the south side of the 87th Precinct. The
deaf man hoped to get through at least fifty of those names before five
o'clock, figuring on the basis of a minute per call, and allowing for a
percentage of no-answers. Hopefully, *all* of the persons called would in turn
call the police. Pessimistically, perhaps ten would report the calls. And,
figuring a rock-bottom return of 10 per cent, at least five would contact the
police.

Even five was a good return for an hour's work if it compounded the
confusion and made the ride to the ferry simpler.

Of the hundred names on the list, four were really in trouble. They were
really in trouble because Chuck and Pop had deposited either incendiary or
explosive bombs in their places of business. These four establishments
would *certainly* call the police, if not immediately upon receipt of the deaf
man's call, then *positively* after the bombs went off. The point of the deaf
man's calls was to provide the police with a list of clues, only four of which
were valid. The trouble was, the police would not know which of the clues
were valid and which were not. And once reports of mayhem began filtering
in, they could not in good conscience afford to ignore *any* tip.

The deaf man pulled the phone to him and dialled the first number on his
list.

A woman answered the phone. 'The Culver Theatre,' she said. 'Good
afternoon.'

'Good afternoon,' the deaf man said pleasantly. 'There is a bomb in a shoe
box somewhere in the orchestra of your theatre,' and he hung up.

At 4.05 p.m., Chuck and Pop boarded the ferry to Majesta and spent the
next ten minutes whispering together like school boys about the conspiracy
they had just committed.

At 4.15 p.m., the first of the bombs exploded.

'Eighty-seventh Squad, Detective Hernandez. What? What did you say?'
He began scribbling on his pad. 'Yes, sir. And the address, sir? When did
you get this call, sir? Yes, sir, thank you. Yes, sir, right away, thank you.'

Hernandez slammed the phone back onto its cradle.

'Pete!' he yelled, and Byrnes came out of his office immediately. 'Another

one! What do we do?'
'A bomb?'
'Yes.'
'A real one, or just a threat?'
'A threat. But, Pete, that last movie theatre . . .'
'Yes, yes.'
'That was just a threat, too. But, damn it, two bombs really went off in the balcony. What do we do?'
'Call the Bomb Squad.'
'I did on the last three calls we got.'
'Call them again! And contact Murchison. Tell him we want any more of these bomb threats to be transferred directly to the Bomb Squad. Tell him –'
'Pete, if we get many more of these, the Bomb Squad'll be hamstrung. They'll dump the squeals right back into our laps, anyway.'
'Maybe we won't get any more. Maybe –'
The telephone rang. Hernandez picked it up instantly.
'Eighty-seventh Squad, Hernandez. Who? Where? Holy Je – *What* did you say? Have you – yes, sir, I see. Have you – yes, sir, try to calm down, will you, sir? Have you called the fire department? All right, sir, we'll get on it right away.'
He hung up. Byrnes was waiting.
'The ball park, Pete. Fires have broken out in the grandstands and bleachers. Hoses on all the extinguishers have been cut. People are running for the exits. Pete, there's gonna be a goddam riot, I can smell it.'
And at that moment, just inside the entrance arch, as people rushed in panic from the fires raging through the stadium, a bomb exploded.

The people on the south side of the precinct did not know what the hell was happening. Their first guess was that the Russians were coming, and that these wholesale explosions and fires were simply acts of sabotage preceding an invasion. Some of the more exotic-minded citizens speculated upon an invasion from Mars, some said it was all that strontium 90 in the air which was causing spontaneous combustion, some said it was all just coincidence, but everyone was frightened and everyone was on the edge of panic.
Not one of them realized that percentages were being manipulated or that a city's preventive forces, accustomed to dealing with the long run, were being pushed into dealing with the short run.
There were 186 patrolmen, 22 sergeants and 16 detectives attached to the 87th Precinct. A third of this force was off duty when the first of the bombs went off. In ten minutes' time, every cop who could be reached by telephone was called and ordered to report to the precinct at once. In addition, calls were made to the adjoining 88th and 89th Precincts which commanded a total of 370 patrolmen, 54 sergeants and 42 detectives and the strength of this force was added to that of the 87th's until a stream of men was pulled from every corner of the three precincts and rushed to the disaster-stricken south side. The ball park was causing the most trouble at the moment, because some forty thousand fans had erupted into a full-scale panic-ridden riot, and the attendant emergency police trucks, and the fire engines, and the patrol cars, and the mounted policemen, and the reporters and the sight-

seeing spectators made control a near-impossibility.

At the same time, a Bomb Squad which was used to handling a fistful of bomb threats daily was suddenly swamped with bomb reports from forty different areas in the 87th Precinct. Every available man was called into action and rushed to the various trouble spots, but there simply weren't enough men to go around and they simply didn't know which trouble spots were going to erupt or when. To their credit, they did catch one incendiary in an office building before it burst into flame, but at the same time a bomb exploded on the fourteenth floor of that same building, an unfortunate circumstance since the bomb had been set in the laboratory of a chemical research company, and the attendant fire swept through three floors of the building even before the fire alarm was pulled.

The Fire Department had its own headaches. The first unit called into action was Engine 31 and Ladder 46, a unit in the heart of the south side, a unit which reportedly handled more damn fires daily than any other unit in the entire city. They connected to a hydrant on Chament Avenue and South Fourth in an attempt to control the blaze that was sweeping through the open-air market on Chament Avenue. Within a few minutes, the fire had leaped across Chament Avenue and was threatening a line of warehouses along the river. Acting Lieutenant Carl Junius in charge of the engine had a brief consultation with Lieutenant Bob Fancher of Ladder 46, and they radioed to Acting Deputy Chief George D'Oraglio who immediately ordered an alarm transmitted with orders to the responsing units to expect counterorders at a moment's notice since he had already received word of a fire in a motion picture theatre not twenty blocks from the market. Engine 81 and Ladder 33 arrived in a matter of minutes and were promptly redispatched to the motion picture theatre, but by this time the hook and ladder company handling the ball park fire had called in for assistance, and Chief D'Oraglio suddenly realized he had his hands full and that he would need every available engine and hook and ladder company in the city to control what was shaping up as a major disaster.

The police emergency trucks with two-way radio numbered fifteen, and the emergency station wagons with two-way radio numbered ten, and all twenty-five of these were dispatched to the scenes of the fires and explosions which were disrupting traffic everywhere on the south side and which were causing all nine of the traffic precincts to throw extra men and equipment into the stricken area.

The north side of the precinct, the area between the new quarters of the Mercantile Trust Company and the waiting-room of the Isola-Majesta ferry, was suddenly devoid of policemen.

Meyer Meyer and Bert Kling, cruising in an unmarked sedan, ready to prevent any crime which occurred against the harassed places of business on their list, received a sudden and urgent radio summons and were promptly off The Heckler Case. The radio dispatcher told them to proceed immediately to a subway station on Grady Road to investigate a bomb threat there.

By 4.30 p.m., six Civil Defence units were thrown into the melee, and the Police Commissioner made a hurried call to the Mayor in an attempt to summon the National Guard. The National Guard *would* eventually be called into action because what started as a simple plot to rob a bank would grow into a threat to the very city itself, a threat to equal the Chicago fire or the San Francisco earthquake, a threat which – when all was said and done – totalled billions of dollars in loss and almost razed to the ground one of the finest ports in the United States. But the wheels of bureaucracy grind exceedingly slow, and the National Guard units would not be called in until 5.40 p.m., by which time the Mercantile Trust Company's vault would be empty, by which time invasion reports had caused panic beyond anything imagined by the deaf man, by which time the river front to the south was a blazing wall of flame, by which time everyone involved knew they were in the centre of utter chaos.

In the meantime, it was only 4.30 p.m., and the deaf man had completed twenty-two of his calls. Smiling, listening to the sound of sirens outside, he dialled the twenty-third number.

Mr Wesley Gannley, manager of the Mercantile Trust Company, paced the marbled floors of his new place of business, grinning at the efficiency of his employees, pleased as punch with the new building. The IBM machines were ticking away behind the counters. Music flowed from hidden wall speakers, and a mural at the far end of the building, washed with rain-dimmed light at the moment, depicted the strength of America and the wisdom of banking. The polished glass-and-steel door of the vault was open, and Gannley could see into it to the rows of safety deposit boxes and beyond that to the barrel steel door, and he felt a great sense of security, he felt it was good to be alive.

Mr Gannley took his gold pocket watch from the pocket of his vest and looked at the time.

4.35 p.m.

In twenty-five minutes they would close up shop for the day.

Tomorrow morning, May 1, everyone would return bright and early, and depositers would come through the bank's marble entrance arch and step up to the shining new tellers' windows, anxious to reap that three and a half per cent, and Mr Gannley would watch from the open door of his manager's office and begin counting the ways he would spend his Christmas bonus this year.

Yes, it was good to be alive.

He walked past Miss Finchley who was bending over a stack of cancelled cheques, and he was seized with an uncontrollable urge to pinch her on the buttocks.

He controlled the urge.

'How do you like the new building, Miss Finchley?' he asked.

Miss Finchley turned toward him. She was wearing a white silk blouse, and the top button had come unfastened and he could see the delicate lace of her lingerie showing where the cream-white flesh ended.

'It's beautiful, Mr Gannley,' she answered. 'Simply beautiful. It's a pleasure to work here.'

'Yes,' he said. 'It certainly is.'

He stood staring at her for a moment, wondering whether or not he should ask her to join him for a cocktail after closing. No, he thought, that would be too forward. But perhaps a lift to the station. Perhaps that might not be misinterpreted.

'Yes, Mr Gannley?' she said.

He decided against it. There was plenty of time for that. In a wonderful new building like this one, with IBM machines and music flowing from hidden speakers, and a bright, colourful mural decorating the far wall, and an impervious steel vault, there was plenty of time for everything.

Recklessly, he said, 'You'd better button your blouse, Miss Finchley.'

Her hand fluttered up to the wayward button. 'Oh, my,' she said, 'I'm practically naked, aren't I?' and she buttoned the blouse quickly without the faintest trace of a blush.

Plenty of time for everything, Wesley Gannley thought, smiling, plenty of time.

The tellers were beginning to wheel their mobile units into the vault. Every day at 4.45 p.m., the tellers performed this ritual. First they took the coin racks from the change machines on the counter and placed these racks into the top drawers of the units. The bottom drawers usually contained folding money. Today, both drawers and coin racks were empty because the bank had not done any business at its new location, and all the money had been transferred directly to the new vault. But nonetheless, it was 4.45 p.m., and so the units were wheeled into the vault and Mr Gannley looked at his watch, went to his desk, and took the key which fit into the three clocks on the inside face of the vault door. The locks were miniscule and were marked with numerals indicating hours. Mr Gannley put his key into the first clock and set it for fifteen hours. He did the same to the other two clocks. He expected to be at work at 7.30 a.m. tomorrow morning, and he would open the vault at 7.45 a.m. It was now 4.45 p.m. – ergo, fifteen hours. If he tried to open the vault door before that time, it would not budge, even if he correctly opened the two combination locks on the front face of the door.

Mr Gannley put the key into his vest pocket and then heaved his shoulder against the heavy vault door. It was a little difficult to close because the carpeting on the floor was new and still thick and the door's friction against it provided an unusual hindrance. But he managed to shove the door closed, and then he turned the wheel which clicked the tumblers into place, and then he spun the dials of the two combination locks. He knew the alarm was automatically set the moment that vault door slammed shut. He knew it would sound at the nearest police precinct should anyone tamper with the door. He knew that the combination locks could not be opened if the time mechanism was not tripped. He further knew that, should the alarm go off accidentally, he was to call the police immediately to tell them a robbery was *not* truly in progress, the alarm had simply gone off by accident. And then, as an added precaution if he made such a call to the police, he was to call them back in two minutes to verify the accident. In short, should a robbery *really* be in progress and should the thief force Gannley into calling the police to say the alarm had been accidental, the police would know something was fishy if he didn't duplicate the call within the next two minutes.

For now, for the moment, there was one thing more to do. Wesley Gannley went to the telephone and dialled FRederick 7-8024.

'Eighty-seventh Precinct, Sergeant Murchison.'

'This is Mr Gannley at the new Mercantile Trust.'

'What is it, Mr Gannley? Somebody call *you* about a bomb, too?'

'I beg your pardon?'

'Never mind, never mind. What is it?'

'I'm about to test this alarm. I wanted you to know.'

'Oh. Okay. When are you going to trip it?'

'As soon as I hang up.'

'All right. Will you call me back?'

'I will.'

'Right.'

Mr Gannley hung up, walked to one of the alarm buttons set behind the tellers' cages, and deliberately stepped on it. The alarm went off with a terrible clanging. Immediately, Mr Gannley turned it off, and then called the police again to tell them everything was working fine. He passed the vault door and patted it lovingly. He knew the alarm was there and working, a vigilant watchdog over all that money.

He did not know that its voice was a tribute to the careful labour which had gone on below the ground for the past two months, or that it would be silenced forever within the next half-hour.

It was 5.05 p.m.

In the new drugstore across the street from the bank, Rafe sat on a stool and watched the bank doors. Twelve people had left so far, the bank guard closing it again behind them. There were three people left inside the bank, including the bank guard. Come on, Rafe thought, get the hell out.

The big clock over the counter read 5.06.

Rafe sipped at his Coke and watched the bank doors.

5.07.

Come on, he thought. We have to catch a goddamn ferry at five minutes after six. That gives us less than an hour. He figures we'll be able to break away that remaining concrete in ten minutes, but I figure at least fifteen. And then ten more minutes to load the money, and another ten – if we don't hit traffic – to get to the ferry slip. That's thirty-five minutes, provided everything goes all right, provided we don't get stopped for anything.

Rafe took off his gold-rimmed glasses, wiped the bridge of his nose, and then put the glasses on again.

The absolute limit, I would say, is five-forty-five. We've got to be out of that vault by five-forty-five. That gives us twenty minutes to get to the ferry slip. We should make it in twenty minutes. Provided everything goes all right.

We should make it.

Unreasonably, the bridge of Rafe's nose was soaked with sweat again. He took off his glasses, wiped away the sweat, and almost missed the bank door across the street opening. A girl in a white blouse stepped out and then shrank back from the drizzle. A portly guy in a dark suit stepped into the rain and quickly opened a big black umbrella. The girl took his arm and they went running off up the street together.

One more to go, Rafe thought.

The bridge of his nose was sweating again, but he did not take off the glasses.

Across the street, he saw the bank lights going out.

His heart lurched.

One by one, the lights behind the windows went dark. He waited. He was getting off the stool when he saw the door opening, saw the bank guard step out and slam the door behind him. The guard turned and tried the automatically locked door. The door did not yield. Even from across the street, Rafe saw the bank guard give a satisfied nod before he started off into the rain.

The clock over the drugstore counter read 5.15.

Rafe started for the door quickly.

'Hey!'

He stopped short. An icy fist had clamped onto the base of his spine.

'Ain't you gonna pay for your Coke?' the soda jerk asked.

The deaf man was waiting at the far end of the tunnel, directly below the bank vault when he heard Rafe enter at the other end. The tunnel was dripping moisture from its walls and roof, and the deaf man felt clammy with perspiration. He did not like the smell of the earth. It was a suffocating, fetid stench which filled the nostrils and made a man feel as if he were being choked. He waited while Rafe approached.

'Well?' he asked.

'They're all out,' Rafe said.

The deaf man nodded curtly. 'There's the box,' he said, and he swung his hand flash up to illuminate the box containing the wiring for the alarm system.

Rafe crawled into the gaping hole in the corroded steel bars and reached up for the exposed alarm box. He pulled back his hands and took off his glasses. They were fogged with the tunnel's moisture. He wiped the glasses, put them back on the bridge of his nose, and then got to work.

In the fevered delirium of his black world, things seemed clearer to Steve Carella than they ever had in his life.

He sat at a nucleus of pain and confusion, and yet things were crystal clear, and the absolute clarity astonished him because it seemed his sudden perception threatened his entire concept of himself as a cop. He was staring wide-eyed at the knowledge that he and his colleagues had come up against a type of planning and execution which had rendered them virtually helpless. He had a clear and startling vision of himself and the 87th Squad as a group of half-wits stumbling around in a fog of laboratory reports, fruitless leg work, and meaningless paper work which in the end brought only partial and miniscule results.

He was certain now that John Smith had been murdered by the same deaf man who had shot and repeatedly battered Carella with the stock of a shotgun. He was reasonably certain that the same weapon had been used in both attacks. He was certain, too, that the blueprint he'd found in the Franklin Street apartment was a construction blue print for the vault of the Mercantile Trust, and that a robbery of that vault had been planned.

Intuitively, and this was what frightened him, he knew that the murder, and his own beating, and the planned bank robbery were tied into the case Meyer Meyer was handling, the so-called Heckler Case.

He did not question the intuition nor its clarity – but he knew damn well it scared him. Perhaps it would have frightened him less if he'd known it wasn't quite intuition. Whether he realized it or not, and despite the fact that he had never openly discussed the supposedly separate cases with Meyer, he *had* unconsciously been exposed to siftings of telephone conversations, to quick glances at reports on Meyer's desk. These never seemed to warrant a closer conversation with the other detective, but they did nonetheless form a submerged layer of knowledge which, when combined with the knowledge he now possessed, welded an undeniable and seemingly intuitive link.

But if the reasoning were correct – and it could hardly be called reasoning – if this *sense* of connection were accurate, it pointed to someone who was not gambling senselessly against the police. Instead, it presented the image of a person who was indeed leaving very little to chance, a person who was *using* the agencies of law enforcement, utilizing them as a part of his plan, making them work for him, joining them instead of fighting them, making them an integral part of a plan which had begun – how long ago?

And this is what frightened Carella.

Because he knew, detective fiction to the contrary, that the criminal mind was not a particularly brilliant one. The average thief with whom the squad dealt daily was of only average intelligence, if that, and was usually handicapped by a severe emotional disturbance which had led him into criminal activities to begin with. The average murderer was a man who killed on the spur of the moment, whether for revenge, or through instant rage, or through a combination of circumstances, which led to murder as the only seemingly logical conclusion. Oh yes, there were carefully planned robberies, but these were few and far between. The average job could be cased in a few days and executed in a half hour. And yes, there were carefully planned murders, homicides figured to the most minute detail and executed with painstaking precision – but these, too, were exceptions. and, of course, one shouldn't forget the confidence men whose stock in trade was guile and wile – but how many *new* con games were there, and how many con men were practising the same tired routines, all known to the police for years and years?

Carella was forced to admit that the police were dealing with a criminal element which, in a very real sense, was amateurish. They qualified for professional status only in that they worked – if you will excuse the term when applied to crime – for money. And he was forced to admit further that the police opposing this vast criminal army were also attacking their job in a somewhat amateurish way, largely because nothing more demanding was called for.

Well, this deaf man whoever he was, *was* making further demands. He was elevating crime to a professional level, and if he were not met on equally professional terms, he would succeed. The entire police force could sit around and the deaf man would run them ragged and carry home the bacon besides.

Which made Carella wonder about his own role as a cop and his own duties as an enforcer of the law. He was a man dedicated to the prevention of crime, or failing that, to the apprehension of the person or persons committing crime. If he totally succeeded in his job, there would be no more crime and no more criminals; and, carrying the thought to its logical conclusion, there would also be no more job. If there was no crime, there would be no need for the men involved in preventing it or detecting it.

And yet somehow this logic was illogical, and it led Carella to a further thought which was as frightening as the sudden clarity he was experiencing.

The thought sprang into his head full-blown: *If there is no crime, will there be society?*

The thought was shocking – at least to Carella it was. For society was predicated on a principle of law and order, of meaning as opposed to chaos. But if there were no crime, if there were in effect no lawbreakers, no one to oppose law and order, would there be a necessity for law? Without lawbreakers, *was* there a need for law? And without law, would there be lawbreakers?

MADAM, I'M ADAM.

Read it forwards or backwards and it says the same thing. A cute party gag, but what happens when you say, 'Crime is symbiotic with society,' and then reverse the statement so that it read, 'Society is symbiotic with crime'?

Carella lay in the blackness of his delirium, not knowing he was up against a logician and a mathematician, but intuitively reasoning in mathematical and logical terms. He knew that something more was required of him. He knew that in this vast record of day-by-day crime, this enormous never-ending account of society and the acts committed against it, something more was needed from him as a cop and as a man. He did not know what that something more was, nor indeed whether he could ever make a quantum jump from the cop and man he now was to a cop and man quite different.

Clarity suffused the darkness of his coma.

In the clarity, he knew he would live.

And he knew that someone was in the room with him, and he knew that this person must be told about the Mercantile Trust Company and the Uhrbinger Construction Company and the blue print he had seen in the Franklin apartment.

And so he said, 'Merc-uh-nuh,' and he knew he had not formed the word correctly and he could not understand why because everything seemed so perfectly clear within the shell of his dark cocoon.

And so he tried the other word, and he said, 'Ubba-nuh coston,' and he knew that was wrong, and he tried again, 'Ubba-nuh . . . ubba . . . Uhrbinger . . . Uhrbinger,' and he was sure he had said it that time, and he leaned back into the brilliant clarity and lost consciousness once more.

The person in the room with him was Teddy Carella, his wife.

But Teddy was a deaf mute, and she watched her husband's lips carefully, and she saw the word 'Uhrbinger' form on those lips, but it was not a word in her vocabulary, and so she reasoned that her husband was delirious.

She took his hand and held it in her own, and then she kissed it and put it to her cheek.

The hospital lights went out suddenly.

The bombs Pop had set at Eastern Electric were beginning to go off.

Rafe, like any good surgeon, had checked his earlier results before making his final incision. He had run a Tong Tester over the wires in the box once more, checking the wires which carried the current, nodding as they tallied with the calculations he had made the first time he looked into the box.

'Okay,' he said apparently to the deaf man who was standing below him, but really to no one in particular, really a thinking out loud. 'Those are the ones carrying the juice, all right. I cross-contact those and cut the others, and it's clear sailing.'

'All right, then do it,' the deaf man said impatiently.

Rafe set about doing it.

He accomplished the cross-contact with speed and efficiency. Then he thrust his hand at the deaf man. 'The clippers,' he said.

The deaf man handed them up to him. 'What are you going to do?'

'Cut the wires.'

'Are you sure you've done this right?'

'I think so.'

'Don't think!' the deaf man said sharply. 'Yes or no? Is that damn alarm going to go off when you cut those wires?'

'I don't think so.'

'*Yes or no?*'

'No,' Rafe said. 'It won't go off.'

'All right,' the deaf man said. 'Cut them.'

Rafe took a deep breath and moved the clippers towards the wires. With a quick, deliberate contraction of his hand, he squeezed the handles of the clippers together and cut the wires.

The alarm did not go off.

At the house in Majesta, Chuck paced the floor nervously while Pop studied the alarm clock sitting on the dresser.

'What time is it?' Chuck asked.

'Five-thirty.'

'They should be out of the bank and on their way by now.'

'Unless something went wrong,' Pop said.

'Yeah,' Chuck answered distractedly, and he began pacing the floor again. 'Put on that radio, will you?' he said.

Pop turned it on.

'. . . raging out of control along a half-mile square of waterfront,' the announcer said. 'Every available piece of fire equipment in the city has been rushed to the disaster area in an effort to control the flames before they spread further. The rain is not helping conditions. Slippery streets seem to be working against the men and apparatus. The firemen and police are operating only from the lights of their trucks, an explosion at the Eastern Electric Company having effectively blinded seventy per cent of the area's streets, homes and businesses. Fortunately, there is still electric power in Union Station where an explosion on track twelve derailed the incoming Chicago train as a bomb went off simultaneously in the waiting-room. The fire in the baggage room there was brought under control, but is still smouldering.'

The announcer paused for breath.

'In the meantime, the Mayor and the Police Commissioner are still in secret session debating whether or not to call out the National Guard in this emergency situation, and there are several big questions that remain unanswered: *What is happening? Who is responsible for this? And why?* Those are the questions in the mind of every thinking citizen as the city struggles for its very survival.'

The announcer paused again.

'Thank you, and good night,' he said.

Pop turned off the radio.
He had to admit he felt a slight measure of pride.

They came out of the vault and through the tunnel at 5.40 p.m. They
made three trips back and forth between the bank vault and the basement of
the store, and then they carried the cartons stuffed with money to the truck.
They opened the door to the refrigerator compartment and shoved the
cartons inside. Then they closed the refrigerator door, and Rafe started the
truck.

'Just a minute,' the deaf man said. 'Look.'

Rafe followed his pointing hand. The sky was ablaze with colour. The
buildings to the south were blacked out, but the sky behind them was an
angry swirl of red, orange and yellow. The flames consumed the entire sky,
the very night itself. Police and fire sirens wailed in the distance to the south;
now and then an explosion touched off by the roaring fire punctuated the
keen of the sirens and the whisper of rain against the pavements.

The deaf man smiled, and Rafe put the truck in motion.

'What time is it?' Rafe asked.

'Five-fifty.'

'So we missed the five-forty-five boat.'

'That's right. And we've got fifteen minutes to make the six-oh-five. I
don't think we'll have any trouble.'

'I hope not,' Rafe said.

'Do you know how much money we have in the ice box?' the deaf man
asked, grinning.

'How much?'

'More than two million dollars.' The deaf man paused. 'That's a lot of
money, Rafe, wouldn't you say so?'

'I would say so,' Rafe answered, preoccupied. He was watching the road
and the traffic signals. They had come eight blocks and there had been no
sign of a policeman. The streets looked eerie somehow. Cops were a familiar
part of the landscape, but every damn cop in the precinct was probably over
on the south side. Rafe had to hand it to the deaf man. Still, he didn't want to
pass any lights, and he didn't want to exceed the speed limit. And, too, the
streets were slippery. He'd hate like hell to crash into a lamppost with all that
money in the ice box.

'What time is it?' he asked the deaf man.

'Five-fifty-six.'

Rafe kept his foot steady on the accelerator. He signalled every time they
made a turn. He panicked once when he heard a siren behind them, but the
squad car raced past on his left, intent on the more important matters at
hand.

'They all seem to be going someplace,' the deaf man said, grinning
securely.

'Yeah,' Rafe said. His heart was beating wildly in his chest. He would not
have admitted it to anyone, but he was terrified. All that money. Suppose
something went wrong? All that money.

'What time is it?' he asked, as he made the turn into the parking lot at the
ferry slip.

'Six-oh-one,' the deaf man said.

'Where's the boat?' Rafe asked, looking out over the river.

'It'll be here,' the deaf man said. He was feeling rather good. His plan had taken into account the probability that some cops would be encountered on the drive from the bank to the ferry slip. Well, they had come within kissing distance of a squad car, and the car had gone merrily along its way, headed for the fire-stricken area. The incendiaries had worked beautifully. Perhaps he could talk the men into voting Pop a bonus. Perhaps . . .

'Where's the damn boat?' Rafe said impatiently.

'Give it time. It'll be here.'

'You sure there *is* a six-oh-five?'

'I'm sure.'

'Let me see that schedule,' Rafe said. The deaf man reached into his pocket and handed him the folder. Rafe glanced at it quickly.

'Holy Je –?' he said.

'What's the matter?'

'It's not running.' Rafe said. 'There's a little notation beside it, a letter *E*, and that letter means it only runs on May thirtieth, July fourth and –'

'You're reading it wrong,' the deaf man said calmly. 'That letter *E* is alongside the seven-fifteen boat. There are no symbols beside the six-oh-five. I know that schedule by heart, Rafe.'

Rafe studied the schedule again. Abashed, he muttered a small Oh,' and then looked out over the river again. 'Then where the hell is it?'

'It'll be here,' the deaf man assured him.

'What time is it?'

'Six-oh-four.'

In the rented house in Majesta, Chuck lighted a cigarette and leaned closer to the radio.

'There's nothing on so far,' he said. 'They don't know what's the hell's happening.' He paused. 'I guess they got away.'

'Suppose they didn't?' Pop said.

'What do you mean?'

'What do we do? If they got picked up?'

'We'll hear about it on the radio. Everybody's just dying for an explanation. They'll flash it the minute they know. And we'll beat it.'

'Suppose they tell the cops where we are?'

'They won't get caught,' Chuck said.

'Suppose. And suppose they tell?'

'They wouldn't do that.'

'Wouldn't they?'

'Shut up,' Chuck said. He was silent for a moment. Then he said, 'No, they wouldn't.'

The patrolman came out of the waiting-room, looked past the ice-cream truck and over the river, sucked the good drizzly air of April into his lungs, put his hands on his hips, and studied the cherry-red glow in the sky to the south. He did not realize he was an instrument of probability. He was one of those cops who, either through accident or design, had been left on his post rather than pulled southward to help in the emergency. He knew there was a big fire on the River Dix, but his beat was the thirty waterfront blocks on the

River Harb, starting with the ferry waiting-room and working east to the water tower on North Forty-first. He had no concept of the vastness of what was happening to the south, and he had no idea whatever that the ice-cream truck standing not ten feet away from him carried two and a half million dollars, more or less, in its ice box.

He was just a lousy patrolmen who had come on duty at 3.45 p.m. and who would go off duty at 11.45 p.m., and he wasn't anticipating trouble here at the ferry slip connecting Isola to the sleepy section called Majesta. He stood with his hands on his hips for a moment longer, studying the sky. Then he casually strolled toward the ice-cream truck.

'Relax,' the deaf man said.

'He's coming over!'

'*Relax!*'

'Hi,' the patrolman said.

'Hello,' the deaf man answered pleasantly.

'I'd like an ice-cream pop,' the patrolman said.

They had managed to control the fire at the stadium, and Lieutenant Byrnes, with the help of three traffic commands, had got the traffic unsnarled and then supervised the loading of the ambulances with the badly burned and trampled victims of the deaf man's plot. Byrnes had tried, meanwhile, to keep pace with what was happening in his precinct. The reports had filtered in slowly at first, and then had come with increasing suddenness. An incendiary bomb in a paint shop, the fire and explosion touching off a row of apartment houses. A bomb left in a bus on Culver Avenue, the bomb exploding while the bus was at an intersection, bottling traffic in both directions for miles. Scare calls, panic calls, *real* calls, and in the midst of all the confusion a goddamn gang rumble in the housing project on South Tenth, just what he needed; let the little bastards kill themselves.

Now covered with sweat and grime, threading his way through the fire hoses snaked across the street, hearing the clang of ambulance gongs and the moan of sirens, seeing the red glow in the sky over the River Dix, he crossed the street and headed for a telephone because there was one call he *had* to make, one thing he *had* to know.

Hernandez followed him silently and stood outside the phone booth while Byrnes dialled.

'Rhodes Clinic,' the starched voice said.

'This is Lieutenant Byrnes. How's Carella?'

'Carella, sir?'

'Detective Carella. The policeman who was admitted with the shotgun wou –'

'Oh, yes, sir. I'm sorry, sir. There's been so much confusion here. People being admitted – the fires, you know. Just a moment, sir.'

Byrnes waited.

'Sir?' the woman said.

'Yes?'

'He seems to have come through the crisis. His temperature's gone down radically, and he's resting quietly. Sir, I'm sorry, the switchboard is –'

'Go ahead, take your calls,' Byrnes said, and he hung up.

'How is he?' Hernandez asked.

'He'll be all right,' Byrnes said. He nodded. 'He'll be all right.'

'I could feel the shadow,' Hernandez said suddenly, but he did not explain his words.

'One of them specials you got advertised on the side of the truck,' the patrolman said. 'With the chopped walnuts.'

'We're all out of the walnut crunch,' the deaf man said quickly. He was not frightened, only annoyed. He could see the ferry boat approaching the slip, could see the captain on the bridge leaning out over the windshield, peering into the rain as he maneouvred the boat.

'No walnut?' the patrolman said. 'That's too bad. I had my face fixed for one.'

'Yes, that's too bad,' the deaf man said. The ferry nudged the dock pilings and moved in tight, wedging toward the dock. A deck hand leaped ashore and turned on the mechanism to lower the dock to meet the boat's deck.

'Okay, let me have a plain chocolate pop,' the patrolman said.

'We're all out of those, too,' the deaf man said.

'Well, what have you got?'

'We're empty. We were heading back for the plant.'

'In Majesta?'

'Yes,' the deaf man said.

'Oh.' The patrolman shook his head again. 'Well, okay,' he said, and he started away from the truck. They were raising the gates on the ferry now, and the cars were beginning to unload. As the patrolman passed the rear of the truck, he glanced at the licence plate and noticed that the plate read IS 6341, and he knew that 'IS' plates were issued to drivers in Isola and that all Majesta plates began with the letters MA. And he wondered what the probability – the word 'probability' never once entered his head because he was not a mathematician or a statistician or a logician, he was only a lousy patrolmen – he wondered what the probability was of a company with its plants on Majesta having a truck bearing plates which were issued in Isola, and he continued walking because he figured *What the hell, it's possible*.

And then he thought of a second probability, and he wondered when he had ever seen an ice-cream truck carrying *two* men in uniform. And he thought, *Well, that's possible, they're both going back to the plant, maybe one is giving the other a lift*. In which case, where had the second guy left *his* truck?

And, knowing nothing at all about the theory of probability, he knew only that it looked wrong, it felt wrong, and so he began thinking about ice-cream trucks in general, and he seemed to recall a teletype he'd read back at the precinct before coming on duty this afternoon, something about an ice-cream truck having been –

He turned and walked back to the cab of the truck. Rafe had just started the engine again and was ready to drive the truck onto the ferry.

'Hey,' the patrolman said.

A hurried glance passed between Rafe and the deaf man.

'Mind showing me the registration for this vehicle, Mac?' the patrolman said.

'It's in the glove compartment,' the deaf man said calmly. There was two and a half million dollars in the ice box of the truck, and he was not going to panic now. He could see fear all over Rafe's face. One of them had to be calm.

He thumbed over the glove compartment and began riffling through the junk there. The patrolman waited, his hand hovering near the holstered ·38 at his side.

'Now where the devil is it?' the deaf man asked. 'What's the trouble anyway, officer? We're trying to catch that ferry.'

'Yeah, well, the ferry can wait, Mac,' the patrolman said. He turned to Rafe. 'Let me see your licence.'

Rafe hesitated, and the deaf man knew exactly what Rafe was thinking – he was thinking his normal operator's licence was not valid for the driving of a commercial vehicle, he was thinking that and knowing that if he showed the patrolman his operator's licence, the patrolman would ask further questions. And yet, there was no sense in *not* producing the licence. If Rafe balked at this point, that holstered ·38 would be in the policeman's hand in an instant. There was nothing to do but play the percentages and hope they could talk their way out of this before the ferry pulled out because the next ferry was not until 8.45, and they sure as hell couldn't sit around here until then, there was nothing to do but bluff the hand; the stakes were certaintly high enough.

'Show him your licence, Rafe,' the deaf man said.

Rafe hesitated.

'Show it to him.'

Nervously, Rafe reached into his back pocket for his wallet. The deaf man glanced toward the ferry. Two sedans had boarded the boat and a few passengers had ambled aboard after them. On the bridge, the captain looked at his watch, and then reached up for the pull cord. The bellow of the foghorn split the evening air. First warning.

'Hurry up!' the deaf man said.

Rafe handed the patrolman his licence. The patrolman ran his flashlight over it.

'This is an operator's licence,' he said. 'You're driving a *truck* Mac.'

'Officer, we're trying to catch that ferry,' the deaf man said.

'Yeah, well ain't that too bad?' the patrolman said, reverting to type, becoming an authoritative son of a bitch because he had them dead to rights and now he was going to play Mr District Attorney. 'Maybe I ought to take a look in your ice box, huh? How come you ain't got no ice cre –'

And the deaf man said, 'Move her, Rafe!'

Rafe stepped on the gas pedal, and the foghorn erupted from the bridge of the boat at the same moment, and the deaf man saw the gates go down on the ferry, and suddenly the boat was moving away from the dock, and the patrolman shouted 'Hey!' behind them, and then a shot echoed on the rain-streaked air, and the deaf man knew that the percentages had run out, and suddenly the patrolman fired again and Rafe screamed sharply and fell forward over the wheel and the truck swerved wildly out of control as the deaf man leaped from the cab.

His mind churning with probabilities. Jump for the ferry? No, because I'm unarmed and the captain will take me into custody. Run for the street? No, because the patrolman will gun me down before I'm halfway across the dock, all that money, all that sweet money, predicted error, I *did* predict the error, damn it, I did take into account the fact that some policemen would undoubtedly be somewhere on our escape route, but an ice-cream pop, God, an ice-cream pop! the river is the only way, and he ran for the fence.

'Halt!' the patrolman shouted. 'Halt, or I'll fire!'

The deaf man kept running. How long can I hold my breath under water? he wondered. How far can I swim?

The patrolmen fired over his head, and then he aimed at the deaf man's legs as the deaf man scrambled over the cyclone fence separating the dock from the water.

He stood poised on the top of the fence for just a moment, as if undecided, as if uncertain that the percentages were truly with him, and then suddenly he leaped into the air and away from the fence and the dock, just as the patrolman triggered off another shot. He hung silhouetted against the grey sky, and then dropped like a stone to the water below. The patrolman rushed to the fence.

Five shots, the deaf man thought. He'll have to reload. Quickly, he surfaced, took a deep, lung-filling breath, and then ducked below the surface again.

All that money, he thought. *Well – next time.*

The patrolman's hammer clicked on an empty chamber. He loaded rapidly and then fired another burst at the water.

The deaf man did not resurface.

There was only a widening circle of ripples to show that he had existed at all.

Chapter Seventeen

It is surprising how co-operative a thief can become when he has a bullet wound in his shoulder and he knows the jig is up. Even before they carted Rafe off to the hospital, he had given them the names of his confederates waiting in the rented house. The Majesta cops picked up Chuck and Pop in five minutes flat.

It is surprising, too, how consistent thieves are. It was one thing to be facing a rap for a bank holdup. It was quite another to be facing charges like wholesale murder, arson, riot and – man, this was the clincher – possible treason. A bright boy in the D.A.'s office looked up the Penal Law and said that these birds had committed treason against the state by virtue of having levied *war* against the people of the state. Now that was a terrifying charge, even if it didn't carry a death penalty. War against the people of the state? *War?* My God!

The three thieves named Rafe, Chuck and Pop were somehow up to their necks in something more than they had bargained for. They didn't mind spending the rest of their lives in Castleview Prison upstate, but there was a certain electrically wired chair up there in which they had no particular desire to sit. And so, in concert, they recognized that a ready-made scapegoat was at hand. Or, if not quite at hand, at least somewhere below the surface of the River Harb.

And, in concert, they consistently repeated that the man in the river was responsible for all the mayhem and all the death, that he and he alone had shot John Smith and set all those bombs, that *he* had waged the war, and that their part in this little caper was confined to the robbery of the bank. Did they look like the kind of men who valued human life so cheaply? Did they look like fellows who would derail trains and set fires in baseball stadiums just for a little money? No, no, the fellow in the river was responsible for all that.

And the fellow's name?

Consistently, and in concert, they identified him solely as 'the deaf man'. More than that, they could not, or would not say.

Their consistency was admirable, to be sure.

And, admirably, they were booked and arranged on *each* of the charges for acting in concert, and it was the opinion of the police and the District Attorney's office that all three of them had a very good chance of frying, or at the very least, spending the rest of their natural lives behind bars at Castleview Prison upstate. The probabilities were good either way, the police felt.

On May 21, Dave Raskin came up to the squadroom. He walked directly to Meyer Meyer's desk and said, 'So what do you think, Meyer?'

'I don't know,' Meyer said. 'What should I think?'

'I'm moving out of that loft.'

'What?'

'Sure. Who needs that cockamamie loft? I tell you the truth, without the bank downstairs, I got nobody to look at out of the window. Before, it was a busy place. Now, nothing.'

'Well,' Meyer said, and he shrugged.

'How's the cop who got shot?'

'He'll be out of the hospital in a few weeks,' Meyer said.

'Good, good. I'm glad to hear that. Listen, if your wife needs some nice dresses, stop around, okay? I'll pick out some pretty ones for her, compliments of Dave Raskin.'

'Thank you,' Meyer said.

Raskin went back to the loft on Culver Avenue where Margarita was packing their stock preparatory to the move, flinging her unbound breasts about with renewed fervour. Raskin watched her for a few moments, pleased with what he saw. The telephone rang suddenly. Still watching Margarita's energetic acrobatics, Raskin picked up the receiver.

'Hello?' he said.

'Raskin?' the voice asked.

'Yes? Who's this?'

'Get out of that loft,' the voice said. 'Get out of that loft, you son of a bitch, or I'll kill you!'

'You!' Raskin said. 'You again!'

And suddenly he heard chuckling on the other end of the wire.

'Who's this?' he asked.

'Meyer Meyer,' the voice said, chuckling.

'You dirty bastard,' Raskin said, and then he began laughing, too. 'Oh, you had me going there for a minute. For a minute, I thought my heckler was back.' Raskin laughed uproariously. 'I got to hand it to you. You're a great comedian. Since your father died, there hasn't been such a comedian. You're just like your father! Just like him!'

Meyer Meyer, at the other end of the wire, listened, exchanged the amenities, and then hung up.

Just like my father, he thought.

Suddenly, he felt a little ill.

'What's the matter?' Miscolo said, coming in from the Clerical Office.

'I don't feel so hot,' Meyer said.

'You're just upset because a patrolman cracked a case you couldn't.'

'Maybe so,' Meyer answered.

'Cheer up,' Miscolo said. 'You want some coffee?'

'Just like my father,' Meyer said sadly.

'Huh!'

'Nothing. But a guy works all his life trying to . . .' Meyer shook his head. 'Just like my father.'

'You want the coffee or not?'

'Yeah. yeah, I'll have the coffee. Stop heckling me!'

'Who's heckling?' Miscolo said, and he went out for the coffee.

From his desk across the squadroom, Bert Kling said, 'It'll be summer soon.'

'So?'

'So there'll be more kids in the streets, and more gang wars, and more petty crimes, and shorter tempers and –'

'Don't be so pessimistic,' Meyer said.

'Who's pessimistic? It sounds like it'll be a lovely summer. Just lovely.'

'I can hardly wait,' Meyer answered.

He pulled a typewritten list closer to the phone, and then dialled the first of a group of eyewitnesses to a burglary.

Outside the squadroom, May seemed impatient for the suffocating heat of July and August.

TEN
PLUS ONE

"Nobody thinks
about death
on a nice
spring day.
Autumn is the
time for dying,
not spring."

This is for Herbert Alexander

Chapter One

Nobody thinks about death on a nice spring day.

Autumn is the time for dying, not spring. Autumn encourages macabre thoughts, invites the ghoulish imagination, tempts the death wish with sere and withered evidence of decay. Autumn is poetic as hell, brief, succinct, stinking of mold and ashes. People die a lot in autumn. Everything dies a lot in autumn.

Nothing is allowed to die in the spring. There's a law that says so – Penal Law 5,0006, DEATH IN THE SPRING: 'Whosoever shall expire, or cause to expire, or conspire to expire, or harbour thoughts of expiring during the vernal equinox shall be guilty of a felony punishable by . . .' It goes on like that. It absolutely forbids death between March 21 and June 21, but there are lawbreakers everywhere, so what can you do?

The man who stepped out of the office building on Culver Avenue was about to become a lawbreaker. Normally, he was a good citizen, a hard-working man, a faithful husband, a devoted father, all that jazz. He had no intention of breaking the law. He didn't know that death was forbidden by legislature, but even if he *had* known, it wouldn't have concerned him, because death and dying were the furthest things from his mind on that bright spring day.

He was, in fact, thinking of life. He was thinking that next week was his birthday, that he would be forty-five years old, that he didn't feel a day over thirty-five. He was thinking that the grey at his temples added a corny but distinguished touch to his noble head, that his shoulders were still broad, that his twice-weekly tennis sessions had eliminated an alarming little potbelly, and that he would lay his wife the moment he saw her, even if they'd never be allowed to eat at Schrafft's again.

He was thinking all these things when the bullet sang across the open, fresh, spring air, spiraling wickedly, unglintingly, unerringly accurate as it traversed the area from the roof of the building across the street, high above the tops of the beetle cars and the heads of the ant people enjoying spring, fast, true, deadly, to the sidewalk opposite, to hit him between the eyes.

Only one thought flashed into his mind the second the bullet struck, and then all thought ceased. He felt a single sharp shattering blow between his eyes and he thought for a split instant that he had walked into the glass doors that separated the building from the street outside. The bullet splintered through the bone, found the soft cushion of his brain, and then blew a hole the size of a baseball through the back of his head as it passed on through. Thought stopped, feeling stopped, there was suddenly nothing. The impact sent him reeling back three feet to collide with a young girl in a yellow cotton frock. He fell backward as the girl reflexively side-stepped, his body seemed to fold in on itself like a battered accordion, the tennis muscles relaxed, he was dead even before he hit the pavement. The large hole below his forehead leaked a tiny trickle of blood while the enormous exit hole at the base of his skull poured blood onto the sidewalk steadily, wetly, redly, a blinding, screaming red still hot with life, flowing swiftly to where the girl stood in shocked and dumb horror, watching the stream of blood as it rushed across the sidewalk.

She pulled back her foot just in time; in another moment, the blood would have touched the toe of her high-heeled pump.

Detective Steve Carella looked down at the body on the sidewalk, and wondered how it could be that ten minutes ago when he left the precinct there were no flies, it was too early in the season for flies, and that now, as he looked down at the dead man whose blood had stopped flowing, the pavement was covered with flies, there was a swarm of flies in the air, and another half-dozen flies were feeding at the open hole between the man's eyes.

'Can't you cover him up?' he snapped at one of the interns, and the intern shrugged and gestured innocently toward the police photographer who was putting another roll of film into his camera in the shade of the ambulance parked at the kerb.

Without looking up, the photographer said, 'Got to take his picture.'

Carella turned away from the body. He was a tall man with a fine-honed muscular appearance, high cheekbones, his brown hair cut sparingly, his brown eyes slanting peculiarly downward to give his face a pained and suffering oriental look as he turned into the sun, squinting, and walked to where the girl in the yellow frock was talking to several newspaper reporters.

'Later, boys,' he said, and the newspapermen, oddly quiescent in the presence of death, faded back into the circle of bystanders beyond the fringe of patrolmen.

'How do you feel?' Carella asked.

'All right. Gee,' she said. 'Gee.'

'Do you feel like answering a few questions?'

'Sure. Gee, I never saw anything like this in my life before. Wait'll I tell my husband.'

'What's your name, ma'am?'

'Mrs Irving Grant.'

'Your first name?'

'Lizanne. With a *z*.'

'And your address, Mrs Grant?'

'Eleven-forty-two Grover.' She paused. 'That's below First.'

'Mmm,' Carella said, jotting the address into his book.

'I mean, in case you thought I lived in a Puerto Rican neighbourhood.'

'No, I didn't think that,' Carella said. He was suddenly very tired. There was a dead man covered with flies on the pavement, and a possible witness to the shooting was worried about whether or not he would think she lived in a Puerto Rican neighbourhood. He wanted to explain that he didn't give a damn whether she lived in a Puerto Rican neighbourhood or a Czechoslovakian neighbourhood, so long as she could tell him, with minimal emotion and maximal accuracy, what she had seen happen to the dead man, who no longer had a nationality. He gave her an over-the-pencil glance that he hoped was withering enough, and then he said, 'Can you tell me what happened?'

'Who is he?' Mrs Grant asked.

'We don't know yet. We haven't looked him over for identification. I'm waiting until the photographer is finished. Can you tell me what happened?'

'I was just walking along when he bumped into me.' She shrugged. 'Then he fell down, and I looked at him, and he was bleeding. Gee, I'm telling you, I never . . .'

'What do you mean he bumped into you?'

'Well, he *backed* into me, really.'

'He'd been shot already, is that it? And he fell backward against you?'

'I don't know if he'd been shot. I guess he had.'

'Well, did he stumble backward, or fall, or what?'

'I don't know. I wasn't paying any attention. I was walking along, that's all, when he bumped into me.'

'All right, Mrs Grant, what happened then?'

'Then he just fell over backward. I moved away from him, and I looked down at him, and that was when I saw he was bleeding, and I knew he was hurt.'

'What'd you do?'

'I don't know what I did. I just kept looking at him, I think.' She shook her head. 'Wait'll I tell my husband about this.'

'Did you hear the shot, Mrs Grant?'

'No.'

'You're certain you didn't hear anything?'

'I was walking along thinking my own thoughts,' Mrs Grant said. 'I didn't expect a thing like this to happen. I mean, maybe there was a shot, maybe there were six shots, I'm only saying I didn't hear anything. He bumped into me all of a sudden, and then he fell down, and there was blood all over his face. Urghh.' Mrs Grant grimaced at the memory.

'I don't suppose you saw anyone with a gun?'

'A gun? No. A what? A gun? No, no.'

'I know you were busy thinking your own thoughts before the man got shot, but *afterward*, Mrs Grant? Did you see anyone in one of the windows across the way, or perhaps on the roof of one of the buildings? Did you notice anything unusual?'

'I didn't look around,' Mrs Grant said. 'I just kept staring at his face.'

'Did the man say anything to you before he fell to the sidewalk?'

'Not a word.'

'*After* he fell?'

'Nothing.'

'Thank you, Mrs Grant,' Carella said. He smiled briefly but pleasantly and then closed his notebook.

'Is that all?'

'Yes, thank you.'

'But . . .' Mrs Grant seemed disappointed. She gave a slight shrug.

'Yes, Mrs Grant?'

'Well . . . won't I have to come to the trial or anything?'

'I don't think so, Mrs Grant. Thank you very much.'

'Well . . . all right,' Mrs Grant said, but she kept watching him in disappointment as he walked away from her and back to the body. The police photographer was dancing his intricate little jig around the corpse, snapping a picture, ejecting a flashbulb, inserting another flashbulb, and then twisting his body and bending his knees to get a shot from another angle. The two interns stood near the ambulance, casually smoking and chatting about an emergency tracheotomy one had performed the day before. Not three feet away from them, talking to a patrolman, stood detectives Monoghan and Monroe, who had been sent over as a matter of form from Homicide North. Carella watched the photographer for a moment, and then walked over to the two Homicide dicks.

'Well, well,' he said, 'to what do we owe the honour?'

Monoghan, wearing a black topcoat and a black derby, looking like a Prohibition cop of the twenties, turned, looked at Carella, and then said to Monroe, 'Why, it's Carella of the Eight-Seven,' as though discovering him in great surprise.

'Upon my soul, I believe it is,' Monroe said, turning away from the patrolman. He, too, wore a black topcoat. A grey fedora was pushed onto the back of his head. He had a nervous tic near one eye that seemed to jerk magically whenever his partner spoke, as though a secret recording mechanism were at work behind his fleshy features.

'I hope we didn't break in on your dinner or anything.' Carella said.

'What I like about the cops of the Eighty-seventh,' Monoghan said while Monroe ticked, 'is that they are always so concerned about their colleagues in the department.'

'Also, they are very funny,' Monroe observed.

'I am always amazed,' Monoghan said, putting his hands in his coat pockets, with the thumbs sticking out, the way he had seen it done by Sydney Greenstreet in a movie once, 'by their concern and their good humour.'

'I am always amazed by it, too,' Monroe said.

'Who's the stiff?' Monoghan asked.

'Don't know yet,' Carella replied. 'I'm waiting for the photographer to get finished there.'

'He takes a good picture,' Monroe said.

'He does portrait work on the side, I hear,' Monoghan said.

'You know what some of these guys are doing now?' Monroe asked.

'Which guys?' Monoghan said.

'The photographers. The ones they send out on homicides.'

'No. What are they doing?'

'They're using these Polaroid cameras to take their pictures.'

'Yeah? What's their hurry?'

'It ain't that they're in a hurry,' Monroe said, 'it's just that when you're working with a stiff, like if the picture don't turn out, you can't call him back for another sitting, you know? By that time, the morgue's got him all cut up. So this way, the photographers can see what they got right off.'

'Boy, what they won't think of next, huh?' Monoghan said, properly awed. 'So what's new, Carella? How's the skipper? How're the boys?'

'Everybody's fine,' Carella said.

'You working on anything interesting?'

'This ought to be an interesting one,' Carella said.

'Yeah, snipers are always interesting,' Monoghan agreed.

'We had a sniper once,' Monroe said, 'when I was just made detective, working out of the Three-Nine. He used to shoot only old ladies. That was his specialty, little old ladies. He used to pick them off with a forty-five. He was a damn good shot, too. You remember Mickey Dunhill?'

'Yeah, I remember him,' Monoghan said.

'You remember Mickey Dunhill?' Monroe asked Carella.

'No. Who's Mickey Dunhill?'

'Detective/first working out of the Three-Nine, Little tiny guy, he could knock you flat on your ass, strong as an ox. We dressed him up like a little old lady. That's how we got the guy. He took a shot at Dunhill, and Dunhill pulled up his skirts and chased him up the roof and nearly beat him to death.'

'Yeah, I remember,' Monoghan said.

'We get the guy downtown, you know? The sniper? We put him in a chair, we try to find out how come he's killing little old ladies. We figure maybe he's got an Oedipus thing, you know? But . . ..'

'A *what*?' Monoghan asked.

'Oedipus,' Monroe said. 'He was this Greek king. He slept with his old lady.'

'That's against the law,' Monoghan said.

'I know. Anyway, we figured maybe this sniper was nuts, you know? So we kept asking him how come little old ladies? Why don't he pick on little old men? Or *anybody*, for that matter? How come he only plugs sweet little old ladies?'

'How come?' Monoghan asked.

Monroe shrugged. 'He wouldn't tell us.'

'What do you mean?'

'He wouldn't tell us.'

'So what's the point of your story?'

'What do you mean, what's the point? Here was a guy, he used to go around shooting little old ladies!' Monroe said indignantly.

'Yeah? So?'

'So? So, what do you mean, what's the point? *That's* the point.'

'What about the other guy?'

'What guy?'

'The Greek guy,' Monoghan said impatiently.

'What Greek guy?'

'The king, the king. Didn't you say there was a Greek king?'

'Oh, for God's sake, he had nothing to do with it,' Monroe said.

'You shoulda looked him up, anyway,' Monoghan insisted. 'You never know.'

'How could we look him up? He was legendary.'

'He was what?' Monoghan asked.

'Legendary. Legendary.'

Monoghan nodded knowingly. 'Well, that could make a difference,' he said. 'Still, it always pays to cover all the angles.'

'I think the photographer's through,' Carella said.

'You need us?' Monroe asked.

'I don't think so. I'll send you a copy of the report.'
'You know what you should do?' Monroe said.
'What?'
'Dress up that big redhead you got up there, what's his name?'
'Cotton Hawes?'
'Yeah, him. Dress him up like a little old lady. Maybe your sniper'll take a crack at him.'
'He seems to favour middle-aged men,' Carella said.
Monoghan turned to look at the corpse. 'He can't be more than forty,' he said, slightly miffed. 'Since when is forty middle-aged?'
'Mature, I meant,' Carella said.
'Yeah, that's better,' Monoghan answered. 'Send us *two* copies, we got a new regulation.'
'Come on, have a heart,' Carella said.
'Do I make the regulations?'
'You mean you *don't?*' Carella said, looking surprised.
'There he goes again. See what I mean? You could wet your pants laughing. Send the two copies, Carella. See who gets the last laugh.'
'You think maybe the Greek guy did it?' Carella asked.
'What Greek guy?'
'I don't know, the one Monroe was talking about.'
'I wouldn't put it past him,' Monoghan said. 'A guy who'd sleep with his own mother is capable of anything.'
Smiling, Carella walked to where the photographer was packing his equipment. 'You all finished here?' he asked.
'Be my guest,' the photographer said.
'I'll want some of those pictures.'
'Sure. What precinct is this, anyway?'
'The Eight-Seven.'
'Right,' the photographer said. 'And your name?'
'Carella. Steve Carella.'
'You'll have them tomorrow.' He glanced at the sedan that pulled to the kerb and then grinned and said, 'Uh-oh.'
'What's the matter?'
'The lab boys. Now you'll have to wait till *they* get through.'
'All I want to do is find out who the hell the guy *is*,' Carella said, and then he turned toward the two technicians who stepped out of the automobile.

Chapter Two

He had found out who the hell the guy was by going through his wallet, and now the hard part lay ahead.

The guy was Anthony Forrest, and his driver's license gave his address as 301 Morrison Drive, his height as five feet eight inches, and his eyes as blue. He carried six credit cards, all made out to Anthony Forrest: the Diner's

Club, American Express, Carte Blanche, the Gulf Oil Corporation, the Mobil Oil Company, and a card for one of the men's department stores in the city. He also carried a business card which repeated his name, Anthony Forrest, and gave the name of his firm, Indian Exports, Inc., and the address, 580 Culver Avenue, which happened to be the address of the building in front of which he'd been shot and killed. The business card also gave him a title, which was vice-president, and a phone number for the company, Frederick 7-4100. There were assorted other cards and scraps of paper in his wallet, and a five-dollar bill folded into his driver's license, apparently there as insurance against traffic tickets. There were seventy dollars in cash in the wallet, three twenties, the five and five singles.

Carella found the photographs in the gatefold.

The woman was perhaps thirty-five years old, with bright youthful eyes and light hair. She smiled happily up at him through the celluloid case. There were pictures of three different children, all with the woman's light hair and light eyes, two boys and a girl. The boys were wearing Cub Scout uniforms. One seemed to be slightly older than the other, but neither one was more than ten or eleven. The girl was perhaps fifteen or sixteen. The picture of her had been taken at a beach someplace. She was holding a large, striped beach ball and grinning over its top. Forrest himself stood behind her, grinning like a teenager, holding up two fingers behind her head so that they resembled horns.

Carella sighed and closed the wallet.

There is a quaint police regulation which requires corpses to be identified, and it is usually a blood relative who makes the positive identification, thereby enabling the police to know they are looking for the murderer of John Smith rather than the murderer of John Doe. The pictures in the wallet seemed to indicate that Forrest had a wife and three children, and it now remained for somebody to go to his home, wait for his door to open, face that wife and those children, and tell them that Anthony Forrest, husband, father, loved one, was stone cold dead.

The somebody was Steve Carella.

The girl who opened the door at 301 Morrison was the same girl Carella had seen grinning over the top of the beach ball in the photograph. The picture, though, had obviously been taken some years before, because the girl seemed to be at least nineteen or twenty. Her hair didn't seem as blond, either, but there was the same lively inquiry in her blue eyes, and she smiled at Carella in polite confusion and said, 'Yes? May I help you?'

'Miss Forrest?' Carella asked.

'Yes?' she said, more confused now, the blond eyebrows rising ever so slightly on her forehead.

'I'm Detective Carella of the Eighty-seventh Precinct,' Carella said. He paused, obligingly showed his shield and his ID card, and then cleared his throat. The girl waited. 'May I speak to your mother, please?'

'She's not in,' the girl said.

'Do you know where I can reach her?'

'She went to meet my father for dinner,' the girl said. 'Why?'

'Oh,' Carella said, and suddenly the girl got the message. Up to that moment she had been only puzzled by his appearance, but something in the way he said the word 'Oh' triggered alarm in her, and her eyes opened wide, and she took a short, quick step toward him and said, 'What is it?'

'May I come in, please?'

'Yes, certainly,' the girl said, but they did not move farther into the house than the entrance foyer. 'What is it?' she said. 'What happened?'

'Miss . . .' Carella said, and he hesitated, wondering if he should tell her, wondering if she was old enough to hear this, and yet realizing he had to locate her mother, had to inform *someone*.

'Do you know where your mother went? Where she was going to meet him?'

'Yes, Schrafft's. I don't know if they were going to have dinner there, but that's where they were meeting. Look, will you please tell me what this is about?'

Carella looked at her for what seemed like a very long time. Then, very gently, he said, 'Miss, your father is dead.'

The girl backed away from him. She stared at him a moment, and then smiled curiously, and then the smile dropped from her mouth, and she shook her head once, briefly, and said, 'No.'

'I'm sorry, miss.'

'There must be some mistake. He was meeting my mother for . . .'

'I don't think there's any mistake, miss.'

'Well . . . well . . . how do you *know*? I mean . . . for God's sake, what happened?'

'He was shot.'

'My *father*?' she asked incredulously. She shook her head again. 'Shot? Are you joking or something?'

'I'm sorry, miss, I'm not joking. I'd like to contact your mother. May I use your phone?'

'Look . . . look . . . what you said is . . . is impossible, don't you see? My father's name is Anthony Forrest. Now, I'm sure you've . . .'

Carella touched her arm gently. 'Miss,' he said, 'the man was carrying identification. We're reasonably certain he was your father.'

'What sort of identification?'

'A wallet.'

'Then someone must have stolen it from him,' the girl said. 'That happens all the time, you know. And the man who got shot was undoubtedly carrying my father's stolen wallet, so naturally you assumed . . .'

'Who is it, Cindy?' a boy's voice yelled from somewhere upstairs.

'It's nothing, Jeff. It's all right,' she answered.

'I'd like to call your mother,' Carella said.

'Why? So you can alarm *her* unnecessarily, too?'

Carella did not answer. He stared at the girl in silence. Tears were gathering behind her eyes; he could see them gathering, but she held on tightly for several moments and then said, 'Go ahead, call. But . . . you better be right, you hear me? That man better be my father. Because . . . you . . . you just better not be making any mistake.' The tears were standing in her eyes now, an opaque film over the clear blue. 'The phone's in here,' she said. As he followed her into the living room, she added, 'I'm sure he's not my father.' A small laugh caught in her throat. 'What would my father be doing getting . . . getting shot?'

Carella picked up the phone book and looked up the number of the Schrafft's restaurant closest to Forrest's business office. He was starting to dial when the girl touched his hand.

'Listen,' she said.

He looked up.

'Listen,' she said, and the tears suddenly began rolling down her face uncontrollably, 'she's not a very strong woman. Please . . . when you tell her . . . please do it gently? Please? When you tell her my father is dead? Please?'

Carella nodded and began dialing the number.

Clara Forrest was thirty-nine years old, a slender woman with a network of tiny wrinkles around her eyes and her mouth. She accompanied Carella into the mortuary silently, her face fixed in that curiously tight, almost angry expression people assume when they are told death has arrived. While the attendant pulled out the drawer on its oiled rollers, she stood by silently and then looked silently into the face of her husband, and nodded only once. She had accepted the knowledge the moment Carella revealed it on the telephone. This now, this looking into the face of the man she had married when she was nineteen, the man she had loved since she was seventeen, the man for whom she had borne three children, the man she had seen through bad times and good, this now, this looking into the dead and sightless face of a man who was now a corpse on an oiled drawer in a mortuary, this was only routine. The heartache had started the moment Carella spoke the words to her, and the rest was only routine.

'Is that your husband, Mrs Forrest?' Carella asked.

'Yes.'

'And his name is Anthony Forrest?'

'Yes.' Clara shook her head. 'Can we get out of here, please?'

They walked out of the big, echoing room and stood outside in the hospital corridor.

'Will they do an autopsy?' she asked.

'Yes, Mrs Forrest.'

'I wish they wouldn't.'

'I'm sorry.'

'Do you think it was painful for him?'

'He probably died instantly, Mrs Forrest.'

'Thank God for that.'

There was a long silence.

'We have clocks,' Clara said. 'Oh, maybe two dozen of them. I knew this would happen.'

'What do you mean?'

'He always wound the clocks. Some of them are very complicated. The older ones. And some of the tricky foreign ones. He used to wind them every week, on Saturday, all the clocks.' She paused and smiled tiredly. 'I was always so afraid this would happen. You see, he . . . I never learned how to wind them.'

'I don't understand,' Carella said.

'Now . . . now that Tony's gone,' she said dully, 'who'll wind the clocks?' And then she began weeping.

The police department is a vast organization, and a detective is only an organization man. He goes to his office each day, and he conducts his business. And, as with any other business, there are company rules and company procedures, and papers to be typed and dictated, and phone calls to be made, and people to be interviewed and visited, and facts to be researched, and other branches of the organization to contact, and specialists to be consulted. And, as with any other business, it is impossible in police work to devote one's full energies to a single pressing matter. There are always calls about something else, there are always unrelated people to see, there are conflicting vacation schedules and shortages of personnel, and overlapping and backslipping, and plain weariness.

Being a detective is something like being an account executive.

There is only one substantial difference, and once the mental adjustment is made, the difference becomes negligible.

An account executive, despite the cutthroat notoriety of his profession, rarely has to look death in the face, and certainly does not have to look it in the face daily.

A detective sees death in all its various forms at least five times a week, and usually more often. He sees it in the street in its elemental form, the slow disintegration of boys and girls, men and women, exposed to the rotting decay of the slums, dying bit by bit, having the life sucked out of them by the relentless city. He sees it more viciously in the junkies, a death that exists only by its negation of life, the slow suffocation of all will, the gradual extinction of any drive save the drive toward heroin. He sees it in convicted thieves, the burglars, the muggers, the con men, the pimps, a death imposed by law, the gradual death of confinement behind bars. He sees it in the whores who have witnessed the death of honour, and daily multiply the death of love, who bleed away their own lives fifty times a day beneath the relentless stabbings of countless conjugations. He sees it in the homosexuals, who have watched their manhood die, and who live a desperate dying life in the shadow of the law. He sees it in the juvenile street gangs, who live in fear of death and who propagate fear by inflicting death to banish fear.

And he sees it at its worst, as the result of violent emotions bursting into the mind and erupting from the hands. He sees gunshot wounds and stab wounds and hatchet wounds and ice-pick wounds and mutilations and eviscerations. And each time, each time he looks at another human body that has been killed and nullified, he is yanked out of his own body, loses his own humanity to become an observer, a visitor from somewhere far in space studying a curious race of insect people who rip each other apart, who tear each other limb from limb and drink each other's blood; he stands appalled, a civilized human who momentarily renounces his citizenship, unable to believe such cruelty can exist in men who have almost reached the stars. And then he blinks his eyes shut, and he opens them again, and there is only a case lying on the pavement, and he is only an organization man, and there are facts to be dug for and information to be had, before this one can be filed away with all the rest.

The ballistics report informed Carella that the bullet dug from the wooden runner of the doors behind Forrest and the discharged shell found on the rooftop of the building across the way were separate parts of a .308-calibre Remington cartridge. The report also stated that the .308 had a full metal case, with a copper-jacketed bullet that had six lands and grooves, a soft point, a right twist, and weighed 191.6 grains. It was suggested that Forrest's murderer must have used a telescopic sight, the distance from the roof to the sidewalk where Forrest was standing being something over a hundred and fifty yards.

Carella studied the report, and then behaved like a man who had not been in this business for a long, long time. He ignored the nagging premonition that had begun the moment he looked down at the dead man, in the hope that if he ignored it, it would go away, thereby making the case easier to cope with. He had caught the squeal, and so the case was officially his. The men of the 87th rarely worked with a fixed partner, rather sharing the case load in a haphazard but effective manner, delegating duty to whoever had time or energy to spare. It was only April, but Meyer Meyer was just returning from his vacation to replace Bert Kling, who was leaving on his. The early vacations were the lieutenant's idea; gang violence and crime in general seemed to enjoy an upswing during the summer months, and he wanted his full squad on duty during July and August. Cotton Hawes and Hal Willis was desperately trying to crack a series of warehouse robberies, Andy Parker was working on a jewellery holdup, and Arthur Brown was working with the Narcotics Squad in an attempt to flush out a known pusher hiding in the precinct. There were sixteen detectives on the squad, and Carella had worked with them all at one time or another, but he enjoyed working with Meyer Meyer and was happy when the lieutenant assigned him to the case.

Meyer, oddly, fell immediately into the pattern Carella had set. He, too, blatantly ignored something that was staring them both in the face. He seemed inordinately glad to discover that they knew who the victim was, where his family lived, and what kind of bullet had killed him. They had often begun cases without the faintest idea of the victim's name or address, without a single clue to his family or friends.

They told each other they were looking for a specific human being who had slain another specific human being. They knew very well that it was impossible to crack every murder case that came their way, but they also knew that the proper amount of patience and legwork, coupled with the right questions posed to the right people, usually brought about the desired results. A man, they told themselves, doesn't get killed unless someone feels he should be killed.

They changed their minds the very next day.

Chapter Three

It was another glorious spring day.

It is almost impossible for the country dweller to understand what such a day can mean to the person living in the city. The city citizen has avidly listened to the television weather reports the night before, and now the first thing he does when he awakens to the jangling of the alarm clock is to walk warily to the window and peer up at the sky. He feels a first real awakening thrill if the sky is blue. He knows immediately that this is going to be a day when nothing can go wrong, and then – winter or summer, spring or fall – he will open the window to test the temperature of the air, basing his wardrobe, his attitude, his entire philosophy of life, on the findings he makes in those few first wakeful moments.

Randolph Norden heard the clock-radio go on at 7:30 A.M. He had bought the clock-radio because he figured it would be nice to awaken to music each morning. But his usual rising time was 7:30, news time, and each and every morning he was awakened by the sound of an announcer giving the latest bad news about Russia. He had tried setting the clock-radio for 7:35, at which time the news had given way to music, but he found that he needed those extra five minutes if he was to get to the office on time. He had also tried setting the clock-radio for 7:25, but then he began resenting the loss of five minutes' sleep. And so, each morning, Randolph Norden listened to the bad news on a clock-radio he had bought to provide music. It was, to his way of thinking, another example of the unfairness of life.

As he got out of bed, he heard the announcer telling him about some offshore islands someplace, and he muttered, 'Go to hell, you *and* your islands,' and then walked wearily to the bedroom window, pulling up his pyjama top and scratching his belly, generally resenting the clock-radio and his wife, Mae, who was sound asleep in the bed, and even his children, who were sound asleep in their separate rooms at the other end of the apartment, and also the maid, who, although he was her employer, slept later than he each morning, making it necessary for him to get his own breakfast. He pulled up the shade, feeling reckless as he hoped sunlight would hit the bed and the face of his wife, and then feeling immediately guilty and turning rapidly to see if sunlight had indeed touched Mae's face. It had not. For a desperate moment, he thought, *No sun today*, but then he looked out and over the rooftops to where the sky curved in robin's-egg-blue artificiality, and a smile touched his mouth, and he gave a short affirmative nod, and then opened the window.

He stuck his head outside. The air was warm, with a gentle balmy breeze blowing south off the River Harb. From his twelfth-floor apartment, he could see the river traffic and the magnificent span of the bridge in the near distance. The smile widened into a grin. He left the window open, walked back to the bed, turned off the clock-radio, and then took off his pyjamas. He dressed swiftly and soundlessly, putting on underwear, trousers, socks and shoes, and then going into the bathroom where he shaved with an electric razor. As he shaved, his convictions about the day began to take firmer, more confident shape. He was a man who was fond of repeating that his best thoughts always came to him while shaving, and he did indeed have some wonderfully inventive – or so they seemed to him – thoughts while he ran the razor over his stubble. By the time he had finished shaving, put on his shirt, tie and jacket, and had gone into the kitchen to pour himself some juice and brew himself some coffee, he was anxious to get to his law office on Hall Avenue, where he would begin putting some of those wonderfully inventive ideas to work. He gulped his juice and coffee, and then marched to the other end of the apartment, where the children were still in bed. Joanie was awake by now, sitting up and reading a Golden Book, wearing the distorted features of half-asleep awareness.

'G'morning, Daddy,' she said, and then went back to her book.

He kissed her and said, 'I'll see you tonight, huh?' and she nodded and continued reading. He went into the other bedroom, where Mike was still asleep. He did not disturb him. He went instead, to the other end of the apartment again and kissed Mae, who mumbled something and then rolled over. He smiled, went to the front door, picked up his attaché case, and stepped into the hallway.

The elevator operator said, 'Good morning, Mr Norden. Beautiful day today.'

'Yes, it is, George,' he answered.

They rode in silence to the lobby. He got out, nodded in answer to George's 'Have a good day, Mr Norden,' and then walked to the mailboxes, which he checked routinely even though he knew it was too early for a mail delivery. He opened the front door of the building, stepped out onto the pavement, looked up at the sky, and grinned again.

He was taking a deep breath of fresh spring air when the bullet struck him between the eyes and killed him.

The detective who caught the squeal at the 65th Precinct was a fairly hip organization man who tried to keep up with anything important happening in the department. Homicide was a rare and unusual occurrence in the posh 65th, and he was somewhat surprised when the beat patrolman called it in. He put on his hat, motioned to his partner, checked out a police sedan with two bald front tires, and drove over to where Randolph Norden was lying dead on the sidewalk. It didn't take him very long to realize that Norden had been shot from somewhere high up in one of the buildings across the street, either a window or a roof; the entrance hole was between Norden's eyes, and the exit hole was low on the back of his neck, indicating a very sharp angle of trajectory. He was not a cop anxious to shirk work; he was, in fact, a little reluctant to let go of a bona-fide murder in a precinct where the biggest crimes were usually burglaries or street muggings. But he had read the morning's newspaper, and he knew that a man named Anthony Forrest had been shot to death on Culver Avenue in the Eight-Seven the day before, and his mind made an automatic connection – but still, he decided to wait before relinquishing the case. He did not have to wait long.

Ballistics told him that the bullet which had passed through Norden's head and flattened itself against the pavement, and the discharged shell found on the roof of the building across the street, were separate parts of a .308-caliber Remington cartridge. The report went on to point out that the .308 had a full metal case, with a copper-jacketed bullet and had six lands and grooves, a soft point, a right twist, and weighed 191.6 grains. And then, because someone at Ballistics was on the ball, there was an additional handwritten note on the bottom of the report:

Better call Detective 2nd/Grade Stephen Carella, 87th Squad, Frederick 7-8024. Investigating similar shooting yesterday, identical cartridge, identical M.O.

G. L.

The detective at the 65th read the report and the additional comment, and then said to no one in particular in the squad room, 'What the hell makes him think he had to tell me?'

He moved the phone into position and began dialing.

The possibility that Carella and Meyer had fastidiously avoided was the possibility that Anthony Forrest had been killed by a sniper.

The sniper is usually a rare breed of murderer who is related to his wartime counterpart only in the methods both employ. The wartime sniper and the peacetime sniper both are hidden, both wait in ambush for their prey. Their success is based on the element of surprise, in combination with a swiftness of action and an accuracy that must be unerring. A wartime sniper hidden in the trees can effectively debilitate and cripple an entire squad, killing several members of it before the squad disperses for cover, pinning down the rest in helpless immobilization. A team of good snipers working in concert can change the outcome of a battle. They are fearful enemies because they rain sudden death from the skies, like the angry wrath of God.

Wartime snipers are trained to kill enemy soldiers. If they kill enough of them, they get medals. A good wartime sniper can even earn the grudging admiration of the men he is trying to kill. They will play a silent game of wits with him, trying to find out where he is, and then trying to discover how they can dislodge him from his vantage point before he slaughters them all. A wartime sniper is a dangerous expert.

A peacetime sniper is anything.

He can be a kid trying out his new BB gun by taking pot-shots at passersby from his bedroom window. He can be a man who shoots at anything wearing red. He can be a Jack the Ripper type who fires at any shapely blonde who passes. He can be an anticleric, an antivegetarian, an antioctogenarian, an anti-Semite, an antipacifist, an anti-any-human-being. The one clear fact about a peacetime sniper would seem to be that he is anti. And yet the police have often arrested snipers who were shooting people for fun, who had disconnected the act of murder from what they considered to be the sport of shooting. To many snipers, the deadly game is only target practice. To others, it is a hunt, and they will sit in ambush the way some men will sit in a duck blind. To some, it is a form of sexual release. The wartime sniper has a reason and a purpose; the peacetime sniper will most often have neither. The wartime sniper is usually pinned to one spot, lashed to a tree, crowded into a bombed-out attic room. If he moves, he will be spotted and hunted down. Lack of mobility is his tactical weakness. The peacetime sniper can shoot and then vanish. He can do this because his victims are almost always unarmed and never expecting violence. Confusion will generally follow the shooting, and in the confusion he will disappear. There is no one to shoot back at him. He has left a dead man, and now he can take a casual stroll like anyone else in the city.

War is dishonourable, but wartime snipers are only trained technicians doing a job.

Peacetime snipers are wholesale murderers.

Neither Carella nor Meyer wanted their man to be a sniper. The 87th Squad had caught the original squeal, which made the case theirs, a nice, fat, snarling baby left in a basket on the doorstep. If their man *was* a sniper, and if he decided to shoot up the entire city, the case was *still* theirs. Oh, yes, there would be additional detectives assigned from other precincts – maybe – and the department would offer whatever help it could – maybe – but the sniper was theirs, and there were ten million people in the city, and any one of them could be either the murderer or the next victim.

How do you play a game without rules?

How do you apply logic to something illogical?

You try.

You start from the beginning.

'*If* he's a sniper,' Meyer said. 'We're not even sure of that yet. There've only been two so far, Steve. You want my opinion, I think this guy at the Sixty-fifth – what's his name?'

'Di Nobile.'

'Yeah, I think he dumped this into our laps prematurely.'

'Same M.O.,' Carella said.

'Yeah, yeah.'

'Same cartridge.'

'All men are bipeds,' Meyer said cryptically, 'therefore, all bipeds are men.'

'So?' Carella said.

'So it may be too early to assume that because two guys were shot from two different rooftops, and the same kind of slug was used in both cases, that . . .'

'Meyer, I wish to God these guys were both shot by my Aunt Matilda because she's named in their insurance policies as beneficiary. It doesn't look that way so far. So far, there's a pattern.'

'What pattern?'

'The obvious one, to begin with. The way it was done, and the weapon used.'

'Could be a coincidence.'

'Could be, I'll grant you that. But the rest seems to add up.'

'It's too early for anything to be adding up,' Meyer said.

'Yeah? Then try this.' Carella picked up a typewritten sheet from his desk. He glanced up at Meyer once, and then began reading. 'Anthony Forrest was almost forty-five years old, married, with three children. Held an important position, vice-president, salary forty-seven thousand dollars a year. Religion Protestant, politics Republican. You got that?'

'Go ahead.'

'Randolph Norden was forty-six years old, married, with two children. Held an important position, junior partner in a law firm, salary fifty-eight thousand dollars a year. Religion Protestant, politics Republican.'

'So?'

'So change their names, and they could almost be the same guy.'

'Are you trying to tell me you think a sniper is after all middle-aged men who are married, with children, and holding important . . .'

'Maybe.'

'Why not carry it further and isolate some of the facts then?' Meyer said. 'Why don't we simply say our sniper is after anybody in this city who is more than forty-five years old?'

'He might be.'

'Or maybe all married men with a couple or more children, huh?'

'Maybe.'

'Or maybe anybody who earns more than forty thousand a year, huh?'

'Maybe.'

'Or all Protestants? Or all Republicans?'

Carella dropped the typewritten sheet on the desk and said, 'Or maybe only people who have *all* those characteristics.'

'Steve, I imagine that description would fit at least – at the *very* least – a hundred thousand people in this city.'

'So? Who says our sniper hasn't got all the time in the world? He just may be out to get each and every one of them.'

'Then that makes him a nut,' Meyer said.

Carella stared at him. 'Meyer,' he said, 'that's exactly why I was hoping this wouldn't turn out to be a sniper.'

'It isn't yet,' Meyer said. 'Just 'cause that guy from the Sixty-fifth jumps the gun . . .'

'I don't think he jumped the gun. I think he was a smart cop who made the only logical deduction. I think this *is* a sniper, and I *hope* it isn't a nut, and I think we'd better start tracking down both Forrest and Norden to find out what other similarities existed or did not exist. That's what I think.'

Meyer shrugged and then put his hands in his pockets and said, 'All we needed right now was a sniper.'

Chapter Four

The president of Indian Exports, Inc., the firm with which Anthony Forrest had been connected, was a balding man in his sixties, somewhat stout, somewhat pompous, somewhat German. He was perhaps five feet eight inches tall, with a protruding middle and flat-footed walk. Meyer Meyer, who was Jewish, felt instantly uncomfortable in his presence.

The man's name was Ludwig Etterman. He stood before his desk in what seemed to be genuine despair and he said, with only the faintest German accent, 'Tony was a good man. I cannot understand why this happened.'

'How long had you been associated with him, Mr Etterman?' Carella asked.

'Fifteen years. That is a long time.'

'Can you give us some of the details, sir?'

'What would you like to know?'

'How you met, what sort of business arrangement you had, what Mr Forrest's function was.'

'He was a salesman when we met. I already had the business. He sold cartons for a company that was downtown at the time – it has since gone out of business. We import from India, you know, and we ship goods all over the United States, so naturally we need cartons in which to ship them. At that time, I bought most of my cartons from Tony's company. I saw him, oh, perhaps twice a month.'

'This was shortly after the war, is that right, sir?'

'Yes.'

'Would you know if Mr Forrest had been in the service?'

'Yes, he was,' Etterman said. 'He was with the artillery. He was wounded in Italy, in a battle with the Germans.' Etterman paused. He turned to Meyer and said, 'I am an American citizen, you know. I was here from nineteen-twelve, my parents came here when I was still a boy. Most of the family left Germany. Some of them went to India, which is how the business started.'

'Do you know what rank Mr Forrest held in the army, sir?' Carella asked.

'He was a captain, I believe.'

'All right, go ahead, please.'

'Well, I liked him from the beginning. There was a nice manner about him. Cartons, after all, are the same no matter where you buy them. I bought from Tony because I liked him personally.' Etterman offered the detectives a cigar, and then lighted one himself. 'My one vice,' he said. 'My doctor says they will kill me. I told my doctor, I would like to die in bed with a young blonde, or else smoking a cigar.' Etterman chuckled. 'At my age, I will have to be content to die smoking a cigar.'

'How did Mr Forrest come to the firm?' Carella said, smiling.

'I asked him one day if he was satisfied with his position, because if he wasn't, I was ready to make him an offer. We discussed it further, and he came to work for the company. As a salesman. That was fifteen years ago. Today, or rather when he died, he was a vice-president.'

'What prompted your offer, Mr Etterman?'

'As I told you, I liked him from the beginning. Then, too . . .' Etterman shook his head. 'Well, it does not matter.'

'What, sir?'

'You see . . .' Etterman shook his head again. 'You see, gentlemen, I lost my son. He was killed in the war.'

'I'm sorry to hear that,' Carella said.

'Yes, well, it was a long time ago, we must go on living, isn't that so?' He smiled a brief, sad smile. 'He was with a bomber squadron, my son. His plane was shot down in the raid on Schweinfurt on April thirteenth, nineteen-forty-four. It was a ball-bearings factory there.'

The room went silent.

'Our family came originally from a town close to Schweinfurt. It is sometimes odd, don't you think, the way life works out? I was born as a German in a town near Schweinfurt, and my son is killed as an American flying over Schweinfurt.' He shook his head. 'It sometimes makes me wonder.'

Again there was silence.

Carella cleared his throat and said, 'Mr Etterman, what sort of a person was Anthony Forrest? Did he get along well with your staff, did he . . .?'

'He was the finest human being I have ever known,' Etterman said. 'I do not know of anyone who disliked him.' He shook his head. 'I can only believe that some maniac killed him.'

'Mr Etterman, did he usually leave the office at the same time each day?'

'We close at five,' Etterman said. 'Tony and I would usually talk for, oh, perhaps another fifteen minutes. Yes, I would say he usually left the building between five-fifteen and five-thirty.'

'Did he get along with his wife?'

'He and Clara were very happily married.'

'How about the children? His daughter is nineteen, is that right, and the two boys are about fifteen?'

'That is correct.'

'Any trouble with them?'

'What do you mean?'

'Well, have they ever been in any kind of trouble?'

'I do not know what you mean.'

'With the law, with other kids, bad company, anything like that.'

'They are fine children,' Etterman said. 'Cynthia was graduated highest in her class from high school, and won a scholarship to Ramsey University. The two boys do very well scholastically. One of them is on his school baseball team, and the other belongs to the debating club. No, there was never any trouble with Tony's children.'

'Do you know anything about his army background, Mr Etterman? Whoever shot him is an expert with a rifle, so the possibility that he's an ex-army man exists. Since Mr Forrest *was* in the army . . .'

'I don't know much about it. I'm sure he was a fine officer.'

'He never mentioned having any trouble with his men, anything that might have carried over into . . .?'

'Gentlemen, he was in the army during the *war*. The war has been over for a long time. Surely, no one would carry a grudge for so many years.'

'Anything's possible,' Carella said. 'We're looking for a place to hang our hats, sir.'

'It must be a maniac,' Etterman said. 'It can only be a maniac.'

'I hope not, sir,' Carella said, and then they rose and thanked him for his time.

On the street outside, Meyer said, 'I always feel funny when I'm around Germans.'

'I noticed that,' Carella said.

'Yeah? Was it really noticeable? Was I too quiet?'

'You didn't say a word all the while we were up there.'

Meyer nodded. 'I kept thinking, "All right, maybe your son was killed flying an Ameican bomber over Schweinfurt, but maybe, on the other hand, one of your nephews was stuffing my relatives into ovens at Dachau."' Meyer shook his head. 'You know, Sarah and I were at a party a couple of weeks ago, and somebody there was arguing with somebody else because he was selling German cars in this country. What it got down to, the guy said that he would like to see all the German people exterminated. So the other guy said, 'There was a German once who wanted to see all the *Jewish* people exterminated.' And I could see his point. What the hell makes it more right for Jews to exterminate Germans than vice versa? I could understand the point completely. But at the same time, Steve, something inside me *agreed* with the first guy. Because, I guess maybe deep down inside, every Jew in the world would like to see the Germans exterminated for what they did to us.'

'You can't hate a people here and now for what another people in another time did, Meyer,' Carella said.

'You're not a Jew,' Meyer said.

'No, I'm not. But I look at a guy like Etterman, and I see only a sad old man who lost his son in the war, and who two days ago lost the equivalent of a second son.'

'I look at him, and I see the film clips of those bulldozers pushing thousands of dead Jews, that's what I see.'

'Do you see the son who died over Schweinfurt?'

'No. I think I honestly hate the Germans, and I think I'll hate them till the day I die.'

'Maybe you're entitled to,' Carella said.

'You know, there are times when I think you're Jewish,' Meyer answered.

'When I think of what happened in Germany, I *am* Jewish,' Carella said. 'How can I be anything else and still call myself a human being? What the hell were they throwing in those ovens? Garbage? Animals? Don't you think I feel what you feel?'

'I'm not sure you do,' Meyer said.

'No? Then go to hell.'

'You getting sore or something?'

'A little.'

'Why?'

'I'll tell you why. I don't think I even knew a Jew until I was twelve years old. That's the God's honest truth. Oh, yeah, there was a guy who used to come around to the door selling stuff, and my mother called him 'The Jew.' She used to say, "The Jew is coming today.' I don't think she meant anything derogatory, or maybe she did, who the hell knows? She was raised in Italy, and she didn't know Jews from a hole in the wall. Maybe, for her, 'Jew' was synonymous with peddler. To me, a Jew was an old man with a beard and a bundle on his back. Until I got to high school. That was where I met Jews for the first time. You have to remember that Hitler was already in power by then. Well, I heard a joke one day, and I repeated it to a Jewish kid in the cafeteria. The joke was built on a riddle, and the riddle was: 'What's the fastest thing in the world?' The answer was: 'A Jew riding through Germany on a bicycle.' The kid I told the joke to didn't think it was very funny. I couldn't understand what I'd said to offend him. So I went home and asked my father, who was also born in Italy, who was running a bakery, well, you know, he still does. I told him the joke, and he didn't laugh either, and then he took me inside, we had a dining room at the time, with one of those big old mahogany tables. We sat at the table, and he said to me in Italian, 'Son, there is nothing good about hatred, and nothing funny about it, either.' I went back to school the next day, and I looked for that kid, I can still remember his name, Reuben Zimmerman, and I told him I was sorry for what I'd said the day before, and he told me to forget it. But he never spoke to me again all the while we were in that high school. Four years, Meyer, and he never spoke to me.'

'What are you saying, Steve?'

'I don't know what the hell I'm saying.'

'Maybe you are Jewish, after all,' Meyer said.

'Maybe I am. Let's stop for an egg cream before we look up Norden's wife.'

Mae Norden was forty-three years old, a brunette with a round face and dark-brown eyes. They found her at the funeral home where Norden's body lay in a satin-lined coffin. The undertaker had done a remarkable job with the front of his face, where the bullet had entered. The casual observer would never have known he'd been shot. The room was filled with relatives and friends, among whom were his wife and his two children, Joanie and Mike. Mike was eight years old and Joanie was five. They both sat on straight-backed chairs near the coffin, looking very old and very bewildered at the same time. Mae Norden was dressed in black, and her eyes looked as if she had cried a lot in the past day, but she was not crying now. She led the detectives outside, and they stood on the sidewalk there and smoked cigarettes and discussed her husband, who lay dead on satin in the silent room beyond.

'I don't know who could have done this,' Mae said. 'I know it's common for a wife to think her husband was well-liked, but I can't think of a single person who disliked Randy. That's the truth.'

'How about business associates, Mrs Norden? He was a lawyer, isn't that right?'

'Yes.'

'Is it possible that one of his clients . . .?'

'Look, anyone who shoots someone has to be a little crazy, isn't that so?'

'Not necessarily,' Meyer said.

'My point is, sure, Randy lost cases. Is there a lawyer who doesn't lose cases? But if you ask me whether or not any of his clients would be . . . be angry enough to do something like this, then I have to say how do I know what a crazy person would do? Where's the basis for . . . for *anything* when you're dealing with someone who's unbalanced?'

'We're not sure the killer was unbalanced, Mrs Norden,' Meyer said.

'No?' She smiled thinly. 'A perfectly normal person went up on that roof and shot my husband when he came out of the building, is that it? Perfectly sane?'

'Mrs Norden, we're not psychiatrists. We're talking about sanity in the eyes of the law. The murderer may not have been what the law considers insane.'

'The hell with the law,' Mae said suddenly. 'Anyone who takes another man's life is insane, and I don't care *what* the law says.'

'But your husband was a lawyer, isn't that right?'

'That's exactly right,' Mae said angrily. 'What are you saying now? That I have no respect for the law, therefore I have no respect for lawyers, therefore I have . . .'

'We didn't say that, Mrs Norden.' Carella paused. 'I feel certain a lawyer's wife would have a great deal of respect for the law.'

'But I'm not a lawyer's wife anymore,' Mae said. 'Didn't you know that? I'm a widow. I'm a widow with two young children, Mr – what was your name?'

'Carella.'

'Yes. I'm a forty-three-year-old widow, Mr Carella. Not a lawyer's wife.'

'Mrs Norden, perhaps you can tell us a few things that might help us to find the man who killed your husband.'

'Like what?'

'Did he usually leave the apartment at the same time each morning?'

'Yes. On weekdays. On Saturdays and Sundays, he slept late.'

'Then anyone who had made a habit of observing him would know that he went to work at the same time each day?'

'I suppose so.'

'Mrs Norden, was your husband a veteran?'

'A veteran? You mean, was he in the service?'

'Yes.'

'He was in the navy for three years during World War Two,' Mae said.

'The navy. Not the army.'

'The navy, yes.'

'He was a junior partner in his firm, is that correct?'

'Yes.'

'How did he feel about that?'

'Fine. How should he have felt about it?'

'How many partners were there, Mrs Norden?'

'Three, including my husband.'

'Was your husband the only junior partner?'

'Yes. He was the youngest man in the firm.'

'Did he get along with the others?'

'Very well. He got along with everyone. I just told you that.'

'No trouble with any of the partners, right?'

'That's right.'

'What sort of law did he practice?'

'The firm handled every kind of case.'

'Criminal?'

'Sometimes.'

'Did your husband ever represent a criminal?'

'Yes.'

'How many?'

'Three or four, I don't remember. Four, I guess, since he's been with the firm.'

'Acquittals or convictions?'

'Two of his clients were convicted, two were acquitted.'

'Where are the convicted men now?'

'Serving jail sentences, I would imagine.'

'Would you remember their names?'

'No. But Sam could probably . . . Sam Gottlieb, one of the partners. He would know.'

'Was your husband a native of this city, Mrs Norden?'

'Yes. He went through the city school system, and also college and law school here.'

'Where?'

'Ramsey.'

'And how did you come to know him?'

'We met in Grover Park one day. At the zoo. We began seeing each other regularly, and eventually we were married.'

'Before he went into the service, or afterward?'

'We were married in nineteen-forty-nine.'

'Had you known him while he was in the service?'

'No. He went into the navy immediately after graduation. He took his bar exams as soon as he was discharged. He passed them and began practicing shortly afterward. When I met him, he had his own small office in Bethtown. He didn't move to Gottlieb and Graham until three years ago.'

'He had his own practice up to that time?'

'No. He'd been with several firms over the years.'

'Any trouble anywhere?'

'None.'

'Criminal cases at those firms, too?'

'Yes, but I can hardly remember what . . .'

'Can you tell us which firms those were, Mrs Norden?'

'You don't really believe this can be someone he lost a case for, do you?'

'We don't know, Mrs Norden. Right now, we have almost nothing to go on. We're trying to find something, anything.'

'I'll write out a list for you,' she said. 'Will you come inside, please?' In the doorway of the funeral home, she stopped and said, 'Forgive me if I was rude to you.' She paused. 'I loved my husband very much, you see.'

Chapter Five

On Monday, April 30, five days after the first murder had been committed, Cynthia Forrest came to see Steve Carella. She walked up the low, flat steps at the front of the grey precinct building, past the green globes lettered with the white numerals 87, and then into the muster room where a sign told her she must state her business at the desk. She told Sergeant Murchison she wanted to talk to Detective Carella, and Murchison asked her her name, and she said, 'Cynthia Forrest,' and he rang Carella upstairs, and then told her to go on up. She followed the white sign that read DETECTIVE DIVISION and climbed the iron-runged steps to the second floor of the building, coming out onto a narrow corridor. She followed the corridor past a man in a purple sports shirt who was handcuffed to a bench, and then paused at the slatted wood railing, standing on tiptoes, searching. When she spotted Carella rising from his desk to come to her, she impulsively raised her arm and waved at him.

'Hello, Miss Forrest,' he said, smiling. 'Come on in.' He held open the gate in the railing, and then led her to his desk. She was wearing a white sweater and a dark-grey skirt. Her hair was hemp-coloured, long, pulled to the back of her head in a ponytail. She was carrying a notebook and some texts, and she put these on his desk, sat, crossed her legs, and pulled her skirt down over her knees.

'Would you like some coffee?' Carella asked.

'Is there some?'

'Sure. Miscolo!' he yelled. 'Can we get two cups of joe?'

From the depths of the clerical office in the corridor, Miscolo's voice bellowed, 'Coming!'

Carella smiled at the girl and said, 'What can I do for you, Miss Forrest?'

'Most everyone calls me Cindy,' she said.

'All right. Cindy.'

'So this is where you work.'

'Yes.'

'Do you like it?'

Carella looked around the room as if discovering it for the first time. He shrugged. 'The office, or what I do?' he asked.

'Both.'

'The office . . .' He shrugged again. 'I guess it's a rat trap, but I'm used to it. The work? Yes, I enjoy it, or I wouldn't do it.'

'One of my psych instructors said that men who choose violent professions are usually men of violence.'

'Oh?'

'Yes,' Cindy said. She smiled faintly, as though enjoying a secret joke. 'You don't look very violent.'

'I'm not. I'm a very gentle soul.'

'Then my psych instructor is wrong.'

'I may be the exception that proves the rule.'

'Maybe.'

'Are you a psych major?' Carella asked.

'No. I'm studying to be a teacher. But I'm taking general psych and abnormal psych. And then later, I'll have to take all the educational psychology courses, ed psych one and two and . . .'

'You've got your work cut out for you,' Carella said.

'I suppose so.'

'What do you want to teach?'

'English.'

'College?'

'High school.'

Miscolo came in from the clerical office and placed two cups of coffee on Carella's desk. 'I put sugar and milk in both of them, is that all right?' he asked.

'Cindy?'

'That's fine.' She smiled graciously at Miscolo. 'Thank you.'

'You're welcome, miss,' Miscolo said, and went back to his office.

'He seems very sweet,' Cindy said.

Carella shook his head. 'A violent man. Terrible temper.'

Cindy laughed, picked up her coffee cup, and sipped at it. She put the cup down, reached into her handbag for a package of cigarettes, was about to put one in her mouth, when she stopped and asked, 'Is it all right to smoke?'

'Sure,' Carella said. He struck a match for her, and held it to the cigarette.

'Thank you.' She took several drags, sipped more coffee, looked around the room a little, and then turned back toward Carella, smiling. 'I like your office,' she said.

'Well, good. I'm glad.' He paused, and then asked, 'What did you have on your mind, Cindy?'

'Well . . .' She dragged on the cigarette again, smoking the way a very young girl smokes, a little too feverishly, with too much obvious enjoyment, and yet at the same time with too much casualness. 'They buried Daddy on Saturday, you know.'

'I know.'

'And I read in the newspapers that another man was killed.'

'That's right.'

'Do you think the same person did it?'

'We don't know.'

'Do you have any ideas yet?'

'Well, we're working on it,' Carella said.

'I asked my abnormal-psych instructor what he knew about snipers,' Cindy said, and paused. 'This *is* a sniper, isn't it?'

'Possibly. What did your instructor say?'

'He said he hadn't read very much about them, and didn't even know whether or not any studies had been done. But he had some ideas.'

'Yes?' Like what?'

'He felt that the sniper was very much like the peeper. The Peeping Tom, do you know?'

'Yes.'

'Yes. He thought the dynamic was essentially the same.'

'And what was that? The dynamic?'

'A response to infantile glimpses of the primal scene,' Cindy said.

'The primal scene?'

'Yes.'

'What's the primal scene?' Carella asked innocently.

Unflinchingly Cindy replied, 'The parents having intercourse.'

'Oh. Oh, I see.'

'My instructor said that every child watches and attempts to pretend he is not watching. The sniper comes equipped with an obvious symbol, the rifle, and usually makes use of a telescopic sight, repeating the furtive way things are carried out in childhood, the looking and not being seen, the doing and not being caught.'

'I see,' Carella said.

'Essentially, my instructor said, sniping is a sexually aggressive act. Witnessing of the primal scene can manifest itself neurotically either through peeping – the voyeur – or through the reverse of peeping, in effect a fear of being peeped *at*. But the dynamic remains essentially the same with both the peeper and the sniper. Both are hidden, furtive, surreptitious. Both find sexual stimulation, and often gratification, in the act.' Cindy put out her cigarette, stared at Carella with wide, young, innocent blue eyes and said, 'What do you think?'

'Well – I don't know,' Carella said.

'Doesn't the department have a psychologist?' Cindy asked.

'Yes, it does.'

'Why don't you ask him what he thinks?'

'They only do that on television,' Carella said.

'Isn't it important for you to know what's motivating the killer?'

'Yes, certainly. But motives are often very complex things. Your abnormal-psychology instructor may be absolutely correct about an individual sniper, or maybe even ten thousand snipers, but it's possible we'll run into ten thousand others who never witnessed the – primal scene, did you call it? – and who . . .'

'Yes, primal scene. But isn't that unlikely?'

'Nothing's unlikely in murder,' Carella said.

Cindy raised her eyebrows dubiously. 'That doesn't sound very scientific, you know.'

'It isn't.' He ended the sentence there with no intention of being rude, and then suddenly realized he had sounded rather abrupt.

'I didn't mean to take up your time,' Cindy said, rising, her manner decidedly cool now. 'I simply thought you might like to know . . .'

'You haven't finished your coffee,' Carella said.

'Thank you, but it's very bad coffee,' she answered, and she stood and looked down at him with her shoulders back and her eyes blazing a challenge.

'That's right,' Carella said. 'It's very bad coffee.'

'I'm glad we agree on something.'

'I wasn't aware we had *dis*agreed on anything.'

'I was only trying to help, you know.'

'I appreciate that.'

'But I suppose I had the mistaken notion that modern police departments might want to know about the psychological forces at work in the criminal mind. My fantasy . . .'

'Come on,' Carella said. 'You're too nice and too young to be getting sore at a dumb flatfoot.'

'I'm not nice, and I'm not young, and you're not dumb!' Cindy said.

'You're nineteen.'

'I'll be twenty in June.'

'Why do you say you're not nice?'

'Because I've seen too much and heard too much.'

'Like what?'

'Nothing!' she snapped.

'I'm interested, Cindy.'

Cindy picked up her books and held them clasped to her breast. 'Mr Carella, this isn't the Victorian age. Just remember that.'

'I'll try to. But suppose you tell me what you mean.'

'I mean that most seventeen-year-olds today have seen and heard everything there is to see or hear.'

'How dull that must be,' Carella said. 'What do you do when you're eighteen? Or nineteen?'

'When you're nineteen,' Cindy said in an icy voice, 'you go looking for the cop who first told you your father was dead. You go looking for him in the hope you can tell him something he might not know, something to help him. And then, the way it always is with so-called adults, you're completely disappointed when you discover he won't even listen.'

'Sit down, Cindy. What did you want to tell me about our sniper? If he *is* a sniper, to begin with.'

'A man who shoots at someone from a rooftop is certainly . . .'

'Not necessarily.'

'He killed two men in the same way!'

'*If* he's the one who killed both men.'

'The newspaper said the same make and calibre of cartridge. . . .'

'That could mean a lot, or it could mean nothing.'

'You're not seriously telling me you think it was a coincidence?'

'I don't know what to tell you, except that we're considering every possibility. Sit down, will you? You make me nervous.'

Cindy sat down abruptly and plunked her books on the desktop. For a nineteen-year-old who had seen and heard all there was to see and hear, she looked very much like a nine-year-old at that moment.

'Well,' Cindy said, '*if* the same man killed my father and that other man, and *if* he's a sniper, then I think you ought to consider the possibility that he may be sexually motivated.'

'We will indeed.'

Cindy rose abruptly and began picking up her books. 'You're putting me on, Detective Carella,' she said, angrily, 'and I don't particularly like it!'

'I'm not putting you on! I'm listening to every word you're saying, but for God's sake, Cindy, don't you think we've ever dealt with snipers before?'

'What?'

'I said don't you think the police department has ever handled a case involving –'

'Oh.' Cindy put her books down again, and again she sat in the chair alongside his desk. 'I never thought of that. I'm sorry.'

'That's all right.'

'I'm truly sorry. Of course. I mean, I suppose you run across all sorts of things. I'm terribly sorry.'

'I'm glad you came up anyway, Cindy.'

'Are you?' Cindy asked suddenly.

'We don't often get nice bright kids in here,' Carella said. 'It's a refreshing change, believe me.'

'I'm just the all-American girl, huh?' Cindy said with a peculiar smile. Then she rose, shook hands with Carella, thanked him, and left.

The woman walking along Culver Avenue was neither a nice bright kid nor an all-American girl.

She was forty-one years old, and her hair was bleached a bright blond, and she wore too much lipstick on her mouth and too much rouge on her cheeks. Her skirt was black and tight, and dusted with powder she had spilled on it while making up her face. She wore a high brassiere and a tight, white, soiled sweater, and she carried a black patent-leather handbag, and she looked very much like a prostitute, which is exactly what she was.

In a day and age when prostitutes in any neighbourhood look more like high-fashion models than ladies of the trade, the woman's appearance was startling, if not contradictory. It was almost as if, by so blatantly announcing her calling, she were actually denying it. Her clothes, her posture, her walk, her fixed smile all proclaimed – as effectively as if the words had been lettered on a sandwich board – I AM A PROSTITUTE. But as the woman walked past, the imaginary back of the sandwich board was revealed, and lettered there in scarlet letters – what else? – were the words: I AM DIRTY! DO NOT TOUCH! The woman had had a rough day. In addition to being a prostitute, or perhaps *because* she was a prostitute, or perhaps she was a prostitute because of *it* – God, there are so many psychological complexes to consider these days – the woman was also a drunk. She had awakened at six A.M. with bats and mice crawling out of the plaster cracks in her cheap furnished room, and she had discovered there was no more booze in the bottle beside her bed, and she had swiftly dressed, swiftly because she rarely wore anything but a bra under her street clothes, and taken to the streets. By twelve noon, she had raised the price of a bottle of cheap whiskey, and by one P.M. she had downed the last drop. She had awakened at four P.M. to find the bats and mice crawling out of the cracks again and to find, again, that the bottle beside the bed was empty. She had put on her bra and sweater, her black skirt and her high-heeled black pumps; she had dusted her face with powder, smeared lipstick on her mouth and rouge on her cheeks, and now she was walking along a familiar stretch of avenue as dusk settled in the sky to the west.

She generally walked this pavement each night along about dusk, drunk or sober, because there was a factory on Culver and North Fourteenth, and the men from the factory quit at five-thirty, and sometimes she was lucky enough to find a quick four-dollar partner or, if her luck was running exceptionally good, even a partner for the night at fifteen dollars in good, hard, American currency.

Tonight she felt lucky.

Tonight, as she saw the men pouring from the factory on the next corner, she felt certain there would be a winner among them. Maybe even someone who would like to do a little honest drinking before they tumbled into the sack. Maybe someone who would fall madly in love with her, the plant superintendent maybe, or even an executive who would love her eyes and her hair and take her home to his large bachelor house in the suburbs of Larksview, where she would have an upstairs maid and a butler and make love only when she felt like it, don't make me laugh.

Still, she felt lucky.

She was still feeling lucky when the bullet smashed through her upper lip, shattering the gum ridge, careening downward through her windpipe, cracking her upper spine, and blowing a huge hole out of her neck as it left her body.

The bullet spent itself against the brick wall of the building against which she fell dead.

The bullet was a Remington .308.

Chapter Six

It is true that in a democracy all men are equal in the eyes of the law, but this does not necessarily apply to all *dead* men. It would be nice to believe that a detective investigating the murder of a Skid Row wino devoted all his time and energy to the case in an attempt to discover the perpetrator. It would be nicer to believe that the untimely demise of a numbers runner or a burglar occasioned anything but relief, an attitude of 'Good riddance' on the part of the police. But there is a vast difference between a murdered millionaire and a murdered criminal. A prostitute, who steals nothing, is nonetheless guilty of a violation, and in the lexicon of the police is a criminal. The death of the Culver Avenue prostitute would have caused little more than slight passing interest, had it not been for the fact that she was slain by a .308-calibre Remington cartridge. As it was, she acquired more status in death than she had ever known in life, either in the eyes of men or in the eyes of the law.

The law is curiously ambiguous concerning prostitutes. The penal law describes prostitution and disorderly houses in detail, but there is nowhere in the code a definition of a prostitute per se. Under the section on prostitution, there are listed:

(1) Abduction of female for purposes of
(2) Compulsory prostitution of women
(3) Compelling prostitution of wife of another
(4) Corroboration of testimony of female compelled or procured
(5) Pimps and procurers
(6) Transporting women for purposes of

Under the section on disorderly houses there are listed:

(1) Abduction of females
(2) Admission of minors
(3) Compulsory prostitution in
(4) Keeping or renting
(5) Sending messenger boys to

. . . and so on. Some of these crimes are felonies. But nowhere in these subdivisions is there reference to the crime of the prostitute herself. There is only one place in the penal law where love for sale is defined. Curiously, it is in Section 722, which defines disorderly conduct: 'Any person who with intent to provoke a breach of the peace, or whereby a breach of the peace may be occasioned, commits any of the following acts shall be deemed to have committed the offense of disorderly conduct.'

The 'following acts' include anything from using threatening language, to causing a crowd to collect, to making insulting remarks to passing pedestrians, and, under Subdivision 9: 'frequents or loiters about any public place soliciting men for the purpose of committing a crime against nature or any other lewdness.'

If one can call going to bed with a man 'a crime against nature,' then that is prostitution. It is not called prostitution in this section. It is called 'soliciting,' but in the section titled 'Solicitation: Lewd or immoral purposes, solicitation for,' there is listed only the following: 'Male persons living on proceeds of prostitution: Every male person who lives wholly or in part on the earnings of prostitution, or who in any public place solicits for immoral purposes, is guilty of a misdemeanor. A male person who lives with or is habitually in the company of a prostitute and has no visible means of support, shall be presumed to be living on the earnings of prostitution.'

So what is an honest, conscientious cop supposed to do when an obvious whore sidles up to him and asks, 'Want some fun, honey?' Left to his own devices, he might accept the offer. Bound by the penal law, he might arrest her for disorderly conduct, the penalty for which can be a jail sentence not to exceed six months, or a fine not to exceed fifty dollars, or both. But the penal law is bolstered by the Code of Criminal Procedure, and every cop in the city knows Section 887, Subdivision 4, by heart. Every prostitute has committed it to memory, too, because this is where they get her by the codes. Section 887 describes, of all things, vagrants. 'The following persons are vagrants,' it states, and then goes on to list everyone including your Uncle Max. When it comes to Subdivision 4, it pulls no punches.

4. A person (*a*) who offers to commit prostitution, or (*b*) who offers to secure for another for the purpose of prostitution or for any other lewd or indecent act; or (*c*) who loiters in or near any thoroughfare or public or private place for the purpose of inducing, enticing or procuring another to commit lewdness, fornication, unlawful sexual intercourse or any other indecent act . . .

That would seem to cover it, man. But those puritan forefathers weren't taking any chances. Section 887, Subdivision 4, goes on to state:

. . . or (*d*) who in any manner induces, entices or procures a person who is
in any thoroughfare or public place or private place, to commit any such
acts; or (*e*) who receives or offers or agrees to receive any person into any
place, structure, house, building or conveyance for the purpose of
prostitution, lewdness or assignation or knowingly permits any person to
remain there for such purposes; or (*f*) who in any way, aids or abets or
participates in the doing of any of the acts or things enumerated in
Subdivision four of Section eight hundred and eighty-seven of the Code
of Criminal Procedure; or (*g*) who is a common prostitute, who has no
lawful employment whereby to maintain herself.

That's a vagrant, sir, madam. And if that is what you are, you can under
Section 891 (*a*) of the same code be sent to a reformatory for as long as three
years, or a county jail, penitentiary, or other penal institution for as long as a
year – so watch yourself!

The man named Harry Wallach was a male person who lived with or was
habitually in the company of the prostitute named Blanche Lettiger, the
woman who had been shot to death on the night of April 30. It did not take
the police long to find him. Everybody knew who Blanche's 'old man' was.
They picked him up the next morning in a poolroom on North Forty-first,
and they brought him to the station house and sat him down in a chair and
began asking their questions. He was a tall, well-dressed man, with hair
greying at the temples, and penetrating green eyes. He asked the detectives if
it was all right to smoke, and then he lighted a fifty-cent cigar and sat back
calmly with a faint superior smile on his mouth as Carella opened the
session.

'What do you do for a living, Wallach?'
'Investment,' Wallach said.
'What kind of investment?' Meyer asked.
'Stocks, bonds, real estate. You know.'
'What's the current quotation on AT&T?' Carella asked.
'Not in my portfolio,' Wallach said.
'What *is* in your portfolio?'
'I don't remember offhand.'
'Do you have a broker?'
'Yes.'
'What's his name?'
'He's in Miami right now on vacation.'
'We didn't ask you where he was, we asked you what his name is.'
'Dave.'
'Dave what?'
'Dave Milias.'
'Where's he staying in Miami?'
'Search me,' Wallach said.
'All right, Wallach,' Meyer said, 'what do you know about this woman
Blanche Lettiger?'
'Blanche *who*?' Wallach said.
'Oh, you want to place this one cool, huh, Wallach? Is that it?'
'It's just the name don't seem to ring a bell.'
'It doesn't, huh? Blanche Lettiger. You share an apartment with her on

Culver and North Twelfth, apartment 6B, rented under the name of Frank Wallace, and you've been living there with her for the past year a half. Does the name ring a bell now, Wallach?'

'I don't know what you're talking about,' Wallach said.

'Maybe he's the guy who plugged her, Steve.'

'I'm beginning to think so.'

'What do you mean?' Wallach asked, unruffled.

'Why the dodge, Wallach? You think we're interested in a crummy pimp like you?'

'I'm not that,' Wallach said with dignity.

'No? What do you call it?'

'Not what you said.'

'Oh, how sweet,' Meyer said. 'He doesn't want to spoil his dainty little lips by saying the word *pimp*. Look, Wallach, don't make this hard for us. You want us to throw the book, we've got it, and we know how to throw it. Make it easy for yourself. We're only interested in knowing about the woman.'

'What woman?'

'You son of a bitch, she was shot down in cold blood last night. What the hell are you, a human being or what?'

'I don't know any woman who was shot down in cold blood last night,' Wallach insisted. 'You're not going to get me involved in a goddamn homicide. I know you guys too good. You're looking for a patsy, and it ain't going to be me.'

'We weren't looking for a patsy,' Carella said, 'but now that you mention it, it's not a bad idea. What do you think, Meyer?'

'Why not?' Meyer said. 'He's as good as anybody to pin it on. Take the heat off us.'

'Where were you last night, Wallach?'

'What time last night?' Wallach answered, still calm, still puffing gently on his cigar.

'The time the woman was killed.'

'I don't know what time any woman was killed.'

'About five-thirty. Where were you?'

'Having dinner.'

'So early?'

'I eat early.'

'Where?'

'The Rambler.'

'Where's that?'

'Downtown.'

'Downtown where? Look, Wallach, if you force us to pull teeth, we know some better ways of doing it.'

'Sure, get out your rubber hose,' Wallach said calmly.

'Meyer,' Carella said calmly, 'get the rubber hose.'

Calmly Meyer walked to a desk on the far side of the room, opened the top drawer, took out a two-foot length of rubber hose, smacked it against his palm, and then walked back to where Wallach was watching him calmly.

'This what you mean, Wallach?'

'You think you're surprising me or something?' Wallach asked.

'Who'd you eat with?' Carella said.

'Alone.'

'We don't need the hose, Meyer. He just cooked his own goose.'

'That's what you think, buddy. The waiter'll remember me.'

'Well, that depends on how much we lean on the waiter, doesn't it?' Carella said. 'We're looking for a patsy, remember? You think we're going to let a lousy waiter stand in our way?'

'He'll say I was there,' Wallach said, but his voice was beginning to lack conviction.

'Well, I certainly hope so,' Carella said. 'But in the meantime, we're going to book you for homicide, Wallach. We won't mention the fact that you're a pimp, of course. We'll save that for the trial. It might impress the hell out of a jury.'

'Listen,' Wallach said.

'Yeah?'

'What do you want from me? I didn't kill her, and you know it.'

'Then who did?'

'How the hell do I know?'

'You know the woman?'

'Of *course* I know her. Come on, willya?'

'You said you didn't.'

'I was kidding around. How did I know you guys were so serious? What's everybody getting so excited about?'

'How long have you known her?'

'About two years.'

'Was she a prostitute when you met her?'

'You getting *me* involved again? I don't know what she worked at. *My* means of earning a living is investment. I *lived* with her, that's all. What she done or didn't do was her business.'

'You didn't know she was a hooker, huh?'

'No.'

'Wallach,' Carella said, 'we're going to take you down and book you for homicide. Because you're lying, you see, and that's very suspicious. So unless we come up with somebody who looks better than you for the rap, you're it. Now, do you want to be it, Wallach? Or do you want to start telling the truth, so we'll know you're an upstanding citizen who only happens to be a pimp? What do you say, Wallach?'

Wallach was silent for a long time. Then he said, 'She was a hooker when I met her.'

'Two years ago?'

'Two years ago.'

'When did you see her last?'

'I was out night before last. I didn't go back to the pad at all yesterday. I didn't see her all day.'

'What time did you leave the apartment the night before?'

'Around eight.'

'Where'd you go?'

'Uptown. Riverhead.'

'To do what?'

Wallach sighed. 'There was a crap game, all right?'

'Was Blanche in the apartment when you left?'

'Yeah.'

'Did she say anything to you?'

'No. She was in the other room with a john.'

'You brought him to her?'

'Yeah, yeah,' Wallach said, and put his cigar in the ashtray. 'I'm playing ball with you, okay?'

'You're playing ball fine, Wallach. Tell us about Blanche.'

'What do you want to know?'

'How old was she?'

'She said she was thirty-five, but she was really forty-one.'

'What's her background? Where's she from?'

'The Middle West someplace. Oklahoma, Iowa, I don't know. One of those hick joints.'

'When did she come here?'

'Years ago.'

'When, Wallach?'

'Before the war. I don't know the exact date. Listen, if you want her life history, you're barking up the wrong tree. I didn't know her that good.'

'Why'd she come here?'

'To go to school.'

'What kind of school?'

'College, what do you think?'

'Where?'

'Ramsey University.'

'How long did she stay there?'

'I don't know.'

'Did she graduate?'

'I don't know.'

'How'd she get to be a hooker?'

'I don't know.'

'Are her parents living?'

'I don't know.'

'Was she married, divorced, would you know?'

'No.'

'What the hell *do* you know, Wallach?'

'I know she was a broad who was over the hill, and I was taking care of her practically as a charity case, okay? I know she was a goddamn lush, and a pain in the ass, and the best thing that coulda happened to her was to get shot in the head, which is what she got, okay? That's what I know.'

'You're a nice guy, Wallach.'

'Thanks, I'm crazy about you, too. What do you want from me? She'da died in the streets a year ago if I hadn't given her a place to stay. I done an act of kindness.'

'Sure.'

'Yeah, sure. What do you think, she made me a millionaire? Who the hell wanted to bang something looked like her? I used to bring her the dregs, that's all. She's lucky she made enough for room and board. Half the time, she never gave me a cent. She had the dough spent on booze before I reached her, and the booze would be gone, too. You think it was a picnic? Try it sometime.'

'How'd a college girl become a hooker?' Carella asked.

'What are you, a cop or a sociologist? There's more hookers in this town who once went to college than I can count. Call the Vice Squad, they'll tell you.'

'Never mind the Vice Squad,' Meyer said. 'You got any idea who killed her?'

'None.'

'You sound very glad to be rid of her.'

'I am. That don't mean I killed her. Look, you guys know I had nothing to do with this. Why are we wasting each other's time?'

'What's your hurry, Wallach? Another crap game?'

'Sure, I'd tell you about it, wouldn't I?'

'Then take your time. We've got all day.'

'Okay, let's shoot the day. What the hell. It's only the taxpayers' money.'

'You never paid a tax in your life, Wallach.'

'I pay taxes every year,' Wallach said indignantly. 'Both federal *and* state, so don't give me that.'

'What do you list as your occupation?'

'We going to go into that again?'

'No, let's get back to Blanche. Did anyone ever threaten her? Would you know that?'

'How would I know? Johns are all different. Some are like little lost kids with their first broad, and some are tough guys who like to smack a girl around. There's something wrong with a guy who goes to a whore in the first place.'

'He's not a pimp,' Meyer said, 'he's a psychologist.'

'I know whores,' Wallach said simply.

'You don't seem to know a hell of a lot about Blanche Lettiger.'

'I told you everything I know. What more can I say?'

'Tell us about her habits.'

'Like what?'

'Like what time she got up in the morning.'

'The morning? You kidding?'

'All right, what then? The afternoon?'

'She usually woke up about one, two in the afternoon and started looking for a bottle.'

'What time did she wake up the day she was killed?'

Wallach smiled, pointed a chiding finger at Carella, and said, 'Ah-ah. Caught you.'

'Huh?' Carella said.

Still smiling, Wallach said, 'I told you I didn't see her at all yesterday, didn't I?'

'I wasn't trying to trip you, Wallach.'

'There ain't a bull in the world who ain't *always* trying to trip guys like me.'

'Look, Wallach,' Carella said, 'we understand you're just a decent, upright, put-upon citizen, okay? So let's send the violinists home and get down to business. You're beginning to get on my nerves.'

'You don't exactly have a calming effect on me,' Wallach replied.

'What the hell is this?' Meyer said, annoyed. 'A vaudeville routine at the

Palace? One more crack out of you, you cheap punk, and I'll bust your head open.'

Wallach opened his mouth and then closed it. He looked at Meyer sourly instead.

'Okay?' Meyer shouted.

'Okay, okay,' Wallach answered, sulking.

'Did she make a habit of leaving the apartment between five and five-thirty every afternoon?'

'Yeah.'

'Where'd she go?'

'There was a factory nearby the pad. Sometimes the guys coming out of work were good for a strike.'

'She did this *every* afternoon?'

'Not every afternoon, but often enough. When you're in the shape she was in, you've got to take them where they come.'

'Where's the factory?'

'Culver and North Fourteenth.'

'So then almost every afternoon, sometime between five and five-thirty, she'd leave the apartment and walk up toward the factory, right?'

'Yeah.'

'Who knew this besides you, Wallach?'

'The cop on the beat knew it,' Wallach answered, unable to repress the crack. 'Maybe *he's* the one who put the blocks to her, huh?'

'Look, Wallach . . .'

'All right, all right, I don't know who knew it. The guy who killed her, I guess. Anybody coulda known it. All they had to do was watch.'

'You've been a great help,' Carella said. 'Get the hell out of here.'

'You only ruined my day,' Wallach said.

He rose, dusted cigar ash off his trousers, and was walking away from the desk when Meyer kicked him square in the behind. Wallach didn't even turn. With great dignity he walked out of the squad room.

Chapter Seven

So far, the police had done only one concrete thing toward solving the multiple murders: nothing.

That morning, after Wallach left, they tried to remedy the situation somewhat by putting in a call to Samuel Gottlieb of Gottlieb, Graham and Norden. They asked the senior partner of the firm how many criminal cases Norden had handled since he'd been with them, and he told them there had been a total of four. He promptly furnished them with the names of all four clients, and then broke the list down into those who had been aquitted, and those who had been convicted. They then took the list Mrs Norden had given them, the one containing the names of the various other firms Norden had worked for over the years, and by eleven o'clock they had called each firm and had a further list of twelve convicted criminals who had once been clients of Norden. They sent the list to the city's BCI with a request for the whereabouts of each man, and then checked out a car and drove downtown to Ramsey University, where they hoped to learn something, anything, about Blanche Lettiger, the dead prostitute.

The university was in the heart of the city, beginning where Hall Avenue ended, sprawling on the fringes of the Quarter, rubbing elbows with Chinatown. An outdoor art exhibition was in full swing on the bordering side streets. Carella parked the car in a no-parking zone, pulled down the sun visor and its hand-lettered sign advising POLICEMAN ON DUTY CALL, and then walked with Meyer past the canvases lined up on the sidewalk. There seemed to be a predominance of seascapes this year. The smiling perpetrators of all this watery art peered hopefully at each passerby, trying to look aloof and not too eager, but placed nonetheless in the uncomfortable position of being merchants as well as creators.

Meyer glanced only cursorily at the seascapes, and then stopped before an 'action' painting, the action consisting of several bold black slashes across a field of white, with two red dots in one corner. He nodded mysteriously, and then caught up with Carella.

'What happened to people?' he asked.

'What do you mean?' Carella answered.

'There used to be a time when you looked at a painting, there were people in it. No more. Artists aren't interested in people. They're only interested in "expression." I read about a guy who covers a nude lady with paint, and then she rolls on a canvas, and what comes out is a painting.'

'You're kidding,' Carella said.

'I swear to God,' Meyer said. 'You can see where she rubbed with her leg or her thigh, or whatever. She's like the guy's paintbrush.'

'Does he clean his brushes at the end of the day?'

'I don't know. The article didn't say. It just told about how he worked, and it showed some examples.'

'That's pretty far-out, isn't it?'

'No, I think it's a return to tradition.'

'How so?'

'The guy is obviously putting people back into painting.'

'There's the school,' Carella said.

Ramsey University sat on the other side of a small park struck with May sunshine. There were several students sitting on the scattered benches discussing the conjugation of the verb *aimer*, discussing too the theory of ratio-mobility. They glanced up momentarily as Meyer and Carella crossed the park and climbed the steps of the administration building. The inside of the building was cool and dim. They stopped a student wearing a white shirt and a loose green sweater and asked him where the records office was.

'What records office?' the student asked.

'Where they keep the records.'

'Records of what? You mean the registrar?'

'We mean records of past students.'

'Alumni, you mean?'

'Well, we're not sure this student ever graduated.'

'Matriculated students, do you mean? Or nonmatriculated?'

'We're not sure,' Carella said.

'Day session or night?' the student asked.

'Well, we're not sure.'

'Which college, would you know that?'

'No,' Carella said.

The student looked at him curiously. 'I'm late for class,' he said at last, and wandered off.

'We get an F,' Meyer said. 'We came to school unprepared.'

'Let's talk to the dean,' Carella said.

'Which dean?' Meyer asked, peering at Carella as the student had done. 'Dean of admissions? Dean of men? Dean of women? Dean Martin?'

'Dean I see you someplace before?' Carella said, and Meyer said, 'Ouch!'

The dean of admissions was a nice lady in her early sixties who wore a starched ruffled blouse and a pencil in her hair. Her name was Dean Agnes Moriarty, and when the detectives said they were from the police, she immediately quipped, 'Moriarty, meet Holmes and Watson.'

'Carella and Meyer,' Carella said, smiling.

'What can I do for you, gentlemen?'

'We're interested in whatever information we can get about a woman who was once a student here.'

'When?' Miss Moriarty asked.

'We don't know. Sometime before the war, we believe.'

'When before the war? This university was founded in eighteen-forty-two, gentlemen.'

'The girl was forty-one years old when she died,' Meyer said. 'We can assume . . .'

'Died?' Miss Moriarty asked, and she raised her eyebrows slightly.

'Yes, ma'am,' Meyer said. 'She was killed last night.'

'Oh,' Miss Moriarty nodded. 'Then this is serious, isn't it?'

'Yes, ma'am.'

'Oh. Well, now, let's see. If she was forty-one years old – most of our students begin at eighteen, which would make this twenty-three years ago. Do you have any idea which college she was enrolled in?'

'No, I'm afraid we haven't.'

'Shall we try the school of liberal arts?'

'We're entirely in your hands, Miss Moriarty,' Carella said.

'Well, then, let's see what we can find out, shall we?'

They found out that Blanche Ruth Lettiger had indeed enrolled in the Liberal Arts College of Ramsey University as a speech and dramatics major in 1940; that she had given her age as eighteen at the time, and her home address as Jonesboro, Indiana, a town with a population of 1,973, close to Kokomo. She had listed her temporary address at 1107 Horsely Road, in the Quarter. She had remained at the school for one term only, a matter of less than five months, and had then dropped out. Her withdrawal was somewhat mysterious, since she was an honour student with a 3.8 index, close to the perfect 4.0. Miss Moriarty had no idea where Blanche Lettiger had gone after her dropout. She had never returned to the school, and had never attempted to contact them in any way.

Carella asked Miss Moriarty if there was anyone at the school now who might remember Blanche Lettiger as a student, and Miss Moriarty

promptly took the detectives to Professor Richardson in the speech and
dramatics department. Richardson was a thin old man with the manner and
bearing of a Shakespearean actor. His voice rolled from his mouth in golden,
rounded tones. He spoke forcefully, as though he were trying to give the
second balcony its money's worth. Carella was certain every word he
projected was heard all the way uptown in the squad room.

'Blanche Lettiger?' he said. 'Blanche Lettiger?'

He put one slender hand to his leonine head, closing the thumb and
forefinger over the bridge of his nose, lost in silent thought. Then he nodded
once, looked up and said, 'Yes.'

'You remember her?' Carella asked.

'Yes.' Richardson turned to Miss Moriarty. 'Do you recall the Wig and
Buskin Society?'

'I do,' she said.

'Then you must also remember *The Long Voyage Home*.'

'I'm afraid I missed that one,' Miss Moriarty said tactfully. 'The school's
drama groups do so *many* shows.'

'Mmm, yes, well,' Richardson said. He turned back to Carella. 'I was
faculty adviser of the group for four successive years. Blanche worked with
us in that play.'

'*The Long Voyage Home?*'

'Yes. A very nice girl. I remember her very well. *And* the play, too. It was
the first production we did in the round. Blanche Lettiger, yes, that's right.
She played one of the . . . ah . . . ladies of easy virtue.'

'What do you mean?' Carella said.

'Well . . .' Richardson paused, glanced at Miss Moriarty, and then said,
'One of the prostitutes.'

Carella glanced at Meyer, but neither of the detectives said anything.

'She was a very nice child,' Richardson said. 'Rather intense, somewhat
brooding, but nice nonetheless. And a very good actress. The play is set in a
London waterfront dive, you know, and the girl Blanche played spoke with a
cockney dialect. Blanche mastered the tones and accent almost immediately.
A remarkable feat, very. She had an excellent memory, too. She had
memorized all of her sides' – Richardson paused here to see whether or not
anyone had caught his use of the professional term 'sides,' and then, getting
no reaction, continued – 'in the first two nights of rehearsal. She had quite
the largest female part in the play, you know. Freda. The girl who has the
long talk with Olson and then is instrumental in drugging him before he's
shanghaied. We did the play in the round, the first time anything of the sort
had been tried at this school. We used the school theatre, of course, but we
banked rows of rented bleachers on the stage, and the performers worked in
the centre of it. Very exciting. In one scene, if you recall the play . . .'

'Mr Richardson, I wonder if . . .'

'. . . one of the sailors, Driscoll, is supposed to throw the beer in his glass
into the face of Ivan, the drunken Russian sailor. Well, when . . .'

'Mr Richardson, do you know if . . .?'

'. . . the actor hurled the contents of his glass, he spattered half a dozen
people sitting in the first row. The immediacy of playing in the round is
difficult to . . .'

'Mr Richardson,' Carella said firmly, 'did Blanche Lettiger . . .?'

'. . . imagine unless you've done it. Blanche was excellent at it. She had a very expressive face, you see. In the scene with Olson, she was required to do a lot of listening, a task even professional actresses find difficult. It was especially difficult here because we were working in the round, where every nuance of expression is clearly visible to the audience. But Blanche carried it off beautifully, a remarkable performance, very.'

'Did she want to . . .?'

'The play isn't one of my particular favourites, you know,' Richardson said. 'Of the *Glencairn* series, I much prefer *The Moon of the Caribbees*, or even *In the Zone*. But *Moon of the Caribbees* has four women, who are all West Indian Negresses, which would rather have limited our female casting; there are, after all, *white* students to consider, too. *In the Zone*, of course, has an all-male . . .'

'Would you know whether Miss Lettiger . . .'

'. . . cast, and this is, after all, a coeducational institution, so we eliminated that one. As a matter of fact, *The Long Voyage Home*, despite its shortcomings, was extremely well suited to our needs. With the exception of two rather small parts at the very end of the play, the parts are rather well . . .'

'Mr Richardson,' Carella said, 'would you know whether or not Miss Lettiger had any idea of becoming a professional actress? Or was this simply another extracurricular activity for her?'

'I honestly don't know how serious she was about the theatre. We discussed it peripherally once or twice, but my notion is she was undecided. Or perhaps intimidated, I'm not sure. I think the city overwhelmed her a bit. She was, after all, only eighteen years old, and from a small town in Indiana, very. The notion of attempting to conquer the professional theatre must have seemed extremely far fetched to her.'

'She *was* a speech and dramatics major, though?'

'Yes. But, of course, she was only here at the school for one term, not even a full semester.'

'Had she spoken to you about leaving school?'

'No.'

'Were you surprised when she left?'

'Mr Canella, the one thing an instructor . . .'

'Carella.'

'Carella, yes, forgive me. The one thing an instructor learns over the years is never to be surprised by anything a student says or does.'

'Does that mean you *were* surprised?'

'Well, she was an excellent student and, as I told you, a talented girl, very. Yes, I suppose I was surprised.'

'Was she in any production besides the O'Neill play?'

'No.'

'Was she in any of your classes?'

'No.'

'Would you know if she had any relatives in this city?'

'I'm sorry, I have no idea.'

'Well, thank you,' Carella said.

'Not at all. My pleasure,' Richardson answered.

They left him in his small office and walked downstairs with Miss

Moriarty. 'He's a crashing bore, *very*,' she said, 'but his memory *is* good, and I'm sure he gave an accurate picture of Blanche Lettiger as she was then. Was it at all helpful?'

'Miss Moriarty,' Carella said, 'the terrible thing about detective work is that you never know what's helpful and what isn't until all the pieces fit together at the end.'

'I'll remember that,' Miss Moriarty said. 'It'll no doubt help me in my sworn and unceasing battle against Holmes.'

'May the best man win,' Carella said.

They shook hands with her and walked out into the sunshine again.

'What do you think?' Meyer asked.

'I don't know what to think. Why'd she drop out of school so suddenly? Good student, good marks, interested in extracurricular stuff.' Carella shrugged.

'It's pretty unusual, isn't it? Especially when she came all the way from Kokomo.'

'No, not Kokomo, some town near it.'

'Yeah, what was the name of that town again?'

'Jonesville, something like that.'

'Jonesboro,' Meyer said.

'That's right.'

'You think we ought to get a flier out?'

'What for?'

'Routine check on her family, relatives, I don't know.'

'What good would it do? I'll tell you what bugs me about this girl, Meyer. She breaks the pattern, you know? Before, there was at least some kind of slender thread. Now . . .' He shrugged. 'This bothers me. It really does.'

'Yeah, well, you don't see *me* grinning from ear to ear, do you?'

'Maybe we *are* up against a nut. If we are, we can just whistle. He'll shoot whoever the hell he wants to, at random, without rhyme or reason.'

'Who's that blonde waving at you?' Meyer said suddenly.

Carella, who thought Meyer was joking, said, 'Blondes always wave at me.'

'Yeah? Even sixteen-year-old ones?'

Carella followed Meyer's gaze to the other end of the park, where a young blond girl wearing a navy skirt and a pale-blue sweater had begun walking quickly toward them. He recognized her immediately, and raised his own arm in greeting.

'You know her?' Meyer asked.

'Sure. Part of my fan club.'

'I keep forgetting you're a big-shot city detective.'

'Try to remember, will you?'

Cindy Forrest was wearing her hair loose around her face. There was a trace of lipstick on her mouth, and a string of tiny pearls around her throat. She was carrying her books hugged against her breasts, carrying also a small secret smile on her face as she approached.

'Hi,' she said. 'Were you looking for me?'

'No,' Carella answered, 'but it's nice to see you, anyway.'

'Why, thank you, sir,' Cindy said. 'What are you doing all the way down here?'

'Looking up some records. What are *you* doing here?'

'I go to school here,' Cindy said. 'Remember? My abnormal-psych instructor? Witness of the primal scene?'

'I remember,' Carella said. 'You're a psychology major, right?'

'Wrong. I'm an education major.'

'And you want to teach college,' he said, nodding.

'High school,' Cindy corrected.

'Some detective,' Meyer said, sighing.

'Meyer, I'd like you to meet Cynthia Forrest. Miss Forrest, this is my partner, Detective Meyer.'

'How do you do, Mr Meyer?' Cindy said, and extended her hand.

Meyer took it, smiled, and said, 'How do you do?'

She turned back to Carella almost immediately. 'Did you find what you were looking for?' she asked.

'Well, we found *something*, but I'm not sure it helps us very much.'

'Weren't the records complete?'

'Yes, fairly complete,' Carella said. 'It's just that . . .'

'Did you talk to Mr Ferguson?'

'Who?'

'Ferguson. The football coach.'

'No, we didn't,' Carella said, puzzled.

'He might have been able to help you. He's been at the school for ages. The team never wins, but they keep rehiring Ferguson because he's such a nice old man.'

'I see,' Carella said.

'You might look him up.'

'Why, Cindy?'

'Well, didn't you come down to . . .?' She stared up into his face. 'I'm sorry, maybe I'm confused.'

'Maybe we're *all* a little confused,' Meyer said, his eyes suddenly narrowing. 'Why do you think we should have looked up the football coach, Miss Forrest?'

'Well, only because he was on the team, you see.'

'*Who* was on the team?' Carella said.

'Why, Daddy.' She paused, her blue eyes wide. 'Didn't you know he went to school here?'

Salvatore Palumbo was fifty-seven years old, a wiry little man who had been born in Naples and who'd come to America in 1938 because he didn't like Mussolini or what he was doing with the country. He did not speak a word of English when he arrived, and he had only forty dollars in American money, plus a wife and two children, and the address of a cousin. He went to see the cousin in Philadelphia, and the cousin made a great show of welcoming him and then promptly let it be known he wasn't really welcome at all. So Palumbo, still not speaking a word of English – this was only a week after he'd arrived – spent twenty of his American dollars for train tickets and took his family to another city, and tried to make a start.

It was not easy to make a start. In Naples, he had been a fruit vendor with a small pushcart. He used to buy his produce from the farmers who drifted into the city from the outlying districts, and he used to shove his pushcart all over the city, sometimes not getting home until nine or ten at night, but nonetheless providing a living for himself and his family. The living was poor, even by Italian standards; in Naples, Salvatore Palumbo and his wife had lived in a slum. In America, he moved from Philadelphia, where his cousin lived in a slum, directly to another city and another slum.

He did not like the slum. In Italian, he said to his wife, 'I did not come to America to live in yet another slum,' and then he set about trying to find work. He thought it might be a good idea to get himself another pushcart, but he didn't speak English at all, and he didn't know where to buy his produce, or how to go about getting a vendor's license, or even that a vendor's license was necessary. He got a job on the waterfront instead. He was always a small man, and lifting bales and crates was difficult for him. He developed a powerful chest and muscular arms, so that he looked like a bandy-legged little wrestler after two years of working the docks.

Well, America is the land of opportunity. That's the God's honest truth, you can take it or leave it. You don't have to stay in a slum, and you don't have to keep working on the docks. If you have the will, determination, and ambition of a man like Salvatore Palumbo, you can in twenty-five years own a little house in Riverhead – in an Italian neighbourhood, yes, but not in a slum or a ghetto – and you can have your own fruit-and-vegetable store seven blocks away on Dover Plains Avenue, and people will call you Sal instead of Salvatore.

At twelve noon on May 1, Detectives Meyer and Carella were in another part of the city making a series of startling discoveries while Sal Palumbo stood on the sidewalk outside his store and polished his fruit. They discovered first of all that Anthony Forrest was a graduate of Ramsey University, a fact they had never known. And then, carried on the wave of this fresh discovery, they remembered that Mae Norden, the wife of the slain lawyer Randolph Norden, had told them her husband had studied at Ramsey Law. Like men who had found the elusive piece of a very tiring jigsaw puzzle when the piece was right there on the table all along, just under the ashtray, they exuberantly tied the first two deaths with the death of the prostitute Blanche Lettiger, who had also been a student at Ramsey, and foolishly and joyously believed the puzzle was almost finished when in actuality it had only just begun.

Sal Palumbo had no such feelings of soaring joy as he polished the fruit. He liked fruit, indeed he loved fruit, but he did not polish it because it gave him any particular pleasure. He was not the kind of person who could go wild over the colour of an apple or a pear. He polished the fruit because when it was polished it looked better to his customers, and when it looked better to his customers, they bought it. One of his customers was walking toward the store now, an Irish lady named Mrs O'Grady. He did not know the Irish lady's first name. He knew that she lived someplace in Riverhead, but not in the immediate neighbourhood. Palumbo's stand was on Dover Plains Avenue, just below the elevated structure, near the corner of 200th Street. There was a station stop on that corner, and every Tuesday afternoon at about this time, Mrs. O'Grady would come down the steps leading from the station and stop first in the candy store on the corner, and then next in the butcher's shop alongside it, and then she would walk to Palumbo's store, which was two stores down from the butcher's shop in the shadow of the station platform.

'Ah, *signora*,' Palumbo said, as she approached, and she promptly answered, 'Don't give me the Eye-talian malarkey, Sal.'

Mrs O'Grady was perhaps fifty-two years old, with a trim, spare figure, and a devilish twinkle in her green eyes. She had been doing business with the merchants along Dover Plains Avenue for five years now because she liked their prices and their goods better than those available in her own neighbourhood. If you had asked either Mrs O'Grady or Sal Palumbo about the casual flirtation that had been going on between them for the past five years, both would have said you were out of your mind. Palumbo was married, with two grown married sons and with three grandchildren. Mrs O'Grady was married, with a married daughter who was pregnant. But Palumbo was a man who liked women in general, not only southern Italian types like his wife, Rose, with her dark hair and her darker eyes, but even trim little types with small compact breasts and tight small backsides and green eyes like Mrs O'Grady. And Mrs O'Grady was a passionate sort who liked nothing better than a good strong man in her arms, and this little fellow Sal Palumbo had good strong arms and a great massive chest with curling black hair showing at the open throat of his shirt. And so the two of them bandied small talk over the fruit, carrying on a flirtation that would never be openly recognized, that would never come to so much as a touch of the hand, but that nonetheless flared once a week every Tuesday over the pears and the apples and the plums and the peaches.

'Well, it don't look so good to me today, Sal,' Mrs O'Grady said. 'Is this all you've got?'

'What's the matter with you?' Palumbo demanded, his voice carrying only the faintest trace of an accent. 'Those are beautiful fruit. What do you want? You want some nice pears today? I got some apricots, too, the first of the season.'

'And bitter as poison, I'll bet.'

'From me? Bitter fruit from Sal Palumbo? Ah, *bella signora*, you know me better than that.'

'What are those melons?'

'What are they but melons? You see them with your eyes, no? You just named them. They're honeydew melons.'

'Good?'

'Beautiful.'

'How do I know?'

'Mrs O'Grady, for you I would slice one open, but only for you, and only because when I slice it open you'll find a melon so sweet, and so ripe, and so green as your own eyes.'

'Never mind my own eyes,' Mrs O'Grady said. 'And you don't have to slice it for me, I'll take your word. No plums yet?'

'We can't rush the summer,' Palumbo answered.

'Well, let me have two pounds of the apples. How much are the apricots?'

'Thirty-nine a pound.'

'That's too high.'

'I'm losing money.'

'I'll just bet you are,' she answered, smiling.

'These have to be shipped in, you know. Refrigerator cars. The grower makes money, the shipper makes money, the railroad makes money, but by the time the apricots get to me, what do I make?'

'Well, give me a couple of pounds, so you can lose some more money.'

'Two?'

'I said a couple, didn't I?'

'*Signora*, in Italy, a couple is always two. In America, a couple can be three, four, a half a dozen. *Ma che?*' He spread his hands and shrugged his shoulders, and Mrs O'Grady laughed.

'Two pounds,' she said.

'You need some lettuce? I got nice iceberg and nice Romaine, whichever your heart desires.'

'The iceberg,' she said. 'You know who has really good fruit?'

'Sal Palumbo has really good fruit,' he answered.

'No, the fruit man in my own neighbourhood. And *his* apricots are cheaper.'

Palumbo, who was reaching over the crates stacked in front of his stand, reaching onto the slanting stand itself to the rear, where his apricots were piled in neat rows, said, 'How much are his apricots?'

'Thirty-five cents a pound.'

'So then go buy *his* apricots,' Palumbo said.

'I would,' Mrs O'Grady replied, 'but he was all out of them when I got there.'

'*Signora*,' Palumbo said, 'if *I* was all out of apricots, they'd be thirty-five cents a pound, too. You want them, *si* or *no*?'

'I'll take them,' Mrs O'Grady said, her green eyes twinkling, 'but it's highway robbery.'

Palumbo opened a brown paper bag and dropped a handful of apricots into it. He put the bag on his hanging scale and was piling more apricots into it when the bullet came from the station platform above him, entering his head at a sharp angle from the top of his skull. He fell forward onto the stand. The fruit and vegetables came tumbling down around him as he collapsed to the sidewalk, the polished pears and apples, the green peppers, the oranges and lemons and potatoes, while Mrs O'Grady looked at him in horror and then began screaming.

Chapter Eight

Carella and Meyer did not learn that an Italian fruit dealer named Salvatore Palumbo had been shot to death until they got back to the squad room at four o'clock that afternoon of May 1. Up to that time, they had been poring over the records of Anthony Forrest and Randolph Norden at the university.

The records were puzzling and contradictory, and supplied them with almost no additional clues as to just what the hell was happening.

Anthony Forrest had entered Ramsey University as a business-administration major in the spring semester of 1937, when he was eighteen years old and a graduate of Ashley High School in Majesta. By the spring of

1940, which was when Blanche Lettiger enrolled at the university, he was entering his senior year. He had been only a fair student, averaging C for almost every semester at the school, barely qualifying academically for the football team. He was graduated two hundred and fifth in his class in January of 1941, with a B.S. degree. He had been a member of the ROTC while at the college, but he was not called to active duty until almost a year after graduation, when the attack on Pearl Harbor startled the world.

Randolph Norden had entered Ramsey University in the fall of 1935, when he was eighteen years old and a graduate of Thomas Hardy High in Bethtown. He enrolled as a liberal-arts major with intentions of eventually going on to Ramsey Law. In the spring of 1937, when Forrest entered the school, Norden was halfway through his sophomore year. In the spring of 1940, when Blanche Lettiger entered the school, Norden had already completed his three-year pre-law requirement and was in his second year of law school. He was graduated from Ramsey Law in June of 1941, and he went into the navy almost immediately after the attack on Pearl Harbor.

His records showed that Norden was an excellent student throughout his entire stay at Ramsey. He had been elected to the student council in his sophomore year, had made Phi Beta Kappa as a junior, was listed in *Who's Who in American Colleges and Universities*, and – in law school – was a member of the Order of the Coif, as well as editor of the *Ramsey Law Review*.

A closer search of the records showed that Randolph Norden had never been in any of Anthony Forrest's classes. Nor did it appear as though either of the men, one of whom was a graduating senior in 1940, the other of whom was in his second year of law school, had shared any classes with the entering freshman named Blanche Ruth Lettiger.

'So what do you make of it?' Carella had asked.

'I'm damned if I know,' Meyer had answered.

Now, entering the squad room at four o'clock in the afternoon, they still did not have the answer. They stopped off in the clerical office and bummed two cups of coffee from Miscolo. A note on Carella's desk told him that the BCI had called. It no longer seemed important to know the names of the criminals Randolph Norden had defended, but he dutifully returned the call anyway, and was talking to a man named Simmons when the other phone rang. Meyer picked it up.

'Eighty-seventh Squad, Meyer,' he said.

'Let me talk to Carella, huh?' the voice on the other end said.

'Who's this, please?'

'This is Mannheim of the One-Oh-Four in Riverhead.'

'Hold on a second, will you?' Meyer said. 'He's on the other line.'

'Sure,' Mannheim said.

Carella looked up.

'The One-Oh-Four in Riverhead,' Meyer whispered. 'Guy named Mannhiem.'

Carella nodded. Into his own phone he said, 'Then all but one of them are still serving prison terms, is that right?'

'That's right,' Simmons told him.

'What's the story on the one who's loose?'

'His name's Frankie Pierce. He's been back with us since last November. He was serving a five-and-dime at Castleview, came up for parole last year,

was granted.'
  'What was the rap?'
  'Burglary Three.'
  'Any other arrests in his record?'
  'He had a J.D. card when he was fifteen, pulled in twice on gang rumbles, but that was all.'
  'Weapons?'
  'A zip gun in one of the rumbles. They threw the Sullivan Act, but his lawyer got him off with a suspended sentence.'
  'He was paroled in November, you say?'
  'That's right.'
  'Where's he living now?'
  'Isola. Three-seven-one Horton. That's down here near the Calm's Point Bridge.'
  'Who's his parole officer?'
  'McLaughlin. You know him?'
  'I think so. Any trouble?'
  'He's been sound as a dollar since he got out. My guess is he'll be back at the old stand pretty soon, though. That's the pattern, ain't it?'
  'Sometimes,' Carella said.
  'You got some burglaries up there, is that it?' Simmons asked.
  'No, this is a homicide.'
  'How does it look?'
  'Pretty cool right now.'
  'Give it time. Homicides work themselves out, don't they?'
  'Not always,' Carella said. 'Thanks a lot, Simmons.'
  'Don't mention it,' he said, and hung up. Carella pressed the extension button.
  'Hello?' he said.
  'Carella?'
  'Yep.'
  'This is Mannheim, the One-Oh-Four in Riverhead.'
  'How are you, Mannheim?'
  'Fine, fine. Listen, you the guy who's handling this sniper case?'
  'I'm the guy. Have you got something for me?'
  'Yeah,' Mannheim said.
  'What is it?'
  'Another stiff.'
Rose Palumbo spoke very bad English even when she was coherent, and she was practically incoherent by the time Carella reached her at the old frame house in Riverhead. They tried sparring in the king's language for a while, with her repeating something about 'atops' that Carella didn't understand at all until one of her sons, a man named Richard Palumbo, told Carella she was worried about them cutting up her husband when they did an autopsy. Carella tried to assure the woman, in English, that all they were interested in establishing was the cause of death, but the woman kept repeating the word 'atops' between her flowing tears and her violent gasps for breath until Carella finally took her shoulders and shook her.
  '*Ma che vergogna, signora!*' he shouted.
  '*Mi dispiace,*' Rose said, '*ma non posso sopportare l'idea che lo taglino.*'

Perchè devono tagliare?'

'*Perchè l'hanno ucciso,*' Carella said, '*e vogliamo scoprire chi è stato.*'

'*Ma che scoprirete tagliandolo?*'

'*La palla è ancora dentro. Dobbiamo trovare la palla perchè ci sono stati altri morti. Altri tre.*'

'*E tagliarono gli altri?*'

'*Sì.*'

'*È peccato contro Dio mutilare i morti.*'

'*È un più grosso peccato contro Dio di uccidere,*' Carella answered.

'What's she saying?' Meyer asked.

'She doesn't want an autopsy.'

'Tell her we don't need her permission.'

'How's that going to help? She's out of her mind with grief.' He turned back to the woman. '*Signora,*' he said, '*è necessario individuare il tipo di pallottola che l'ho uccise. La palla è ancora dentro, non comprende? Doddiamo sapere che tipo.*'

'*Sì, sì, capisco.*'

'*È per questo che dobbiamo fare un'autopsia. Comprende? Così potremo trovare l'assassino.*'

'*Sì, sì, capisco.*'

'*La prego, signora. Provi.*' He patted her on the shoulder, and then turned to the son, Richard. Richard was perhaps thirty years old, a strapping man with broad shoulders and a dancer's narrow waist. 'We'd like to ask you a few questions, Mr Palumbo, is that all right?'

'You have to excuse my mother,' Palumbo said. 'She doesn't speak English too well.'

'That's all right,' Carella said.

'My father spoke pretty good English, though not when he first came here. He really worked at it. But my mother . . .' Richard shook his head. 'I guess she always felt America was a temporary thing, a stop along the way. I think she always planned to go back to Naples, you know? But not my father. This was it. For him, this was it. He'd really found the place. So he learned the language. He really learned it pretty good. A little accent, but not too noticeable. He was quite a guy.'

Richard said all this looking at a point somewhere above Carella's shoulders, not looking into Carella's eyes or even his face. He delivered the words as though he were saying a prayer over Palumbo's open grave. There were no tears in his eyes, but his face was white, and he kept focusing on that imaginary point somewhere above Carella's shoulder, staring.

'He worked hard all his life,' Richard said. 'When we first came to this country, I was just a little kid. That was in nineteen-thirty-eight, that was a long time ago. I was eight years old. My brother was only three. We didn't have nothing to eat then, you know? My father worked like a horse on the docks. He was a skinny little guy then, you shoulda seen him. Then he got all these muscles from lifting all that heavy stuff, you know? He was quite a guy, my father.' He gestured toward the small framed picture of Palumbo where it stood on the living room mantlepiece. 'He made all this himself, you know – the house, the store. From nothing. Saved up his pennies, learned English, got himself a pushcart at first with the money he saved from the docks. Just like when he was in Naples, he used to push that damn pushcart all over the city, he used to be exhausted when he got home at night. I remember he used to yell at me, and once he even slapped me, not because he was sore at me, but only because he was so damn tired. But he made it, huh? He got his own store, didn't he? He had a good business, my father. He was a real good man.'

Carella looked at Meyer, and neither said a word.

'So somebody kills him,' Richard said. 'Somebody shoots him from up there on the train station.' He paused. 'What did he do to anybody? He never hurt anybody in his entire life. Only once did he ever slap even me, his own son, and that was because he was so tired, not because he was sore, he never hit anybody in anger, he never hit anybody at all. So he's dead.'

Richard gave a slight shrug, and his hands moved in a futile, bewildered gesture.

'How do you figure it? I don't know. How do you make any sense out of it? He worked all his damn life to have his store, to take care of his family, and then somebody just shoots him, like as if he was . . . *nothing*. That's my *father* that guy shot, don't he know that? That's my father they took away in the ambulance. For Christ's sake, don't he realize that, the guy who shot him? Don't he realize this is my father who's dead now?'

Tears were welling into his eyes. He kept staring at the spot above Carella's shoulder.

'Ain't *he* got a father, that guy? How could he just . . . just *shoot* him like that, how could he make himself pull the trigger? This is a man who was standing down there, a man, my *father*, for Christ's sake! Don't he know what he done? Don't he know this man is never gonna go to his store again, he's never gonna argue with the customers, he's never gonna laugh or nothing? How could he do that, will you tell me?'

Richard paused. His voice lowered. 'I didn't even see him today. He left the house before I got up this morning. My wife and I, we live right upstairs. Every morning I usually meet him, we leave about the same time to go to work. I work in an aircraft-parts factory on Two Thirty-third. But this morning, I had a little virus, I was running a small fever, my wife said stay in bed, so she called in sick. And I didn't get to see my father. Not even to say, "Hello, Pop, how's it going?" So today, somebody kills him. The day I didn't see him.'

'Have you got any idea who might have done this?' Carella asked.

'No.'

'Has anyone been threatening your father? Had he received any notes or phone calls, or . . .?'

'No.'

'Any trouble with any of the businessmen along the avenue?'

'None.' Richard shook his head again. 'Everybody liked him. This don't make sense. Everybody liked him.' He rubbed at his nose with his forefinger, sniffed, and said again, 'I didn't even see him today. Not even to say hello.'

Chapter Nine

The next morning, Wednesday, May 2, Steve Carella went in to see Detective Lieutenant Byrnes. He told the lieutenant that the case was taking some unexpected twists, that he and Meyer thought they'd had at least something to go on, but that they weren't quite so sure of that anymore, and that there was a strong possibility the killer was a nut. In view of the circumstances, Carella told the lieutenant, he would like additional help from whomever Byrnes could spare on the squad, and he would also like to request that Byrnes put in for help from the other squads in the city, since the killer seemed to be moving from place to place, and since legwork alone was taking up a considerable amount of time that could just possibly go into deduction, if there was anything to deduce, which there didn't seem to be at the moment.

Byrnes listened to everything Carella had to say, and told him he would do everything he could as soon as he had a chance to look over his duty schedules and to call the Chief of Detectives downtown at headquarters. But Carella had to wait until much later that day before he got the help he requested. And then, unexpectedly, the help came from the District Attorney's office.

Andrew Mulligan was an assistant district attorney who wanted to be governor of the state one day, and after that – now that Kennedy had broken the ground for Catholics – he figured it might be nice to be president. His office was downtown on High Street adjacent to the Criminal Courts Building, just across the street from Police Headquarters. Byrnes had placed his call to the Chief of Detectives at precisely 11:15 A.M., but Mulligan didn't know that, since he'd been in court at the time. In fact, Mulligan had no notion that the men of the 87th Squad were working on four possibly related murders, nor did he have any idea that he would soon be helping them with the case. At the moment, he was working with the D.A. himself on a case involving income-tax evasion. Mulligan didn't know that the D.A. himself wanted to be governor of the state, too, but even if he had known, it wouldn't have bothered him. The particular case they were trying together involved a very big-shot racketeer and was getting a lot of headlines in the local press. Mulligan liked headlines. It annoyed him that there was a jazz musician named Gerry Mulligan, who wasn't even a relation. He felt that when anyone mentioned the name Mulligan, or whenever the name Mulligan appeared in print, it should instantly bring to mind the image of a fighting assistant district attorney, and not some crumby bongo drummer, or whatever this other Mulligan was.

He had, in fairness to the case he would soon become a part of, tried four murder cases since he'd begun working with the D.A.'s office. He liked murder cases because they usually guaranteed a lot of newspaper coverage. His first murder case had been brought to him by the detectives of the 49th Squad, an open-and-shut Murder One that anyone fresh out of law school could have tried successfully. Mulligan milked the case for all it was worth. The trial should have been over and done with in two weeks at the most. Mulligan stretched it to a month, with headlines screaming every day, and would have stretched it even further if the judge hadn't begun issuing some subtle hints about the 'seemingly inexhaustible supply of rhetoric at this trial.' Mulligan got his headlines, and he also got his conviction, and then – because nothing succeeds like success, that's how the saying goes, go tell it to Larry Parks – he was assigned another murder case shortly thereafter, and then another, and then yet another, the number of murders committed in that fair city being almost as inexhaustible as the supply of rhetoric at his first trial.

As he left the courthouse and walked down the broad flat steps in front of the building, he was wondering what he'd be working on after they had demolished this cheap racketeer with his phony meat market covering up a multimillion-dollar vice ring. He did not know he would become involved in the case the 87th was now working on, but he certainly hoped his next one would be another murder trial. He was also thinking about what he would order for lunch.

The restaurant he habitually frequented was off on one of the side streets bordering the financial district. Most of the lawyers who had any traffic with the downtown courts lunched there, and he enjoyed the quiet buzz that usually accompanied his entrance into the place. He had no idea what any of the attorneys were whispering about him behind their hands, but he was sure it was good. As he entered the restaurant that afternoon, he saw two young lawyers interrupt their conversation and turn in his direction. He did not acknowledge their stares in any way. He stood unobtrusively immense just inside the doorway, the courtroom dynamo in his civilian disguise, and waited for the proprietress of the restaurant to discover him.

She discovered him almost immediately.

'Oh, Mr Mulligan,' she said, distressed. 'I did not know you were coming today. Your table is taken.'

'Oh?' Mulligan said, his eyebrows raising just a trifle, an only faintly interested expression on his face. 'Didn't my secretary call?'

'No, Mr Mulligan, I'm sorry. She didn't.'

'Well . . .' Mulligan said, and he turned a gently anticipatory inquiring look on the flustered proprietress, a look that firmly demanded, 'Well, what do you propose to do about this intolerable set of circumstances?'

The proprietress knew how to read looks, because she'd been dealing with lawyers both here and in the old country, and they were all the same, they all stank.

'I'll get you another table, Mr Mulligan,' she said, 'a very nice table in the other room. Come with me, I'll take care of you.'

She started to turn, and then stopped in her tracks, and a smile flowered on her face, and she said, 'Wait, they're leaving. Look, they're just paying their check. See, Mr Mulligan? It all turned out all right, after all. You can have your own table.'

'I appreciate that,' Mulligan said. 'Sincerely, I do.'

The two gentlemen sitting at Mulligan's customary table paid the check, rose, lighted their cigars, and left the restaurant. The waiter changed the tablecloth, and held the chair for Mulligan as he sat. Mulligan pulled the chair close to the table and, without looking at the waiter, said, 'Dewar's on the rocks, please,' and then relaxed and looked through the huge plate-glass window at the street outside. He enjoyed sitting in the same spot each day, because it made him easier to identify. He particularly enjoyed this table immediately adjacent to the window because it enabled him to be identified from *outside* the restaurant as well as inside. A fellow attorney passed the table, said, 'Hello, Andy, how are you?' and touched him on the shoulder. Mulligan smiled in response and wondered where the hell his Scotch was. The waiter brought it almost instantly.

'Would you like to order now, Mr Mulligan?' the waiter asked.

'I'll look over the menu,' Mulligan said. The waiter brought the card, and Mulligan picked up his glass of Scotch, took a sip of it, and began reading. The menu rarely changed. He almost knew it by heart.

He was wondering whether he should have the crabmeat au gratin when suddenly the plate-glass window alongside the table shattered.

Mulligan didn't have time to react to the falling glass because it had been shattered by a bullet, and the next thing the bullet shattered was the bone just below his right temple.

If there had been a scale of importance for homicide, ranging from zero for the least important to ten for the most important, Blanche Lettiger would have clocked in at zero, Sal Palumbo would have registered a resounding two, and both Anthony Forrest and Randolph Norden would have fallen somewhere between the three and four mark.

Andrew Mulligan fell snoot-first into his glass of Dewar's on the rocks and promptly sent the murder meter soaring to seven-point-eight. There were two leading afternoon newspapers in the city, one big, one small, you paid your money and you took your choice. They both stank. The big one always printed its headline-above-the-headline in red type. The tabloid-sized one always printed its headline-above-the-headline in blue type, because it was a very liberal newspaper and didn't want people to think it was *too* liberal, in fact didn't want even the slightest association with the colour red. The big newspaper's headline that afternoon read SNIPER SLAYS D.A. The headline-above-the-headline was printed in red and it said: MULLIGAN'S TRIUMPHS, p. 5. The tabloid-sized newspaper's headline that afternoon read MULLIGAN MURDERED, and across the top of the page, in blue, THE FIGHTING D.A., A Study by Agnes Lovely, p. 33. Agnes Lovely's study had been composed in fifteen minutes by backtracking through the paper's morgue shortly before press time. The *news* story, on the other hand, read more like a study, because it was a policy of the blue-headline tabloid to make every item of news sound like a piece of fiction in a popular magazine. If President Kennedy sent a new tax bill to Congress, the blue-headline tabloid started the story something like this: *These ancient halls were still with contemplation today. There was a paper to be considered, a decision to be made. The paper had come down to them from above, a document that could change the lives of everyone in the nation, a document that . . .* and so on. Somewhere

toward the end of the news story, the reporter usually revealed what the hell
he was talking about. Up to that time, he was writing for atmosphere and
suspense.

There were many people in the city who felt that the rifle death of an
assistant district attorney contained enough atmosphere and suspense all by
itself. These people foolishly felt that all a newspaper was supposed to do in a
news story was tell the facts, ma'am. But the blue-headline newspaper, you
see, was really running a disguised school for fiction writers, someone
having told the city editor that Ernest Hemingway had once been a
newspaper correspondent. The city editor also felt that most of the people in
the city were illiterate. He would have liked to fill his newspaper with a lot of
photographs beneath which would be short, sharp captions, but a morning
newspaper in the city had been using that format for a good many years now,
and the city editor of the blue-headline tabloid didn't want to seem like a
copycat. So instead, he decided that illiterate people would rather not have
their news straight from the shoulder, but would instead prefer reading each
story as if it were a chapter of a long novel about life.

> The tall man was drinking Scotch.
> He sat by the restaurant window
> watching the rush of humanity out-
> side, thinking private thoughts of
> a crusader who has foolishly and
> momentarily taken off all his arm-
> or. He could have been a Columbus in
> other times, he could have been an Es-
> sex at the side of Elizabeth. He was,
> instead, a tall and impressive man
> drinking his Scotch. He was soon to
> be a dead man.

This was the way the reporter on the blue-headline newspaper started his
story. But in addition to a city editor who had the notion that everyone was
an illiterate except maybe himself, the paper also had a typesetter who
thought that people enjoyed working out cryptograms while reading their
newspapers. When you were dealing with illiterates, it wasn't necessary to
give the facts in the first place, and in the second place it was always
necessary to garble every line of type so that the story became even more
mystifying and, in many cases, practically unintelligible.

The story on page 3 of that afternoon's edition read like this:

> Thet allman was drinking Scotch. He sat by the
> restaurant window watching the Russian hu-
> manity outside, thinking private thoughts of sex
> at the side of Elizabeth. He was, a crusader who
> has foolishly and momentarily taken off his arm.
> Or he could have been a Columbus in other
> times, he could have been an Es DRINKING
> HIS SCOTCH. He was soon to be a dead man.
> instead, a tall and impressive man.

It really didn't matter what the blue-headline tabloid said, because the
assistant district attorney named Andrew Mulligan was inconsiderately

turning a little blue on a slab in the morgue, and the district attorney himself, a man named Carter Cole, turned a very deep shade of blue mixed with red and bordering on purple when he found out that a man from his office had been inconveniently knocked off in the middle of a trial while drinking a glass of Scotch.

The D.A. himself picked up a telephone and put in a call to the Police Commissioner, wanting to know what the hell was happening in this city when a respected and much-needed assistant district attorney couldn't even go to a restaurant without having his brains blown out while drinking a glass of Scotch. The Police Commissioner told him that he was doing everything in his power to get at the facts, after which he hung up and called the Chief of Detectives.

He asked the Chief of Detectives what the hell was happening in this city when a respected and much-needed assistant district attorney couldn't even go into a restaurant without having his brains blown out while drinking a glass of Scotch. The Chief of Detectives told him that he was doing everything in his power to get at the facts, after which he hung up and called Detective Lieutenant Peter Byrnes of the 87th Squad.

Detective Lieutenant Peter Byrnes informed the Chief of Detectives that he had called him only this morning in an attempt to solicit some assistance on this case, which was getting a little out of hand, what with people dying like flies, and what with respected and much-needed assistant district attorneys getting their brains blown out and all. The Chief of Detectives told Lieutenant Byrnes that he would certainly see to it that Capello, or whatever his name was, got all the help he needed on this case, because, and here his voice lowered, and he actually said, 'Just between you and me, Pete, the D.A. himself was a little burned up over the situation.'

Andrew Mulligan, meanwhile, was being sliced up nicely and neatly, and being searched for a stray bullet, which, when it was found, turned out to be a Remington .308, of all things. Being dead, he still had no idea that Carella and Meyer of the 87th Squad were working on a case involving someone who was putting bullets through people's heads, nor had he any idea how much his own death had helped the investigating cops.

By midnight that night, Carella had been assigned teams of detectives from every section of the city to assist in running down the sniper. He had, in effect, a small army to work with.

Now all the army had to do was find the enemy.

Chapter Ten

The enemy, like all good enemies everywhere, vanished from sight.

There were no subsequent killings that week, and it seemed indeed as though detectives from all over the city had been mobilized to combat a ghost. Thursday, Friday, and Saturday passed uneventfully. The cruelest month was gone, taking part of May with it, and the murderer seemed to have disappeared.

On Sunday, May 6, two detectives from the 12th Precinct, near the Calm's Point Bridge downtown, decided it would be a good idea to look up Frankie Pierce. Carella had mentioned the name casually to them, as that of an ex-con who had once been a client of Randolph Norden. He had also mentioned that, in view of later developments, it seemed to him Pierce was clean, and not worth picking up. But the two detectives from the 12th were Detectives/1st Grade, and Carella was only a Detective/2nd Grade, and they didn't much like being told how to investigate a homicide by someone whom they outranked, even if the squeal happened to be Carella's. Besides, the two detectives from the 12th were bulls.

One was named Masterson, and the other was named Brock. The two had been working together as a pair for a long time, and they had a long series of arrests and convictions to their credit, but they were nonetheless bulls. On that first Sunday in May, with the carnelian cherry blossoms bursting in the park, and a mild breeze blowing in off the River Dix from the south, Masterson and Brock got a little restless in the stuffy squad room of the 12th, and decided they could use a little fresh air. And then, since they were simply cruising around the streets in the vicinity of the Calm's Point Bridge, they decided to look up Frankie Pierce, who lived at 371 Horton in the bridge's shadow.

Frankie Pierce had no idea he was about to be visited by detectives, or by detectives who were bulls. He was in constant touch with his parole officer, and he knew he had done nothing to break parole. He was, in fact, working at a garage as a mechanic and he had every intention of going straight, like they say in the movies. His employer was a fair-minded man who knew Frankie was on parole, but who felt that a man deserves a chance at rehabilitation. Frankie was a good worker and a hard worker. His employer was satisfied with him and had given him a raise only the month before.

But Frankie made a couple of mistakes on that first Sunday in May when the bulls named Masterson and Brock visited him. The first mistake he made was in assuming the two detectives were only detectives and not bulls. The second mistake he made was in believing that people are understanding.

He had a date that afternoon with a girl who was the cashier in a restaurant near the garage. He had told the girl he was an ex-con because he wanted to get things straight with her from the start. The girl had looked him over very carefully and then said, 'What do I care what you used to be?' and that was that. He was going to take her over to the park, where they would go rowing for a while, and then have dinner at the outdoor restaurant, and then maybe walk up the Stem and take in a movie later. He was standing before the mirror putting on his tie when the knock sounded on his door.

'Who is it?' he asked.

'Police. Open up, Frankie.'

A puzzled look crossed his face. He looked at himself in the mirror, as though expecting an answer from his own image, then shrugged and walked to the door.

Masterson and Brock stood in the hallway. They were both well over six feet tall, each weighing about two hundred pounds, both wearing slacks and short-sleeved sports shirts that showed the bulge of their chest and arm muscles. Frankie, standing in front of them in the open door, looked very small, even though he was five feet ten inches tall and weighed a hundred and sixty-five pounds.

'Frankie Pierce?' Masterson asked.

'That's right,' he answered.

'Get your hat, Frankie,' Masterson said.

'What's the matter?'

'We want to talk to you.'

'What about?'

'Get your hat.'

'I don't wear a hat. What's the matter?'

'We want to ask you a few questions, Frankie.'

'Well . . . well, why don't you ask them then?'

'You gonna be a wise guy?' Brock asked suddenly. It was the first time he had spoken, and the effect of his words was chilling. He had slate-grey eyes and a thick nose, and a mouth drawn across his face with a draftsman's pen, tight and hard, and barely moving when he spoke.

'No, look,' Frankie said. 'I don't mind answering some questions. It's just I have a date, that's all.'

'You want to finish tying your tie, Frankie?' Masterson asked. 'Or do you want to come along the way you are?'

'Well . . . well, I'd like to tie my tie and . . . you know, I want to polish my shoes and . . .' He hesitated. 'I told you, I have a date.'

'Yeah, you told us. Go tie your tie.'

'Is this gonna take long?'

'That depends on you, don't it, Frankie?'

'What do you mean?'

'Tie your tie.'

He went to the mirror and finished the Windsor knot he had started. He was annoyed when he noticed his hands were trembling. He looked in the mirror at the two detectives who waited for him just inside the door, wondering if they had noticed, too, that his hands were trembling.

'You want to shake a leg, Frankie?' Masterson said.

'Sure, be right with you,' Frankie said pleasantly. 'I wish you guys would tell me what this is all about.'

'You'll find out, Frankie.'

'I mean, if you think I broke parole or something, you can give my parole officer a call, his name's McLaughlin, he can tell you . . .'

'We don't have to give nobody a call,' Brock said in that same chilling voice.

'Well . . . well, okay, let me just put on my jacket.'

He put on his jacket, and then walked to the door, and followed the detectives out, and locked the door behind him. There were a lot of people on the front stoop of the building and hanging around the candy store, and he was embarrassed because he knew everybody in the neighbourhood could smell a cop from away the hell across the street, and he didn't want anybody to think he was in trouble again. He kept telling himself all the way crosstown to the station house that he wasn't in trouble, this was probably some kind of routine pickup, somebody done something, so they were naturally rounding up all the ex-cons in the neighbourhood, something like that. It would just be a matter of explaining to them, of making them understand he was going straight, had a good job with a good salary, wasn't even seeing any of the guys he used to run with before he got busted.

The two detectives said hello to the desk sergeant on their way into the building, and then Brock said in his chilling voice, 'No calls, Mike,' and they walked him to the back of the building where the detective squad room was, and then into the squad room itself, and then into a small room with the word INTERROGATION lettered on the frosted glass door. Brock closed the door, took a key out of his pocket, locked the door, and put the key in his pocket.

'Sit down, Frankie,' Masterson said.

Frankie sat. He had heard what Brock said to the desk sergeant, and he had seen Brock lock the door and put the key in his pocket, and he was beginning to think that maybe something very serious had been done, and he wanted no part of it, whatever the hell it was. At the same time, he knew he was an ex-con, and he knew that it was only natural for them to go looking up a guy with a record if something was done, but once he explained, once they understood he was straight now . . .

'How long you been out, Frankie?' Masterson asked.

'Since November fifteenth.'

'Castleview?'

'Yeah.'

'What were you in for?'

'Third-degree burglary.'

'You were a good boy, huh?'

'Well, yeah, I didn't give nobody any trouble.'

'That's nice, Frankie,' Masterson said.

'How long you been living down there on Horton?' Brock asked.

'Since I got out.'

'You working?'

'Yeah. I got a job.'

'Where?'

'The Esso station near the bridge. Right where the approach . . .'

'What do you do there?'

'I'm a mechanic.'

'Yeah?'

'Yeah, I worked in the automobile shop up at Castle –'

'Doing what? Making license plates?' Masterson said, and Brock laughed. His laugh was a curious thing. It never made a sound. It came into this throat and erupted there only as a series of muscular apasms.

'No, I learned a trade,' Frankie said. 'Listen, I was good enough for the garage to hire me.'

'That's nice, Frankie,' Masterson said.

'What's this all about?' Frankie asked. 'Somebody pull a job?'

'Yeah, somebody pulled a job.'

'Well, it wasn't me,' Frankie said. 'I learned my lesson.'

'Did you?'

'Five years was enough for me,' He shook his head. 'No more. Never again.'

'It's good to hear that, Frankie,' Masterson said.

'Well, I happen to mean it. I'm making eighty bucks a week now, and I work like a dog for it, but it's clean, you know. They deduct all the taxes from it, and what's left is mine, earned honest, no problems. I report once a week to my parole . . .'

'Yeah, Frankie, you know a guy named Randolph Norden?'

'Sure I do. He was my lawyer.'

'*Was?*'

'Yeah. When I had the trouble. Was. Why? What's the matter?'

'How do you feel about him, Frankie?'

'He's a good lawyer. Why?'

'A good lawyer? He got you sent up, didn't he?'

'That wasn't his fault. He wanted me to plead not guilty, but this guy I knew, he was a kid in and out of jail since he could walk, he told me I should cop out, that maybe I'd get a suspended sentence. So I argued with Norden, and he kept saying not guilty, not guilty, but I told him I'd decided to cop out. So I copped out, and got ten years. Some jerk I was, huh?'

'So you liked Norden, huh?'

'Yeah, he was okay.'

'Maybe he shoulda argued a little more, don't you think? Convinced you? Don't you think that's what a good lawyer shoulda done?'

'He tried to, but I wouldn't listen. I figured all I had on my record so far was juvenile stuff, you know, rumbles, and once when I was carrying a zip gun, the Sullivan Act. But I figured, what it amounted to, the burglary rap was a first offense really, and I figured if I copped out they'd go easy, maybe make it a suspended sentence. Instead, we got a judge he figured I'd learn a lesson behind bars for a little while." Frankie shrugged. 'Maybe he was right.'

'You're a pretty nice fellow, ain't you, Frankie? You forgive Norden for steering you wrong, and now you're forgiving the judge for sending you away. That's real nice of you, Frankie.'

'A judge only has a job to do,' Frankie said, and he shrugged again. 'Listen, I don't understand what this is all about. What's this got to do with . . .?'

'With *what*, Frankie?'

'With . . . well, with *whatever*. With . . . with why you dragged me up here. What's the story?'

'You read the papers, Frankie?'

'Sometimes.'

'When's the last time?'

'I don't know. I go to work early, and I ain't got time to stop for them. Anyway, I don't read so good. That's why I got in all that trouble when I was still in high school. Everybody else was reading . . .'

'Yeah, let's never mind the underprivileged-kid bit, Frankie,' Masterson said. 'When's the last time you read a newspaper?'

'I don't know. I just told you . . .'

'You listen to the radio?' Brock asked in his even, emotionless voice.

'Sure I do.'

'You heard about the guy who's going around shooting people?'

'What guy?'

'The sniper.'

'Yeah, I think I heard something about it. Yeah, that's right, he shot some guy up in Riverhead, didn't he? A fruit man or something. Yeah, I heard that.' Frankie looked up at the detectives, puzzled. 'I don't get it. What . . . what . . . ?'

'All right, let's cut the crap,' Brock said, and the room went silent.

Frankie looked up at them expectantly, and they looked down at him patiently, waiting. Frankie wasn't sure what crap he was expected to cut, but he suddenly wanted that door to be unlocked, suddenly wanted the telephone to ring. The two detectives stood over him silently, and he looked up at them silently, each waiting, he not knowing what he was expected to say or do, they seemingly possessed of infinite patience. He wiped his upper lip. He shrugged, the silence lengthened unbearably. He could hear the clock ticking on the wall.

'Look,' he said at last, 'could you tell me what . . . ?' and Brock hit him. He hit him suddenly and effortlessly, his arm coming up swiftly from its position at his side, his hand open, his palm catching Frankie noisily on the cheek. Frankie was more surprised than hurt. He brought his hands up too late, felt the stinging slap, and then looked up at Brock with a puzzled expression.

'What'd I do?' he asked plaintively.

'Randolph Norden is dead, Frankie,' Masterson said.

Frankie sat still for several moments, looking up at the detectives, sweating freely now, feeling trapped in this small room with its locked door. 'What . . . what do you want from me?'

Brock hit him again. He hit him very hard this time, drawing back his fist and smashing it full into Frankie's face. Frankie felt the hard knuckles colliding with his nose, and he said, 'What are you doing?' and started to come out of the chair, when Masterson put both meaty hands on his shoulders and slammed him down again, so hard that the shock rumbled up his spine and into his neck. 'Hey!' he said, and Brock hit him once more, and this time Frankie felt something break in his nose, heard the terrible crunching sound of his own nose breaking, and then immediately touched his upper lip and felt the blood pouring onto his hand.

'Why'd you do it, Frankie?' Brock said tightly.

'I didn't do nothing. Listen, will you listen . . . ?'

Brock bunched his fist and raised it over his head as if he were holding a hammer in it, and then brought it down as if the fist itself were the head of the hammer, onto the bridge of Frankie's nose, and Frankie screamed in pain and fell out of the chair. Masterson kicked him in the ribs, once, sharply.

'Get up,' Brock said.

'Look, look, will you please . . . ?'

'*Get up!*'

He struggled to his feet. There was an unbearable pain in his nose, and blood was dripping onto his lip and all over his white shirt and the new tie he had bought for his afternoon date.

'Listen,' he said, 'listen to me. I've got a job, I'm working, I'm straight, can't you understand . . . ?' and Brock hit him. 'Listen!' he screamed. '*Listen to me!* I didn't do anything! You hear me? Can you understand me?' and Brock hit him again, because Brock did not understand him at all. Brock understood only that Frankie Pierce was a punk who had been cutting up other punks in street rumbles since the time he was twelve. He understood only that the punk named Frankie Pierce had graduated into the cheap thief who was Frankie Pierce, and then into the jailbird, and then into the ex-con, all of which still made him a punk, that was the understanding Brock had. So he kept following him around the room while Frankie backed against the walls trying to explain that he was straight now, he was honest, he was working, kept hitting the broken nose over and over again until it was only a sodden shapeless mass plastered to his face, don't you understand, hit him as Frankie reached for the phone and tried to pick up the receiver, won't you please understand, kicked him when he fell to the floor whimpering in pain, please, please, understand, and then stood over him with his fists bunched and ready and yelled, 'Why'd you kill him, you little son of a bitch?' and hit him again when he couldn't answer.

The girl waited for Frankie in the park for two hours. He never showed up for the date because Brock and Masterson kept him in the locked interrogation room for six hours, alternately rousing him and then beating him senseless again, while asking why he had killed a man he hadn't seen in five years. At the end of their session, they were convinced he was clean. They wrote out a report stating he had broken parole by assaulting a police officer during a routine interrogation.

Frankie Pierce was removed to the criminal ward of the hospital on Walker Island in the River Dix, to recuperate before he was shipped back to the penitentiary at Castleview, upstate.

Chapter Eleven

A sure sign that nothing was happening on this case – oh, yeah, maybe a cheap hood was being beaten up and made to realize you can't go home again – was the fact that time was passing. It was true that there had been no murders since Andrew Mulligan drank his last drink, but time was nonetheless flitting by, and there was no greater proof of this than the reappearance of Bert Kling at the squad room, looking tanned and healthy and very blond from the sun after his vacation. Lieutenant Byrnes, who didn't like to see anyone looking so well-rested, immediately assigned him to the Sniper Case.

On the afternoon of May 7, while Meyer and Carella were uptown requestioning Mrs O'Grady, the nice little woman who had been present when Salvatore Palumbo called it quits, Bert Kling was in the office looking over the Sniper file and trying to acquaint himself with what had gone before. When the blond young lady walked into the squad room, he barely looked up.

Meyer and Carella were sitting in the living room of a two-story clapboard dwelling in Riverhead while Mrs O'Grady poured them coffee and tried to recall the incidents preceding the death of Salvatore Palumbo.

'I think he was weighing out some fruit. Do you take cream and sugar?'

'Black for me,' Meyer said.

'Detective Carella?'

'A little of each.'

'Should I call you Detective Carella, or Mr Carella, or just what?'

'Whichever is most comfortable to you.'

'Well, if you don't mind, I'll call you Mr Carella. Because calling you Detective Carella sounds as if you should be calling me Housewife O'Grady. Is that all right?'

'That's fine, Mrs O'Grady. He was weighing out some fruit, you said.'

'Yes.'

'And then what? I know we've been over all this, but . . .'

'Then he just fell onto the stand and slid down to the sidewalk. I guess I began screaming.'

'Did you hear the shot, Mrs O'Grady?'

'Yes.'

'When?'

'Just before the train pulled in.'

'What train?'

'The train. Upstairs.'

'The elevated?'

'Yes.'

'It was coming into the platform when Mr Palumbo got shot?'

'Well, to tell you the truth,' Mrs O'Grady said, 'I'm not too clear about the sequence. I mean, I heard the shot, but at the time I didn't think it was a shot, I figured it was a backfire or a blowout – who expects to hear a gun go off while you're buying fruit from a man? So, although I heard the shot, I didn't realize Sal . . . Mr Palumbo . . . had been shot. I thought he was suffering a heart attack or something, him falling like that, and the fruit all tumbling off the stand. But then, of course, I saw the blood at the back of his head, and I guess my mind made the connection between the explosion I had heard and the fact that Sal was . . . well, I didn't know he was dead . . . but certainly hurt.'

'And the train?'

'Well, what I'm trying to say is that everything happened so fast. The train coming in . . . I think it was coming in, though it may have been leaving . . . and the shot, and Sal falling down hurt. It all happened so fast that I'm not sure of the time sequence, the poor man.'

'You're not sure, then, whether the train was pulling into the station or leaving it.'

'That's right. But it was moving, that's for sure. It wasn't just standing still in the station.'

'Did you see anyone on the station platform, Mrs O'Grady?'

'No, I didn't even look up there. I thought it was a backfire at first, you see, or something like that. It never crossed my mind that somebody was shooting a gun. So I had no reason to look around to see who or what it was. Besides, I was buying fruit, and to tell you the truth, the shot didn't register on my mind at all, either as a backfire or *anything*, it just didn't register until I began thinking about it afterward, *after* Sal was dead, do you know what I mean? It's hard to explain, but there are so *many* noises in the city, and you just don't listen to them anymore, you just go about your business.'

'Then, in effect, you really *didn't* hear the shot at the time. Or at least, you didn't react to it.'

'That's right. But there was a shot.' Mrs O'Grady paused. 'Why are you asking? Do they make silencers for rifles?'

'They're not manufactured, Mrs O'Grady, no. There are both state and federal regulations against the use of silencers. But any fairly competent machinist could turn one out in his own garage, especially if he had something like murder on his mind.'

'I always thought silencers were very complicated things. They always look so complicated in the movies.'

'Well, they're really very simple in principle. When you put a silencer on a gun or a rifle, you're closing a series of doors, in effect. You're muffling the sound.'

'Doors?' Mrs O'Grady asked.

'Try to visualize a piece of tubing, Mrs O'Grady, perhaps an inch and a half in diameter, and about eight inches long. Inside this tube is a series of separated eight-inch baffling plates, the closed 'doors' that absorb the sound. That's a silencer. A man can fashion one on a home lathe.'

'Well, I heard a shot,' Mrs O'Grady said.

'And yet you didn't turn, you didn't look up, you didn't comment upon it to Mr Palumbo.'

'No.'

'The rifle that fired a three-oh-eight-calibre bullet would have been a high-powered rifle, Mrs O'Grady. Powerful enough to have felled a charging lion.'

'So?'

'It would have made a pretty loud noise.'

'So?'

'I'm only suggesting, Mrs O'Grady, that your reconstruction of what happened may only be a result of your later thoughts about the incident.'

'I heard a shot,' Mrs O'Grady insisted.

'Did you? Or is it only now, now that you know Mr Palumbo was shot and killed, that you think you remember hearing a shot? In other words, Mrs O'Grady, is logic interfering with your memory?'

'Logic?'

'Yes. If a bullet was fired, and if a man was killed, there must have been a shot. And if there was shot, you must have heard it. And if you heard it, you must have dismissed it as a backfire or a blowout.'

'I'm sure that's what happened.'

'Have you ever heard a blowout, Mrs O'Grady?'

'Yes, I think so.'

'And what happened? Did you ignore it, or were you momentarily startled?'

'I suppose I was startled.'

'Yet when Mr Palumbo was killed with a high-powered rifle, which would have made a very loud noise, you only *later* remembered hearing a shot. Does that sound valid?'

'Well, I *think* I heard a shot,' Mrs O'Grady said.

Carella smiled. 'Maybe you did,' he answered. 'We'll check with the man in the change booth on the platform. In any case, Mrs O'Grady, you've been extremely cooperative and most helpful.'

'He was a nice man,' Mrs O'Grady said. 'Sal. He was really a very nice man.'

The man in the change booth at the station platform above Palumbo's store was not a very nice man at all. He was a crotchety old grouch who began giving the detectives trouble the moment they approached the booth.

'How many?' he asked immediately.

'How many what?' Meyer asked.

'Can't you read the sign? State how many tokens you want.'

'We don't want any tokens,' Meyer said.

'Map of the system is on the wall right there,' the attendant said. 'I'm not paid to give out travel information.'

'Are you paid to cooperate with the police?' Carella asked amiably.

'The what?'

'Police,' Meyer said, and he flashed the tin.

'What's that say? I'm a little nearsighted.'

'It says "Detective,"' Meyer answered.

'Yeah?'

'Yeah.'

'Well, what do you want?'

'We want to know the best way to get to Carruthers Street in Calm's Point,' Carella said.

'What?'

'You heard me.'

'I never heard of Carruthers Street.'

'That's because I just made it up,' Carella said.

'Listen, what are you, a bunch of wise guys?' the attendant asked.

'We're two college kids on a scavenger hunt,' Meyer said. 'We're supposed to bring back a hibernating bear, and you're the first one we've seen all day.'

'Haha,' the attendant said mirthlessly. 'That's very funny.'

'What's your name?' Carella asked.

'Quentin. You going to give me trouble? I'm a civil-service employee, too, you know. It ain't nice to give your own kind trouble.'

'What's your first name, Mr Quentin?'

'Stan.'

'Stan Quentin?' Meyer asked incredulously.

'Yeah, what's the matter with that?' The old man peered into Meyer's face. 'What's *your* name?'

Meyer, whose full name was Meyer Meyer, the legacy of a practical-joking father, hastily said, 'Let's never mind the names, okay, Mr Quentin? We only want to ask you some questions about what happened downstairs last week, okay?'

'The wop who was killed, you mean?' Quentin asked.

'Yeah, the wop who was killed,' Carella said.

'So what about him? I didn't even know him.'

'Then how do you know he was a wop?'

'I read his name in the papers.' He turned to Meyer again. 'What's wrong with Stan Quentin, would you mind telling me?'

'Nothing. They almost named a prison after you.'

'Yeah? Which one?'

'Alcatraz,' Meyer said.

The old man stared at him blankly. 'I don't get it,' he said.

'Tell us about the day of the murder.'

'There's nothing to tell. The guy downstairs got shot, that's all.'

'He got shot from this platform, Mr Quentin,' Meyer said. 'For all we know, *you* could have done it.'

'Haha,' Quentin said.

'Why not?'

'Why not? Because I can't even read what your shield says from a distance of three feet. How the hell could I shoot a man who's all the way down in the street?'

'You could have used a telescopic sight, Mr Quentin.'

'Sure. I could also be governor of the state.'

'Did you see anyone come onto the platform carrying a rifle?'

'Look,' Quentin said, 'maybe you don't understand me. I don't see too good, you get that? I am the most cockeyed guy you'll ever meet in your life.'

'Then why aren't you wearing glasses?' Carella asked.

'What, and spoil my looks?' Quentin said seriously.

'How do you know how much money a person is giving you?' Meyer asked.

'I hold the bill up to my face.'

'So, let's get this straight, all right? Even if somebody had come up here with a rifle, you wouldn't have seen what he was carrying. Is that what you're saying?'

'I thought I said it pretty plain,' Quentin said. 'What do you mean, Alcatraz? How's that named after me?'

'You work on it, Mr Quentin,' Meyer said. 'Have you got a train schedule here?'

'The company don't issue schedules. You know that.'

'I know the company doesn't, but isn't there one issued to employees? Don't *you* know when the trains come in and out of this platform?'

'Sure I know.'

'Do you think you might be willing to tell us?'

'Sure.'

'When, Mr Quentin? We're sort of anxious to get back to the party.'

'What party?'

'The one we're out on the scavenger hunt from.'

'Haha,' Quentin said.

'So how about it?'

'You want to know every train that comes in and out of here?'

'No. We only want to know the trains that come in and out on the uptown side at about twelve noon. That's what we'd like to know. Do you think you can supply us with the information?'

'I think so,' Quentin said. 'Alcatraz, huh? Where's that?'

'In the water off San Francisco.'

'They made a picture of that once, didn't they?'

'That's right.'

'What'd they do? Use my name in the picture?'

'Why don't you write to the movie company?' Carella suggested.

'I will. Who made the picture?'

'It was an M-G-M musical,' Meyer said.

'Haha,' Quentin said. 'Come on, who made the picture?'

'A couple of convicts,' Carella said. 'It was part of the prison therapy programme.'

'Can I sue a convict?'

'Nope.'

'Then what's the use?'

'There's no use. Just be grateful they named the joint after you, that's all. And as a gesture of your gratefulness, tell us about the trains, okay?'

'You're just a bunch of wise guys,' Quentin said sourly. 'I knew that the minute you came up to the booth.'

'The trains,' Meyer prompted.

'Okay, okay. Weekdays?'

'Weekdays.'

'Around noon?'

'Around noon.'

'There's one gets in at eleven-fifty-seven, pulls out about thirty seconds later.'

'And the next one?'

'Gets in at twelve-oh-three.'

'And leaves?'

'Same thing. Thirty seconds or so. They only open the doors, let the people off and on, and shove right off. What do you think this is? A first-class coach to Istanbul? This is the elevated system.'

'How are your ears, Mr Quentin?'

'My what?'

'Your ears. Did you hear a shot at about twelve noon on the day Mr Palumbo was killed?'

'What day was that?'

'It was May first.'

'That's only a date. What was the day? I only remember days by days.'

'It was a Tuesday.'

'A week ago?'

'A week ago tomorrow.'

'Nope, I didn't hear no shot on a week ago tomorrow.'

'Thanks, Mr Quentin,' Meyer said. 'You have been extremely helpful.'

'You know those guys at Alcatraz?'

'We know a lot of guys at Alcatraz,' Carella said.

'Tell them to take my name off it, you hear?'

'We will,' Carella said.

'Damn right,' Quentin said.

In the street downstairs, Meyer said, 'So?'

'I think our man used a silencer.'

'Me, too.'

'That's a lot of help, isn't it?'

'Oh, yes. Oh, my, yes, that's a great deal of help.'

'This case is making me giddy, you know that?'

'You want some coffee?'

'No, spoil my appetite. I want to go see the elevator operator at Norden's apartment building again, and then I want to talk to the woman who witnessed Forrest's death again, and then . . .'

'Let's send some of our little helpers.'

'I want to talk to them myself.'

'Why?'

'I don't trust cops,' Carella said, grinning.

The young blonde who walked into the squad room while Bert Kling was poring over the files was Cindy Forrest. She was carrying a black tote bag in one hand and a manila folder under her arm, and she was looking for Detective Steve Carella, ostensibly to give him the material in the folder. Cindy – by her own admission – was a nineteen-year-old girl who would be twenty in June and who had seen it all and heard it all, and also done a little. She thought Steve Carella was an attractive man in a glamour profession – listen, some girls have a thing for cops – and whereas she knew he was married and suspected he had four dozen kids, she nonetheless thought it might be sort of interesting to see him again, the marriage contract being a remote and barely understood cultural curiosity to most nineteen-year-olds going on twenty. She didn't know what would happen with Carella when she saw him again, though she had constructed a rather elaborate fantasy in her own mind and knew exactly what she *wished* would happen. The fact that he was married didn't disturb her at all, nor was she very troubled by the fact that he was almost twice her age. She saw in him a man with an appealing animal vitality, not too dumb for a cop, who had just possibly seen and heard even more than she had, and who had most certainly *done* more than she had, her own experience being limited to once in the back seat of an automobile and another time on a bed at a party in New Ashton. She could remember the names of both boys, but they were only boys, that was the thing, and Steve Carella seemed to her to be a man, which was another thing again and something she felt she ought to experience *now*, before she got married herself one day and tied down with kids.

She hadn't consulted Carella on the possibility as yet, but she felt this was only a minor detail. She was extremely secure in her own good looks and in an undeniable asset called youth. She was certain that once Carella understood her intentions, he would be happy to oblige, and they would then enter into a madly delirious and delicious love affair which would end some months from now because, naturally, it could never be; but Carella would remember her forever, the nineteen-year-old going on twenty who had shared those tender moments of passion, who had enriched his life, who had rewarded him with her inquiring young mind and her youthful, responsive body.

Feeling like Héloïse about to keep an assignation with Abelard, she walked into the squad room expecting to find Carella – and instead found Bert Kling.

Kling was sitting at his own desk in a shaft of sunlight that came through the grilled window and settled on his blond head like a halo. He was suntanned and muscular, and he was wearing a white shirt open at the throat, and he was bent over the papers spread on his desk, the sun touching his hair, looking very healthy and handsome and young.

She hated him on sight.

'I beg your pardon,' she said.

Kling looked up. 'Yes, miss?'

'I'd like to see Detective Carella, please.'

'Not here right now,' Kling answered. 'Can I help you?'

'Who are *you*?' Cindy asked.

'Detective Kling.'

'How do you do?' She paused. 'You did say *Detective* Kling?'

'That's right.'

'You seem so' – she hesitated on the word, as if it were loathsome to her – 'young. To be a detective, I mean.'

Kling sensed her hostility immediately, and immediately reacted in a hostile manner. 'Well, you see,' he said, 'I'm the boss's son. That's how I got to be a detective so fast.'

'Oh, I see.' She looked around the squad room, obviously annoyed by Kling, and the room, and Carella's absence, and the world. 'When will he be back? Carella?'

'Didn't say. He's out making some calls.'

With a ghoulishly sweet grin, Cindy said, 'And they left *you* to mind the store. How nice.'

'Yeah,' Kling answered, 'they left me to mind the store.' He was not smiling, because he was not enjoying this little snotnose who came up here with her *Saturday Evening Post* face and her college-girl talk. 'So since I'm minding the store, what is it you want, miss? I'm busy.'

'Yes, I can see that.'

'What can I do for you?'

'Nothing. I'll wait for Carella, if you don't mind.' She was opening the gate in the slatted rail divider when Kling came out of his chair swiftly and abruptly.

'Hold it right there!' he snapped.

'Wh-what?' Cindy asked, her eyes opening wide.

'Just *hold* it, miss!' Kling shouted, and to Cindy's shocked surprise, he pulled a pistol from a holster clipped to his belt and pointed it right at her heart.

'Get in here,' he said. 'Don't reach into that bag!'

'What? Are you . . .?'

'*In*!' Kling shouted.

She obeyed him instantly, because she was certain he was going to shoot her dead in the next moment. She had heard stories about cops who lost their minds and went around shooting anything that moved. She was also beginning to wonder whether he really was a cop, and not simply a stray hoodlum who had wandered up here.

'Empty your bag on the desk,' Kling said.

'Listen, what the hell do you think you're . . .?'

'Empty it, miss,' he said menacingly.

'I'm going to *sue* you, you know,' she said coldly, and turned over her bag, spilling the contents onto the desk.

Kling went through the pile of junk rapidly. 'What's in that folder?' he asked.

'Some stuff for Detective Carella.'

'On the desk.'

She put the folder down. Kling loosened the ties on it, and stuck his hand into it. He kept the gun trained at Cindy's middle, and she watched him with growing exasperation.

'All right?' she asked at last.

'Put your hands up over your head as high as you can get them.'

'Listen, I don't have to . . .'

'Miss,' he said warningly, and she raised her hands.

'Higher. Stretch.'

'Why?'

'Because I'd really like to frisk you, but this'll have to do.'

'Oh, boy, are you getting in trouble,' she said, and she reached up for the ceiling. He studied her body minutely, looking for the bulge of a gun anywhere under her clothes. He saw only a trim, youthful figure in a white sweater and a straight black skirt. No unexplainable bulges.

'All right, put your hands down. What do you want with Carella?'

'I want to give him what's in that folder. Now, suppose you explain . . .'

'Miss, a couple of years back we had a girl come in here asking for Steve Carella, who happened to be out making a call. None of us could help her. She said she wanted to wait for Steve. So she marched through that gate, just the way you were about to do, and then she pulled out a thirty-eight, and the next thing we knew, she told us she was here to *kill* Carella.'

'What's that got to do with . . .?'

'So, miss. I'm only the boss's son and a very dumb cop, but that dame put us through hell for more hours than I care to remember. And I know enough to come in out of the rain. Especially when there's lightning around.'

'I see. And is this what you do with every girl who comes into the squad room? You frisk them?'

'I didn't frisk you, miss.'

'Are you finished with me?'

'Yes.'

'Then go frisk yourself,' Cindy said, and she turned away from him coldly and began putting the junk back into her bag.

'Let me help you with that,' Kling said.

'Mister, you'd better just stay as far away from me as possible. I don't have a thirty-eight, but if you take one step closer to me, I'll clonk you right on the head with my shoe.'

'Look, you weren't exactly radiating . . .'

'I've never in my entire life dealt with anyone as . . .'

'. . . sunshine when you came in here. You looked sore, and I automatically . . .'

'. . . suspicious, or as rude, or as overbearing in his manner . . .'

'. . . assumed you . . .'

'Shut up when I'm talking!' Cindy shouted.

'Look, miss,' Kling said angrily. 'this happens to be a police station, and I happen to be a policeman, and I . . .'

'*Some* policeman!' Cindy snapped.

'You want me to kick you out of here?' Kling said menacingly.

'I want you to apologize to me!' Cindy yelled.

'Yeah, you've got a fat chance.'

'Yeah, I'm going to tell you something, Mister Big Shot Boss's Son. If you think a citizen . . .'

'I'm not the boss's son,' Kling yelled.

'You said you were!' Cindy yelled back.

'Only because you were so snotty!'

'*I* was snotty? *I was* . . .'

'I'm not used to seventeen-year-old brats . . .'

'I'm nineteen! Damn you, I'm *twenty*!'

'Make up your mind!' Kling shouted, and Cindy picked up her bag by the straps and swung it at him. Kling instinctively put up one of his hands, and the black leather collided with the flat palm, and all the junk Cindy had painstakingly put back into the bag came spilling out again, all over the floor.

They both stood stock-still, as if the spilling contents of the bag were an avalanche. Cigarettes, matches, lipstick, eyeshadow, sunglasses, a comb, an address and appointment book, a bottle of APC tablets, a book of twenty-five gummed parcel-post labels, a chequebook, a compact, more matches, a package of Chiclets, an empty cigarette package, a scrap of yellow paper with the handwirtten words 'Laundry, Quiz Philosophy,' a hairbrush, an eyelash curler, two more combs, a package of Kleenex, several soiled Kleenex tissues, more matches, a pillbox without any pills in it, a box of Sucrets, two pencils, a wallet, more matches, a ball-point pen, three pennies, several empty cellophane wrappers, and a peach pit all came tumbling out of the bag and fell onto the floor to settle in a disorderly heap between them.

Kling looked down at the mess.

Cindy looked down at the mess.

Silently, she knelt and began filling the bag again. She worked without looking up at him, without saying a word. Then she rose, picked up the manila folder from the desk, put it into Kling's hands, and frostily said, 'Will you please see that Detective Carella gets this?'

Kling accepted the folder. 'Who shall I say left it?'

'Cynthia Forrest.'

'Listen, I'm sorry about . . .'

'Detective Kling,' Cindy said, enunciating every word sharply and distinctly, 'I think you are the biggest bastard I've ever met in my life.'

Then she turned and walked out of the squad room.

Kling stared after her a moment, and then shrugged. He carried the manila folder to Carella's desk, remembered abruptly that the name Cynthia Forrest had been in at least two of the D.D. reports he'd read, realized immediately that she was the daughter of the dead Anthony Forrest, almost started out of the squad room in an attempt to catch up with her, said 'The hell with it' aloud, and plunked the folder down on Carella's desktop.

The folder did not contain as much junk as Cindy's bag had contained, but it did hold a great deal of material on the man who had been her father. Most of the stuff dealt with his days as a student at Ramsey University – some of his old term papers, pictures of him with the football squad, several report cards, a notebook he had kept, and, oh, stuff like that. Carella would not see the contents of the folder until the next morning, because he would be occupied uptown all that day, and would go directly home to dinner with his wife and two kids afterward.

Actually, there wasn't much in the folder that would have helped him or the case. Except perhaps one thing.

The one thing was a frayed and yellowing theatre programme.

The front of the programme read:

The Wig and Buskin Society

PRESENTS

THE LONG VOYAGE HOME

A ONE ACT PLAY BY

Eugene O'Neill

The programme sat on top of Carella's desk, inside the manila folder. The inside of the programme listed the past activities of the drama group on the left-hand page, together with a well-wishing half-page ad from the graduating class of June 1940. The back of the programme carried a full-page ad for Harry's Luncheonette, Ice Cream Treats Our Specialty, near the school.

The inside right-hand page of the programme contained the following printed information:

CAST IN ORDER OF APPEARANCE

FAT JOE	*Thomas Di Pasquale*
NICK	*Andrew Mulligan*
MAG	*Margaret Buff*
OLSON	*Randolph Norden*
DRISCOLL	*Anthony Forrest*
COCKY	*David Arthur Cohen*
IVAN	*Peter Kelby*
KATE	*Helen Struthers*
FREDA	*Blanche Ruth Lettiger*
FIRST ROUGH	*Salvatore Palumbo*
SECOND ROUGH	*Rudy Fenstermacher*

That night, while Detective Steve Carella was sitting down to dinner with his wife, Teddy, and the twins, Mark and April, a man named Rudy Fenstermacher was walking from the subway to his home in Majesta.

He never made it, because a .308-calibre bullet hit him right in the head and killed him instantly.

Chapter Twelve

Carella started the next morning by yelling.

He was not a yelling man by nature, and he was very fond of Bert Kling, at whom he was directing his tirade. But he was roaring anyway, so loud that the cops downstairs in the locker room could hear him.

'You call yourself a cop?' he shouted. 'What kind of a cop . . .?'

'I didn't think to look, okay?' Kling said patiently. 'She said it was for you, so . . .'

'I thought you'd been assigned to this case.'

'That's right,' Kling said patiently.

'Then why didn't . . .?'

'How the hell was I supposed to know what was in that folder?'

'She gave it to you, didn't she?'

'She said it was for you.'

'So you didn't even look to see what . . .'

'I *felt* inside it,' Kling said. 'When she first came up.'

'You what?'

'I felt inside it.'

'You *felt*? Did you say 'felt'?'

'That's right.'

'What the hell for?'

'To see if she was carrying a gun.'

'Who?'

'Cynthia Forrest.'

'Carrying a *what*?'

'A gun.'

'Cynthia Forrest?'

'Yes.'

'What could have possibly given you the idea that Cynthia Forrest . . .?'

'Because she came up here asking for you, and when I told her you weren't here, she said she'd wait and then began coming through that gate. And I remembered what happened with Virginia Dodge that time, and I figured maybe this one wanted to put a hole in your head, too. That's why. Okay?'

'Oh, boy,' Carella said.

'So I felt in the folder, and I looked in her purse, and when I saw she wasn't heeled, I just took the folder and dumped it on your desk, after I had an argument with her.'

'Without looking inside it.'

'That's right.'

'Oh, boy,' Carella said.

'Look, I know I'm just a stupid amateur when it comes to the mastermind . . .'

'Cut it out,' Carella said

'. . . of the squad, but I'm new on this case, and I don't know who half these people are, and I'm not in the habit of opening something that was specifically . . .'

'Go get him a crying towel, will you, Meyer?'

'. . . left for someone else. Now, if you want to make a big federal case out of this . . .'

'*A man was killed last night!*' Carella shouted.

'I know that, Steve,' Kling said. 'But there are a lot of other names on that college programme. And while we're arguing here about what I did or didn't do, our man might be out taking a potshot at another one of them.' Kling paused. 'You want to argue, or shall we hit the phone book and try to locate some of the others?'

'For your information, Junior G-man, Meyer and I got to the squad room at seven o'clock this morning, after spending all night with the family of Rudy Fenstermacher, who was killed last night because . . .'

'Steve, get off my back,' Kling said. 'I'm not responsible for what happened last night!'

'Maybe you're not!' Carella shouted.

'No maybes!'

'Okay! I'm trying to tell you we began checking out the names on that programme the minute I found it on my desk. There were eleven people in that play, and six of them are already dead. Of the remaining five, we've been able to trace only two of the men. The third man isn't listed in the phone book, and the women are probably married, with new names. We've already contacted the university, and they're going to call back if they have any luck. In the meantime, we've called both of the men whose whereabouts are known, and they're expecting our visit. Now, do you think if I gave you a name and address you could find your way to the right house and manage to ask the man some questions about . . .?'

'Listen, Steve,' Kling said, 'you're beginning to burn me up, you know that?'

'The man's name is Thomas Di Pasquale. He played Fat Joe in the O'Neill play. His address is four-one-nine Servatius, right here in Isola. He's expecting you.'

'What do you want to know from him?' Kling asked.

'I want to know just what happened back in nineteen-forty.'

Thomas Di Pasquale lived in a luxurious apartment building on the city's South Side. When Kling rang his doorbell that morning, he shouted, 'Come in, come in, it's open,' and Kling tried the knob and opened the door onto a wide, thickly carpeted entrance foyer, beyond which was a sunken living room, and a man on a telephone.

The man who had played Fat Joe in a college production years ago was now tall and slim, and somewhat over forty years old. He was wearing a silk dressing gown and had the telephone to his ear as Kling entered the apartment and closed the door and stood waiting in the foyer. Without looking in Kling's direction, and without stopping his telephone conversation, Di Pasquale gestured to an easy chair opposite him, lighted a cigarette, paused for a moment to allow whoever was on the other end to say something, and then said, 'Hold it, Harry, hold it right there. That's where we stop doing business. There's nothing more to talk about.'

Kling took the seat opposite Di Pasquale, and pretended not to be listening to the conversation.

'No, Harry, but when you start talking in terms of forty G's for someone of this guy's standing and reputation, we got nothing further to say. So if you don't mind, Harry, I'm very busy, and I'm late for the office now, so . . .'

Kling lighted a cigarette while Di Pasquale listened for a few seconds. 'Yeah, well, then, let me hear you *really* talking, Harry. Who? That's a screen writer by you? That's a French fag by me. He can't even speak English, you expect him to do a screenplay about the West? For Chrissake, Harry, make sense.'

He covered the mouthpiece, looked up at Kling, said, 'Hi, there's some coffee in the kitchen, if you want some,' and then immediately said into the phone, 'What do I care if he won the French Academy Award? You know what you can do with the French Academy Award, don't you? Look, Harry, I'm not interested in who you can get for forty G's. If you want to hire a French fag to write a screenplay about the West, then go right ahead. And good luck to you.' Di Pasquale paused. 'What do you mean, how much am I asking? Make me a sensible offer, for Chrissake! Start around a hundred, and then maybe I'll listen a little.' He covered the mouthpiece again. 'There's coffee in the kitchen,' he said to Kling.

'I've already had breakfast.'

'Well, if you want a cup, there's some in the kitchen. What do you mean, he never got a hundred in his life? He got a hundred and a quarter from Metro the last time out, and the time before that he got a hundred and five from Fox! Now, you want to talk, Harry, or you want to waste my time? Well, what is it? Who? Harry, what do I care about Clifford Odets? I don't represent Clifford Odets, and anyway, can Clifford Odets write a Western? Well, then, fine. If Clifford Odets can write *anything*, then you just go get Clifford Odets. Yeah, and see what *he* costs you! What? No. No, we're starting at a hundred thousand, that's where we start to talk. Well, you think about it, Harry, and give me a ring back. I'll be leaving for the office in a little while. Please, Harry, don't start with the old song and dance again. I don't care if you're gonna have Liz *Taylor* in the picture, which you're not anyway. Stick Liz Taylor in front of the camera without lines to say, and see how long she can ad-lib, go ahead. Will you call me back? What? *How* much? Seventy-five? Don't be ridiculous. If I even called him up and told him seventy-five, you know what he'd do? He'd go right over to William Morris tomorrow. That's the truth. I wouldn't insult him. Well, you think about it, I've got company. What? Yeah, yeah, *six* naked blonds, what do you think? We know how to live here in the East. Call me back, baby, huh? I wouldn't steer you wrong, believe me, baby, have I ever sold you a lox? This guy writes like a dream, you could shoot the movie right off the paper it's written on, you don't even need actors, huh, baby? Good, good, I'll hear from you, fine, good-bye, baby, yeah, at the office, so long, sure, baby, think about it, right, good-bye now, yeah, nice talking to you, so long, baby.'

He hung up and turned to Kling.

'Big jerk, he never made a good movie in his life. You want some coffee?'

'Thanks, I've had breakfast.'

'So have a cup of coffee, it'll kill you?'

Di Pasquale turned and walked toward the kitchen. Over his shoulder he said, 'What's your name?'

'Detective Kling,' Kling yelled after him.

'You're a little young to be a detective, ain't you?'

'No, there are men my age who've . . .'

'Where'd you get that tan?' Di Pasquale shouted from the kitchen.

'I was on vacation. Just got back to work yesterday.'

'Looks terrific on you, kid. Blond guys look great with tans. Me, I turn red like a lobster. You take cream and sugar?'

'Yes.'

'All right, I'll bring the works out. Seventy-five grand, he offers. I wasn't kidding him. I call the writer with an offer like that, he'll tell me to go straight to hell.' Di Pasquale came back into the living room carrying a tray with the coffee pot, the cups, and the cream and sugar. He put the tray down and said, 'You wouldn't prefer a drink, would you? No, too early in the morning, huh? What the hell time is it, anyway?'

'It's nine-thirty, Mr Di Pasquale.'

'Yeah. You know what time that guy called me? The guy working with you?'

'Carella?'

'Yeah, him. He called me at seven-thirty, the middle of the night! I woke up, it was so dark I thought I went blind.' Di Pasquale laughed and poured from the coffeepot. 'So what's up, kid?'

'Mr Di Pasquale, were you in a play called *The Long Voyage Home* in nineteen-forty at Ramsey University in this city?'

'Whaaaat?' Di Pasquale said.

'Were you in a play . . .?'

'Yeah, yeah, I heard you, but my God, where did you find *that* out? That was before the beginning of time, almost. That was when dinosaurs were still roaming the earth.'

'*Were* you in that play, Mr Di Pasquale?'

'Sure I was. I played Fat Joe, the bartender. I did a pretty good job, too. I wanted to be an actor then, but I was too fat, you see? When I got out of college, I used to go around making my calls, and all the casting directors told me I was too fat. So I went on a crash diet, look at me now, a ninety-seven-pound weakling, people kick sand in my face. But the funny part was, once I slimmed down, I didn't want to be an actor anymore. So what am I now? An agent! And I do more acting on that telephone every day of the week than I did all the while I was a professional actor. So what about the play, kid, drink your coffee.'

'Do you remember any of the other people who were in that play, Mr Di Pasquale?'

'Only one, this broad named Helen Struthers. Boy, boy, boy, boy, was she something! Beautiful girl, beautiful. I wonder if she ever made it.'

'Do you remember a man named Anthony Forrest?'

'No.'

'Randolph Norden?'

'Randolph Norden . . . yeah, yeah, wait a minute, he played the Swede, yeah, I remember him.'

'Mr Di Pasquale, do you read the newspapers?'

'Sure, I do. *Variety, Hollywood Reporter* . . .'

'Any of the dailies?'

'*Hollywood Reporter* is a daily,' Di Pasquale said.

'I meant outside of the trade papers.'

'Sure I do.'

'Mr Di Pasquale, have you read any of the newspaper coverage on the sniper who's killed six people to date?'

'Sure.'

'Do you know that Randolph Norden was . . .?'

'Oh, my God, Randolph Norden!' Di Pasquale said, and he slapped his forehead. 'Holy Jesus, how come it didn't ring a bell? Of course! Of course, for God's sake! He was killed by this nut, wasn't he? So *that's* why you're here. What happened? Who did it?'

'We don't know yet. I mentioned Randolph Norden only because you said you remembered him. But, Mr Di Pasquale, there seems to be a pattern to the killings . . .'

'Don't tell me,' Di Pasquale said, and he rolled his eyes toward the ceiling.

'What?'

'He's after all of us who were in the play.'

'We think that's a possibility, sir.'

'I knew it.'

'How did you know it, Mr Di Pasquale?'

'What else could it be? Kid, I been selling stories to the movies since before you could walk. What else could it be? Some nut has taken it in his head to knock off everybody who was in that crumby play. Naturally. It stands to reason. Did he get Helen Struthers yet? Because that would be a real shame, believe me. This was a beautiful girl. Though who knows, she may have grown up to be a beast, huh? Who knows?'

'You don't seem particularly frightened by the idea of . . .'

'Frightened? What do you mean?'

'Well, if he's killing everyone who was in that play . . .'

'Me? You mean me?'

'You were in the play, Mr Di Pasquale.'

'Yeah, but . . .'

'So, you see . . .'

'Nah,' Di Pasquale said. He looked at Kling seriously for a moment, and then asked, 'Yeah?'

'Maybe.'

'Pssssss,' Di Pasquale said.

'Do you have any idea who might be doing this, Mr Di Pasquale?'

'Have some more coffee.'

'Thanks.'

'Who could be doing this, huh? Six, you say, huh? Who? Who were the ones killed?'

'Anthony Forrest. I believe you said you didn't know him.'

'No, it doesn't register.'

'Randolph Norden.'

'Yeah.'

'Blanche Lettiger.'

'Blanche Lettiger, no, don't remember her.'

'Salvatore Palumbo.'

'Oh, sure.'

'You know him?'

'Yeah, little Italian immigrant, hot stuff. He was studying English at night session, you know? So he wandered into a rehearsal one night after his class, and it happened we needed somebody for one of the bit parts, I forget which it was. So this little guy who could barely speak English, he took the part. He's supposed to be British, you know? It was a hot sketch, him walking in and talking like a cockney with an Italian accent a mile long. Funny guy. He got killed, huh? That's too bad. He was a nice little man.' Di Pasquale sighed. Who else?'

'A man named Andrew Mulligan.'

'Yeah, I read that. The district attorney. I didn't realize it was the same guy from the play.'

'And last night, a man named Rudy Fenstermacher.'

'That makes five,' Di Pasquale said.

'No, six,' Kling said.

'Norden, right?'

'Yes, and Forrest, and Lettiger . . .'

'And the little Italian guy . . .'

'Right, that's four. And Mulligan and Fenstermacher. That's six.'

'That's right, six. You're right.'

'Can you tell me a little about the play?'

'We did it in the round,' Di Pasquale said. 'We were all kids, you know how these amateur things are. All of us except the little Italian guy, what was his name?'

'Palumbo.'

'Yeah, he must've been maybe thirty-five years old. But the rest of us were all kids, and I guess the play stunk. I can hardly remember it, tell you the truth. Except for this Helen Struthers, who played one of the whores, she wore one of these very low-cut peasant blouses. I wonder what ever happened to her.'

'We're trying to locate her now. You wouldn't know whether she got married, would you? Or left the city?'

'Never saw her before the play, or after it. Oh, yeah, maybe in the halls, you know, between classes, hello, goodbye, like that.'

'Did you graduate from Ramsey, Mr Di Pasquale?'

'Sure. I don't sound like a college graduate, do I?'

'You sound fine, sir.'

'Look, you don't have to snow me. I know what I sound like. But the movie business is full of pants pressers. If I sounded like a college graduate, they'd all get nervous. They want me to sound like *I* work in a tailor shop, too. So that's the way I sound.' He shrugged. 'Listen, I can still quote Chaucer, *Whan that Aprille with his shoures sote*, but who wants to hear Chaucer in the movie business? You quote Chaucer in a producer's office, he'll send for the guys in the white jackets. Yeah, I graduated, class of June nineteen-forty-two.'

'Were you in the service, Mr Di Pasquale?'

'Nope. Punctured eardrum.'

'Tell me some more about the play.'

'Like what? It was a little college play. We cast it, we rehearsed it, we performed it, we struck it. End of story.'

'Who directed it?'

'The faculty adviser, I forget his na – no, wait a minute. Richardson. Professor Richardson, that was it. Boy, the things you remember, huh? This was more than twenty years ago.' Di Pasquale paused. 'You sure somebody's trying to . . .?' He shrugged. 'You know, twenty years is a long, long time. I mean, like, man, that has to be one hell of a grudge to carry for twenty years.'

'Was there any trouble during rehearsals, sir, would you remember?'

'Oh, the usual junk. You know actors. Even the pros are disgusting, all ego and a mile high. Well, amateurs are worse. But I can't remember any big fight or anything like that. Nothing that would last twenty years.'

'How about Professor Richardson? Did everyone in the cast get along with him?'

'Yeah, a harmless guy. Nothing on the ball, but harmless.'

'Then you can't remember anything that might have caused this kind of extreme reaction.'

'Nothing.' Di Pasquale paused reflectively. 'You think this guy is *really* out to get all of us?'

'We're going on that assumption, Mr Di Pasquale.'

'So where does that leave me? Do I get police protection?'

'If you want it.'

'I want it.'

'You'll get it.'

'Pssssss,' Di Pasquale said.

'There's just one other thing, Mr Di Pasquale,' Kling said.

'Yeah, I know. Don't leave town.'

Kling smiled. 'That's just what I was going to say.'

'Sure, what else could you say? I've been in this movie business a long time, kid. I've read them all, I've seen them all. It don't take too much brains to figure it.'

'To figure what?'

'That if somebody's out to get all of us who were in the play, well, kid, figure it. The somebody who's out to get us *could* be somebody who was in the play, too. Right? So, okay, I won't leave town. When are you sending the protection?'

'I'll get a patrolman here within the half-hour. I should tell you, Mr Di Pasquale, that so far the killer has struck without warning and from a distance. I'm not sure what good our protection will . . .'

'Anything's better than nothing,' Di Pasquale said. 'Look, baby, you finished with me?'

'Yes, I think . . .'

'Well, then, good, kid,' he said, leading him to the door. 'If you don't mind, I'm in a hell of a hurry. That guy's gonna call me back at the office, baby, and I've got a million things on my desk, so thanks for coming up and talking to me, huh? I'll be looking for the cop, kid, send him over right away before I'm gone, huh, baby? Good, it was nice seeing you, take it easy, baby,

so long, huh?'
And the door closed behind Kling.

Chapter Thirteen

David Arthur Cohen was a sour little man who made his living being funny.

He operated out of a one-room office on the fourteenth floor of a building on Jefferson, and it was in this office that he greeted the detectives sourly, offered them chairs sourly, and then said, 'It's about these killings, isn't it?'

'That's right, Mr Cohen,' Meyer said.

Cohen nodded. He was a thin man with a pained and suffering look in his brown eyes. He was almost as bald as Meyer, and the two men, sitting on opposite sides of the desk, with Carella standing between them at one end of the desk, looked like a pair of billiard balls waiting for a careful shooter to decide how he would bank them.

'It dawned on me when Mulligan was murdered,' Cohen said. 'I'd recognized the other names before then, but when Mulligan got killed, the whole thing suddenly fell into place. I realized he was after all of us.'

'You realized this when Mulligan was killed, huh?' Meyer said.

'That's right.'

'Mulligan was killed on May second, Mr Cohen. This is May eighth.'

'That's right.'

'That's almost a full week, Mr Cohen.'

'I know that.'

'Why didn't you call the police?'

'What for?'

'To tell us what you suspected.'

'I'm a busy man.'

'We understand that,' Carella said. 'But surely you're not too busy to bother trying to save your own life, are you?'

'Nobody's going to shoot me,' Cohen said.

'No. You have a guarantee of that?'

'Did you guys come up here to argue? I'm too busy to argue.'

'Why didn't you call us, Mr Cohen?'

'I told you. I'm busy.'

'What do you do, Mr Cohen? What makes you so busy?'

'I'm a gag writer.'

'What do you mean?'

'I write gags.'

'For what? For whom?'

'For cartoonists.'

'Comic strips?'

'No, no, single-box stuff. Like you see in the magazines. I write captions for them.'

'Let me get this straight, Mr Cohen,' Carella said. 'You work with a cartoonist who . . .'

'I work with a *lot* of cartoonists.'

'All right, you work with a lot of cartoonists who send you drawings to which you write captions? Is that it?'

'No. I send them the caption, and they make the drawing.'

'From the caption?'

'From a lot more than the caption.'

'I still don't understand.'

'Do you see these filing cabinets?' Cohen asked, waving his arm toward the wall behind him. 'They're full of cartoon ideas. I write up the gag, and then I send a batch of them to any one of the cartoonists on my list. They read the gags. If they like four, or five, or even one, they'll hold it and draw up a rough sketch to show the humour editor of the magazine or newspaper. If the editor okays it, the cartoonists draws up a finish, gets his cheque, and sends me my cut.'

'How much is your cut?'

'I get ten percent of the purchase price.' Cohen looked at the detectives, saw that they were still puzzled, and said, 'Here, let me show you.' He turned in his swivel chair, opened one of the files at random, and pulled out a thick sheaf of small white slips measuring about three by five. 'There's a gag typed on each one of these slips,' Cohen said. 'See? That's the number in the right-hand corner – each gag has a different number – and my name on the bottom of the slip.' He spread several of the slips on the desktop. Meyer and Carella leaned over the desk and read the nearest one.

```
                                          #702

A picket on strike outside the Excelsior Match
Company is being stopped by a passer-by. The
passer-by says:

"Got a match, buddy?"


                         David Arthur Cohen
                         1142 Jefferson Avenue
                         Isola
```

'That's what you send the cartoonist?' Carella asked.

'Yeah,' Cohen said. 'Here's a good one. Look at this one.'

Carella looked.

```
                                                    #708

A barroom. Two men are having a violent fist
fight. In the background are the usual men stand-
ing at the bar. They are all watching a fight on
the television set.

No caption.

                              David Arthur Cohen
                              1142 Jefferson Avenue
                              Isola
```

'That's pretty funny,' Meyer said.

Cohen nodded sourly. 'Here's the one right after it. This is called snowballing. You write one gag, and another one along similar lines suggests itself, and you write that one. Here, look at it.'

```
                                                    #709

Cleanup woman in television studio standing with
surprised look on her face. She is watching a tele-
vision set and the picture is one of her cleaning
up the studio.

No caption.

                              David Arthur Cohen
                              1142 Jefferson Avenue
                              Isola
```

'I don't get it,' Meyer said.

'Well, you either get them or you don't,' Cohen answered, shrugging. 'Here's one of my favourites.'

```
                                                          #712

Car with a telephone. On the back seat, a drunk
in a tuxedo is sprawled out, dead to the world.
Chauffeur, speaking into phone, says:

"He's out just now. Can you call later?"


                              David Arthur Cohen
                              1142 Jefferson Avenue
                              Isola
```

'Is this what you do all day long?' Carella asked.

'All day long,' Cohen said.

'How many of these do you write every day?'

'It depends on how it's going,' Cohen answered. 'Sometimes I can turn out twenty or thirty a day. Other times I'll just sit at the typewriter, and nothing'll come to mind at all. It runs in cycles.'

'Do all cartoonists use gag writers?'

'Not all of them. But a great many. I send to about a dozen of them regularly. I've got . . . oh . . . maybe two hundred gags at market right this minute. I mean, gags they've held and drawn up to show around. I make a pretty good living at it.'

'I'd go out of my mind,' Meyer said.

'Well, it's not bad, really it isn't,' Cohen said.

'Do you enjoy doing it?' Carella asked.

For a moment the three men had forgotten why they were in that office. They were in that office to discuss six murders, but for the moment Cohen was a professional explaining his craft, and Meyer and Carella were two quite different professionals who were fascinated by the details of another man's work.

'Sometimes it gets a little dull,' Cohen said. 'When the ideas aren't coming. But I usually enjoy it, yes.'

'Do your jokes make *you* laugh?' Carella asked.

'Hardly ever.'

'Then how do you know whether they're funny or not?'

'I don't. I just write them and hope somebody else'll think they're funny.' He shrugged. 'I guess they must be, because I sell an awful lot of them. To the best magazines, too.'

'I never met a gag writer before,' Meyer said, cocking his head to one side appreciatively.

'I never met a detective before,' Cohen said, and suddenly the visit came back into focus, suddenly there were two detectives in a small office with a man who was linked to six homicides. In deference to the pleasant tangent, there were perhaps thirty seconds of silence. Then Meyer said, 'Can you tell us anything about that play in nineteen-forty, Mr Cohen?'

'There isn't much to tell,' Cohen said. 'I went into it for kicks. I was a liberal-arts major, and I hadn't yet made up my mind what I wanted to do, so I was experimenting. I fooled around with the drama group for about a year, I guess.'

'Acting?'

'Acting, yes, and I also wrote some skits for a revue we did.'

'When was that?'

'After *The Long Voyage Home*; nineteen-forty-one, I think.'

'What about the people who were in the O'Neill play? What do you remember about them?'

'Gee, that was a long time ago,' Cohen said.

'Was there anything out of line? An incident of some kind? A fight? Even a heated argument?'

'Not that I can recall. It seemed like a pretty smooth production. I think everyone got along pretty well.'

'There were three girls in the play,' Carella said. 'Was there any trouble with them?'

'What kind of trouble?'

'Two guys falling for the same girl, anything like that?'

'No, nothing,' Cohen said.

'Then nothing out of the ordinary happened?'

'I can't remember anything. It was just a routine college show. We all got along pretty well.' Cohen hesitated. 'Even had a party after the show.'

'Anything out of line happen at the party?'

'No.'

'Who was there?'

'The cast, and the crew, and Professor Richardson, the faculty adviser. He left early.'

'How late did you stay?'

'Until it was over.'

'And when was that?'

'Oh, I don't remember. Early in the morning sometime.'

'Who else was there when it broke up?'

'Five or six of us.' Cohen shrugged. 'Six, I guess.'

'Who were the six?'

'Three guys and three girls.'

'Who were the girls?'

'The three who were in the show. Helen Struthers, and the other two.'

'And the guys?'

'Tony Forrest, Randy Norden, and me.'

'Any trouble?'

'No. Look, we were kids. We were all in separate rooms, necking.'

'And then what, Mr Cohen?'

'Then we all went home.'

'All right, what'd you do after you got out of college? Were you in the service?'

'Yes.'

'What branch?'

'The army. The infantry.'

'What was your rank?'

'I was a corporal.'

'And your job?'

Cohen hesitated. 'I . . .'' He shrugged. 'I told you. I was in the infantry.'

'What'd you do in the infantry?'

'I was a sniper,' Cohen said.

The room went silent.

'I know how that sounds.'

'How does it sound, Mr Cohen?'

'Well, I'm not exactly an idiot, and I know the man who's been doing these killings is a . . . a sniper.'

'Yes, that's right.'

'I haven't seen a rifle since I was discharged in nineteen-forty-six,' Cohen said. 'I never want to see another rifle as long as I live.'

'Why?'

'Because I didn't like killing people from ambush.'

'But you were an expert marksman, is that right?'

'Yes.'

'Do you shoot at all now?'

'I told you . . .'

'Hunting, I mean. For sport.'

'No.'

'Do you own a rifle, Mr Cohen?'

'No.'

'A pistol?'

'No.'

'Any kind of a weapon?'

'No.'

'Have you ever used a telescopic sight?'

'Yes, in the army.' Cohen paused. 'You're barking up the wrong tree,' he said. 'Nowadays, when I talk about killing somebody, I mean I've written a gag that'll knock him dead.'

'And that's all you mean?'

'That's all.'

'Mr Cohen,' Meyer said, 'where do you live?'

'Uptown. Near the Coliseum.'

'We'd like to take a look at your apartment, Mr Cohen, if that's all right with you.'

'And if it isn't?'

'We'll be forced to swear out a search warrant.'

Cohen reached into his pocket and threw a ring of keys on the desk. 'I've got nothing to hide,' he said. 'The key with the round head opens the vestibule door. The brass key opens the apartment door.'

'The address?'

'One hundred and twenty-seven North Garrod.'

'And the apartment number?'

'Four C.'

'We'll give you a receipt for the keys, Mr Cohen,' Carella said.

'Will you be out of there by six?' Cohen asked. 'I've got a date.'

'I imagine so. We appreciate your cooperation.'

'I just have one question,' Cohen said. 'If this guy *is* out to get us, how do I know I'm not next?'

'Would you like police protection?' Carella asked. 'We can provide it, if you like.'

'What kind of protection?'

'A patrolman.'

Cohen considered this for a moment. Then he said, 'Forget it. There's no protection against a sniper. I used to be one.'

In the street outside, Carella asked, 'What do you think?'

'I think he's clean,' Meyer said.

'Why?'

'Well, I'll tell you. I've been watching television, and going to the movies, and reading books, and I discovered something about homicide.'

'What's that?'

'If there's a Jew, or an Italian, or a Negro, or a Puerto Rican, or a guy with any foreign-sounding name, he's never the one who did it.'

'Why not?'

'It ain't permitted, that's why. The killer has to be a hunnerd-percent white American Protestant. I'll bet you ten bucks we don't find anything bigger than a slingshot in Cohen's apartment.'

Chapter Fourteen

#1841

A detective squadroom. Two detectives are sitting on opposite sides of a desk, looking through the window at the beautiful May sunshine outside. A big black bomb is on the desk, and the fuse is burning furiously, but neither of the detectives sees it. One of them says:

"It's hard to think about crime on a day like this, isn't it?"

David Arthur Cohen
1142 Jefferson Avenue
Isola

The big black bomb with the furiously burning fuse was an unknown sniper somewhere out there in a city of ten million people. The two detectives sitting in a shoddy detective squad room were drinking coffee from cardboard containers and looking out at the May sunshine streaming through the grilled window. They had searched David Arthur Cohen's apartment from transom to trellis – the apartment boasted a small outdoor terrace overlooking a beautiful view of the River Harb – and found nothing at all incriminating. This did not mean that Cohen wasn't a very clever murderer who had hidden his rifle in an old garage somewhere. It simply meant that, for the time being, the detectives had found nothing in his apartment.

At three-thirty that afternoon, long after they had returned Cohen's keys to him, the telephone on Carella's desk rang, and he picked the receiver from its cradle and said, 'Eighty-seventh Squad, Carella.'

'Mr Carella, this is Agnes Moriarty.'

'Hello, Miss Moriarty. How are you?'

'Fine, thank you. Suffering a bit of eyestrain, but all right otherwise.'

'Did you find anything?'

'Mr Carella, I've been searching through our files since you called this morning. I am a very weary woman.'

'We certainly appreciate your help,' Carella said.

'Well, don't get too appreciative until I tell you what I've found.'

'What's that, Miss Moriarty?'

'Nothing.'

'Oh.' Carella paused. 'Nothing at all?'

'Well, *next* to nothing, anyway. I couldn't find the slightest bit of information on the two girls. I had home addresses for both of them here in the city, but that was twenty-three years ago, Mr Carella, and when I called the numbers, the people who answered had never heard of Margaret Buff or Helen Struthers.'

'That's understandable,' Carella said.

'Yes,' Miss Moriarty answered. 'Then I called Mrs Finch, who heads our alumni association, and asked her if *she* had any information on them. Apparently they had both come back to the college for the five-year reunion, but neither was married at the time, and they dropped out of the association shortly thereafter.' Miss Moriarty paused. 'Reunions can be very frightening things, you know.'

'Did she know whether or not they're married now?'

'She had not heard from either of them since that reunion.'

'Well, that's too bad,' Carella said.

'Yes. I'm sorry.'

'What about the man? Peter Kelby.'

'Again, I went over his records with a fine-tooth comb, and I called the phone number he had listed, and I spoke to a very irate man who told me he worked nights and didn't like being awakened by a maiden lady in the middle of the day. I asked him if he was Peter Kelby, and he said he was Irving Dreyfus, if that means anything to you.'

'Nothing at all.'

'He said he had never heard of Peter Kelby, which didn't surprise me in the least.'

'What did you do then?'

'I called Mrs Finch. Mrs Finch went through the records, and called back to tell me that apparently Peter Kelby had never graduated from Ramsey and therefore she could find nothing on him as an alumnus. I thanked her very much, and hung up, and then went back to my own records again. Mrs Finch was right, and I chastised myself for having missed the fact that Peter Kelby dropped out of school in his junior year.'

'So you got nothing on him either, is that it?'

'Well, I'm a very persevering woman, Mr Carella. For a maiden lady, that is. I discovered that Peter Kelby had been a member of a fraternity called Kappa Kappa Delta, and I called the local chapter and asked them whether or not they knew anything about his current whereabouts, and they referred me to the national chapter, and I called them, and the last known address they had for Peter Kelby was one he registered with them in nineteen-fifty-seven.'

'Where?'

'Minneapolis, Minnesota.'

'Did you try to reach him there?'

'I'm afraid the school authorites would have frowned upon a long-distance call, Mr Carella. But I do have the address, and I will give it to you if you promise me one thing.'

'What's that, Miss Moriarty?'

'I want you to promise that if I ever get a speeding ticket, you'll fix it for me.'

'Why, Miss Moriarty!' Carella said. 'Don't tell me you're a speeder!'

'Would I admit something like that to a cop?' Miss Moriarty asked. 'I'm waiting for you to promise.'

'What makes you think I can fix a ticket?'

'I have heard it bruited about that one can fix anything but narcotics or homicide in this city.'

'And do you believe that?'

'Assault costs a hundred dollars on the line, I've been told. Burglary can be fixed for five hundred.'

'Where do you get your information, Miss Moriarty?'

'For a maiden lady,' Miss Moriarty said, 'I get around.'

'I can arrest you for attempting to bribe an officer, and also for withholding information,' Carella said, smiling.

'What information? I don't know what you're talking about.'

'Peter Kelby's last-known address.'

'Who's Peter Kelby?' Miss Moriarty said, and Carella burst out laughing.

'Okay, okay,' he said, 'you've got my promise. No guarantees, you understand, but I'll certainly try. . . .'

'Have you got a pencil?' Miss Moriarty asked.

The telephone operator supplied Carella with a number listed to the address of Peter Kelby in Minneapolis, Minnesota. He asked her if she would try the number for him, and then he listened to a series of clickings and bongs and chimes on the line, and finally he heard the phone ringing on the other end, lo, those many miles away, and then a woman answered the phone and said, 'Kelby residence.'

'May I speak to Mr Kelby, please?' Carella said.

'Who's calling, please?' the voice asked.

'Detective Stephen Carella.'

'Just a minute, please.'

Carella waited. He could hear a voice calling to someone on the other end, and then he heard someone asking 'Who?' and the original voice saying, 'A *Detective* Carella,' and then the sound of footsteps approaching the phone, and the sound of the phone being lifted from the tabletop, and then a different woman's voice saying, 'Hello?'

'Hello,' Carella said. 'This is Detective Carella of the Eighty-seventh Squad in Isola. I'm calling . . .'

'Yes? This is Mrs Kelby speaking.'

'Mrs *Peter* Kelby?'

'Yes, that's right. What is it?'

'May I speak to your husband, please, Mrs Kelby?' Carella said.

There was a long pause on the line.

'Mrs Kelby?'

'Yes?'

'May I . . .?'

'Yes, I heard you.'

There was another pause.

Then Mrs Kelby said, 'My husband is dead.'

Which, of course, explained only one thing.

Peter Kelby had been shot to death on May 4. He had been killed while driving to the country club for a drink, as was his habit, after a long week of labour in the insurance office he headed. The Remington .308 slug had smashed through the windshield and entered his throat, and the automobile had swerved out of control and hit a milk truck going in the opposite direction. Peter Kelby was dead before the vehicles struck each other. But the murderer now had a few residual benefits to his credit, since there were two men in the cab of the milk truck and when Kelby's car hit it, one of the men went through the windshield and had his jugular severed by a shard of glass, and the other wrenched at the wheel in an attempt to keep the truck on the road, and suddenly discovered that the steering shaft was pushing up into his chest. That was the last discovery he ever made, because he was dead within the next ten seconds.

The three deaths explained only one thing.

They explained why there had been no murders in the city between May 2, when Andrew Mulligan was killed, and May 7, when Rudy Fenstermacher was killed.

It is very difficult for someone to be in two places at the same time.

The woman walked into the squad room at exactly 5:37, just as Carella and Meyer were leaving for home. Carella was in the middle of a sentence containing a choice bit of profanity, the words 'Now why the f –' stopping immediately in his throat when the woman appeared at the slatted rail divider.

She was a tall redhead, with a creamy pale complexion and slanted green eyes. She wore a dark-green suit that captured the colour of her eyes and captured, too, the mold of her body, classically rounded, narrow-waisted, wide-hipped. She was pushing forty, but there was contained voluptuousness in the woman who stood at the railing, and Meyer and Carella – both married men – caught their breaths for an instant, as though a fantasy had suddenly materialized. Down the corridor, and behind the woman, Miscolo – who had caught a glimpse of her as she passed his open door – peeked around the jamb of the clerical office for a better look, and then rolled his eyes toward the ceiling.

'Yes, miss?' Carella said.

'I'm Helen Vale,' she said.

'Yes, Miss Vale?' Carella said. 'What can we do for you?'

'*Mrs* Vale,' she corrected.

'Yes, Mrs Vale?'

'Helen *Struthers* Vale.'

She spoke in a normally deep voice that carried the unmistakable stamp of elocution lessons. She kept both hands on the slatted rail divider, clinging to it as if it were a lover. She waited patiently, as though embarrassed by her surroundings, and embarrassed, too, by the mature ripeness of her own body. And yet, her own awareness seemed to heighten the awareness of the observer. She was a potential rape victim expecting the worse, and inviting it through dire expectation. It took several seconds for the detectives to extract the maiden name 'Struthers' from the names fore and aft, and then to separate it from the heavy miasma of sensuality that had suddenly smothered the room.

'Come in, Mrs Vale,' Carella said, and he held open the gate in the railing for her.

'Thank you,' she said. She lowered her eyes as she passed him, like a novice nun who has reluctantly taken a belated vow of chastity. Meyer pulled a chair out from one of the desks and held it for her while she sat. She crossed her legs, her skirt was short, it rode up over splendid knees, she tugged at it but it refused to yield, she sat in bursting provocative awareness.

Meyer wiped his brow.

'We've been trying to locate you, Mrs Vale,' Carella said. 'You *are* the Helen Struthers who . . .'

'Yes,' she said.

'We assumed you were married, but we didn't know to whom, and we had no idea where to begin looking because this is a very large city, and although we tried . . .' He abruptly stopped speaking, wondering why he was talking so rapidly and so much.

'Anyway, we're glad you're here,' Meyer said.

Carella wiped his brow.

'Yes, I thought I should come,' Helen said, 'and now I'm glad I did.' She delivered these last words as if she were paying tribute to the two most handsome, charming, gallant, intelligent men in the world. Both detectives smiled unconsciously, and then, catching the smile on the other's face, frowned and tried to become businesslike.

'Why *did* you come, Mrs Vale?' Carella said.

'Well . . . because of the shootings,' Helen answered, opening her eyes wide.

'Yes, what about them?'

'He's killing everyone in the play, don't you see?' she said.

'*Who* is, Mrs Vale?'

'Well, I don't know,' she said, and she lowered her eyes again, and again tugged at her skirt, but her skirt didn't budge. 'I thought so at first when I connected the names Forrest and Norden, but then I thought, 'No, Helen, you're imagining things.' I have a very good imagination,' she explained, raising her eyes.

'Yes, Mrs Vale, go on.'

'Then the girl got killed, I forget her name, and then Sal Palumbo, the nice Italian man who was studying English in night school, and then Andy Mulligan, and Rudy, and I knew for certain. I said to my husband: "Alec, somebody's killing everyone who was in *The Long Voyage Home* in nineteen-forty at Ramsey University." That's what I said.'

'And what did your husband say?'

'He said, "You're crazy, Helen."'

'I see.'

'Crazy like a fox,' Helen said, her eyes narrowing. 'So I decided to come up here.'

'Why? Do you have some information for us, Mrs Vale?'

'No.' Helen wet her lips. 'I'm an actress, you see.'

'I see.'

'Yes. Helen Vale. Do you think "Struthers" would be better?'

'I beg your pardon?'

'Helen Struthers. My maiden name. Does that sound better?'

'Well, no, this is fine.'

'Helen Vale sounds very good,' Meyer agreed, nodding.

'Pure,' she said. 'Classical.'

'What?'

'Helen. It sounds pure and classical.'

'Yes, it does.'

'And Vale adds mystery, don't you think? Vale. V-a-l-e. Which is my husband's real name. But it can also be spelled V-e-i-l, which is what gives it the mystery. Helen Vale. A veil is very mysterious, you know.'

'It certainly is.'

'Being an actress, I decided I should come up here.'

'Why?'

'Well, what good is a dead actress?' Helen said. She shrugged and then spread her hands in utter simplicity.

'That's true,' Meyer said.

'So here I am.'

'Yes,' Carella said.

Miscolo sauntered casually into the squad room and said, 'Anybody want some coffee? Oh, excuse me, I didn't know you had a visitor.' He smiled graciously at Helen, and she returned the smile demurely and tugged at her skirt. 'Would you like some coffee, miss?' he asked.

'No, thank you,' she said. 'But thank you for asking.'

'Not at all,' Miscolo said, and he went out of the squad room humming.

'I almost married a man named Leach,' Helen said. 'Helen Leach, wouldn't that have been terrible?'

'Awful,' Meyer agreed.

'Still, he was a nice fellow.'

'Miss Lea . . . Miss . . . uh . . . Mrs Vale,' Carella said, 'what do you remember about *The Long Voyage Home*?'

'I played Kate,' she said. She smiled.

'What else do you remember about it?'

'Nothing.'

'Nothing at all?'

'It was lousy, I think. I don't remember.'

'What do you remember about the other people in the cast?'

'The boys were all very sweet.'

'And the girls?'

'I don't remember them.'

'Would you happen to know whether Margaret Buff ever married?'

'Margaret *who*?'

'Buff. She was in the play, too.'

'No. I don't remember her.'

Two patrolmen wandered into the squad room, went to the files, opened them, looked at Helen Vale where she sat with her legs crossed, and then went to the water cooler, where they drank three cups of water each while watching Helen Vale where she sat with her legs crossed. As they were leaving the squad room, four more patrolmen wandered into the room. Carella frowned at them, but they all went about finding busywork that only happened to take Helen into their direct line of view.

'Have you been an actress ever since you got out of college, Mrs Vale?' Carella asked.

'Yes.'

'Have you appeared on the stage here in this city?'

'Yes. I'm Equity, and AFTRA, and also SAG.'

'Mrs Vale, has anyone ever made any threats on your life?'

'No.' Helen frowned. 'That's a very funny question. What's this got to do with me alone, if the killer is after *all* of us?'

'Mrs Vale, the wholesale slaughter may be just a smoke screen. He may be after *one* of you, and he may be killing the others to throw us off the track, to make it seem he has a different motive, other than what may be the real motive.'

'Really?'

'Yes,' Carella said.

'I didn't understand a word of that,' Helen said.

'Oh. Well, you see . . .'

'Besides, that's not what interests me. I mean, his motives or anything.'

There were fourteen patrolmen in the room now, and the word was spreading throughout the building, and perhaps the entire precinct, very rapidly. Only once during his entire career as a detective could Carella remember seeing so many patrolmen in the squad room at one time, and that was when the commissioner had issued his edict against moonlighting, and every uniformed cop in the precinct had come upstairs to bellyache about it in a sort of open forum.

'What *does* interest you, Mrs Vale?' he asked, and five more patrolmen came down the corridor and into the room.

'I think I need protection,' she said, and she lowered her eyes at that moment, as if she were talking not about the sniper who was going around shooting people, but about the patrolmen who were crowding into the room like migrating sardines.

Carella stood up suddenly and said, 'Fellows, it's getting a little stuffy in here. Why don't you go have your meeting in the locker room?'

'What meeting?' one of the patrolmen asked.

'The meeting you're going to have in the locker room in three seconds flat,' Carella said, 'before I pick up the phone and have a talk with Captain Frick downstairs.'

The patrolmen began to disperse. One of them, in a very loud *sotto voce*, muttered the word 'Chicken,' but Carella ignored it. He watched them as they left, and then he turned to Helen and said. 'We'll assign a man to you, Mrs Vale.'

'I *would* appreciate that,' she said. 'Who?'

'Well . . . I'm not sure yet. It depends on who's available and what . . .'

'I'm sure he'll be dependable,' she said.

'Mrs Vale,' Carella said. 'I wonder if you can try remembering about the play. I know it was a long time ago, but . . .'

'Actually, I have a very good memory,' Helen said.

'I'm sure you do.'

'Actresses *need* to have good memories, you know.'

'I know that.'

'Otherwise we'd never learn our lines,' Helen said, and she smiled.

'Good. What do you remember about the play?'

'Nothing,' Helen said.

'Everyone got along fine with each other, is that right?' Carella prodded.

'Oh, yes, it was a very nice group.'

'At the party, too, right? No trouble?'

'Oh, no, it was a lovely party.'

'You stayed late, is that right?'

'That's right.' Helen smiled. 'I always stay late at parties.'

'Where was this party, Mrs Vale?'

'What party?' Helen asked.

'The one after the play.'

'Oh, that one. At Randy's house, I think. Randy Norden. He was a regular rip. Very smart in school, you know, but oh what a rip! His parents were away in Europe, so we all went up there after the show.'

'And you and the other two girls stayed late, is that right?'

'That's right, yes. It was a lovely party.'

'With three of the boys.'

'Oh no, there were a lot of boys.'

'I meant you stayed late. With three of the boys.'

'Oh. Yes, that's right. We did.'

'Was there any trouble?'

'No,' Helen said. She smiled sweetly. 'We were making love.'

'You were necking, you mean.'

'No, no. We were diddling.'

Carella cleared his throat and looked at Meyer.

'It was a very nice party,' Helen said.

'Mrs Vale,' Carella said, 'What do you mean by "didling"?'

Helen lowered her eyes. 'Well, you know,' she said.

Carella looked at Mayer again. Meyer shrugged in confusion.

'With the boys, do you mean? The three boys?'

'Yes.'

'You . . . you were in separate rooms, is that right?'

'Yes. Well, in the beginning, anyway. There was an awful lot to drink, you know, and Randy's parents were in Europe, so we just had a lot of fun.'

'Mrs Vale,' Carella said, taking the bull by the horns, 'do you mean that you and the other two girls were *intimate* with these boys?'

'Oh, yes, very intimate,' she said.

'And the three boys were Anthony Forrest, Randolph Norden, and David Arthur Cohen, is that right?'

'That's right. They were all very nice boys.'

'And you . . . you were sort of wandering around from room to room, is that right? All of you?'

'Oh, yes,' Helen said delightedly. 'It was a regular orgy.'

Carella began coughing, and Meyer hit him on the back.

'You're coming down with something,' Helen said pleasantly. 'You ought to get to bed.'

'Yes, yes, I will,' Carella said, coughing. 'Thank you very much, Mrs Vale, you've been very helpful.'

'Oh, I enjoyed talking with you,' Helen said. 'I'd almost forgotten that party, and it was really one of the nicest parties I've ever been to.'

She rose, picked up her purse, opened it, and placed a small white card on the desk. 'My home address and number,' she said, 'and also my service, if you can't reach me.'

She smiled and walked to the railing. Carella and Meyer sat rooted to the desk, watching her move across the room. At the railing, she turned and said, 'You *will* do your best to see that I'm not killed, won't you?'

'We will, Mrs Vale,' Carella said fervently. 'We most certainly will do our very utmost best.'

'Thank you,' she murmured, and then walked down the corridor. They could hear her high heels clatterng on the iron-runged steps to the floor below.

'Because, lady,' Meyer whispered, 'it would be a *crime* to kill you, I swear to God, it would be a heinous crime.'

They knew when she reached the street outside because a tumultuous cheer went up from the patrolmen waiting there for her.

Chapter Fifteen

Well, things were certainly looking up.

Not only did they now know that the seven murder victims had all been in a college production of *The Long Voyage Home* back in 1940, but they further knew there had been a party after the play, and that all the members of the cast and crew had been present at it, as well as Professor Richardson, the faculty adviser. They further knew that the faculty adviser had stopped advising some time during the night, and that the party had dwindled down to six people of opposite sexes who had taken advantage of the fact.

The next morning, they decided to have another chat with David Arthur Cohen, who, by his own admission, had been a sniper during the war, and who had also been present at the midnight revelry those many years ago. They called him and asked him to come up to the squad room. He complained bitterly because he said he'd lose a whole day's work in a week when the gags were coming fast and good, but they told him this happened to be a homicide case and if he came to the squad room of his own volition, it would save them the trouble of sending a patrolman after him.

Cohen arrived at ten A.M.

They sat him in a chair, and then they stood around him, Kling, Carella, and Meyer. Cohen was rushing the season a bit with a seersucker suit. He looked cool and unruffled. He sat in the chair with his habitual sour expression, and waited for one of the detectives to start the questioning. Meyer threw the first pitch.

'We're primarily interested in the party that took place after the play, Mr Cohen,' he said.

'Yeah, what about it?'

'We want to know what happened.'

'I told you what happened.'

'All right, Mr Cohen,' Carella said, 'first of all, who was there?'

'Everybody in the show.'

'In the show, or *connected* with the show?'

'Connected with it.'

'And by "everybody," who exactly do you mean?'

'The cast, the crew, and some hangers-on.'

'Like who?'

'Like some guys brought girls, and also some of the kids who weren't really in the group, but who were on the fringes of it.'

'And who else?'

'Professor Richardson.'

'Was it a good party?' Kling asked.

'Yeah, it was okay. This was more than twenty years ago, for God's sake. Do you expect me to remember . . .'

'Helen Struthers was in here yesterday, Mr Cohen,' Meyer said. 'She seems to remember the party pretty well.'

'Oh yeah?'

'Yeah. She says it was one of the best parties she'd ever been to. How about it?'

'She's entitled to her opinion, I guess.' Cohen paused. 'How'd she look? Helen?'

'Very nice. How was the party in your opinion, Mr Cohen?'

'Pretty good.'

'Helen seemed to think it was better than pretty good,' Carella said.

'Yeah?'

'Yeah. She seemed especially to remember what happened after most of the people went home.'

'Yeah? What does she remember?'

'Well, what do *you* remember, Mr Cohen?'

'We were necking around a little.'

'That's all?'

'That's all. We were only kids.'

'Well, for kids, Mr Cohen, Helen seems to think a little more than necking took place.'

'What does she seem to think?'

'She seems to think you all crawled into the sack.'

'Yeah?'

'Yeah. In fact, she seems to think you all crawled into the sack *together* at one point.'

'Yeah?'

'Yeah. In fact, Mr Cohen, she described what happened as "a regular orgy."'

'Yeah?'

'Yeah. Funny you should forget an event of such proportions, don't you think, Mr Cohen? Unless, of course, you're in the habit of attending org –'

'All right,' Cohen said.

'Is that what happened?'

'Yeah, yeah, that's what happened.'

'You remember it now?'

'Remember it?' Cohen said. 'I've been trying to forget it for twenty-three years. I've been in analysis for six years, trying to forget what happened that night.'

'Why?'

'Because it was disgusting. We were drunk. It was disgusting. It warped my entire life.'

'How?'

'What do you mean, how? Because we turned a . . . a private thing into a . . . circus. That's how. Look, do we have to talk about this?'

'Yes, we have to talk about it. Was everyone drunk?'

'Yeah. Randy Norden was a kind of wild kid. He was older than most of us, you know, in his twenties, already in law school. His parents had this big penthouse apartment on Grover, and they were away in Europe, so we all went up there after the show. The girls got pretty high. I guess Helen was setting the pace. Well, you've seen her, you know the kind of girl she is. She was the same then.'

'Hold it right there, Mr Cohen!' Meyer said sharply.

'What? What's the matter?'

'How do *you* know what kind of girl she is, Mr Cohen? When did *you* see her last?'

'I haven't seen anybody connected with that show since I got out of college.'

'Then how do you know what she looks like now?'

'I don't.'

'Then why'd you say she's the same now as she was then?'

'I just assumed she'd be. She was a wild one then, and the wild ones don't change.'

'How about the other girls?'

'They . . . were just nice kids. They got drunk, that's all.'

'And what happened?'

'Well, we . . . it was Randy's idea, I guess. He was older, you know, and with Helen, and naturally . . . well, we all split up . . . there were a lot of bedrooms in the house . . . and well . . . that's what happened.'

'*What* happened?' Meyer insisted.

'I don't want to talk about it!' Cohen shouted.

'Why?'

'Because I'm ashamed of it, that's why. Okay?'

'Tell us about being a sniper, Mr Cohen,' Carella said.

'That was a long time ago.'

'So was the party. Tell us about it.'

'What do you want to know?'

'What theatre of operations?'

'The Pacific.'

'Where?'

'Guam.'

'What'd you use?'

'A BAR with a telescopic sight.'

'Smokeless powder?'

'Yes.'

'How many men did you kill?'

'Forty-seven,' Cohen said without hesitation.

'How'd you feel about it?'

'I hated every minute of it.'

'Then why didn't you get out?'

'I asked for a transfer, but they said no. I was a good sniper.'

'These were Japanese you killed?'

'Yeah, Japanese.'

'How much did you drink at that party?'

'A lot.'

'How much?'

'I don't remember. We *really* began drinking after Richardson left. There was a lot of booze. Tony was in charge of tickets . . .'

'Tony?'

'Forrest. Tony Forrest. He was in charge of tickets for the show, and I think he took some money from the till to pay for the party. It wasn't illegal or anything, I mean everybody in the group knew he was doing it. It was for the party. But there was a lot of booze.' Cohen paused. 'Also, there was a climate of . . . well, the war had already started in Europe, and I guess most students at the time knew America would get into it sooner or later. So it was a kind of kiss-me-my-sweet attitude. We didn't care what the hell happened.'

'Did you shoot from a tree or what?' Kling asked suddenly.

'What?'

'When you were on Guam.'

'Oh. Usually. Yeah.'

'What happened afterward?' Carella asked.

'It depended on the operation. Usually, I was supposed to pin down . . .'

'After Helen and Randy started the ball rolling, I mean.'

'We all got involved.'

'And after that?'

'We wound up in one room.'

'Which room?'

'Randy's mother's room. The bedroom. The big one.'

'Where were you on Friday, May fourth?' Meyer asked.

'I don't know.'

'Try to remember.'

'When was that?'

'It was Friday, May fourth. This is Wednesday, May ninth. Where were you, Cohen?'

'I think I was out of town.'

'Where?'

'Upstate. That's right. I left Friday morning. Just to take a long weekend, you know?'

'You wouldn't have been in Minneapolis on May fourth, would you?'

'Minneapolis? No. Why should I go there? I've never been there in my life.'

'Do you remember a man named Peter Kelby?'

'Yeah, he was in the play.'

'Did he come to the party?'

'He came to the party.'

'Where'd you stay last weekend? On your trip upstate?'

'I went fishing.'

'We didn't ask you what you did, we asked you where you stayed.'

'I camped out.'

'Where?'

'In the reservation. Up near Cattawan.'

'In a rent?'

'Yes.'

'Alone?'

'Yes.'

'Anyone else on the campsite?'

'No.'

'Stop for gas anywhere along the way?'

'Yes.'

'Use a credit card?'

'No.'

'You paid cash?'

'Yes.'

'The same in any restaurants you might have stopped at?'

'Yes.'

'In other words, Mr Cohen, we have only your word that you were up in Cattawan and not in Minneapolis, Minnesota, killing a man named Peter Kelby.'

'Whaaat!'

'Yes, Mr Cohen.'

'Look, I . . .'

'Yes, Mr Cohen?'

'Look . . . why would I . . . how the hell would I even know where Peter

Kelby *was?* I mean . . .'

'Somebody knew where he was, Mr Cohen, because somebody put a bullet in his head. We rather suspect it was the same somebody who killed six people right here in this city.'

'I haven't seen Peter Kelby since we were in school together!' Cohen protested. 'I had no idea he was in Minneapolis.'

'Ah, but, Mr Cohen, *somebody* found out he was there. In fact, Mr Cohen, it couldn't have been too difficult, because even a nice lady named Agnes Moriarty at Ramsey University was able to find out where Kelby lived – and she wasn't even interested in murdering him.'

'Neither was I!' Cohen shouted.

'But that party still bugs you, huh, Cohen?'

'Why does it bug you?'

'Too much sex there?'

'You enjoy firing a rifle?'

'How does it feel to kill a man?'

'Which girl were you with, Cohen?'

'What else did you do that night?'

'*Shut up, shut up, shut up!*' Cohen shouted.

The squad room was very silent. Into the silence Carella said, 'What's your analyst's name, Cohen?'

'Why?'

'We want to ask him some questions.'

'Go to hell,' Cohen said.

'Maybe you don't realize how tight your position is, Cohen.'

'I realize, all right. But whatever is said between me and my analysist is *my* business, and not yours. I had nothing to do with any of these goddamn murders. You can go around opening whatever closets you want to, but some of my closets are going to stay *closed*, you hear me? Because they've got nothing to do with you *or* your case, they've only got to do with *me*. You hear that? Me, David Arthur Cohen, a crumby gag writer who doesn't know how to laugh, all right? I don't know how to laugh, all right, that's why I'm going to an analyst, okay? And maybe I didn't know how to laugh even back in nineteen-forty when I was eighteen years old and at a wild party that should have knocked me out, but that doesn't mean I'm going around killing people. I killed enough people. I killed forty-seven people in my life, and they were all Japanese, and I cry every night for every goddamn one of them.'

The detectives stared at him for several moments, and then Meyer nodded his head at the other men, and they walked to one corner of the room and stood shoulder to shoulder in a tight huddle.

'What do you think?' Meyer asked.

'I think this is real meat,' Carella said.

'Yeah, it looks that way to me, too.'

'Shall we book him?'

'I'm not sure,' Kling said.

'We've got nothing that'll stick.' Carella said.

'We don't have to book him for homicide. Let's throw something else at him, just to keep him here awhile. I think he'll crack if we can keep at him.'

'What can we book him for? Vagrancy? He's gainfully employed.'

'Dis cond.'

'What did he do?'

'He used abusive language just a little while ago.'

'What do you mean?'

'He told you to go to hell.'

'Jesus, that's slim,' Carella said.

'We just gonna let him walk out of here?'

'How long can we hold him without booking him?'

'If the thing comes to trial, it's up to the court to decide what was a proper and reasonable length of time. But, man, if this comes up zero, he'll sue for false arrest before we can bat an eyelash.'

'If we don't book him, we're not arresting him, are we?' Kling asked.

'Sure we are. If we keep him from leaving here, that amounts to arrest. He'd have a bona-fide case against the city, and against the arresting officer.'

'So what the hell do we do?'

'I think we ought to ring in the D.A.'s office,' Carella said.

'You think so?'

'Absolutely. Call the Homicide Bureau, tell them we've got what looks like real meat, and we want a D.A. in on the questioning. Let them make the decision.'

'I think that's best,' Meyer said. 'Bert?'

'Let's work him for another ten minutes, see what we can get on our own.'

'I don't think so.'

'Okay, do what you like.'

'Steve, you want to call the Bureau?'

'Yeah, sure. What do we do with him meanwhile?'

'I'll take him downstairs.'

'Not in the cells, Meyer!'

'No, no, I'll phony it up, stall him. I don't think he knows anything about booking, anyway.'

'All right,' Carella said.

Meyer walked across the room. 'Come on, Cohen.'

'Where are you taking me?'

'Downstairs. I want you to look at some pictures.'

'What kind of pictures?'

'Of the people killed by the sniper.'

'Why?'

'I think you ought to see them. We want to make sure they're the same people who were in that play.'

'All right,' Cohen said. He seemed immensely relieved. 'Then can I go?'

'You better look at the pictures first.'

He started out of the squad room with Meyer and Kling, passing another man in the corridor outside. The man was perhaps forty-five years old, small and round with sad brown eyes and a rumpled brown suit. He walked to the railing and stood just outside it, holding his hat in his hands, waiting to be discovered.

Carella, who had already dialed the Bureau and was at the desk nearest the railing, glanced up at the man, and then turned his attention back to the telephone conversation.

'No, we haven't booked him,' Carella said. 'We've got nothing that'll stick yet.' He paused, listening. 'No, he hasn't said a thing, denies the whole business. But I think we can get him to crack if we work on him. Right. Can you get a man down right away? Well, how long can we legally hold him here? That's just my point. I think the decision should come from someone in the D.A.'s office. Well, when's the soonest? That's too late. Can't you get someone here this morning? Okay, fine, we'll be waiting.'

He hung up and turned to the man.

'Yes, sir, can I help you?'

'My name is Lewis Redfield,' the man said.

'Yes, Mr. Redfield?'

'I hate to bother you this way . . .'

'Yes?'

'. . . but I think my wife may be in danger.'

'Come in, Mr Redfield,' Carella said.

Redfield nodded, took a hesitant step toward the railing, searched it for an opening, and then stopped dead in his tracks, bewildered. Carella went to the gate and opened it for him.

'Thank you,' Redfield said, and then waited for Carella to lead him to the desk.

When they were seated, Carella asked, 'What makes you think your wife is in danger, Mr Redfield? Has she received any threatening . . .?'

'No, but I . . . this may sound silly to you.'

'What is it, Mr Redfield?'

'I think this fellow may be after her.'

'What fellow?'

'The sniper.'

Carella wet his lips and stared at the small round man opposite him. 'What makes you think that, Mr Redfield?'

'I've been reading the papers,' Redfield said. 'The people who've been killed . . . they were all in a play with Margaret many years ago.'

'Margaret *Buff*? Is that you wife's maiden name?'

'Yes, sir.'

'Well!' Carella smiled and extended his hand. 'It's certainly good to see you, Mr Redfield. We've been trying to locate your wife.'

'I would have come sooner, but I wasn't sure.'

'Where *is* your wife, sir? We'd like very much to talk to her.'

'Why?'

'Because we have what looks like a good suspect, and any information . . .'

'You've found the killer?'

'We're not sure, Mr Redfield, but we think we have.'

Redfield sighed heavily. 'I'm certainly relieved to hear that. You have no idea the strain I've been through. I was certain that at any moment Margaret would . . .' He shook his head. 'I certainly am relieved.'

'*Could* we talk to her, sir?'

'Yes, of course.' Redfield paused. 'Who did you arrest? Who's the man?'

'His name is David Arthur Cohen,' Carella said. 'But he hasn't been arrested as yet, sir.'

'Was he in the play, too?'

'Yes.'

'Why was he doing it? Why was he killing all those people?'

'We're not sure yet. We think it had something to do with a party he went to.'

'A party?' Redfield asked.

'Well, it's pretty complicated, sir. That's why I'd like to talk to your wife.'

'Of course,' Redfield said. 'The number is Grover 6–2100. I think you can reach her there now.'

'Is that your home number, sir?'

'Yes, it is.'

'Will she be able to come down here right away?'

'I think so, yes.'

'You have no children, sir?'

'What?'

'Children. Will she have to make arrangements? If so, I can go . . .'

'No. No children.' Quickly Redfield added, 'We've only been married a short time.'

'I see,' Carella said. He pulled the phone to him and began dialing.

'Two years, actually. I'm Margaret's second husband.'

'I see.'

'Yes, she divorced her first husband in nineteen-fifty-six.'

Carella put the receiver to his ear and listened to the ringing on the other end. 'We're anxious to get her down here, because we've either got to book Cohen for homicide or let him go. A man from the D.A.'s office is coming up soon, and anything concrete we can provide him with will be a big help. Your wife just might be able to . . .'

'Hello?' a woman's voice said.

'Hello, Mrs Redfield?'

'Yes?'

'This is Detective Carella of the Eighty-seventh Squad. Your husband is here with me, Mrs Redfield. We've been trying to locate you on these sniper killings.'

'Oh. Oh, yes,' she said. Her voice was curiously toneless.

'I wonder if you could come down to the station house. We have a suspect, and we're very anxious to talk to you.'

'All right.'

'Can you come down right now?'

'All right.'

'Fine, Mrs Redfield. When you get here, just tell the desk sergeant you want to see me, Detective Carella, and he'll pass you through.'

'All right. Where is it?'

'On Grover Avenue, right opposite the park's carousel entrance.'

'All right. Is Lewis there?'

'Yes. Do you want to speak to him?'

'No, that's all right.'

'We'll see you soon, then.'

'All right,' Margaret Redfield said, and then she hung up.

'She's coming over,' Carella said.

'Good,' Redfield answered.

Carella smiled and put the phone back onto its cradle. It rang almost instantly. He pulled the receiver up again and said, 'Eighty-seventh Squad, Carella.'

'Carella, this is Freddie Holt, the Eight-Eight across the park.'

'Hi, Freddie,' Carella said cheerfully. 'What can I do for you?'

'You still working on the sniper case?'

'Yeah.'

'Good. We got your boy.'

'What?' Carella said.

'Your boy, the guy who's been doing it.'

'What do you mean?'

'We picked him up maybe ten minutes ago. Shields and Durante made the collar. Got him on a rooftop on Rexworth. Shot two ladies in the street before we could pin him down.' Holt paused. 'Carella? You with me?'

'I'm with you,' Carella said wearily.

Chapter Sixteen

The man in the cage in the squad room of the 88th Precinct was a raving lunatic. He was wearing dungarees and a tattered white shirt, and his hair was long and matted, and his eyes were wild. He climbed the sides of the small mesh prison like a monkey, peering out at the detectives in the room, snarling and spitting, rolling his eyes.

When Carella came into the room, the man in the cage shouted, 'Here's another one! Shoot the sinner!'

'That's the man?' Carella asked Holt.

'That's him, all right. Hey, Danny!' Holt called, and a detective sitting at one of the desks rose and walked to where Carella and Holt were standing.

'Steve Carella, Danny Shields.'

'Hi,' Shields said. 'I think we met once, didn't we? That fire over on Fourteenth?'

'I think so, yeah,' Carella said.

'Don't go too near the cage,' Shields warned. 'He spits.'

'Want to fill me in on it, Danny?' Carella said.

Shields shrugged. 'There's not much to tell. The beat cop called in about a half-hour ago – it was about a half-hour, huh, Freddie?'

'Yeah, about that,' Holt said.

'Told us some nut was up on the roof shooting down into the street. So Durante and me, we took the squeal, and he was still blasting away when we got there. I went up the hallway, and Durante took the building next door, to go up the roof, you know, catch him by surprise. By the time we got up there, he'd plugged two dames in the street. One was an old lady, the other was a pregnant woman. They're both in the hospital now.' Shields shook his head. 'I just spoke to the doctor on the phone. He thinks the pregnant one's gonna die. The old lady has a chance, he says. That's the way it always is huh?'

'What happened on the roof, Danny?'

'Well, Durante opened fire from the next building, and I come in and got him from behind. He was some bundle, believe me. Look at him. He thinks he's Tarzan.'

'Shoot the sinners!' the man in the cage yelled. 'Shoot all the filthy sinners!'

'Did you get his weapon?'

'Yeah. It's over there on the desk, tagged and ready to go.'

Carella glanced at the desk. 'That looks like a twenty-two,' he said.

'That's what it is.'

'You can't fire a three-oh-eight slug from that,' Carella said.

'Who said you could?'

'Well, what makes you think this is my boy?'

'We figured it was a chance. We been getting a lot of heat on this, Carella. The loot got a call from downtown only yesterday, asking if we was really helping you guys or just fooling around up here.'

'I don't think he's connected with it,' Carella said.

'Well, what do you want us to do?'

'Have you checked his apartment yet?'

'What apartment? He probably sleeps in the park.'

'Where'd he get a rifle?'

'We're checking our stolen guns list now. There was a couple of hockshops busted into, night before last. Maybe he done it.'

'Have you questioned him yet?'

'Questioned him? He's got a screw loose, all he does is yell about sinners and spit at anybody who goes near him. Look at him, the crazy bastard.' Shields looked at him, and then burst out laughing. 'Jesus,' he said, 'just like a monkey, look at him.'

'Well, if you find out where he lives, run a check for me, will you? We're looking for any gun that might have fired a three-oh-eight Remington.'

'That's a lot of guns, buddy,' Shields said.

'Yeah, but it's not a twenty-two.'

'That's for sure.'

'You'd better call Buenavista and tell them to warm up a bed in the psycho ward.'

'I already done it,' Shields said. 'Not your boy, huh?'

'I don't think so.'

'Too bad. I'll tell you the truth, Carella, we were a little anxious to get rid of him.'

'Why? Nice sweet old guy like that.'

'Well, we got a problem, you see.'

'What's the problem?'

'Who's gonna take him out of that cage?' Shields asked.

Margaret Buff Redfield was waiting for Carella when he got back to the squad room.

She was thirty-nine years old, and she looked tired. Her hair was brown, and her eyes were brown, and she wore a shade of lipstick too red for her complexion, and a dress that hung limply from her figure.

She took Carella's hand wearily when her husband introduced them, and then looked at him expectantly, as if waiting for him to crack her across the face. Suddenly Carella had the notion that the woman had been hit before, and often. He glanced at the soft-spoken Redfield, and then turned his attention back to Margaret.

'Mrs Redfield,' he said, 'there are some questions we'd like to ask you.'

'All right,' Margaret said.

Intuitively Carella turned to Redfield and said, 'Sir, if you don't mind, I'd like to talk to your wife privately.'

'Why?' Redfield said. 'We're married. We have no secrets.'

'I know that, sir, and I respect it, believe me. But we've found that people will often be very nervous in the presence of their husbands or wives, and we try to conduct an interview privately, if it's at all possible.'

'I see,' Redfield said.

'Yes, sir.'

'Well . . .'

'If you don't mind, sir, I'll ask Miscolo to show you to a room down the hall. There are some magazines in there, and you can smoke if you . . .'

'I don't smoke,' Redfield said.

'Or perhaps Miscolo can bring you a cup of coffee.'

'Thank you, I don't want a . . .'

'Miscolo!' Carella yelled, and Miscolo came running at the double. 'Would you show Mr Redfield down the hall, please, and make him comfortable?'

'Right this way, sir,' Miscolo said.

Reluctantly, Redfield got out of his chair and followed Miscolo out of the squad room. Carella waited until he was certain Redfield was out of earshot, and then he turned to Margaret and quickly said, 'Tell me about the party in nineteen-forty.'

'What?' she said, startled.

'The party at Randy Norden's house.'

'How . . . how did you know about that?' she asked.

'We know about it.'

'Does my husband know?' she asked quickly.

'We didn't ask him, Mrs Redfield.'

'You won't tell him, will you?'

'Of course not. We only want to know about David Arthur Cohen, Mrs Redfield. Can you tell me how he behaved that night?'

'I don't know,' she said. She moved back on the seat of the chair, and her voice came from her throat like a whine, as though he were holding a club and were threatening her with it. Her eyes had widened, and she visibly moved deeper into the chair, her back climbing it, her shoulders pulling away from him.

'What did he do, Mrs Redfield?'

'I don't know,' she said, and again the words were a whine, and her eyes were beginning to blink uncertainly now.

'Mrs Redfield, I'm not asking you what *you* did that night. I only want to know . . .'

'I didn't do anything!' she shouted, and she gripped the sides of the chair with both hands, as though knowing he would hit her now, and bracing herself for the shock.

'No one said you did, Mrs Redfield. I only want to know if anything happened that might have caused Cohen to . . .'

'Nothing happened,' she said. 'I want to go home now. I want my husband.'

'Mrs Redfield, we think we have a murderer downstairs. He claims he had nothing to do with the murders, but if we can find something, anything, that'll start him talking . . .'

'I don't know anything. I want to go home.'

'Mrs Redfield, I don't want to have to . . .'

'I don't know anything.'

'. . . embarrass you, or make this difficult for you. But unless we can find something concrete to . . .'

'I told you, I don't know. I want to go home. I don't know.'

'Mrs Redfield,' Carella said evenly, 'we know everything that happened that night at Randy Norden's. *Everything*. Helen Struthers told us about it, and so did Cohen.'

'I didn't do anything. They did it.'

'Who?'

'The . . . the others.'

'What others?'

'Helen and Blanche. Not me Not me.'

'What did they do?'

'They couldn't get me to do it,' Margaret said. 'I wouldn't, and they couldn't force me. I knew what was right. I was only seventeen, but I certainly knew what was right and what was wrong. It was the others, you see.'

'You had no part of anything that happened, is that right?'

'That's right.'

'Then why didn't you leave, Mrs Redfield?'

'Because they . . . they held me. All of them. Even the girls. They held me while . . . listen, I didn't even want to be in the *play*. I was Mag, the barmaid, she was a barmaid, not a girl like the others, my mother wouldn't let me be in the play at first because of the kind of girls they were supposed to be, I was only in the play because Randy talked me into it. But I didn't know the kind of boy Randy was until the night of the party, when he was with Helen. That's what started it all, his being with Helen, and everybody drinking so much . . .'

'Were you drunk, Mrs Redfield?'

'No, yes, I don't know. I must have been drunk. If I'd been sober, I wouldn't have let them . . .'

Margaret stopped.

'Yes?'

'Nothing.'

'Mrs Redfield, do you want to tell this to a policewoman?'

'I have nothing to tell.'

'I'll get a policewoman.'

'I have nothing to say to her. What happened wasn't my fault. I've never . . . do you think I *wanted* what happened?'

'Miscolo, get me a policewoman, on the double!' Carella yelled.

'The others did, but not me. I was drunk, or they wouldn't have been able to hold me. I was only seventeen. I didn't know about such things, because I came from a good home. If I hadn't been drunk . . . I wouldn't have let them ruin my life. If I'd known the kind of boy Randy was, the kind of filth in him, in his body, and the others, Helen especially, if I'd known what she was, I wouldn't have stayed at the party, I wouldn't have had a single drink, I wouldn't even have been in the play, if I'd known what kind of boys they were, and girls, if I'd known what they could do to me, if I'd only known. But I was seventeen, I didn't even think about such things, and when they said they were going to have a party after the show, I thought it would be a nice party, after all Professor Richardson was going to be there, but they were drinking even with him in the room, and then when he left, it must have been about midnight, they really began drinking. I'd never even drunk anything stronger than beer before that, and here they were pouring drinks, and before I knew it, only the six of us were left . . .'

Alf Miscolo saw the policewoman going down the corridor toward the squad room, and he figured it wouldn't be long before he could stop the pretense of entertaining Lewis Redfield. Redfield had tired quickly of even the new *Saturday Evening Post*, and he fidgeted uneasily in his chair now in the sparsely furnished, loosely titled 'reception room,' which was really a small cubicle off the clerical office. Miscolo wished both Redfield and his wife would go home so that he could get back to typing and filing, but instead the policewoman vanished down the corridor, and Redfield sat in his chair and fidgeted as though his wife were in the hands of heartless torturers.

Miscolo was a married man himself, so he said, 'Don't worry about her, Mr Redfield. They're only asking a few questions.'

'She's a nervous woman,' Redfield answered. 'I'm afraid they might upset her.' He did not look at Miscolo as he spoke. His eyes and his complete attention were riveted to the open doorway leading to the corridor. He could not see the squad room from where he sat, nor could he hear a word spoken there, but his eyes stayed on the hallway, and he seemed to be straining to catch stray snatches of sound.

'How long you been married, sir?' Miscolo asked, making conversation.

'Two years,' Redfield said.

'You're practically newlyweds, huh?' Miscolo said, grinning. 'That's why you're so worried about her. Me, I been married . . .'

'I don't think we fall into the "newlywed" category,' Redfield said. 'We're not exactly teenagers.'

'No, I didn't mean . . .'

'Besides, this is my wife's second marriage.'

'Oh,' Miscolo said, and couldn't think of anything to add to it.

'Yes,' Redfield said.

'Well, plenty of people get married late in life,' Miscolo said lamely. 'Lots of times, those turn out to be the best marriages. Both parties are ready to accept family responsibility, ready to settle . . .'

'We don't have a family,' Redfield said.

'I beg your pardon?'

'We don't have any children.'

'Well, sooner or later,' Miscolo said, smiling. 'Unless, of course, you don't want any.'

'I'd like a family,' Redfield said.

'Nothing like it,' Miscolo answered, warming to his subject, 'I've got two kids myself, a girl and a boy. My daughter's studying to be a secretary at one of the commercial high schools here in the city. My son's up at MIT. That's in Boston, you know. You ever been to Boston?'

'No.'

'I was there when I was in the navy, oh, this was way back even before the Second World War. Were you in the service?'

'Yes.'

'What branch?'

'The army.'

'Don't they have a base up near Boston someplace?'

'I don't know.'

'Seems to me I saw a lot of soldiers when I was there.' Miscolo shrugged. 'Where were you stationed?'

'How much longer will they be with her?' Redfield asked suddenly.

'Oh, coupla minutes, that's all. Where were you stationed, Mr Redfield?'

'In Texas.'

'Doing what?'

'The usual. I was with an infantry company.'

'Ever get overseas?'

'Yes.'

'Where?'

'I was in the Normandy invasion.'

'No kidding?'

Redfield nodded. 'D-Day plus one.'

'That musta been a picnic, huh?'

'I survived,' Redfield said.

'Thank God, huh? Lotsa guys didn't.'

'I know.'

'I'll tell you the truth, I'm a little sorry I missed out on it. I mean it. When I was in the navy, nobody even dreamed there was gonna be a war. And then, when it *did* come, I was too old. I'd have been proud to fight for my country.'

'Why?' Redfield asked.

'*Why?*' For a moment, Miscolo was stunned. Then he said, 'Well . . . for . . . for the future.'

'To make the world safe for democracy?' Redfield asked.

'Yeah. That, and . . .'

'And to preserve freedom for future generations?' There was a curiously sardonic note in Redfield's voice. Miscolo stared at him.

'I think it's important my kids live in freedom,' Miscolo said at last.

'I think so, too,' Redfield answered. 'Your kids and my kids.'

'That's right. When you have them.'

'Yes, when I have them.'

The room went silent.

Redfield lighted a cigarette and shook out the match. 'What's taking them so long?' he asked.

The policewoman who spoke privately to Margaret Redfield was twenty-four-years old. Her name was Alice Bannion, and she sat across the desk from Mrs Redfield in the empty squad room and listened to every word she said, her eyes saucer-wide, her heart pounding in her chest. It took Margaret only fifteen minutes to give the details of that party in 1940, and during that time Alice Bannion alternately blushed, turned pale, was shocked, curiously excited, repulsed, interested, and sympathetic. At one o'clock, Margaret and Lewis Redfield left the squad room, and Detective 3rd/Grade Alice Bannion sat down to type her report. She tried to do so unemotionally, with a minimum of involvement. But her spelling became more and more uncontrolled as she typed her way deeper into the report and the past. When she pulled the report out of the typewriter, she was sweating. She wished she hadn't worn a girdle that day. She carried the typewritten pages into the lieutenant's office, where Carella was waiting. She stood by the desk while Carella read what she had written.

'That's it, huh?' he asked.

'That's it,' she said. 'Do me a favour next time, will you?'

'What's that?'

'Ask your own questions,' Alice Bannion said, and she left the office.

'Let me see it,' Lieutenant Byrnes said, and Carella handed him the report:

DETECTIVE DIVISION SUPPLEMENTARY REPORT	SQUAD	PRECINCT	PRECINCT REPORT NUMBER	DETECTIVE DIVISION REPORT NUMBER	PAGE NUMBER
	87	87	87-934	RL-4105	1

DETAILS

   Mrs. Redfield highly disturbed, did not wish to discuss matter at all. Claimed she had only told this to one other person in her life, her family doctor, and that because of urgency of matter, and need to do something about it. Has retained doctor over the years, general practitioner, Dr. Andrew Fidio, 106 Ainsley Avenue, Isola.

   Mrs. Redfield claims drinks were forced upon her against will night of party Randolph Norden's home, circa April 1940. Claims she was intoxicated when other students left at one or two in morning. Knew party was getting wild, but was too dizzy to leave. She refused to take part in what she knew was happening in other rooms, staying in living room near piano. Other two girls, Blanche Lettiger and Helen Struthers, forced Mrs. Redfield into bedroom, held her with assistance of boys while Randy Norden "abused" her. She tried to get out of room, but they tied her hands and one by one attacked her until she lost consciousness. She says all the boys participated in attack, and she can remember girls laughing. She seems to recall something about a fire, one of drapes burning, but memry is hazy. Someone took her home at about five a.m., she does not remember who. She did not report incident to sole living parent, mother, out of fear.

In circa October 1940, she went to Dr. Fidio
with what seemed routine irritation of cervix.
Blood test showed she was venereally infects,
and that gonorrhea had entered chronic stage
with internal scarring of female organs. She
told Dr. Fidio about party in April, he suggested prosecution. She refused, not wanting
mother to know about incident. But severity of
symptoms indicated hysterectomy to Fidio, and
she was admitted hospital in November, when he
performed operation. Mother was told operation was appendectomy.

Mrs. Redfield feels to this day Randy Norden
was boy who "diseased" her, but does not kniw
for sure because each boy was attacker in turn.
She stronly implies unnatural rlations with
girls as well, but will not bring self to discuss it. She saed she was glad the boys were
dead. When told that ·Blanche Lettiger had
later became a prostitute, she said, "I'm not
surprised." She ended interview by saying,
"I wish Helen was dead, too. She started it
all."

DATE OF THIS REPORT   *May 9th*

Det/3rd Bennion Alice R.   7045   *87th Squad*
RANK   SURNAME   INITIALS   SHIELD NUMBER   COMMAND

SIGNATURE OF COMMANDING OFFICER

They worked on David Arthur Cohen for four hours, putting him
through a sort of crash therapy his analyst would never have dreamed of.
They had him tell and retell the details of that party long ago, read him
sections of the report on Margaret Redfield, reread it, asked him to tell what
had happened in his own words, asked him to explain the drapes being on
fire, asked him what the girls had done, went over it and over it until,
weeping, he could bear it no longer and simply repeated again and again,
'I'm not a murderer, I'm not a murderer.'

The assistant district attorney, who had been sent up from downtown,
had a small conference with the detectives when they were finished with
Cohen.

'I don't think we can hold him,' the assistant D.A. said. 'We've got
nothing that'll stick.'

Carella and Meyer nodded.

'We'll put a tail on him,' Carella said. 'Thanks for coming up.'

They released David Arthur Cohen at four o'clock that afternoon. The
detective assigned to his surveillance was Bert Kling. He never got to do any
work, because Cohen was shot dead as he came down the precinct steps into
the afternoon sunshine.

Chapter Seventeen

There were no buildings across the street from the station house: there was only a park. And there were no trees behind the low stone wall that bordered the sidewalk. They found a discharged shell behind the wall, and they assumed that the killer had fired from there, at a much closer range than usual, blowing away half of Cohen's head. Kling had immediately run out of the muster room, and down the precinct steps, and across the street into the park, chasing aimlessly along paths and into bushes, but the killer was gone. There was only the sound of the whirling carousel in the distance.

The precinct patrolmen were beginning to think this was all very funny. A guy getting killed on the steps of the station house was a pretty macabre piece of humour, but they enjoyed the fun of it nonetheless. They were all aware that the detectives upstairs had called in the D.A. that afternoon, and they were also aware that Cohen had been held in the squad room for a damn long time, and they joked now about the fact that he could no longer bring charges of false arrest since someone had very conveniently murdered him. One of the patrolmen jokingly said that all the detectives had to do was wait long enough and then everybody who'd been in that play would be dead, and the killings would automatically stop, and they could all go home to sleep. Another of the patrolmen had a better idea. He figured it was simply a process of elimination. As soon as the killer had murdered everybody but *one*, why then the remaining person was obviously the murderer of all the others.

Carella didn't think it was so funny. He knew that neither Thomas Di Pasquale nor Helen Vale had put that bullet in Cohen's head because they both were being escorted around the city by patrolmen who never let them out of sight. On the other hand, Lewis and Margaret Redfield had left the squad room at one o'clock, some three hours before Cohen walked down those steps and into a Remington .308 slug. Detective Meyer Meyer was sent promptly to the Redfield apartment on the corner of Grover and Forty-first in Isola, where he was told that Margaret Redfield had gone directly to the beauty parlour after leaving the squad room, apparently feeling in need of treatment after her cathartic experience. Lewis Redfield told Meyer he had gone to his office on Curwin Street after leaving the squad room, and stayed there until five P.M., at which time he had come home. He could remember, in fact, dictating some letters to his secretary, and then attending a meeting at three P.M. A call to the office verified the fact that Redfield had come to work at about one-thirty and had not left until five. They could not say where he was specifically at four o'clock when Cohen was murdered, but there seemed little doubt he was somewhere in the office. Nonetheless, because that narrow margin of doubt did exist, Meyer phoned Carella at the squad room to tell him he was going to stick to the Redfields for a while. Carella agreed that the tail was a good idea, and then he went home to dinner. Neither he nor Meyer thought the case was very funny. In fact, they were sick to death of it.

And then, oddly, considering how lightly the patrolmen were taking all this grisly slaughter, it was a patrolman who provided the next possibility for action in the case, and then only indirectly through a call from Captain Frick at eleven o'clock that night, while Carella was home and trying to read the newspaper.

When he heard the phone ring, he glanced at it sourly, rose from his easy chair in the living room, and quickly walked into the foyer. He picked the receiver from the cradle and said, 'Hello?'

'Steve, this is Captain Frick. I didn't wake you, did I?'

'No, no. What is it?'

'I hate to bother you on this, but I'm still here at the office trying to get these time sheets straightened out.'

'What time sheets are those, Marshall?'

'On my patrolmen.'

'Oh, yes. Well what is it?'

'Well, I've got Antonino listed as being with this Helen Vale woman from eight this morning until four this afternoon, when he was relieved by Boardman, who'll be on until midnight. That right?'

'I guess so,' Carella said.

'Okay. And Samalman was supposed to be with this guy Di Pasquale from eight this morning until four this afternoon, but I see here on his sheet he left at three. And I see that Canavan, who was supposed to relieve him at four, called in at nine P.M. to say he had just relieved on post. Now, I don't get that, Steve. Did you give these guys permission for this?'

'What do you mean, Marshall? Are you saying nobody was with Di Pasquale from three o'clock this afternoon to nine o'clock tonight?'

'That's what it looks like. Judging from these time sheets.'

'I see,' Carella said.

'Did you give them permission?'

'No,' Carella said. 'I didn't give them permission.'

Thomas Di Pasquale had a patrolman at his door and a woman in his apartment when Carella arrived that night. The patrolman moved aside to allow his superior to ring the doorbell. Carella rang it with dispatch, and then waited for Di Pasquale to answer the ring. Di Pasquale's dispatch did not equal Carella's, since he was all the way in the bedroom at the other end of the apartment, and he had to put on a robe and slippers and then come trotting through six rooms to the front door. When he opened the door, he looked out at a face he had never seen before.

'Okay, what's the gag?' he asked.

'Mr Di Pasquale?'

'Yeah?'

'I'm Detective Carella.'

'That's very nice. Do you know it's eleven-thirty at night?'

'I'm sorry about that, Mr Di Pasquale, but I wanted to ask you some questions.'

'Can't they wait till morning?'

'I'm afraid not, sir.'

'I don't have to let you in, you know. I can tell you to go whistle.'

'You can do that, sir, that's true. In which case I'd be forced to swear out a warrant for your arrest.'

'Hey, sonny boy, you think you're dealing with a hick?' Di Pasquale said. 'You can't arrest me for anything, because I haven't *done* anything.'

'How about suspicion of murder?'

'How about it? There's no such crime as *suspicion* of anything. Murder? Don't make me laugh. Who am I supposed to have killed?'

'Mr Di Pasquale, can we discuss it inside?'

'Why? You afraid of waking the neighbours? You already woke *me* up, what difference will a few dozen others make? Argh, come in, come in. No damn manners, the police in this lousy town. Come around the middle of the night. Come in, for Chrissake, don't stand there in the hall.'

They went into the apartment. Di Pasquale turned on a light in the living room, and they sat facing each other.

'So?' he said. 'You're here, you got me out of bed, so say what's on your mind.'

'Mr Di Pasquale, a man was shot and killed this afternoon at four o'clock as he was leaving the police station.'

'So?'

'Mr Di Pasquale, we checked with the patrolman who was assigned to "protect" you, and he tells us you let him go at three o'clock this afternoon. Is that right?'

'That's right.'

'Is it also true that you told him you wouldn't be needing him again until nine o'clock this evening? Is that also true, Mr Di Pasquale?'

'That's true. So what? Is that why you come knocking on my door in the middle of the night? To check on whether or not your patrolman is telling the truth? Is that all you've got to do with your time? You're the guy who called me up at seven-thirty one morning, ain't you? You *like* waking people up, don't you?'

'Mr Di Pasquale, why'd you tell the patrolman you wouldn't need him?'

'For the very simple reason that I was up at Columbia Pictures today talking a deal with the head of the story department. I went up there at three o'clock, and I expected to be there with him until six, at which time I knew we would both go downstairs where a chauffeured Cadillac would be waiting to take us to a very fancy restaurant where I wouldn't be sitting near any windows. We would have a couple of drinks at the bar, and at seven o'clock we would be joined by a writer who would give a story line to the head of the story department, and then we would eat dinner, also not sitting near any windows. Then we would get right into the Cadillac again, and they would drive me home, where I asked that fathead patrolman to meet me – I see he isn't even here, there's some other jerk outside – and where also the young lady who is now asleep in the other room would be waiting for me. So you see, Mr Carella who likes to wake up people in the middle of the night, I thought I would save the city a little money and also release a cop for active duty in spots all over the city where teenagers are bashing each other's heads in, instead of hanging around me when I knew I'd be absolutely safe, *that's* why, Mr Carella. Does that answer your question?'

'Were you anywhere near the precinct today, Mr Di Pasquale?'

'I was up at Columbia all afternoon, and then I went straight to dinner, and then I came straight here.'

'Mr Di Pasquale, do you own any guns?'

'No.' Di Pasquale stood up angrily. 'What is all this, would you mind telling me? How come I'm suddenly a suspect in this thing? What's the matter? You running out of people?'

He had delivered his words in anger, but he had struck very close to the truth. They *were* running out of people. They had begun the case by grasping at straws, and they were still grasping at straws.

Carella sighed heavily. 'I suppose the head of Columbia's story department can corroborate . . .'

'You want to call him from here? I'll give you his home number. Go ahead, why don't you call him? You might as well wake up the whole goddamn city while you're at it.'

'I think that can wait until morning,' Carella said. 'I'm sorry I disturbed you. Good night, Mr Di Pasquale.'

'Can you find your way out?' Di Pasquale asked sarcastically.

It was close to the witching hour.

Meyer Meyer stood on the corner opposite the Redfields' apartment building, and wondered if he should call it a day. He had positioned himself on the street corner at six that evening, and it was now eleven-forty, and he was certain the Redfields would turn out their lights soon and go to sleep. But at seven that evening, Margaret Redfield had come down into the street with a Welsh terrier on a leash, and she had walked around the block and then returned to the building at seven-twenty-five. Meyer did not own a dog, but he was sure a seven-o'clock constitutional would not be the final promenade for a terrier kept in a city apartment. And yet, it was now eleven-forty – he glanced at his watch, no, eleven-forty-five – and there was no indication that either Margaret or Lewis Redfield would take the pooch down for another stroll before retiring, and besides, it was beginning to rain.

It was not a heavy rain at first; it was only a light, sharp drizzle that penetrated directly to the marrow. Standing on the corner, Meyer looked up again at the lighted third-floor apartment window. He swore mildly under his breath, decided to go home, changed his mind, and crossed the street to stand under the awning outside a bakery. The bakery was closed. It was nearing midnight, and the streets were deserted. A strong wind suddenly came in off the river, pushing heavier rain clouds ahead of it. The deluge covered the street. The drizzle turned to a teeming downpour in a matter of seconds. Lightning streaked the sky over the tops of the buildings. Meyer stood under the awning and thought of a warm bed with Sarah beside him. He cursed the Redfields again, decided to go home, remembered that damn Welsh terrier, convinced himself the dog would be going for another walk, pulled up the collar of his coat, and again looked up at the lighted third-floor window. The awning leaked. He glanced up at the tear in the canvas, and then switched his scrutiny back to the window.

The light went out.

There was what seemed like a half-hour of blackness, and then another light went on, the bedroom, he figured, and then a light came up behind a smaller window. The bathroom, Meyer thought. Thank God, they're finally going to sleep. He waited. Both lights stayed on. On impulse, he walked across the street rapidly and into the building. The elevator was directly opposite the entrance doorway. He walked halfway into the lobby and looked up at the indicator over the closed elevator doors. The needle was stopped at the number six. He watched patiently for several moments, and suddenly the needle began to move. Five, four, three . . . the needle stopped again.

Three, he thought. The Redfields live on the third floor.

The needle was moving again.

He raced out of the building and crossed the street, taking up his position under the leaking awning, certain now that either Lewis or Margaret Redfield was coming downstairs with the dog before going to bed, and then wondering what the hell difference it made, and then wishing again *he* were home in bed. He kept his eyes on the doorway to the building. Margaret Redfield came out of the doorway, leading the terrier on a leash, just as the patrolman rounded the corner.

It was five minutes to midnight.

The patrolman glanced at Meyer as he passed him, took in the hatless, bald-headed man with the jacket collar turned up, standing outside a closed bakery, five to midnight, rain, empty streets . . .

The patrolman turned back.

The sniper was out of breath.

He had leaped the airshaft between the two buildings and taken up his position behind the parapet, looking down into the street now, the street empty and deserted, but knowing that she would soon turn the corner, knowing she would soon stroll leisurely up the block, leading the dog, knowing she would soon be dead, breathing hard, waiting.

The rifle felt long and lethal in his hands, more lethal because of the telescopic sight, bringing the street below into sharp focus. He sighted along the barrel at the lamppost in the middle of the block, far below, close to him because of the sight; she would make a good target.

He wondered if he should stop.

He wondered if she should be the last one, and then wondered if she shouldn't have been the first one. He knew the dog would lead her to the lamppost. He knew she would stop there. He fixed the lamppost in the crossed hairs of the sight, and cursed the rain. He had not supposed the rain would make that much difference, and yet he could not see too clearly; he wondered if he should wait until another time.

No.

You bastards, he thought.

You, he thought.

I should have taken care of you first.

The rain drummed on his shoulders and his head. He was wearing a black raincoat, wearing the night around him, hidden by the night, he felt a thrill of anticipation as he waited for her. Where are you, he thought, come walk into my rifle, come walk into my sight, come let me kill you, come, come, come.

The dog stopped alongside the fire hydrant on the corner. He sniffed, hesitated, sniffed again. Meyer, who was watching Margaret and the dog intently, didn't even see the patrolman approaching.

'What's the trouble, mister?' the patrolman said.

'Huh?' Meyer answered, startled.

'What are you standing around here for?'

A grin came onto Meyer's face. Of all times for a cop to get conscientious, he thought, and then he said, 'Look, I'm . . .'

The patrolman shoved him. The patrolman had just come on duty, he had a little heartburn, and he wasn't ready to take any crap from a suspicious character who looked as if he was planning a burglary. 'Move along,' he said angrily. 'Go on, move along.'

'Look,' Meyer said, the grin dropping from his face. 'I happen to be a . . .'

'You gonna give me trouble?' the patrolman asked, and he grabbed Meyer's right sleeve, twisting it in his fist.

At that moment, Margaret Redfield disappeared around the corner.

He saw her turn into the block. She was partially obscured by the rain, but he recognized her and the dog immediately.

He wiped the palms of his hands on his coat, realizing only afterward that the coat was wetter than his hands.

I'm going to kill you better than the others, he thought.

You bitch, I am going to kill you better.

He was no longer out of breath, but his heart was pounding furiously, and his hands had begun to tremble. He glanced over the parapet again, saw that she was coming steadily down the block.

There was a lot of wind. He would have to compensate for the wind.

He wiped the rain from his eyes.

He put the rifle to his shoulder.

He sighted again on the lamppost, waiting.

Come on, he thought.

Come on.

Goddamn you to hell, *come on*!

'I'm a detective,' Meyer said. 'Let go of my sleeve!'

Instead of letting go of Meyer's sleeve, the patrolman twisted his arm up behind his back and began frisking him for a gun, which of course he found immediately.

'You got a permit for this?' he asked, while across the street Meyer could see nothing, could hear only the clatter of Margaret's heels around the corner.

'You goddamn fool,' Meyer said to the patrolman. 'You want to find yourself walking a beat in Bethtown? Give me that gun!'

The patrolman suddenly recognized something in Meyer's voice, a note of authority, a no-nonsense attitude that told him he might indeed be walking a beat in Bethtown if he didn't cooperate with this bald bastard. He handed back the .38 immediately. Lamely he said, 'You can understand . . .' But Meyer wasn't in an understanding mood, nor did he even hear the patrolman's words. He ran to the corner and turned it immediately. He could see Margaret Redfield halfway up the street, the dog hesitating near the lamppost, close to the kerb. He began walking after her, ducking into doorways. He was perhaps a hundred feet from her when she suddenly collapsed on the sidewalk.

He had heard no shot.

She fell swiftly and soundlessly, and the absence of sound magnified the event, because he knew she had been shot, and yet there was no clue to the sniper's hiding place. He began running toward her, and then stopped, and then looked up at the rooftops on either side of the street, and realized suddenly that the shot could have come from any one of them. The terrier was barking now, no, not barking but wailing, a lonely terrible wail like the mournful sound of a coyote.

The woman, Meyer thought. Get to the woman.

The roof, he thought, get to the roof.

Which roof?

Where?

He stopped dead in the middle of the street.

The killer is up there somewhere, he thought, and his mind stopped working for a moment. The rain drumming around him, Margaret Redfield lying on the sidewalk ahead of him, the dog wailing, the patrolman coming around the corner curiously, Meyer's mind clicked shut, he did not know what to do or where to turn.

He ran to the doorway of the building closest to the lamppost, ran reflexively, passing Margaret Redfield, who poured blood into the gutter while the dog wailed, ran without stopping to think it through, going there automatically because that was where the shot had most likely come from. Then he stopped on the sidewalk and shut his eyes for a moment, forced reason into his mind, forced himself to realize the killer would not come down on this block, he would leap the airshaft, cross over to one of the other buildings and try to make his escape on the avenue or the next cross street.

He ran for the corner. He almost slipped on the slick, wet asphalt, regained his balance, ran with the gun in his right fist, pumping the air with both arms, reaching the corner and turning it, and running past the fire hydrant, and stopping before the entrance to the Redfields' apartment building, and looking up at the still-lighted windows, and then turning his eyes back to the street, and seeing nothing.

Where? he thought. Where are you?

He waited in the rain.

The patrolman discovered the body of Margaret Redfield around the corner. The terrier snapped at him when he tried to pick up her wrist to feel for a pulsebeat. He kicked the dog in the chops with the side of his shoe, and then lifted her wrist. Blood was pouring down her arm from the wound in her shoulder. She was one hell of a mess, and it was raining, and the patrolman had heartburn.

But he had sense enough to know she wasn't dead, and he immediately phoned the nearest hospital for an ambulance.

The sniper did not come down into the street where Meyer was waiting for him. Nor did Meyer suppose he was still on one of the roofs up there. No, he had guessed wrong, and that was that. The sniper had made his escape elsewhere, swallowed by the rain and the darkness, free to kill again.

As he holstered his gun, Meyer wondered how many mistakes a cop is allowed. Then, dejectedly, he looked up as he heard the sound of the approaching ambulance.

Chapter Eighteen

The hospital was shrouded in a slow, steady drizzle that echoed the greyness of its walls. They arrived there at one A.M., parked the car, and then went to the admissions desk, where a nurse told them Mrs Redfield was in Room 407.

'Has Mr Redfield arrived yet?' Meyer asked.

'Yes, he's upstairs,' the nurse said. 'Mrs Redfield's doctor is with her, too. You'll have to check with him before talking to the patient.'

'We'll do that,' Carella said.

They walked to the elevator. Carella pressed the call button, and then said, 'Redfield got here fast enough.'

'He was in the shower when I went up to the apartment to tell him his wife had been wounded,' Meyer said. 'Takes a shower every night before going to bed. That explains the bathroom light going on.'

'What'd he say when you told him?'

'He came to the door in a bathrobe, dripping water all over the floor. He said, "I should have taken the dog down myself."'

'That's all?'

'That's all. Then he asked where his wife was, and said he'd dress and get right over here.'

They took the elevator up to the fourth floor, and waited in the corridor outside Margaret's room. In ten minutes' time, a white-haired man in his sixties came out of Room 407. He looked at his watch and was hurrying toward the elevators when Carella stopped him.

'Sir?' he said.

The man turned. 'Yes?'

'Sir, are you Mrs Redfield's doctor?'

'I am,' the man said. 'Dr Fidio.'

'I'm Detective Carella of the Eighty-seventh Squad. This is my partner, Detective Meyer.'

'How do you do?' Fidio said, and he shook hands with the men.

'We'd like to ask Mrs Redfield some questions,' Carella said. 'Do you think she's up to it?'

'Well,' Fidio said sceptically, 'I just gave her a sedative. I imagine it'll begin working any minute. If this won't take too long . . .'

'We'll try to keep it short,' Carella promised.

'Please,' Fidio answered. He paused. 'I can appreciate the gravity of what has happened, believe me, but I wish you'd try not to overtax Margaret. She'll live, but she'll need every ounce of strength she can summon.'

'We understand, sir.'

'And Lewis as well. I know you've got to ask questions, but he's been through a great deal in the past month, and now this thing with . . .'

'The past month?' Carella said.

'Yes.'

'Oh, worrying about Margaret, you mean.'

'Yes.'

'Well, we can understand the strain he's been under,' Carella said. 'Knowing a sniper was at large and wondering when . . .'

'Yes, yes, that too, of course.'

Meyer looked at Fidio curiously. He turned to Carella, and saw that Carella was also staring at the doctor. The corridor outside Room 407 was suddenly very silent.

'That *too*?' Carella said.

'What do you mean?' Meyer said instantly.

'What *else* was bothering him?' Carella asked.

'Well, the entire business with Margaret.'

'*What* entire business, Dr Fidio?'

'I hardly think this is germane to your case, gentlemen. Margaret Redfield was shot and almost killed tonight. This other thing is a private matter between her and her husband.' He looked at his watch again. 'If you're going to question her, you'd better hurry. That sedative . . .'

'Dr Fidio, I think *we* ought to decide what's germane to the case, don't you? What was troubling Lewis Redfield?'

Dr Fidio sighed deeply. He looked into the detectives' faces, sighed again, and then said. 'Well . . .' and told them what they wanted to know.

Margaret Redfield was asleep when they entered the room. Her husband was sitting in a chair beside her, a round-faced man with sad brown eyes and a dazed expression on his face. A black raincoat was draped over a chair on the other side of the room.

'Hello, Mr Redfield,' Carella said.

'Hello, Detective Carella,' Redfield answered. Behind his chair, rain stained the window, crawling over the glass, dissolving the pane in globs of running light.

'Dr Fidio tell us your wife is going to pull through.'

'Yes, I hope so,' Redfield said.

'It's no fun getting shot,' Meyer said. 'In the movies, it all looks so clean and simple. But it isn't any fun.'

'I don't imagine it is,' Redfield said.

'I take it you've never been shot,' Carella said.

'No.'

'Were you in the service?'

'Yes.'

'What branch, Mr Redfield?'

'The army.'

'Did you see combat?'

'Yes.'

'Then you know how to use a rifle?'

'Oh, yes,' Redfield said.

'Our guess is you know how to use it pretty well, Mr Redfield.'

Redfield looked suddenly alert. 'What do you mean?' he asked.

'Our guess is you were an expert shot during the war, is that right, Mr Redfield?'

'I was only fair.'

'Then you must have learned an awful lot since.'

'What do you mean?' Redfield asked again.

'Mr Redfield,' Meyer said, 'where did you go tonight when your wife left the apartment with the dog?'

'I went into the shower.'

'Which shower?'

'What . . . what do you mean . . . the *shower*,' Redfield said. 'The shower.'

'In your bathroom . . . or on the roof?'

'What?'

'It's raining, Mr Redfield. Is that why you missed killing her? Is that why you only hit her in the shoulder?'

'I don't know what you . . . who are you . . . my *wife*, do you mean? Are you talking about *Margaret*?'

'Yes, Mr Redfield. We are talking about your knowing your wife would take the dog down sometime before midnight. We are talking about your going up to the roof the moment she left the apartment, and crossing over to a building around the corner, and waiting for her to come around the block. That is what we are talking about, Mr Redfield.'

'I . . . that's the silliest thing I've ever heard in my life. Why, I . . . I was in the shower when it . . . when it all happened. I even came to the door in my bathrobe. I . . .'

'How long does it take to shoot someone, get back down to the apartment, and hop into the tub, Mr Redfield?'

'No,' Redfield said. He shook his head. 'No.'

'Yes, Mr Redfield.'

'No.'

'Mr Redfield,' Carella said, 'we just had a chat with Dr Fidio in the hall outside. He told us that you and Mrs Redfield have been trying to have a baby since you were married two years ago. Is that right?'

'Yes, that's right.'

'He also told us that you came to see him at the beginning of April because you thought perhaps something was wrong with you, that you were the one who was responsible.'

'Yes,' Redfield said.

'Instead, Dr Fidio told you that your wife, Margaret, had had a hysterectomy performed in November of nineteen-forty, and that she could never have a child. Is that also true, Mr Redfield?'

'Yes, he told me that.'

'And you didn't know about it before?'

'No, I didn't.'

'Surely your wife must have a scar. Didn't you ever ask her about it?'

'Yes. She said it was an appendectomy scar.'

'But when Dr Fidio told you the real nature of the operation, he also told you about a party that had taken place in April of nineteen-forty, and about your wife's subsequent venereal . . .'

'Yes, yes, he told me,' Redfield said impatiently. 'I don't see what . . .'

'How old are you, Mr. Redfield?'

'I'm forty-seven.'

'Have you ever had any children?'

'No.'

'You must have wanted them pretty badly.'

'I . . . I wanted children.'

'But they made it impossible, didn't they?'

'I . . . I . . . don't know who you mean, what you mean.'

'The people who were at that party, Mr Redfield. The ones who caused the hysterectomy, the ones . . .'

'I don't know who those people were. I don't know what you mean.'

'That's right, Mr Redfield. You *didn't* know who they were. You only knew there had been a party following a production of *The Long Voyage Home*, and you properly assumed all the members of the cast had been to that party. What did you do? Find Margaret's old theatre programme and just start going down the list?'

Redfield shook his head.

'Where's the rifle, Mr Redfield?' Carella said.

'Who was next on your list?' Meyer said.

'I didn't do any of this,' Redfield said. 'I didn't kill any of them.'

'If that's your raincoat,' Carella said, 'you'd better put it on.'

'Why? Where are you taking me?'

'Downtown.'

'What for? I'm telling you I didn't . . .'

'We're booking you for homicide, Mr Redfield,' Carella said.

'Homicide? I didn't kill anyone, how can you . . .?'

'We think you did.'

'You thought Cohen did, too.'

'There's one difference, Mr Redfield.'

'What's that?'

'This time we're sure.'

It was two A.M. by the time they got back to the precinct. He tried to brazen it through at first, but he did not know a patrolman was going through his apartment while the detectives were questioning him in the squad room. He refused to admit a thing. He kept repeating that he was in the shower when his wife was shot, he hadn't known a thing about it until Meyer knocked on his door to report the shooting, and then he'd put on a robe and come to answer it. How could he have been on the roof? And when Cohen was killed on the precinct steps, he had been at work in his office, how could they hold him responsible for *that* death? True, no one had seen him after the time the office meeting broke up at three-thirty, true, he could have left the office by the back stairs and come over to the precinct to wait for Cohen, but wasn't that the wildest sort of speculation, by those rules *anyone* could be convicted of murder, he had nothing to do with any of this.

'Where were you on Friday, May fourth?' Carella asked.

'I was home,' Redfield answered.

'You didn't go to work?'

'No, I had a cold.' He paused. 'Ask my wife. She'll tell you. I was home all day.'

'We *will* ask her, believe me, Mr Redfield,' Carella said. 'As soon as she's able to talk to us.'

'She'll tell us you weren't in Minneapolis, huh?'

'I've never been there in my life. I had nothing to do with any of this. You're making a terrible mistake.'

And that was when the patrolman walked into the squad room. Maybe Redfield would have told it all, anyway. It is a convention that they tell it all in the end, and besides, human beings will reach a point where hope is balanced against despair, where they see the scale slowly tilting against them. They recognize this point when it arrives, they stare at it with wise, discovering eyes, and they know there is nothing left for them. There is relief in confession. If there is any hope at all in despair, it is the hope of confession, so perhaps he would have told it all, anyway.

The patrolman walked directly to Carella's desk. He put down the long leather case and said, 'We found this at the back of his bedroom closet.'

Carella opened the case.

The rifle was a bolt-action Winchester Model 70.

'This your gun, Mr Redfield?' Carella asked.

Redfield stared at the rifle and said nothing.

'These were on the shelf, behind his hats,' the patrolman said. He put the box of Remington .308 cartridges on the desk top. Carella looked at the cartridges, and then looked at Redfield, and then said, 'Ballistics'll give us the answer in ten minutes' time, Mr Redfield. You want to save us the trouble?'

Redfield sighed.

'Well?'

Redfield sighed again.

'Call Ballistics, Meyer,' Carella said. 'Tell them a patrolman's on his way down with a rifle. We want a comparison test made with the bullets and discharged shells we've got on . . .'

'Never mind,' Redfield said.

'You want to tell us about it?' Carella said.

Redfield nodded.

'Stenographer!' Carella yelled.

'I didn't plan to kill any of them,' Redfield said. 'Not at first.'

'Just a second,' Meyer said. 'Miscolo, you got a stenographer coming?'

'You see,' Redfield said, 'when Dr Fidio told me about Margaret, I . . . I was shocked, of course, I thought . . . I don't know what I thought . . .'

'Miscolo! Goddamnit!'

'Coming, coming!' Miscolo shouted, and he ran into the squad room and began taking the confession himself, his open pad poised on his lap.

'Sadness, I suppose,' Redfield said. 'I wanted a family, you see. I'm not a young man. I wanted a family before it was too late.' He shrugged. 'Then . . . as I . . . as I began thinking about it, I guess I . . . I began to get . . . angry. My wife couldn't have a baby, you see. She could never have a baby. Because of the hysterectomy. And they were responsible, you see. The ones who had done this to her. The ones who had been at that party Dr Fidio described to me. Only, I . . . I didn't know who they were.'

'Go on, Mr Redfield.'

'I came upon the theatre programme by accident. I was looking for something in one of the closets, and I found the trunk, covered with dust, all covered with dust, and the programme was inside it. So you see, I . . . I knew their names then. I knew the people who had done it to her, the ones who were at the party, and I . . . I began looking for them, not intending to kill them at first, but only wanting to see them, wanting to get a good look at the people who had . . . who had made it impossible for me to have children, my wife to have children. Then, I don't know when, I think it was the day I found Blanche Lettiger, traced her to that dingy neighbourhood, followed her, and she . . . she stopped me on the street and propositioned me, I think it was that day, seeing the filth she had become, and knowing the filth that had poisoned Margaret, I think it was that day I decided to kill them all.'

Redfield paused. Miscolo looked up from his pad.

'I killed Anthony Forrest first, not for any special reason, only because he was the one I decided to kill first, and maybe in the back of my mind I thought it would be better not to kill them in the order they appeared on the programme, but just at random, you know, so it wouldn't seem they were connected, just to kill them, you know, as if . . . as if there were no connection.'

'When did you decide to kill your own wife, Mr Redfield?' Meyer asked.

'I don't know when. Not at the beginning. After all, she'd been a victim of the others, hadn't she? But then, I . . . I began to realize how dangerous my position was. Suppose a connection was made between the murder victims? Suppose you discovered all ten of them had been members of the same college drama group? Why, if I killed them all but allowed Margaret to live, well . . . well, wouldn't you wonder about this? Wouldn't you want to know why she alone hadn't been killed? Of the entire group? My position was very dangerous, you see.'

'So you decided to kill her, too? To protect yourself?'

'Yes. No. More than that. Not only that.' Redfield's eyes suddenly flared. 'How did I know she'd really been such an innocent? Was she really a victim that night? Or had she gone along with the others willingly in their . . . their dirty . . . I didn't know, you see. So I . . . I decided to kill her, too, along with the other ten. That was why I came here to talk with you. To throw off suspicion. I figured if I'd already been to the police to warn them of possible danger to Margaret, why, then, when she was actually killed, I wouldn't be suspect, don't you see? That was what I figured.'

'*Were* you in Minneapolis on May fourth, Mr Redfield?'

'Yes. Oh, yes, I killed Peter Kelby.'

'Tell us about Cohen.'

'What do you want to know?'

'How you managed the timing on it.'

'That was risky. I shouldn't have attempted it. But it worked, so maybe . . .'

'*How*, Mr Redfield?'

'I left here at about one yesterday, and was back in my office by one-thirty. I dictated some letters to my secretary, and then attended a meeting at two-forty-five. I said it started at three, but it really started at two-forty-five and was over by three-fifteen. I left the office through the back stairs. My own private office has a back door opening on a corridor, you see, and I took the steps down . . .'

'No one saw you?'

'No.'

'Did you tell anyone you were leaving?'

'No. I thought of telling my secretary not to disturb me for the next hour or so, but then I decided against it. I thought if anyone started asking questions later, it would be better if everyone simply said they knew I was in the building somewhere, but not exactly where.'

'You did quite a bit of planning, didn't you, Mr Redfield?'

'I was murdering,' Redfield said simply.

'You realize you were murdering?'

'Of course I realize it!'

'Go on. What'd you do when you left the office?'

'I took a cab to my apartment. To get the rifle.'

'Is that where you usually stored it?'

'Yes. In the closet. Where your man found it.'

'Your wife never saw it?'

'Once.'

'Didn't she ask you what you were doing with a rifle?'

'She didn't know it was a rifle.'

'What do you mean?'

'It was in the case. I told her it was a fishing rod.'

'And she *believed* you?'

'I don't think she has ever seen a rifle *or* a fishing rod. The gun was in its case. She had no way of knowing what was inside the case.'

'Go ahead. You went to pick up the rifle . . .'

'Yes. I took a cab. I was uptown in twenty minutes, and in another ten minutes, I was across the street, waiting in the park. Cohen came out at four o'clock, and I shot him.'

'Then what?'

'I ran south across the park, and took a cab on the other side.'

'Did you take the rifle back to the office with you?'

'No. I left it in a pay locker at Central Station.'

'And picked it up again on your way home last night?'

'Yes. Because I planned to kill Margaret last night, you see. The rain. I missed because of the rain.'

'Where'd you get the rifle, Mr Redfield?'

'I bought it.'

'When?'

'The day I decided to kill them all.'

'And the silencer?'

'I made it from a piece of copper tubing. I was afraid it might injure the barrel of the rifle after a single firing, but it didn't. I think I was lucky. Aren't silencers supposed to ruin guns?'

'Mr Redfield, you killed eight people, do you know that?' Carella said.

'Yes, I know that.'

'Why didn't you adopt children, Mr Redfield? You could have done that, you know. You planned all these murders, but you couldn't see your way clear to going to an adoption agency! Why the hell . . .?'

'It never occurred to me,' Redfield said.

After the confession was typed and signed, after they led Redfield downstairs to the detention cells to await transportation downtown later in the morning, Carella picked up the phone and called Thomas Di Pasquale to tell him he could stop worrying.

'Thanks,' Di Pasquale said. 'What the hell time is it?'

'Five A.M.,' Carella said.

'Don't you *ever* sleep?' Di Pasquale said, and hung up.

Carella smiled and replaced the phone in its cradle. He did not call Helen Vale until later in the day. When he told her the good news, she said, 'Oh, that's wonderful. Now I can go away without that on my mind.'

'Away, Mrs Vale?'

'For summer stock. The season starts next month, you know.'

'That's right,' Carella said. 'How could I forget a thing like that?'

'I want to thank you again,' Helen said.

'For what, Mrs Vale?'

'For the patrolman,' she answered. 'I really enjoying having him.'

Cynthia Forrest came up to the squad room that afternoon to pick up the material she had left, the old newspaper clippings, the report cards, the theatre programme. Bert Kling met her in the corridor as she was leaving.

'Miss Forrest,' he said, 'I want to apologize for the way . . .'

'Drop dead,' Cynthia said, and went down the iron-runged steps to the street.

The three detectives were alone in the squad room. May was dying, the long summer lay ahead. Outside on the street, they could hear the sound of a city rushing by, ten million people.

'I keep thinking about what you told me,' Meyer said suddenly.

'What was that, Meyer?'

'When we were leaving Etterman's office, the German guy, the one whose son was shot down over Schweinfurt.'

'Yeah, what about it?'

'You said, "You can't hate a people here and now for what another people in another time did."'

'Mmm,' Carella said.

'Redfield hated them here and now,' Meyer answered.

The telephone rang.

'Here we go,' Kling said, and picked up the receiver.